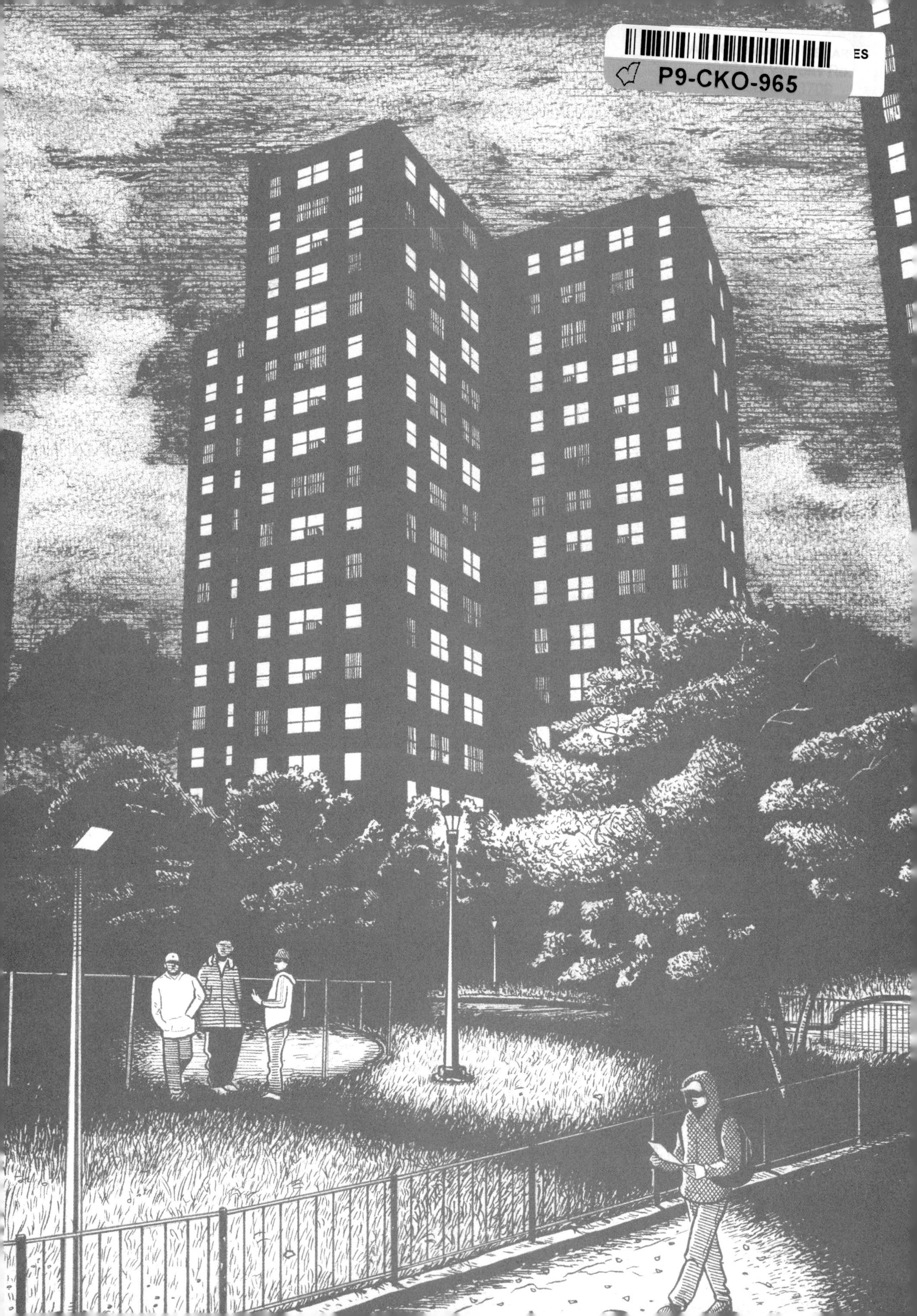

Designer: Keeli McCarthy
Editor: Gary Groth
Editorial Assistance: Conrad Groth
Production: Christina Hwang
Associate Publisher: Eric Reynolds
Publisher: Gary Groth

Fantagraphics Books, Inc.
7563 Lake City Way NE
Seattle, WA 98115

www.fantagraphics.com
@fantagraphics

ISBN: 978-1-68396-322-6
Library of Congress Control Number: 2019953946
First Fantagraphics Books edition: May 2020
Printed in China

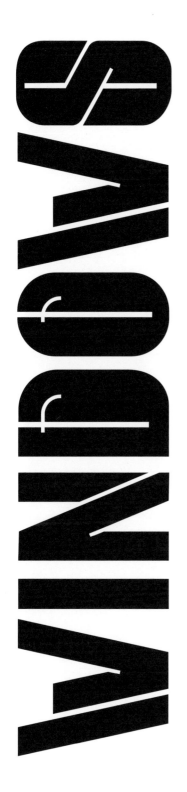

WINDOWS ON THE WORLD

Written by Robert Mailer Anderson
and Zack Anderson

Illustrated by Jon Sack

FANTAGRAPHICS BOOKS

MAZATLAN, MEXICO
SEPTEMBER, 2001

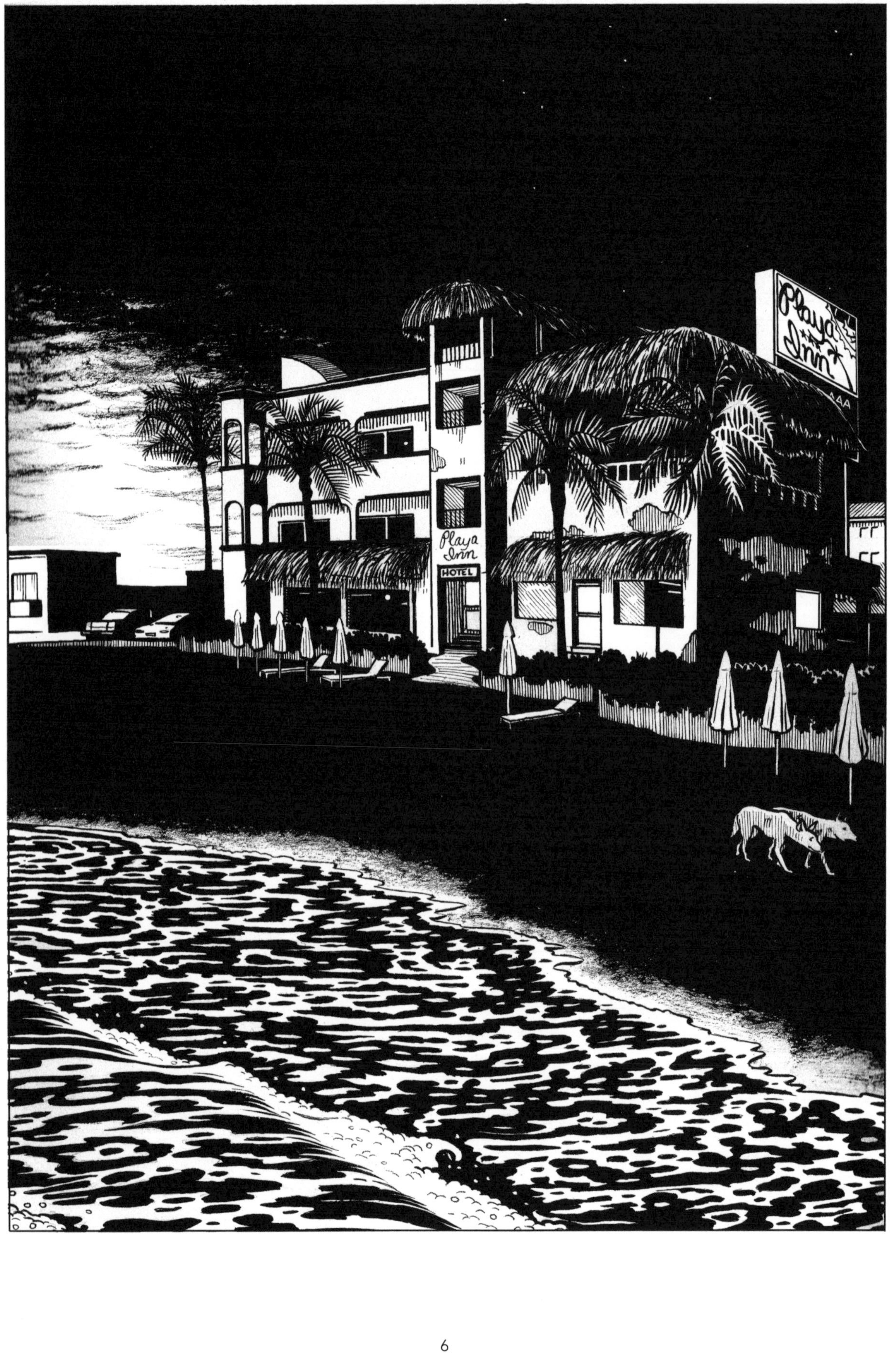
Playa Inn
Playa Inn
HOTEL

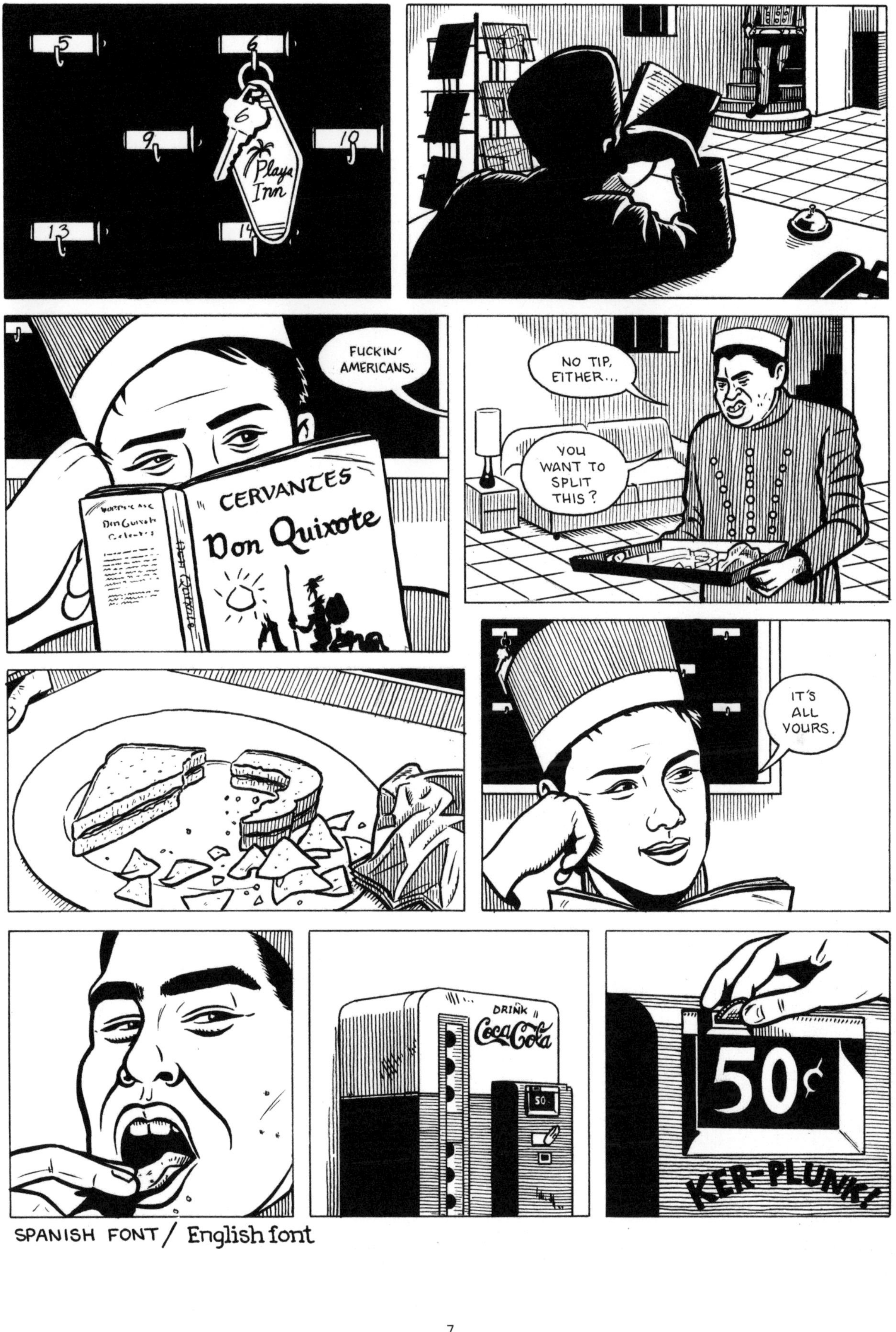

Playa Inn
FUCKIN' AMERICANS.
CERVANTES
Don Quixote
NO TIP, EITHER...
YOU WANT TO SPLIT THIS?
IT'S ALL YOURS.
DRINK
Coca-Cola
50¢
KER-PLUNK!

SPANISH FONT / English font

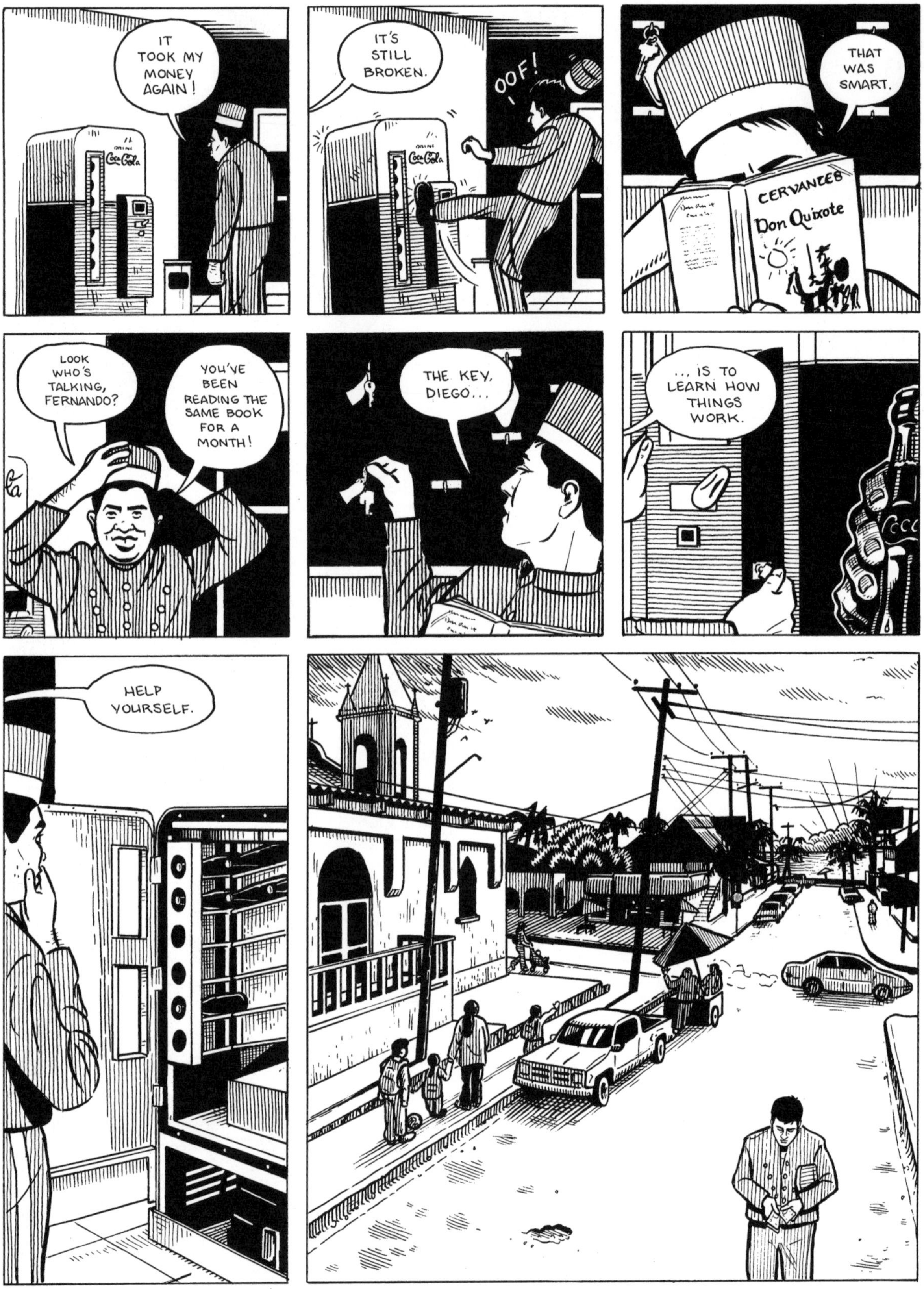
IT TOOK MY MONEY AGAIN!
DRINK Coca-Cola
IT'S STILL BROKEN.
OOF!
DRINK Coca-Cola
THAT WAS SMART.
CERVANTES Don Quixote
LOOK WHO'S TALKING, FERNANDO?
YOU'VE BEEN READING THE SAME BOOK FOR A MONTH!
THE KEY, DIEGO...
..., IS TO LEARN HOW THINGS WORK.
HELP YOURSELF.

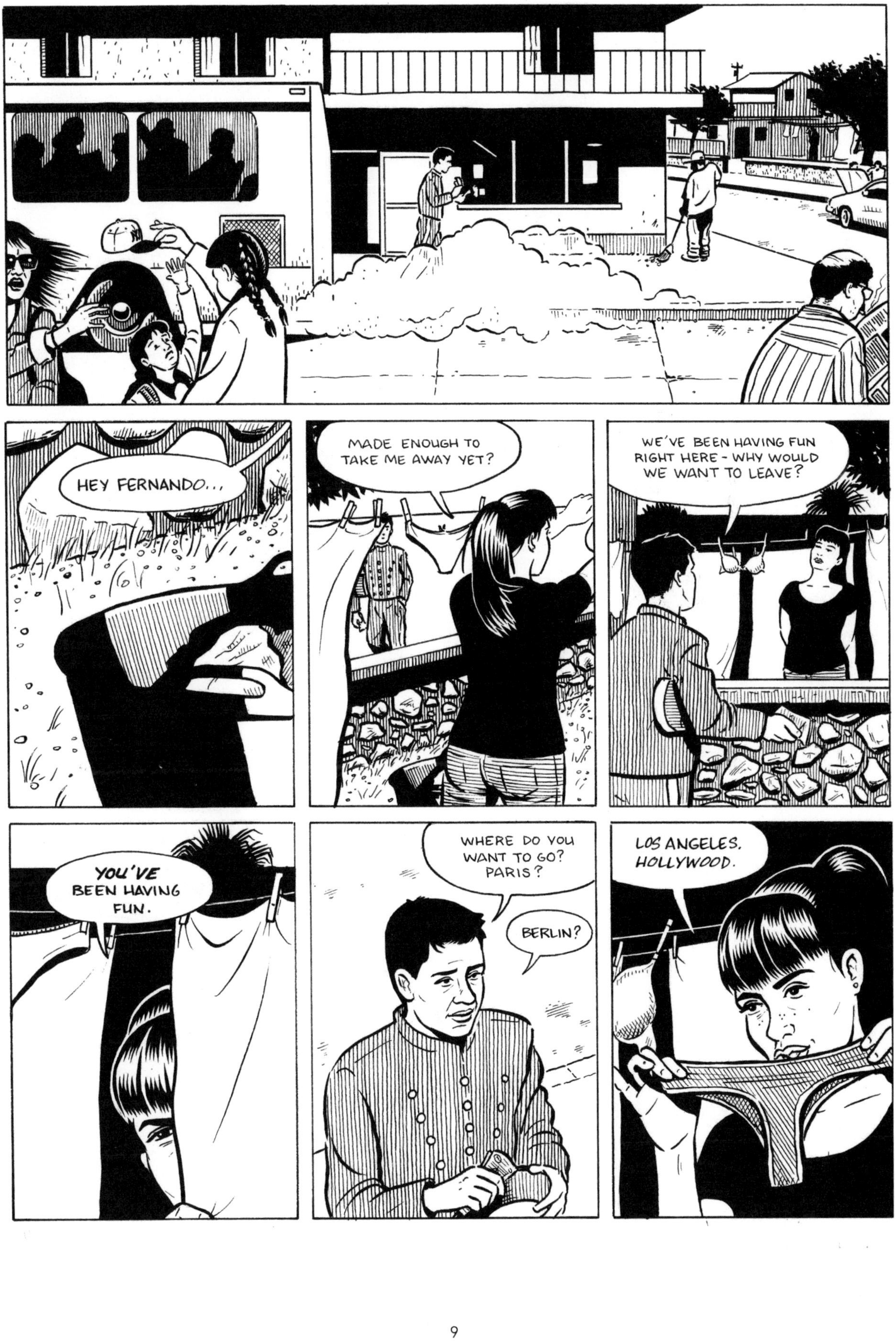
HEY FERNANDO...
MADE ENOUGH TO TAKE ME AWAY YET?
WE'VE BEEN HAVING FUN RIGHT HERE - WHY WOULD WE WANT TO LEAVE?
YOU'VE BEEN HAVING FUN.
WHERE DO YOU WANT TO GO? PARIS?
BERLIN?
LOS ANGELES. HOLLYWOOD.

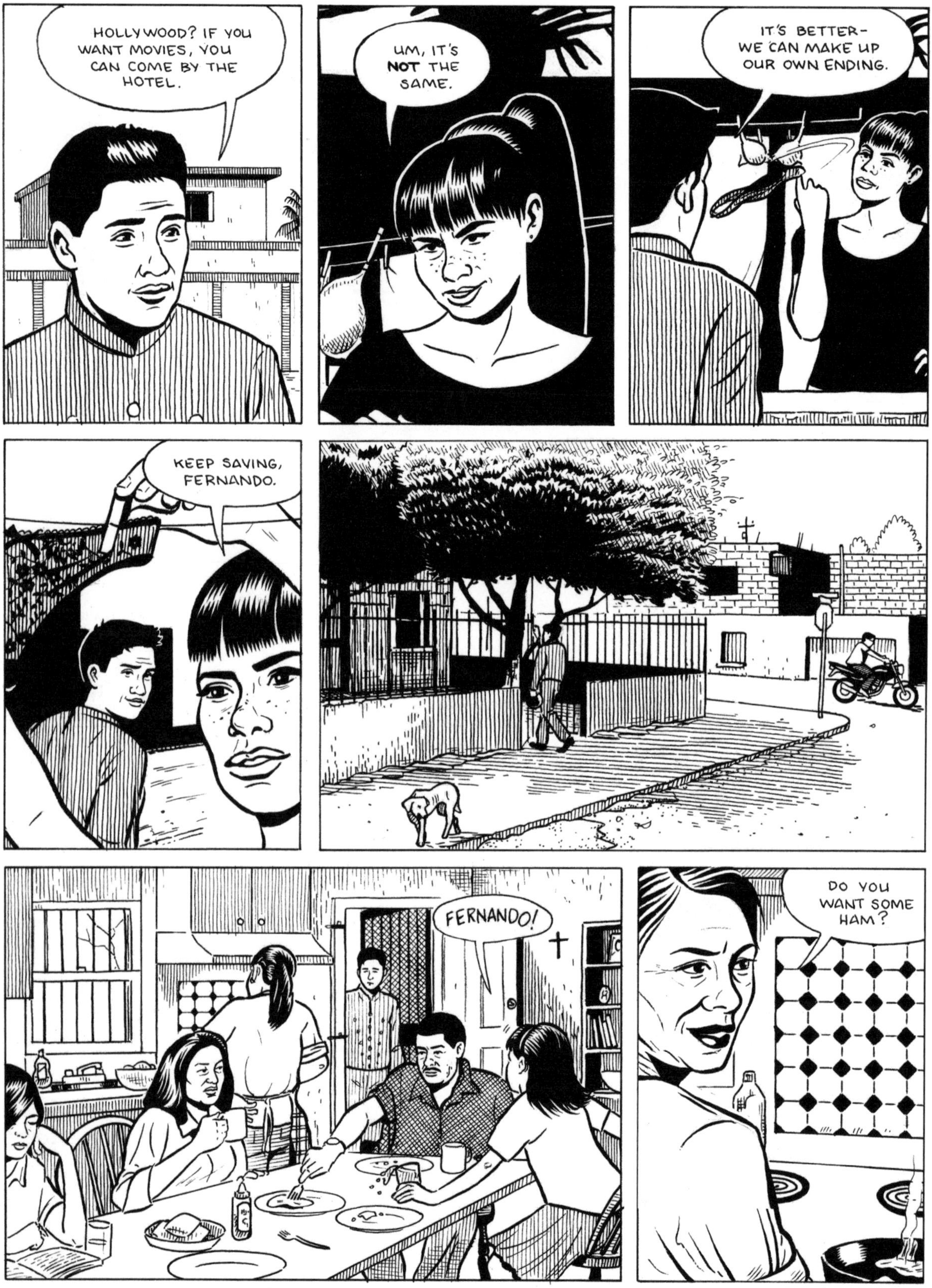
HOLLYWOOD? IF YOU WANT MOVIES, YOU CAN COME BY THE HOTEL.
UM, IT'S **NOT** THE SAME.
IT'S BETTER- WE CAN MAKE UP OUR OWN ENDING.
KEEP SAVING, FERNANDO.
FERNANDO!
DO YOU WANT SOME HAM?

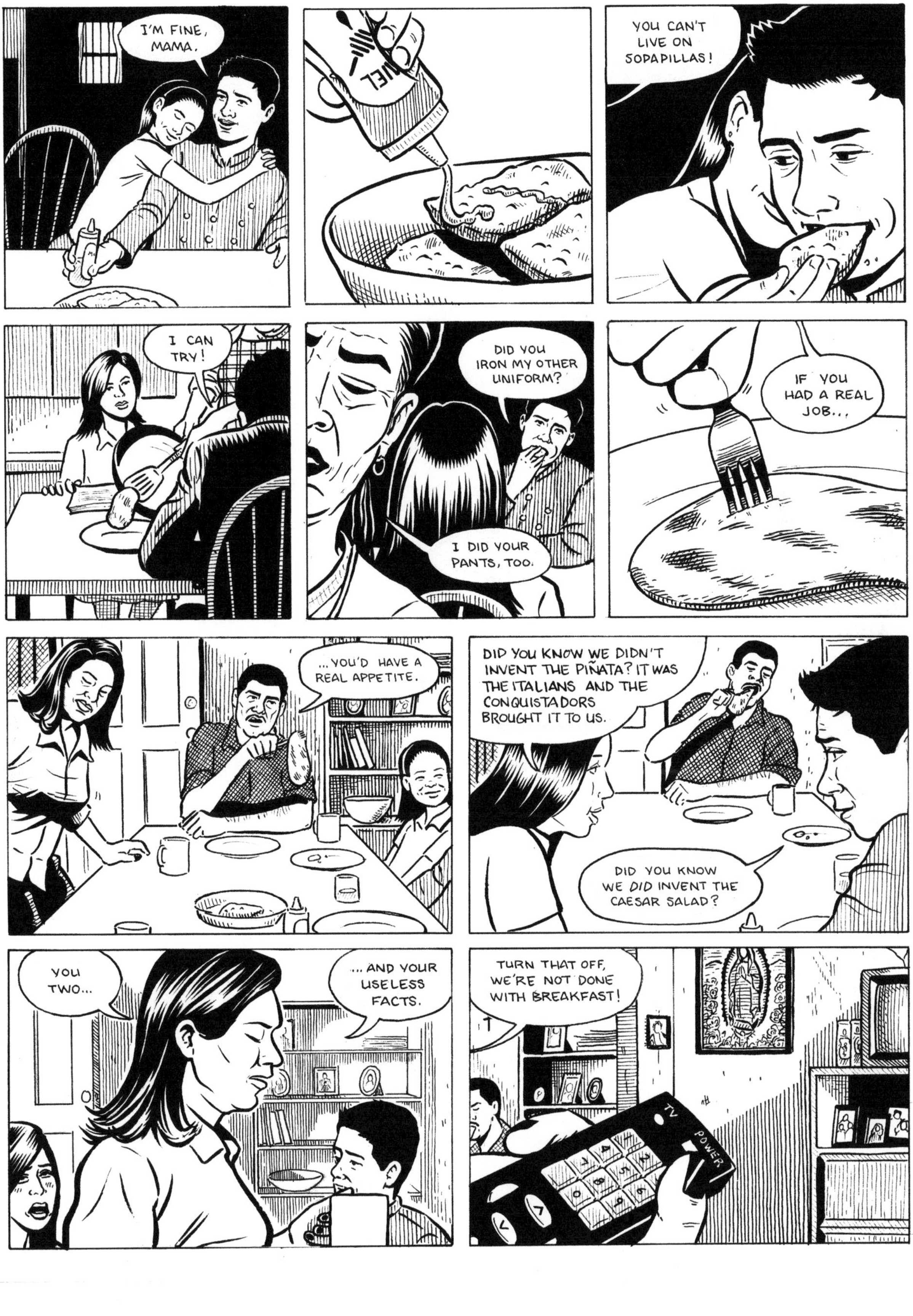
I'M FINE, MAMA.
YOU CAN'T LIVE ON SOPAPILLAS!
I CAN TRY!
DID YOU IRON MY OTHER UNIFORM?
I DID YOUR PANTS, TOO.
IF YOU HAD A REAL JOB...
...YOU'D HAVE A REAL APPETITE.
DID YOU KNOW WE DIDN'T INVENT THE PIÑATA? IT WAS THE ITALIANS AND THE CONQUISTADORS BROUGHT IT TO US.
DID YOU KNOW WE *DID* INVENT THE CAESAR SALAD?
YOU TWO...
...AND YOUR USELESS FACTS.
TURN THAT OFF, WE'RE NOT DONE WITH BREAKFAST!
TV
POWER

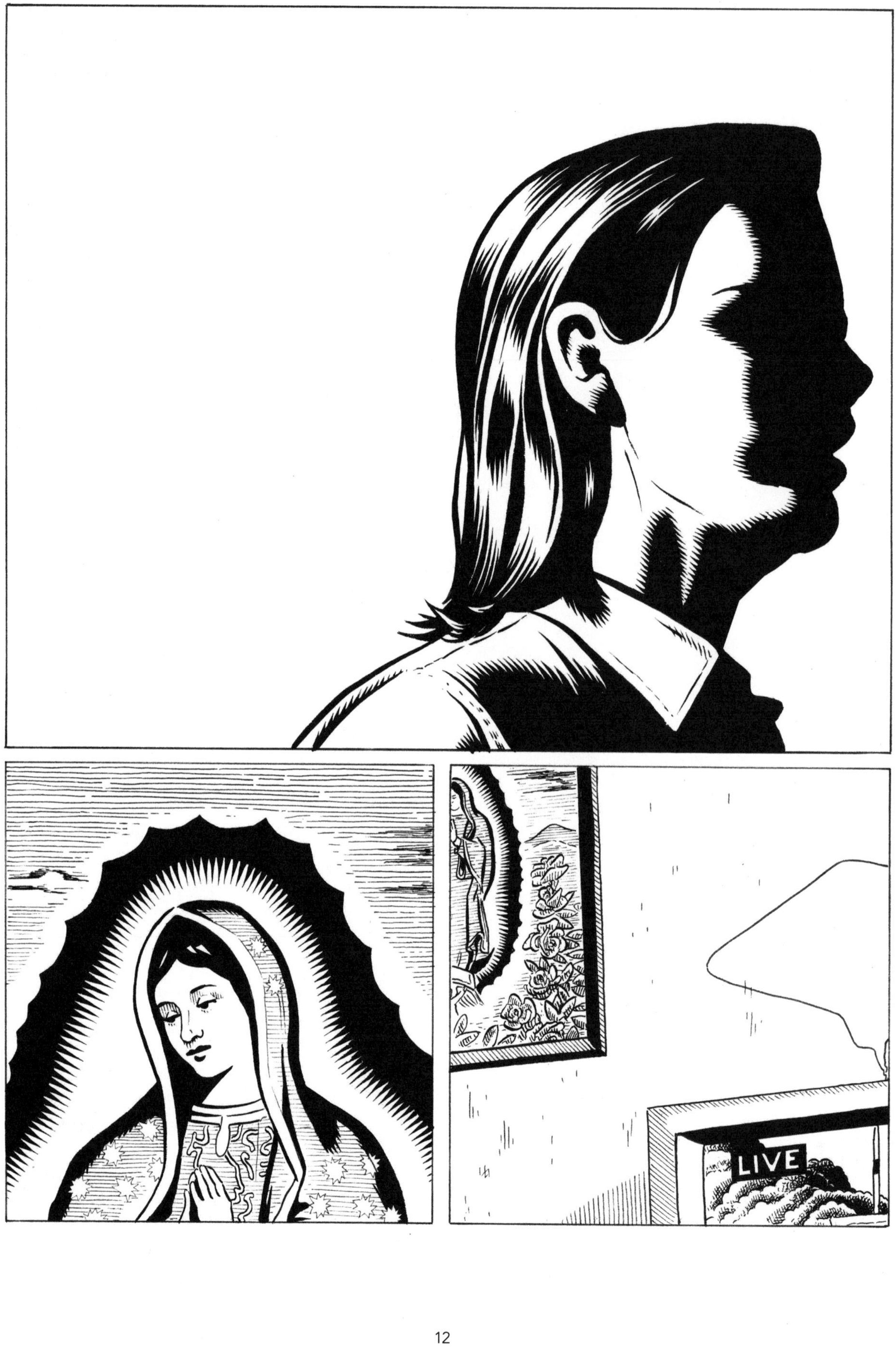
LIVE

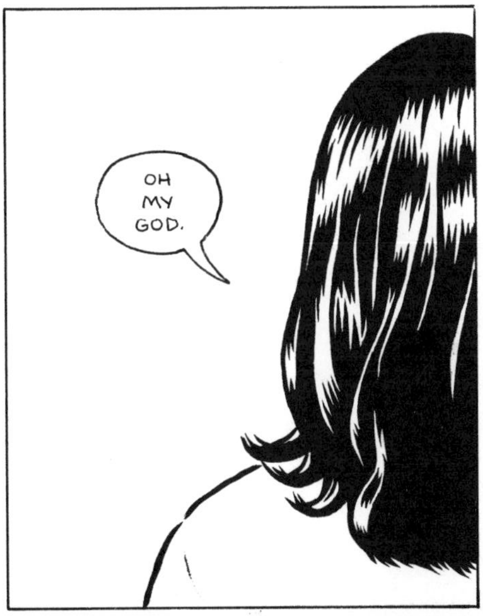
OH
MY
GOD.
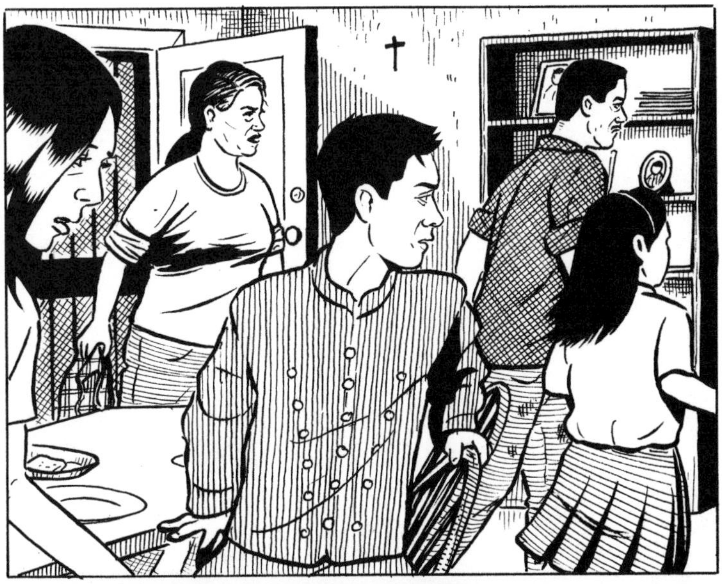
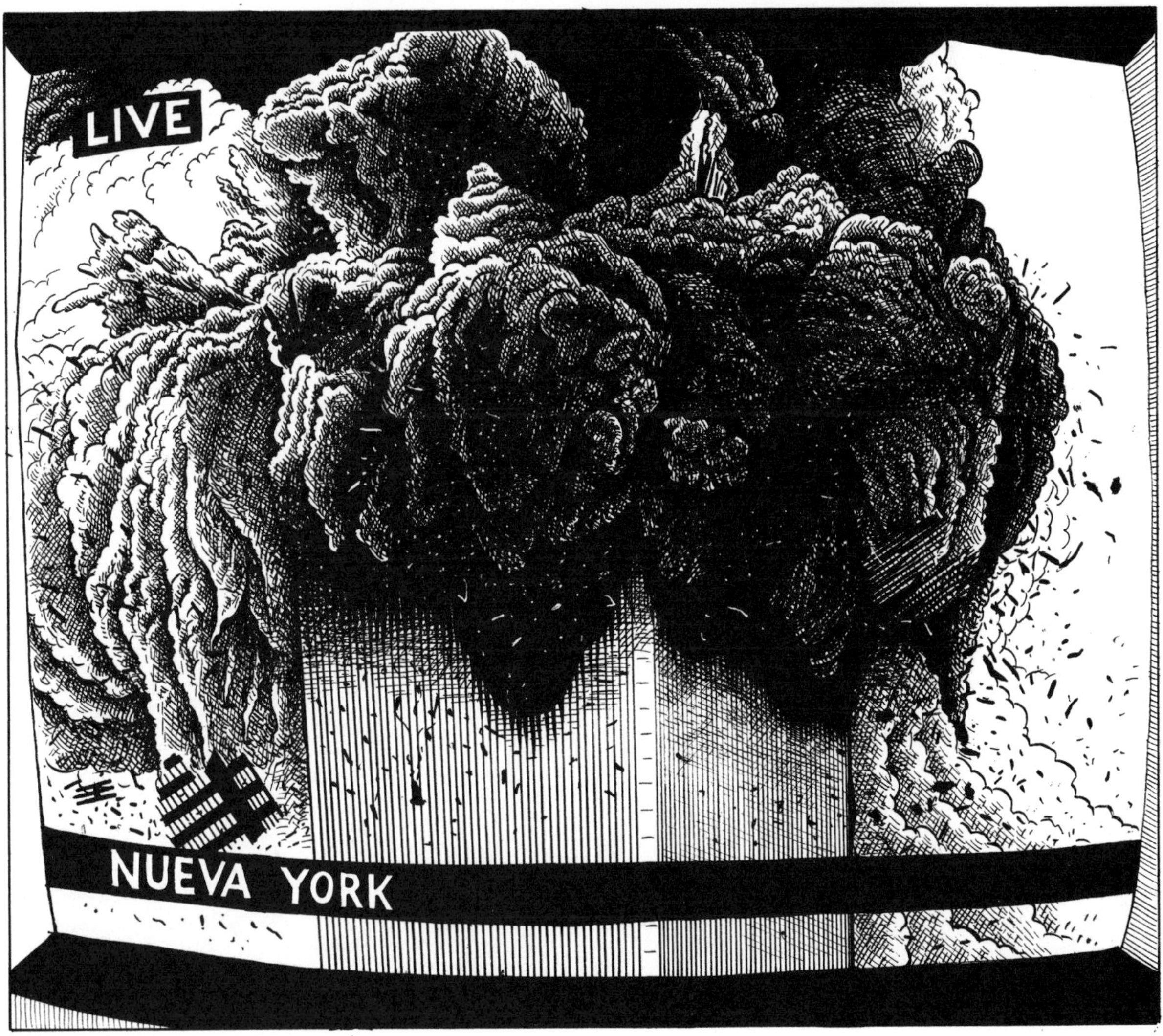
LIVE
NUEVA YORK

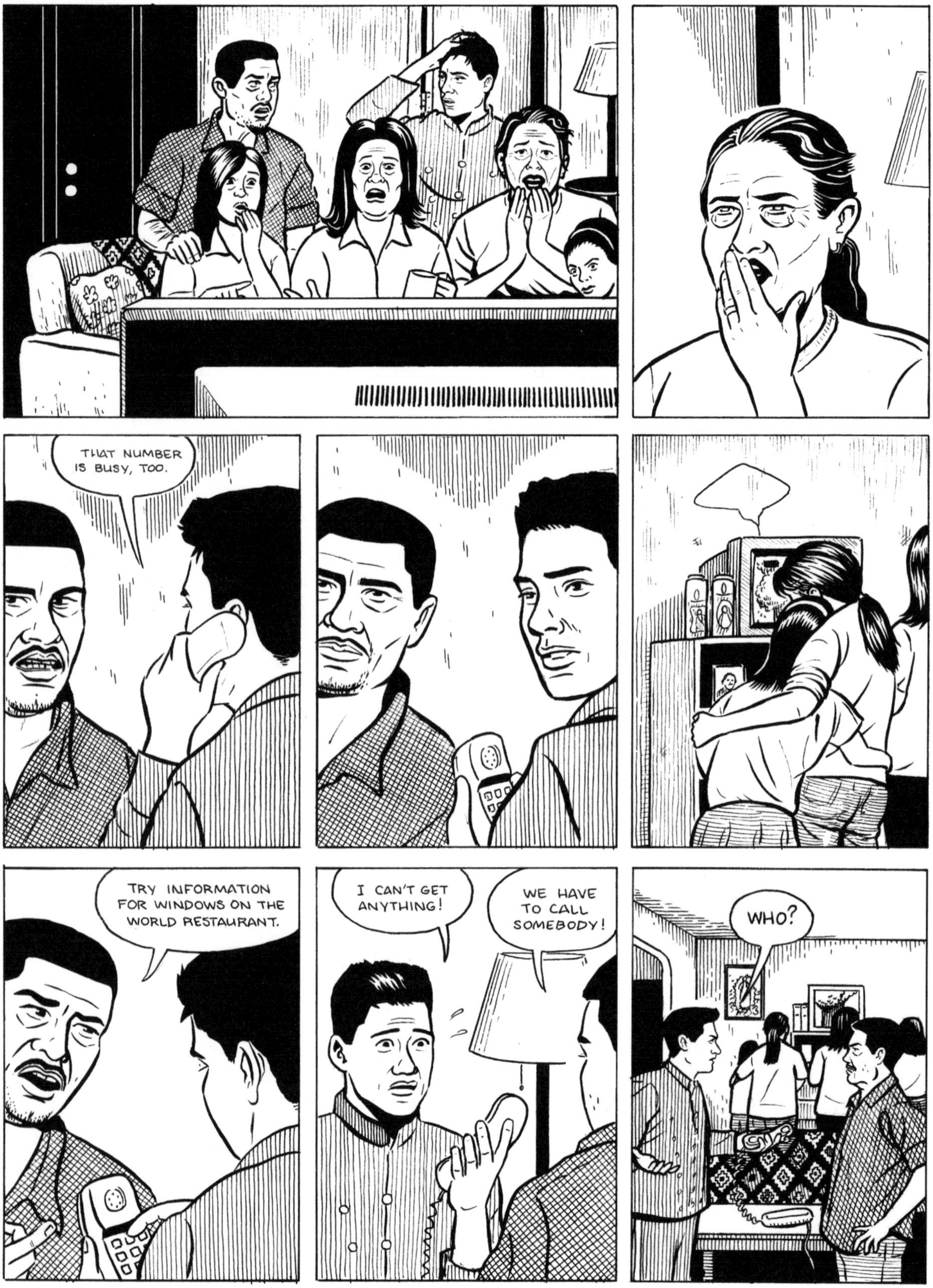
THAT NUMBER IS BUSY, TOO.
TRY INFORMATION FOR WINDOWS ON THE WORLD RESTAURANT.
I CAN'T GET ANYTHING!
WE HAVE TO CALL SOMEBODY!
WHO?

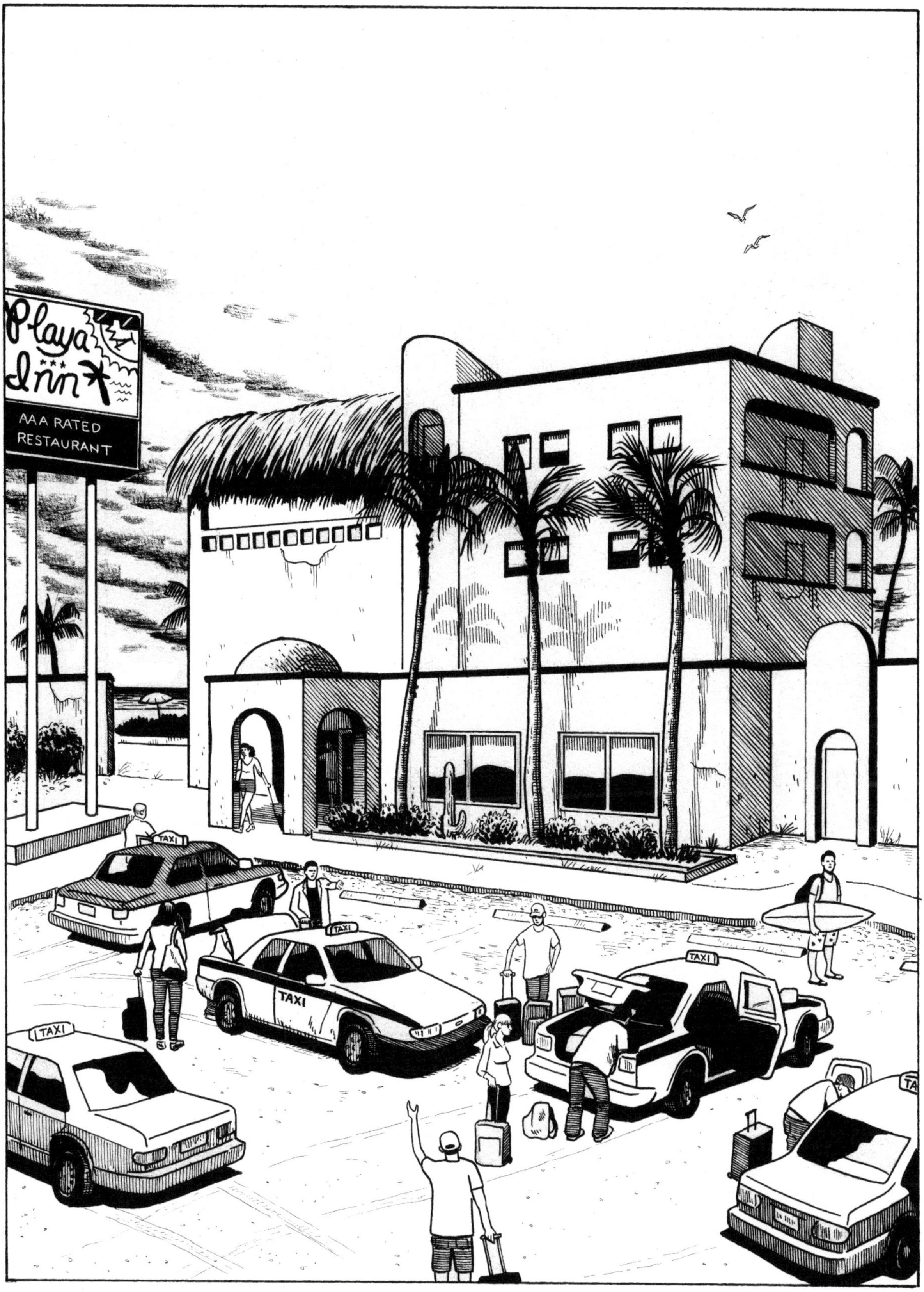
Playa Inn
AAA RATED RESTAURANT
TAXI
TAXI
TAXI
TAXI
TAXI

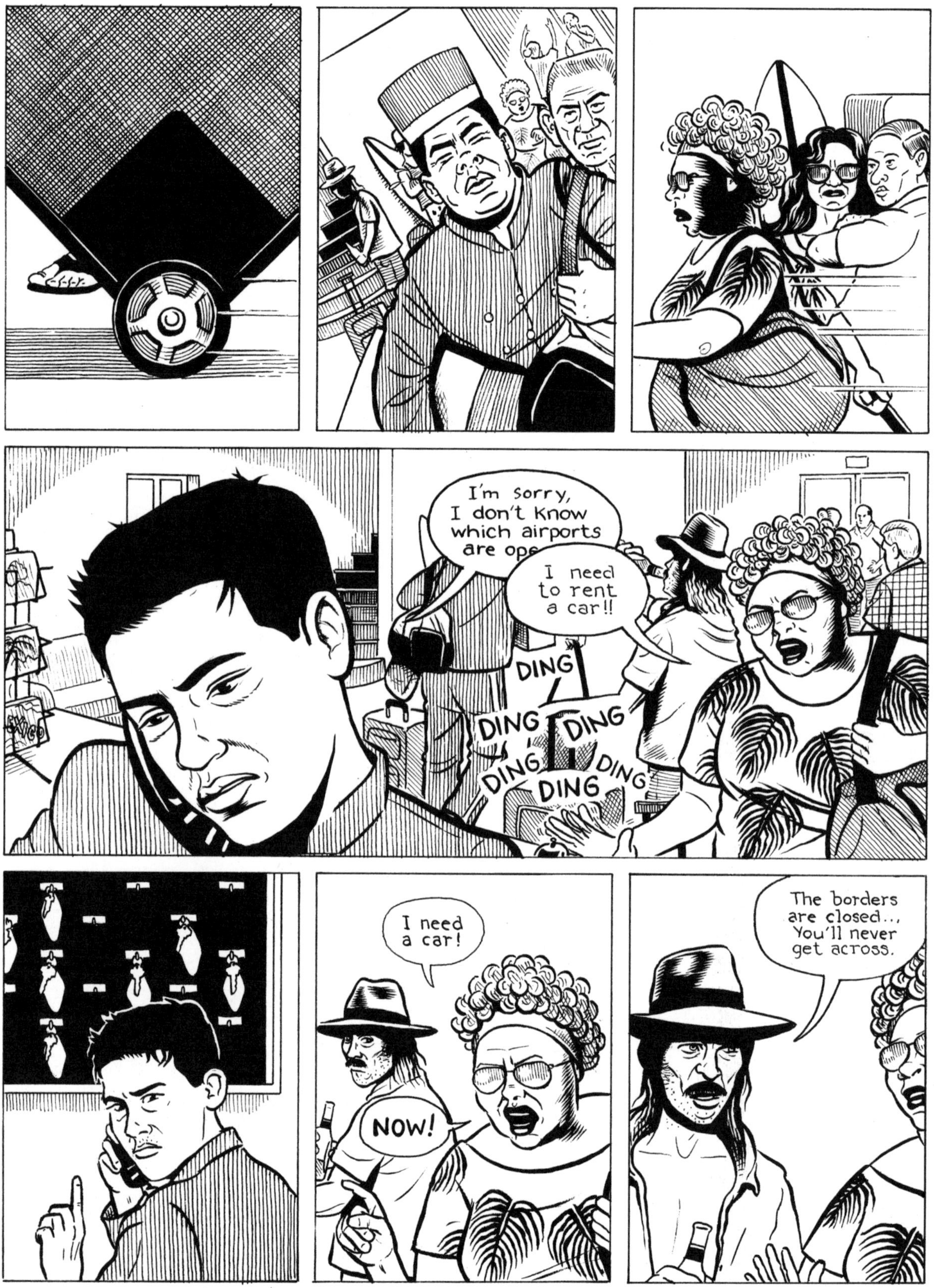
I'm sorry, I don't know which airports are ope
I need to rent a car!!
DING
DING DING
DING DING
DING
I need a car!
NOW!
The borders are closed.., You'll never get across.

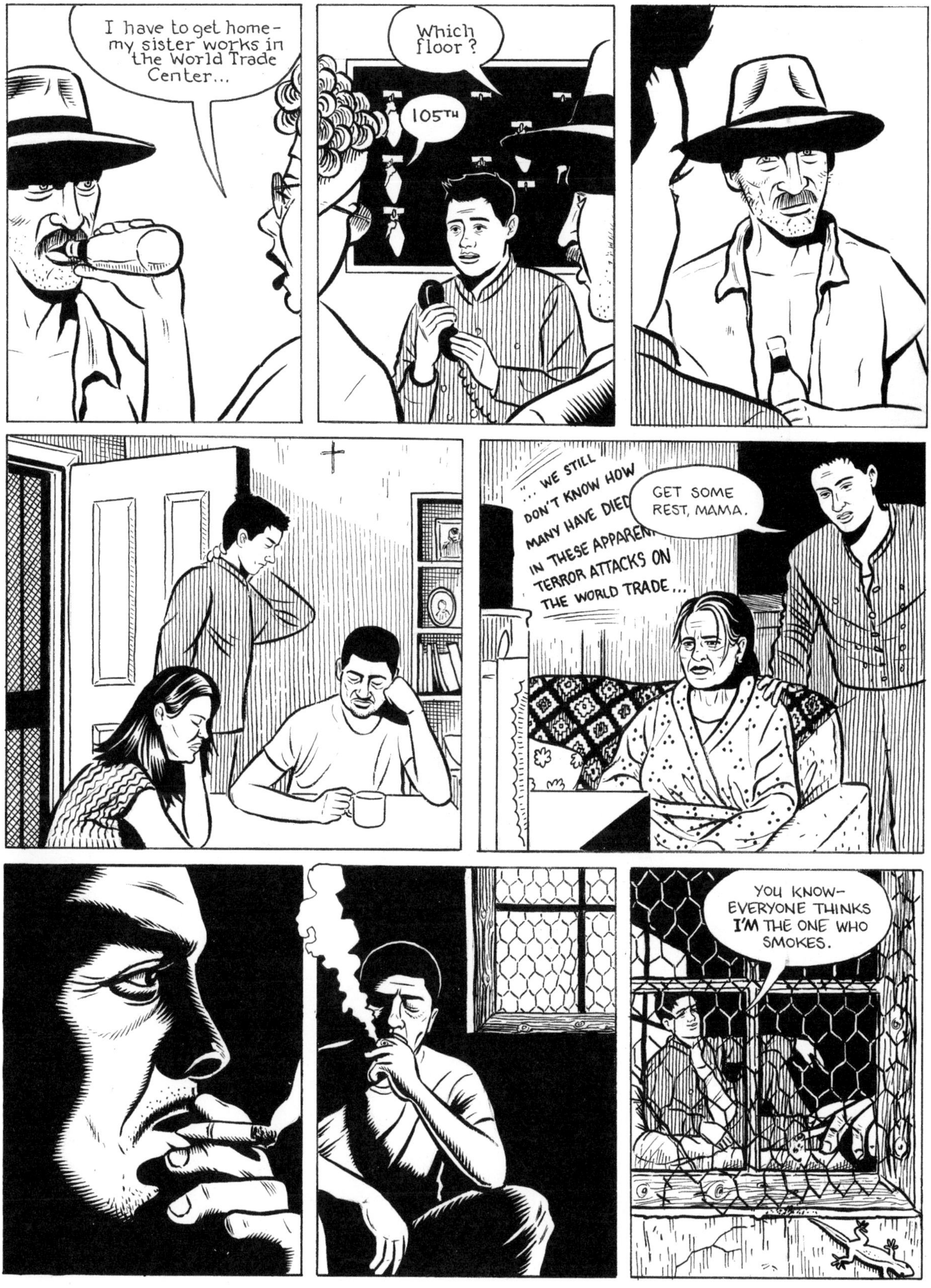

I have to get home - my sister works in the World Trade Center...
Which floor?
105TH
... WE STILL DON'T KNOW HOW MANY HAVE DIED IN THESE APPARENT TERROR ATTACKS ON THE WORLD TRADE...
GET SOME REST, MAMA.
YOU KNOW- EVERYONE THINKS I'M THE ONE WHO SMOKES.

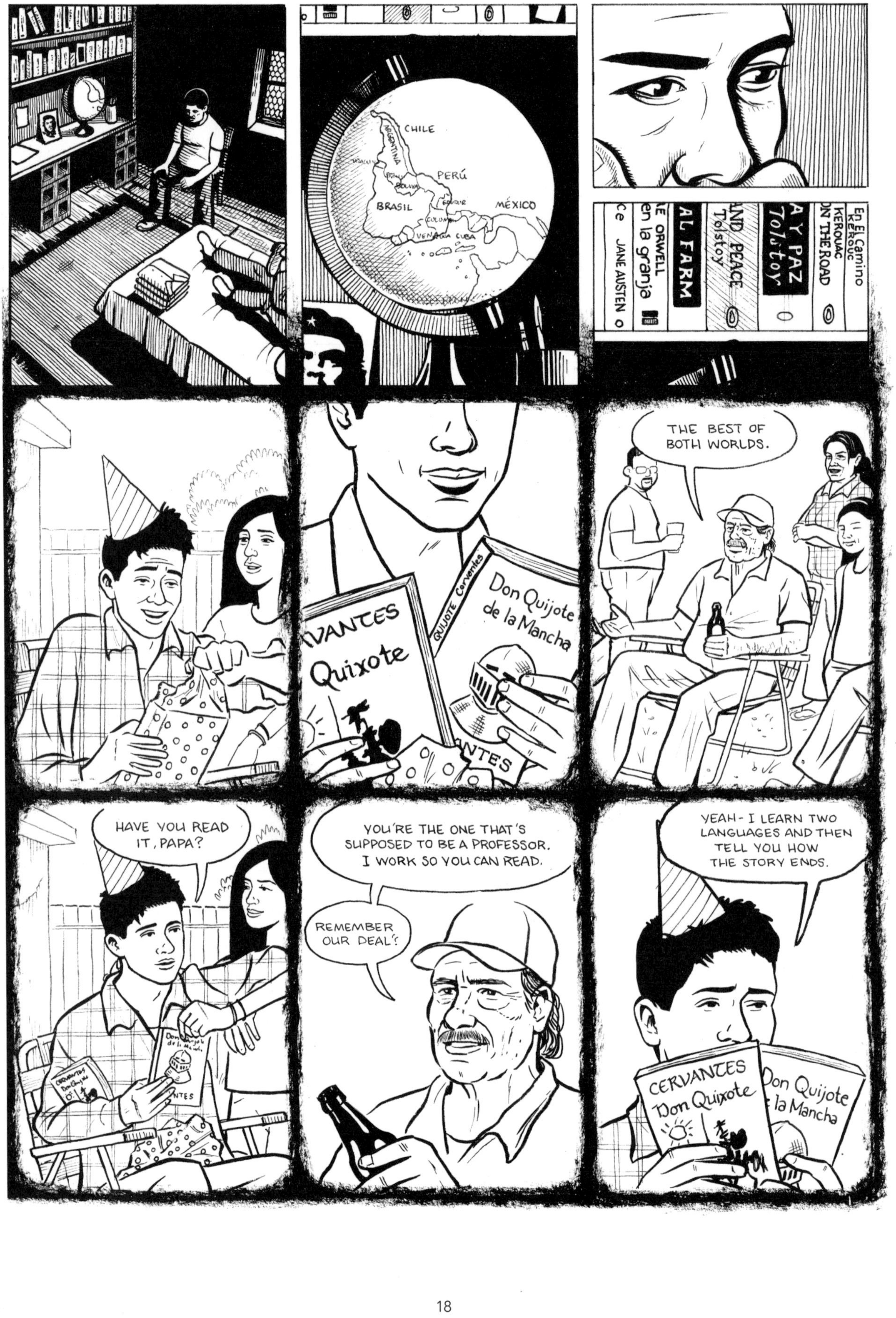
CHILE
ARGENTINA
PERÚ
BRASIL
MÉXICO
CUBA
En El Camino
KEROUAC
ON THE ROAD
A Y PAZ
Tolstoy
AND PEACE
Tolstoy
AL FARM
E ORWELL
en la granja
JANE AUSTEN
VANTES
Quixote
QUIJOTE Cervantes
Don Quijote
de la Mancha
NTES
THE BEST OF BOTH WORLDS.
HAVE YOU READ IT, PAPA?
YOU'RE THE ONE THAT'S SUPPOSED TO BE A PROFESSOR. I WORK SO YOU CAN READ.
REMEMBER OUR DEAL?
YEAH- I LEARN TWO LANGUAGES AND THEN TELL YOU HOW THE STORY ENDS.
CERVANTES
Don Quixote
Don Quijote
la Mancha

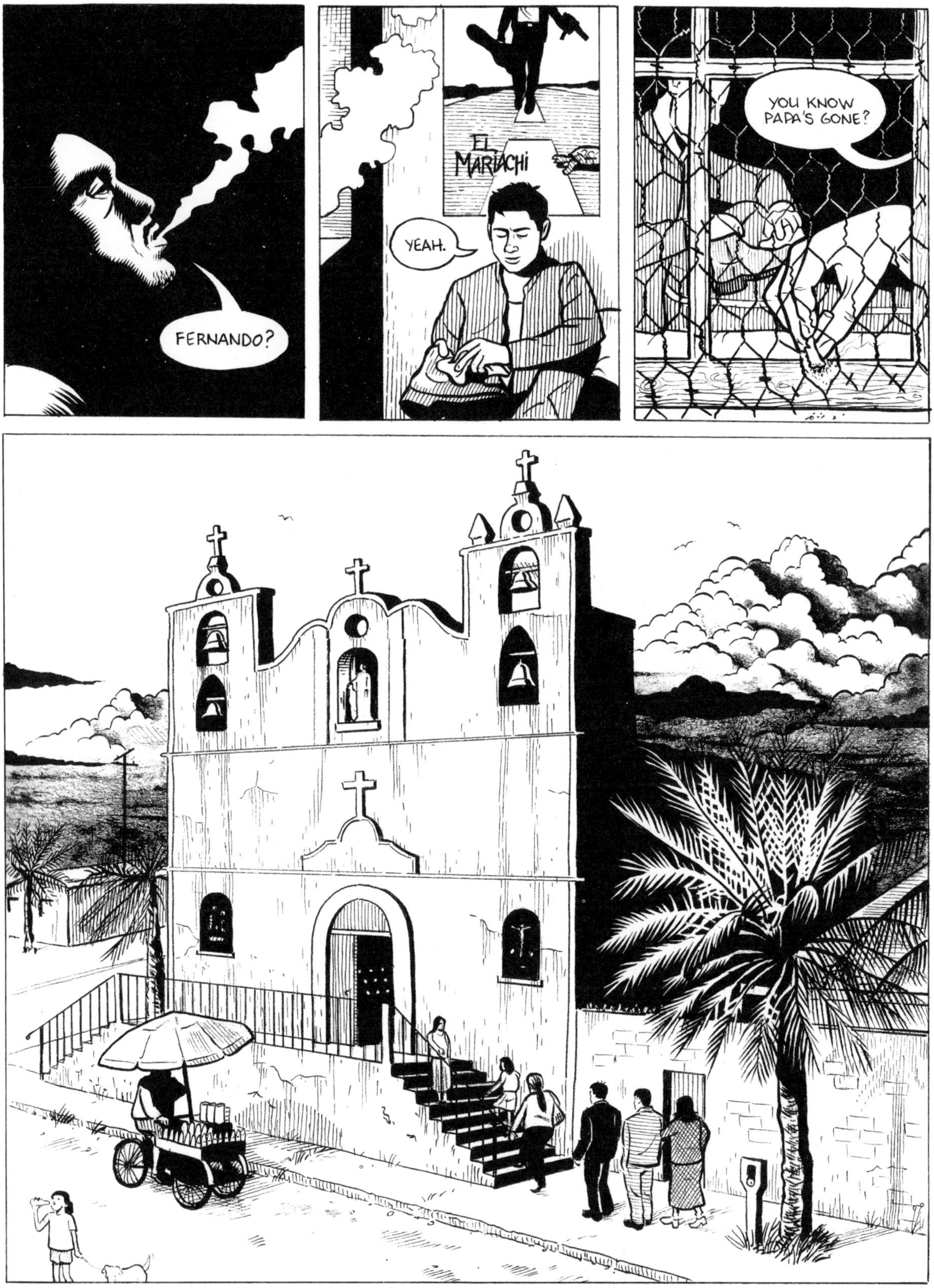
FERNANDO?
EL MARIACHI
YEAH.
YOU KNOW PAPA'S GONE?

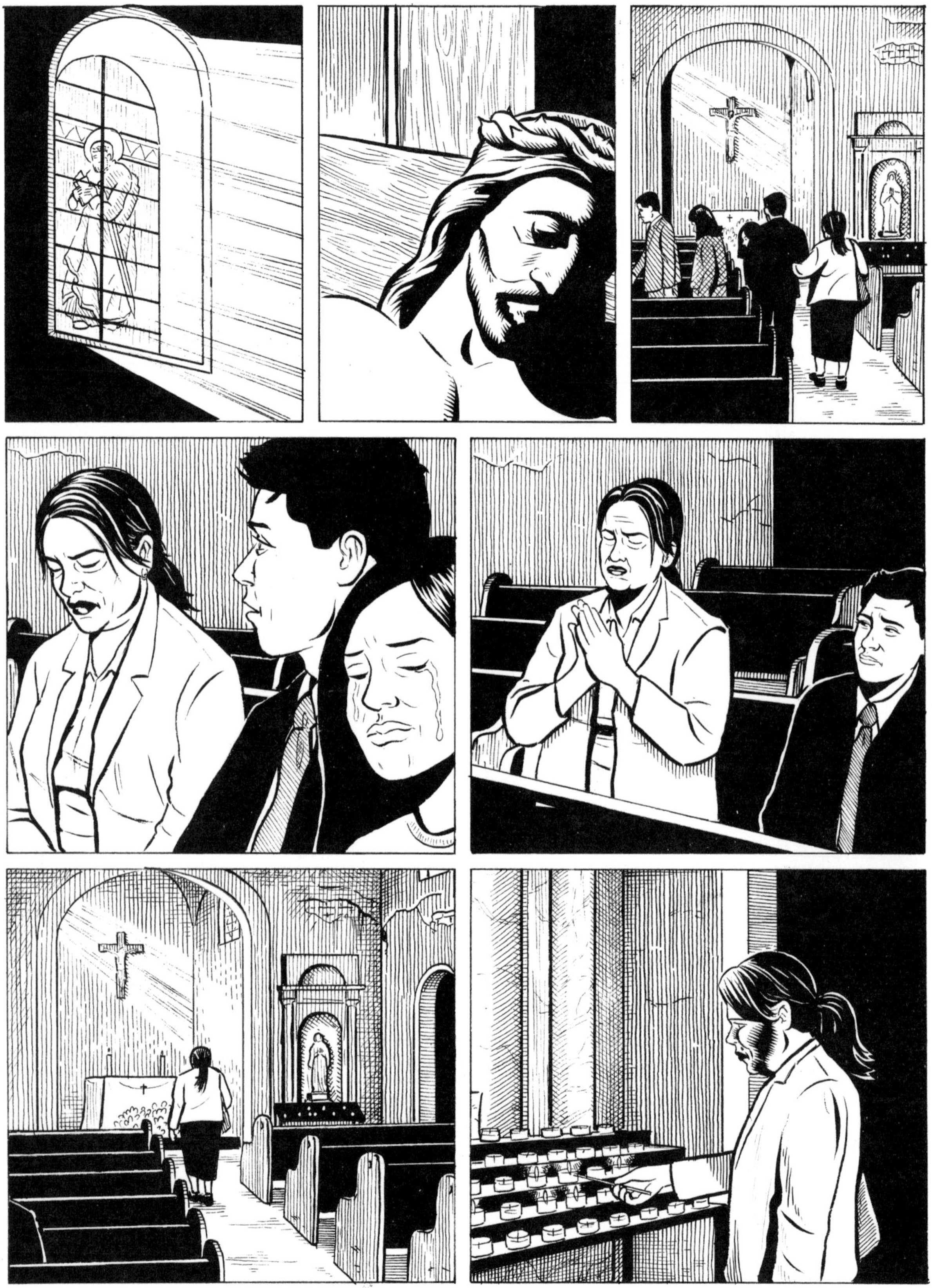

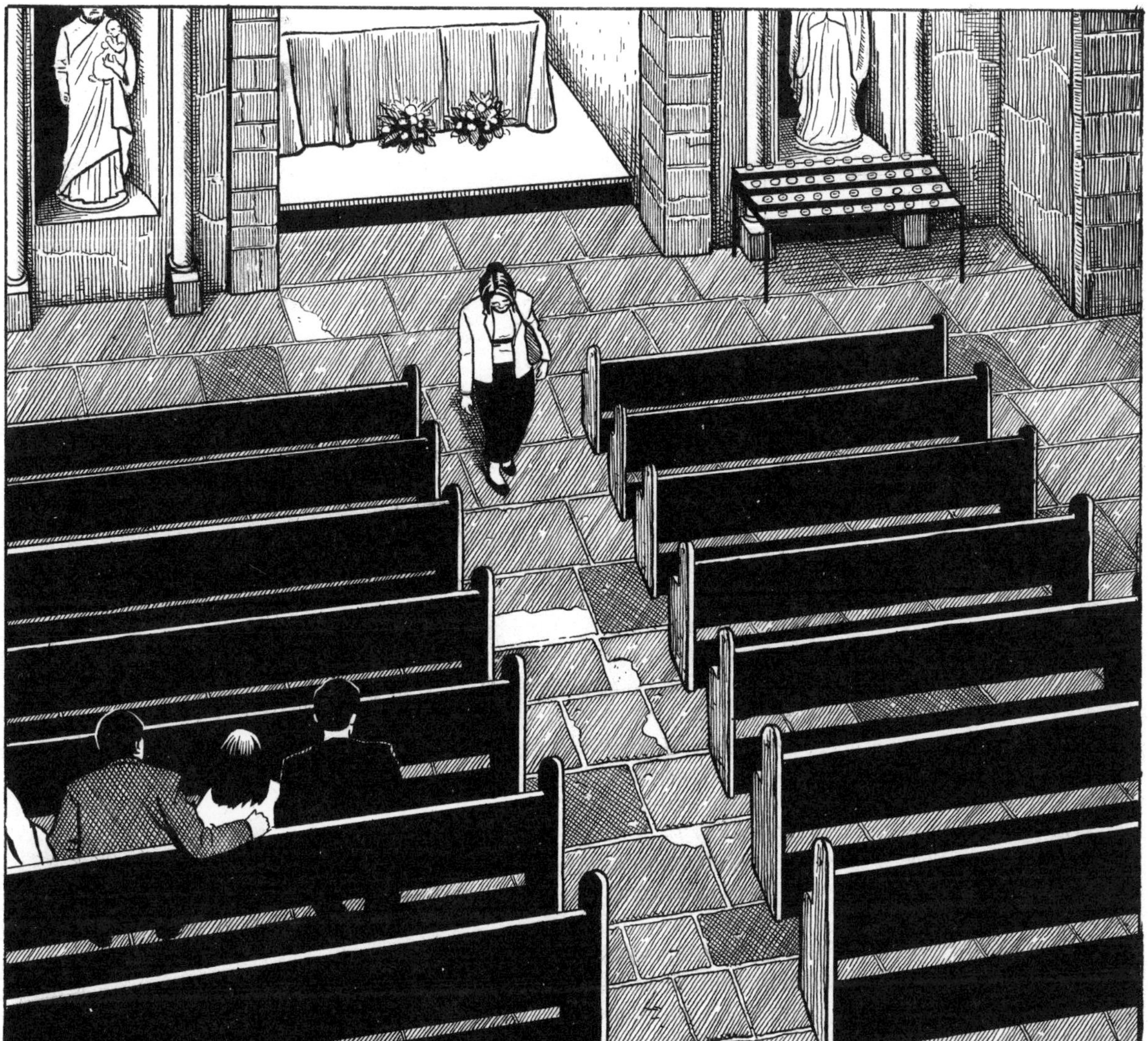

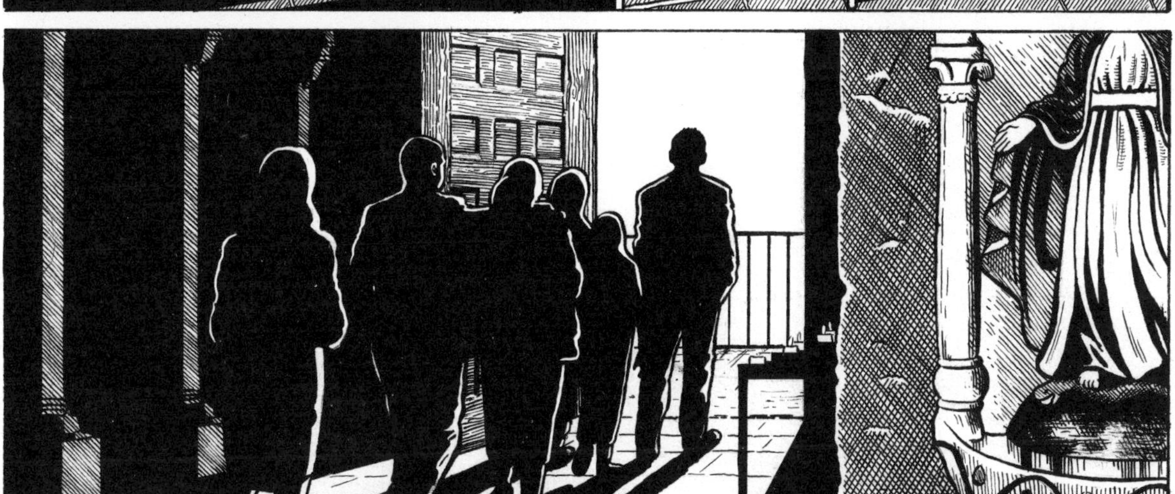

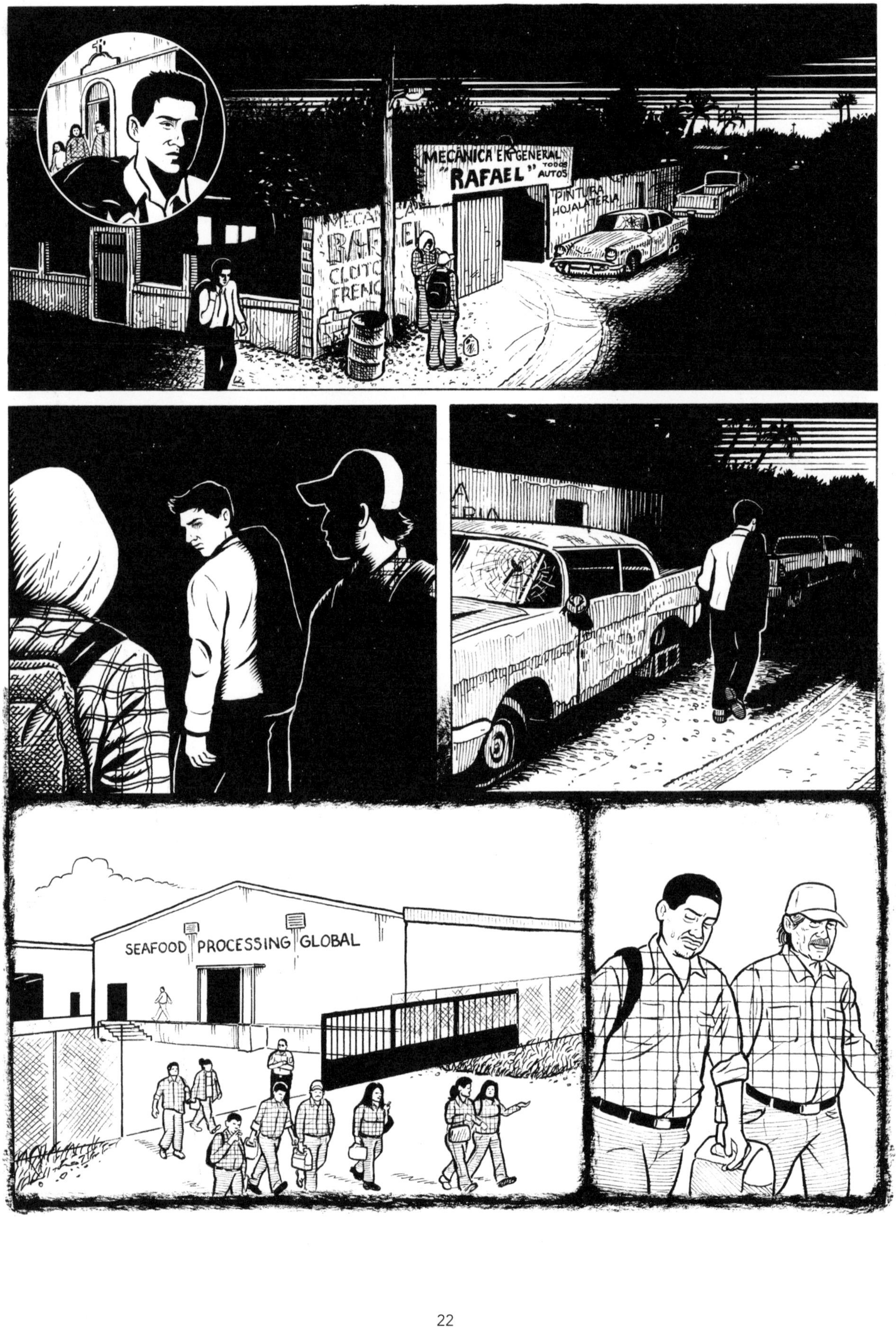

MECÁNICA EN GENERAL
"RAFAEL" TODOS AUTOS
PINTURA
HOJALATERIA
SEAFOOD PROCESSING GLOBAL

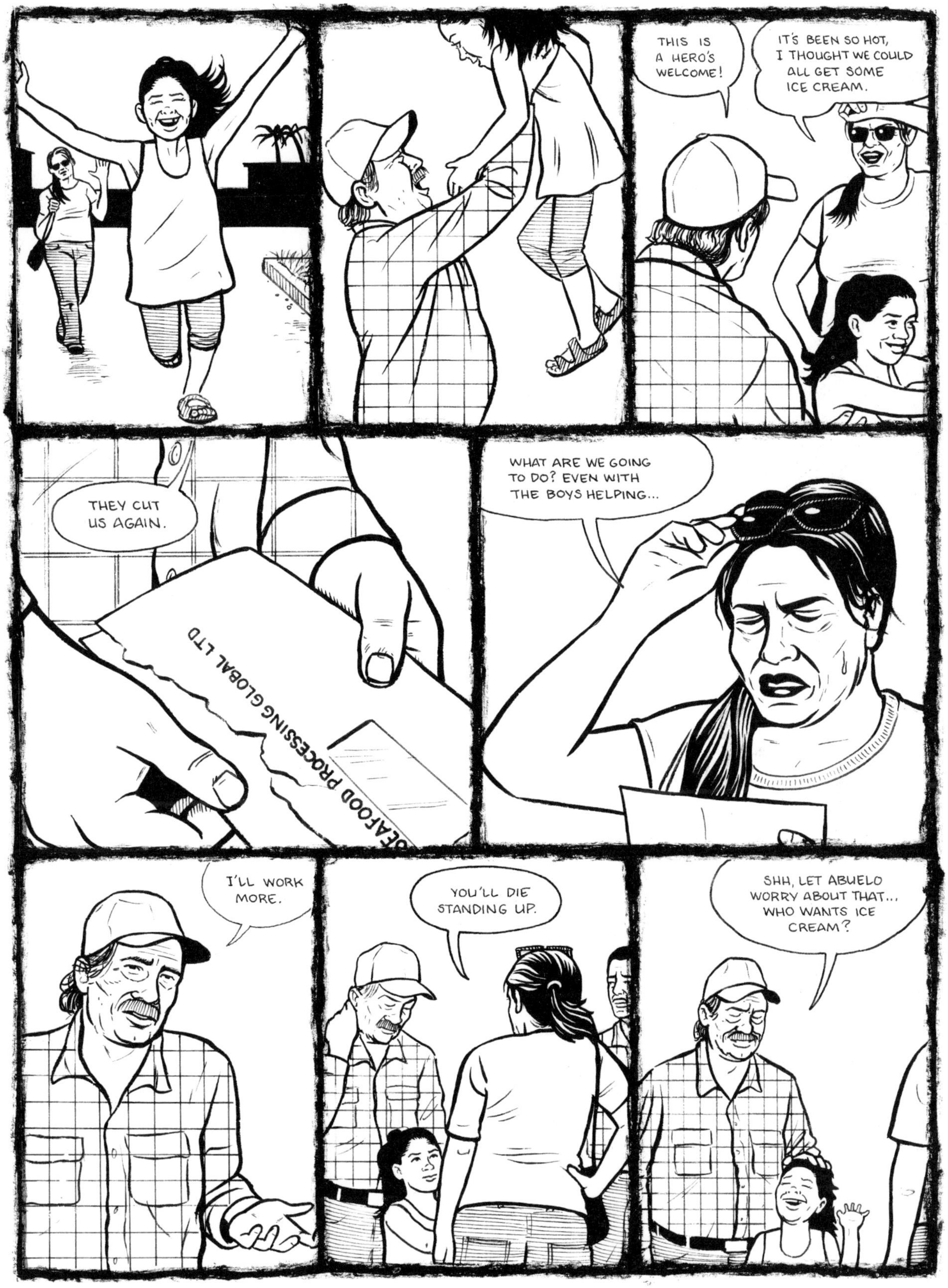
THIS IS A HERO'S WELCOME!
IT'S BEEN SO HOT, I THOUGHT WE COULD ALL GET SOME ICE CREAM.
THEY CUT US AGAIN.
SEAFOOD PROCESSING GLOBAL LTD
WHAT ARE WE GOING TO DO? EVEN WITH THE BOYS HELPING...
I'LL WORK MORE.
YOU'LL DIE STANDING UP.
SHH, LET ABUELO WORRY ABOUT THAT... WHO WANTS ICE CREAM?

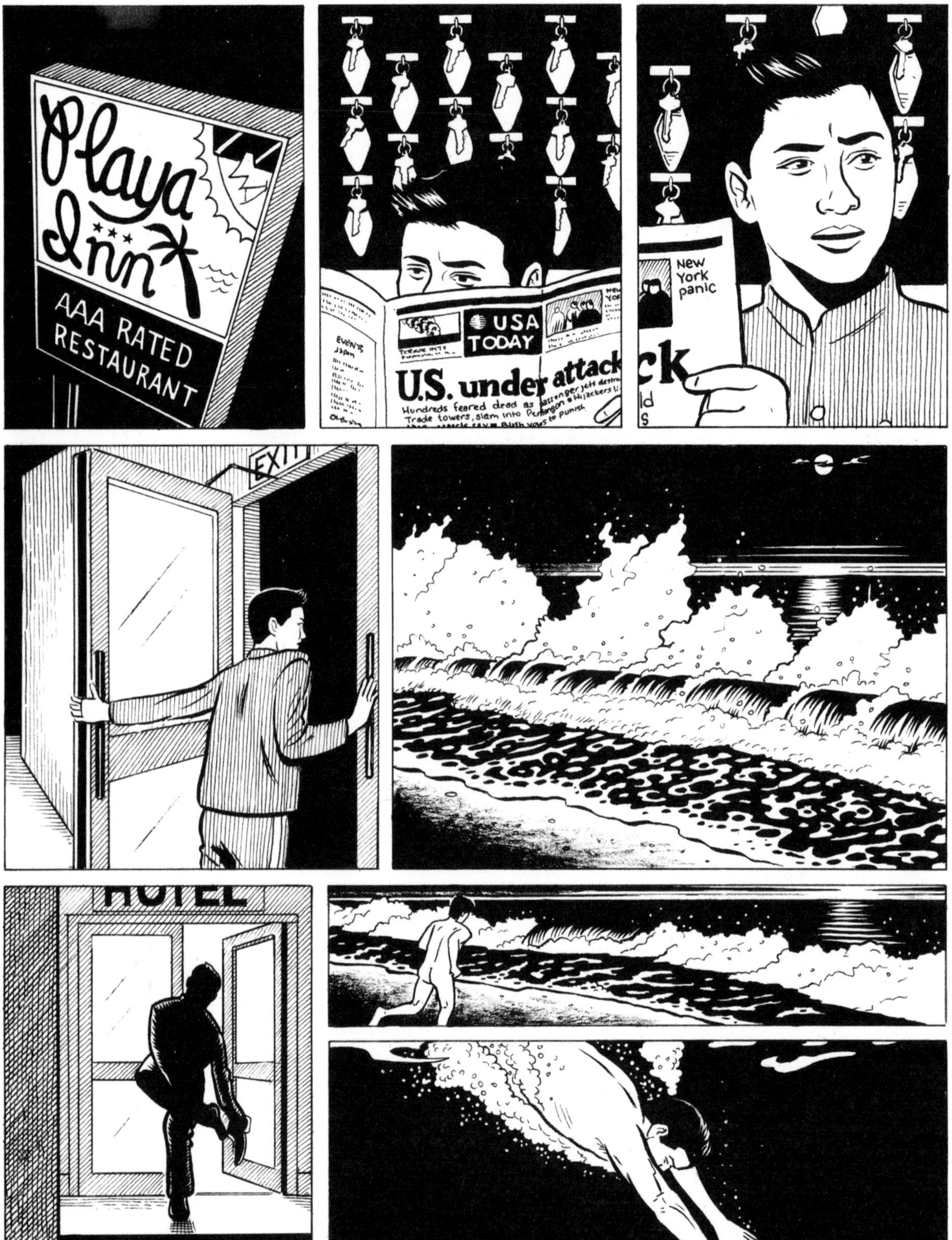
Playa Inn
AAA RATED RESTAURANT
USA TODAY
U.S. under attack
Hundreds feared dead as
New York panic
EXIT
HOTEL

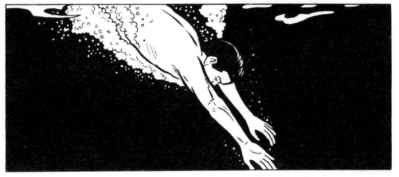

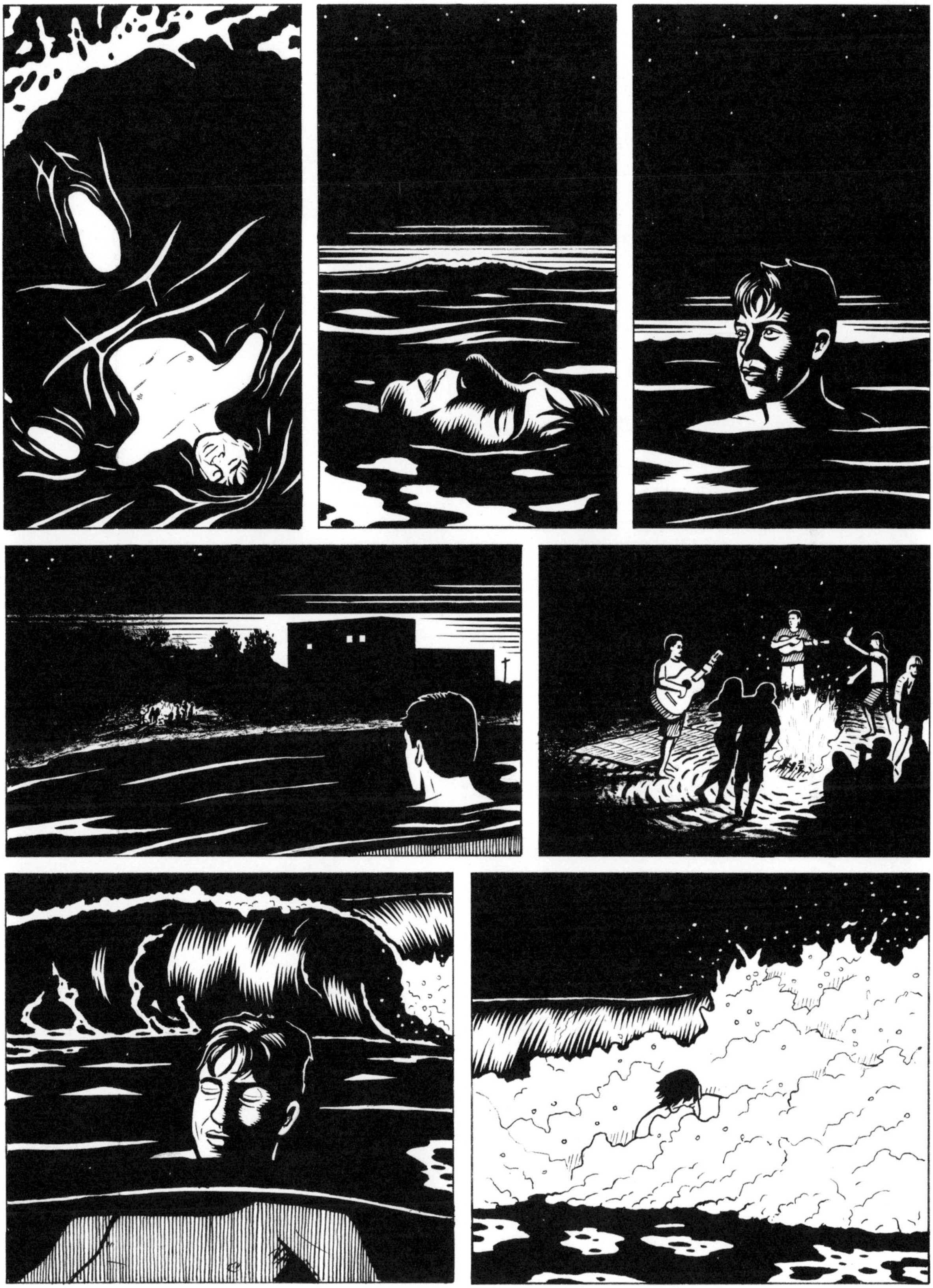

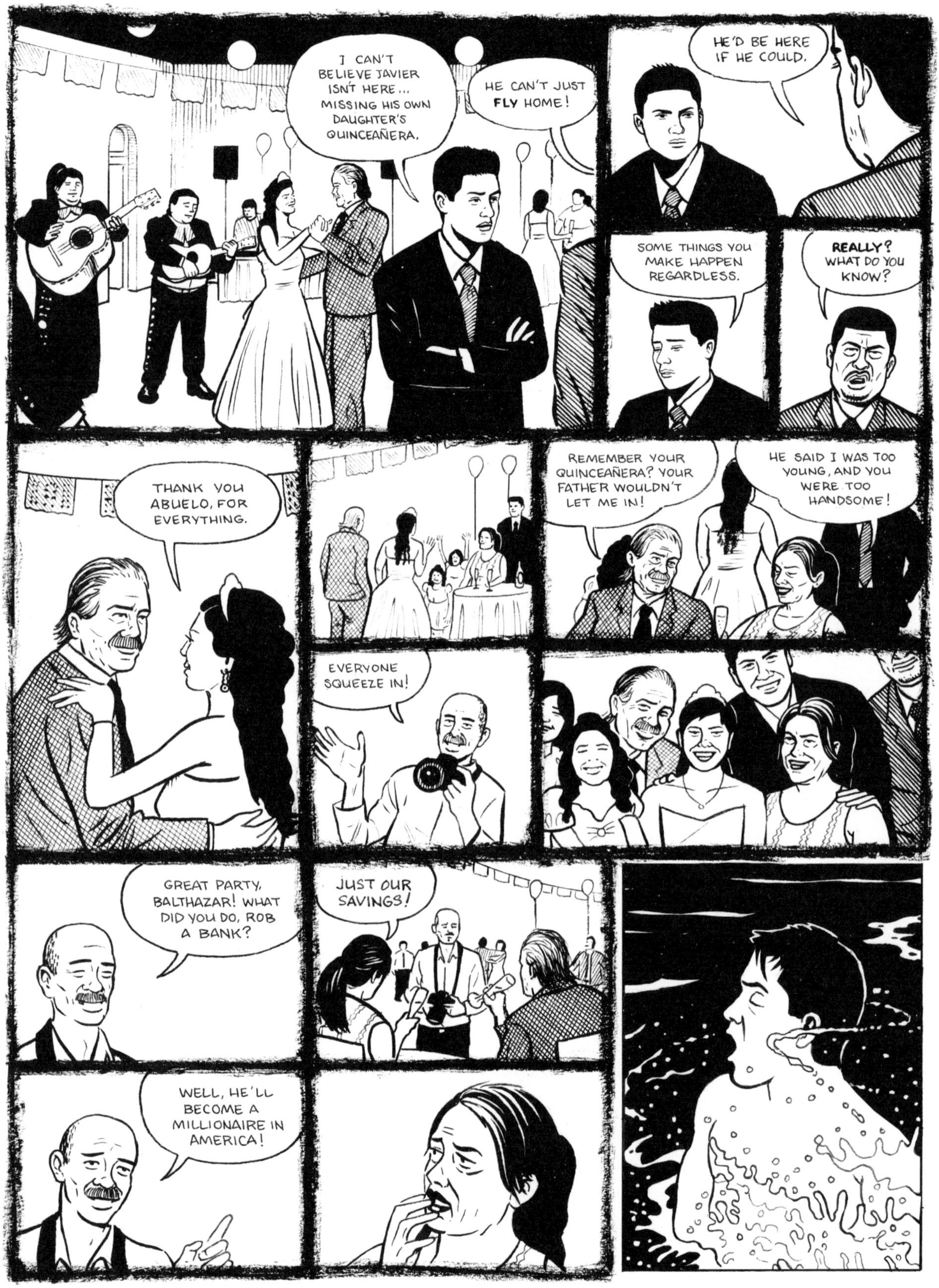
I CAN'T BELIEVE JAVIER ISN'T HERE... MISSING HIS OWN DAUGHTER'S QUINCEAÑERA.
HE CAN'T JUST **FLY** HOME!
HE'D BE HERE IF HE COULD.
SOME THINGS YOU MAKE HAPPEN REGARDLESS.
REALLY? WHAT DO YOU KNOW?
THANK YOU ABUELO, FOR EVERYTHING.
REMEMBER YOUR QUINCEAÑERA? YOUR FATHER WOULDN'T LET ME IN!
HE SAID I WAS TOO YOUNG, AND YOU WERE TOO HANDSOME!
EVERYONE SQUEEZE IN!
GREAT PARTY, BALTHAZAR! WHAT DID YOU DO, ROB A BANK?
JUST OUR SAVINGS!
WELL, HE'LL BECOME A MILLIONAIRE IN AMERICA!

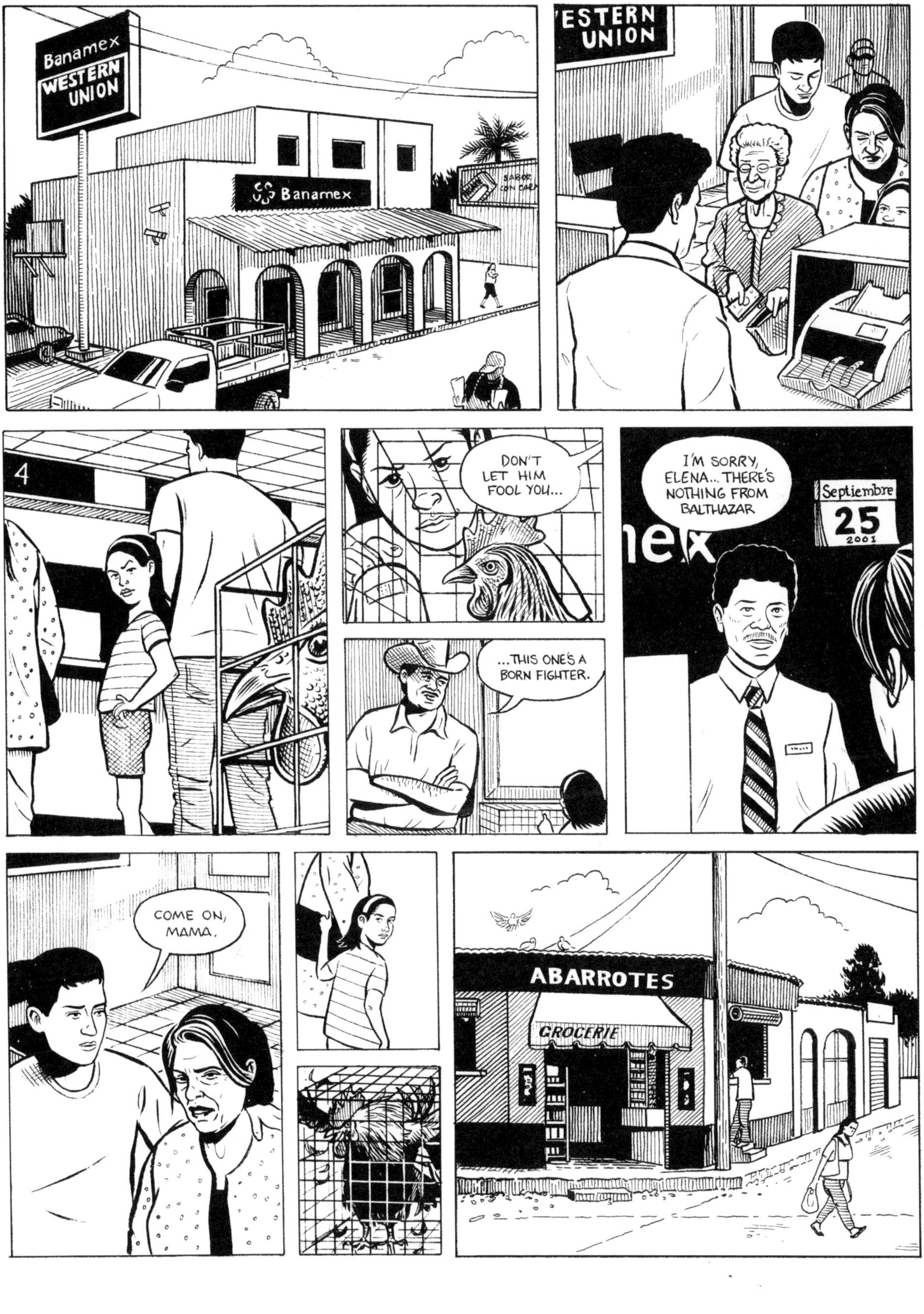
Banamex
WESTERN UNION
Banamex
WESTERN UNION
DON'T LET HIM FOOL YOU...
...THIS ONE'S A BORN FIGHTER.
I'M SORRY, ELENA... THERE'S NOTHING FROM BALTHAZAR
Septiembre
25
2001
COME ON, MAMA.
ABARROTES
GROCERIE

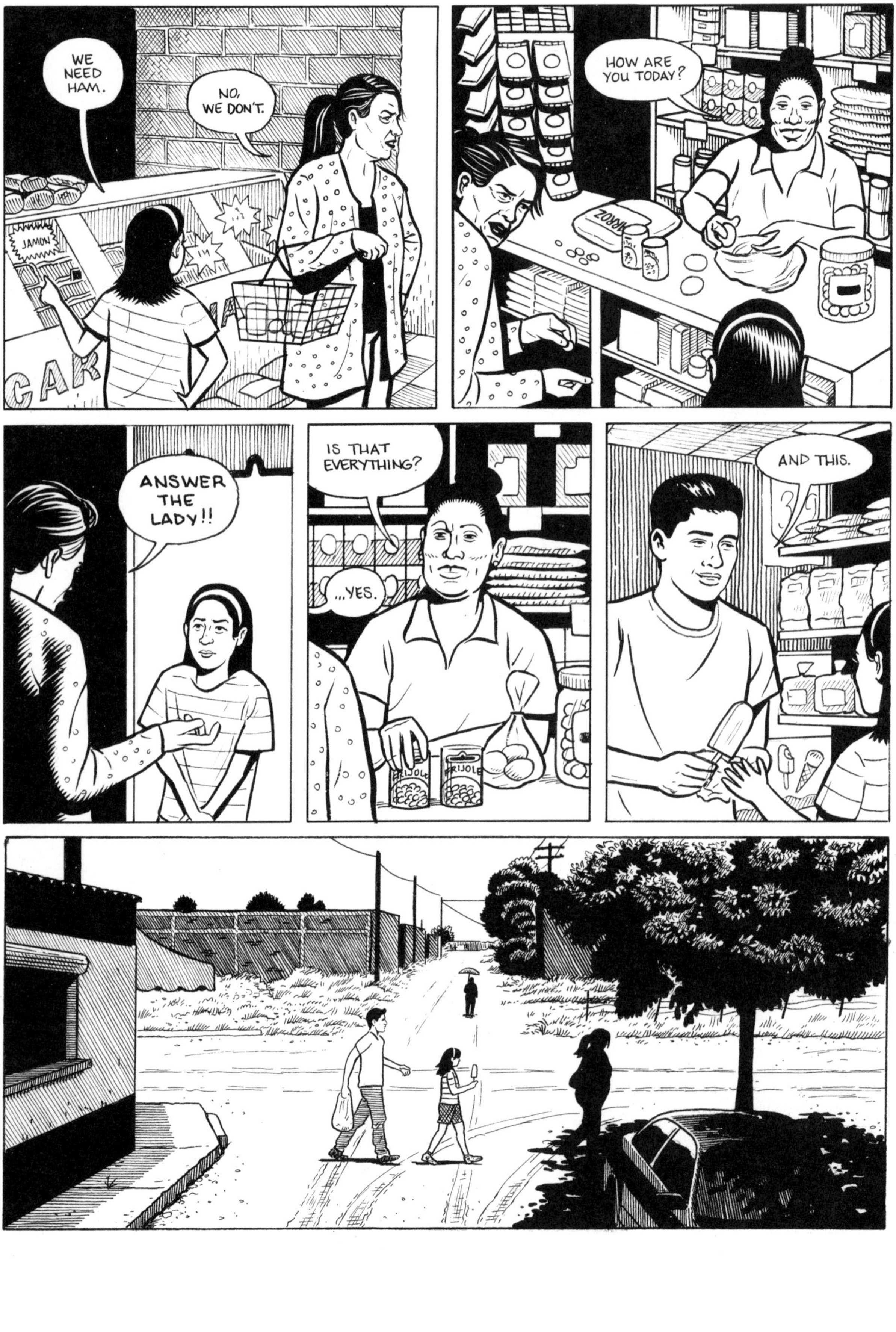
WE NEED HAM.
NO, WE DON'T.
JAMON
HOW ARE YOU TODAY?
ANSWER THE LADY!!
IS THAT EVERYTHING?
...YES.
FRIJOLE
FRIJOLE
AND THIS.

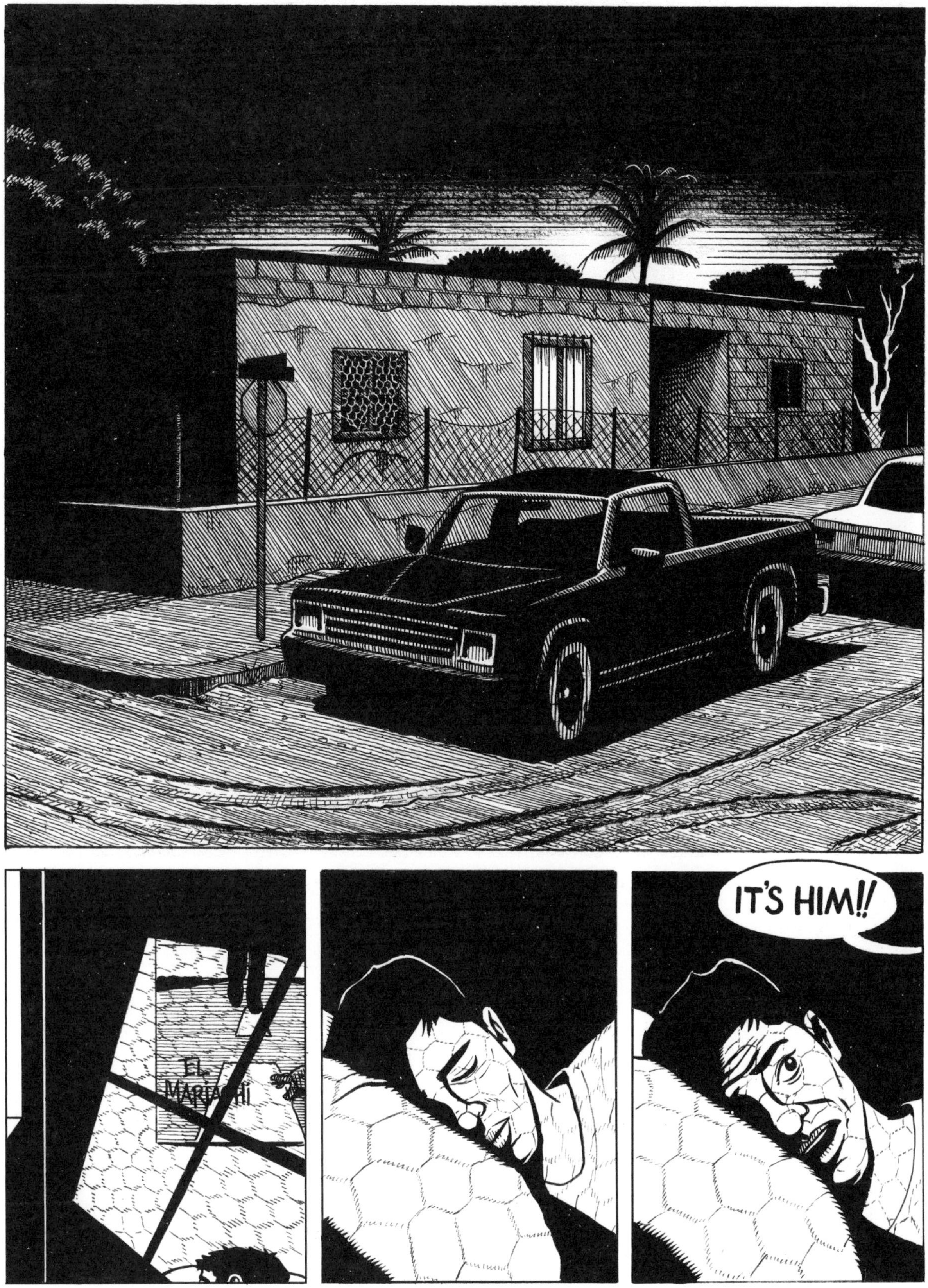
EL MARIACHI
IT'S HIM!!

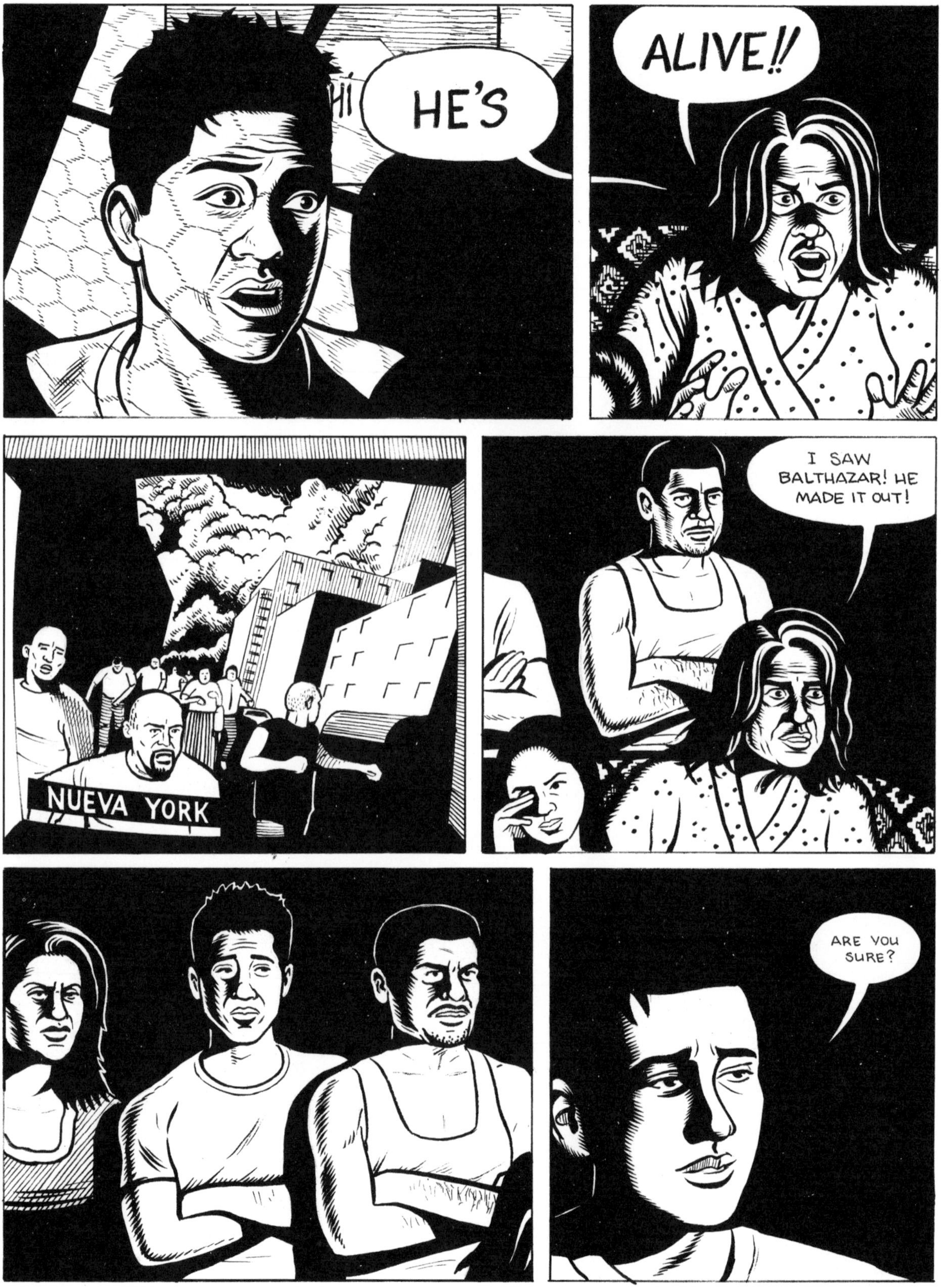
HE'S
ALIVE!!
NUEVA YORK
I SAW BALTHAZAR! HE MADE IT OUT!
ARE YOU SURE?

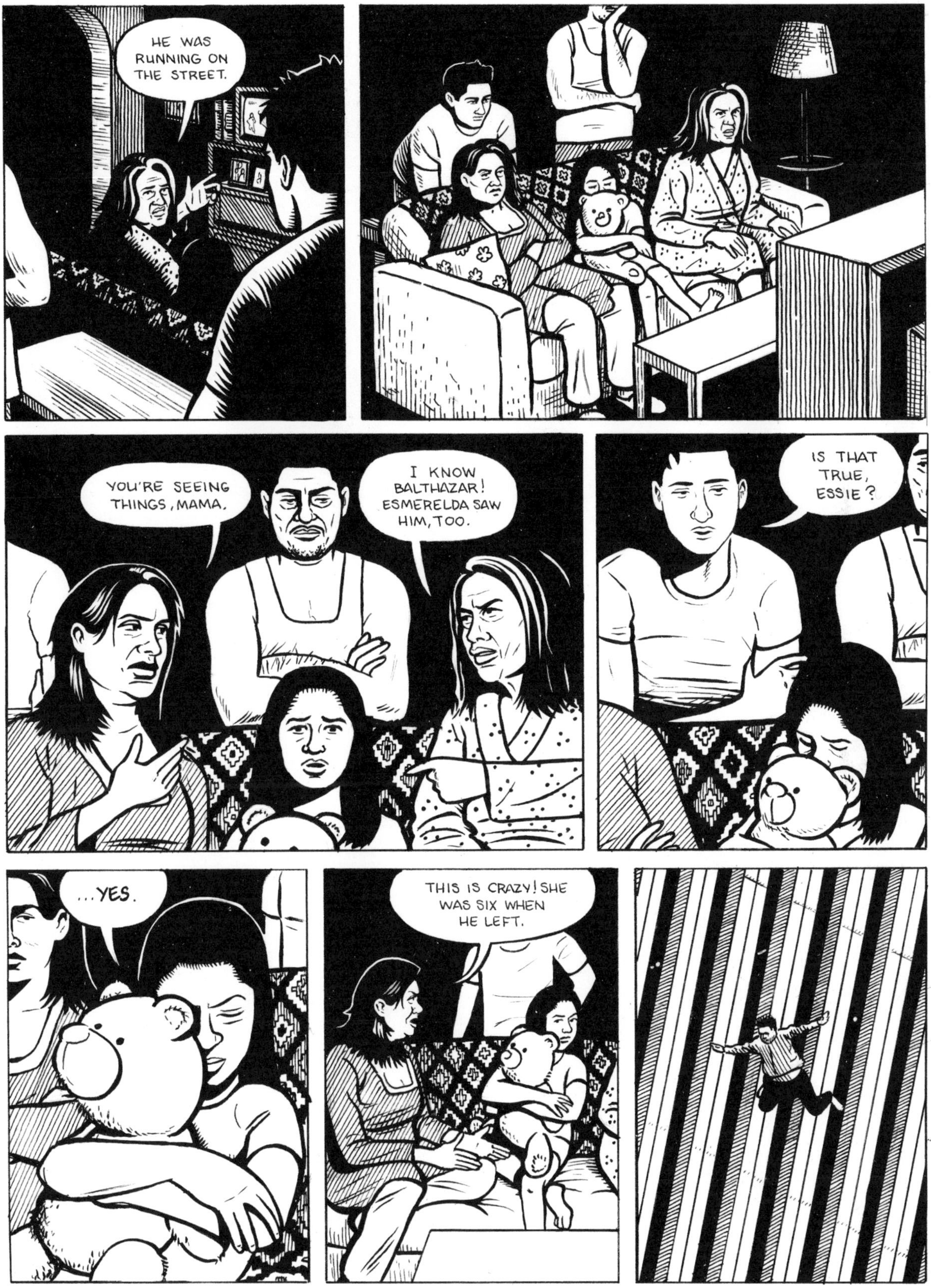
HE WAS RUNNING ON THE STREET.
YOU'RE SEEING THINGS, MAMA.
I KNOW BALTHAZAR! ESMERELDA SAW HIM, TOO.
IS THAT TRUE, ESSIE?
...YES.
THIS IS CRAZY! SHE WAS SIX WHEN HE LEFT.

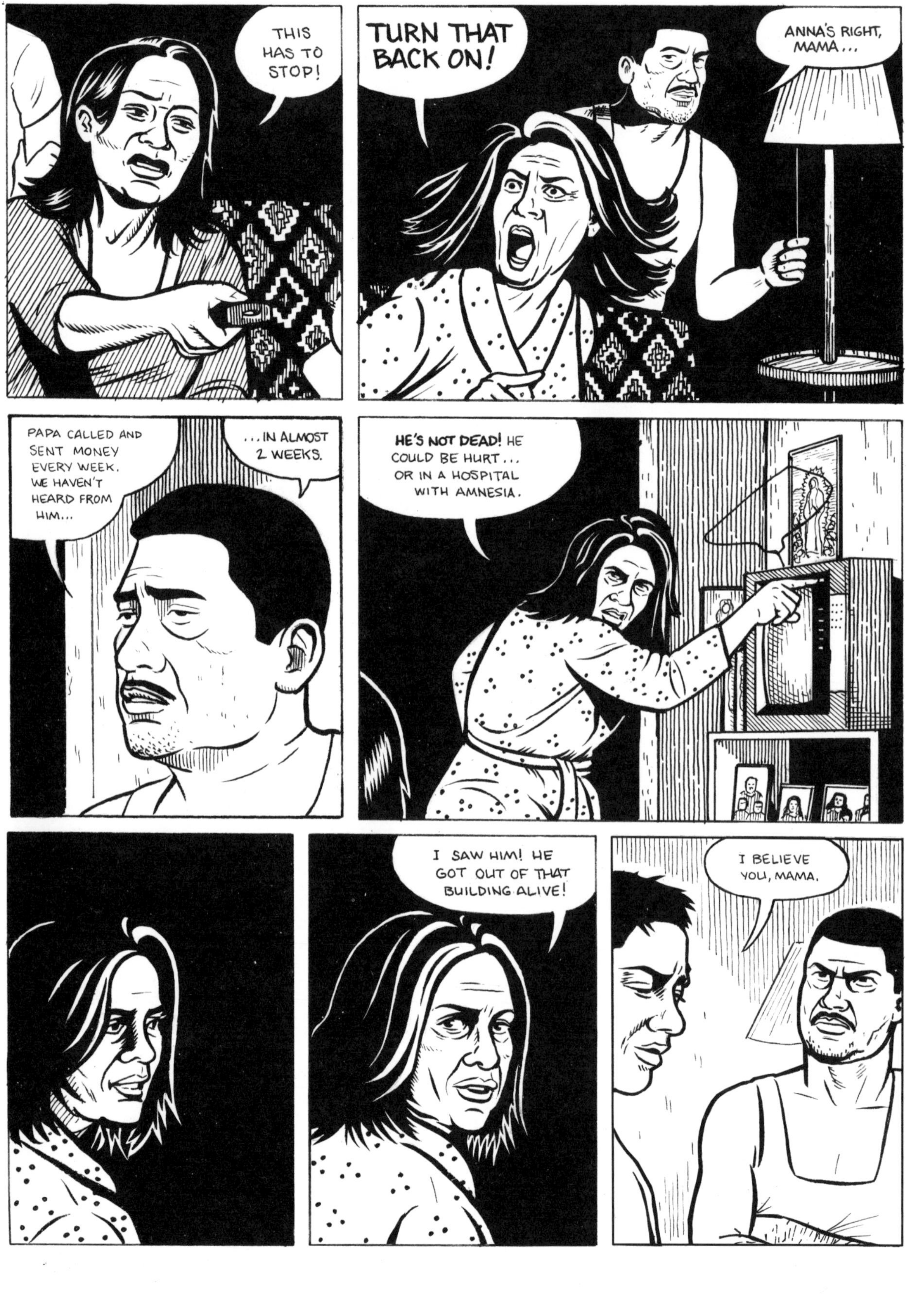
THIS HAS TO STOP!
TURN THAT BACK ON!
ANNA'S RIGHT, MAMA...
PAPA CALLED AND SENT MONEY EVERY WEEK. WE HAVEN'T HEARD FROM HIM...
...IN ALMOST 2 WEEKS.
HE'S NOT DEAD! HE COULD BE HURT... OR IN A HOSPITAL WITH AMNESIA.
I SAW HIM! HE GOT OUT OF THAT BUILDING ALIVE!
I BELIEVE YOU, MAMA.

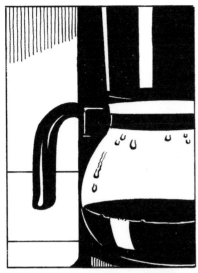

WHERE'S LUIS AND ANNA?

THEY LEFT EARLY.

TO GET MOM A JOB.

WHAT?

AT THE FACTORY. PAPA SAID WE NEEDED THE MONEY FOR OUR SCHOOL.

I DON'T KNOW WHY. NONE OF US ARE GOING TO COLLEGE ANYWAY...

WHAT? YOU QUIT! AND YOU'RE THE SMART ONE!

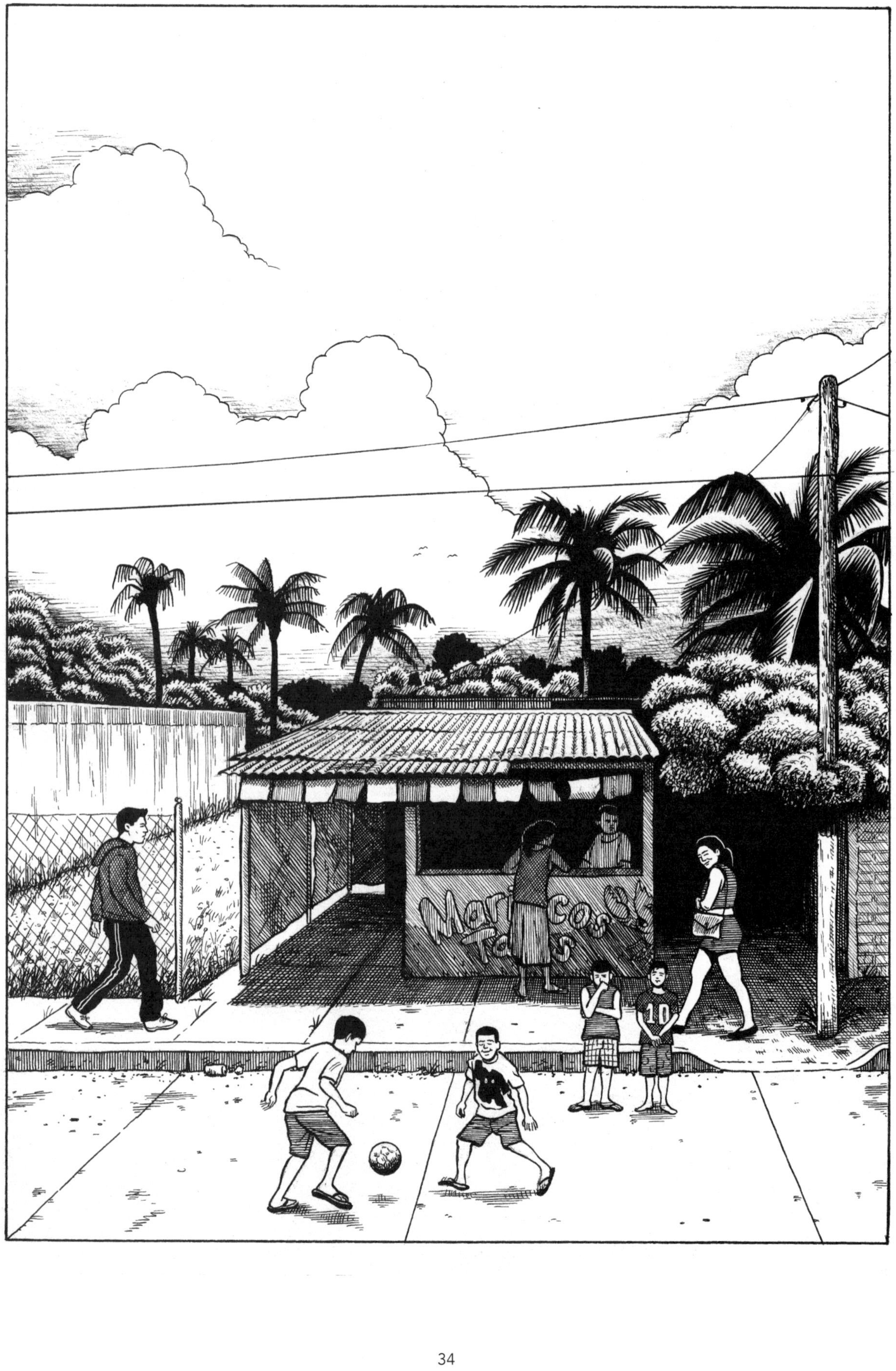
10

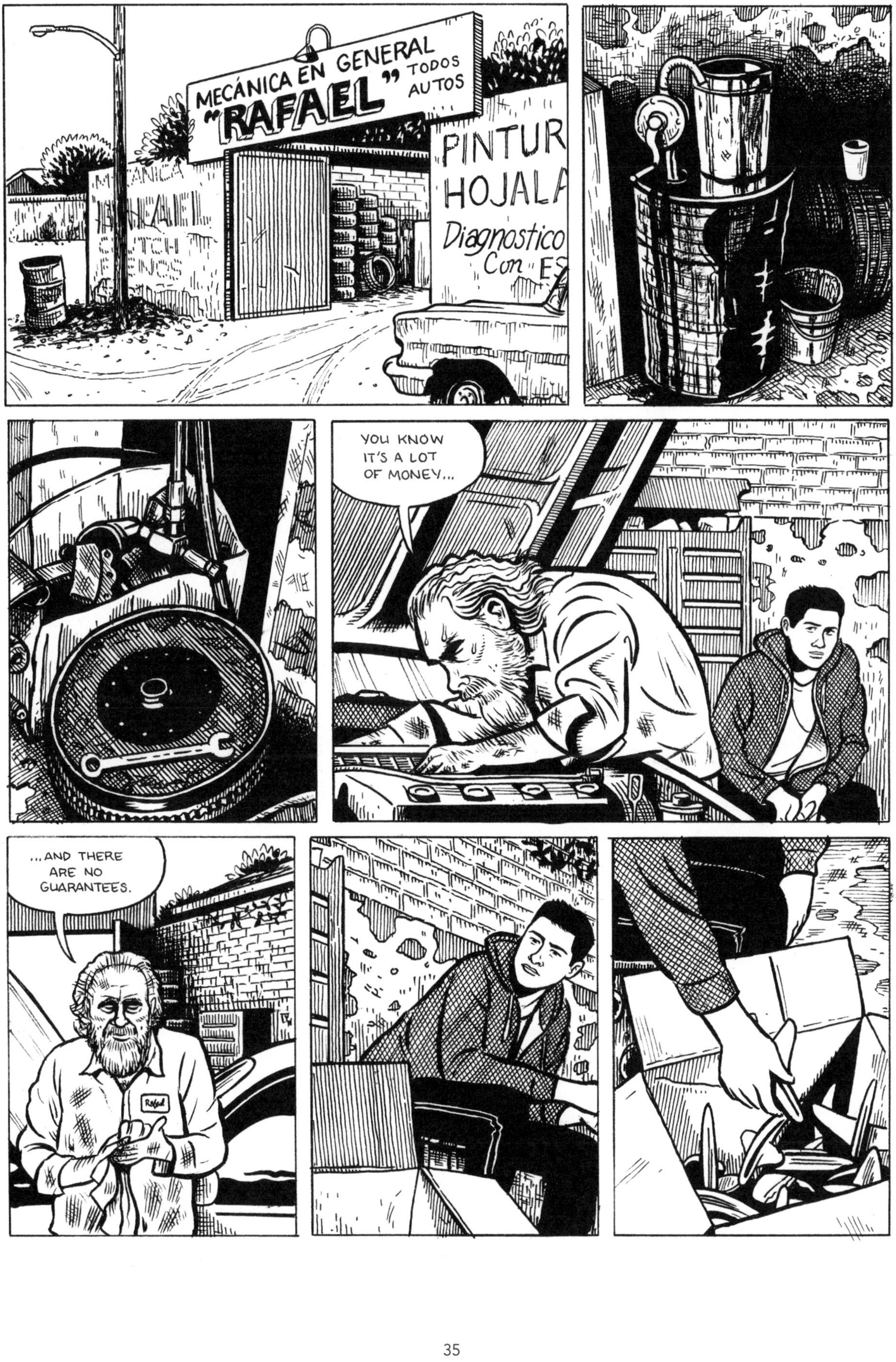
MECÁNICA EN GENERAL
"RAFAEL"
TODOS AUTOS
PINTUR
HOJALA
Diagnostico
Con ES
YOU KNOW IT'S A LOT OF MONEY...
...AND THERE ARE NO GUARANTEES.
Rafael

THAT'S OFF A '54 FORD.

HOW COME THEY DON'T MAKE THINGS THIS BEAUTIFUL ANYMORE?

NO MONEY IN IT.

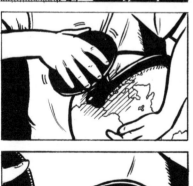

I'M THE OLDEST, I SHOULD GO.

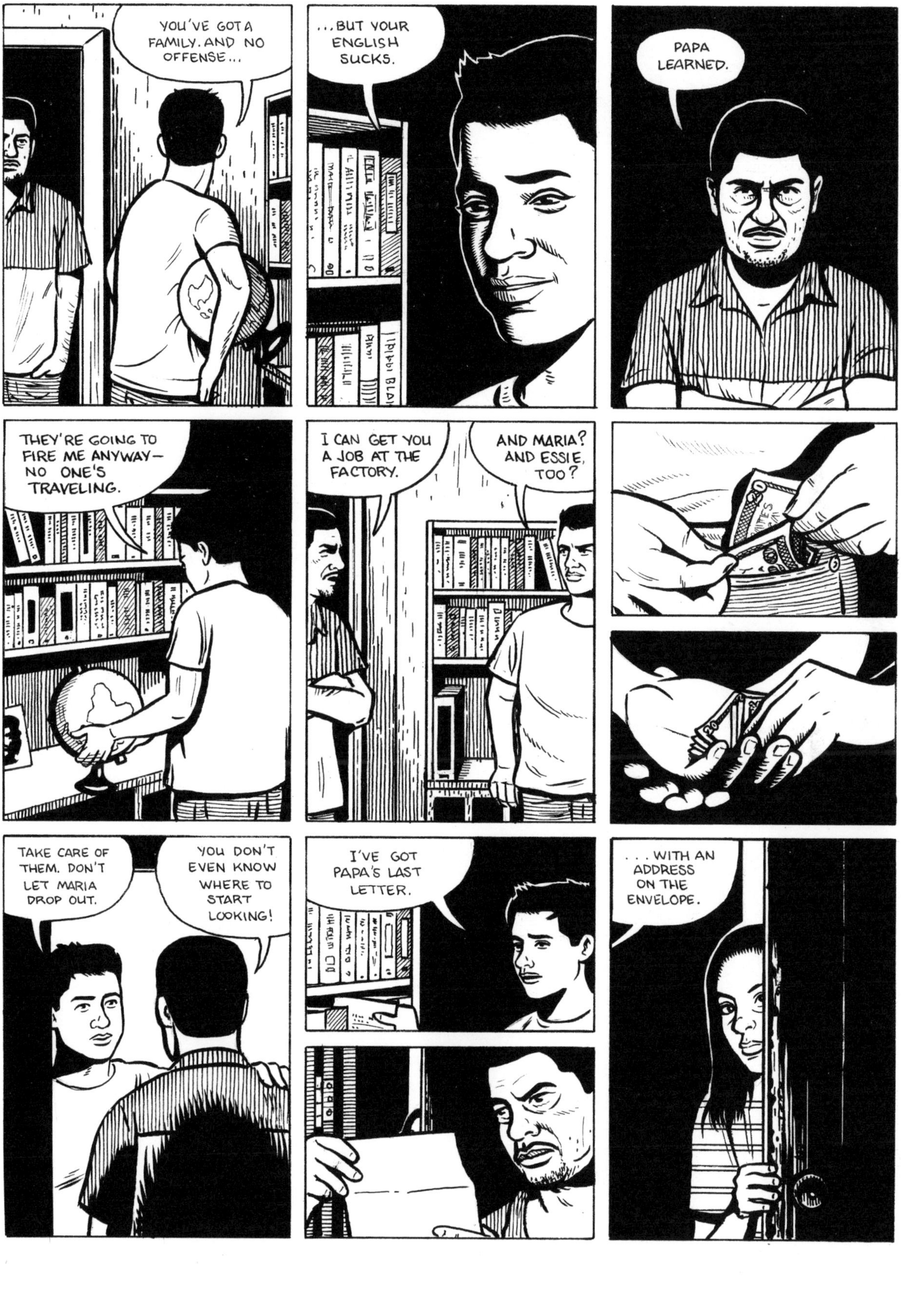
YOU'VE GOT A FAMILY. AND NO OFFENSE...
...BUT YOUR ENGLISH SUCKS.
PAPA LEARNED.
THEY'RE GOING TO FIRE ME ANYWAY— NO ONE'S TRAVELING.
I CAN GET YOU A JOB AT THE FACTORY.
AND MARIA? AND ESSIE, TOO?
TAKE CARE OF THEM. DON'T LET MARIA DROP OUT.
YOU DON'T EVEN KNOW WHERE TO START LOOKING!
I'VE GOT PAPA'S LAST LETTER.
...WITH AN ADDRESS ON THE ENVELOPE.

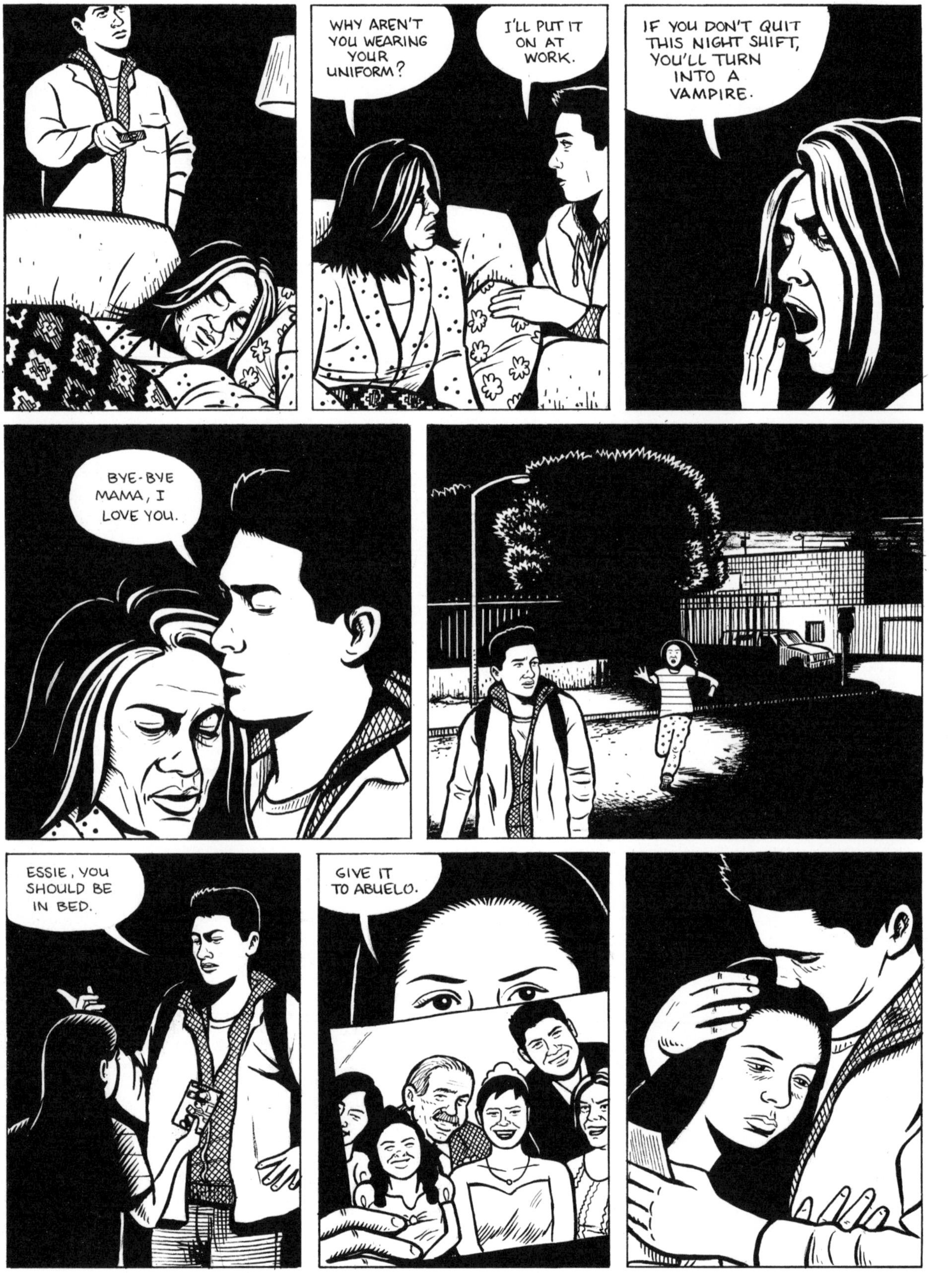
WHY AREN'T YOU WEARING YOUR UNIFORM?
I'LL PUT IT ON AT WORK.
IF YOU DON'T QUIT THIS NIGHT SHIFT, YOU'LL TURN INTO A VAMPIRE.
BYE-BYE MAMA, I LOVE YOU.
ESSIE, YOU SHOULD BE IN BED.
GIVE IT TO ABUELO.

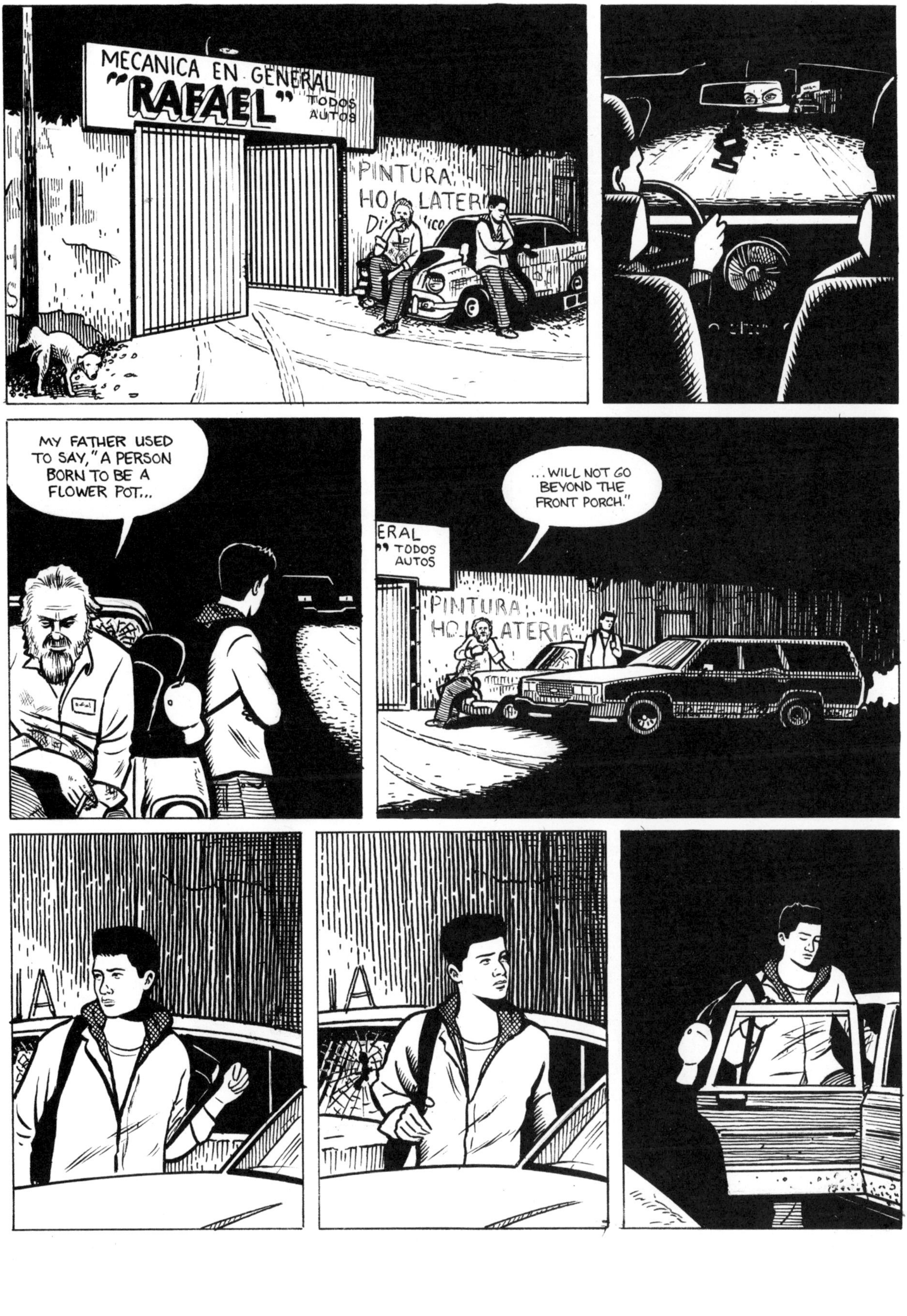
MECANICA EN GENERAL
"RAFAEL" TODOS AUTOS
PINTURA
HOJALATERIA
MY FATHER USED TO SAY, "A PERSON BORN TO BE A FLOWER POT...
...WILL NOT GO BEYOND THE FRONT PORCH."
ERAL
" TODOS AUTOS
PINTURA
HOJALATERIA

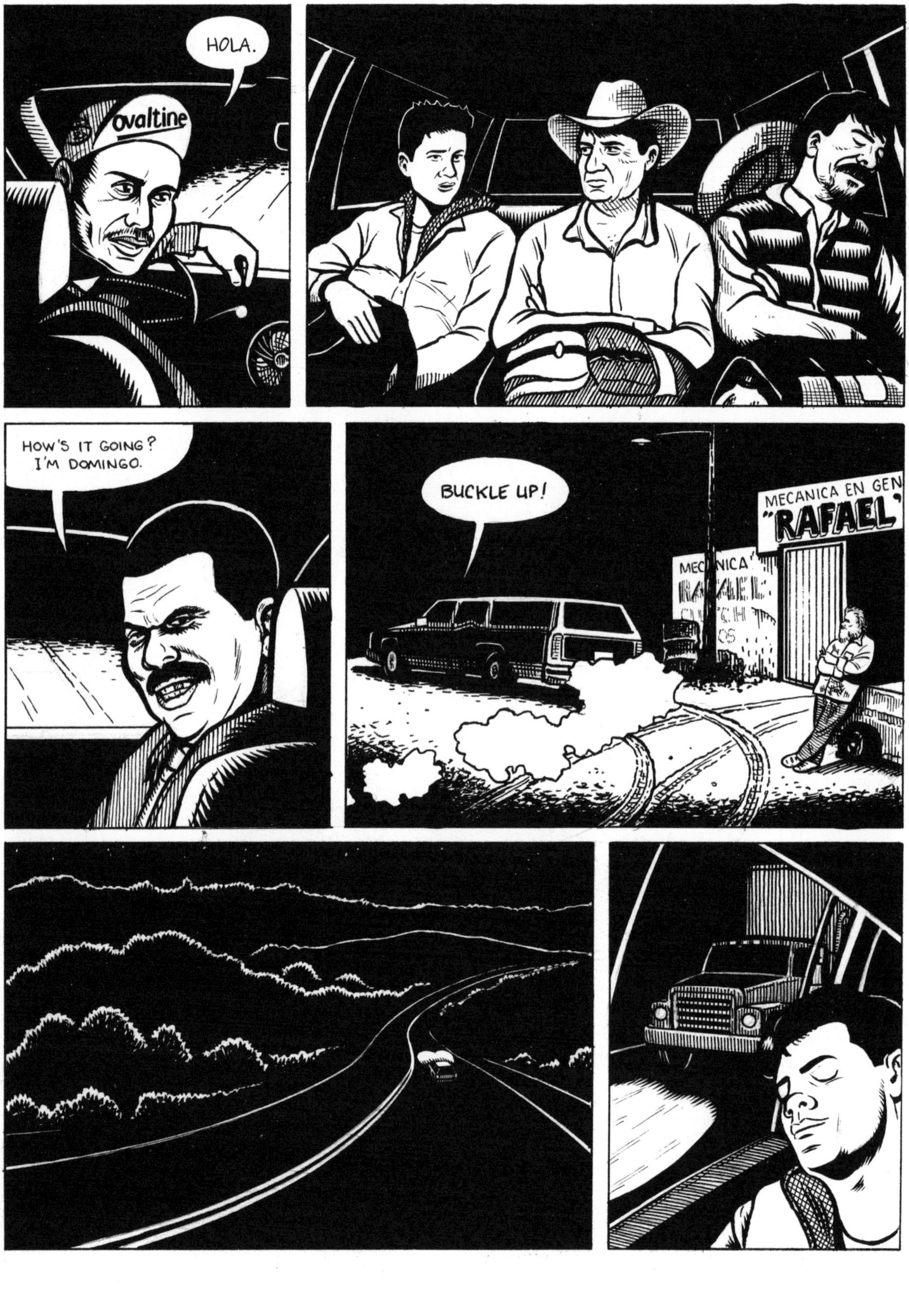
HOLA.
ovaltine
HOW'S IT GOING? I'M DOMINGO.
BUCKLE UP!
MECANICA EN GEN
"RAFAEL"

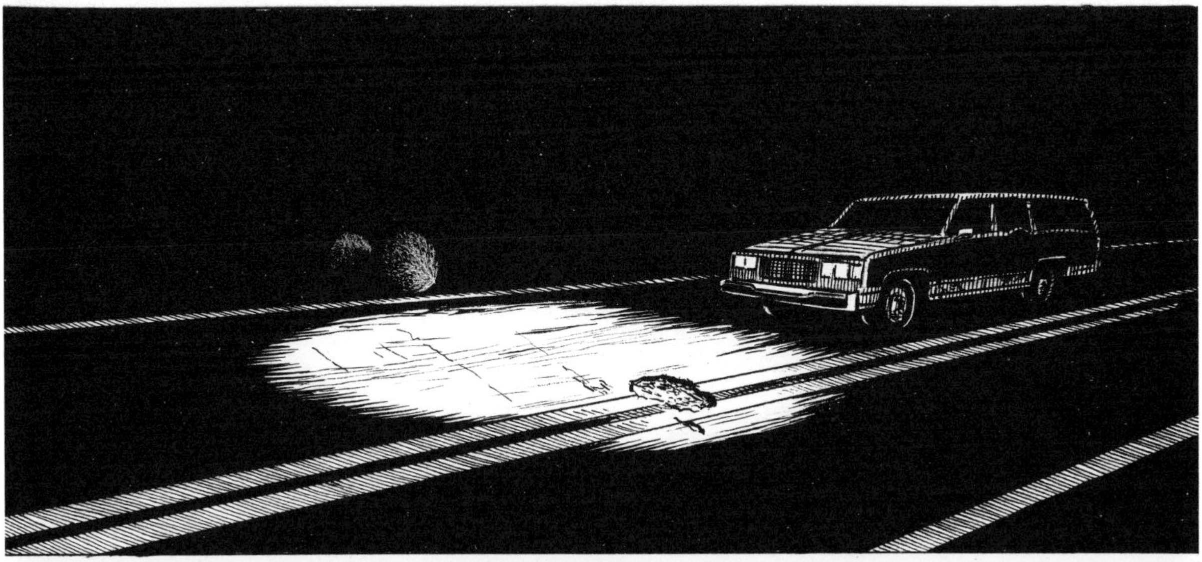

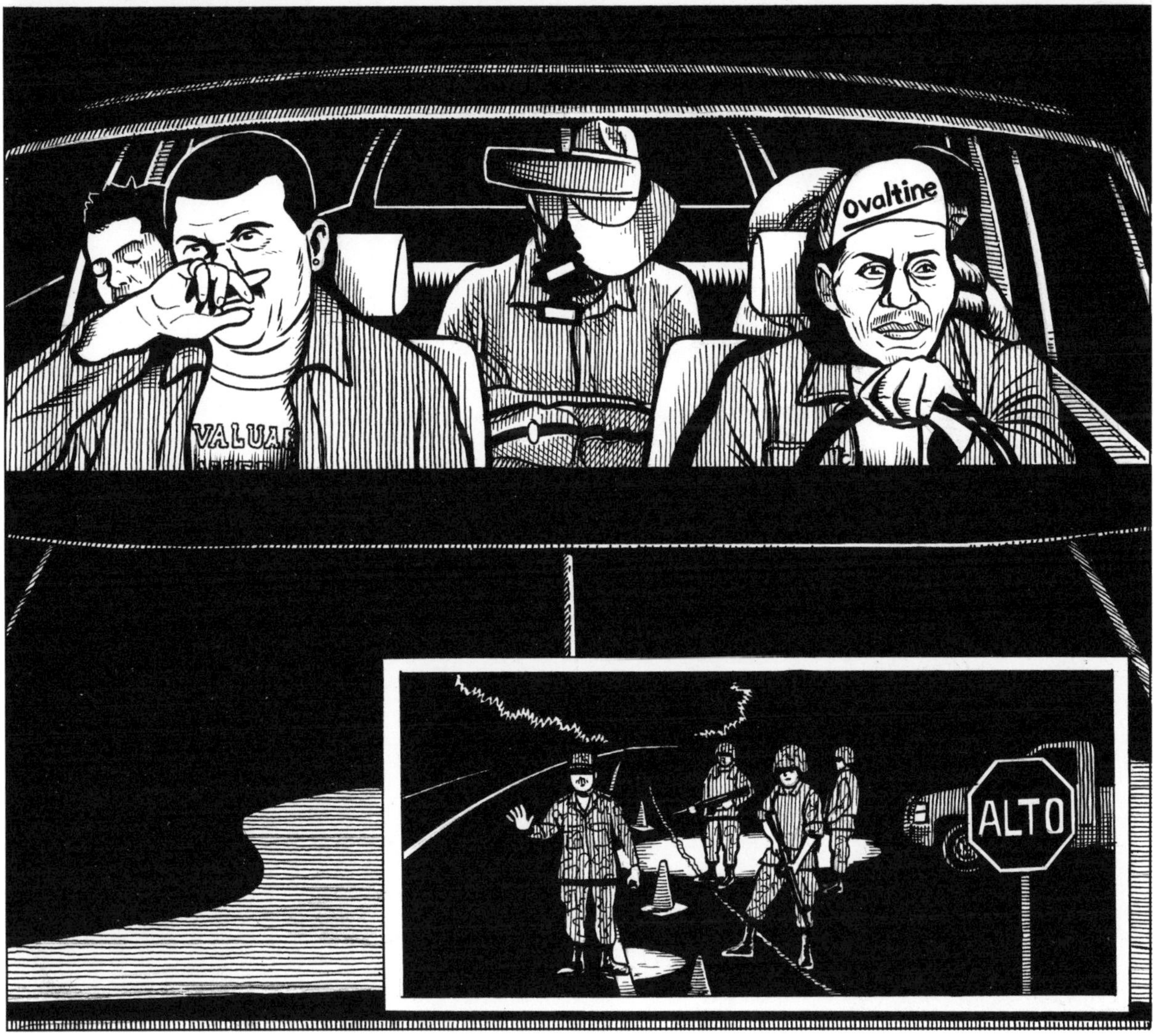
Ovaltine
ALTO

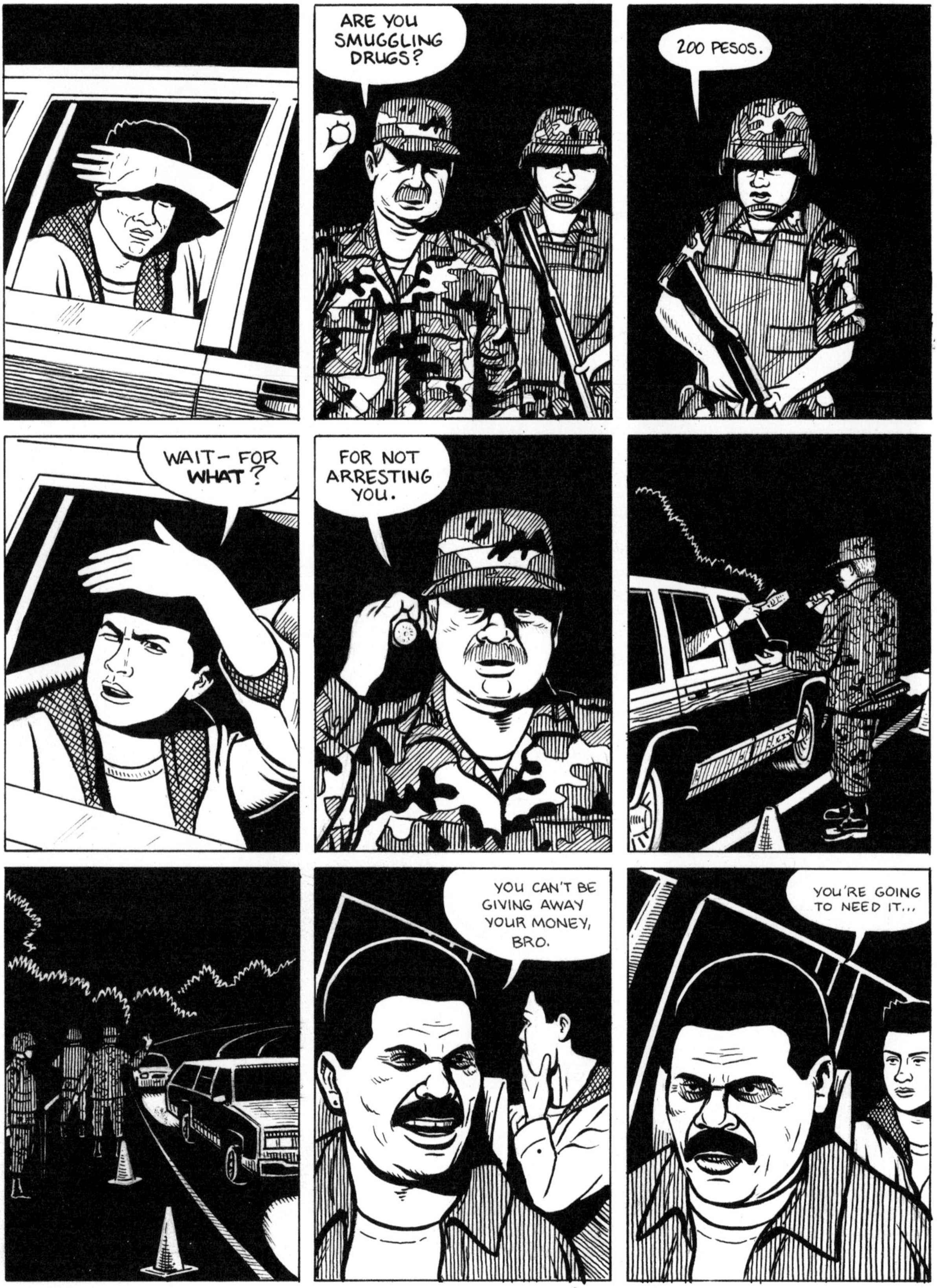
ARE YOU SMUGGLING DRUGS?
200 PESOS.
WAIT- FOR WHAT?
FOR NOT ARRESTING YOU.
YOU CAN'T BE GIVING AWAY YOUR MONEY, BRO.
YOU'RE GOING TO NEED IT...

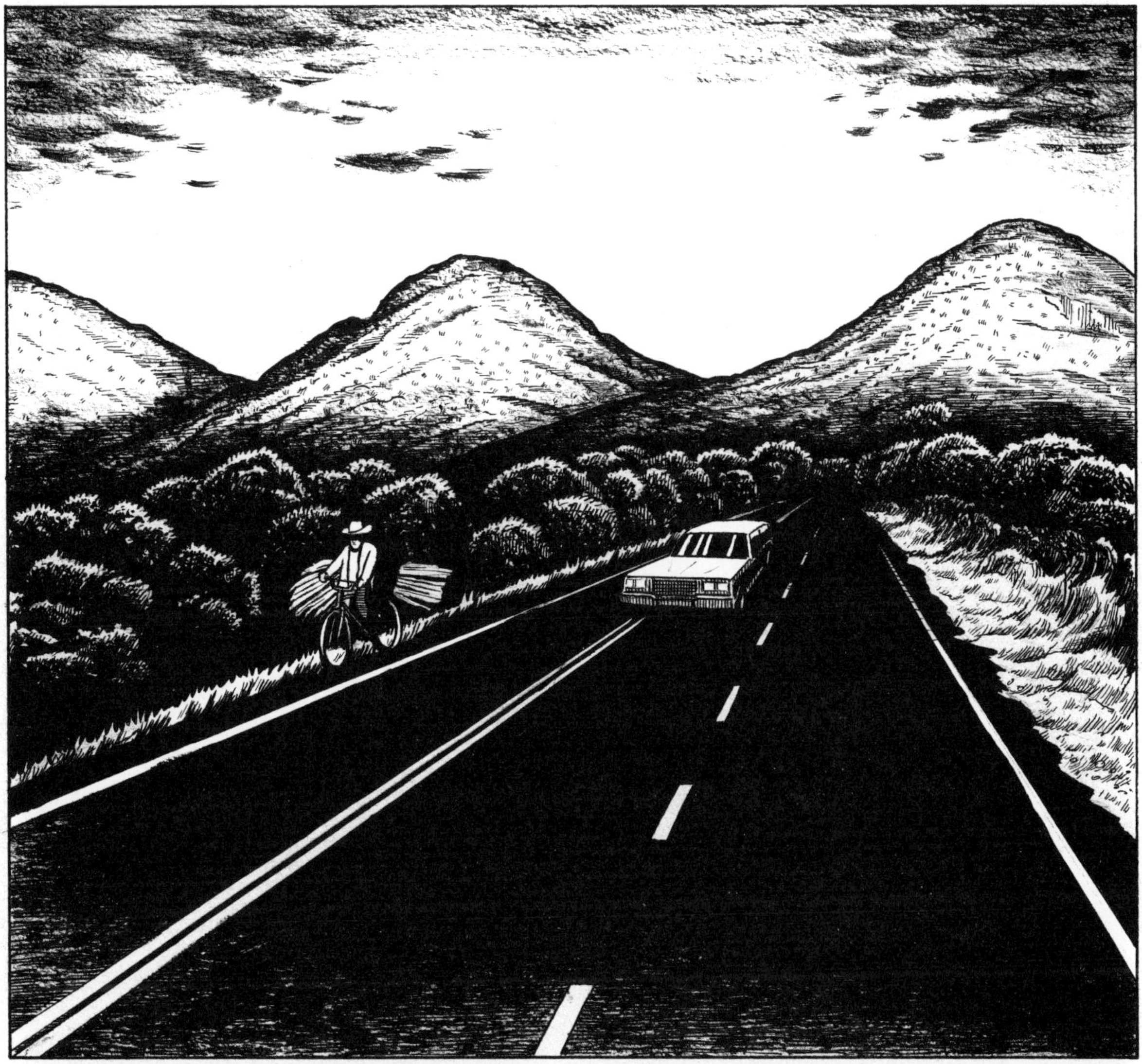

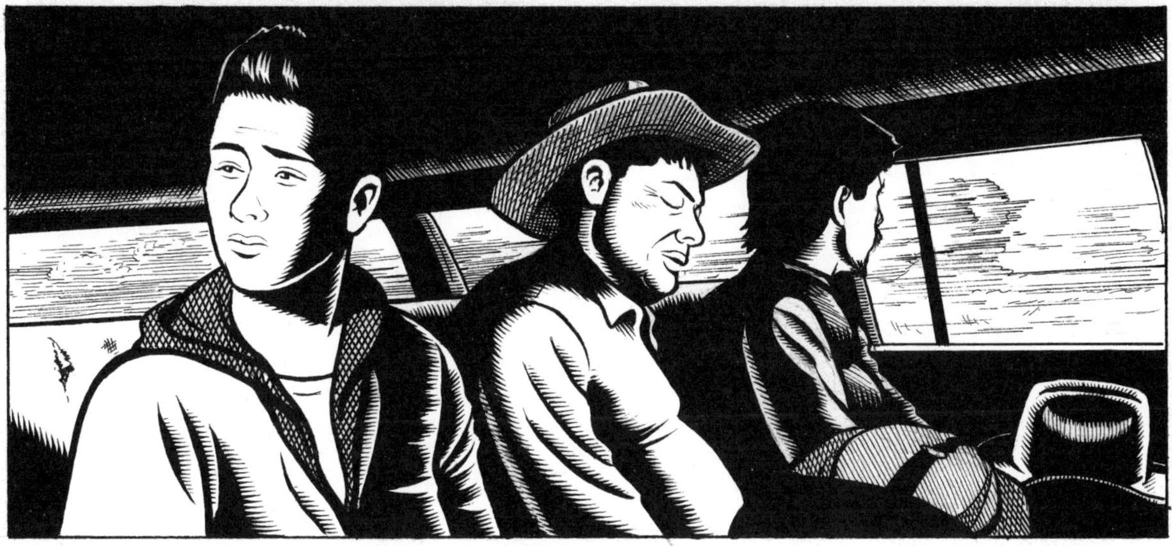

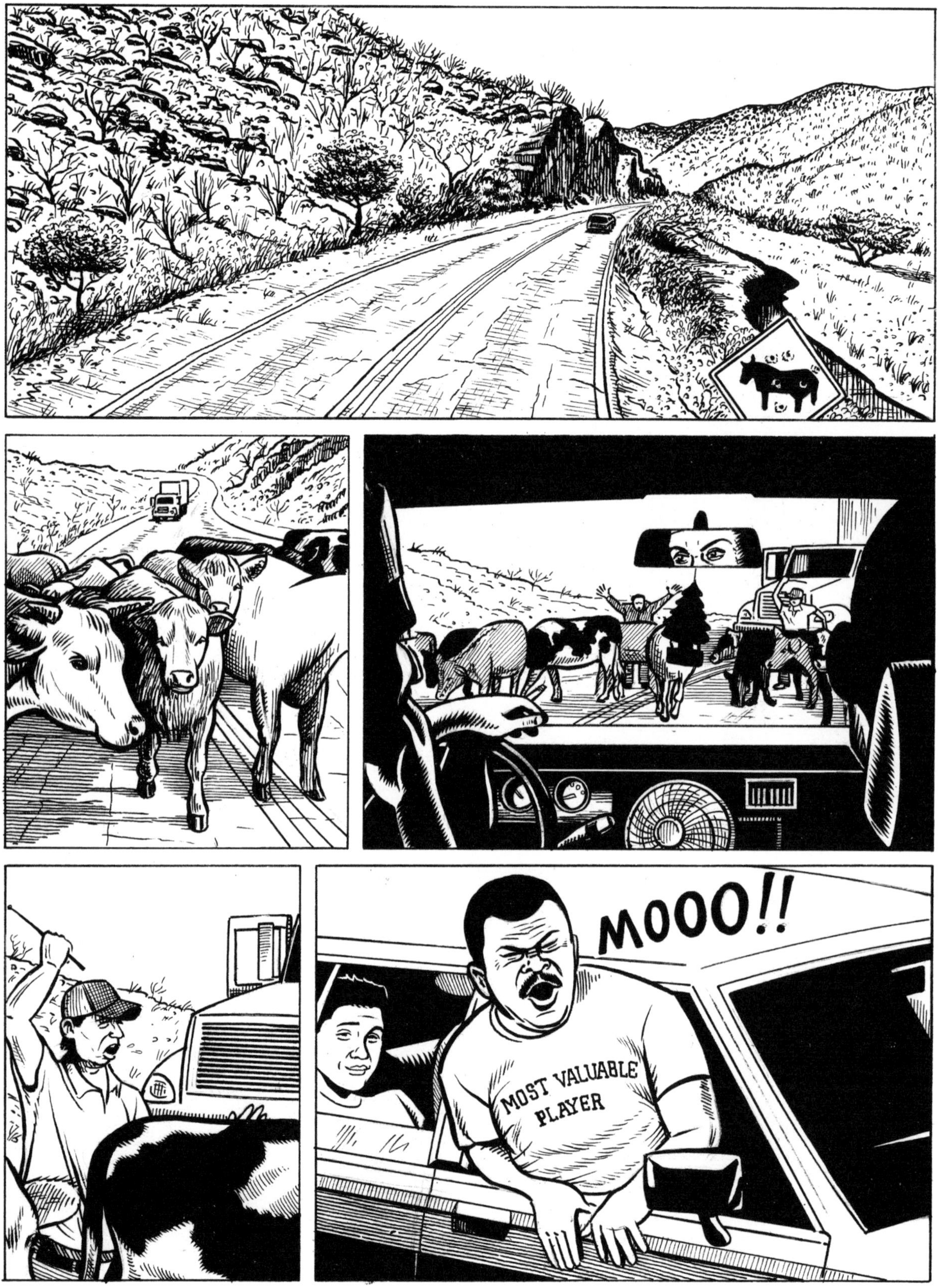
MOOO!!
MOST VALUABLE PLAYER

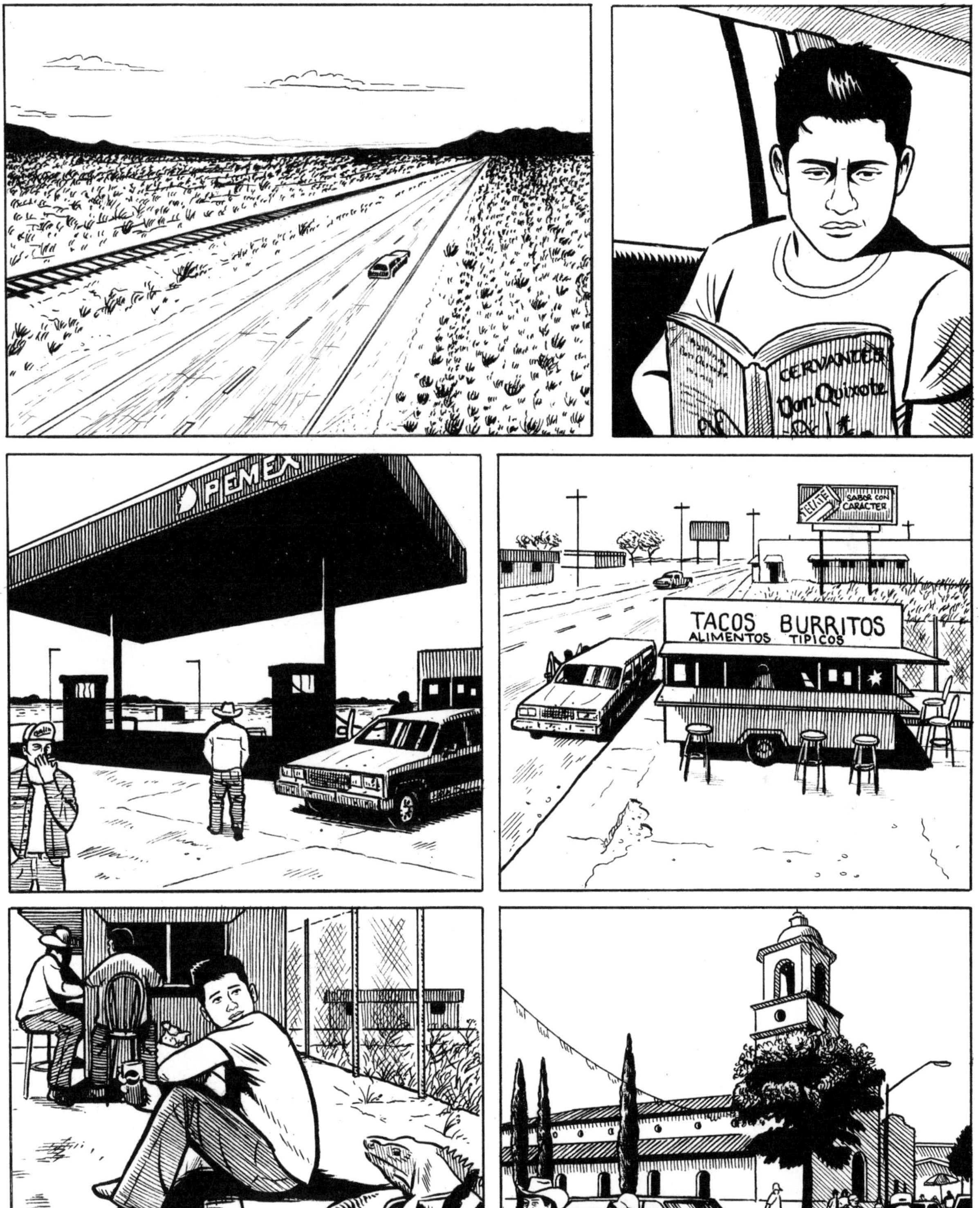
CERVANTES
Don Quixote
PEMEX
TECATE
SABOR CON CARACTER
TACOS BURRITOS
ALIMENTOS TIPICOS

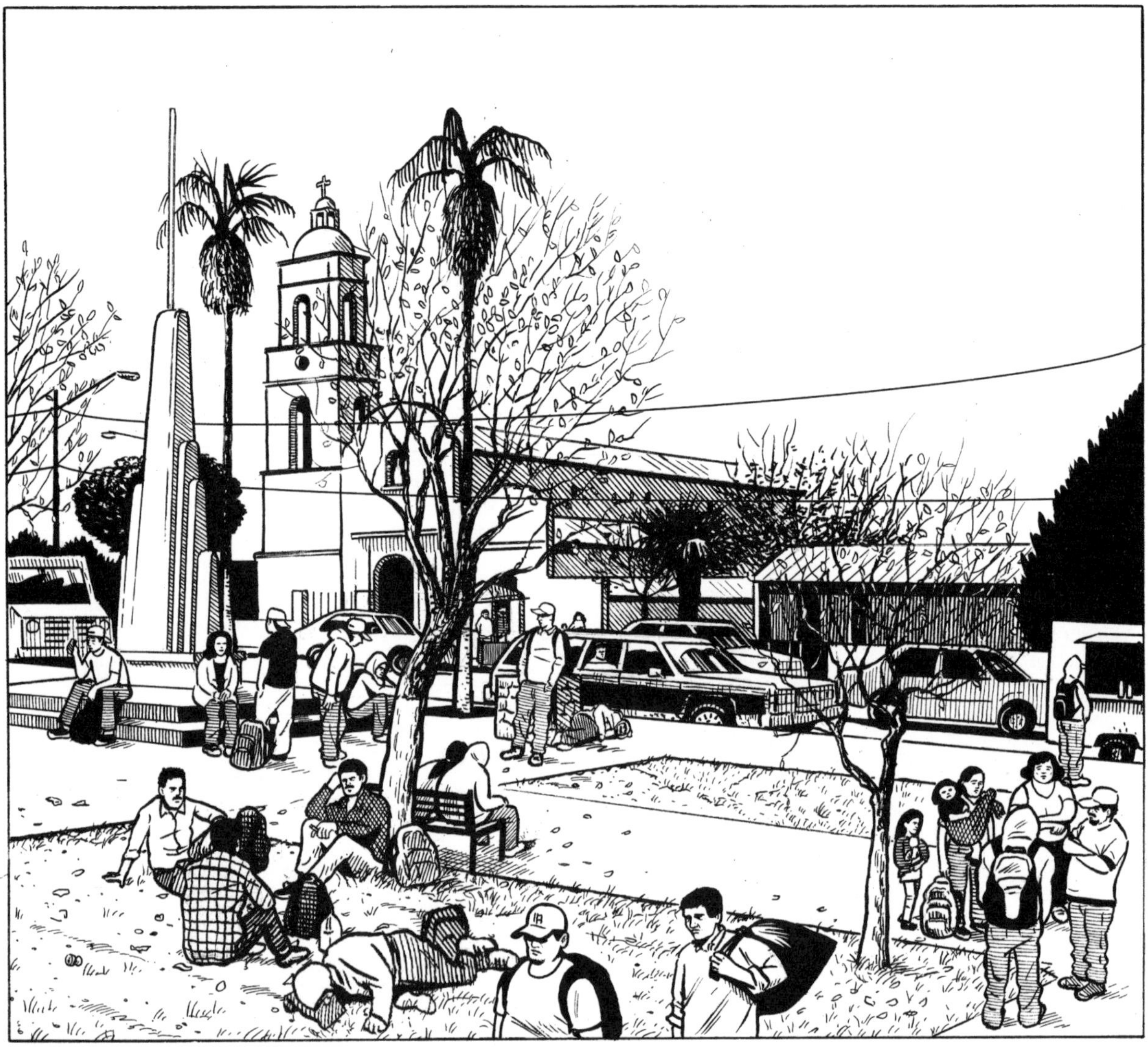

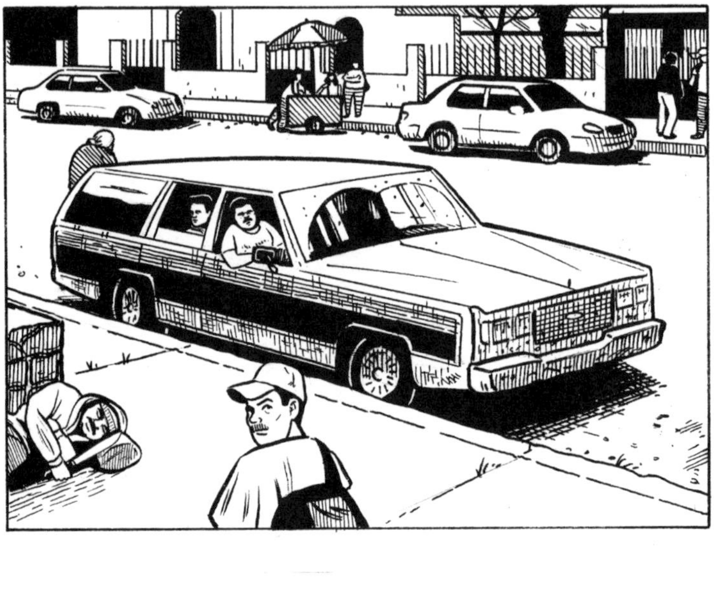

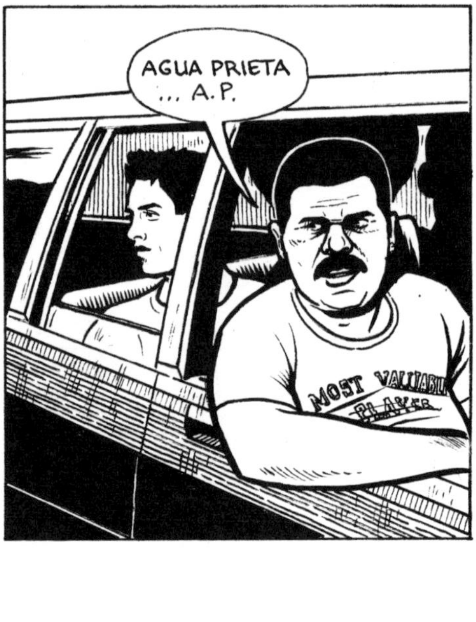
AGUA PRIETA ... A.P.

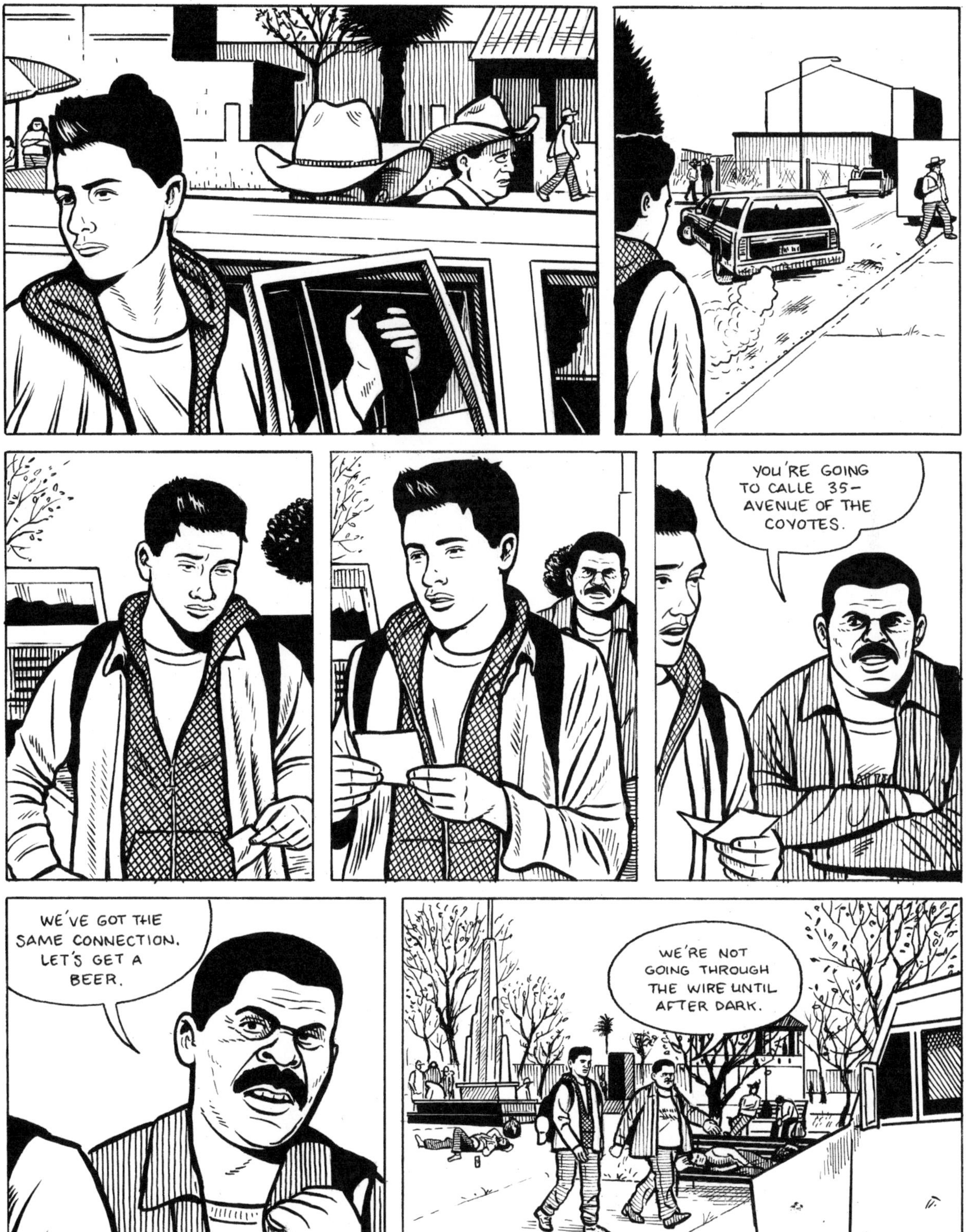
YOU'RE GOING TO CALLE 35— AVENUE OF THE COYOTES.
WE'VE GOT THE SAME CONNECTION. LET'S GET A BEER.
WE'RE NOT GOING THROUGH THE WIRE UNTIL AFTER DARK.

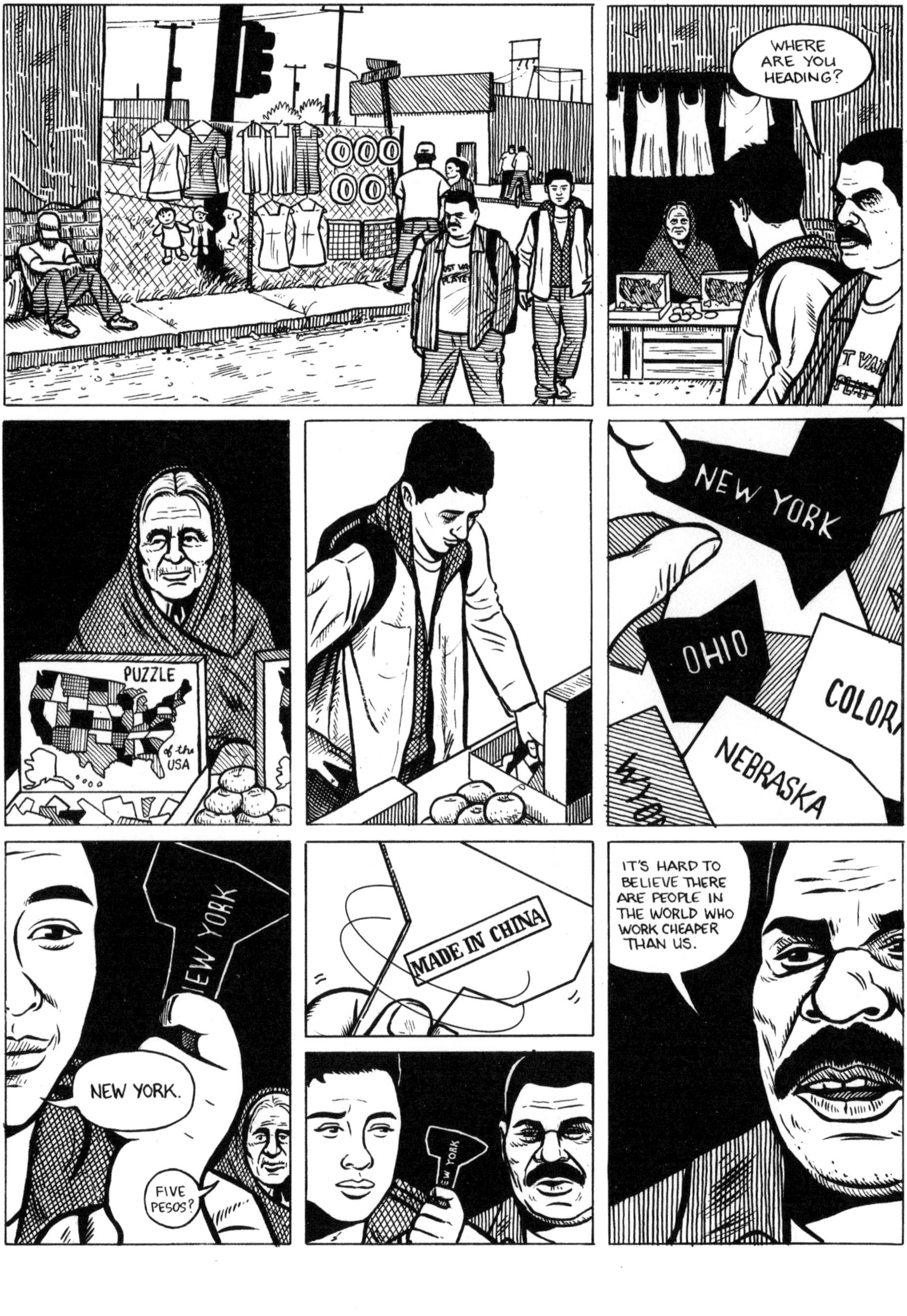
WHERE ARE YOU HEADING?
PUZZLE of the USA
NEW YORK
OHIO
NEBRASKA
NEW YORK.
FIVE PESOS?
MADE IN CHINA
IT'S HARD TO BELIEVE THERE ARE PEOPLE IN THE WORLD WHO WORK CHEAPER THAN US.

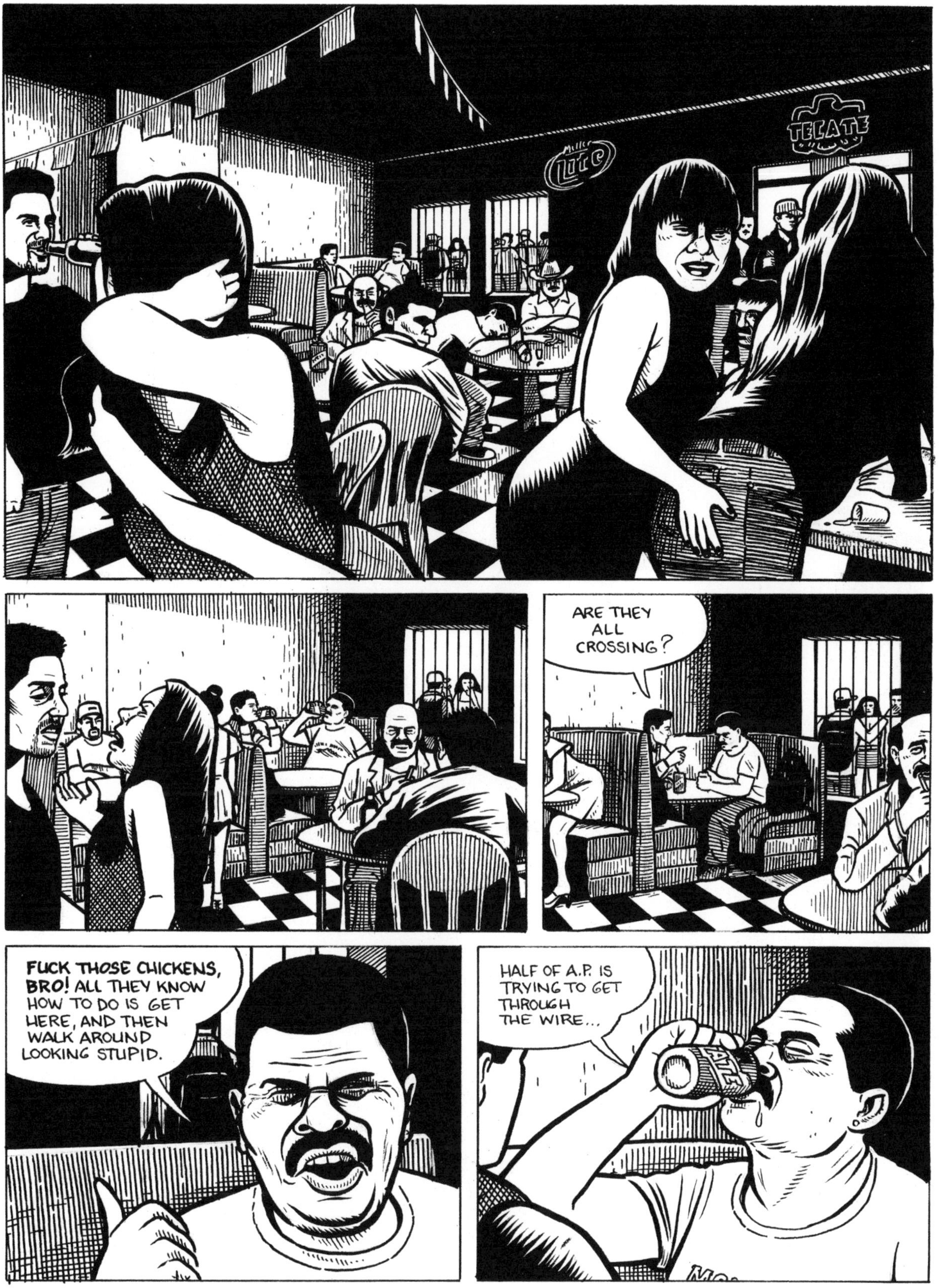
Miller Lite
TECATE
ARE THEY ALL CROSSING?
FUCK THOSE CHICKENS, BRO! ALL THEY KNOW HOW TO DO IS GET HERE, AND THEN WALK AROUND LOOKING STUPID.
HALF OF A.P. IS TRYING TO GET THROUGH THE WIRE...

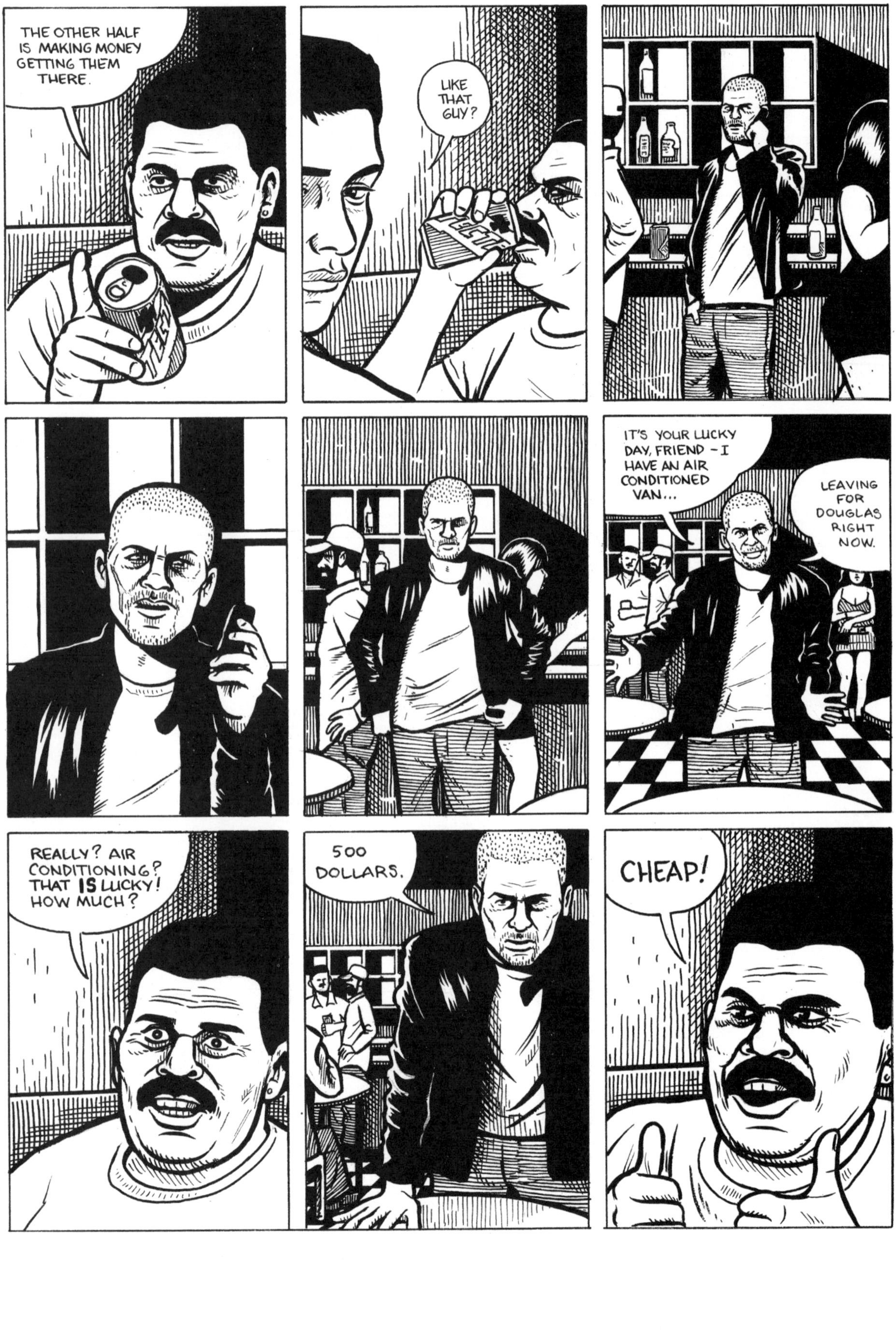
THE OTHER HALF IS MAKING MONEY GETTING THEM THERE.
LIKE THAT GUY?
IT'S YOUR LUCKY DAY, FRIEND - I HAVE AN AIR CONDITIONED VAN...
LEAVING FOR DOUGLAS RIGHT NOW.
REALLY? AIR CONDITIONING? THAT IS LUCKY! HOW MUCH?
500 DOLLARS.
CHEAP!

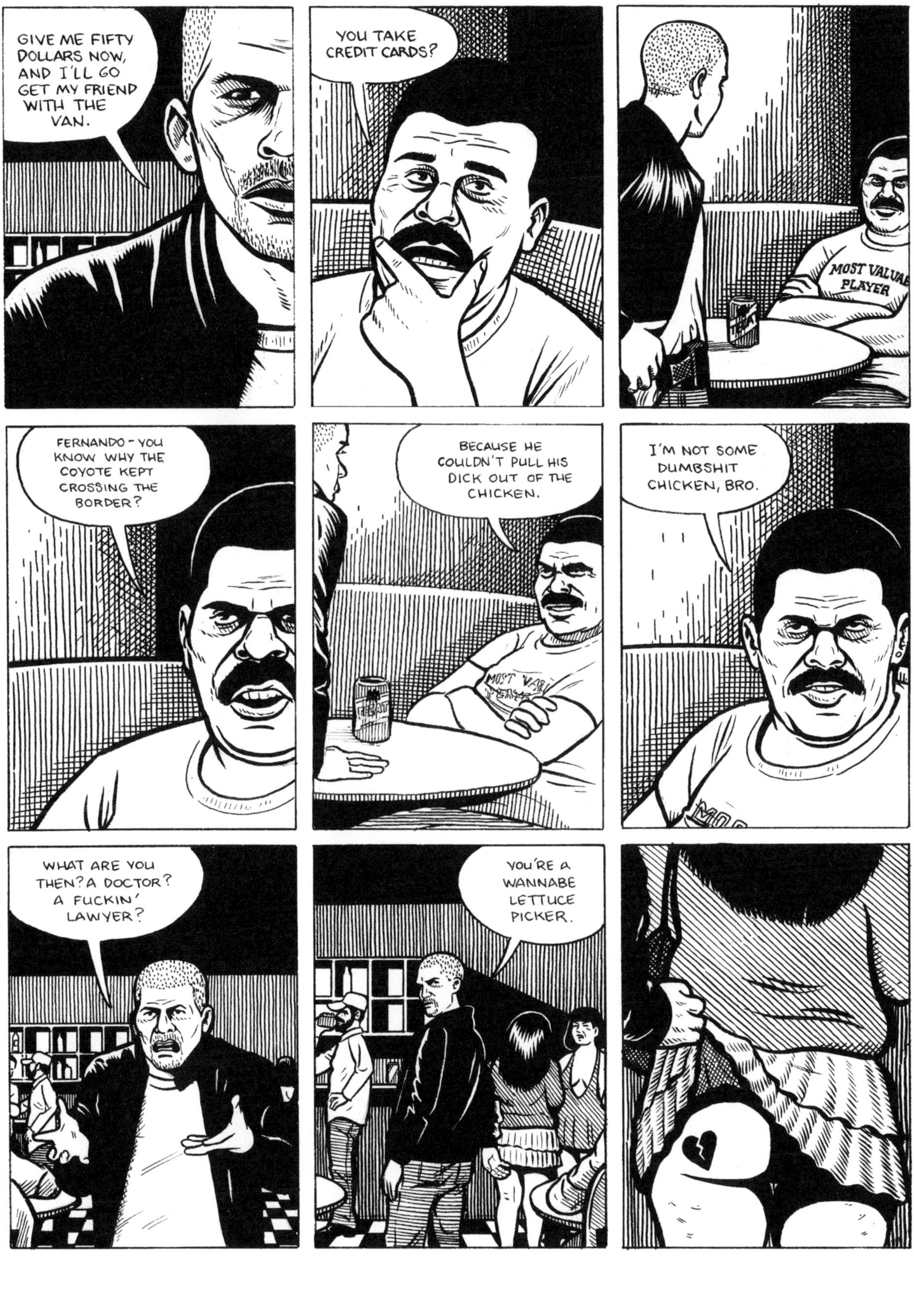
GIVE ME FIFTY DOLLARS NOW, AND I'LL GO GET MY FRIEND WITH THE VAN.
YOU TAKE CREDIT CARDS?
MOST VALUAB PLAYER
FERNANDO - YOU KNOW WHY THE COYOTE KEPT CROSSING THE BORDER?
BECAUSE HE COULDN'T PULL HIS DICK OUT OF THE CHICKEN.
I'M NOT SOME DUMBSHIT CHICKEN, BRO.
WHAT ARE YOU THEN? A DOCTOR? A FUCKIN' LAWYER?
YOU'RE A WANNABE LETTUCE PICKER.

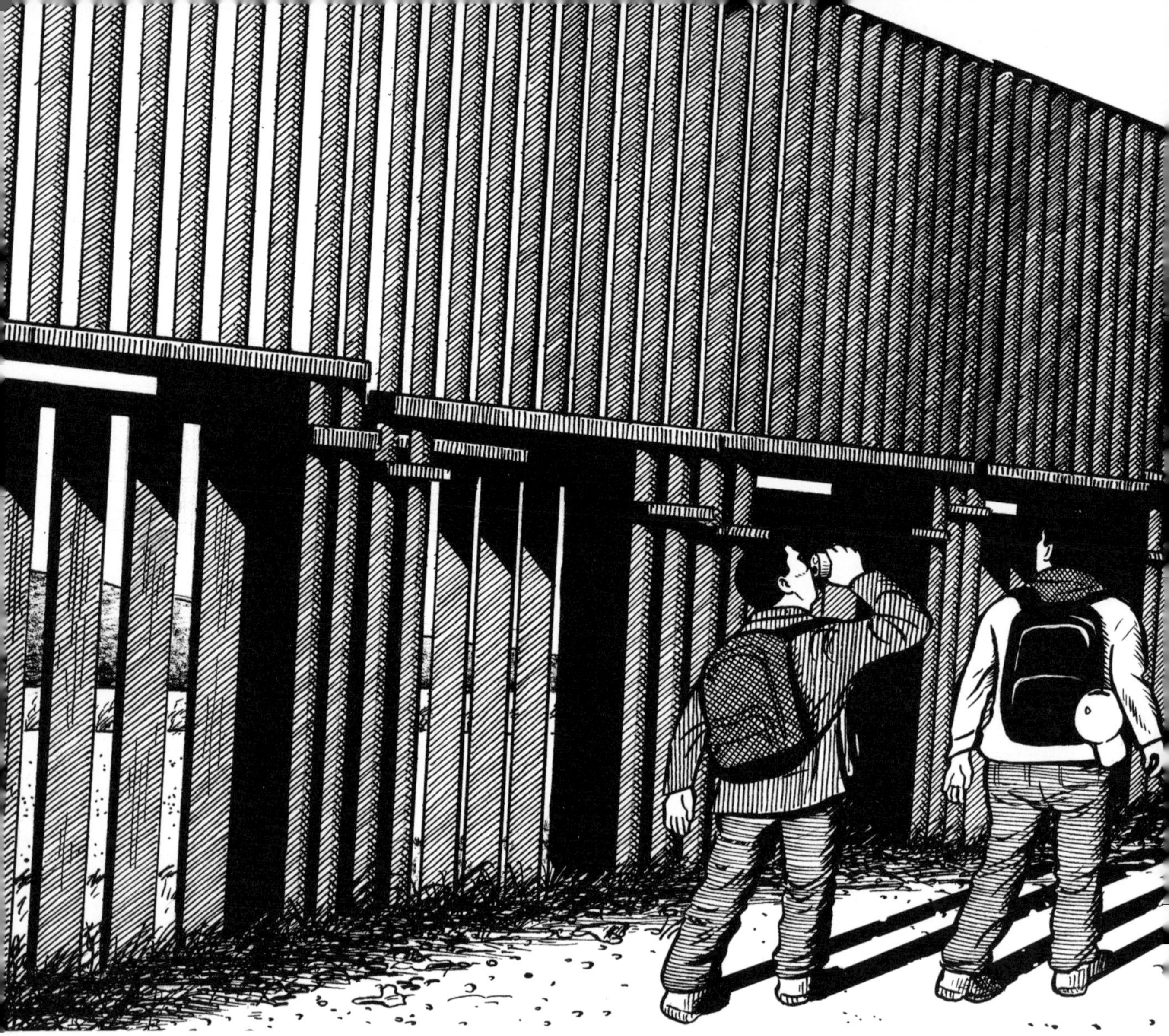

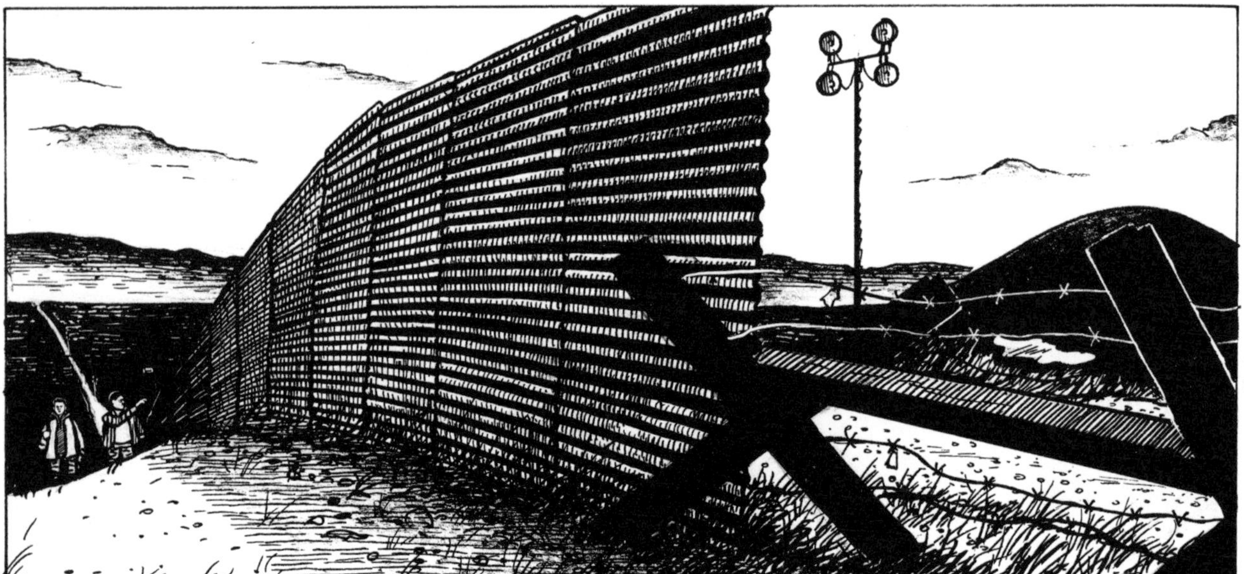

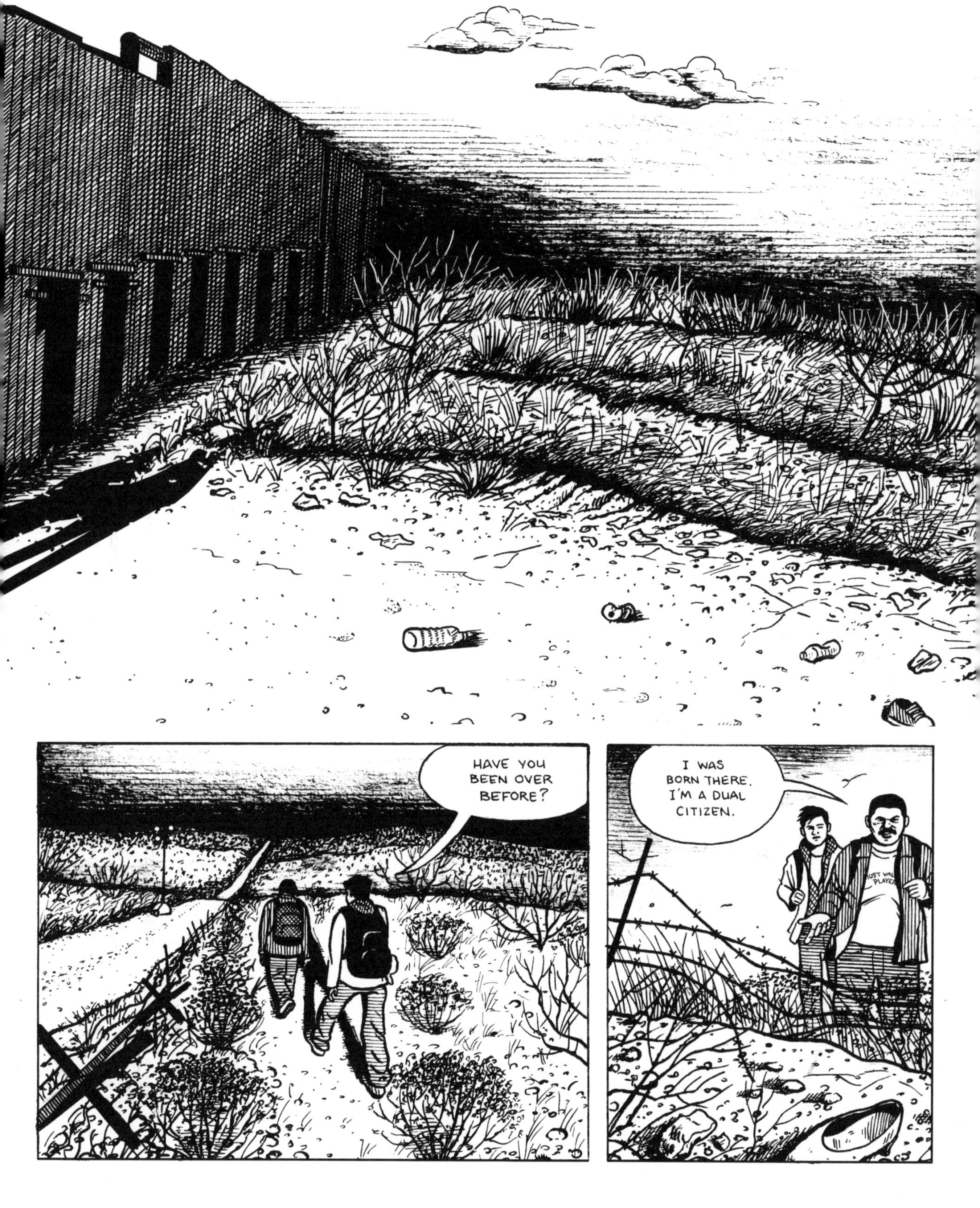
HAVE YOU BEEN OVER BEFORE?
I WAS BORN THERE. I'M A DUAL CITIZEN.

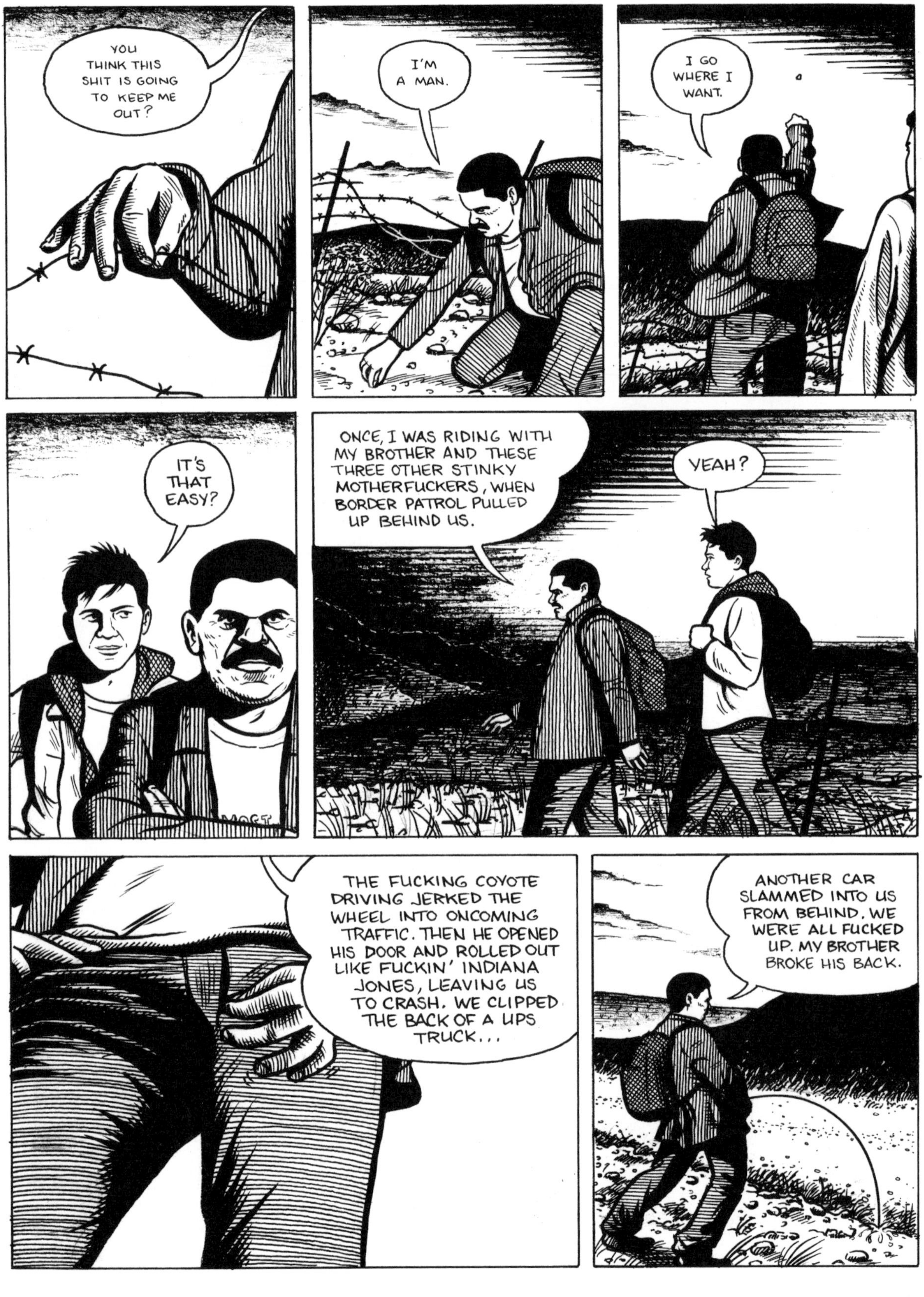
YOU THINK THIS SHIT IS GOING TO KEEP ME OUT?
I'M A MAN.
I GO WHERE I WANT.
IT'S THAT EASY?
ONCE, I WAS RIDING WITH MY BROTHER AND THESE THREE OTHER STINKY MOTHERFUCKERS, WHEN BORDER PATROL PULLED UP BEHIND US.
YEAH?
THE FUCKING COYOTE DRIVING JERKED THE WHEEL INTO ONCOMING TRAFFIC. THEN HE OPENED HIS DOOR AND ROLLED OUT LIKE FUCKIN' INDIANA JONES, LEAVING US TO CRASH. WE CLIPPED THE BACK OF A UPS TRUCK...
ANOTHER CAR SLAMMED INTO US FROM BEHIND. WE WERE ALL FUCKED UP. MY BROTHER BROKE HIS BACK.

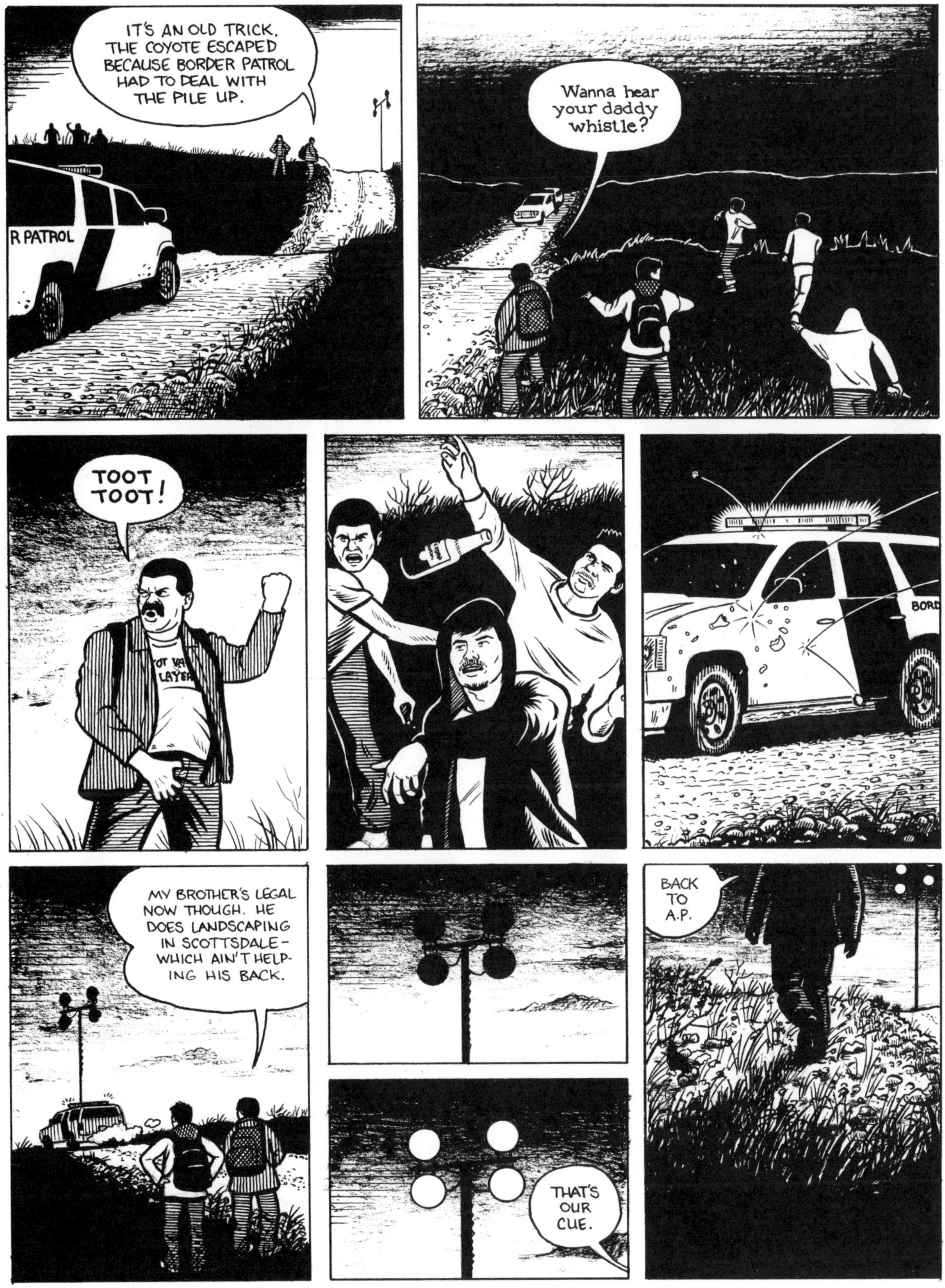
IT'S AN OLD TRICK. THE COYOTE ESCAPED BECAUSE BORDER PATROL HAD TO DEAL WITH THE PILE UP.
R PATROL
Wanna hear your daddy whistle?
TOOT TOOT!
BORD
MY BROTHER'S LEGAL NOW THOUGH. HE DOES LANDSCAPING IN SCOTTSDALE- WHICH AIN'T HELPING HIS BACK.
THAT'S OUR CUE.
BACK TO A.P.

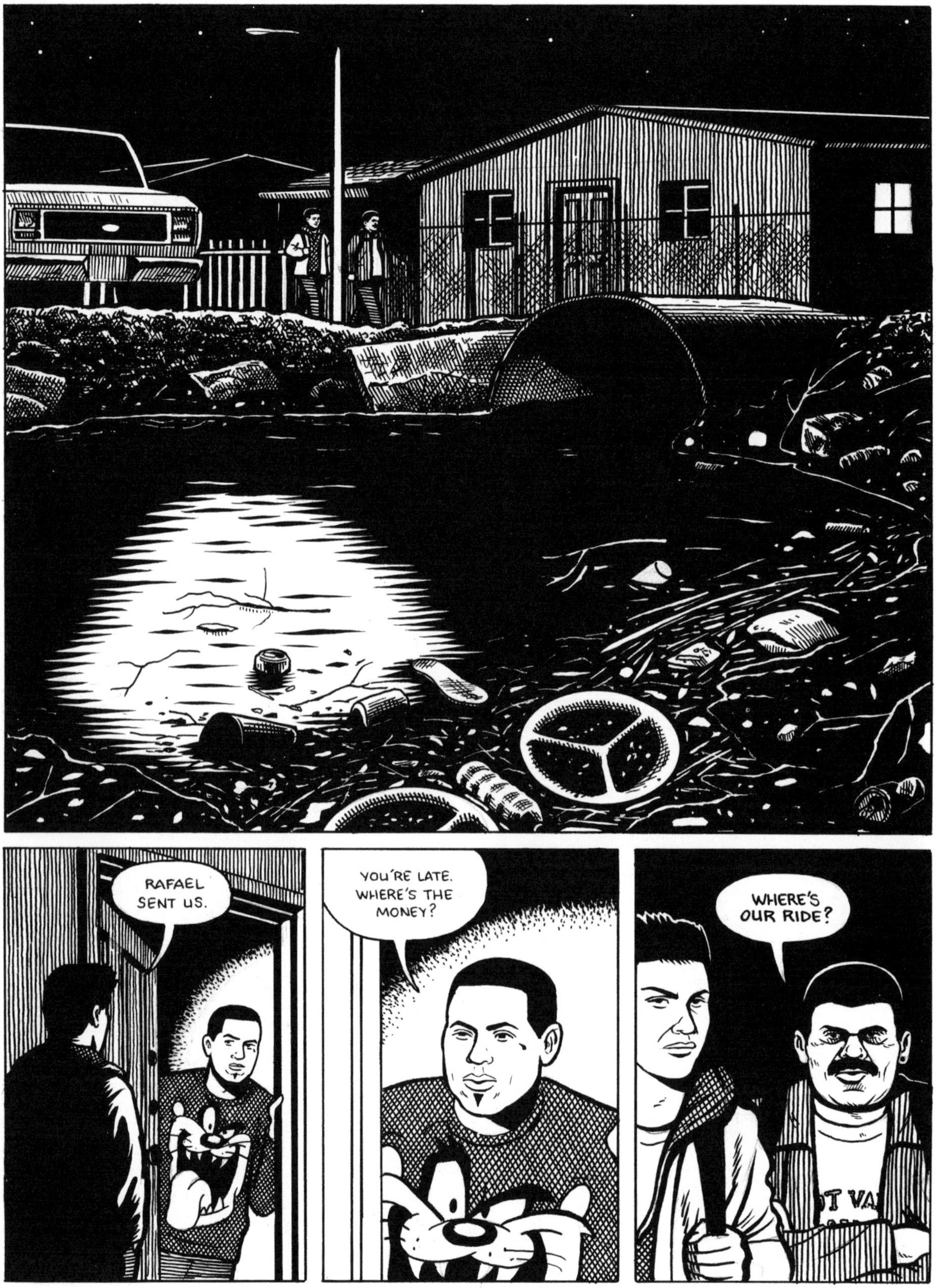
RAFAEL SENT US.
YOU'RE LATE. WHERE'S THE MONEY?
WHERE'S OUR RIDE?

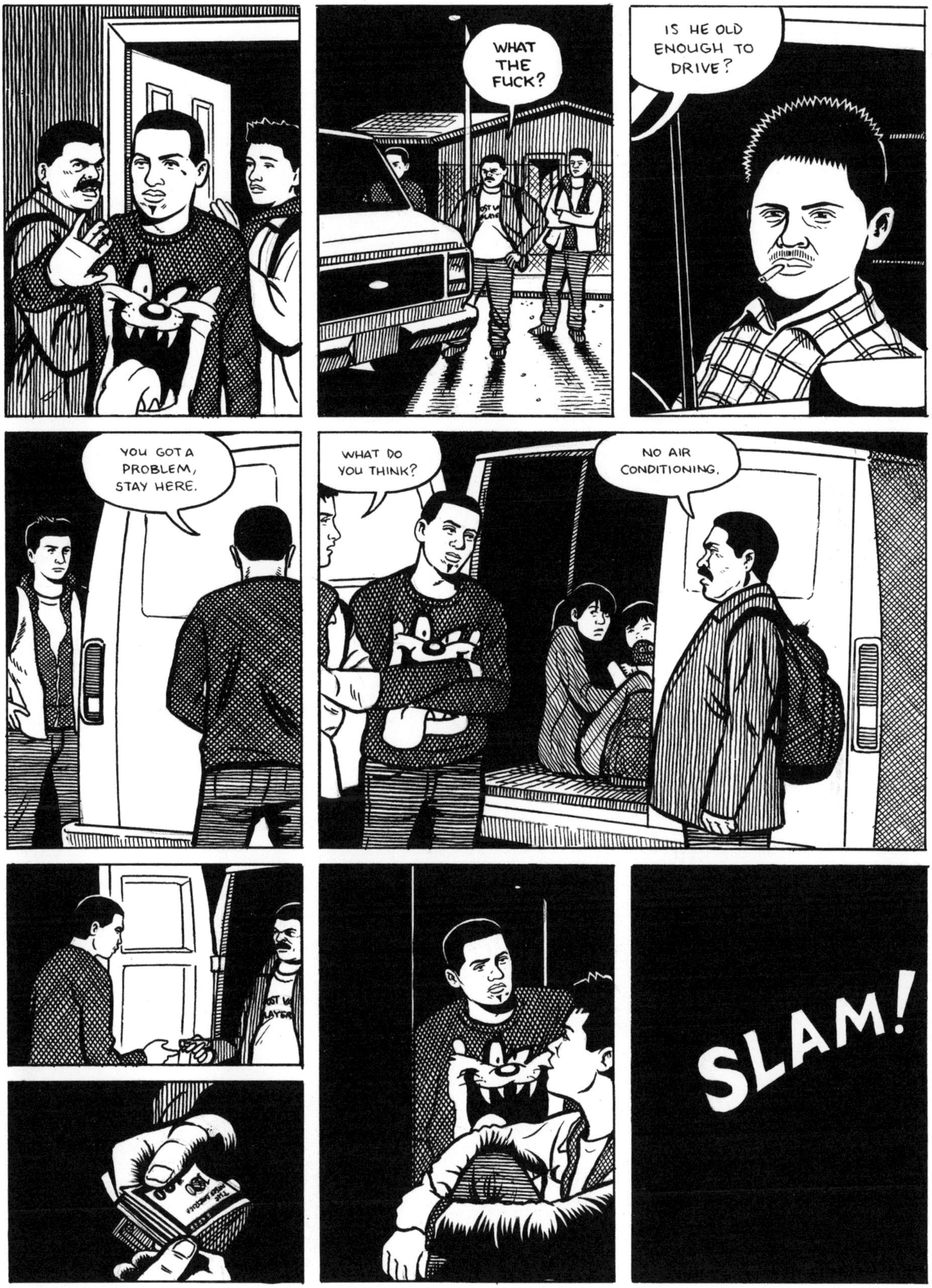
WHAT THE FUCK?
IS HE OLD ENOUGH TO DRIVE?
YOU GOT A PROBLEM, STAY HERE.
WHAT DO YOU THINK?
NO AIR CONDITIONING.
SLAM!

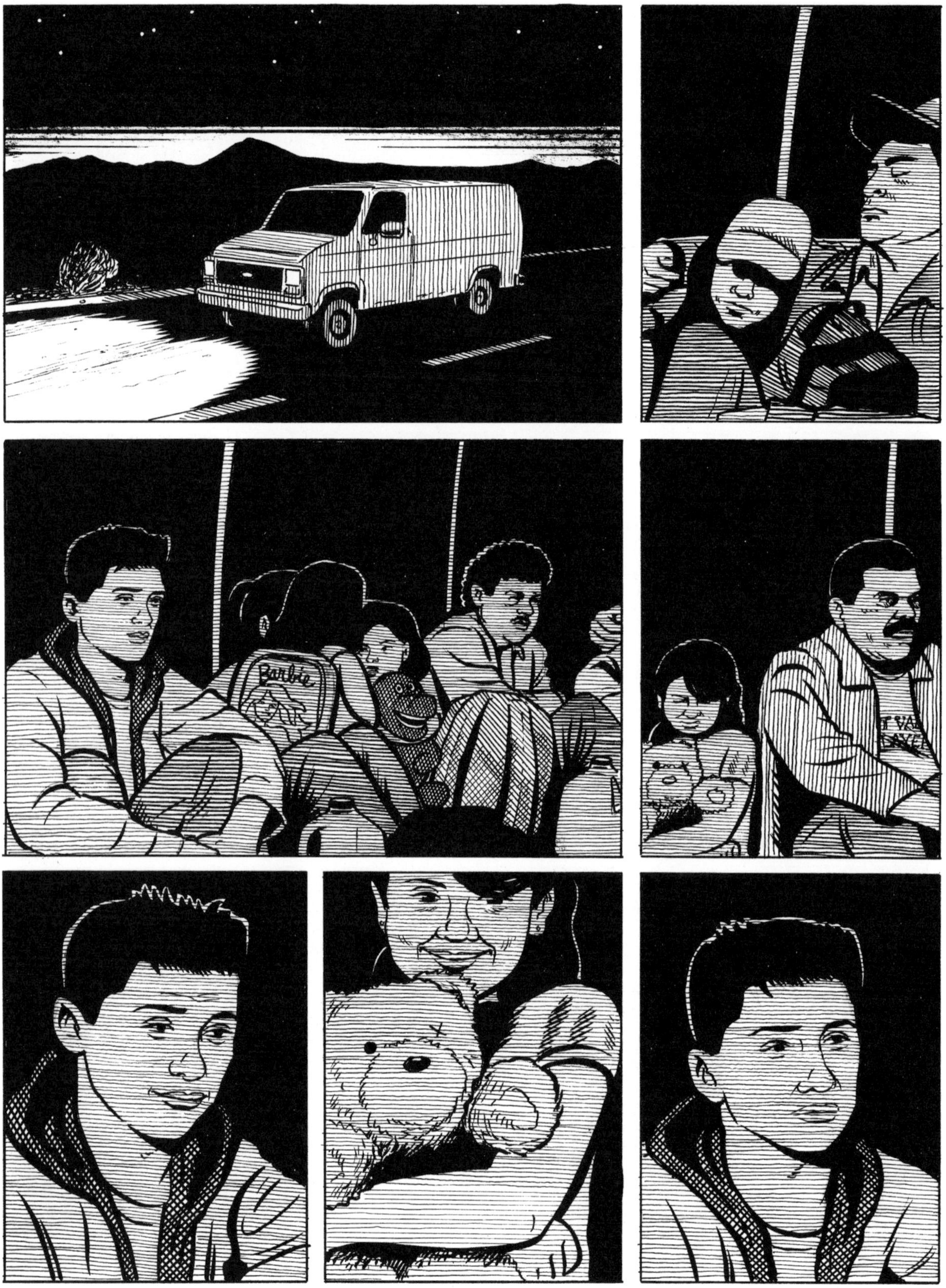
Barbie

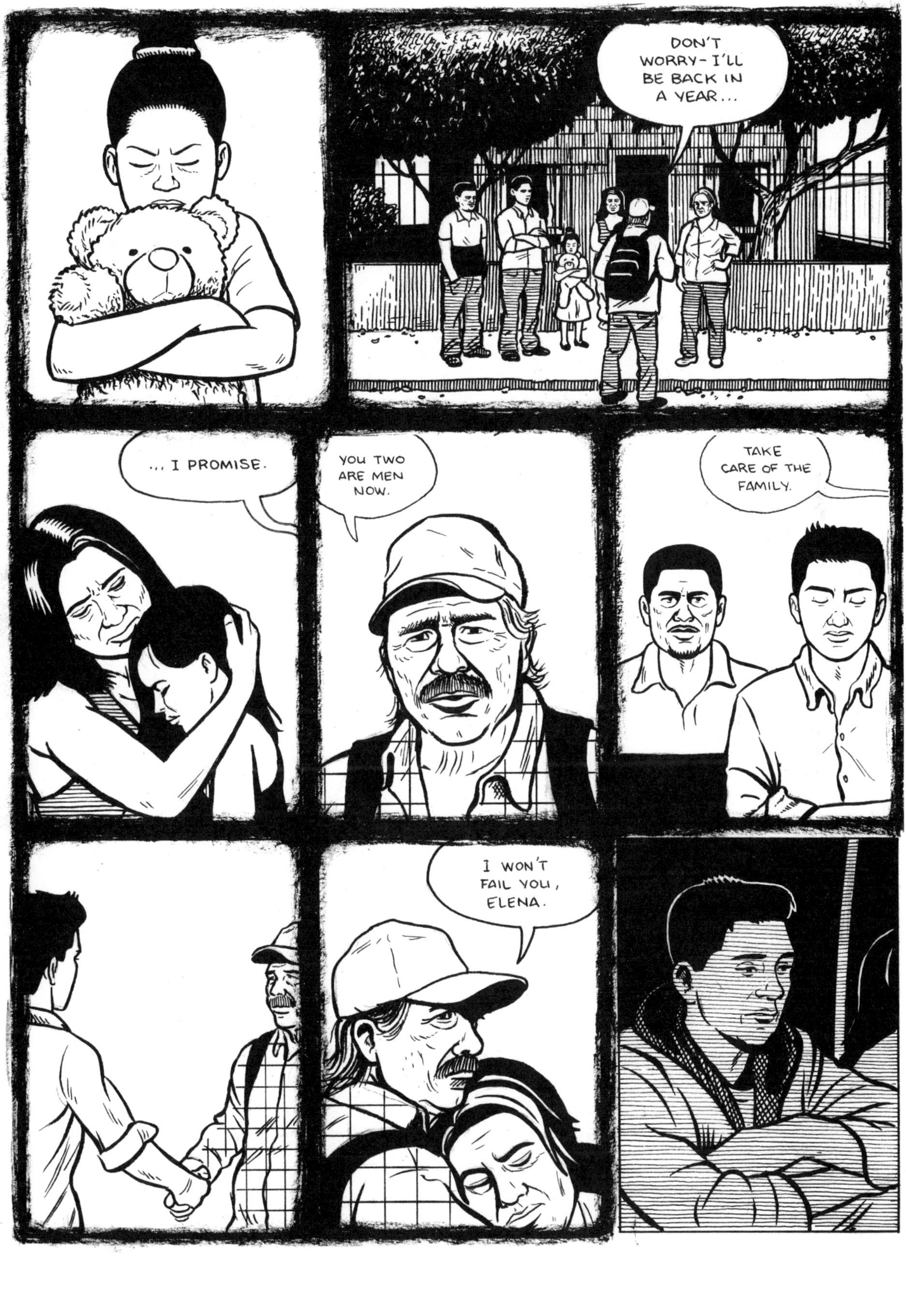
DON'T WORRY- I'LL BE BACK IN A YEAR...
... I PROMISE.
YOU TWO ARE MEN NOW.
TAKE CARE OF THE FAMILY.
I WON'T FAIL YOU, ELENA.

SCREECH!

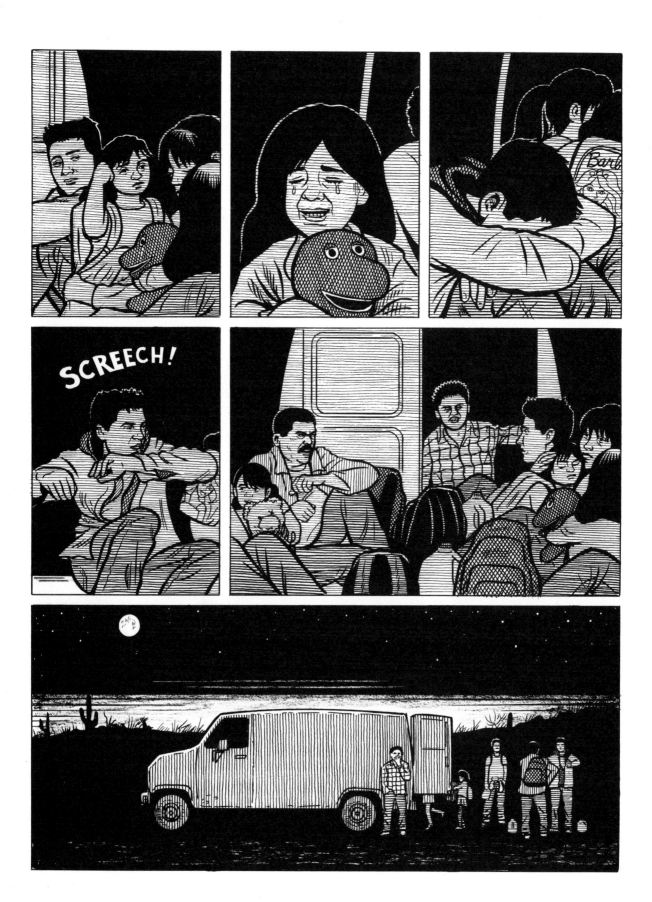

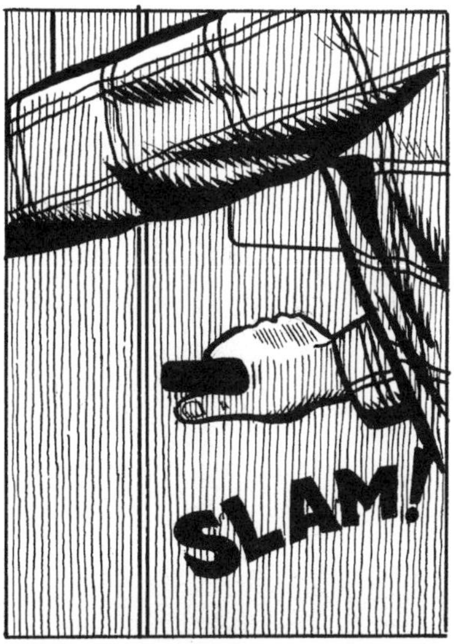
SLAM!
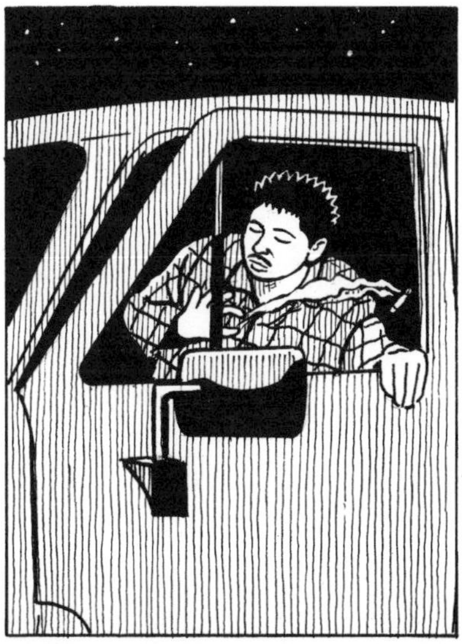
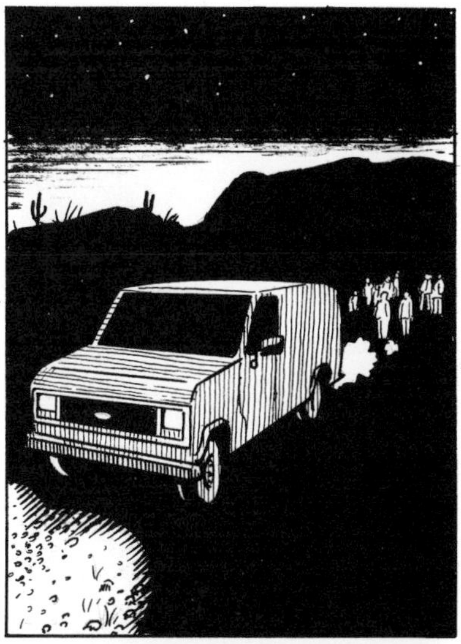
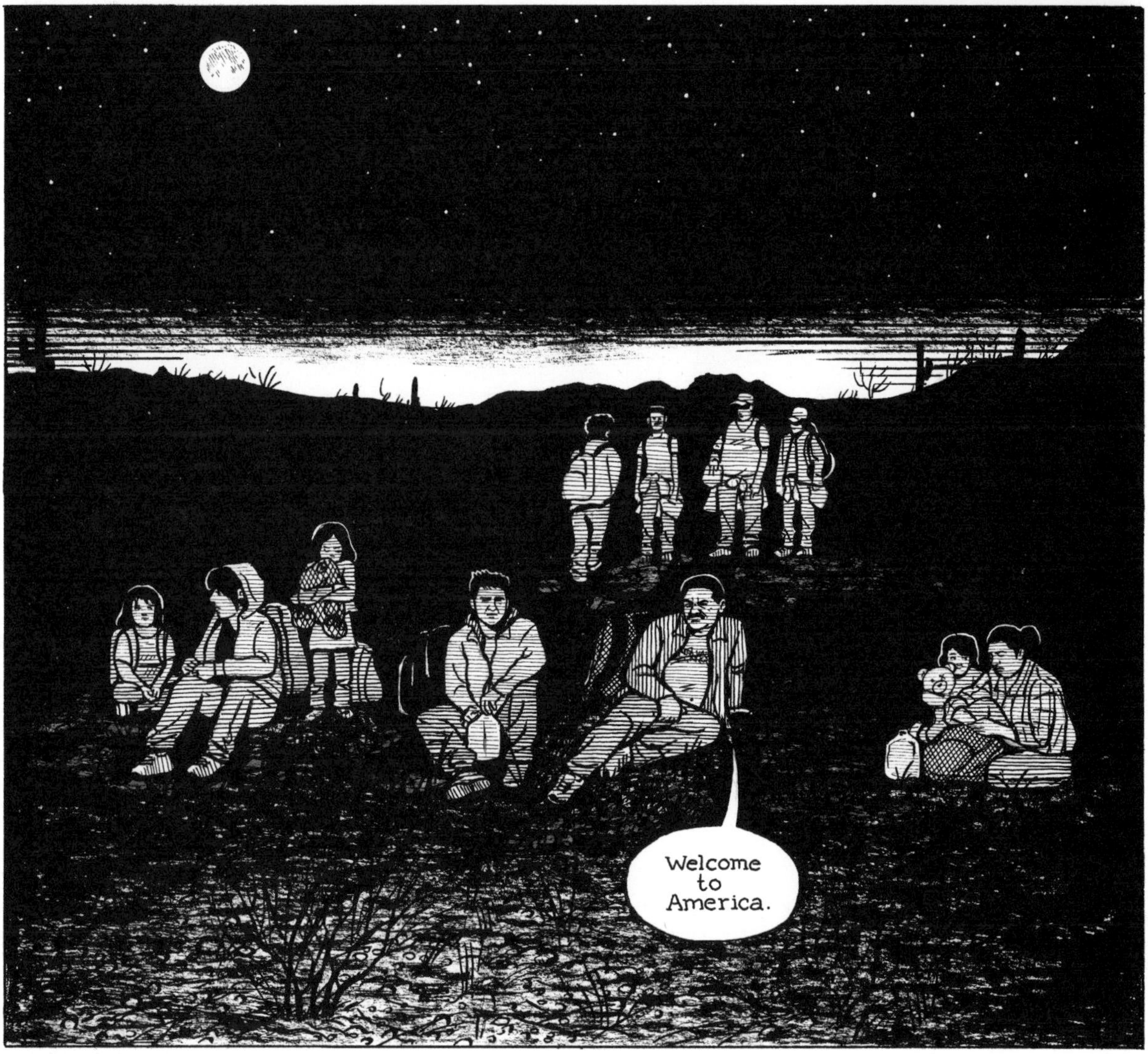
Welcome to America.

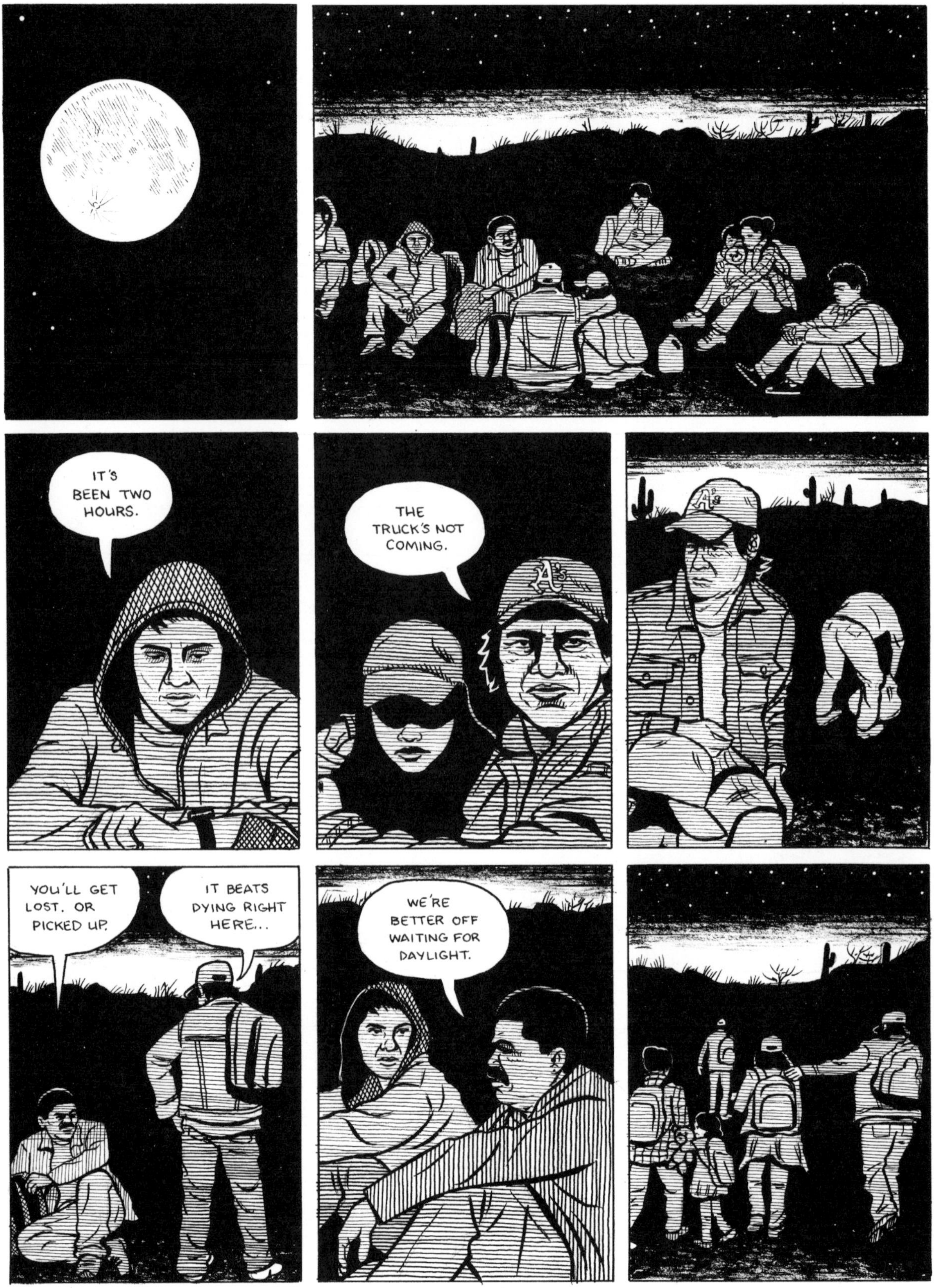
IT'S BEEN TWO HOURS.
THE TRUCK'S NOT COMING.
YOU'LL GET LOST. OR PICKED UP.
IT BEATS DYING RIGHT HERE...
WE'RE BETTER OFF WAITING FOR DAYLIGHT.

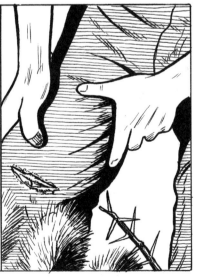

HOW MUCH FARTHER?

UNTIL WE SEE THE PEARLY GATES.

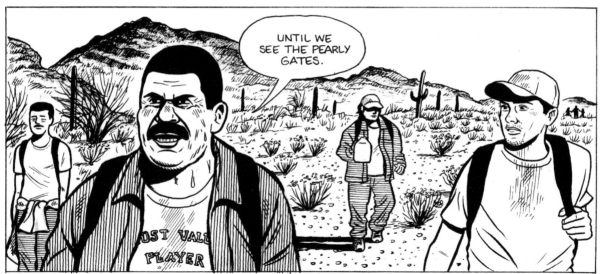

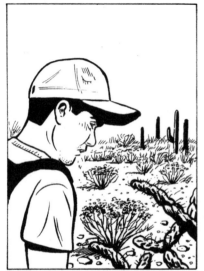

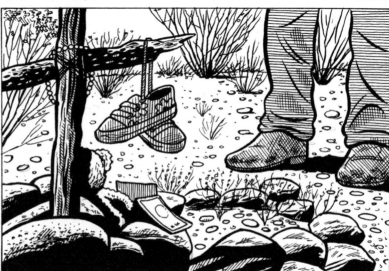

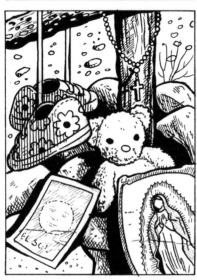

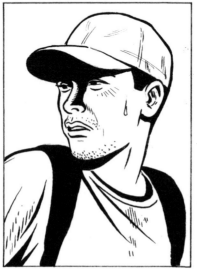

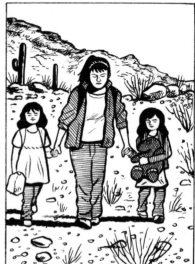

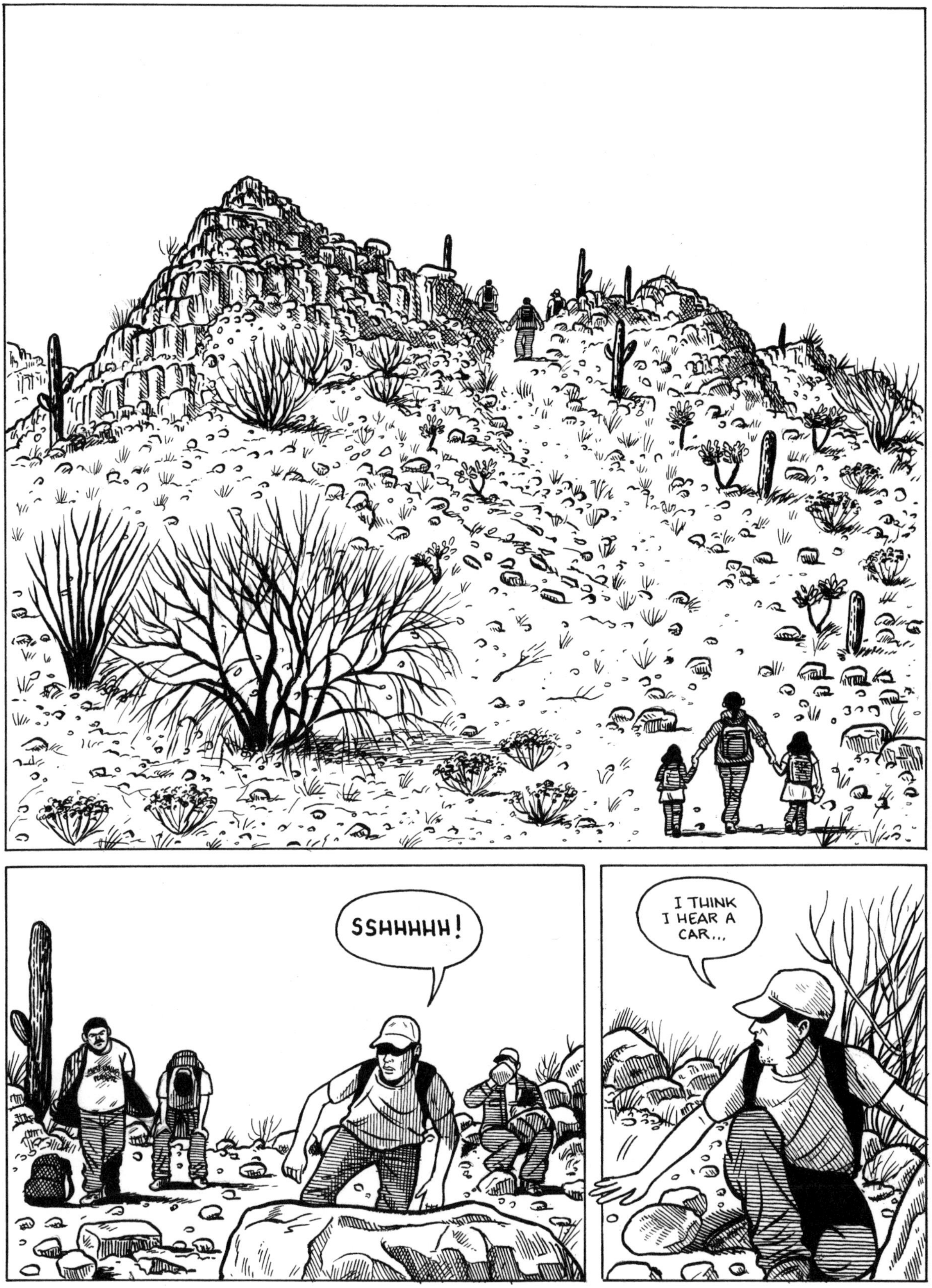
SSHHHHH!
I THINK I HEAR A CAR...

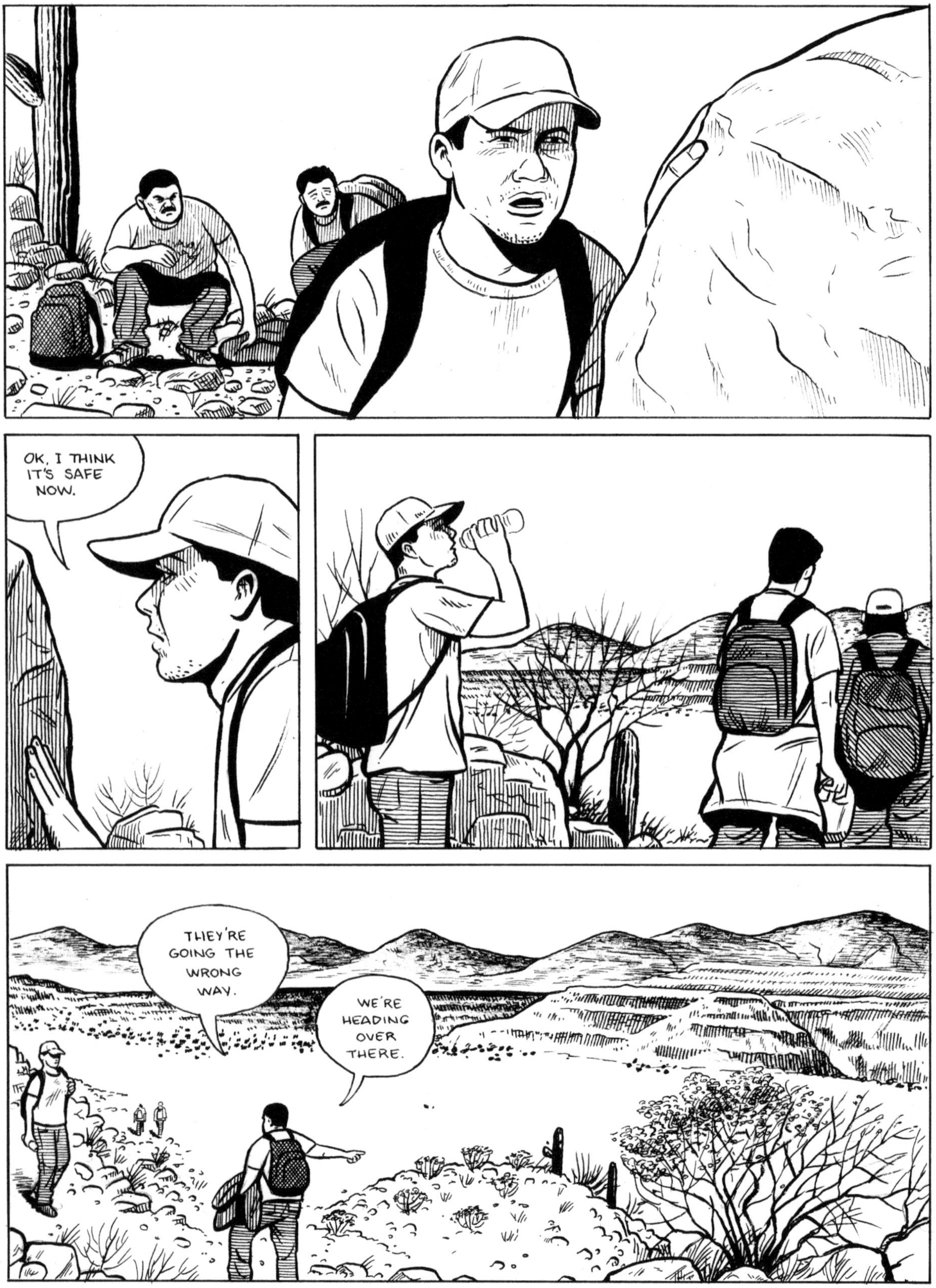
OK, I THINK IT'S SAFE NOW.
THEY'RE GOING THE WRONG WAY.
WE'RE HEADING OVER THERE.

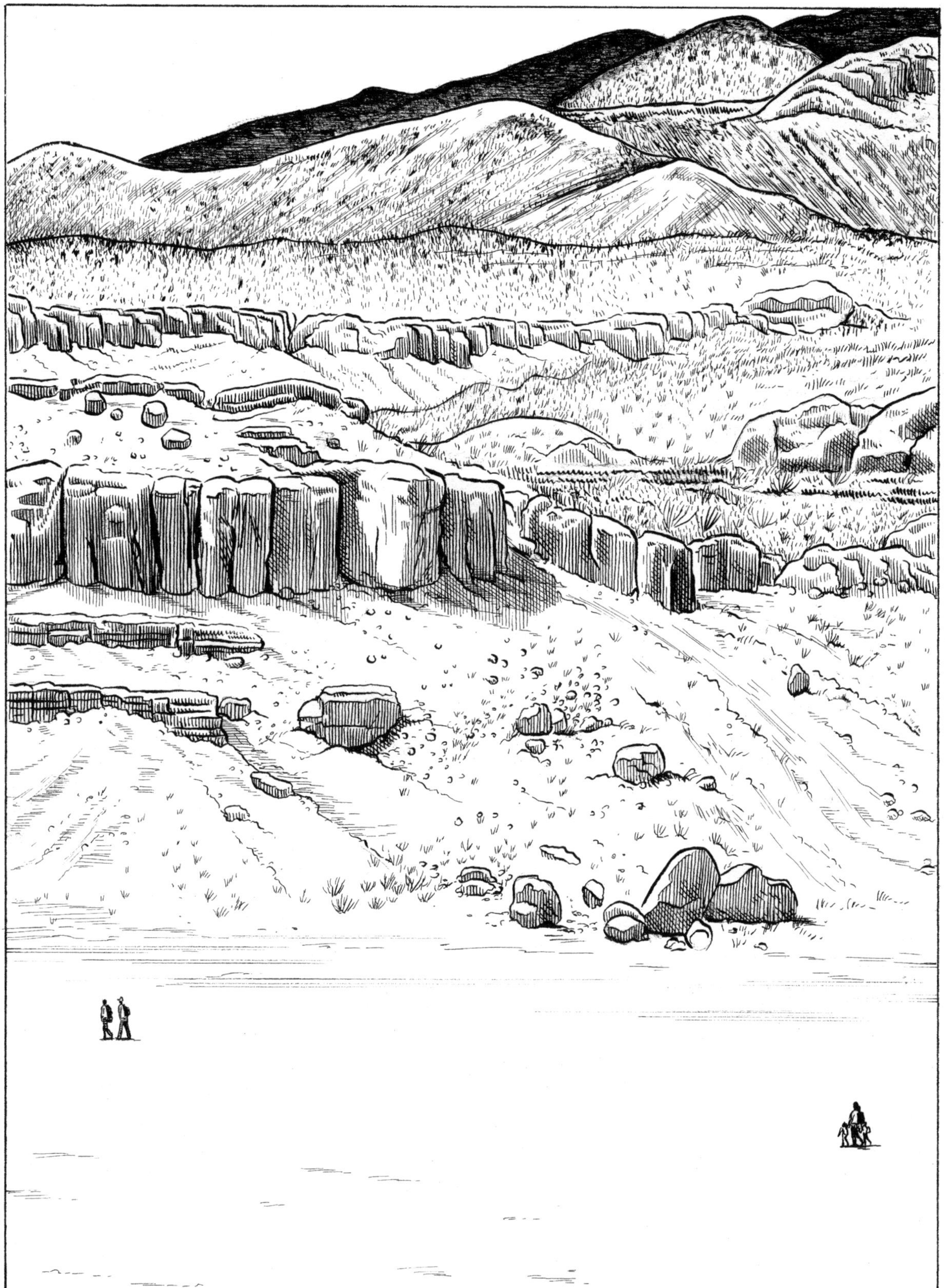

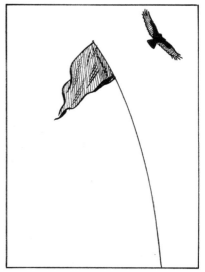

WATER STATION.

WHO PUT IT THERE?

GRINGO GUILT.

THEY DON'T ALL FEEL GUILTY...

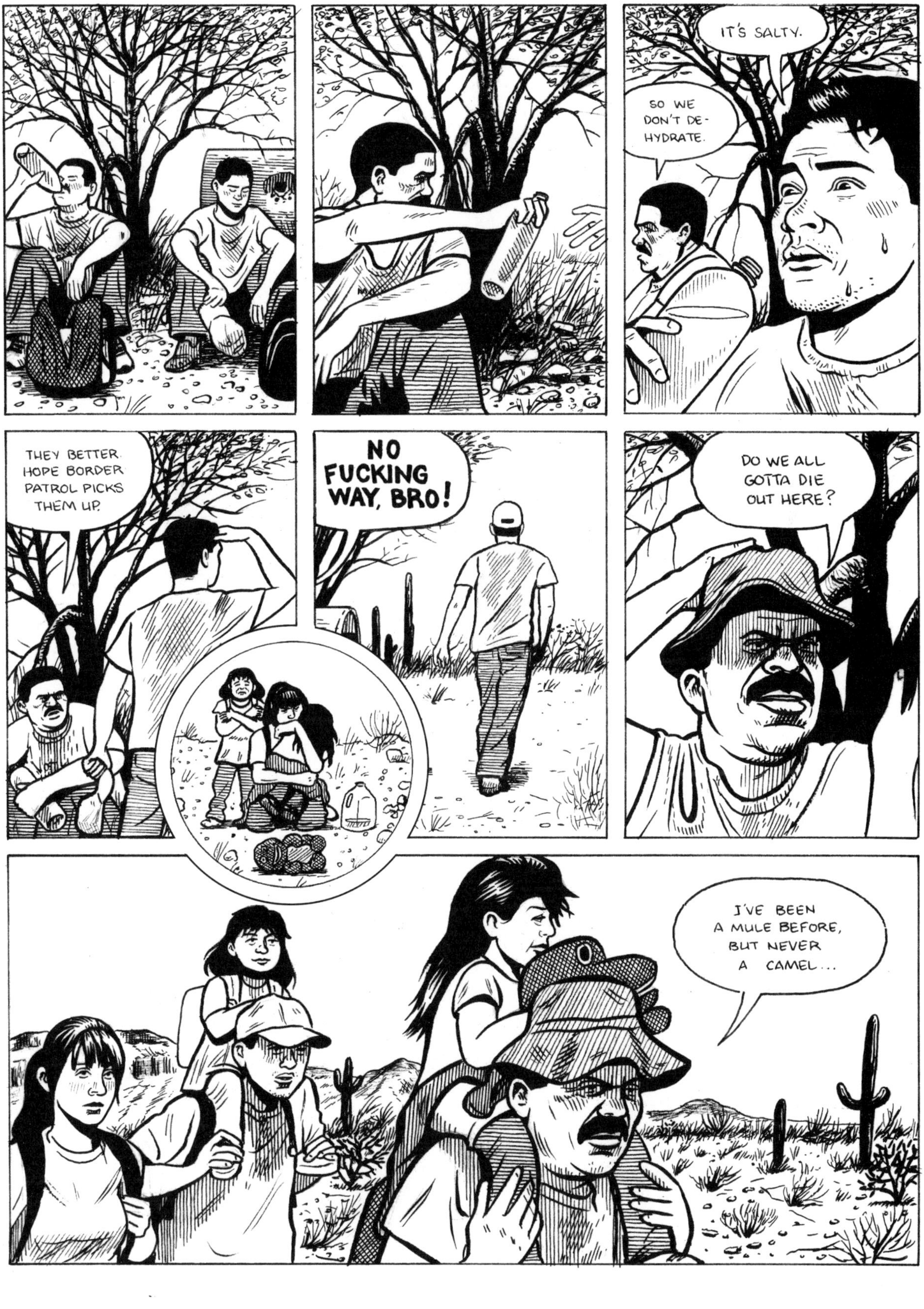
IT'S SALTY.
SO WE DON'T DE-HYDRATE.
THEY BETTER HOPE BORDER PATROL PICKS THEM UP.
NO FUCKING WAY, BRO!
DO WE ALL GOTTA DIE OUT HERE?
I'VE BEEN A MULE BEFORE, BUT NEVER A CAMEL...

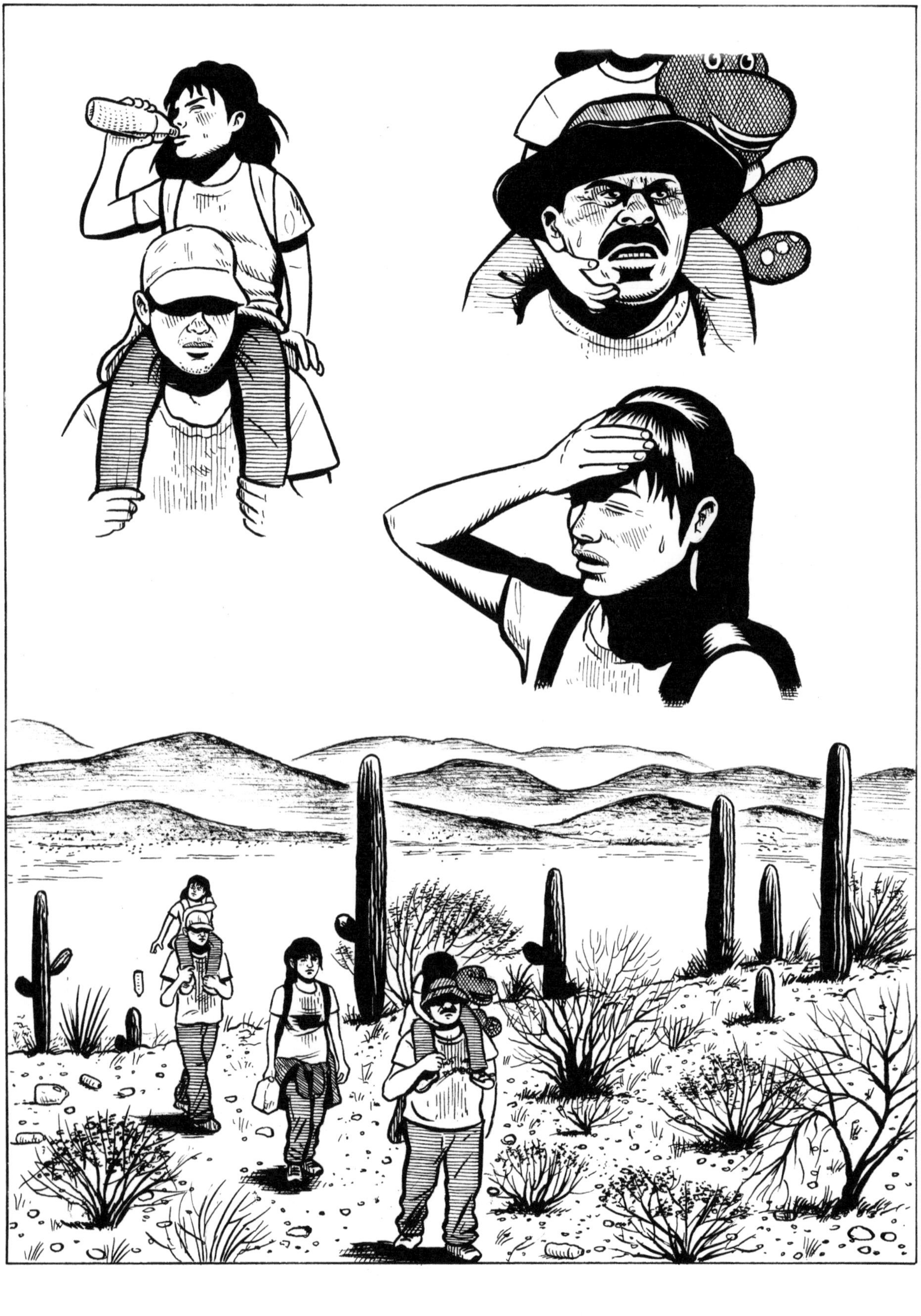

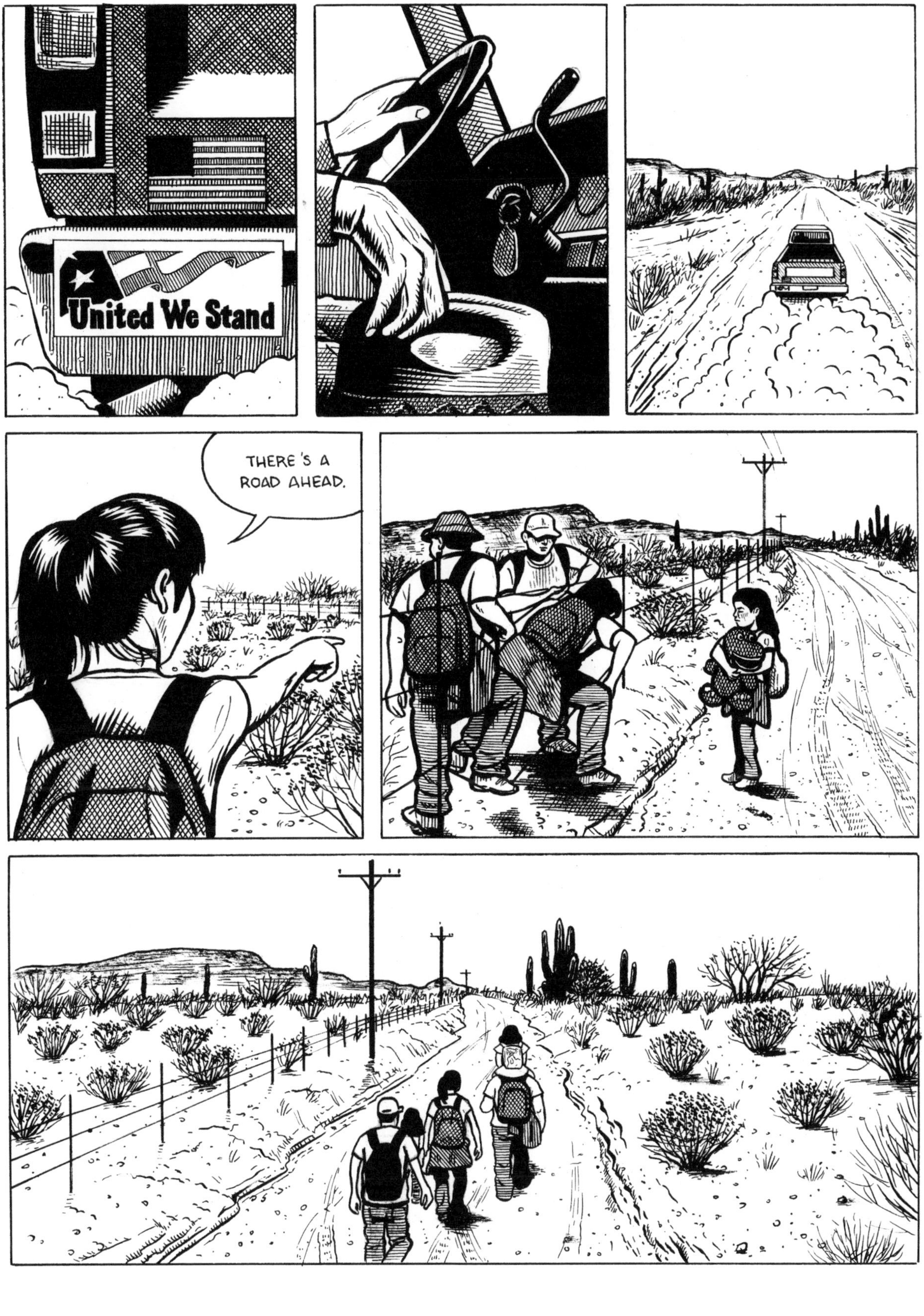
United We Stand
THERE'S A ROAD AHEAD.

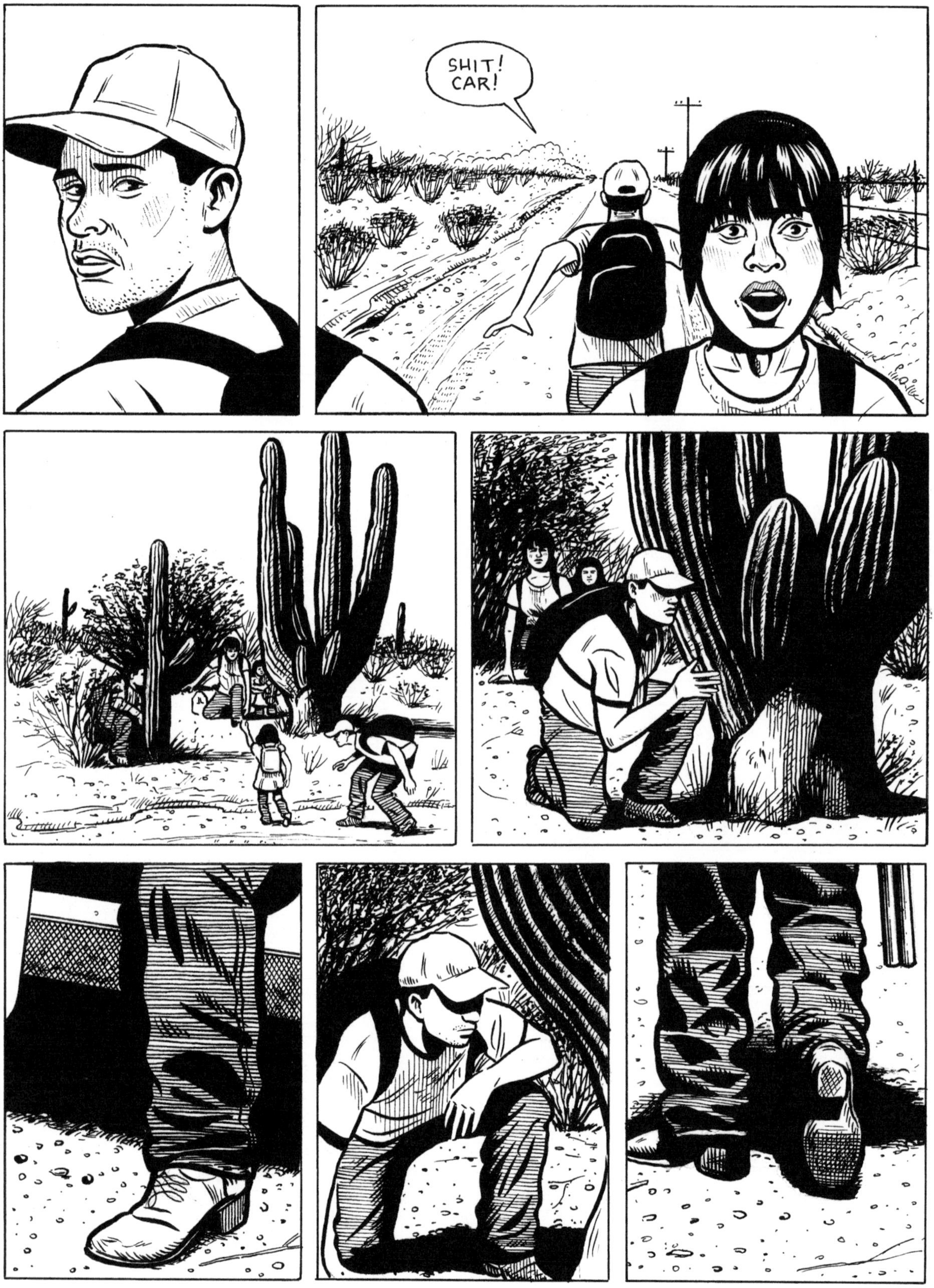
SHIT!
CAR!

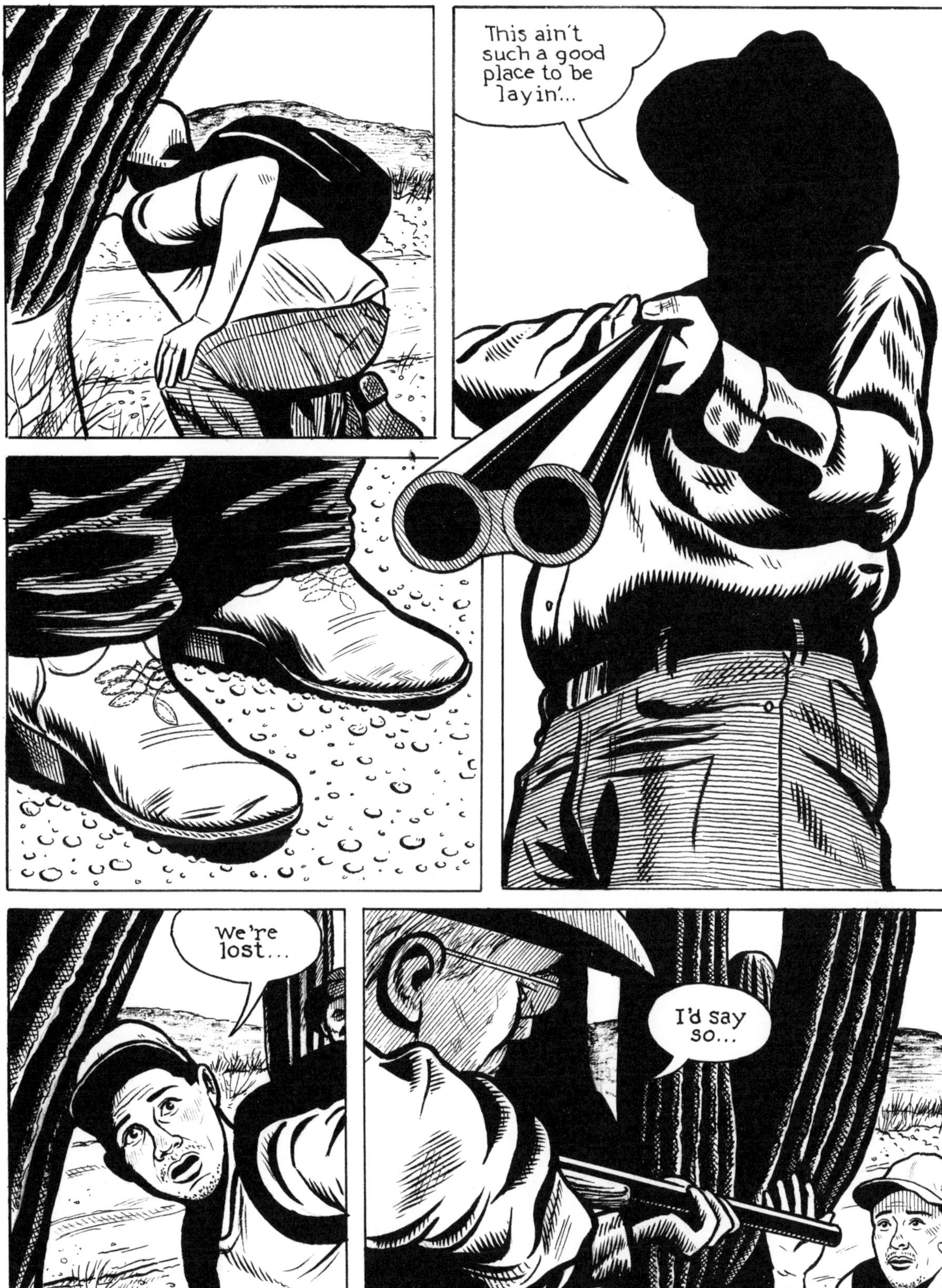
This ain't such a good place to be layin'...
We're lost...
I'd say so...

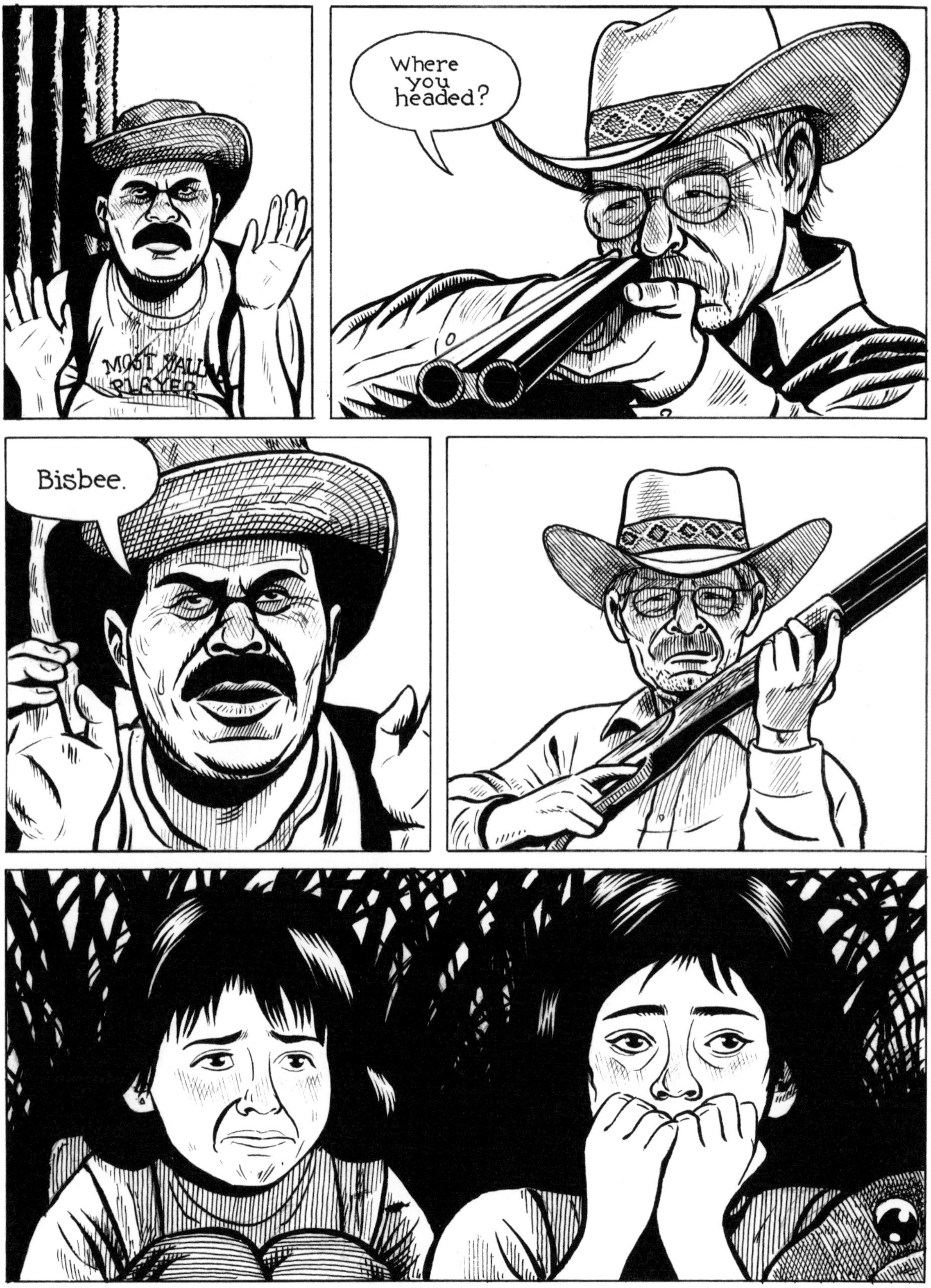
Where you headed?
Bisbee.

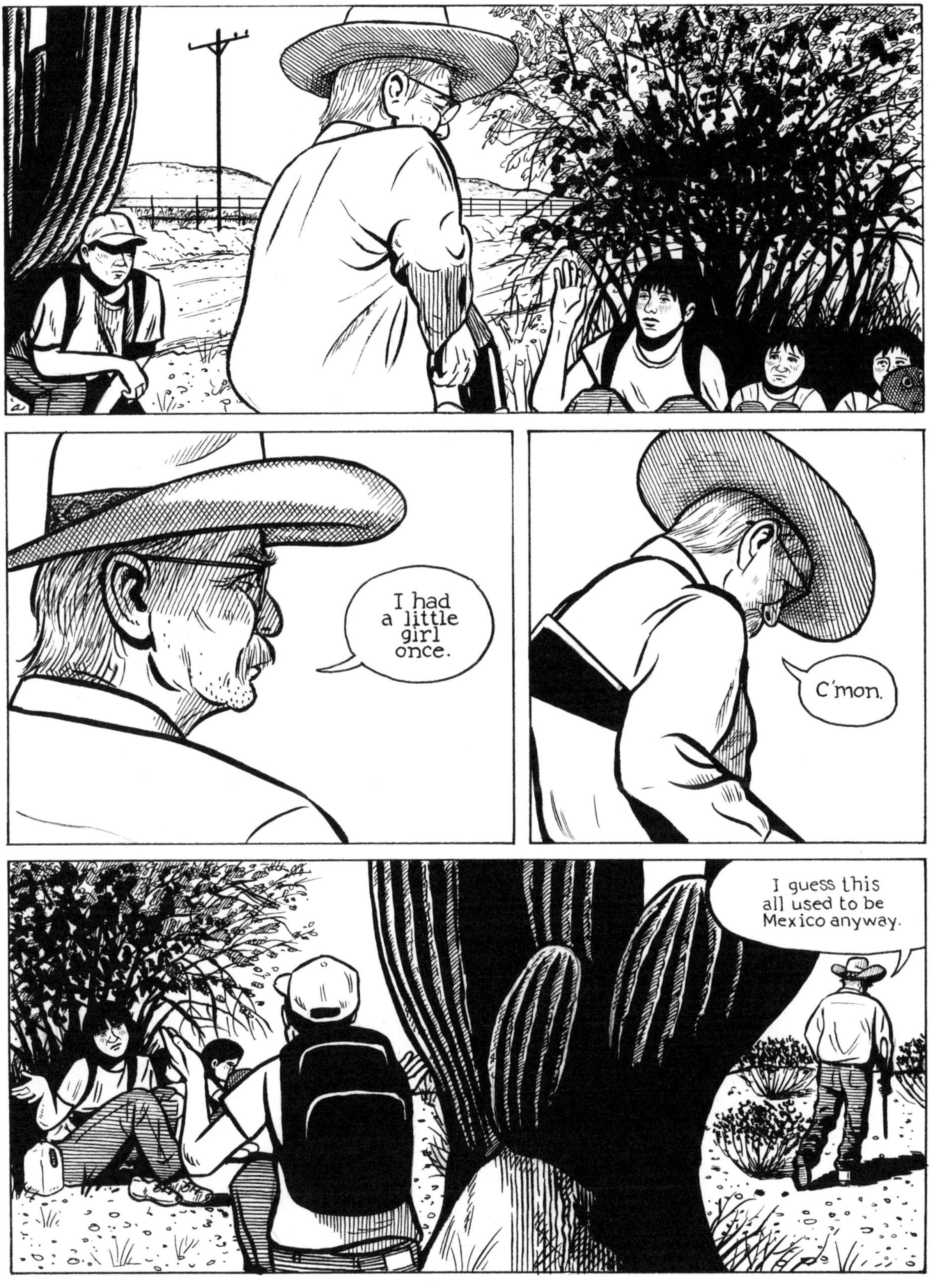
I had a little girl once.
C'mon.
I guess this all used to be Mexico anyway.

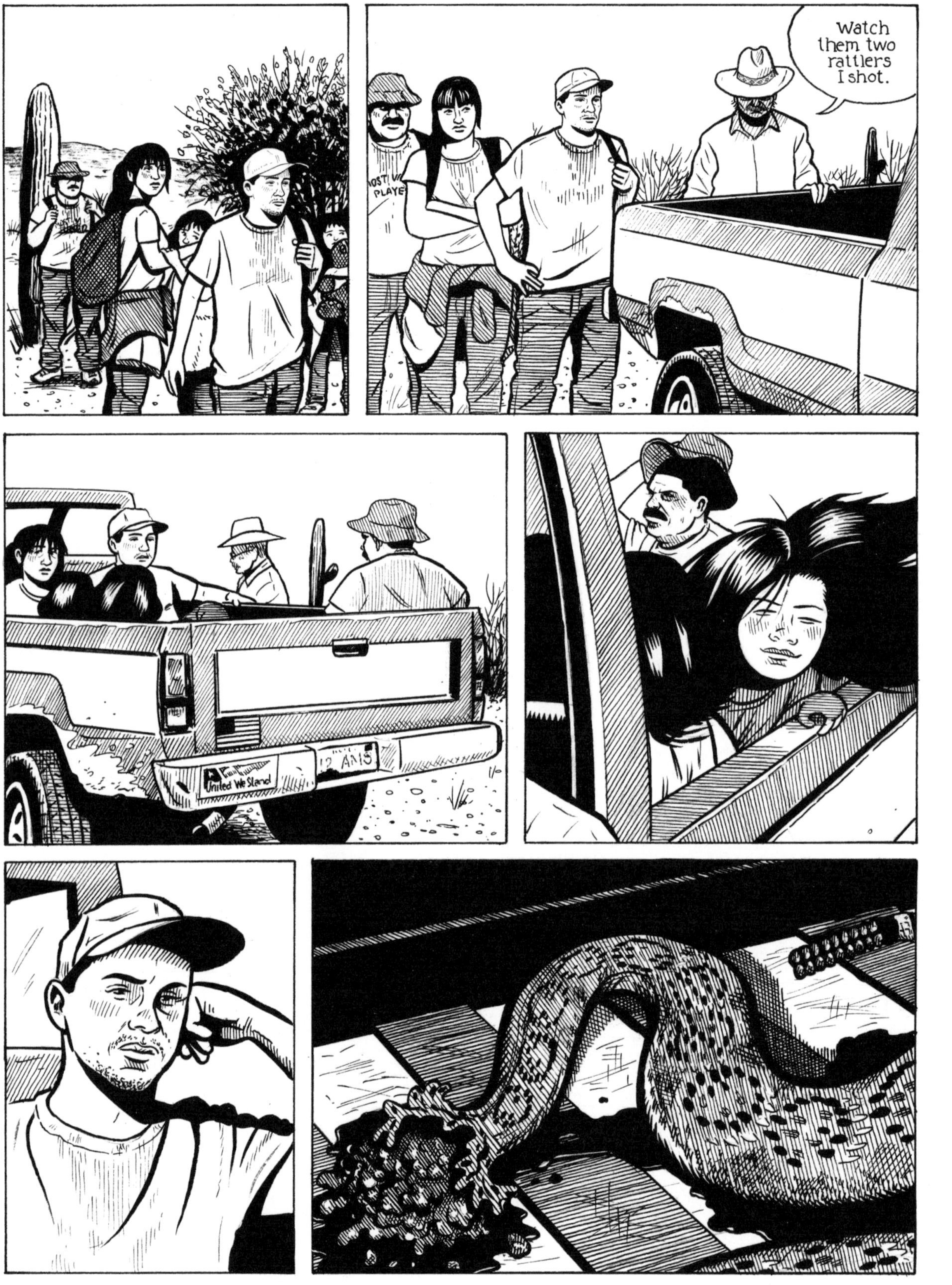
Watch them two rattlers I shot.
United We Stand

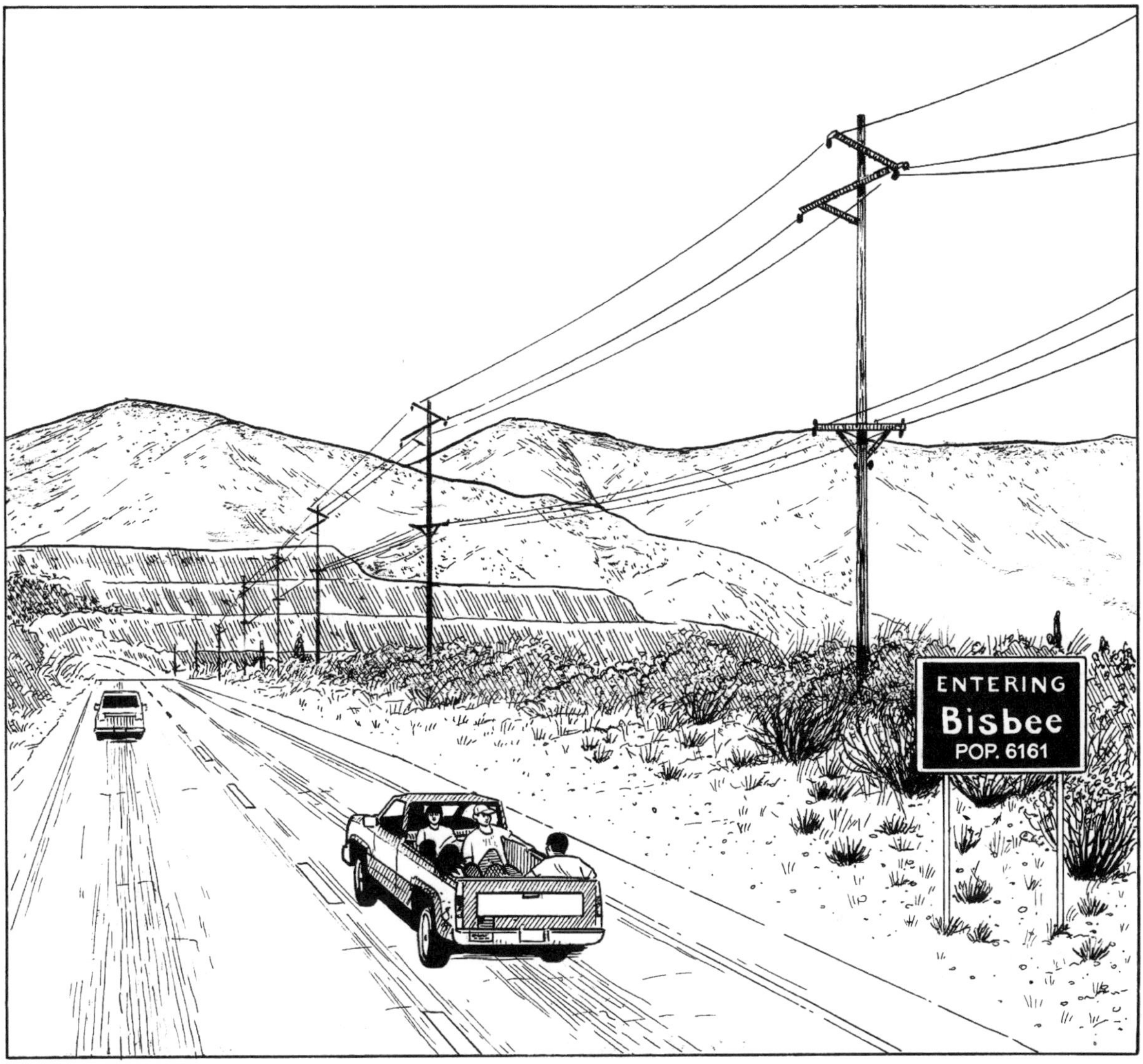
ENTERING
Bisbee
POP. 6161

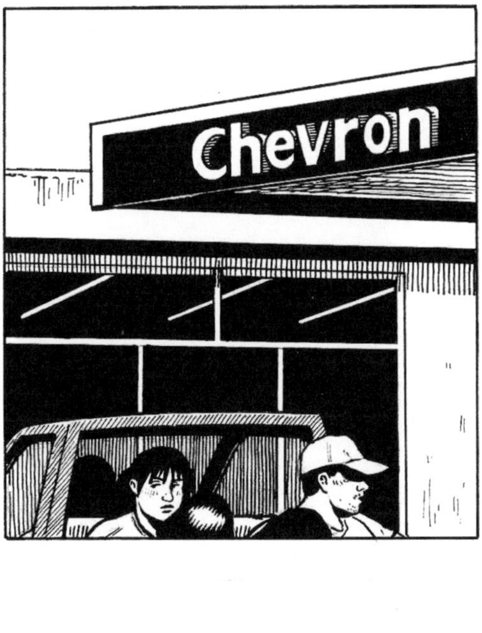
Chevron

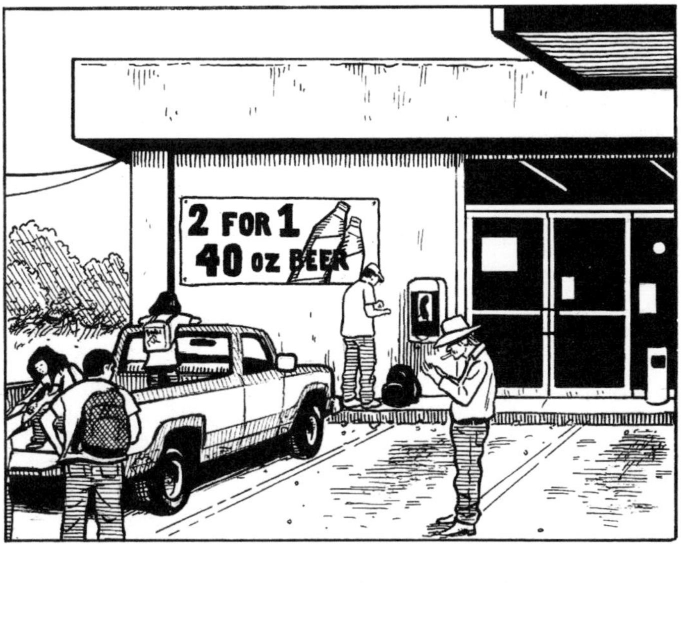
2 FOR 1
40 OZ BEER

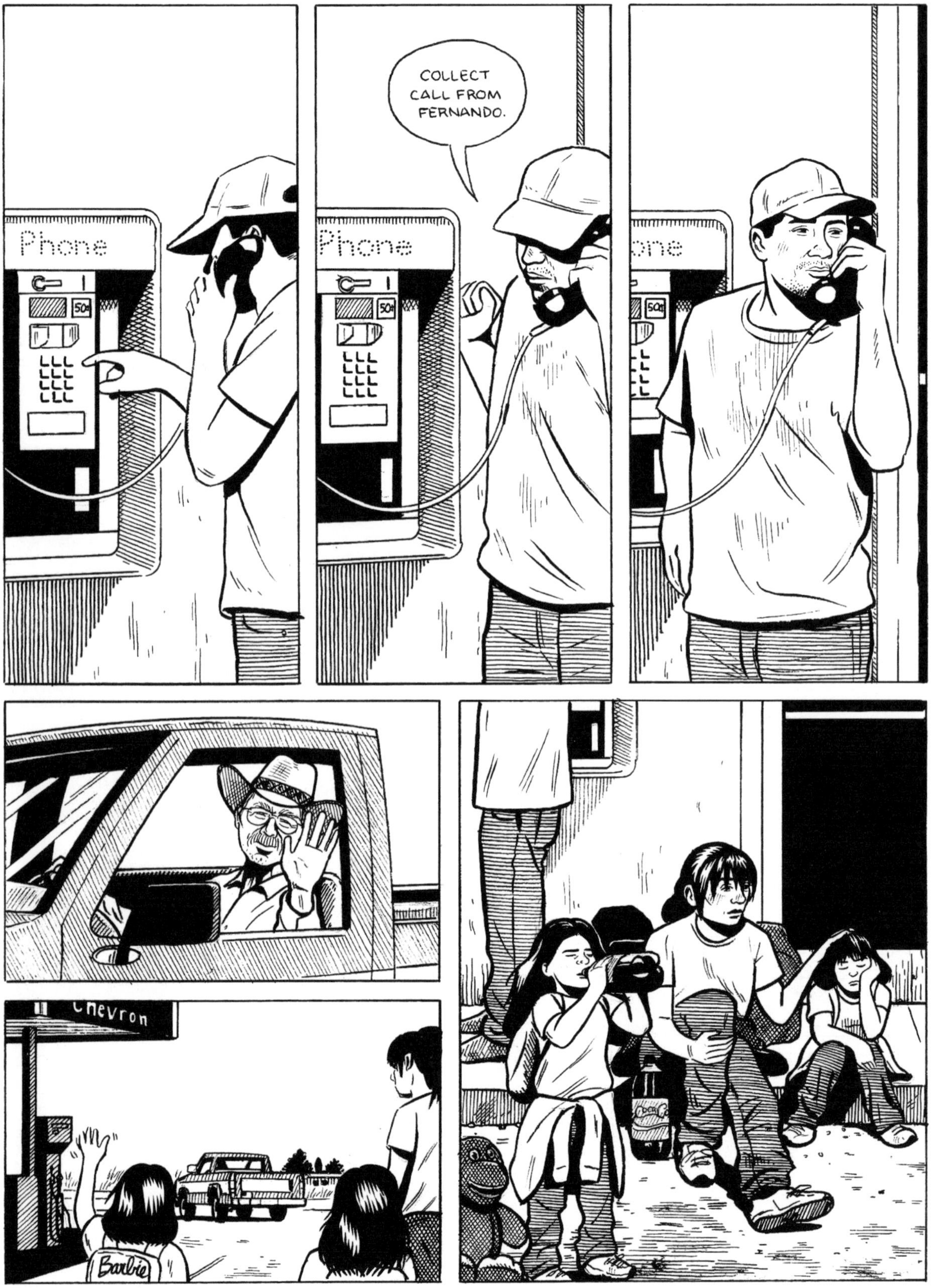
Phone
Phone
COLLECT CALL FROM FERNANDO.
Phone
Chevron
Barbie
Coca-Cola

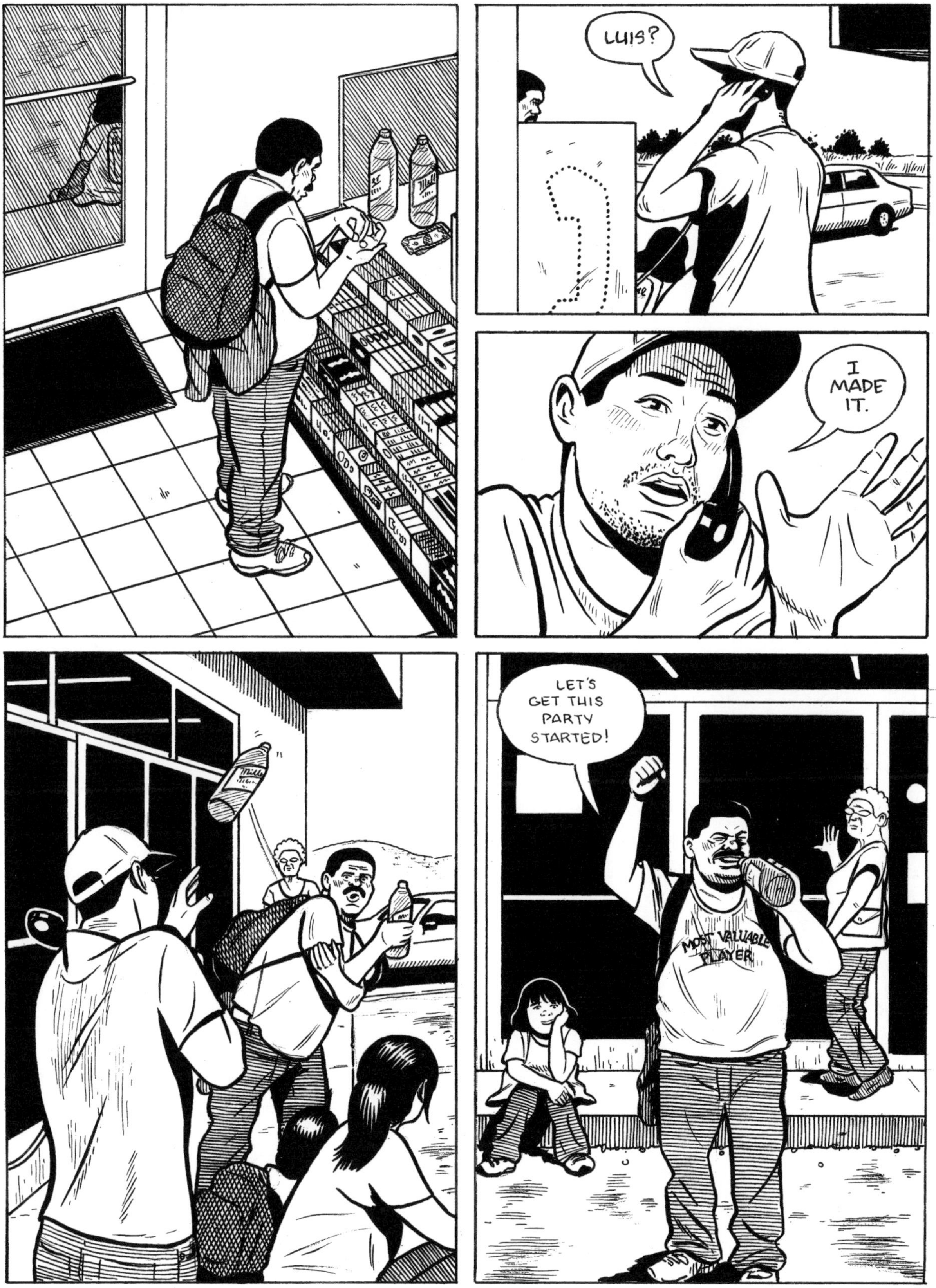
LUIS?
I MADE IT.
LET'S GET THIS PARTY STARTED!
MOST VALUABLE PLAYER

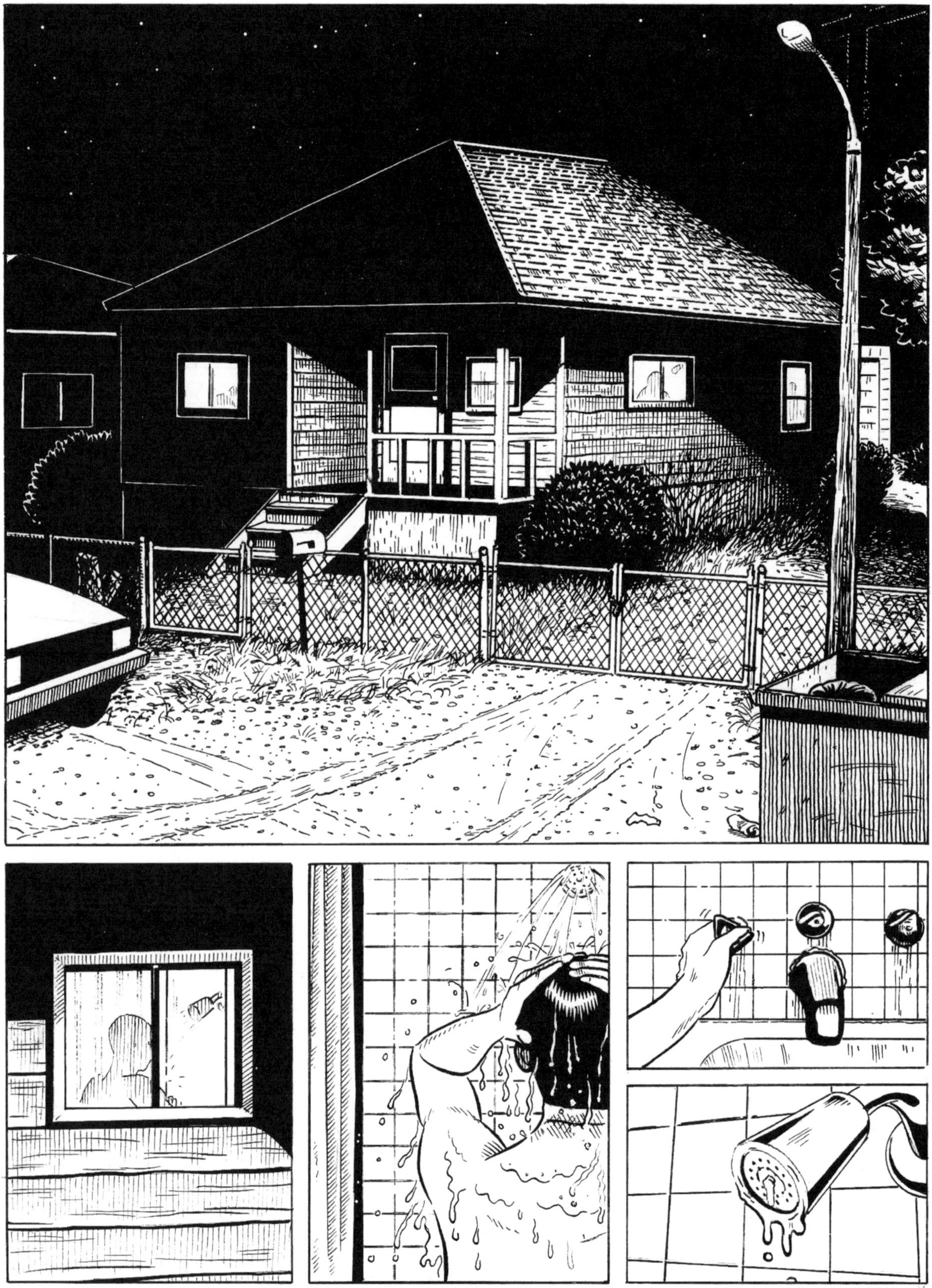

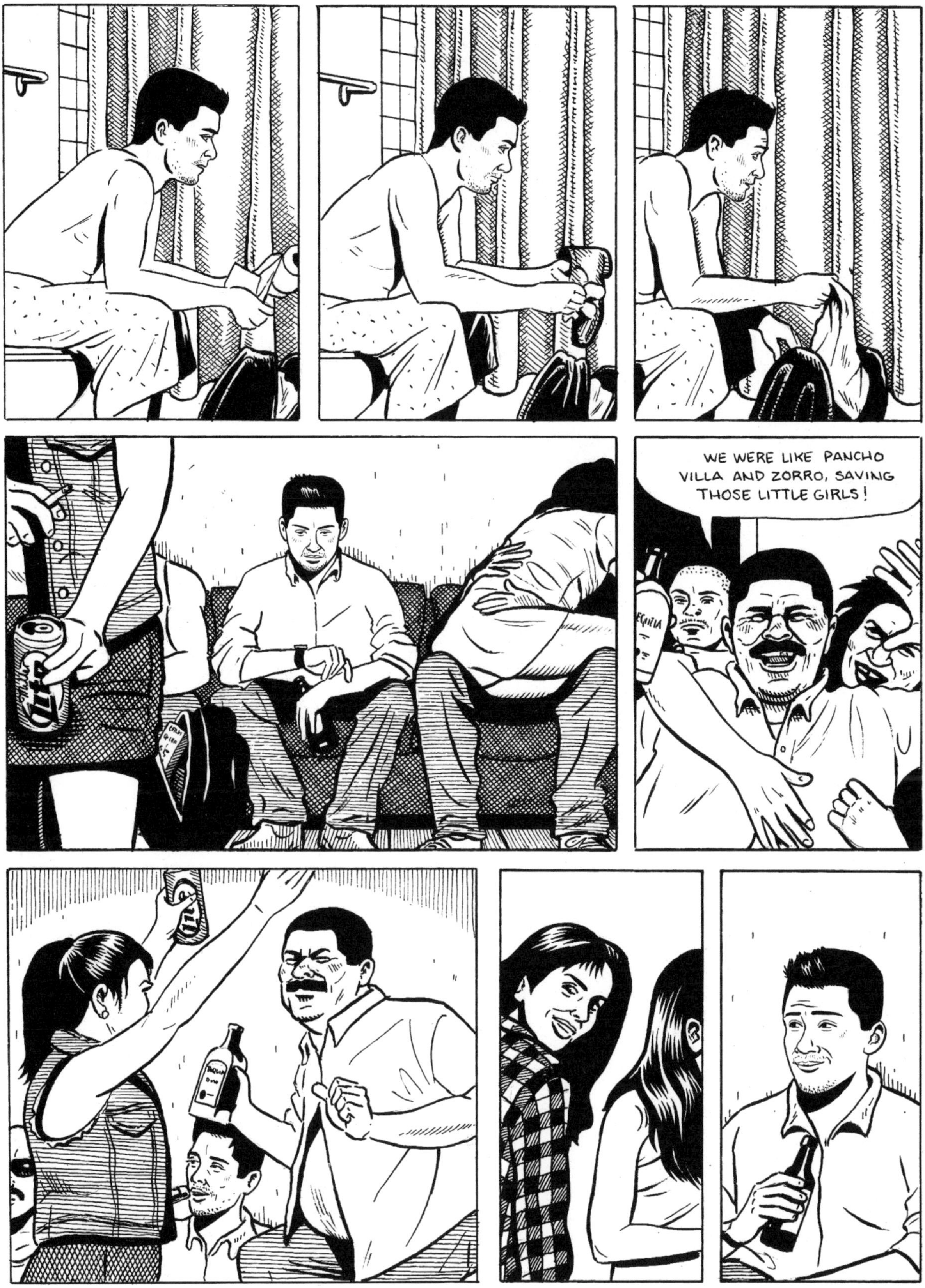
WE WERE LIKE PANCHO VILLA AND ZORRO, SAVING THOSE LITTLE GIRLS!

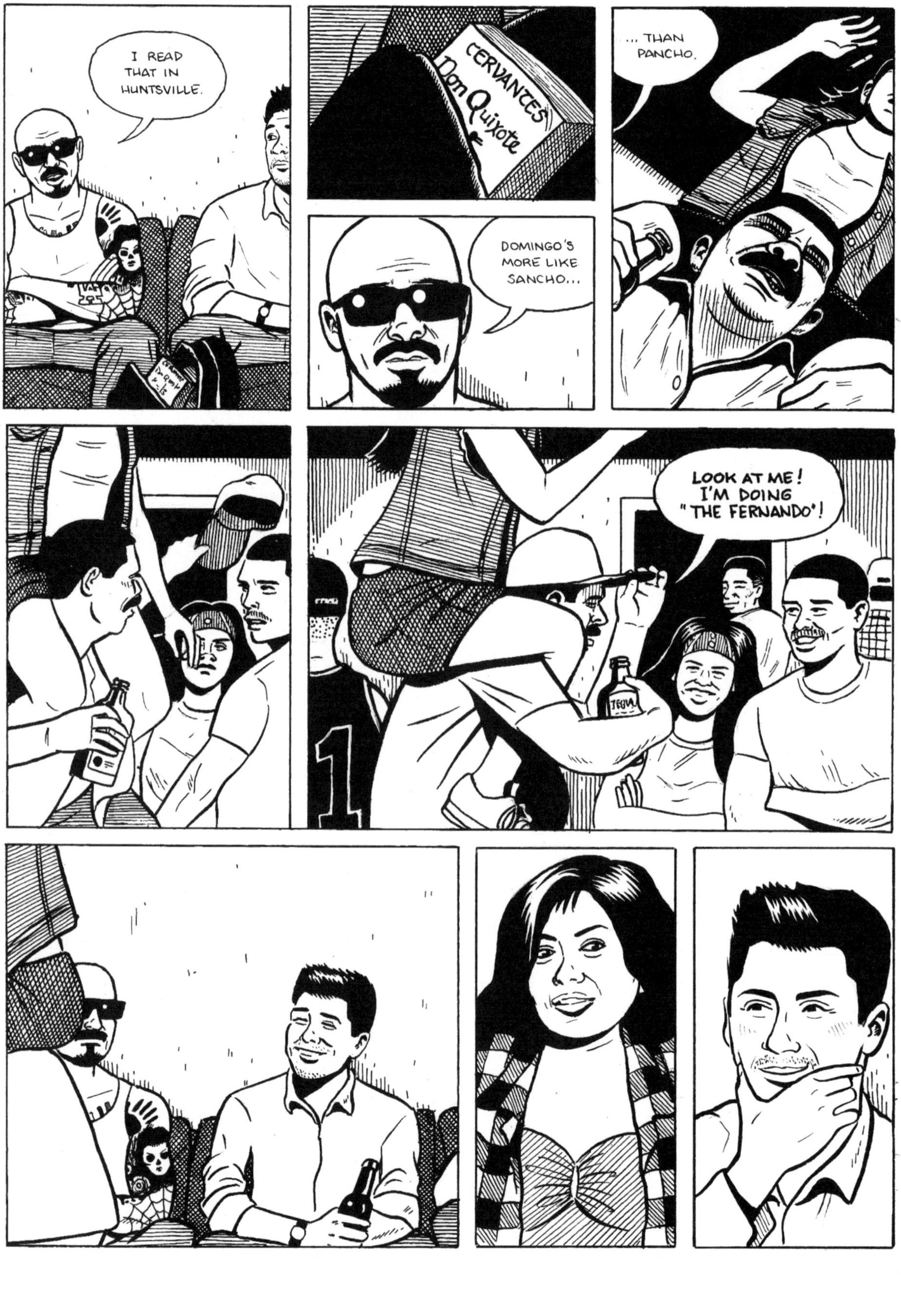
I READ THAT IN HUNTSVILLE.
CERVANTES Don Quixote
DOMINGO'S MORE LIKE SANCHO...
... THAN PANCHO.
LOOK AT ME! I'M DOING "THE FERNANDO"!

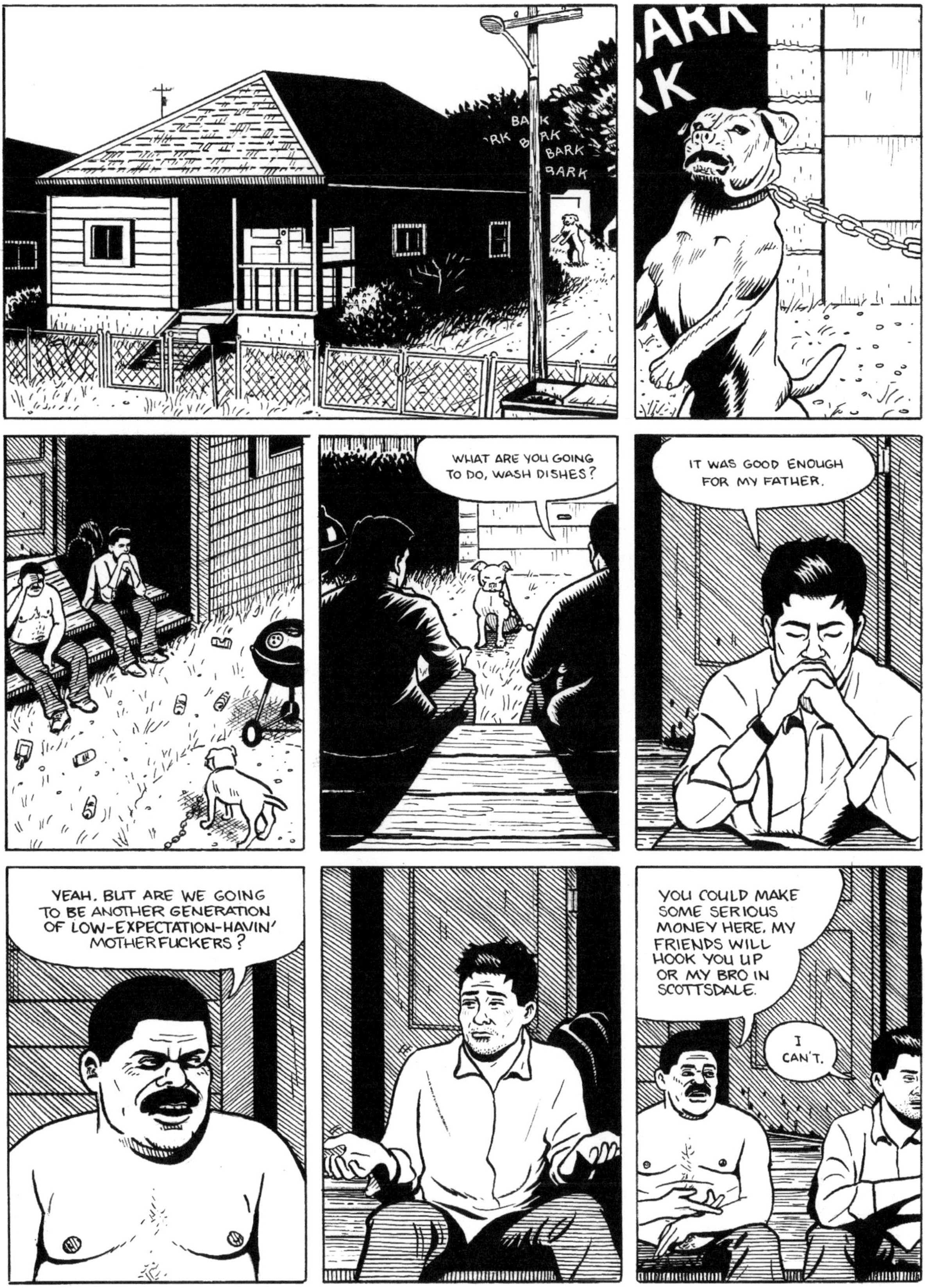
BARK
BARK
BARK
BARK
WHAT ARE YOU GOING TO DO, WASH DISHES?
IT WAS GOOD ENOUGH FOR MY FATHER.
YEAH. BUT ARE WE GOING TO BE ANOTHER GENERATION OF LOW-EXPECTATION-HAVIN' MOTHERFUCKERS?
YOU COULD MAKE SOME SERIOUS MONEY HERE. MY FRIENDS WILL HOOK YOU UP OR MY BRO IN SCOTTSDALE.
I CAN'T.

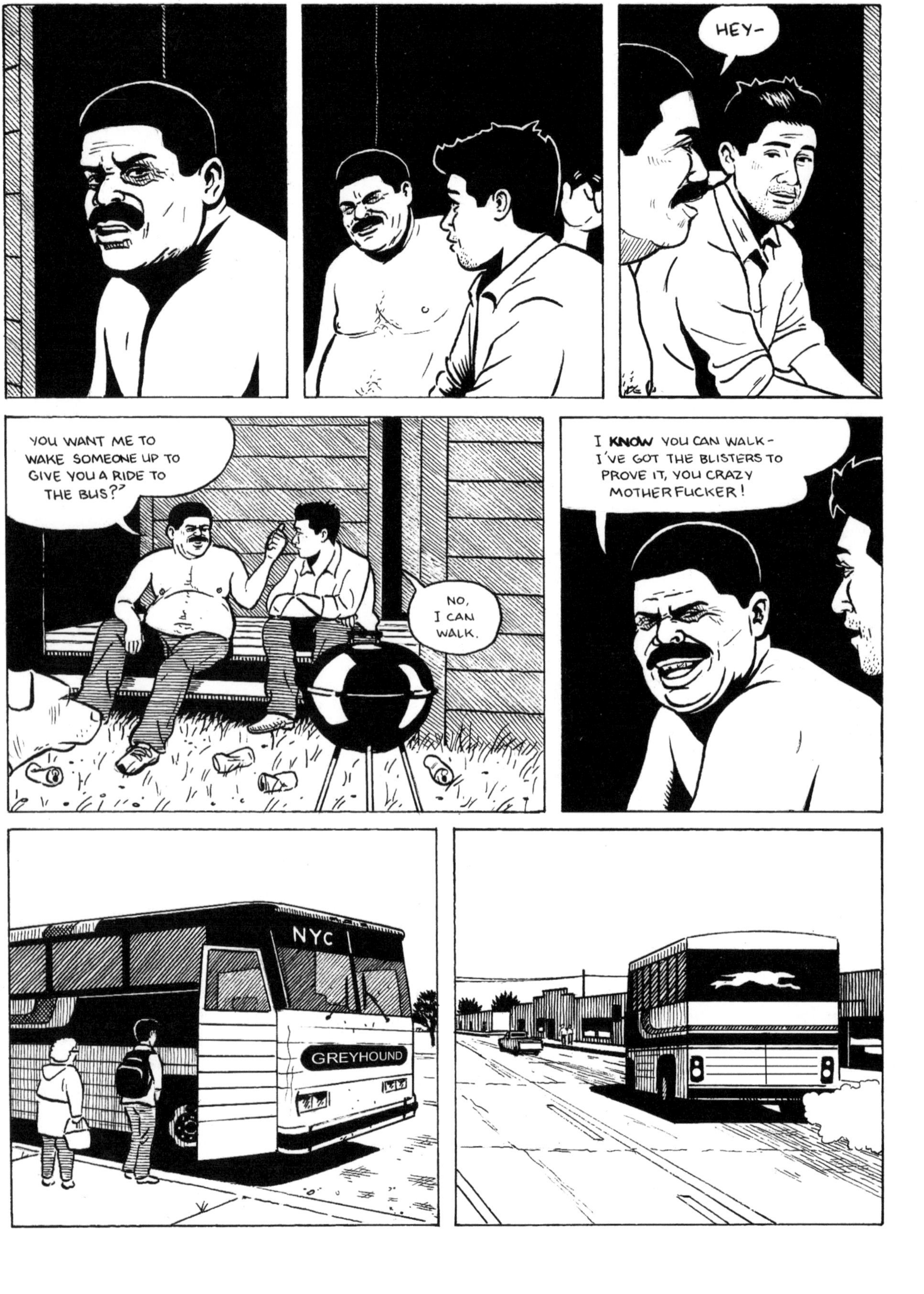
HEY-
YOU WANT ME TO WAKE SOMEONE UP TO GIVE YOU A RIDE TO THE BUS?
NO, I CAN WALK.
I **KNOW** YOU CAN WALK- I'VE GOT THE BLISTERS TO PROVE IT, YOU CRAZY MOTHERFUCKER!
NYC
GREYHOUND

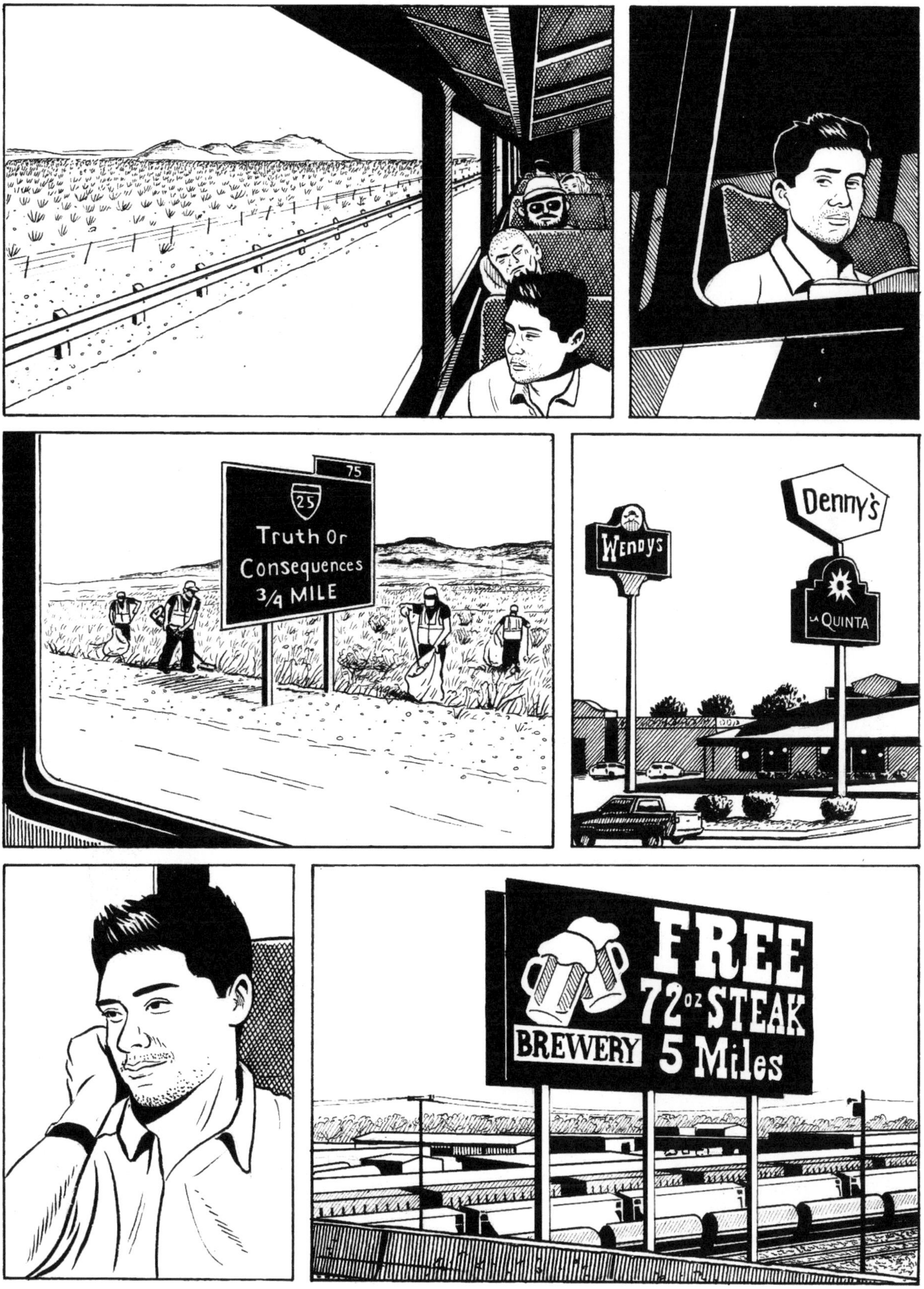
75
25
Truth Or
Consequences
3/4 MILE
Wendys
Denny's
LA QUINTA
FREE
72 OZ STEAK
BREWERY
5 Miles

GREYHOUND
NYC
GREYHOUND
GREYHOUND

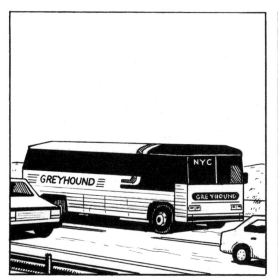

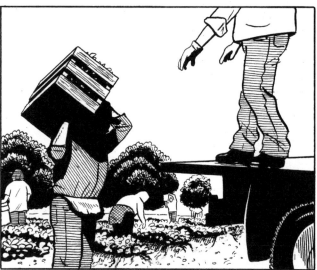

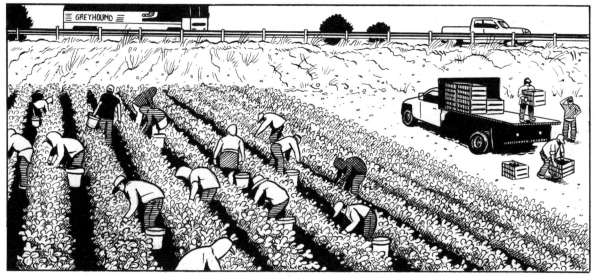

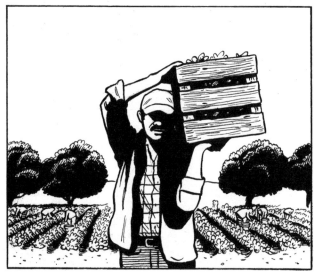

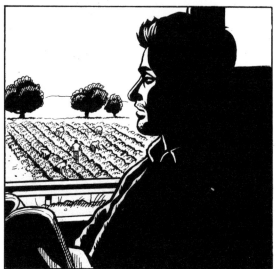

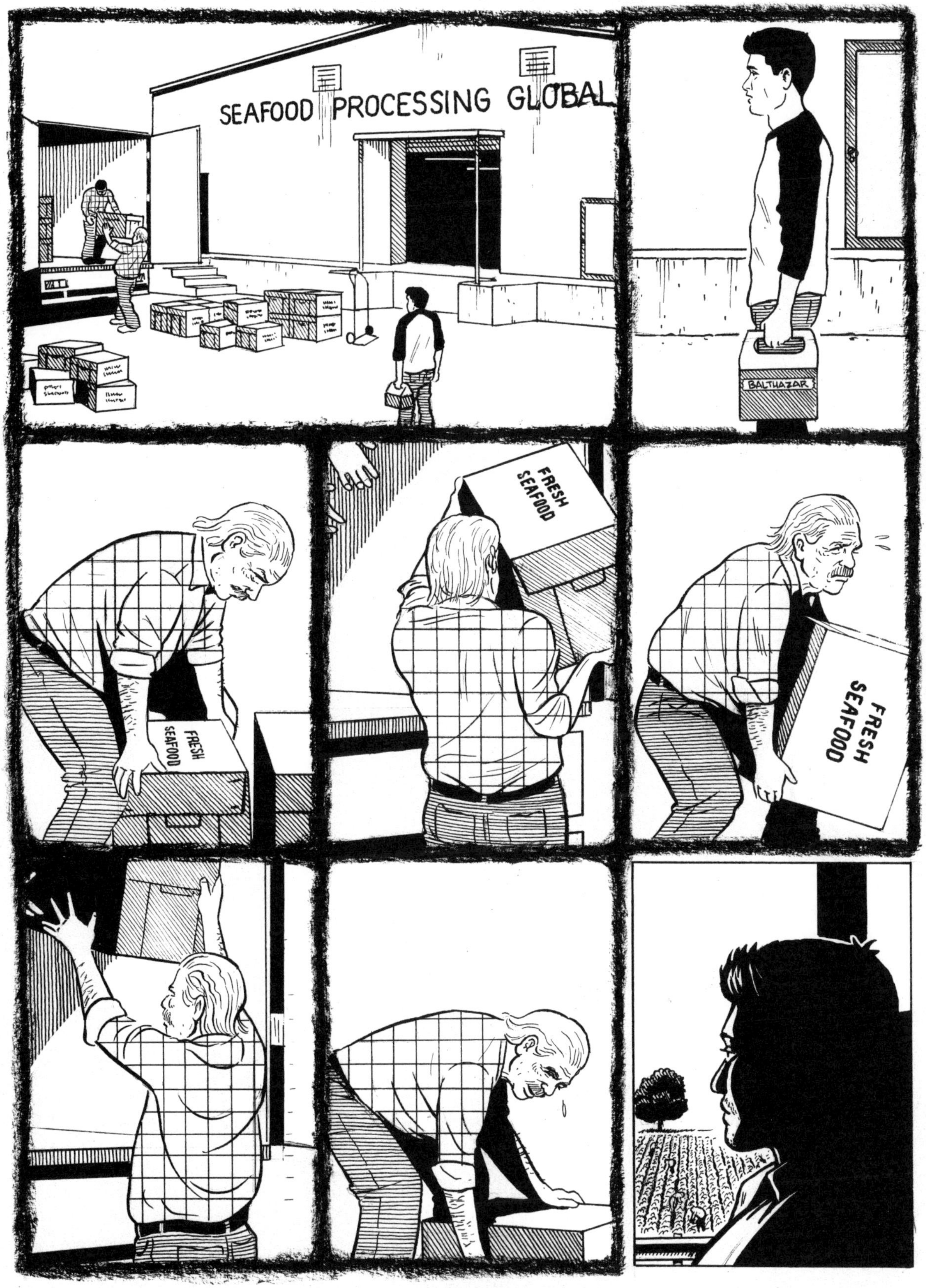
SEAFOOD PROCESSING GLOBAL
BALTHAZAR
FRESH SEAFOOD
FRESH SEAFOOD
FRESH SEAFOOD

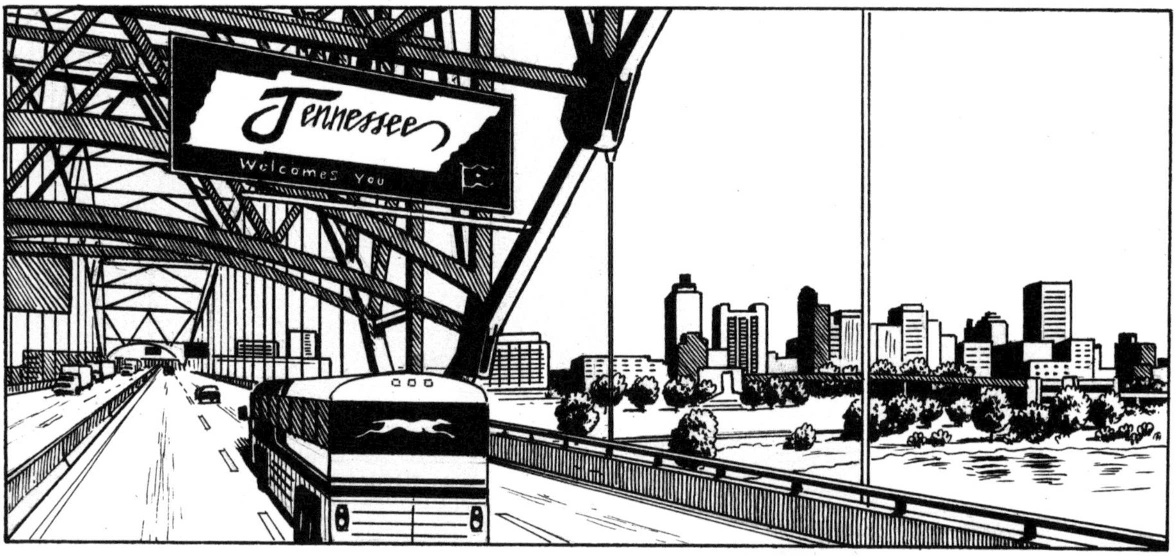
Tennessee
Welcomes You

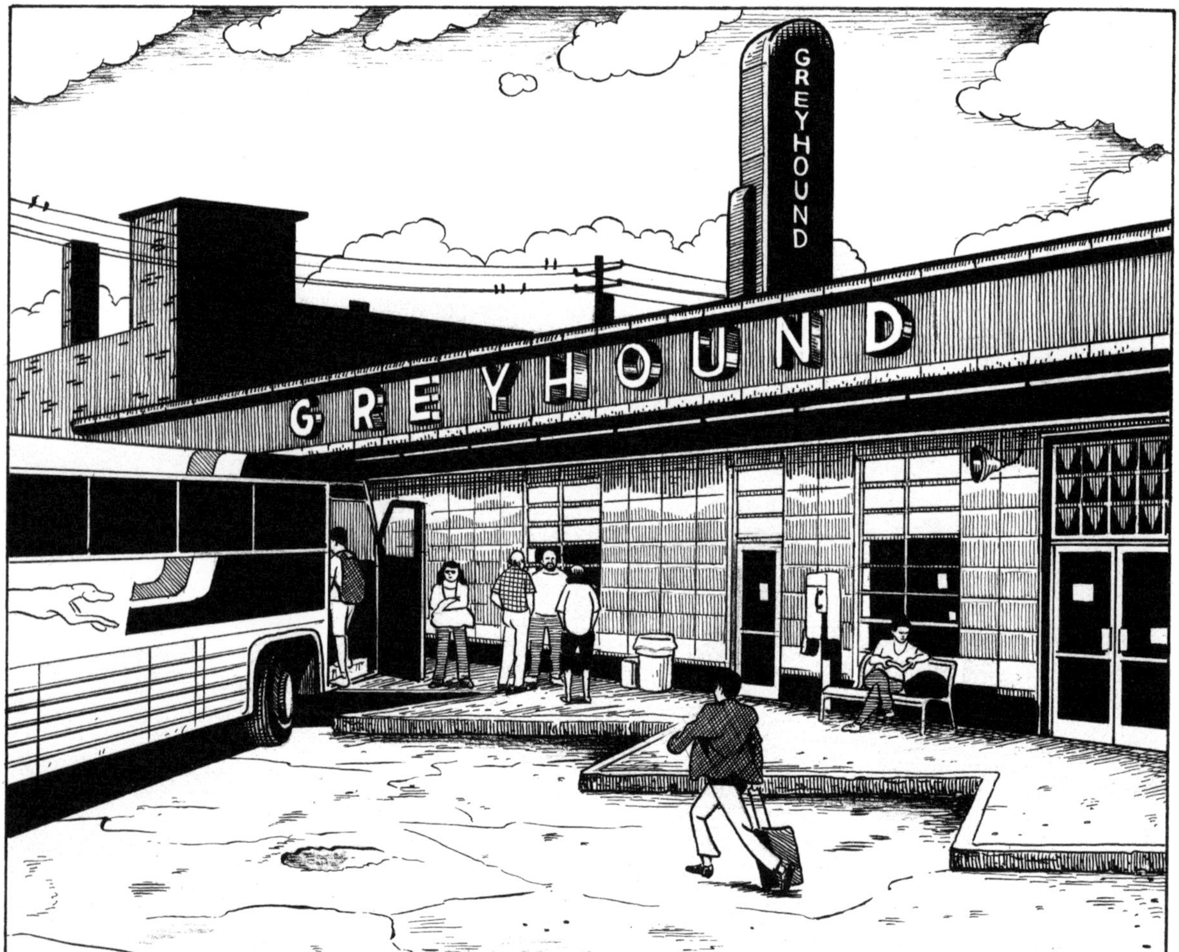
GREYHOUND
GREYHOUND

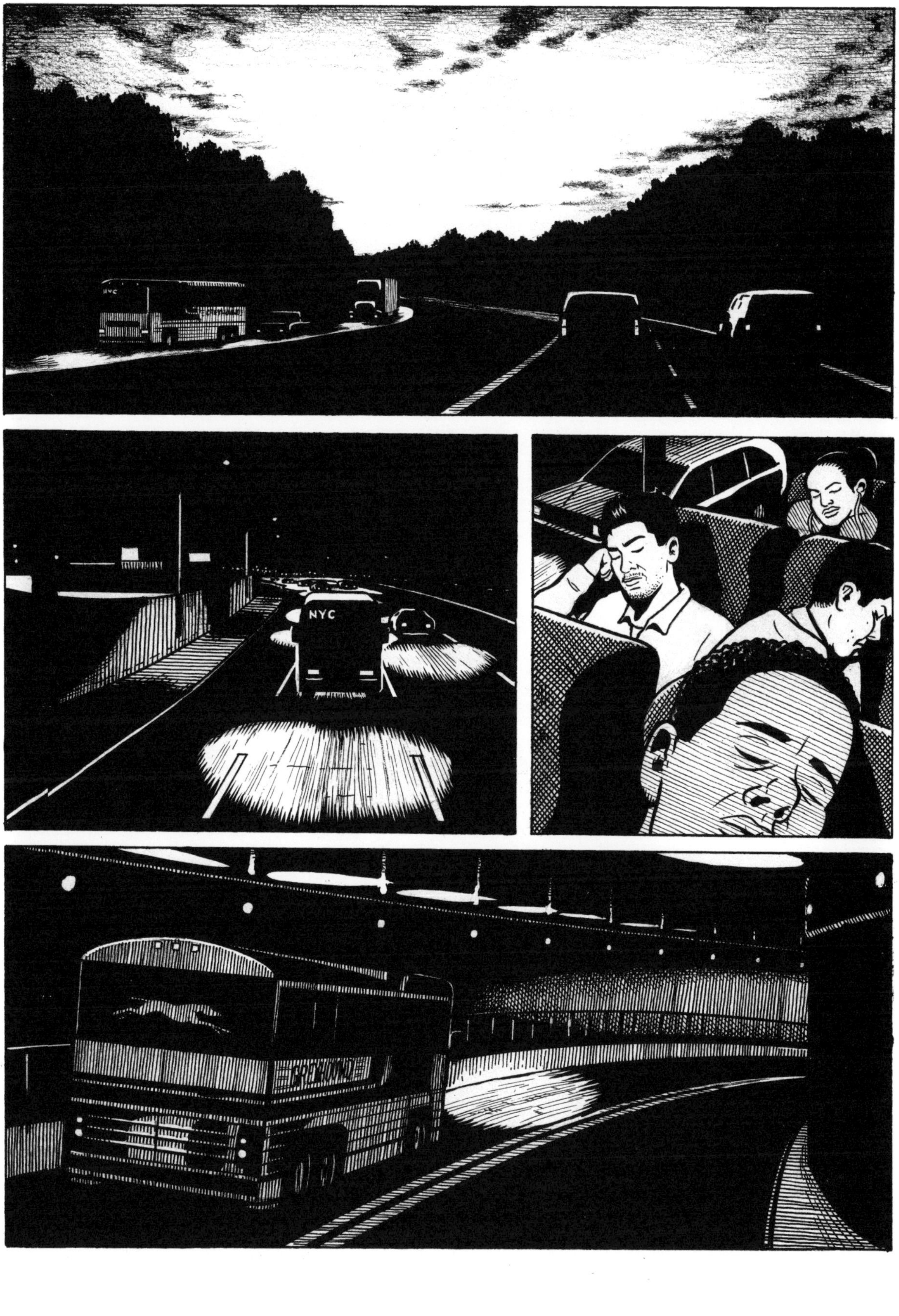
NYC
NYC

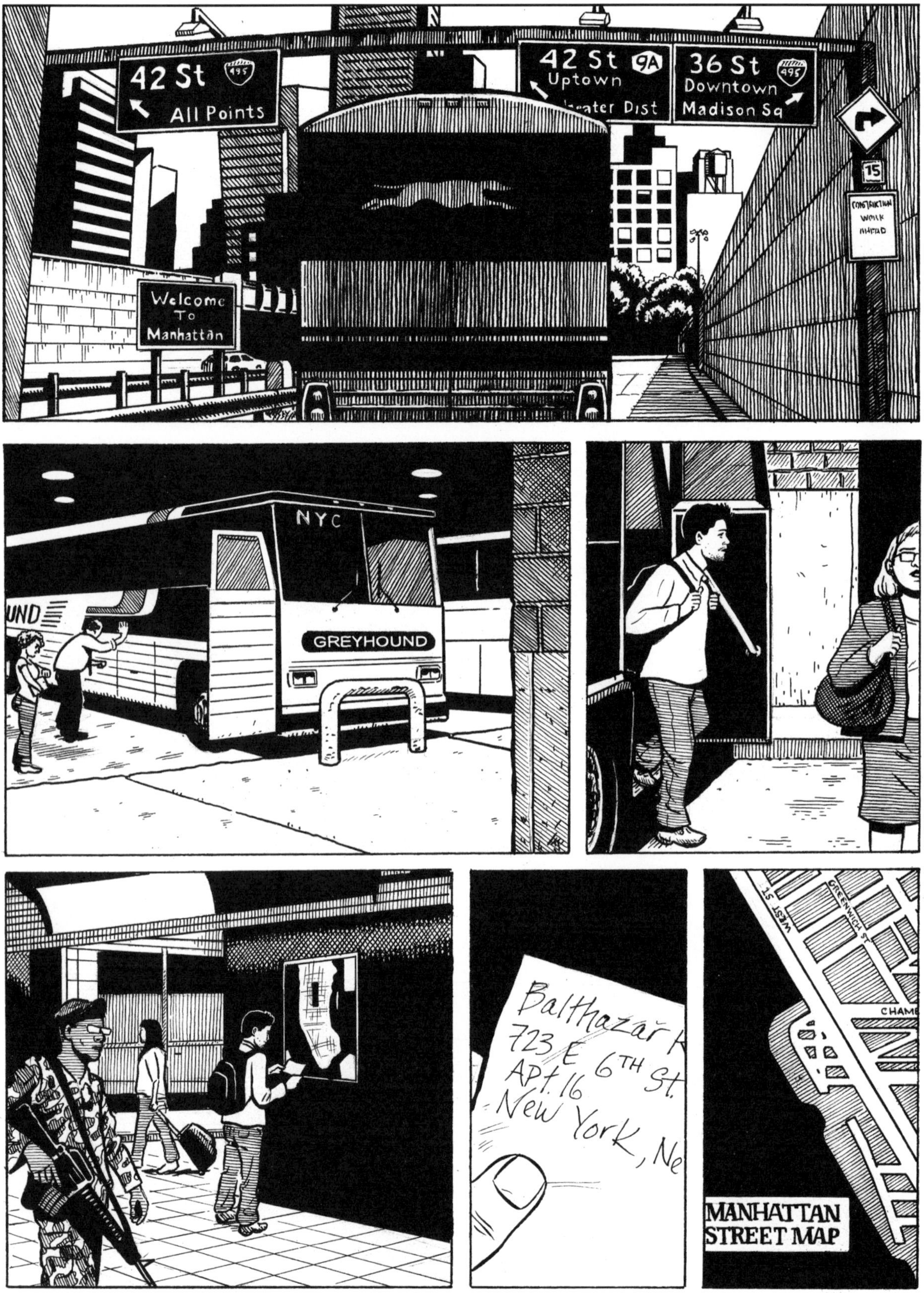
42 St
495
All Points
Welcome To Manhattan
42 St
9A
Uptown
36 St
495
Downtown
Madison Sq
15
NYC
GREYHOUND
Balthazar
723 E 6TH St.
Apt. 16
New York,
WEST ST
GREENWICH ST
MANHATTAN STREET MAP

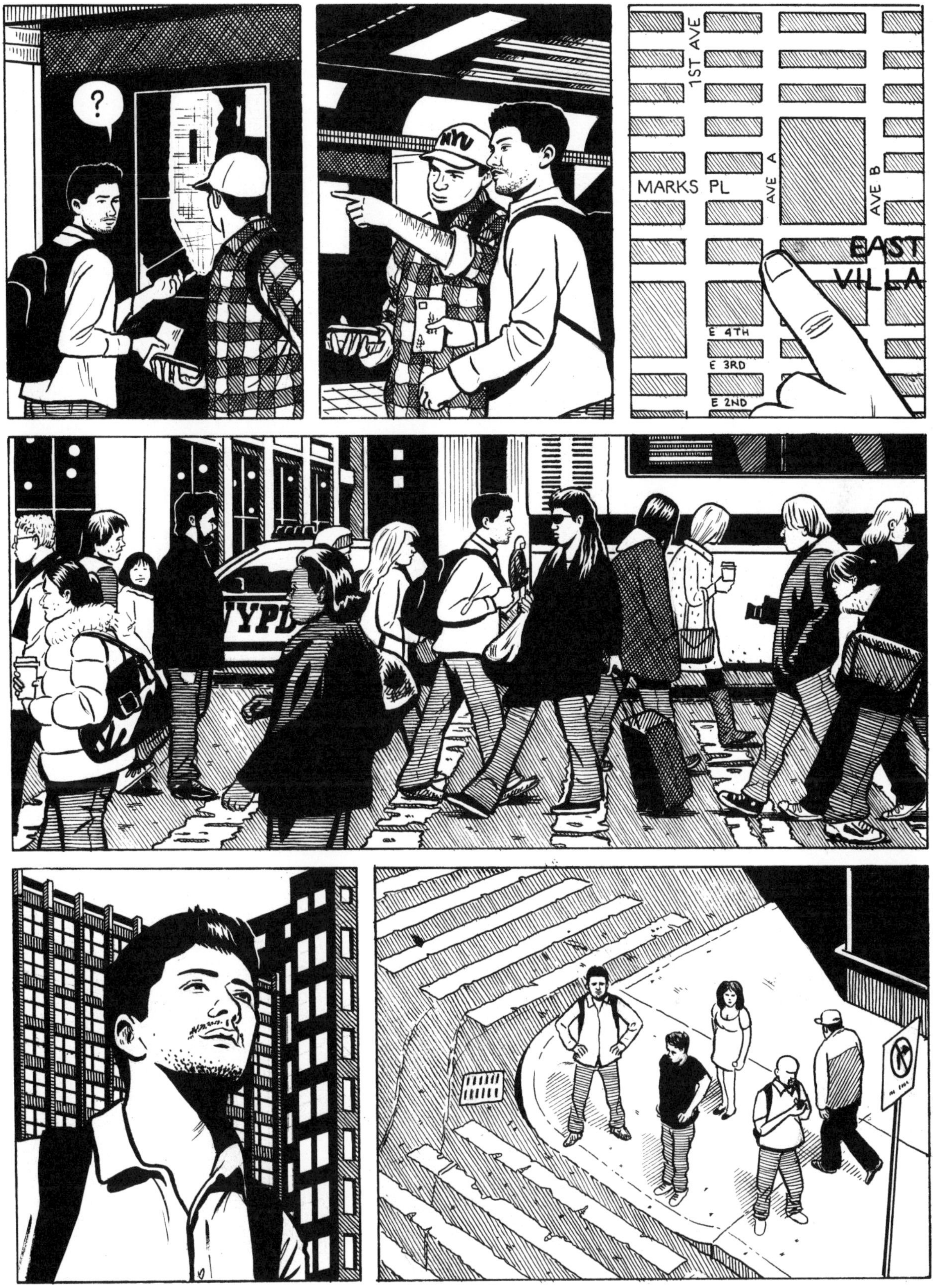
?
NYU
1ST AVE
MARKS PL
AVE A
AVE B
EAST
VILLA
E 4TH
E 3RD
E 2ND
YPD

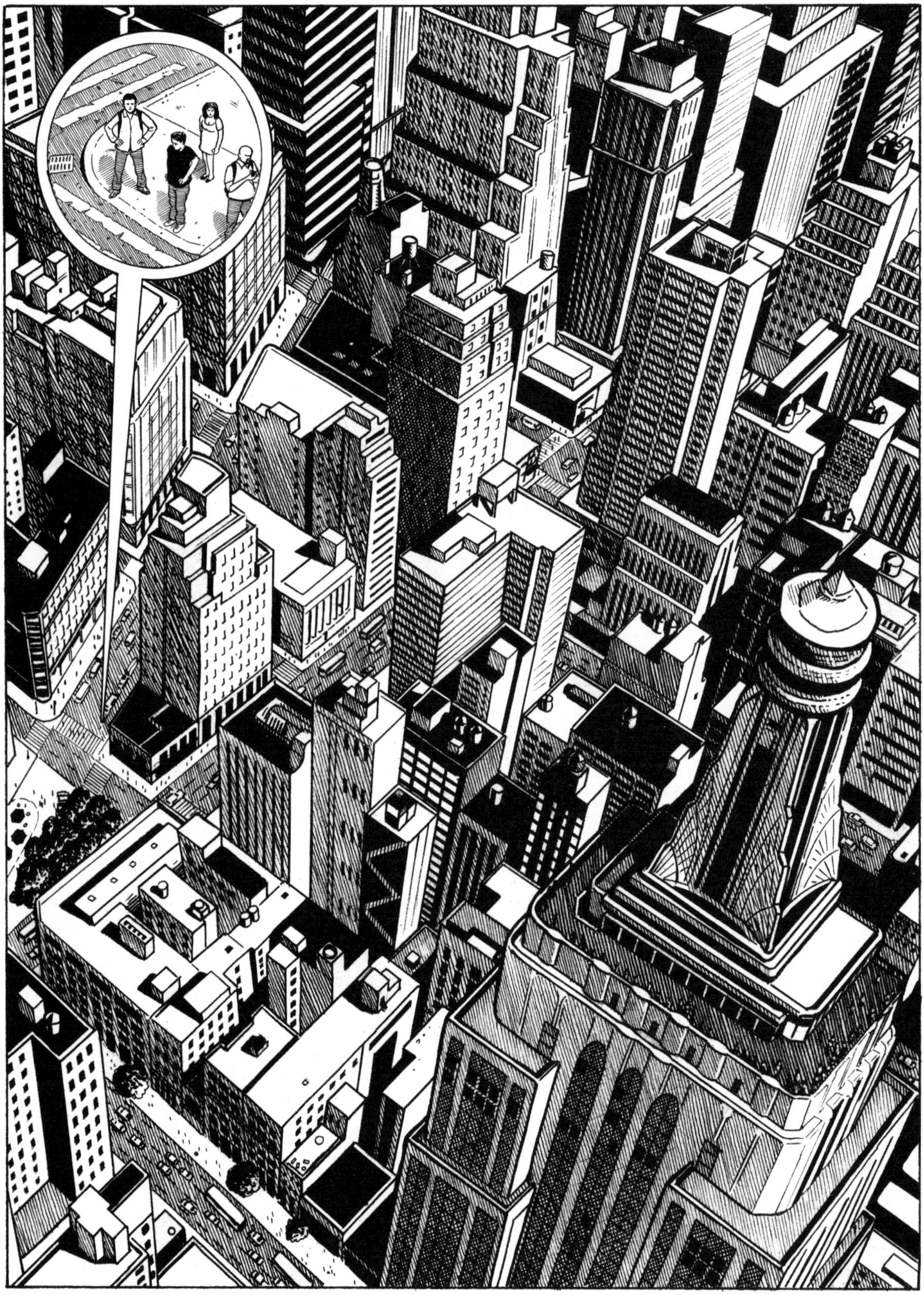

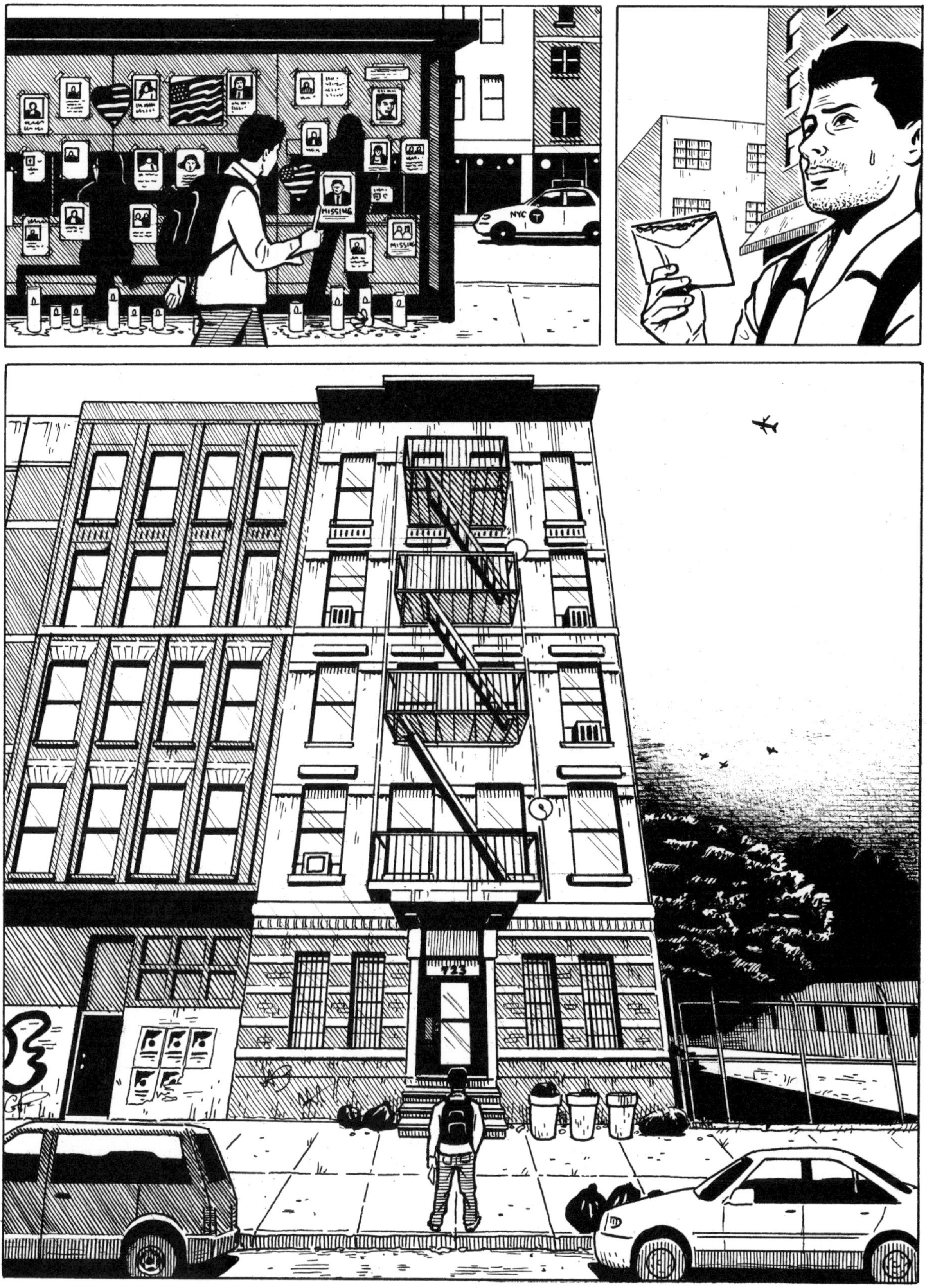
MISSING
MISSING
NYC
723

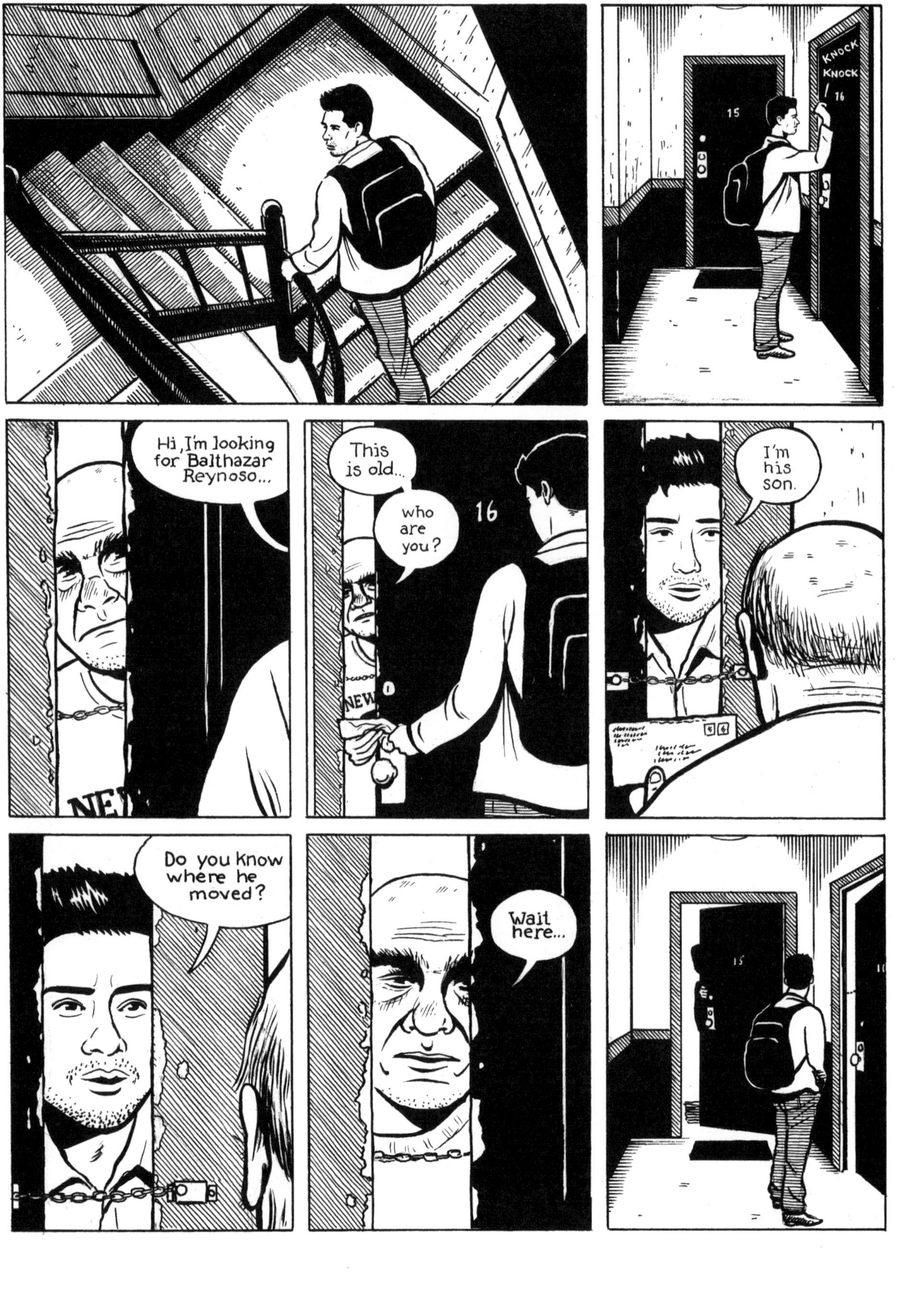
KNOCK KNOCK
16
15
Hi, I'm looking for Balthazar Reynoso...
This is old...
who are you?
16
NEW
I'm his son.
Do you know where he moved?
Wait here...
15

SLAM!
15

Tell them to stop writing.

NEW YORK
JETS

Elena Reynoso
Av. Colina
Mazatlan
México

Balthazar Reynoso
Apt. 16
723 E. 6th Street
New York, NY
U.S.A.

SLAM!

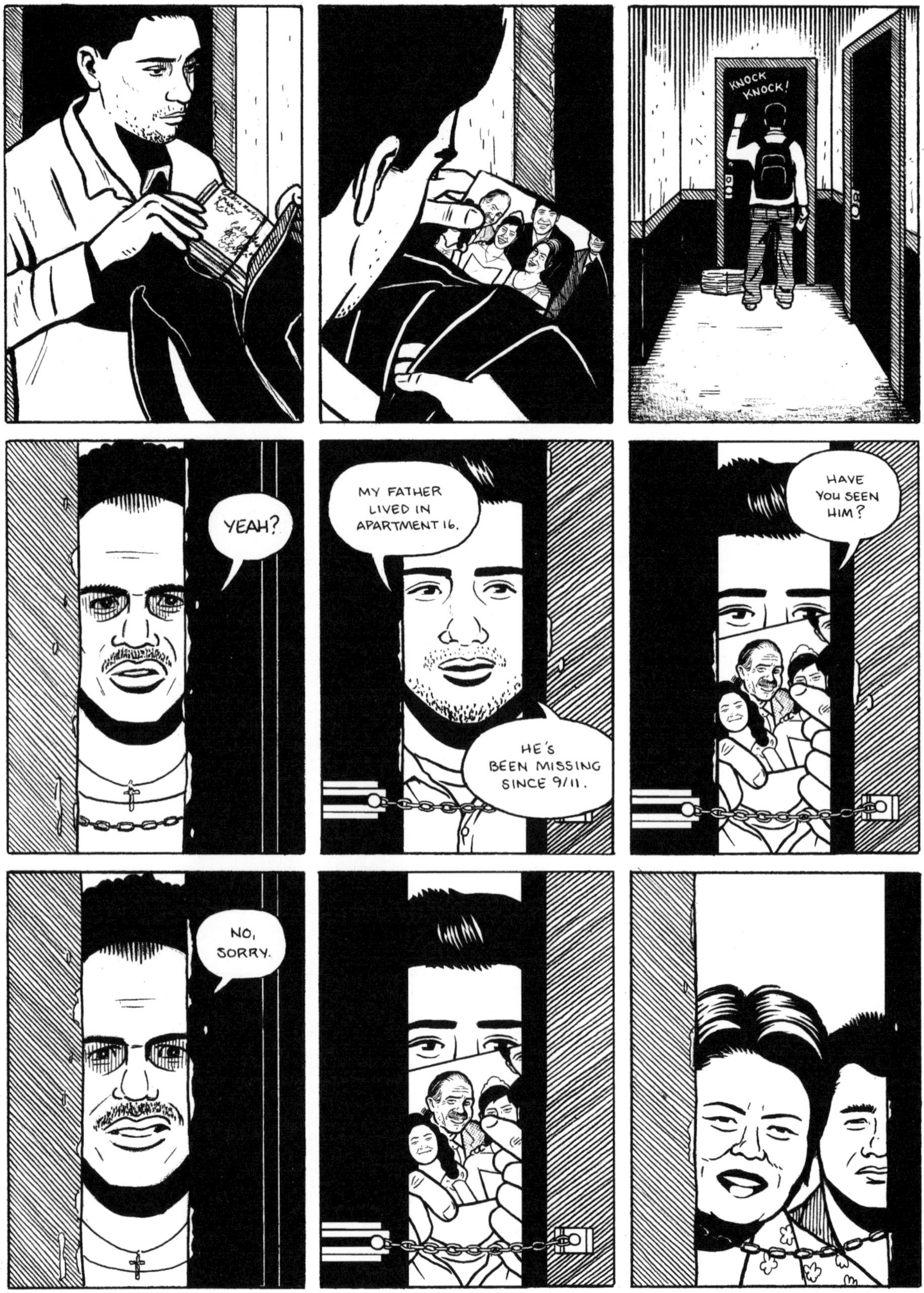
KNOCK KNOCK!
YEAH?
MY FATHER LIVED IN APARTMENT 16.
HE'S BEEN MISSING SINCE 9/11.
HAVE YOU SEEN HIM?
NO, SORRY.

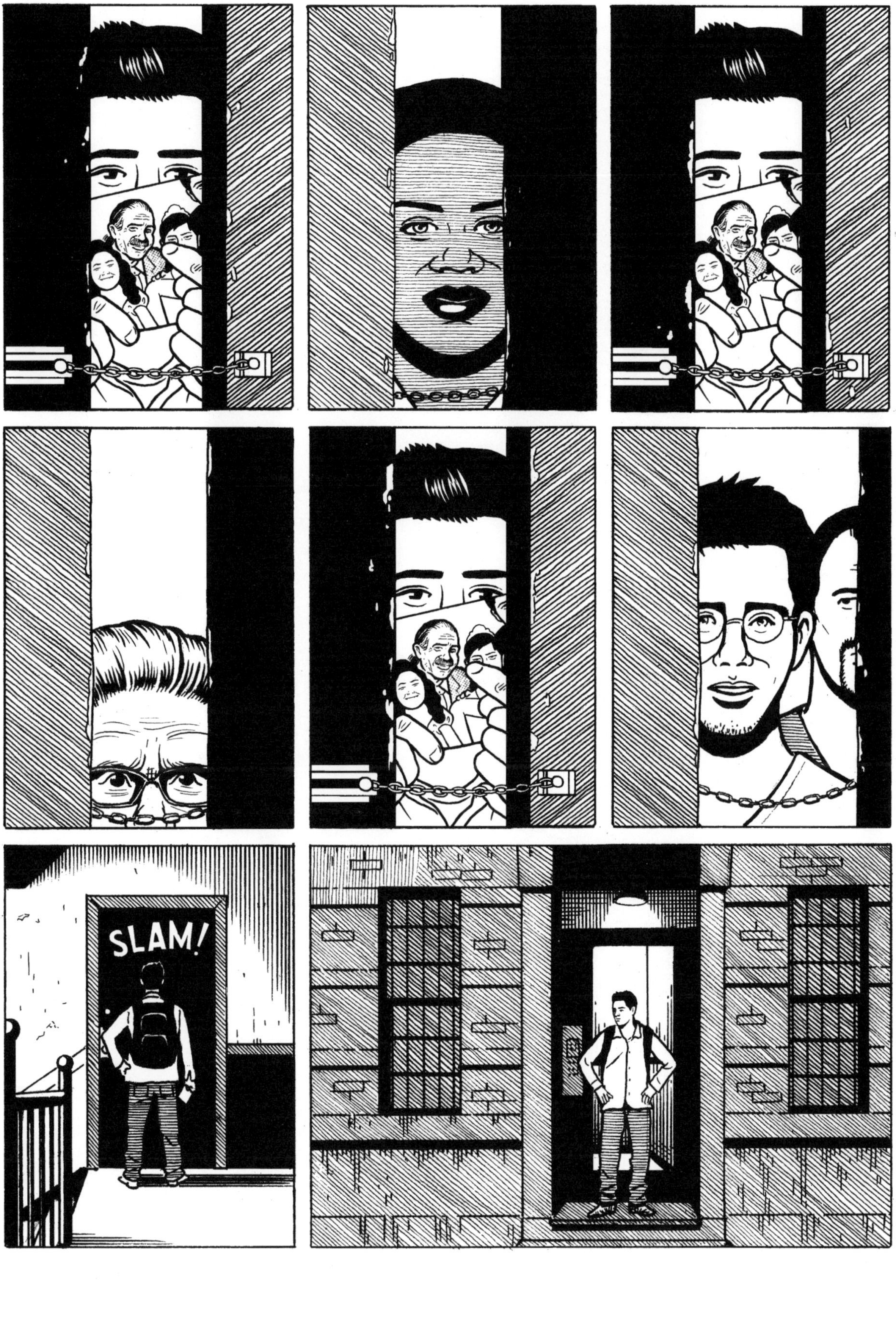
SLAM!

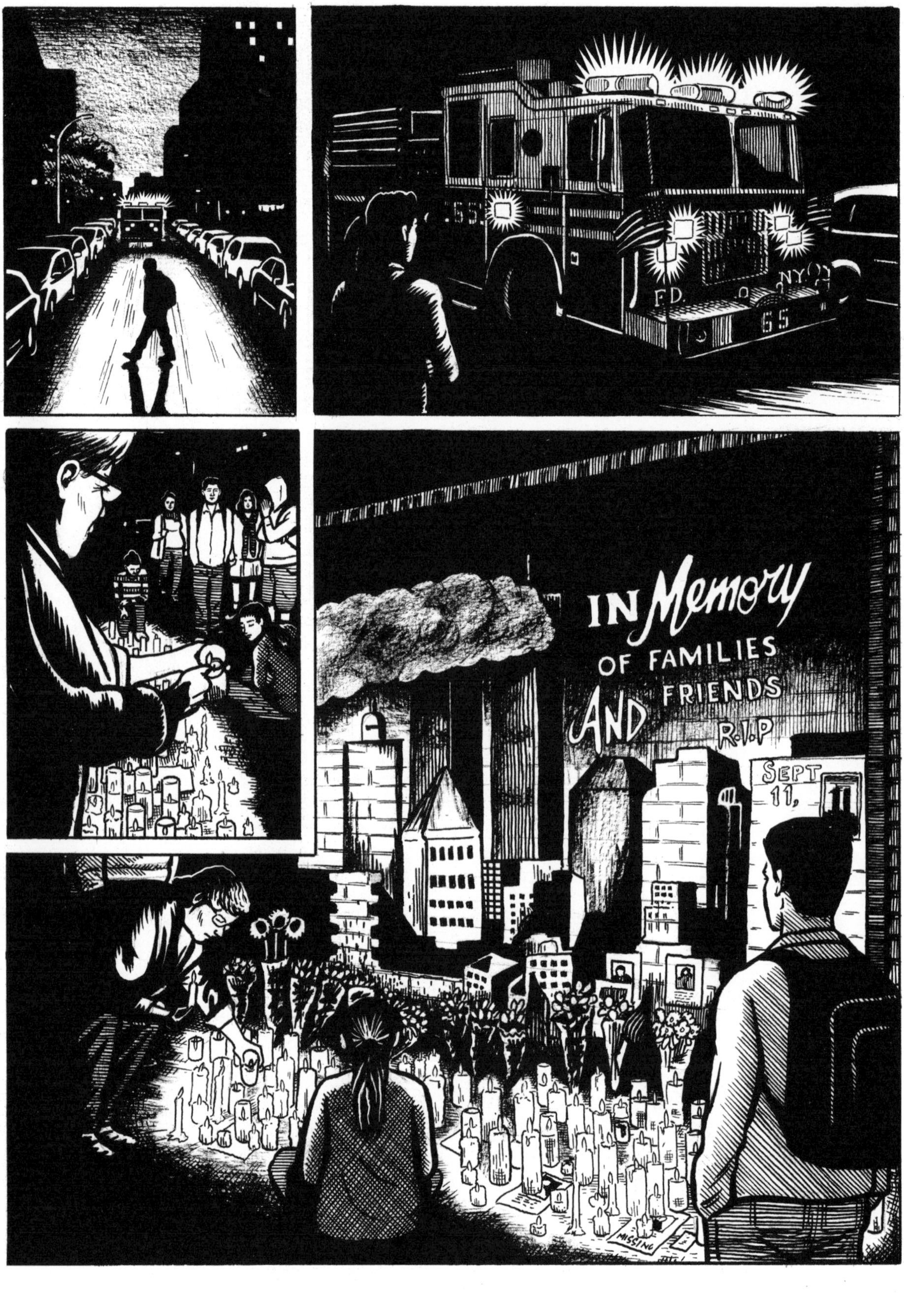
F.D.
NY
65
IN Memory OF FAMILIES AND FRIENDS R.I.P
SEPT 11,
MISSING

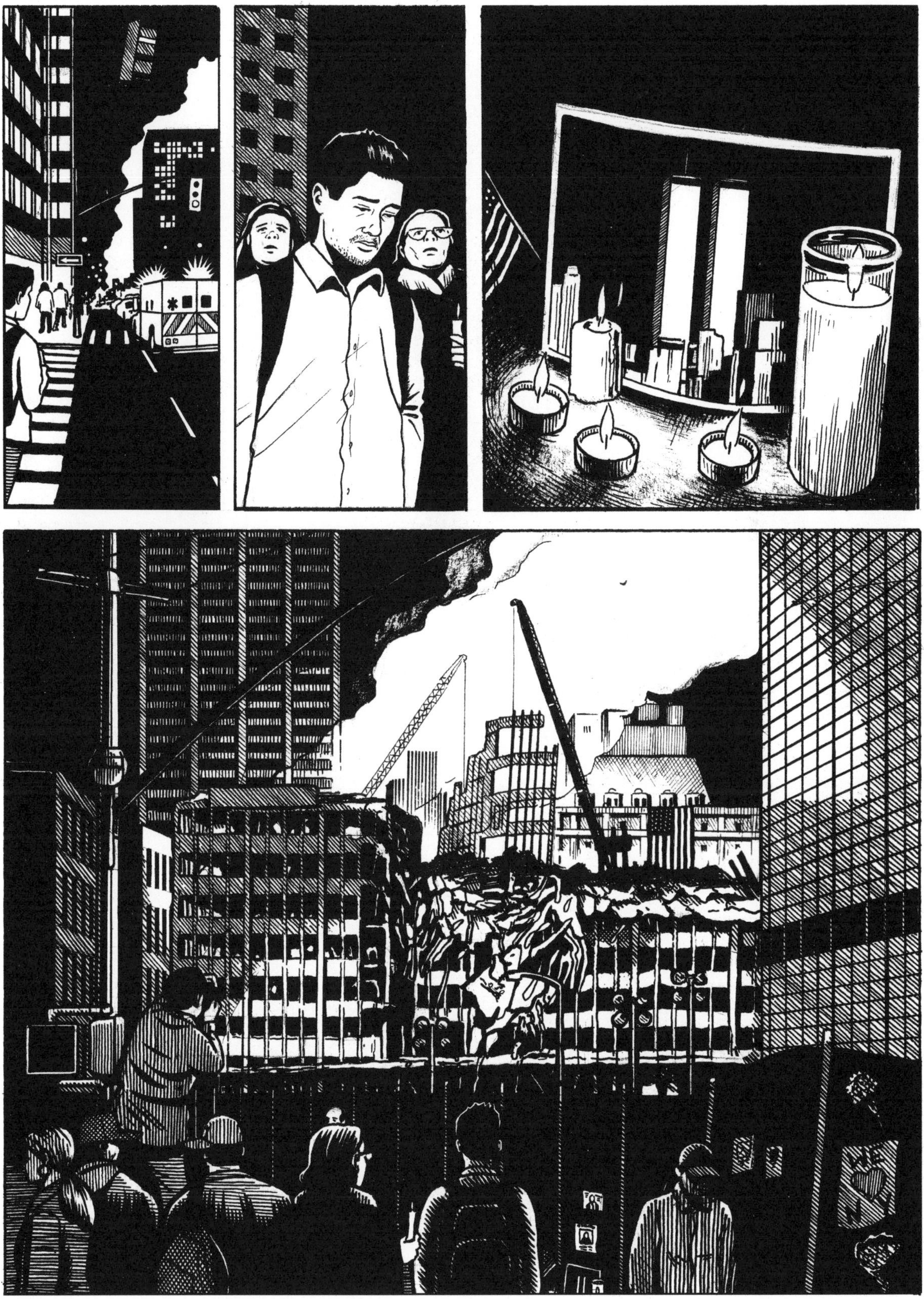

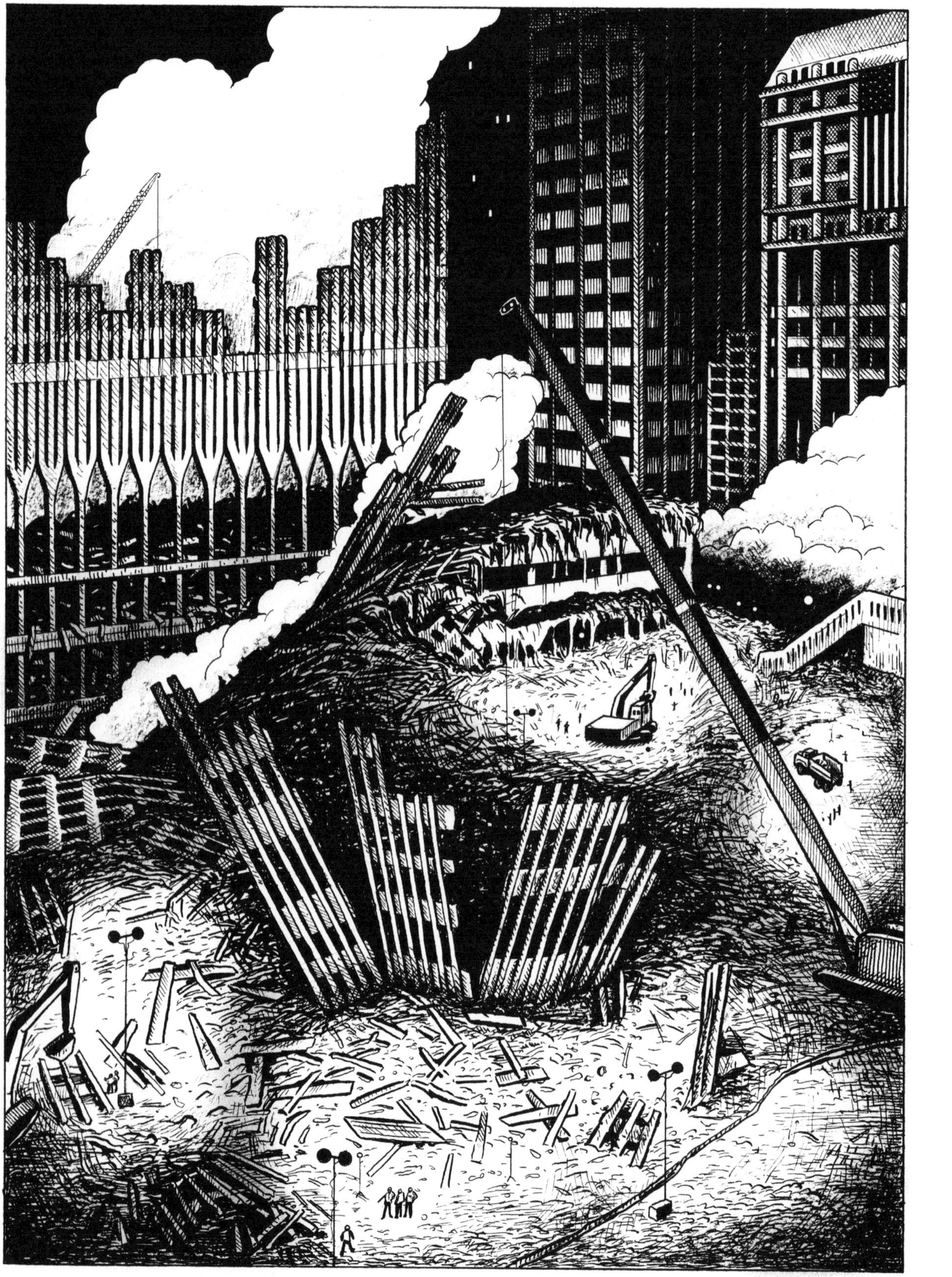

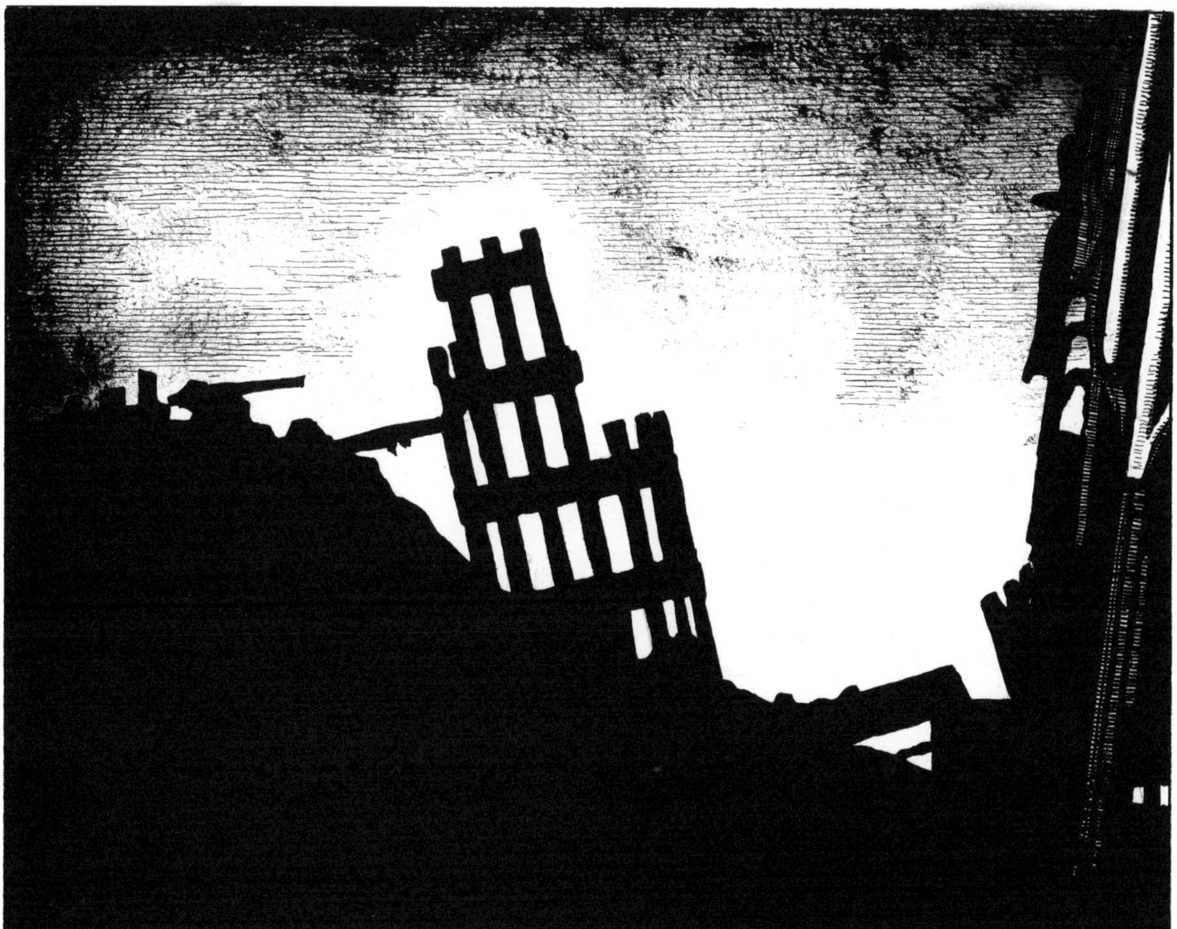

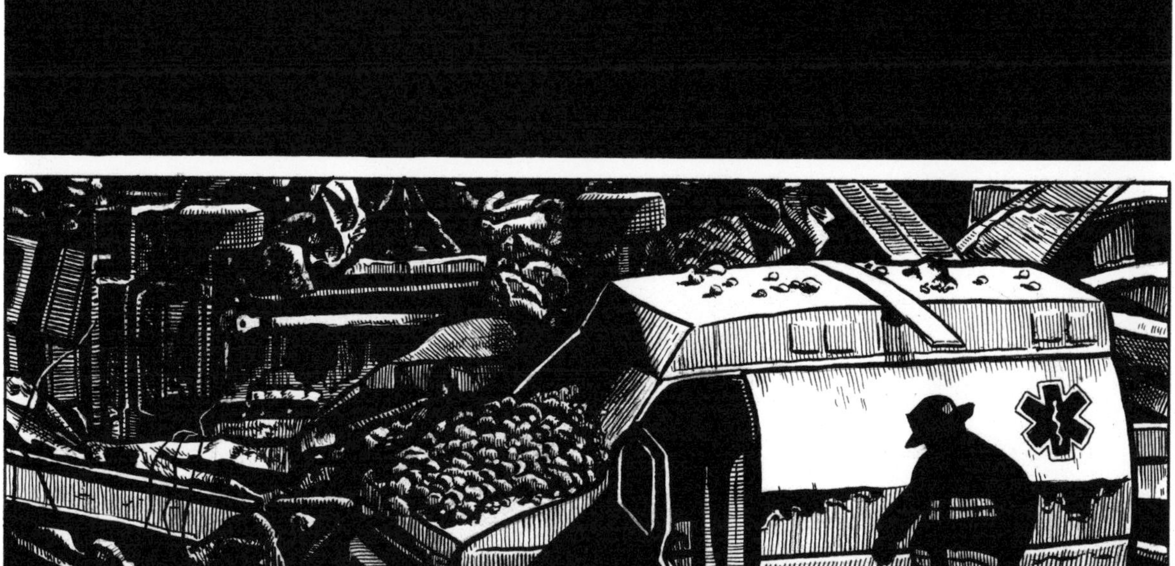

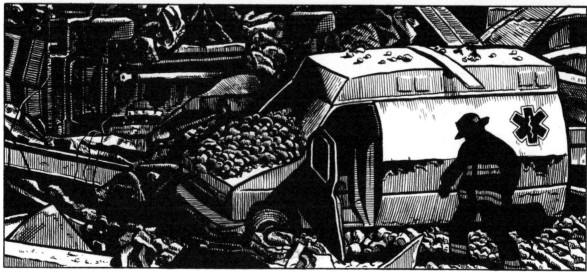

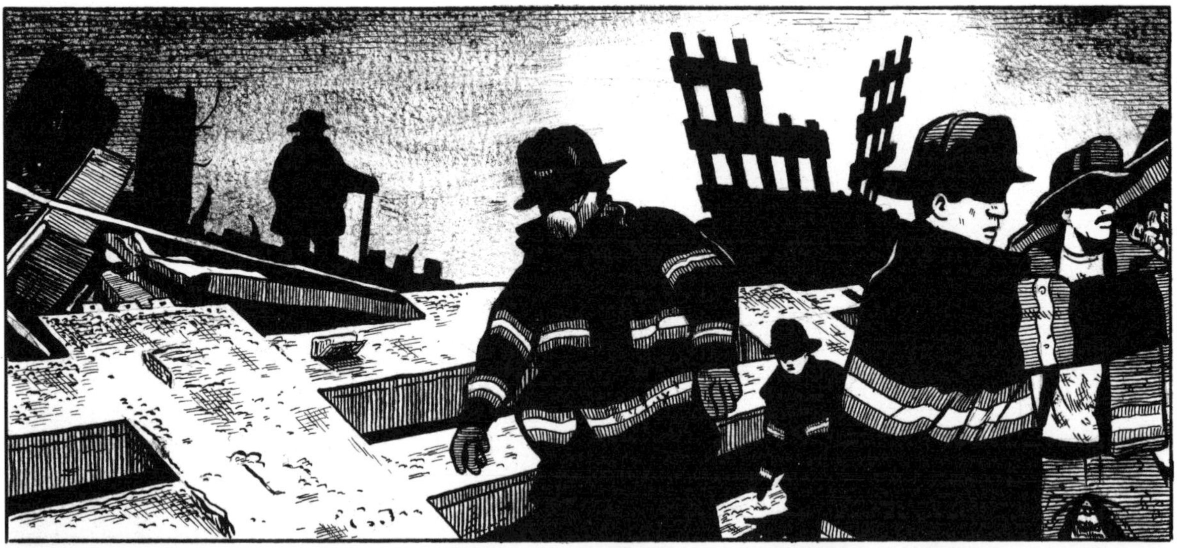
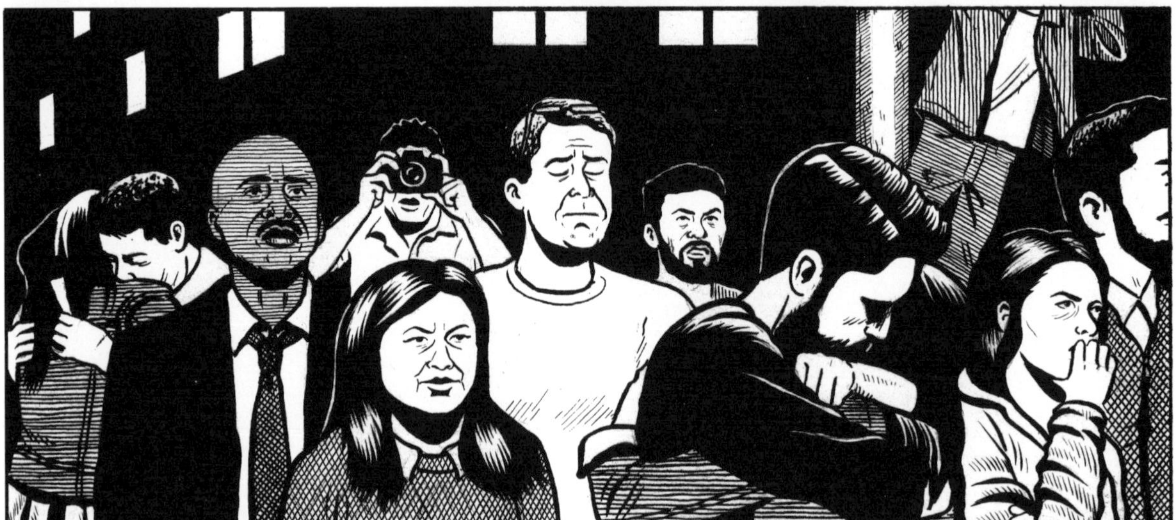
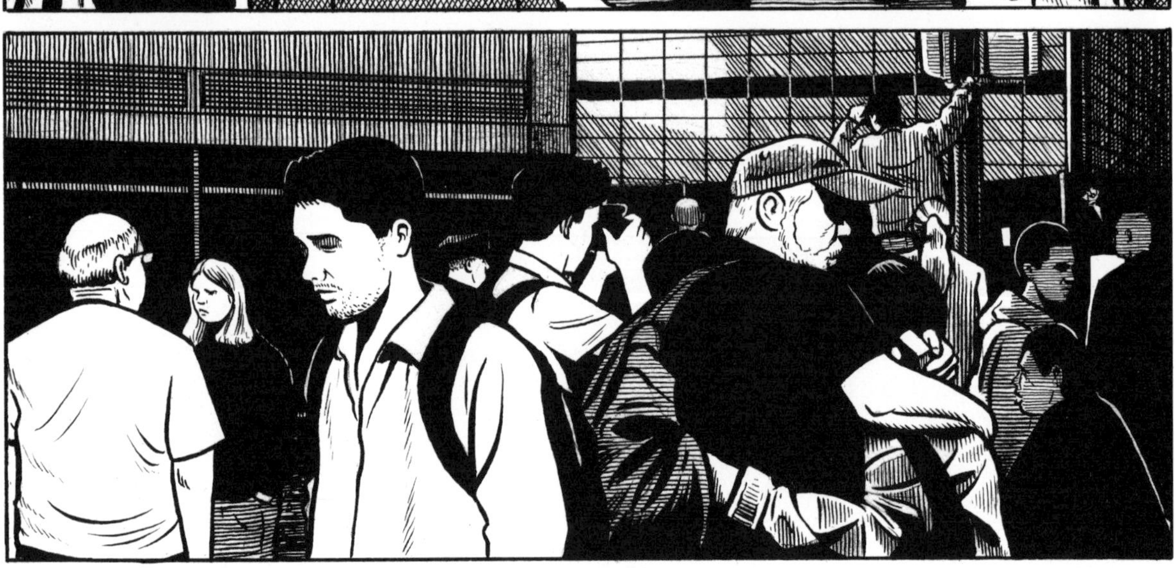

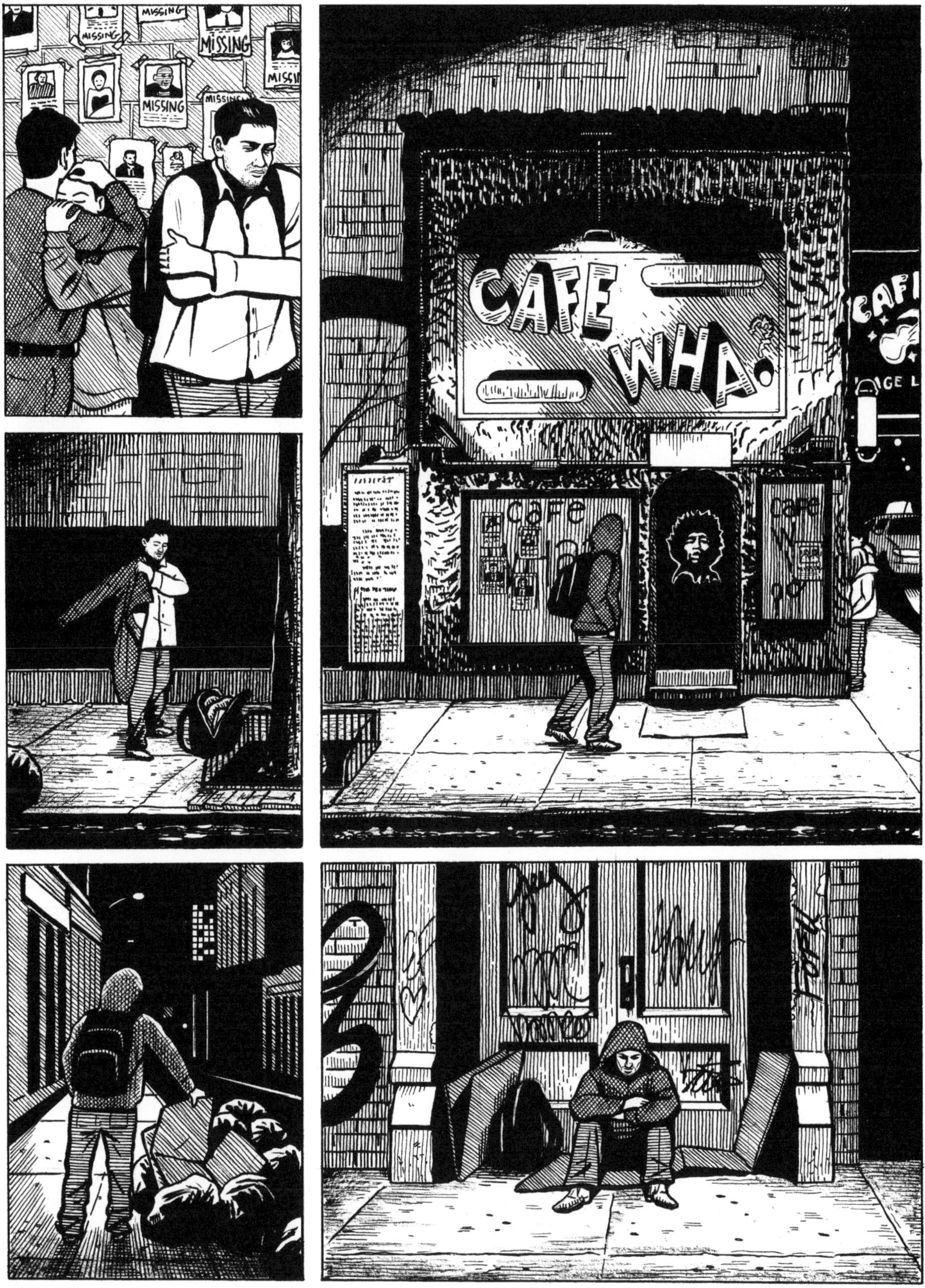
MISSING
MISSING
MISSING
MISSING
CAFE
WHA
cafe
Cafe

SNIFF
SNIFF
1984
SNIFF
SNIFF
YAP!
YAP!
YAP!
YAP!
YAP!
YAP!
YAP!
YAP!
YAP!
YAP!

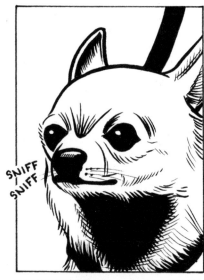

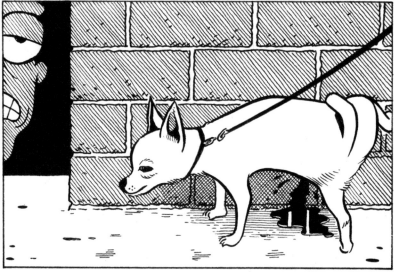

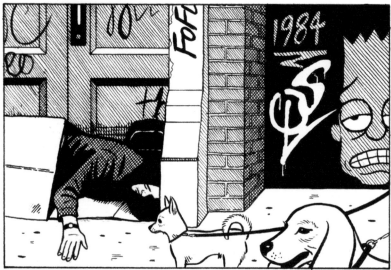

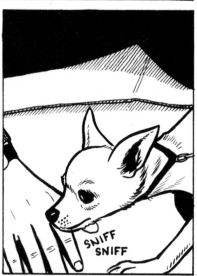

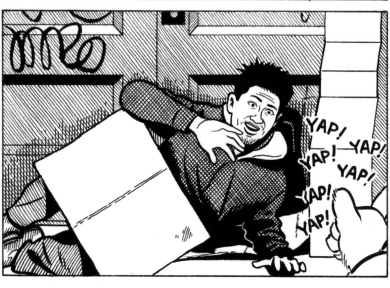

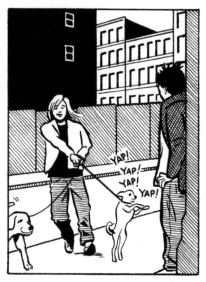

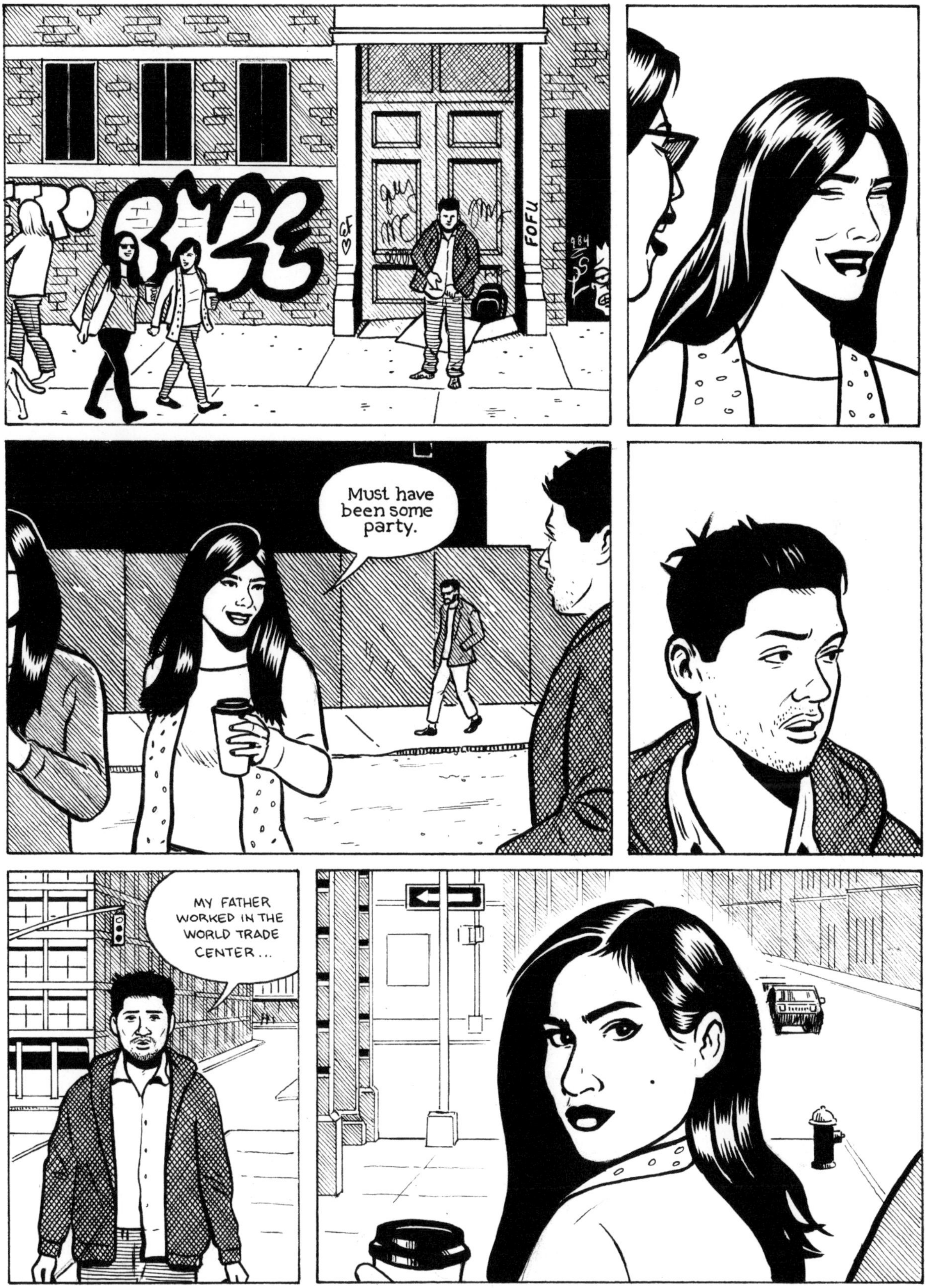
Must have been some party.
MY FATHER WORKED IN THE WORLD TRADE CENTER ...

FINE ART
L.M. DELI

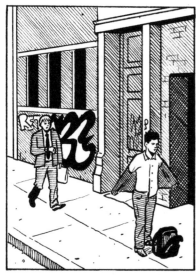

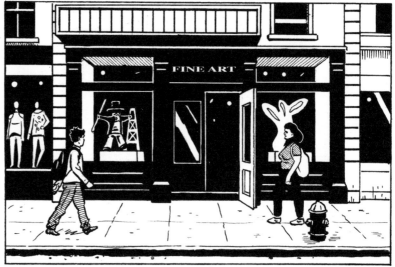

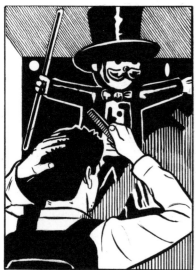

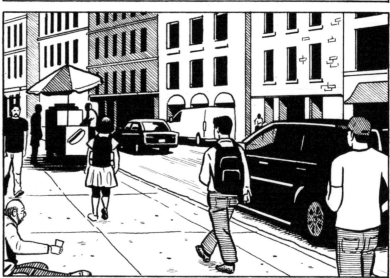

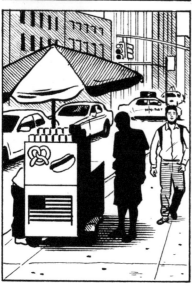

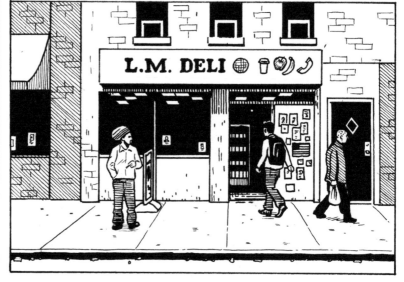

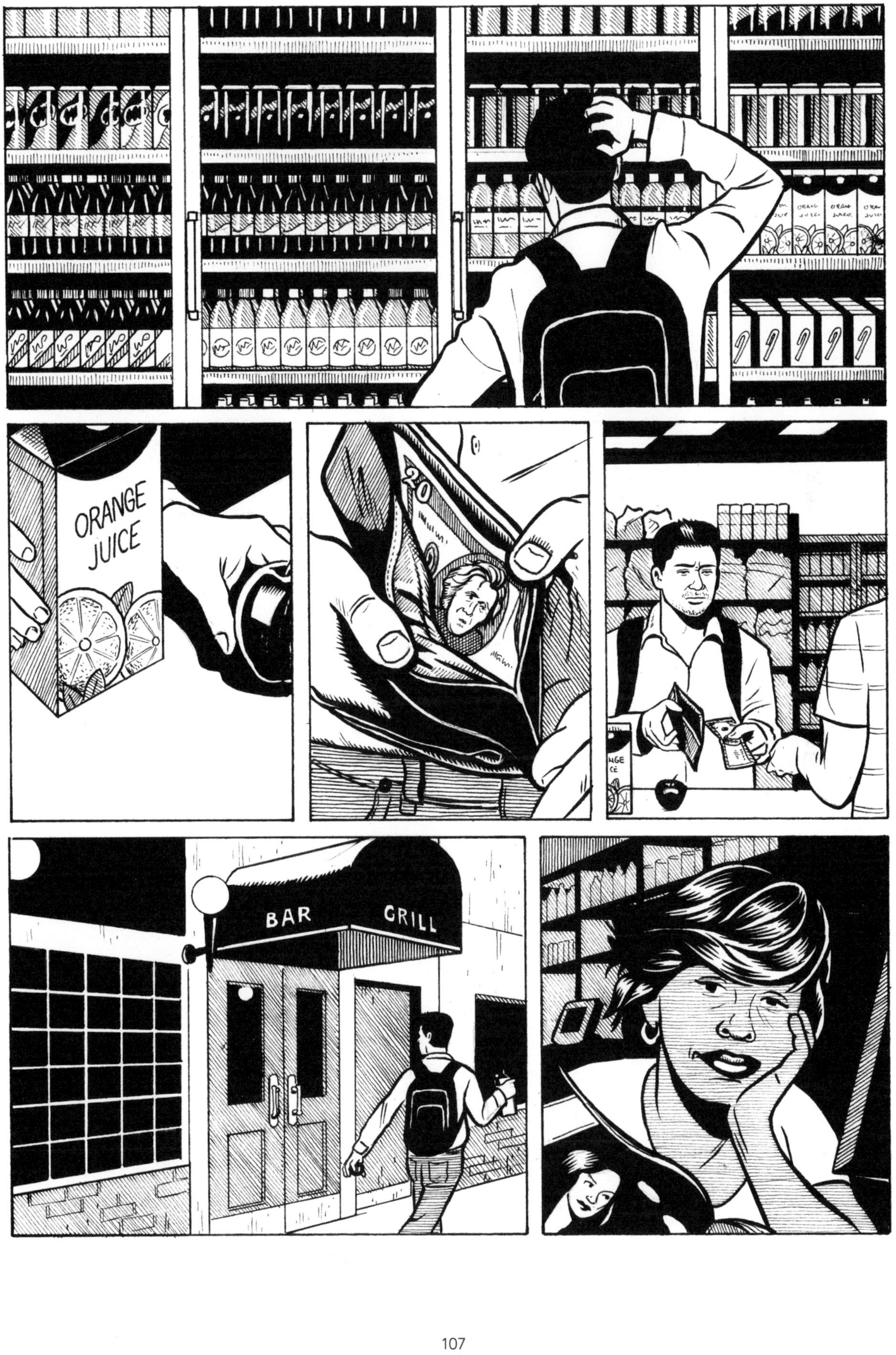
ORANGE JUICE
20
BAR
GRILL

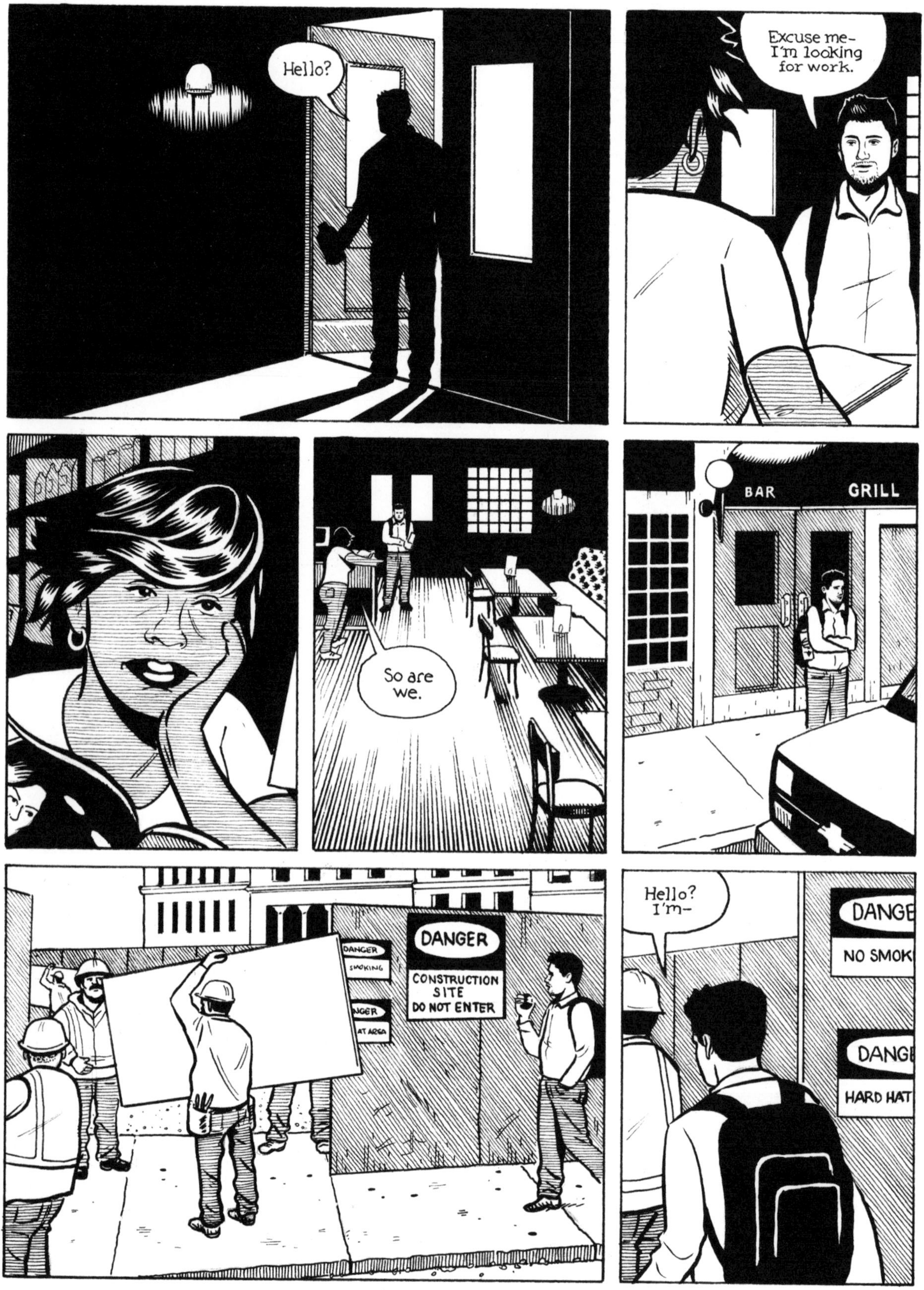

Hello?
Excuse me- I'm looking for work.
So are we.
BAR
GRILL
DANGER
SMOKING
DANGER
CONSTRUCTION SITE DO NOT ENTER
Hello? I'm-
DANGE
NO SMOK
DANGE
HARD HAT

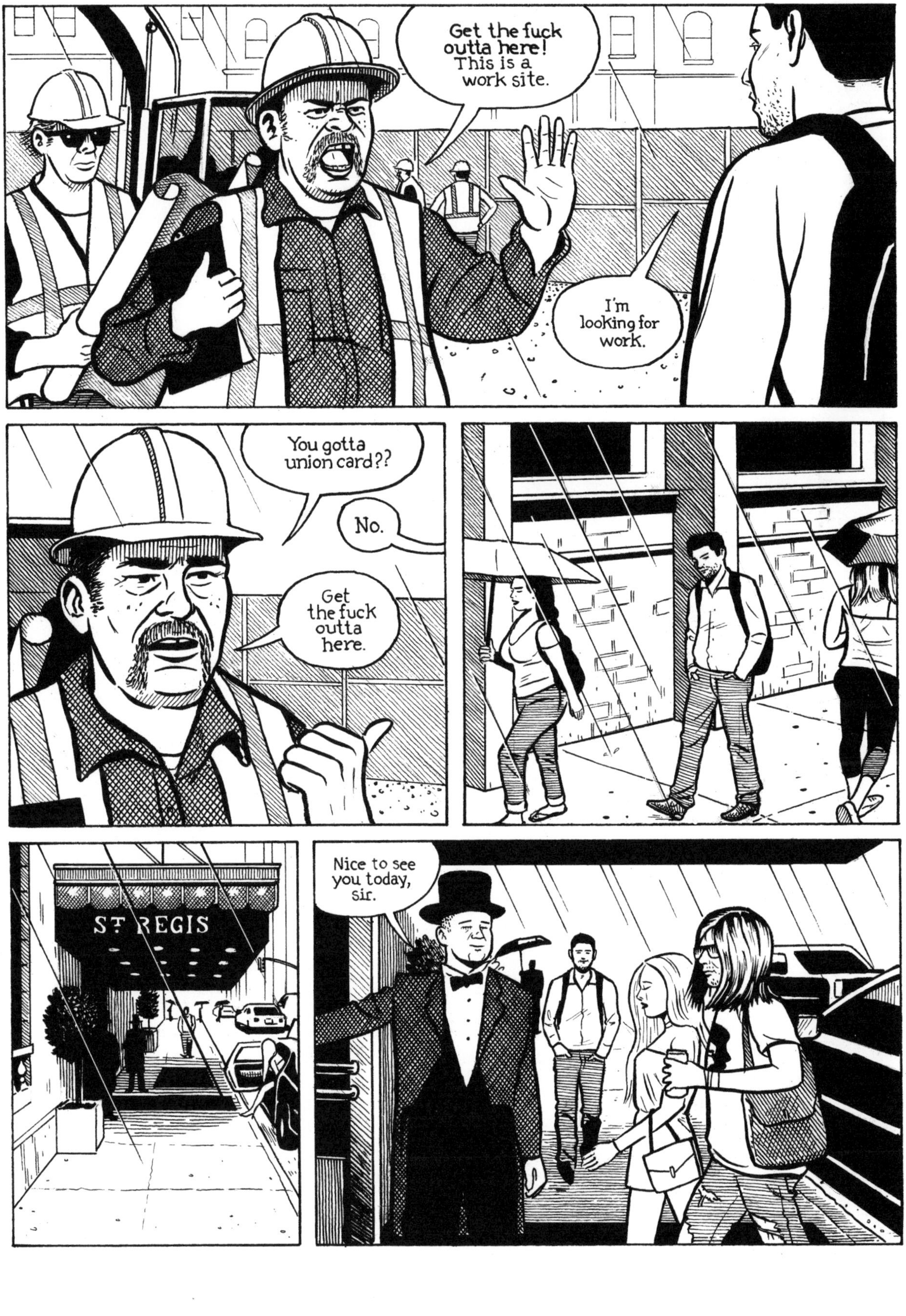
Get the fuck outta here! This is a work site.
I'm looking for work.
You gotta union card??
No.
Get the fuck outta here.
ST REGIS
Nice to see you today, sir.

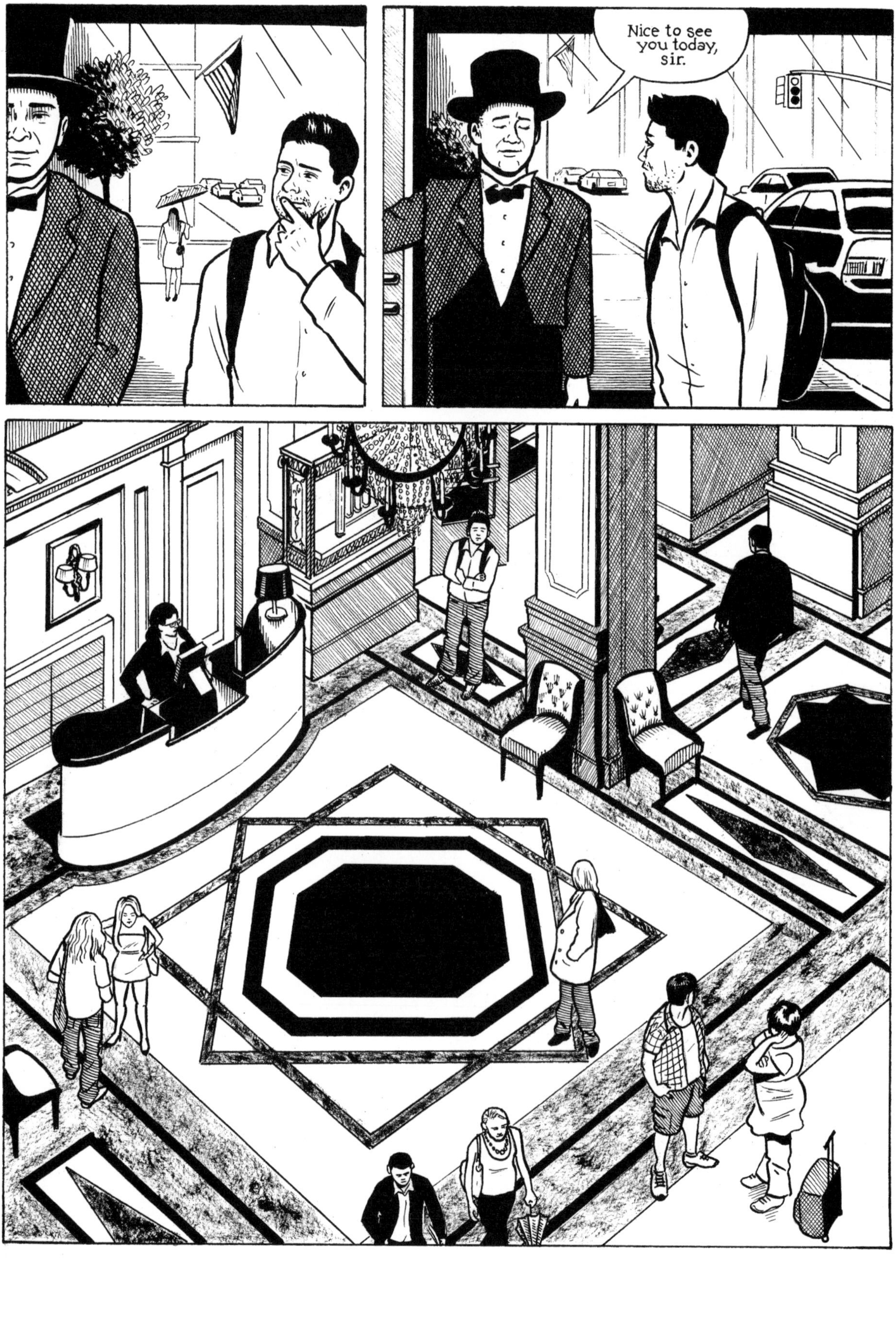
Nice to see you today, sir.

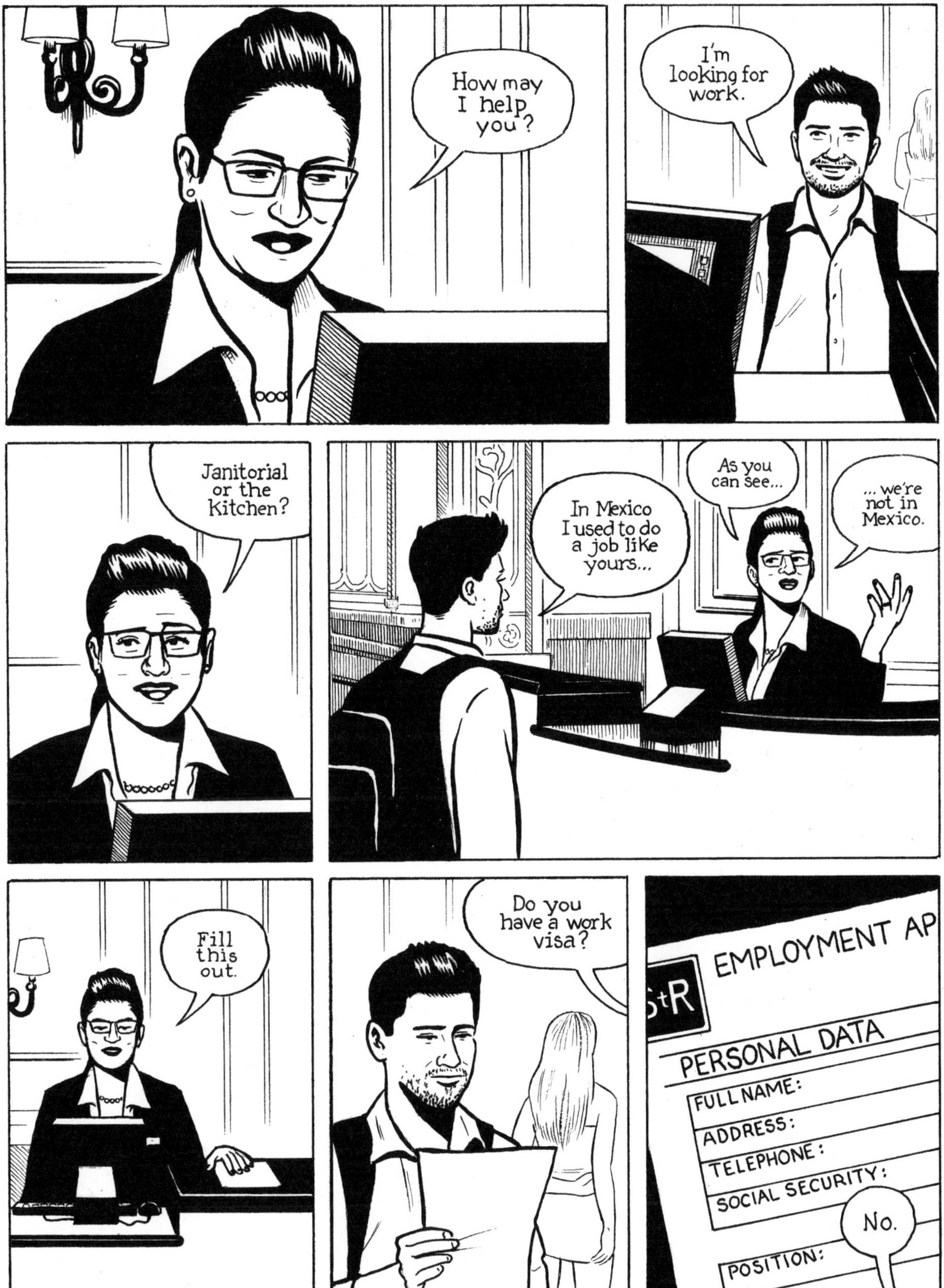
How may I help you?
I'm looking for work.
Janitorial or the Kitchen?
In Mexico I used to do a job like yours...
As you can see...
... we're not in Mexico.
Fill this out.
Do you have a work visa?
EMPLOYMENT AP
PERSONAL DATA
FULL NAME:
ADDRESS:
TELEPHONE:
SOCIAL SECURITY:
No.
POSITION:

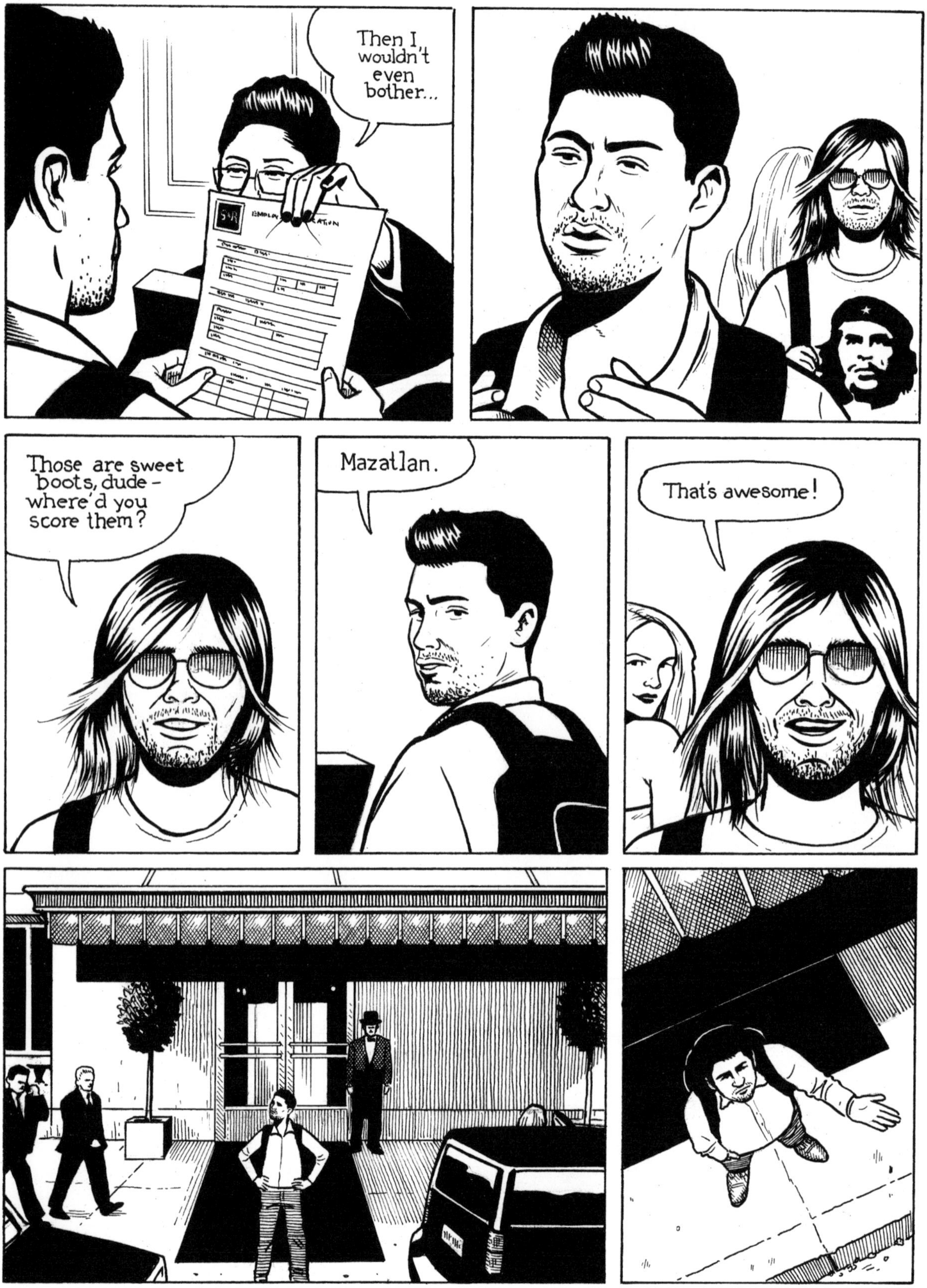
Then I, wouldn't even bother...
Those are sweet boots, dude - where'd you score them?
Mazatlan.
That's awesome!

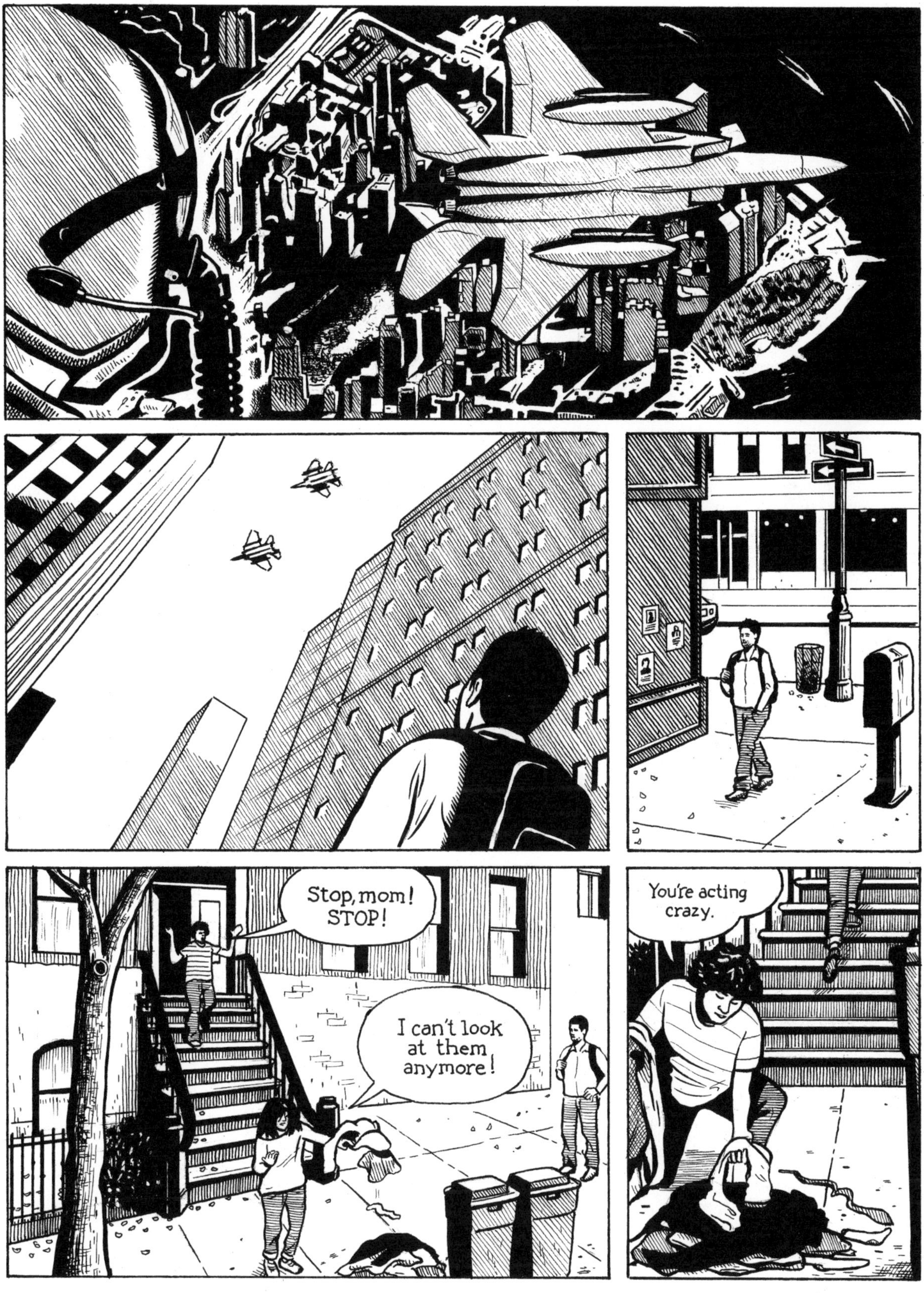
Stop, mom! STOP!
I can't look at them anymore!
You're acting crazy.

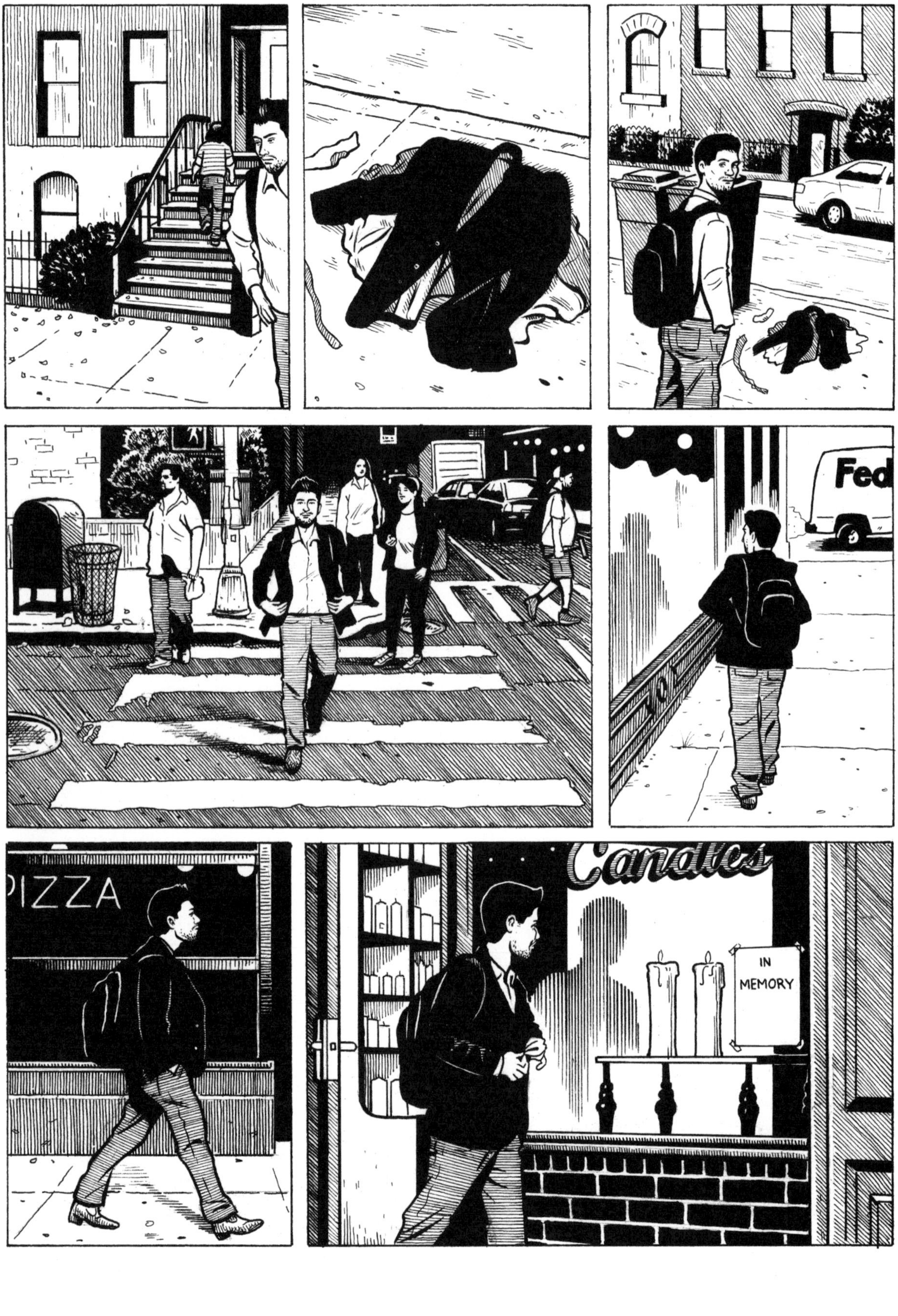
Fed
PIZZA
Candles
IN MEMORY

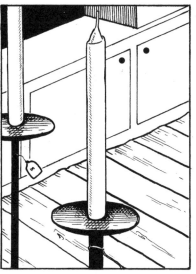
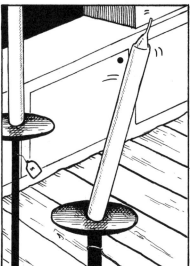

SNAP!
May I help you?
May I help *you*?

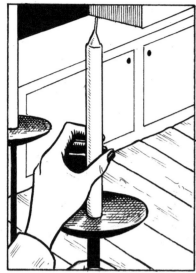

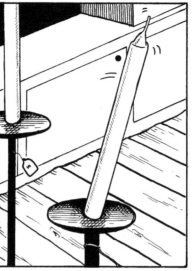

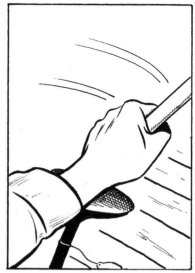

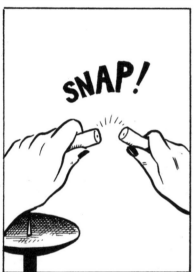

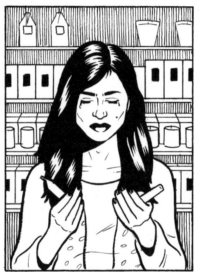

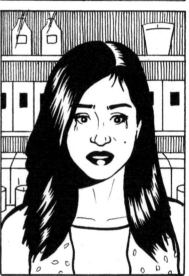

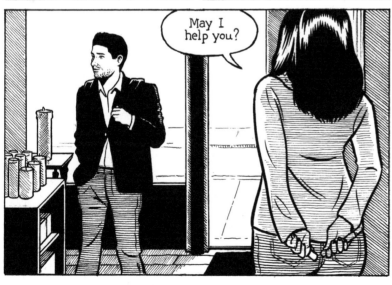

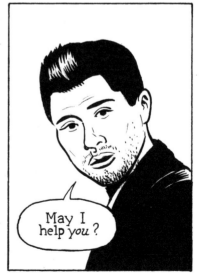

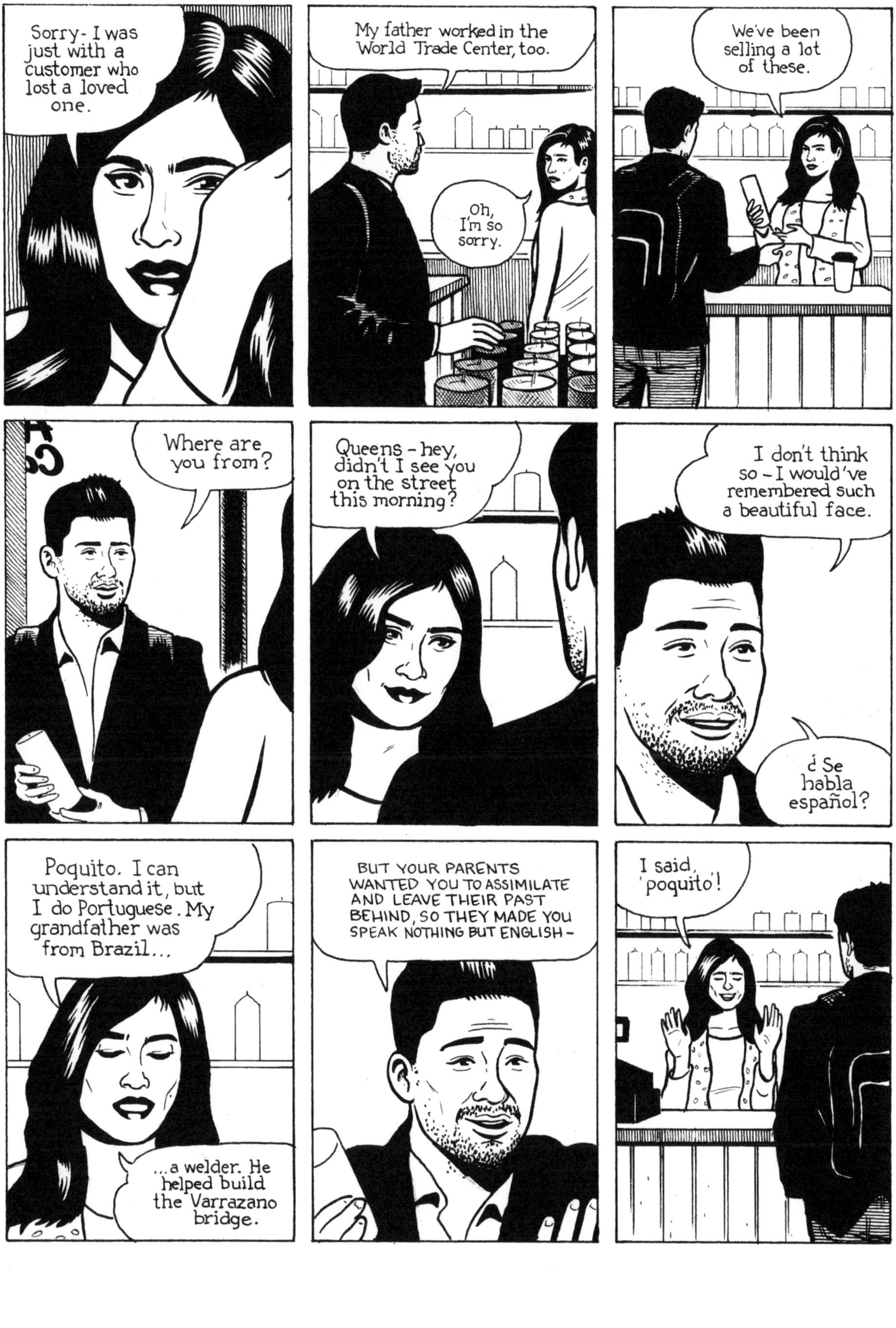
Sorry- I was just with a customer who lost a loved one.
My father worked in the World Trade Center, too.
Oh, I'm so sorry.
We've been selling a lot of these.
Where are you from?
Queens - hey, didn't I see you on the street this morning?
I don't think so - I would've remembered such a beautiful face.
¿ Se habla español?
Poquito. I can understand it, but I do Portuguese. My grandfather was from Brazil...
...a welder. He helped build the Varrazano bridge.
BUT YOUR PARENTS WANTED YOU TO ASSIMILATE AND LEAVE THEIR PAST BEHIND, SO THEY MADE YOU SPEAK NOTHING BUT ENGLISH -
I said, 'poquito'!

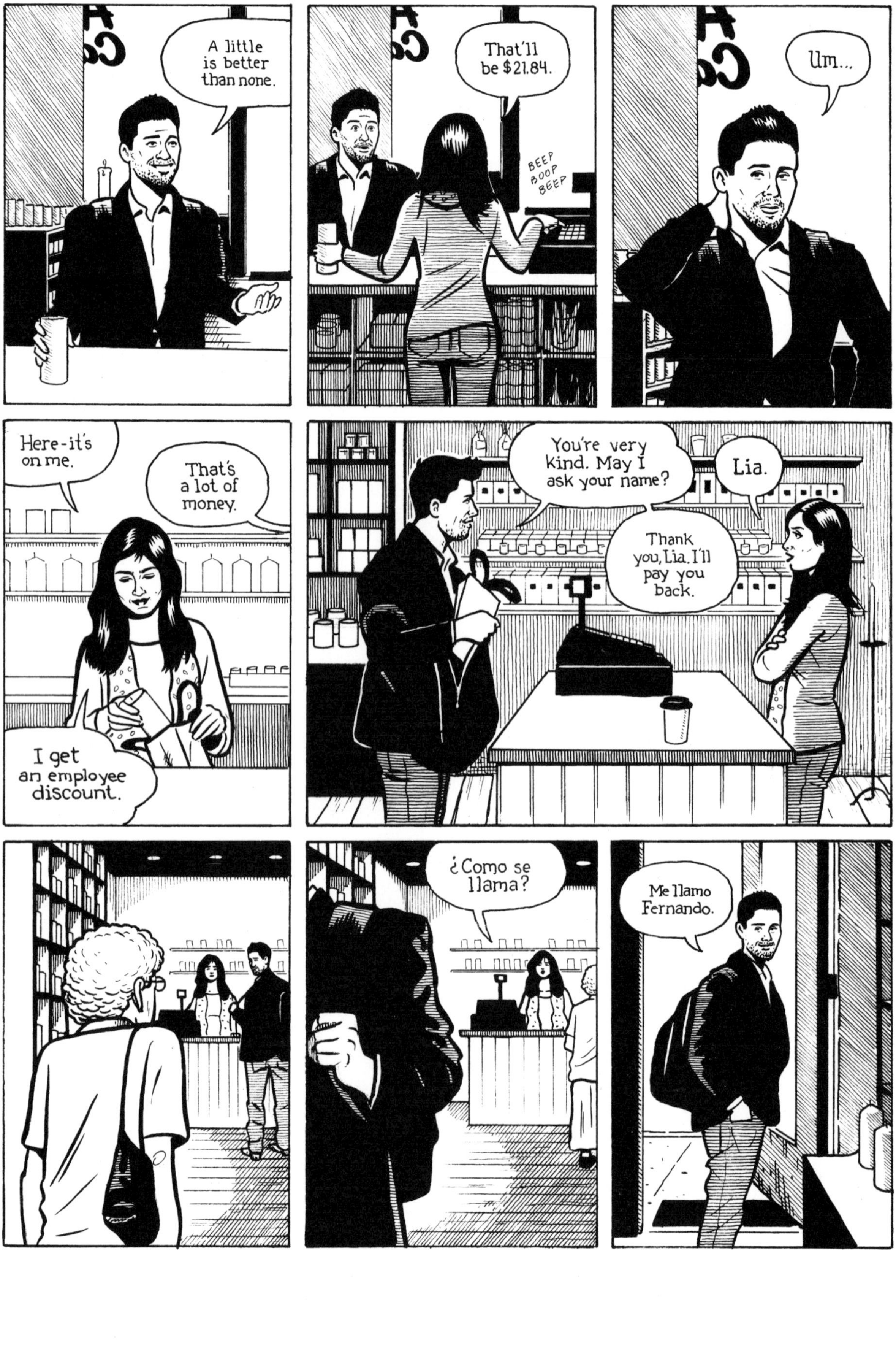
A little is better than none.
That'll be $21.84.
BEEP BOOP BEEP
Um...
Here-it's on me.
That's a lot of money.
I get an employee discount.
You're very kind. May I ask your name?
Lia.
Thank you, Lia. I'll pay you back.
¿Como se llama?
Me llamo Fernando.

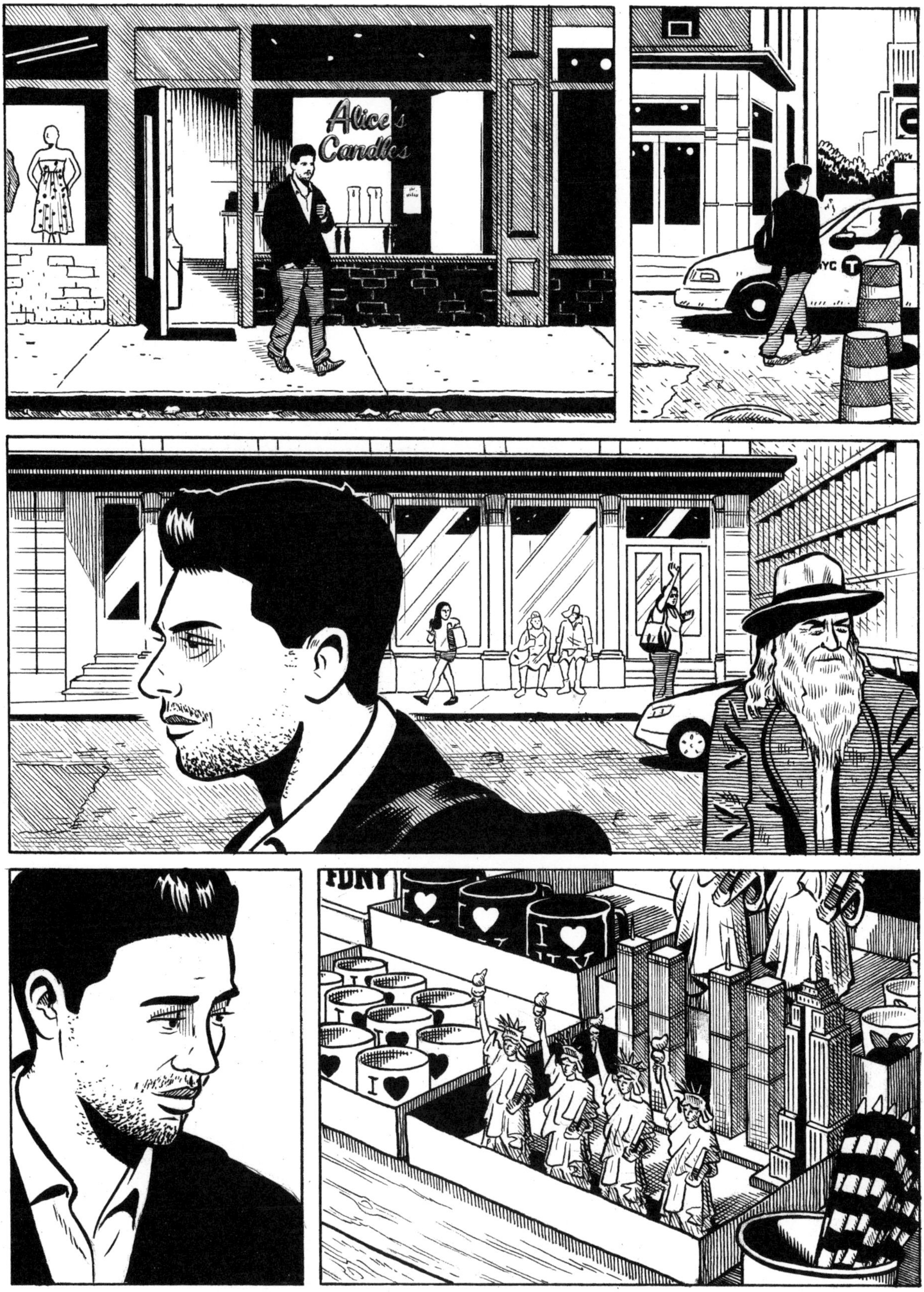
Alice's Candles
NYC

NY NY
BROADWAY
WALL ST
NY
MADISON
9/11 FAMILY ASSISTANCE CENTER
ARE YOU MISSING A LOVED ONE? LET US KNOW
PLEASE BRING:
- RECENT PHOTO
- ADDRESS
- SSN
MISSING SINCE 9/11
FAMILY ASSIST CENTE
I'm sorry to ask, but was your father working in this country illegally?

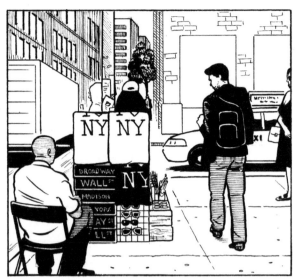

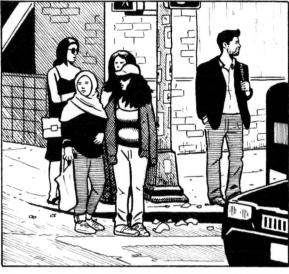

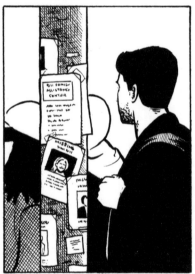

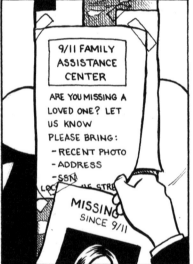

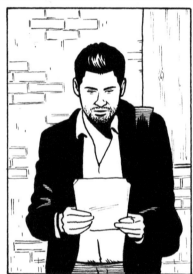

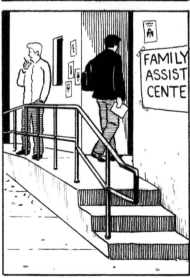

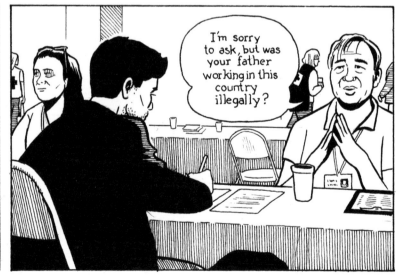

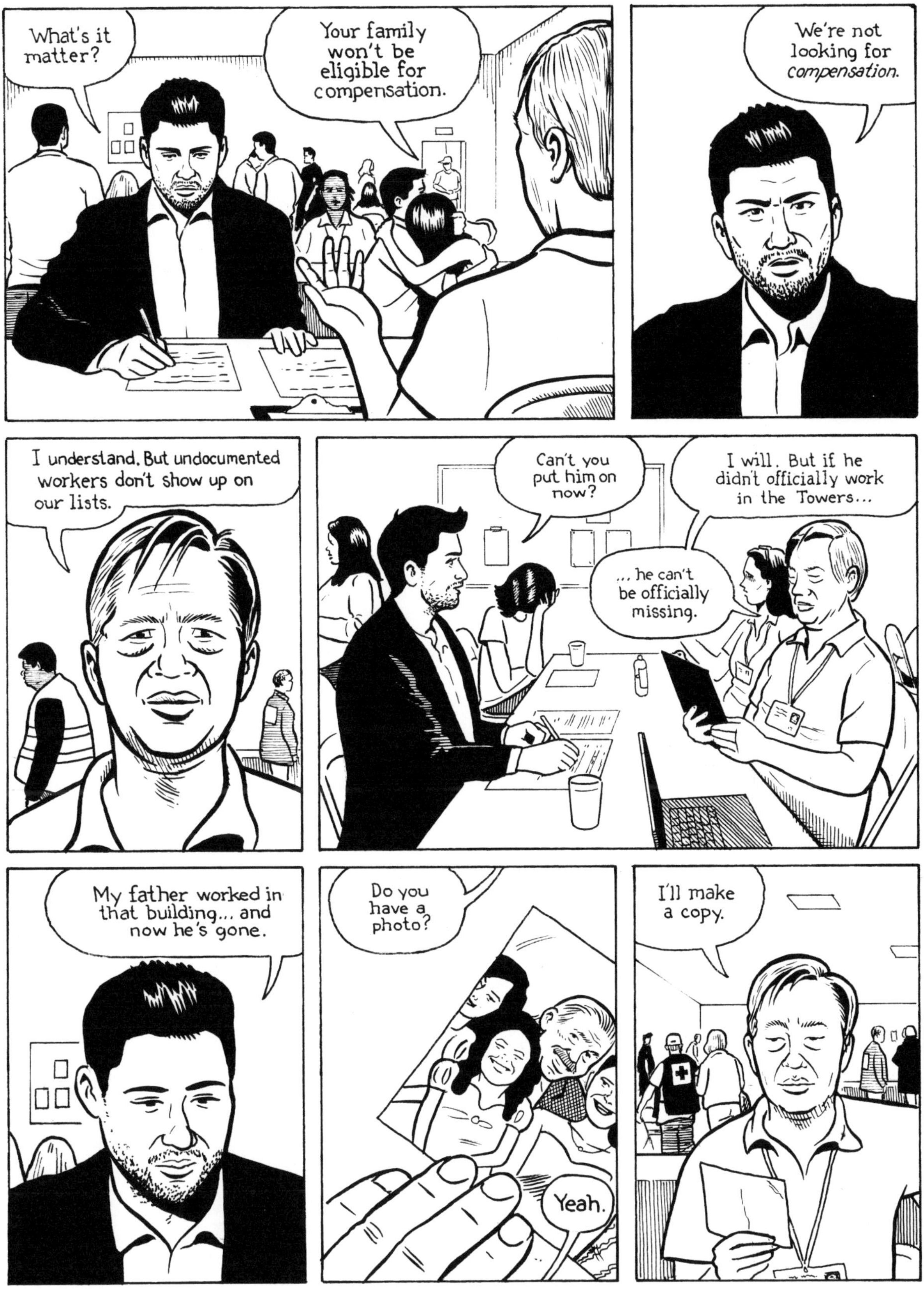
What's it matter?
Your family won't be eligible for compensation.
We're not looking for *compensation*.
I understand. But undocumented workers don't show up on our lists.
Can't you put him on now?
I will. But if he didn't officially work in the Towers...
... he can't be officially missing.
My father worked in that building... and now he's gone.
Do you have a photo?
Yeah.
I'll make a copy.

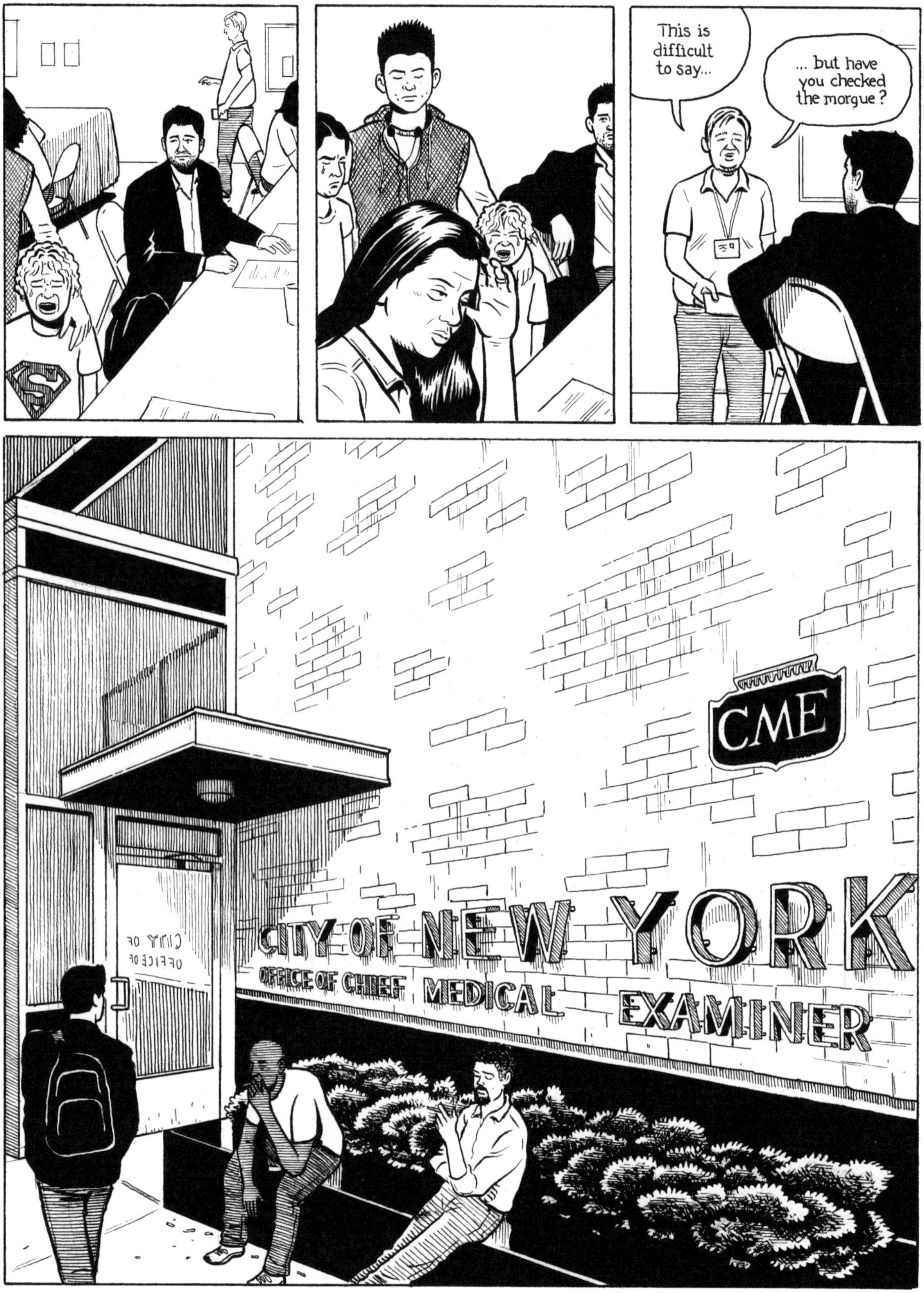
This is difficult to say...
... but have you checked the morgue?
CME
CITY OF NEW YORK
OFFICE OF CHIEF MEDICAL EXAMINER

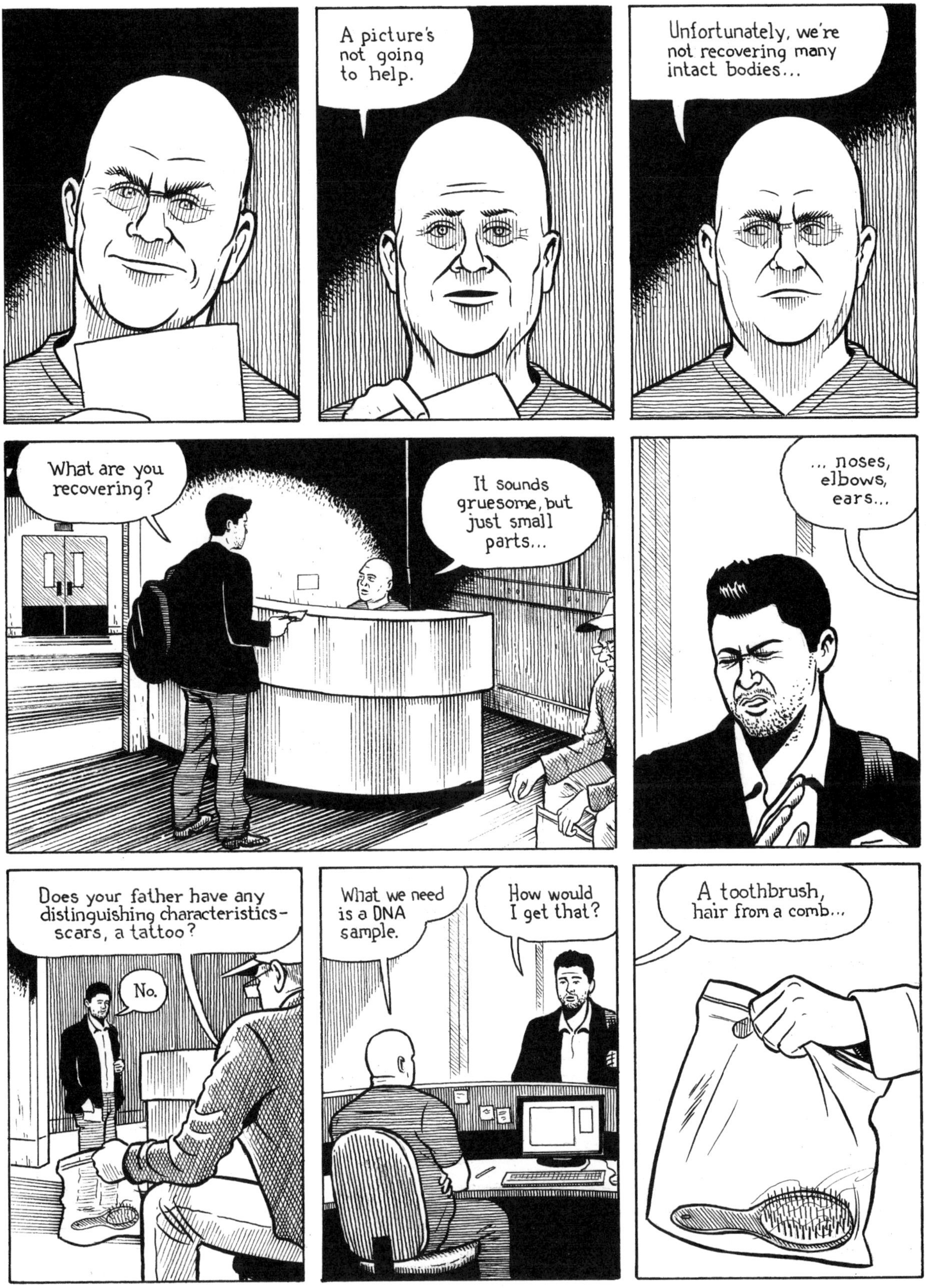
A picture's not going to help.
Unfortunately, we're not recovering many intact bodies...
What are you recovering?
It sounds gruesome, but just small parts...
... noses, elbows, ears...
Does your father have any distinguishing characteristics - scars, a tattoo?
No.
What we need is a DNA sample.
How would I get that?
A toothbrush, hair from a comb...

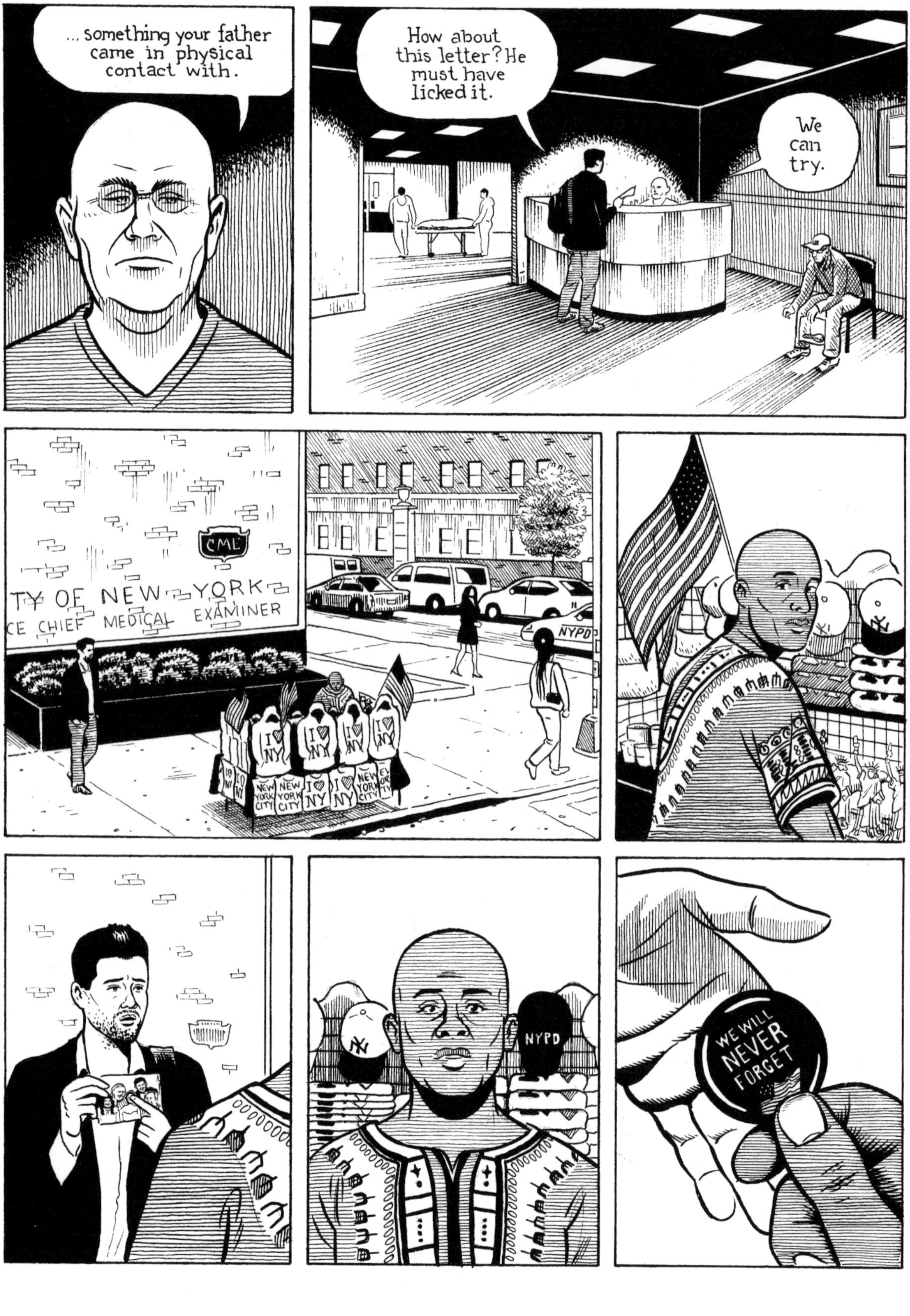
... something your father came in physical contact with.
How about this letter? He must have licked it.
We can try.
TY OF NEW YORK
CE CHIEF MEDICAL EXAMINER
NYPD
I ♥ NY
NEW YORK CITY
NYPD
WE WILL NEVER FORGET

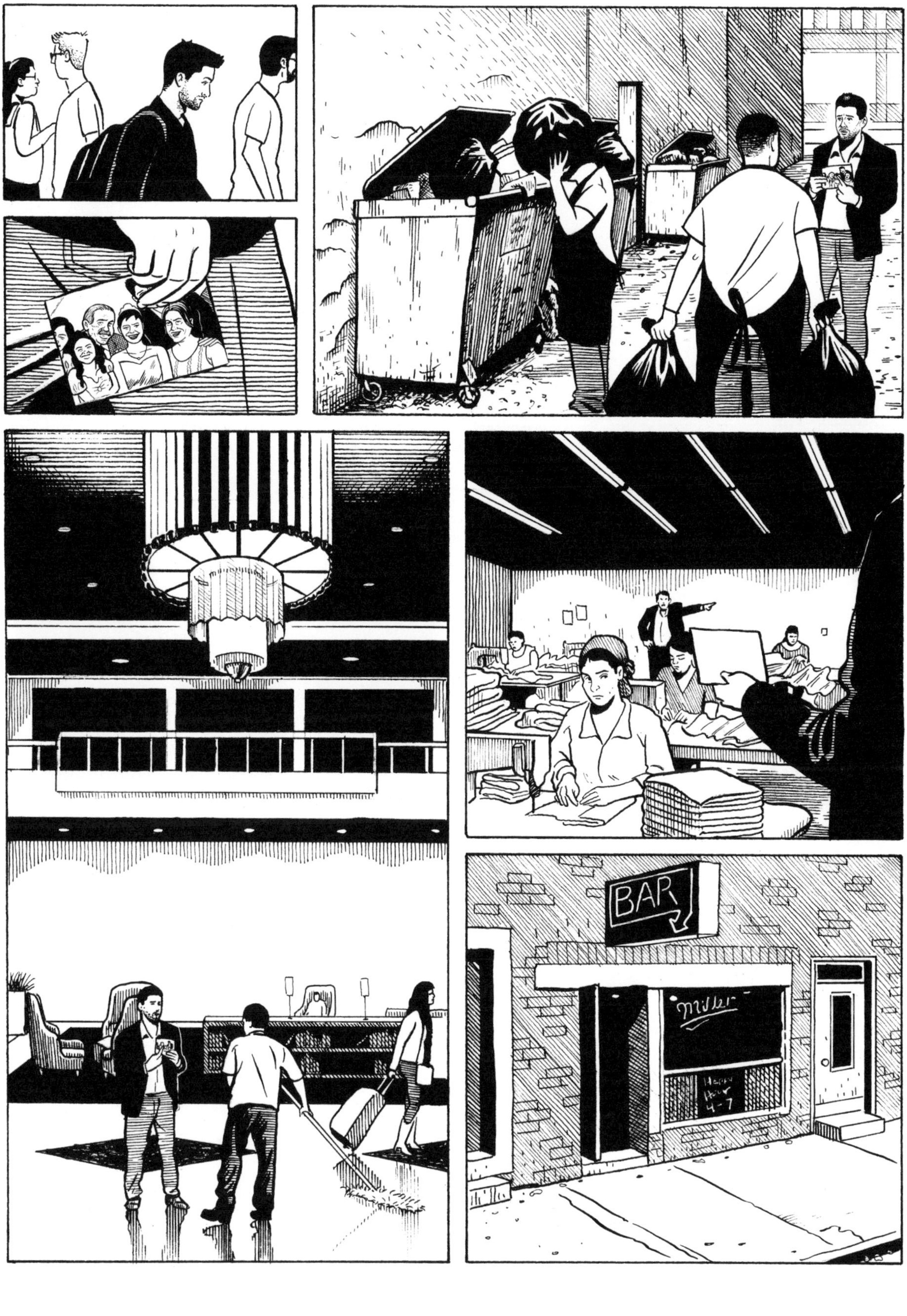
BAR
Miller
Happy Hour 4-7

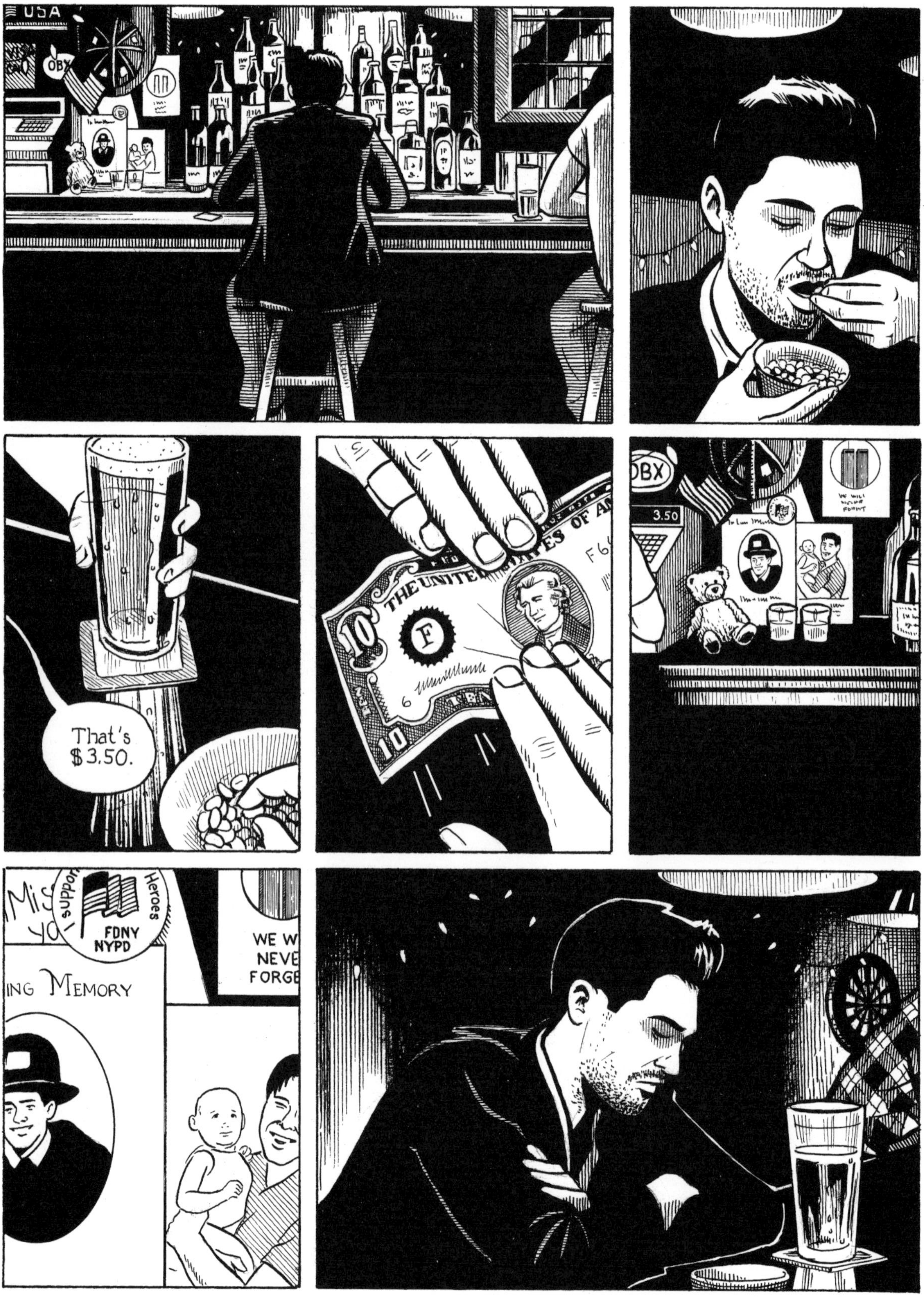
USA
OBX
That's $3.50.
THE UNITE STATES OF A
10
F
OBX
3.50
I support Heroes
FDNY
NYPD
WE W
NEVE
FORGE
ING MEMORY

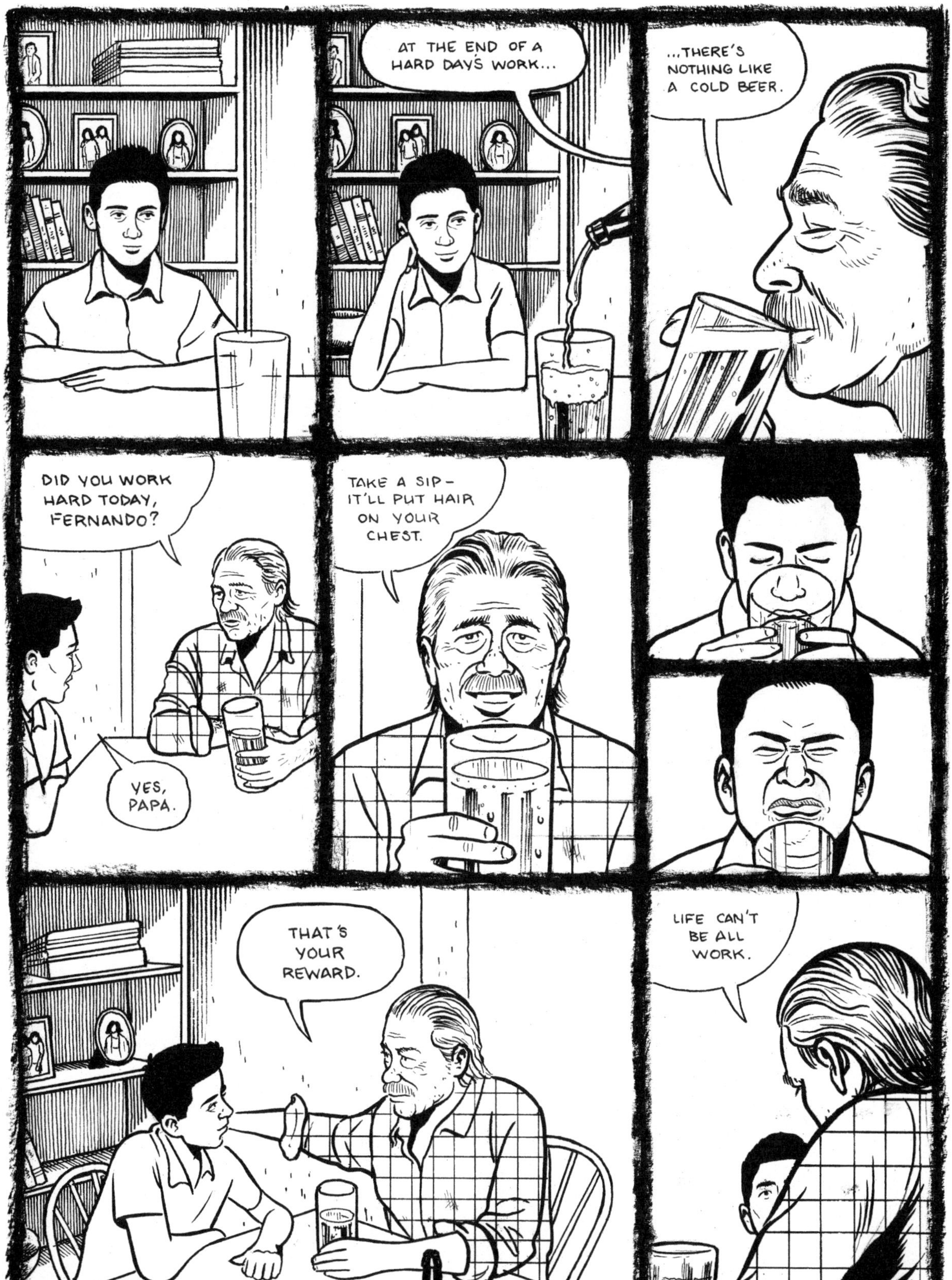
AT THE END OF A HARD DAY'S WORK...
...THERE'S NOTHING LIKE A COLD BEER.
DID YOU WORK HARD TODAY, FERNANDO?
YES, PAPA.
TAKE A SIP- IT'LL PUT HAIR ON YOUR CHEST.
THAT'S YOUR REWARD.
LIFE CAN'T BE ALL WORK.

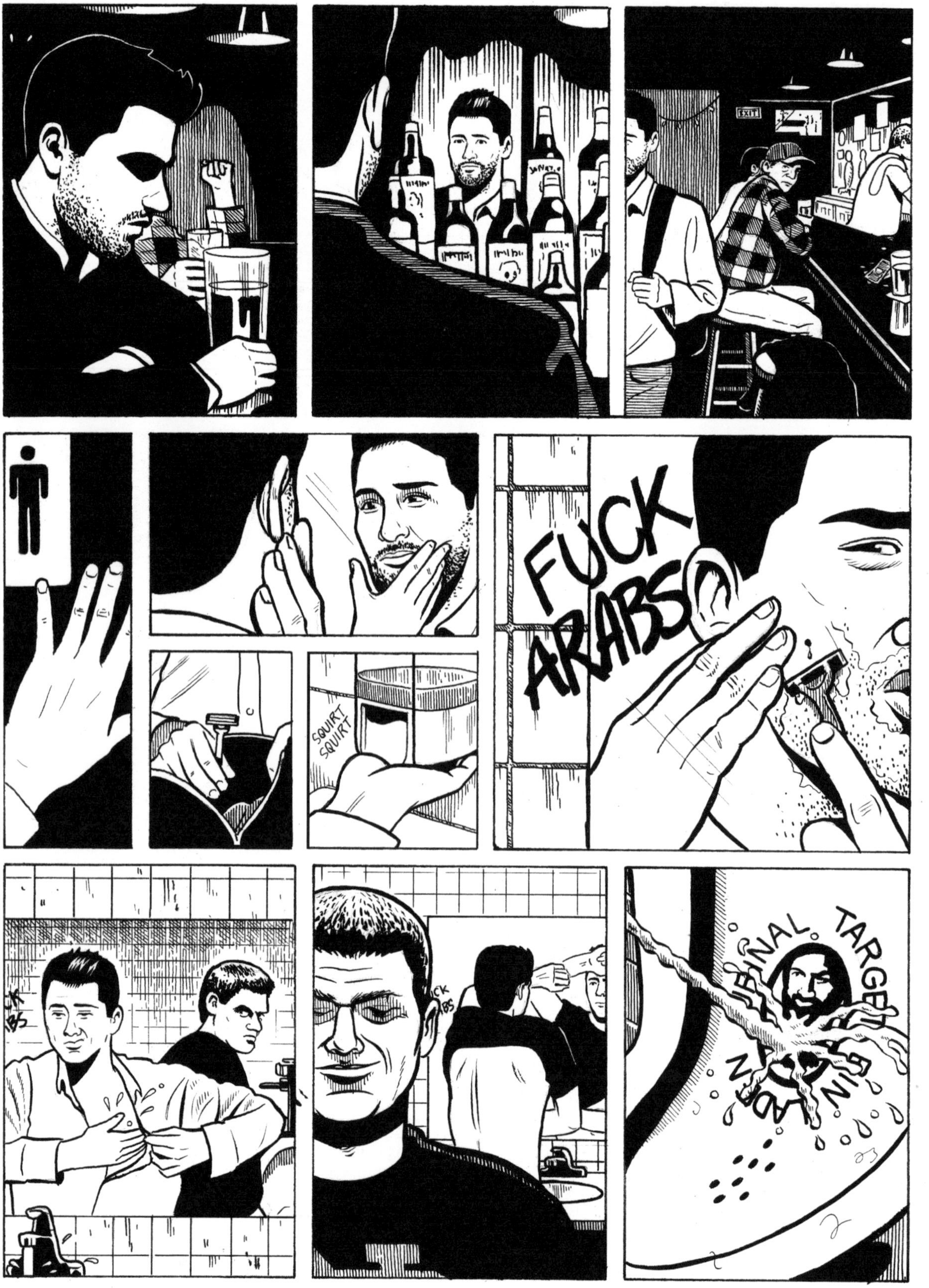
EXIT
FUCK ARABS
SQUIRT SQUIRT
INAL TARGE
IN LADEN

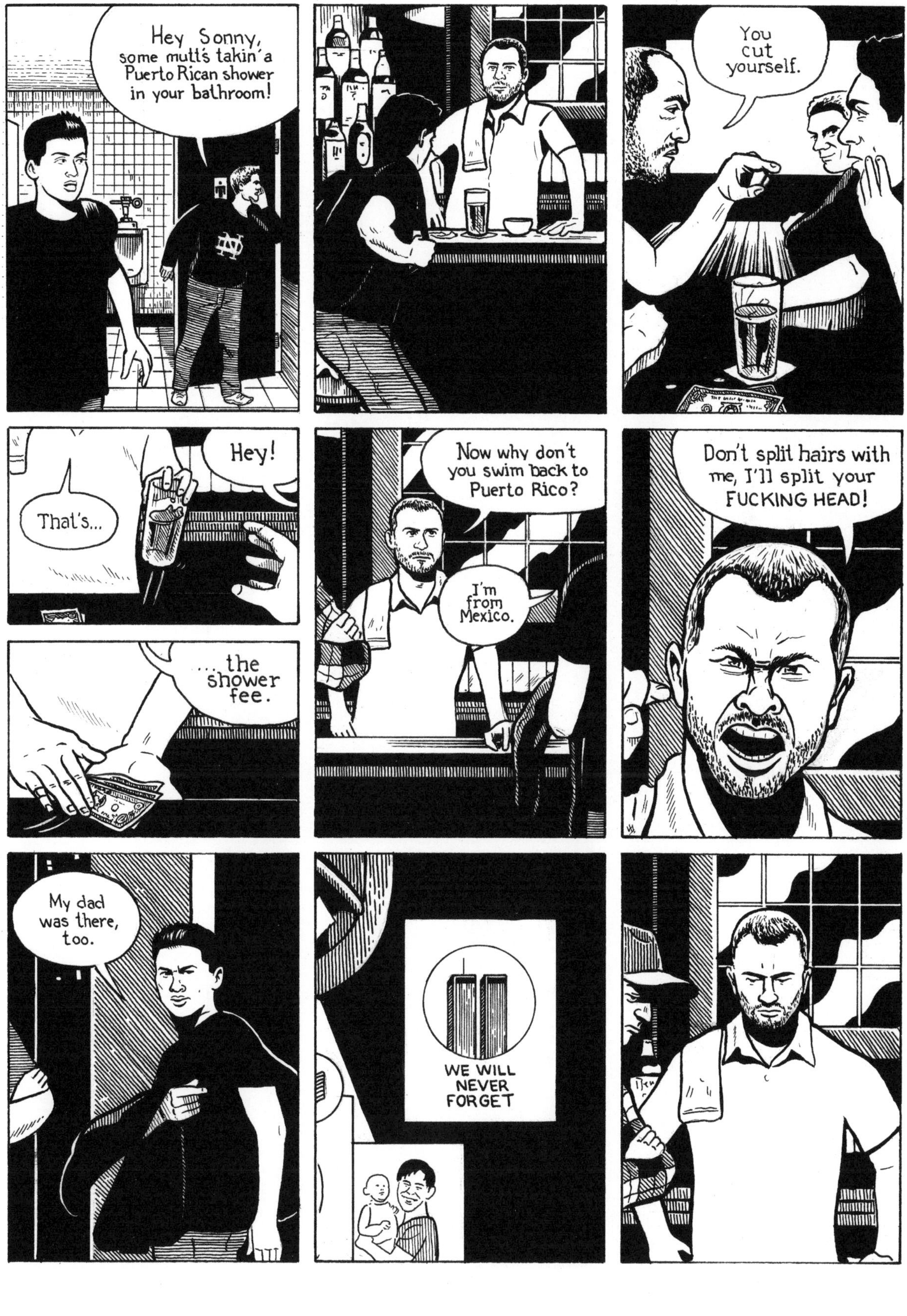
Hey Sonny, some mutt's takin' a Puerto Rican shower in your bathroom!
You cut yourself.
Hey!
That's...
... the shower fee.
Now why don't you swim back to Puerto Rico?
I'm from Mexico.
Don't split hairs with me, I'll split your FUCKING HEAD!
My dad was there, too.
WE WILL NEVER FORGET

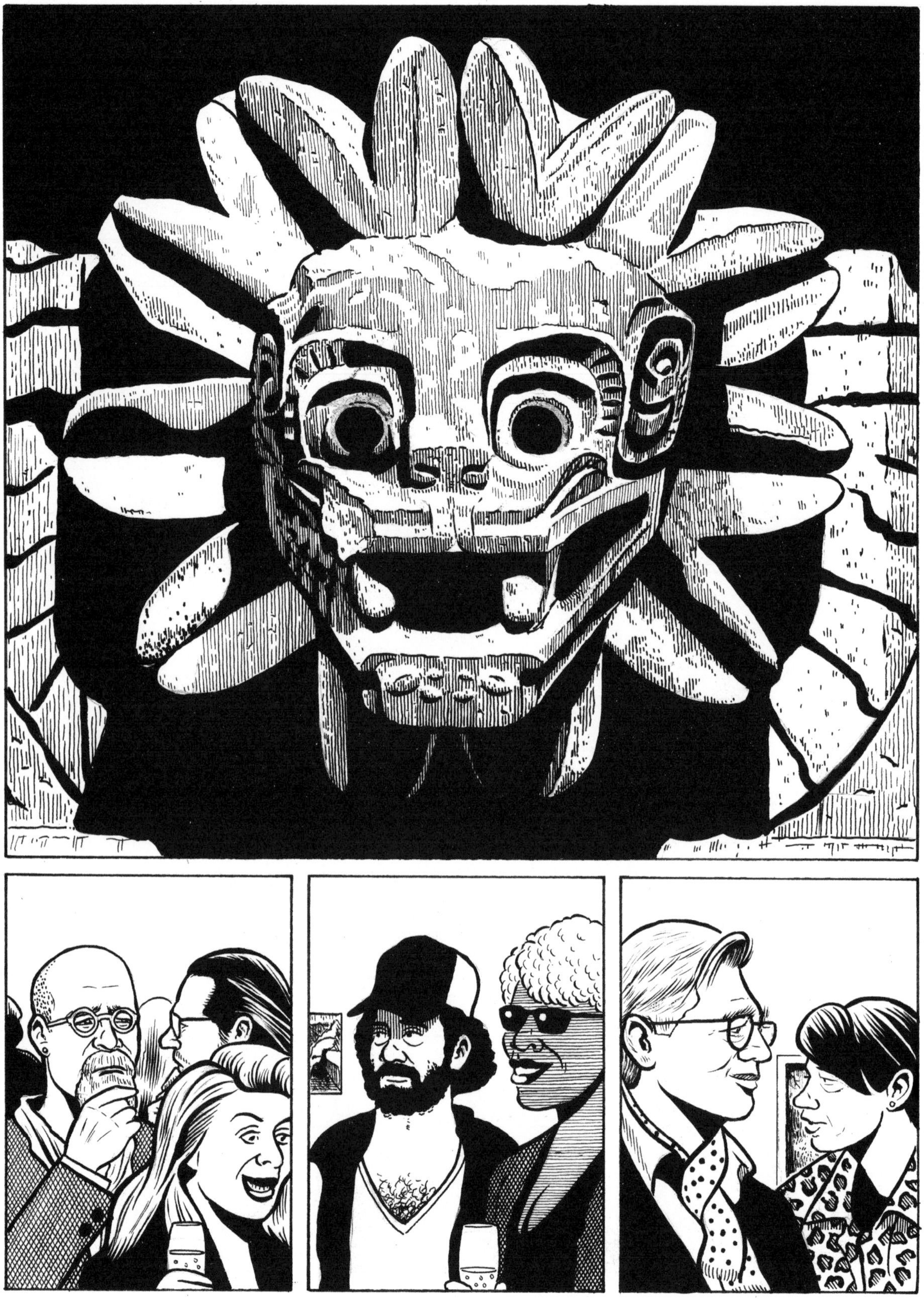

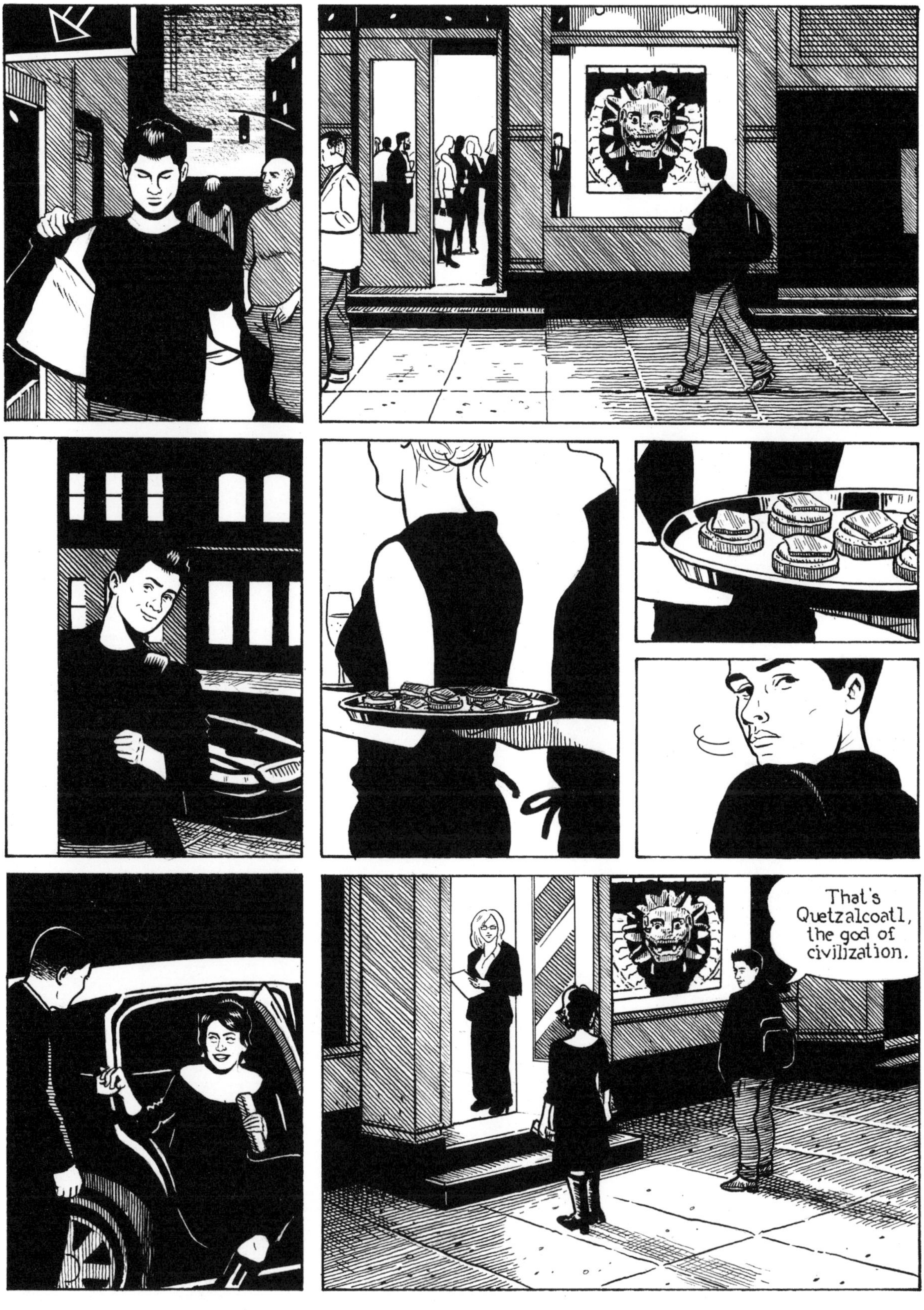
That's Quetzalcoatl, the god of civilization.

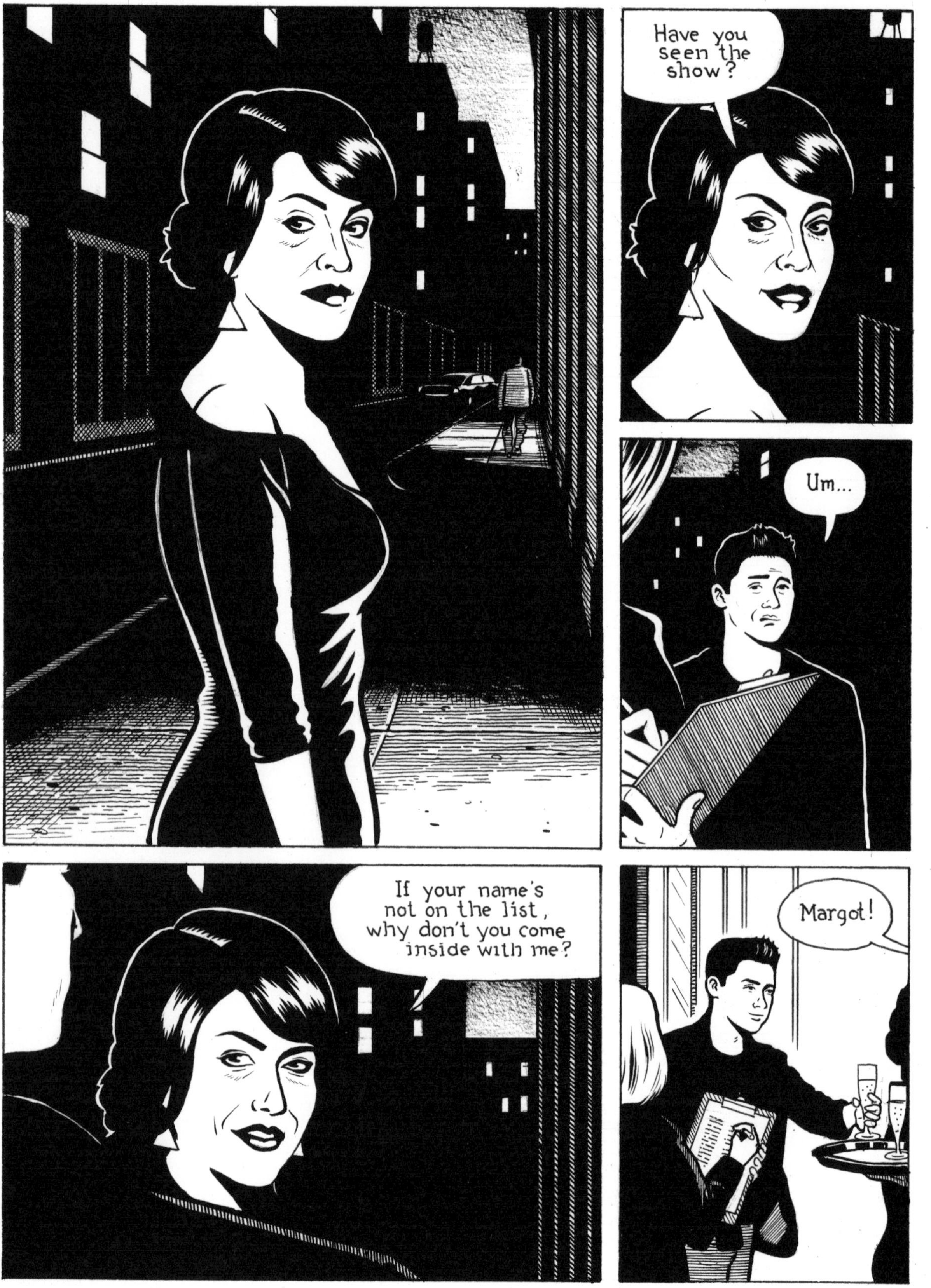
Have you seen the show?
Um...
If your name's not on the list, why don't you come inside with me?
Margot!

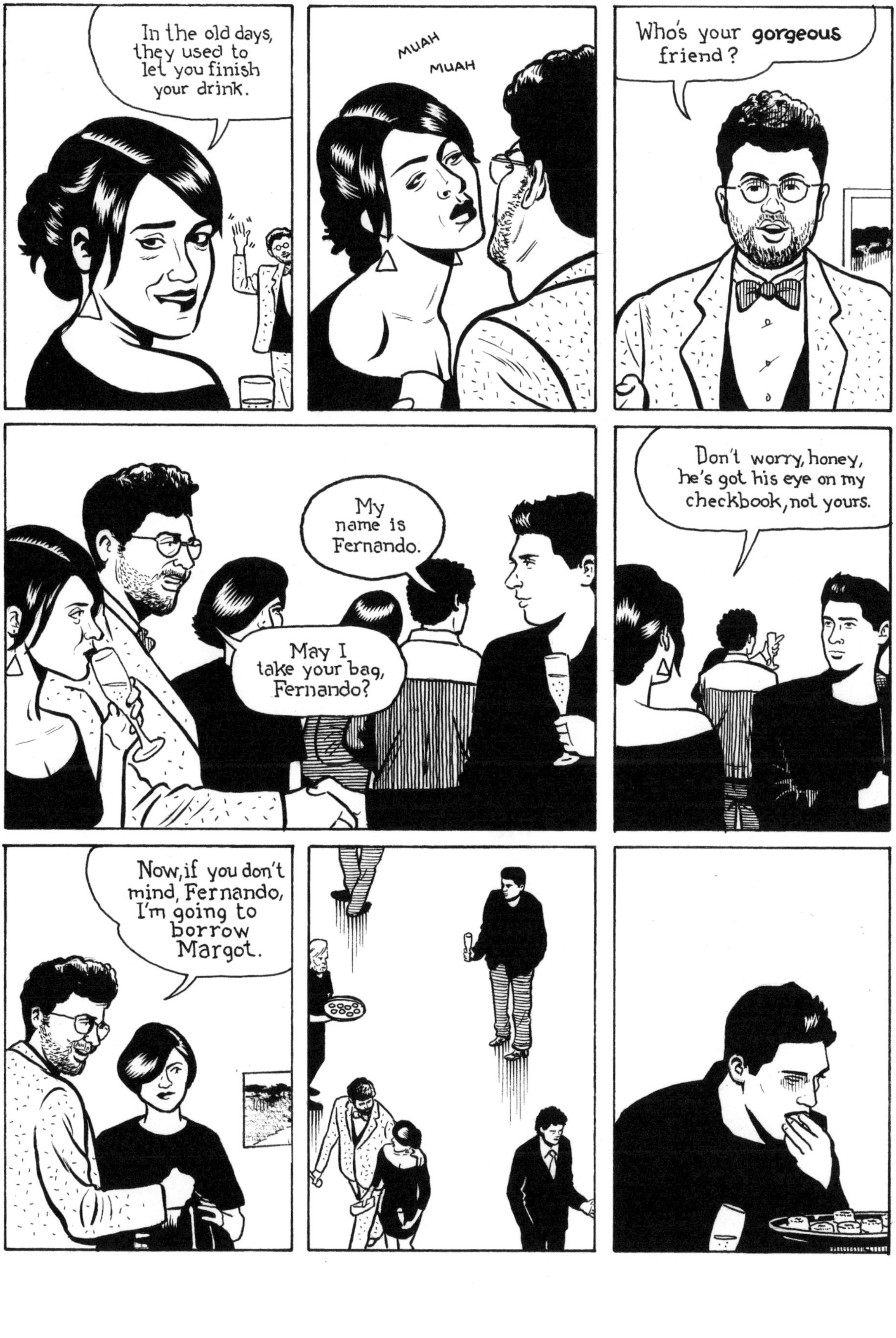

In the old days, they used to let you finish your drink.
MUAH
MUAH
Who's your **gorgeous** friend?
My name is Fernando.
May I take your bag, Fernando?
Don't worry, honey, he's got his eye on my checkbook, not yours.
Now, if you don't mind, Fernando, I'm going to borrow Margot.

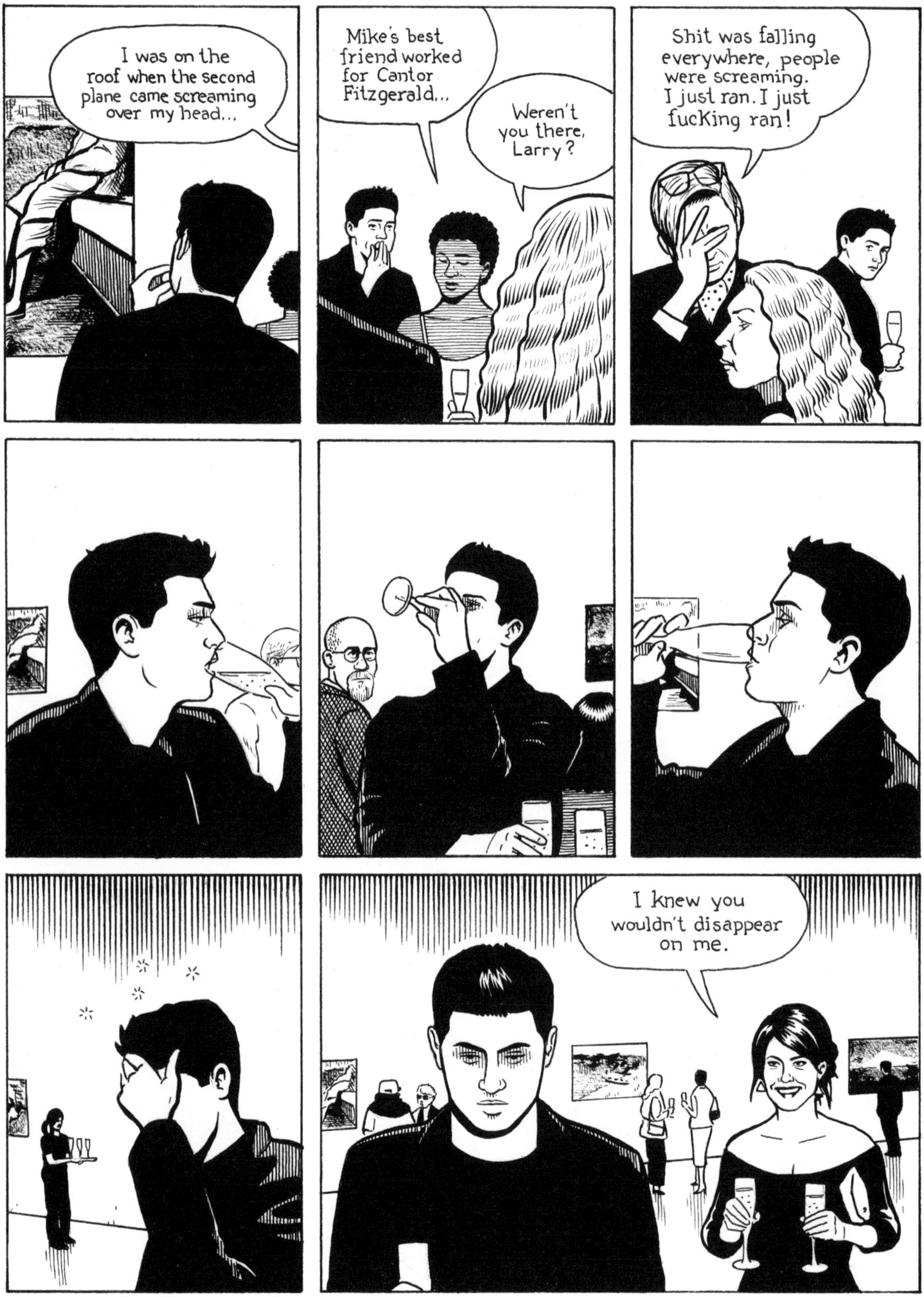
I was on the roof when the second plane came screaming over my head...
Mike's best friend worked for Cantor Fitzgerald...
Weren't you there, Larry?
Shit was falling everywhere, people were screaming. I just ran. I just fucking ran!
I knew you wouldn't disappear on me.

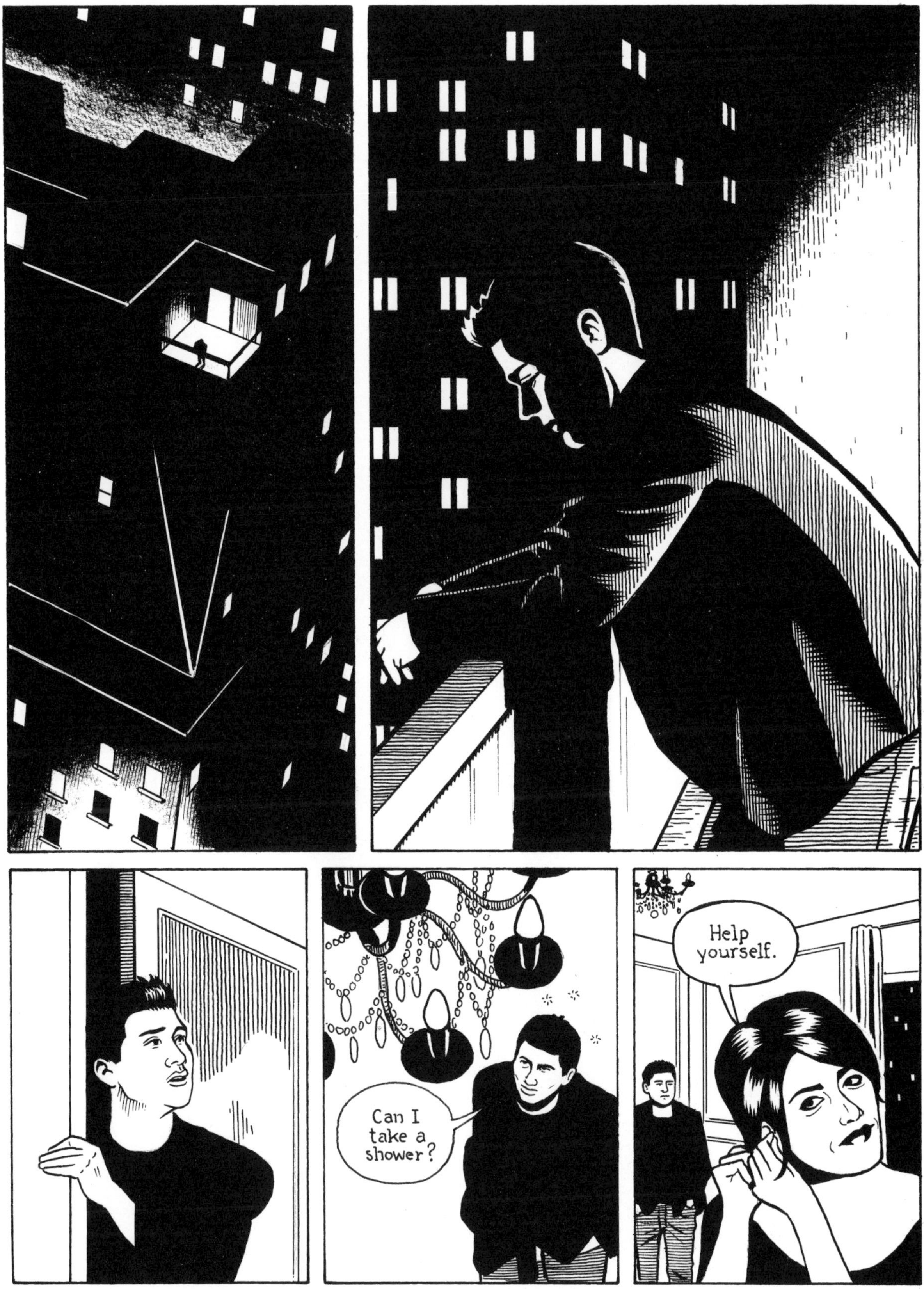
Can I take a shower?
Help yourself.

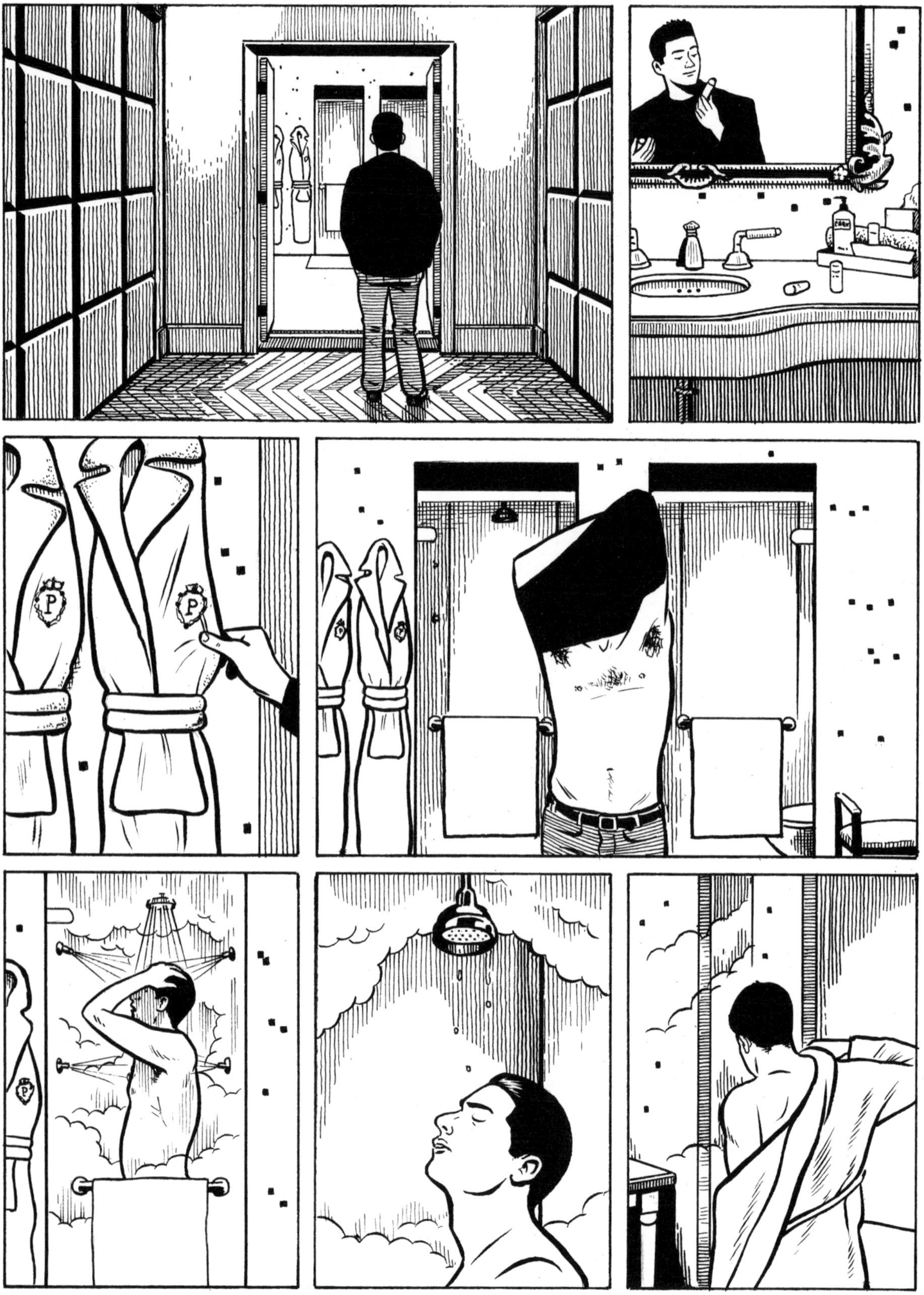

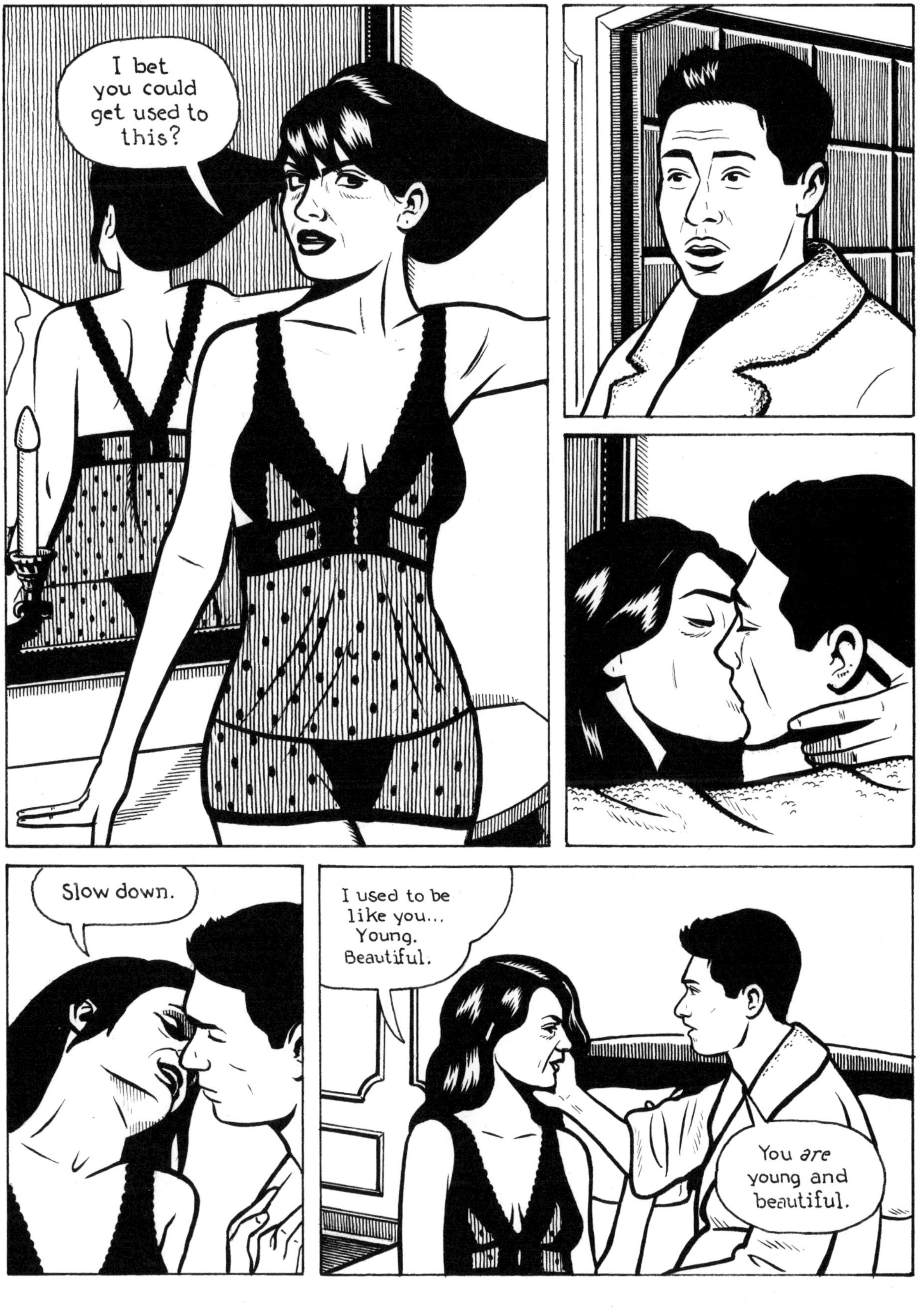
I bet you could get used to this?
Slow down.
I used to be like you... Young. Beautiful.
You *are* young and beautiful.

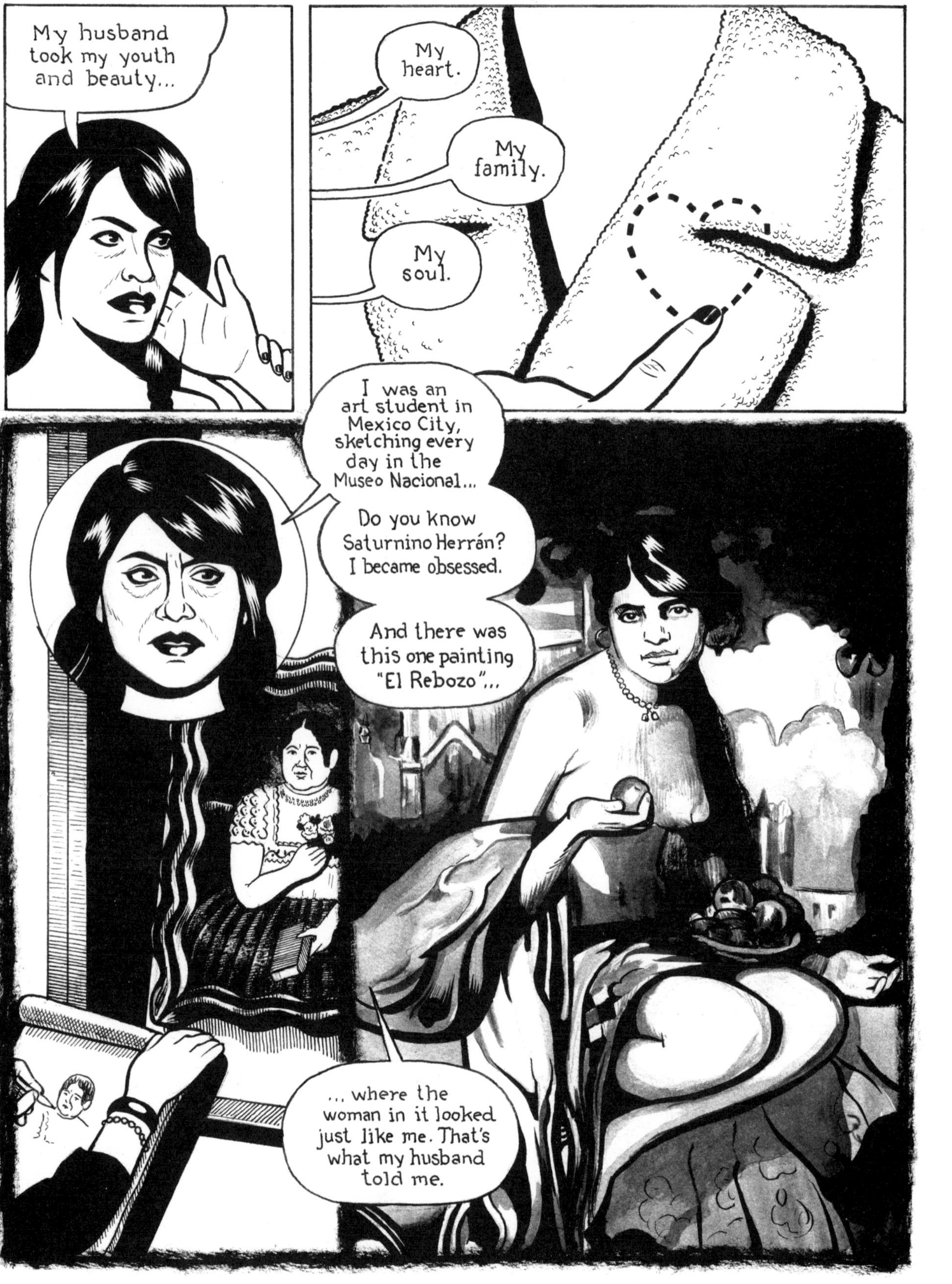
My husband took my youth and beauty...
My heart.
My family.
My soul.
I was an art student in Mexico City, sketching every day in the Museo Nacional...
Do you know Saturnino Herrán? I became obsessed.
And there was this one painting "El Rebozo"...
... where the woman in it looked just like me. That's what my husband told me.

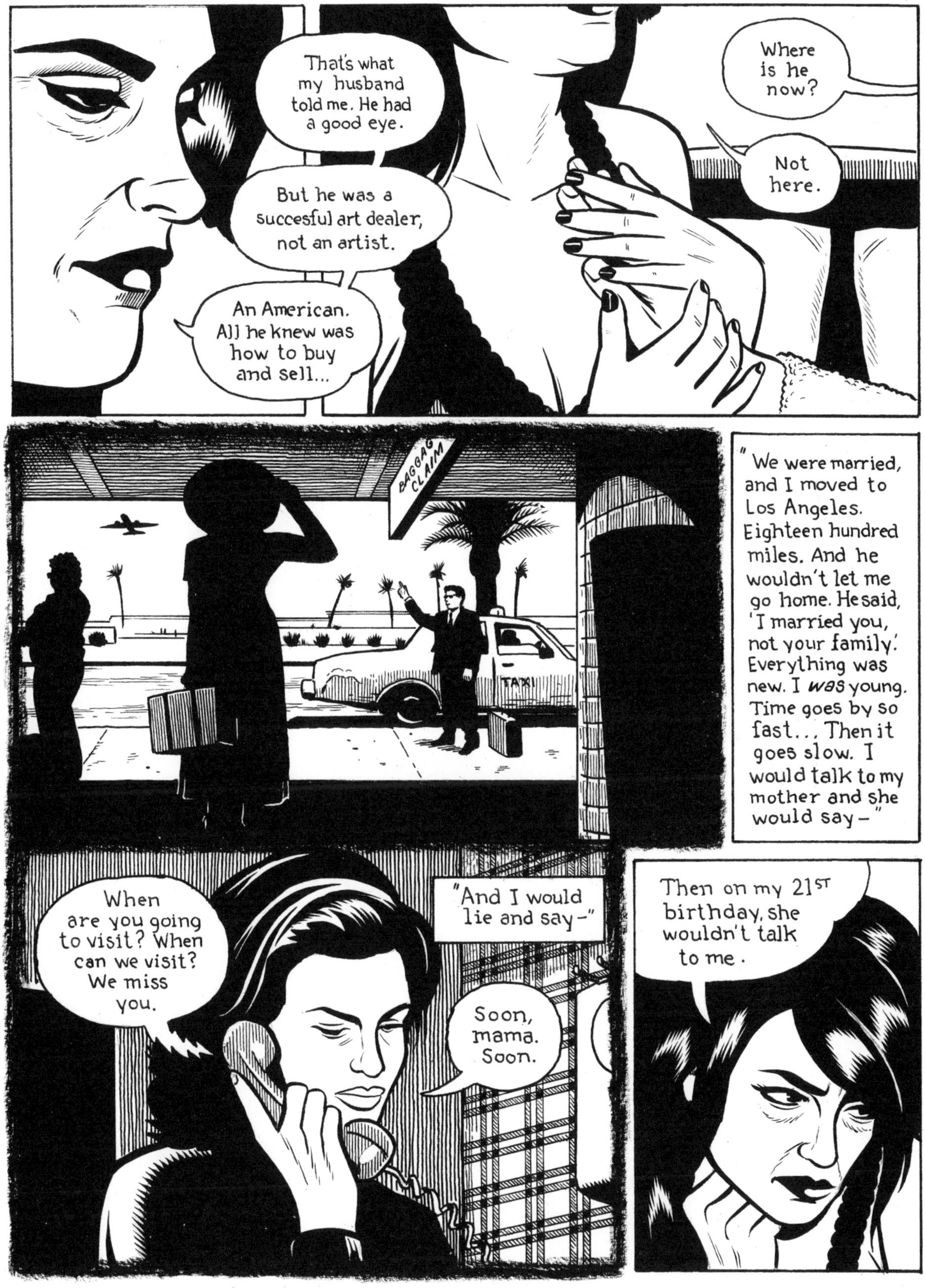
That's what my husband told me. He had a good eye.
But he was a succesful art dealer, not an artist.
An American. All he knew was how to buy and sell...
Where is he now?
Not here.
BAGGAGE CLAIM
TAXI
"We were married, and I moved to Los Angeles. Eighteen hundred miles. And he wouldn't let me go home. He said, 'I married you, not your family.' Everything was new. I *was* young. Time goes by so fast... Then it goes slow. I would talk to my mother and she would say –"
When are you going to visit? When can we visit? We miss you.
"And I would lie and say –"
Soon, mama. Soon.
Then on my 21ST birthday, she wouldn't talk to me.

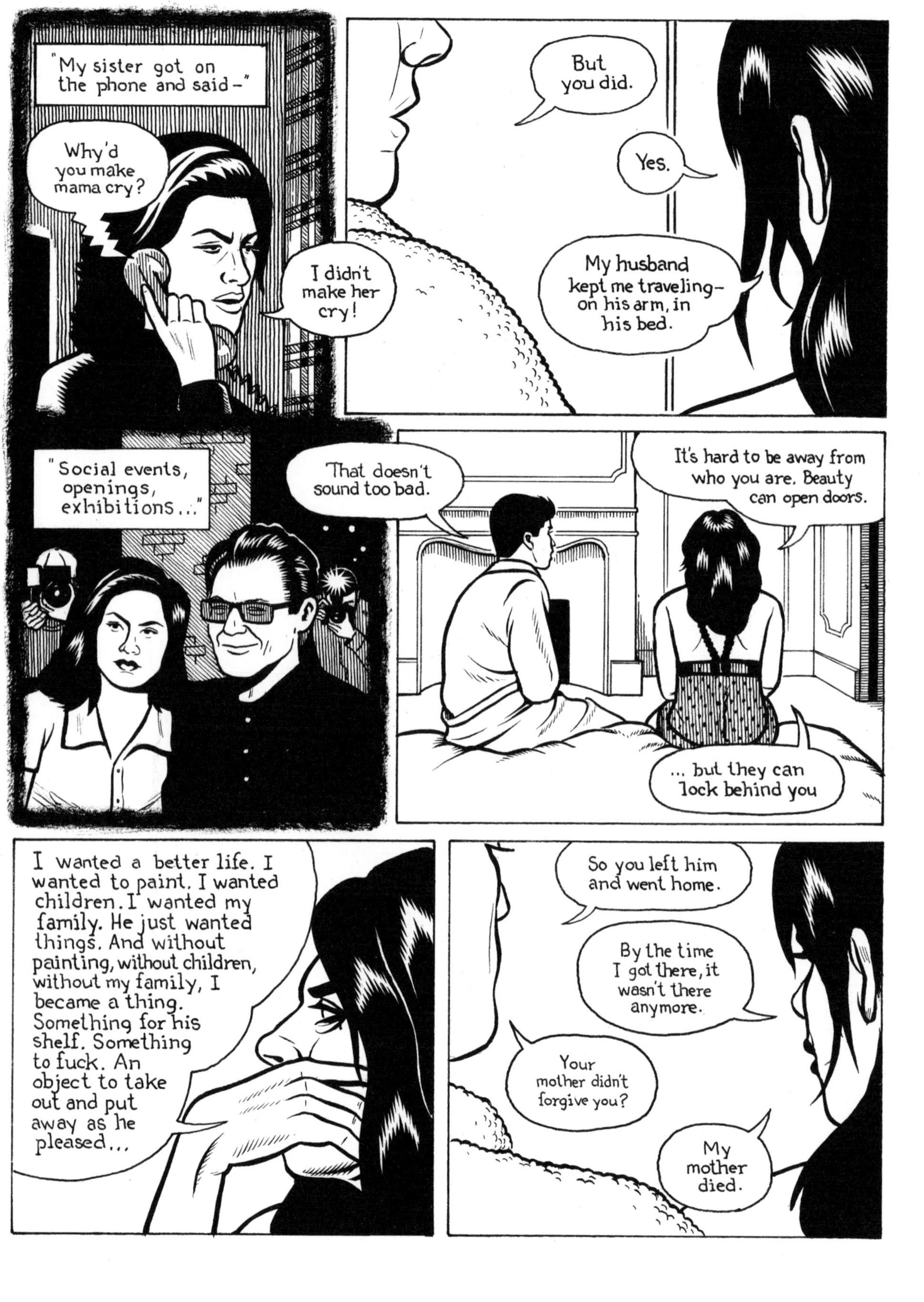
"My sister got on the phone and said –"
Why'd you make mama cry?
I didn't make her cry!
But you did.
Yes.
My husband kept me traveling– on his arm, in his bed.
"Social events, openings, exhibitions..."
That doesn't sound too bad.
It's hard to be away from who you are. Beauty can open doors.
... but they can lock behind you
I wanted a better life. I wanted to paint. I wanted children. I wanted my family. He just wanted things. And without painting, without children, without my family, I became a thing. Something for his shelf. Something to fuck. An object to take out and put away as he pleased...
So you left him and went home.
By the time I got there, it wasn't there anymore.
Your mother didn't forgive you?
My mother died.

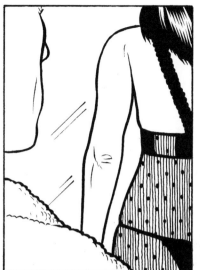

GO HOME!

GO HOME

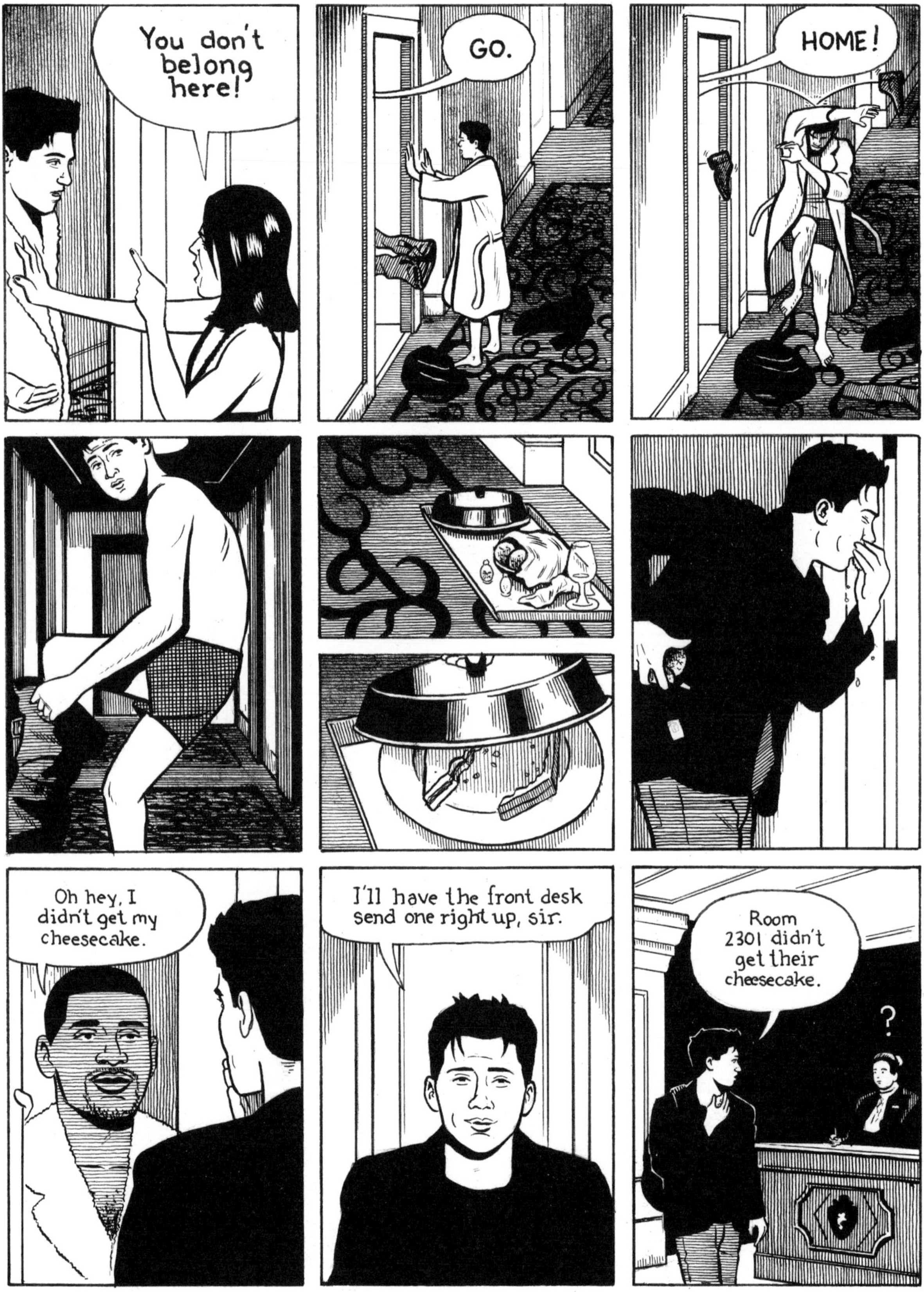
You don't belong here!
GO.
HOME!
Oh hey, I didn't get my cheesecake.
I'll have the front desk send one right up, sir.
Room 2301 didn't get their cheesecake.
?

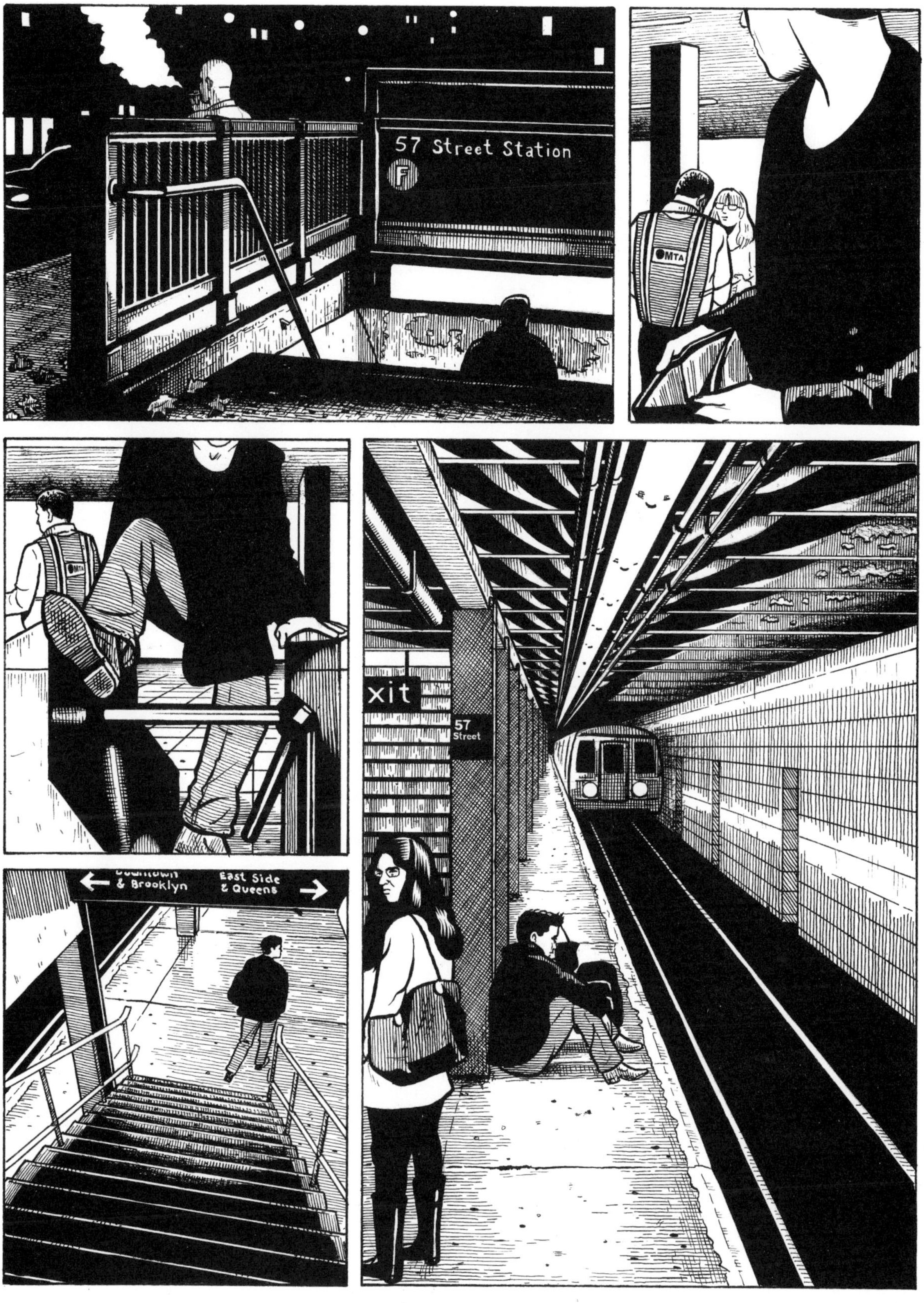
57 Street Station
F
MTA
MTA
xit
57 Street
& Brooklyn
East Side & Queens

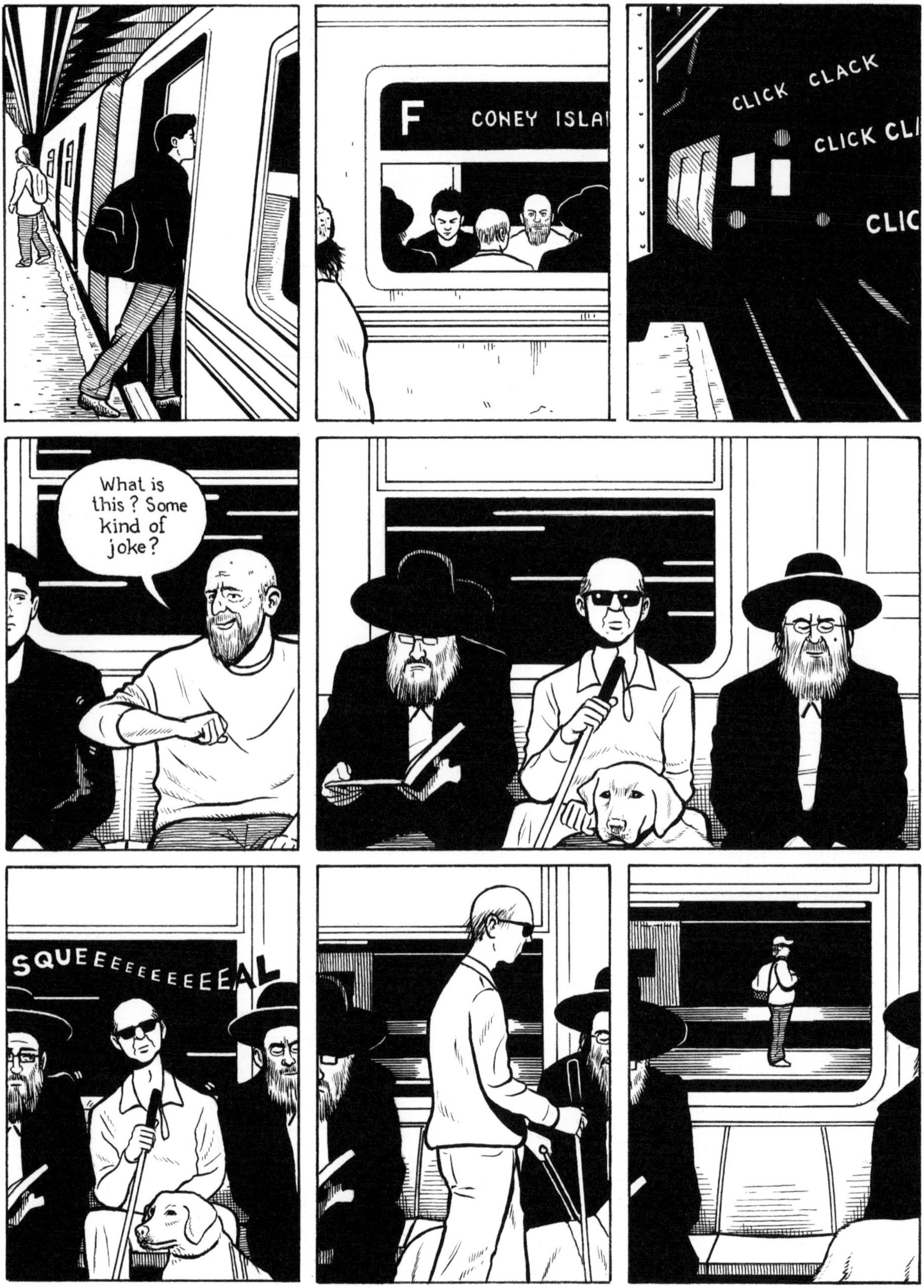
F
CONEY ISLA
CLICK CLACK
CLICK CL
CLIC
What is this? Some kind of joke?
SQUEEEEEEEEEEEAL

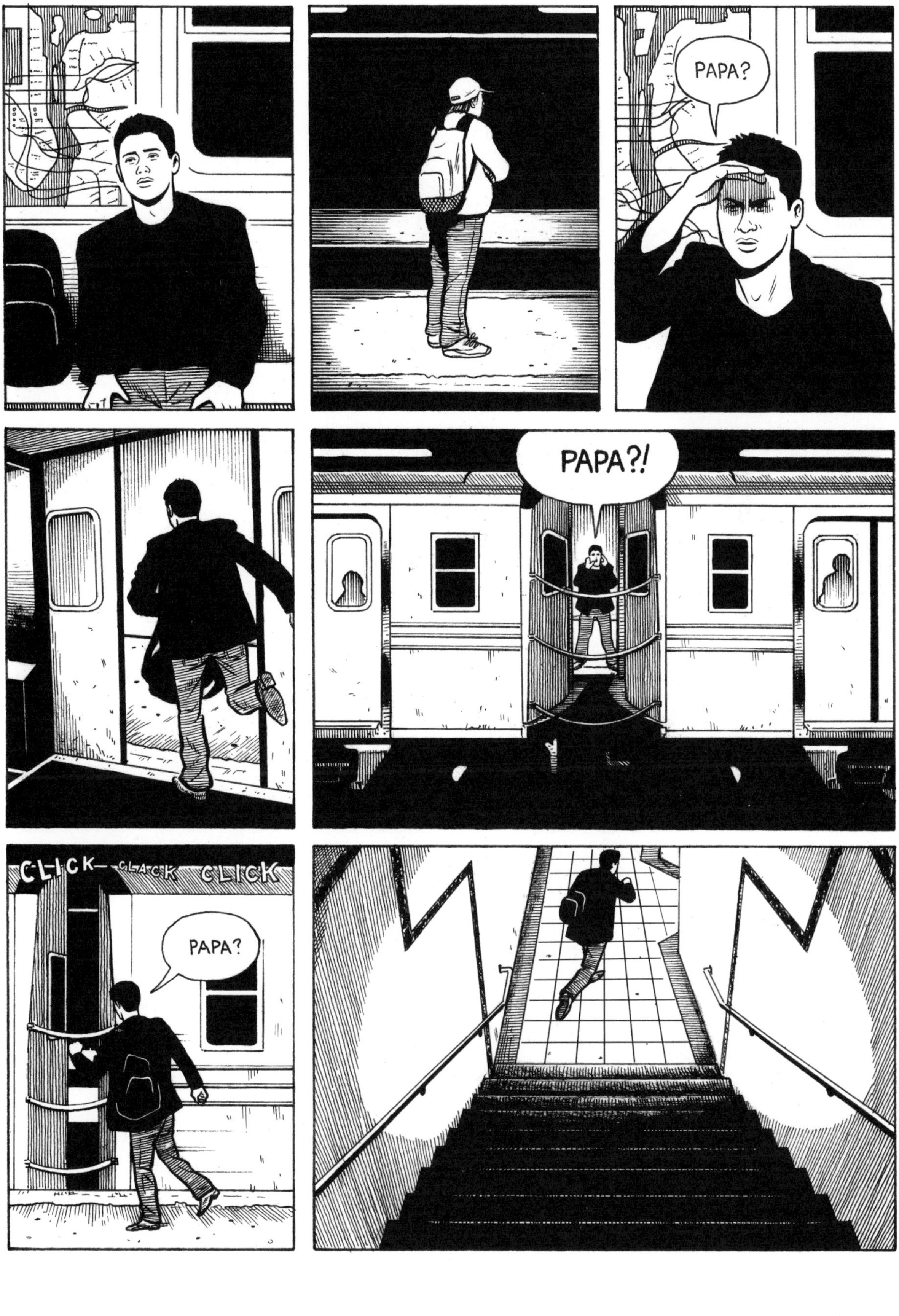
PAPA?
PAPA?!
CLICK—CLACK CLICK
PAPA?

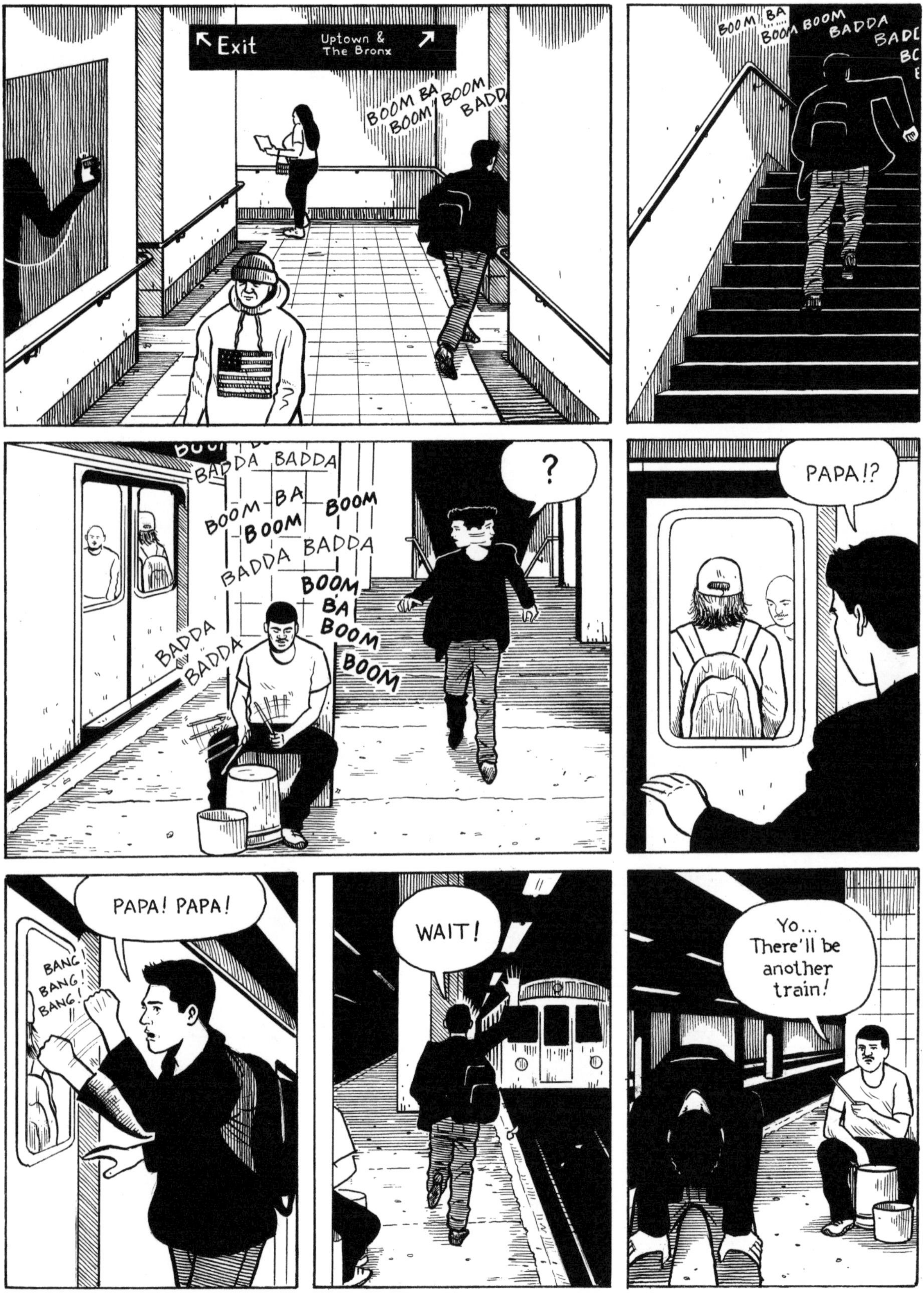
Exit
Uptown & The Bronx
BOOM BA BOOM BOOM BADDA
BOOM BA BOOM BOOM BADDA
BADDA BADDA
BOOM BA BOOM BOOM
BADDA BADDA
BOOM BA BOOM BOOM
BADDA BADDA
?
PAPA!?
PAPA! PAPA!
BANG! BANG! BANG!
WAIT!
Yo... There'll be another train!

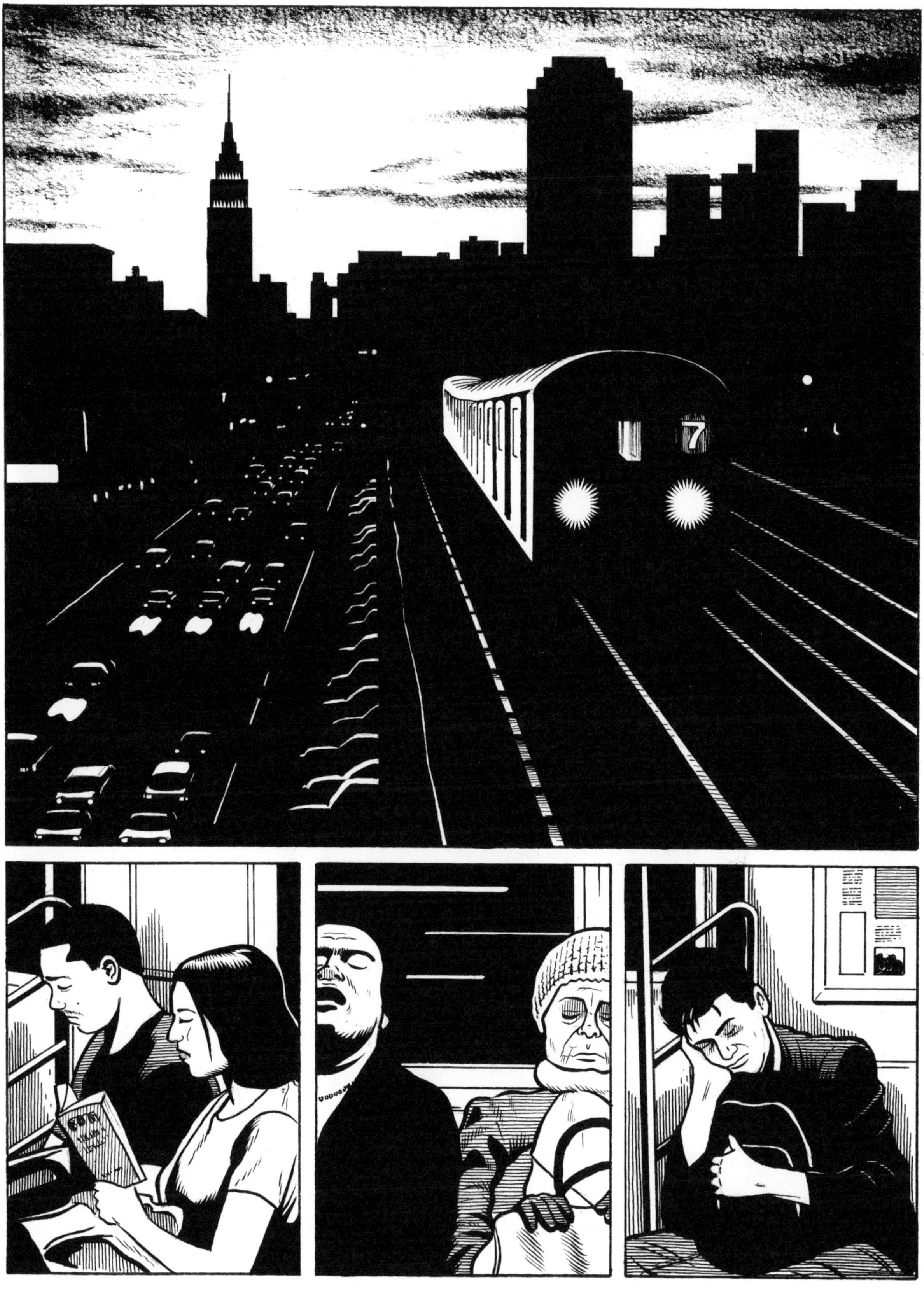
7

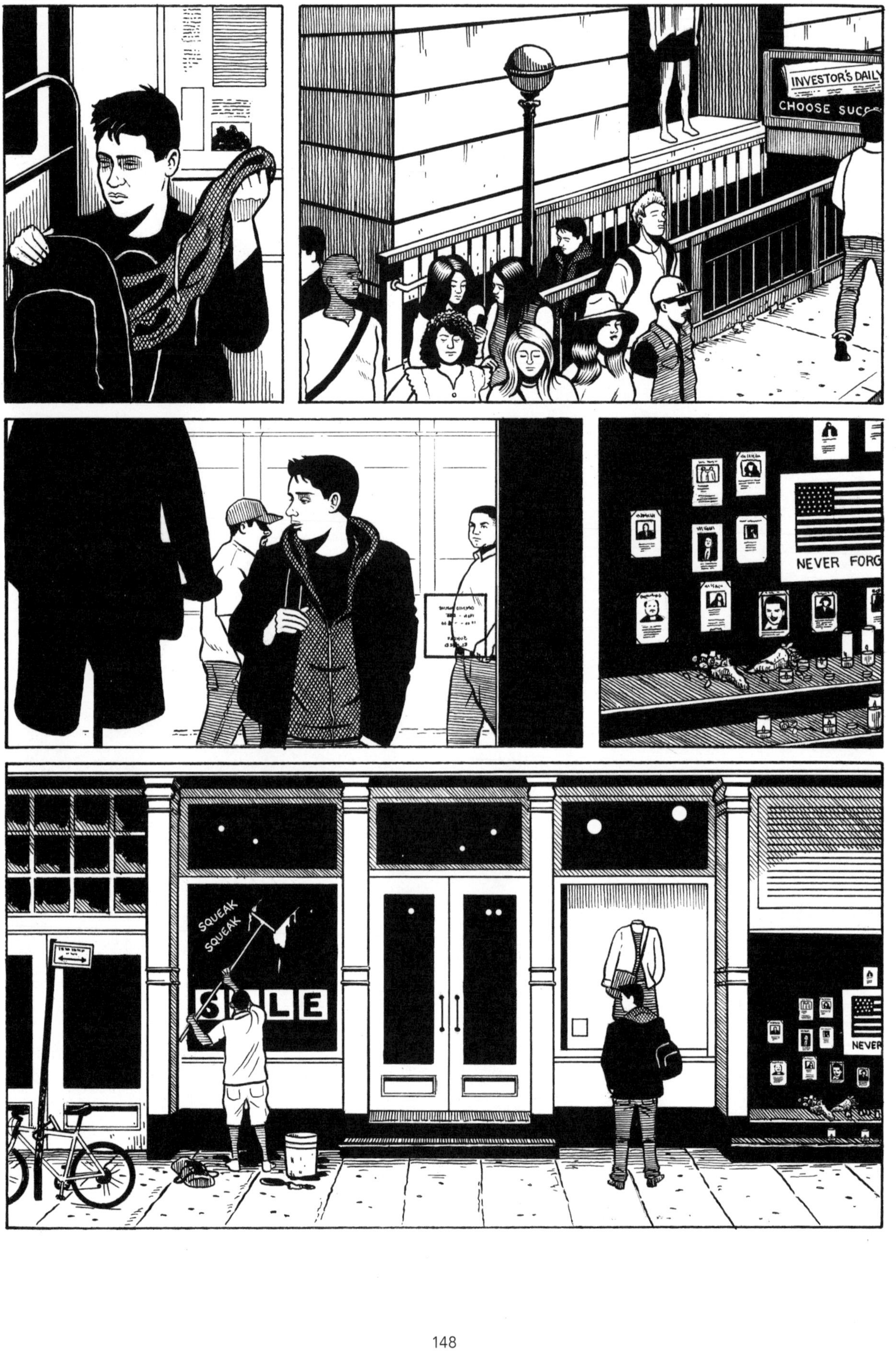
INVESTOR'S DAILY
CHOOSE SUCC
NEVER FORG
SQUEAK
SQUEAK
NEVER

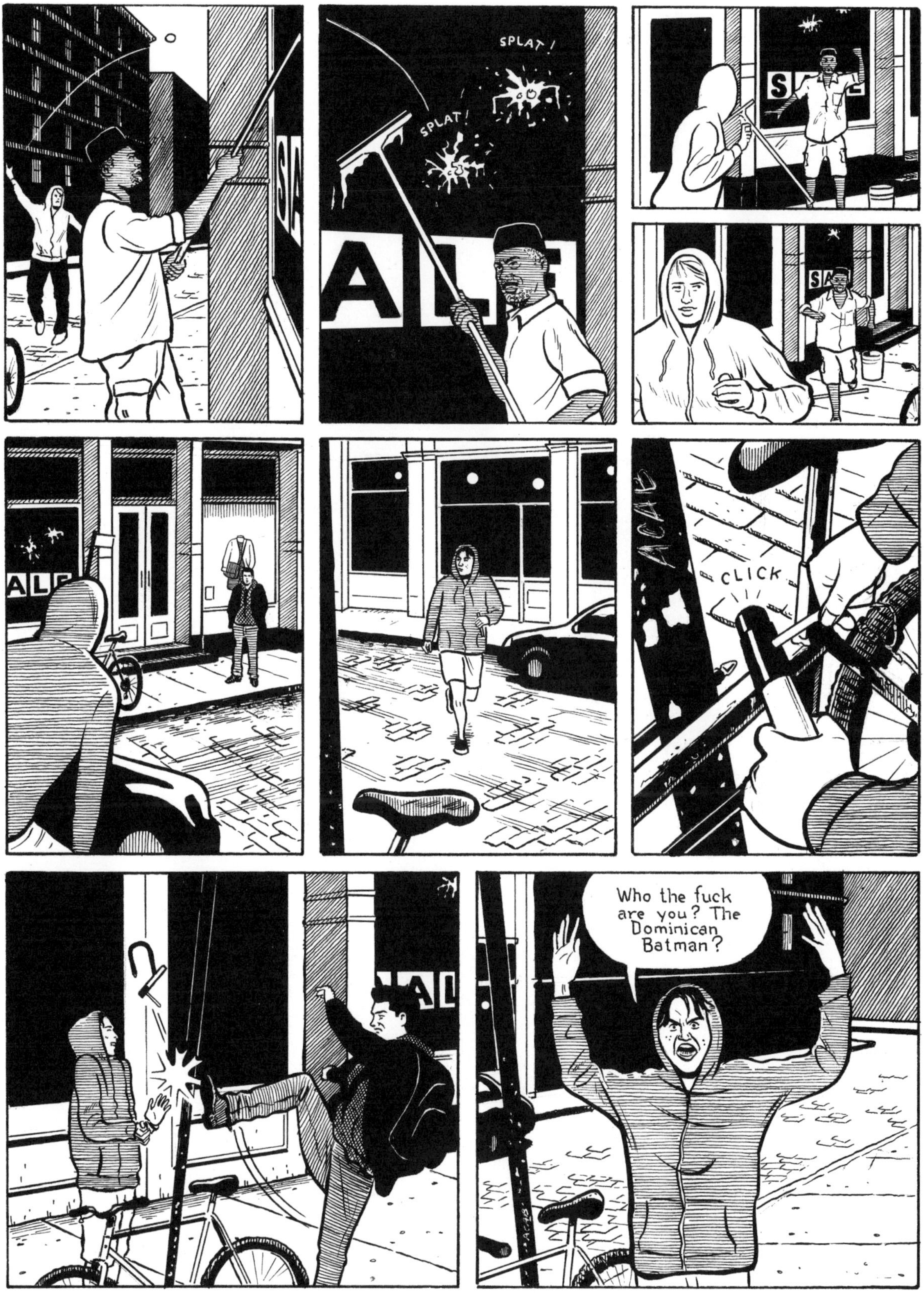
SPLAT!
SPLAT!
ACAB
CLICK
Who the fuck are you? The Dominican Batman?

The pen is mightier than the sword...

...and my lock.

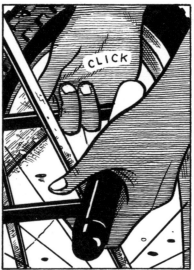

CLICK

I may have to steal it back one day!

Thank you.

It's getting to be as bad as Lagos out here...

Nigeria. Lagos is as big as New York. And getting bigger...

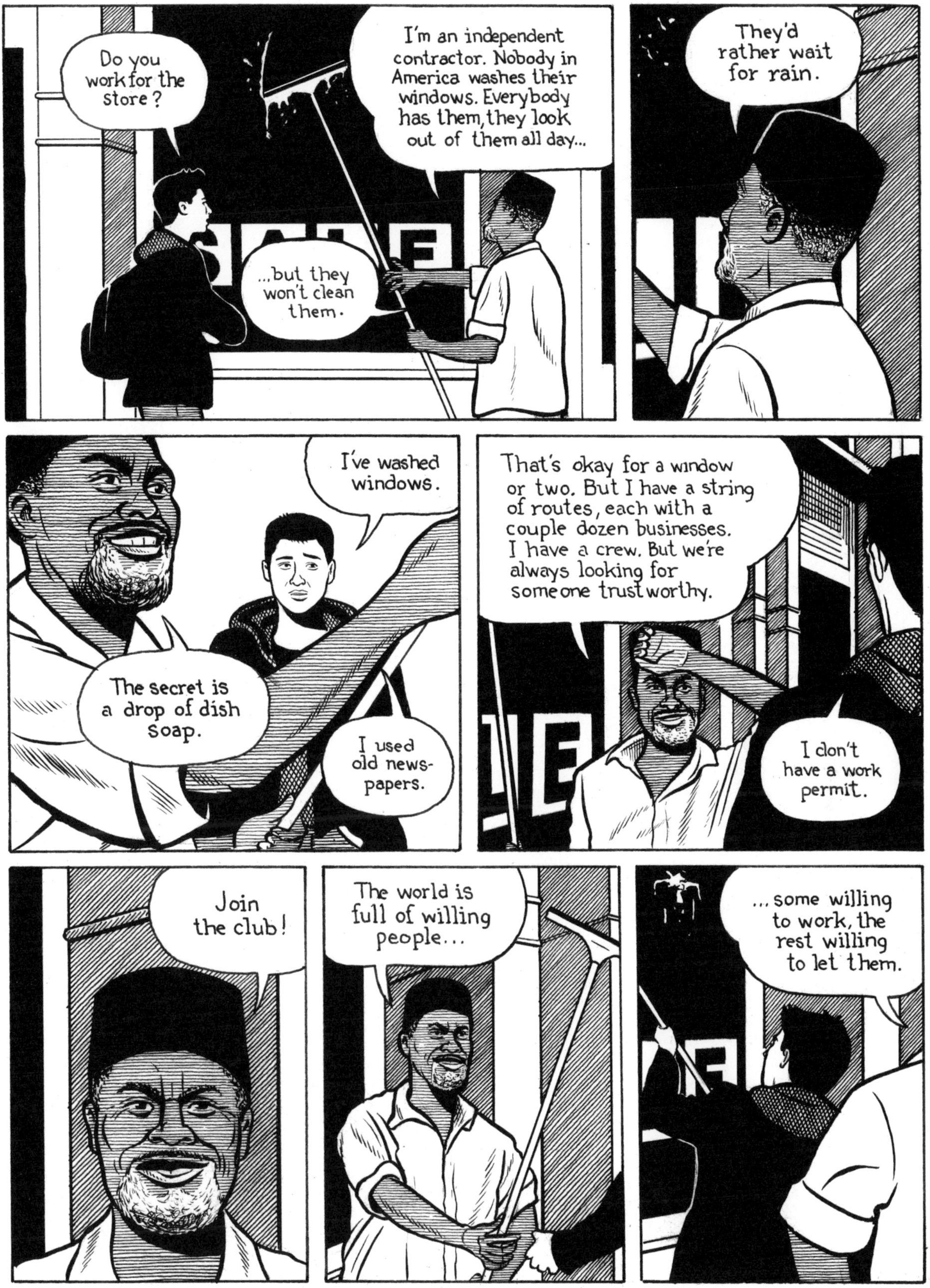
Do you work for the store?
I'm an independent contractor. Nobody in America washes their windows. Everybody has them, they look out of them all day...
...but they won't clean them.
They'd rather wait for rain.
I've washed windows.
The secret is a drop of dish soap.
I used old news-papers.
That's okay for a window or two. But I have a string of routes, each with a couple dozen businesses. I have a crew. But we're always looking for someone trustworthy.
I don't have a work permit.
Join the club!
The world is full of willing people...
...some willing to work, the rest willing to let them.

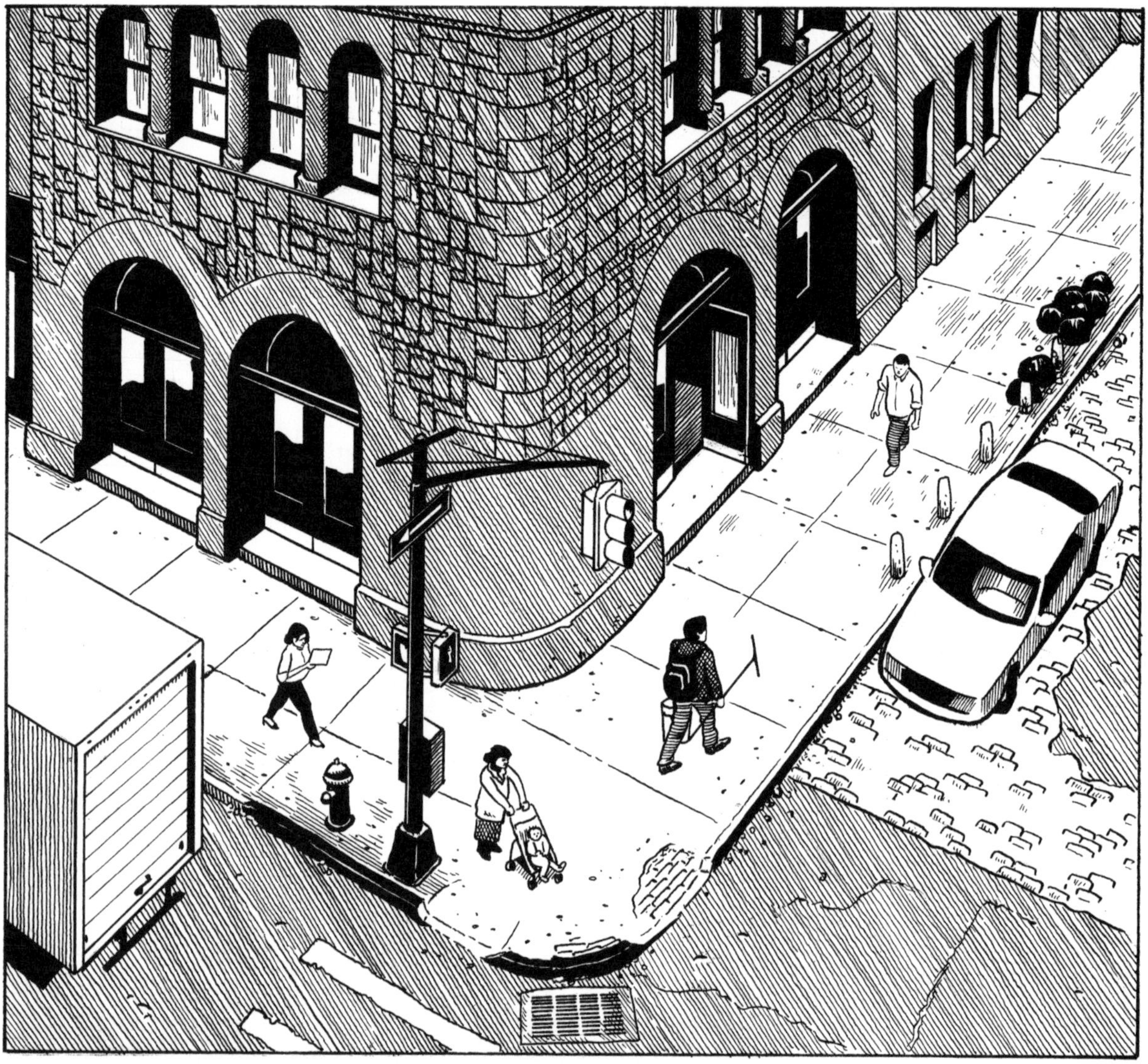

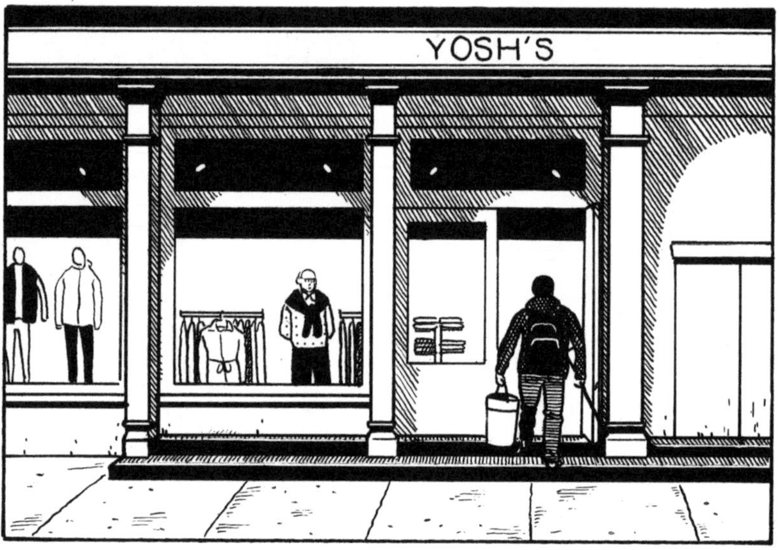
YOSH'S

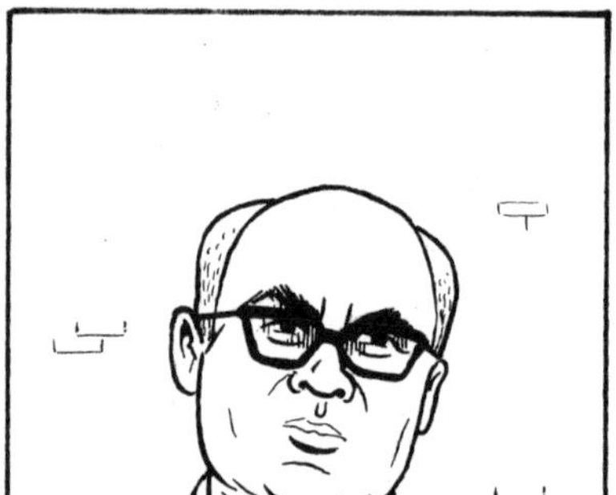

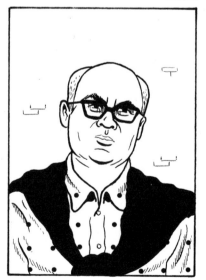

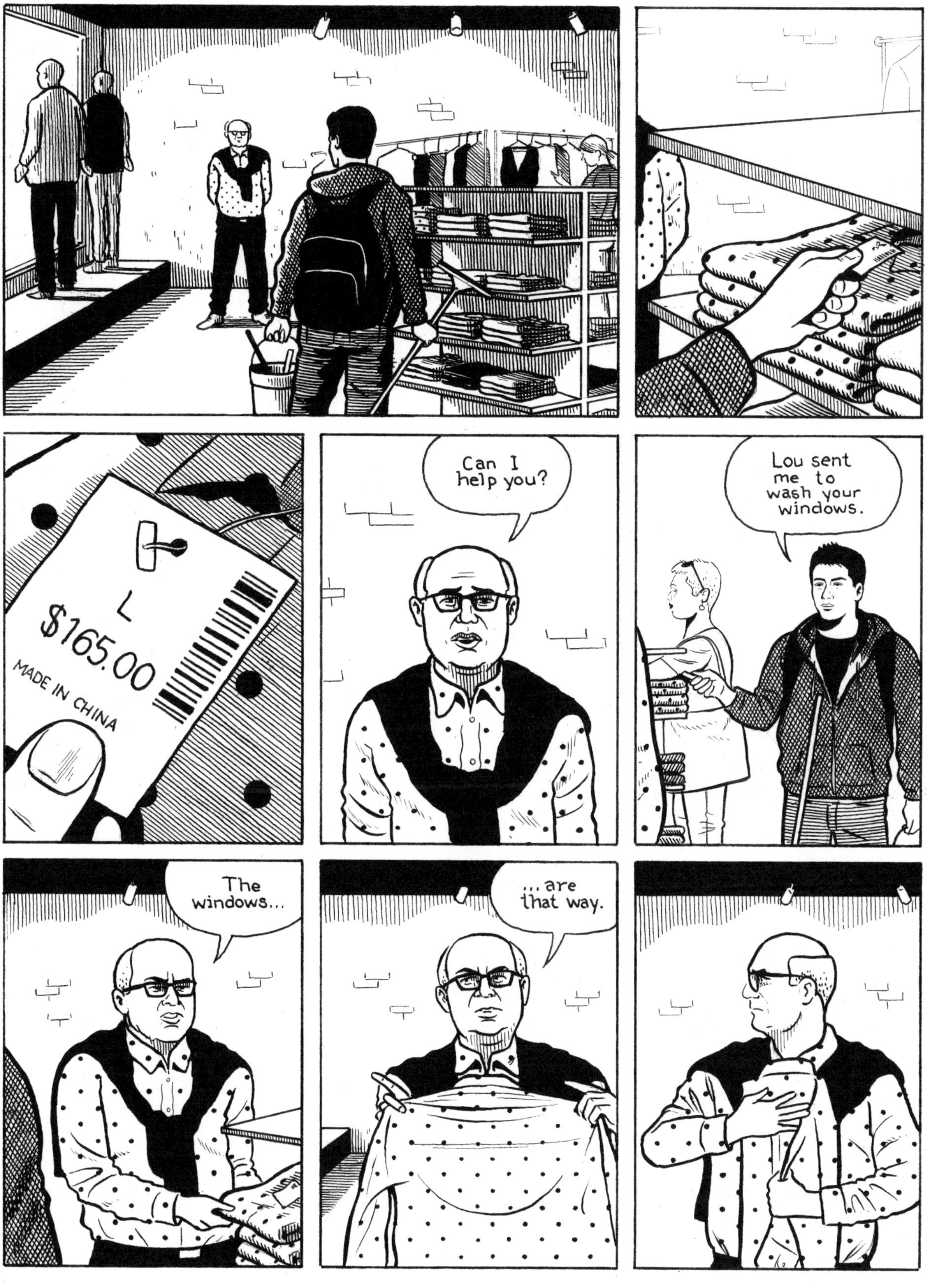
L
$165.00
MADE IN CHINA
Can I help you?
Lou sent me to wash your windows.
The windows...
...are that way.

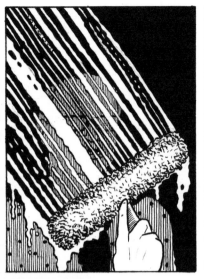

You missed a spot...

SALE
SALE

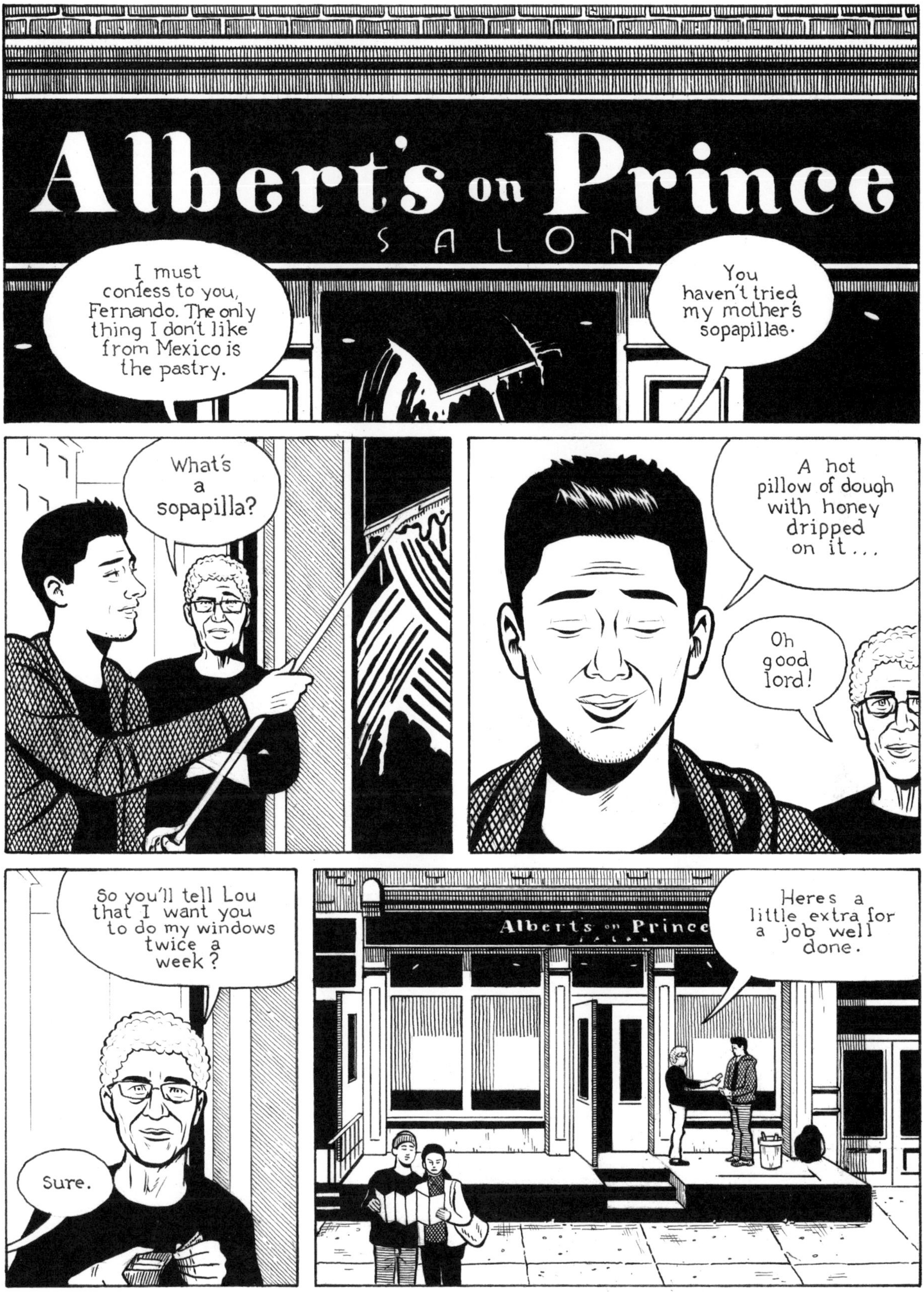
Albert's on Prince
SALON
I must confess to you, Fernando. The only thing I don't like from Mexico is the pastry.
You haven't tried my mother's sopapillas.
What's a sopapilla?
A hot pillow of dough with honey dripped on it...
Oh good lord!
So you'll tell Lou that I want you to do my windows twice a week?
Sure.
Albert's on Prince
Heres a little extra for a job well done.

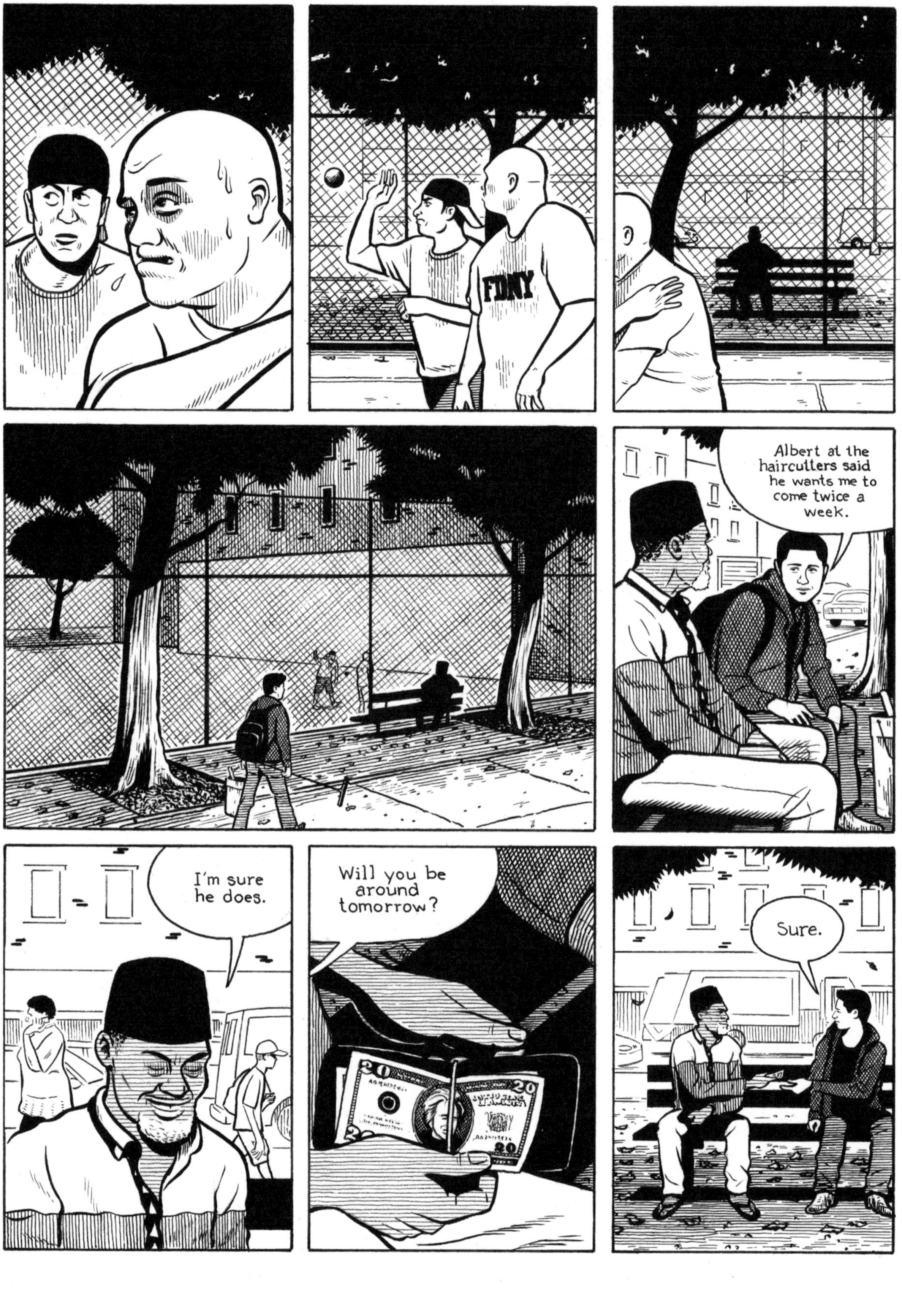
FDNY
Albert at the haircutters said he wants me to come twice a week.
I'm sure he does.
Will you be around tomorrow?
Sure.

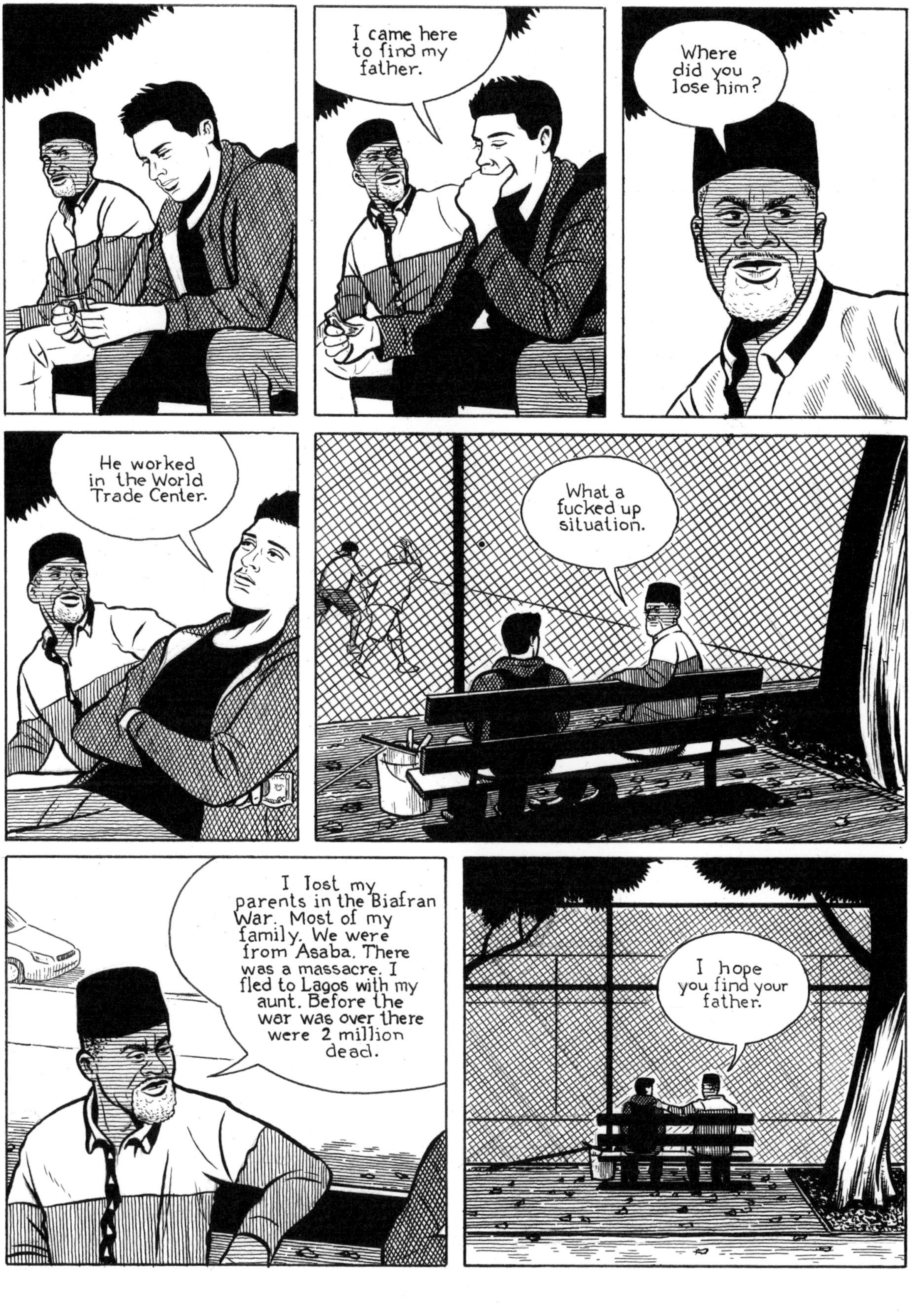
I came here to find my father.
Where did you lose him?
He worked in the World Trade Center.
What a fucked up situation.
I lost my parents in the Biafran War. Most of my family. We were from Asaba. There was a massacre. I fled to Lagos with my aunt. Before the war was over there were 2 million dead.
I hope you find your father.

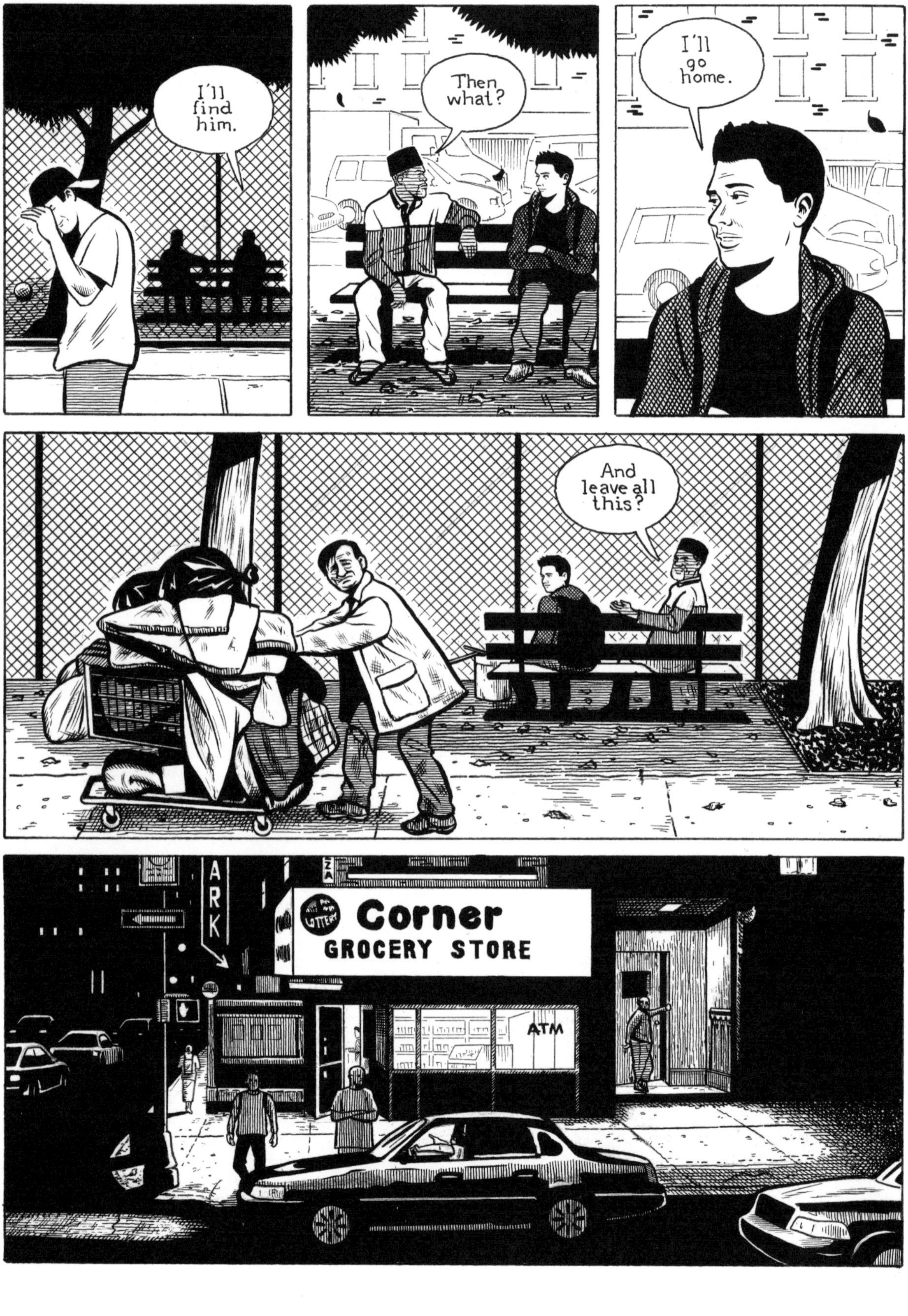
I'll find him.
Then what?
I'll go home.
And leave all this?
Corner
GROCERY STORE
LOTTERY
ATM
ARK

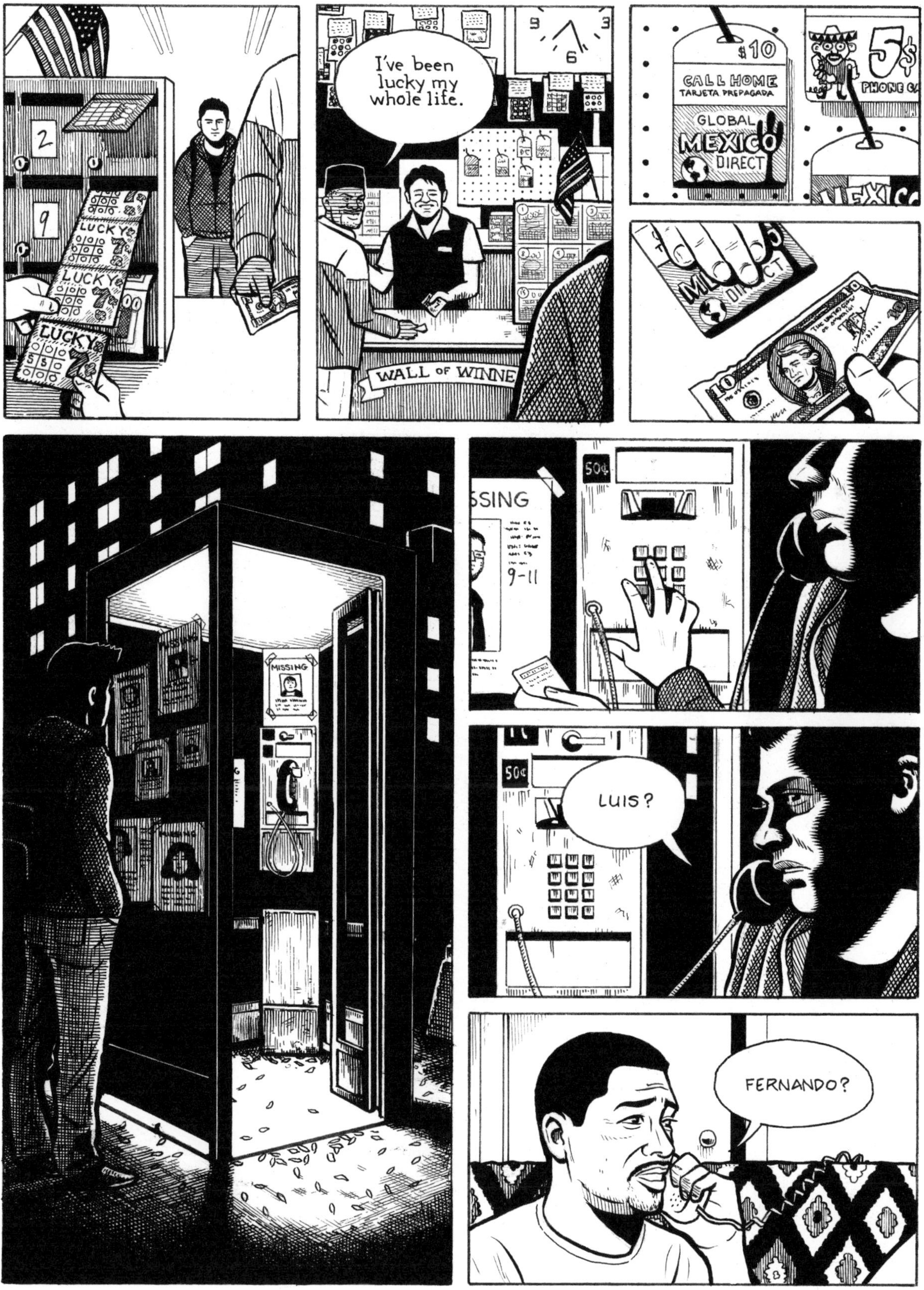
LUCKY
I've been lucky my whole life.
WALL OF WINNE
$10
CALL HOME
TARJETA PREPAGADA
GLOBAL
MEXICO
DIRECT
5$
MISSING
50¢
9-11
50¢
LUIS?
FERNANDO?

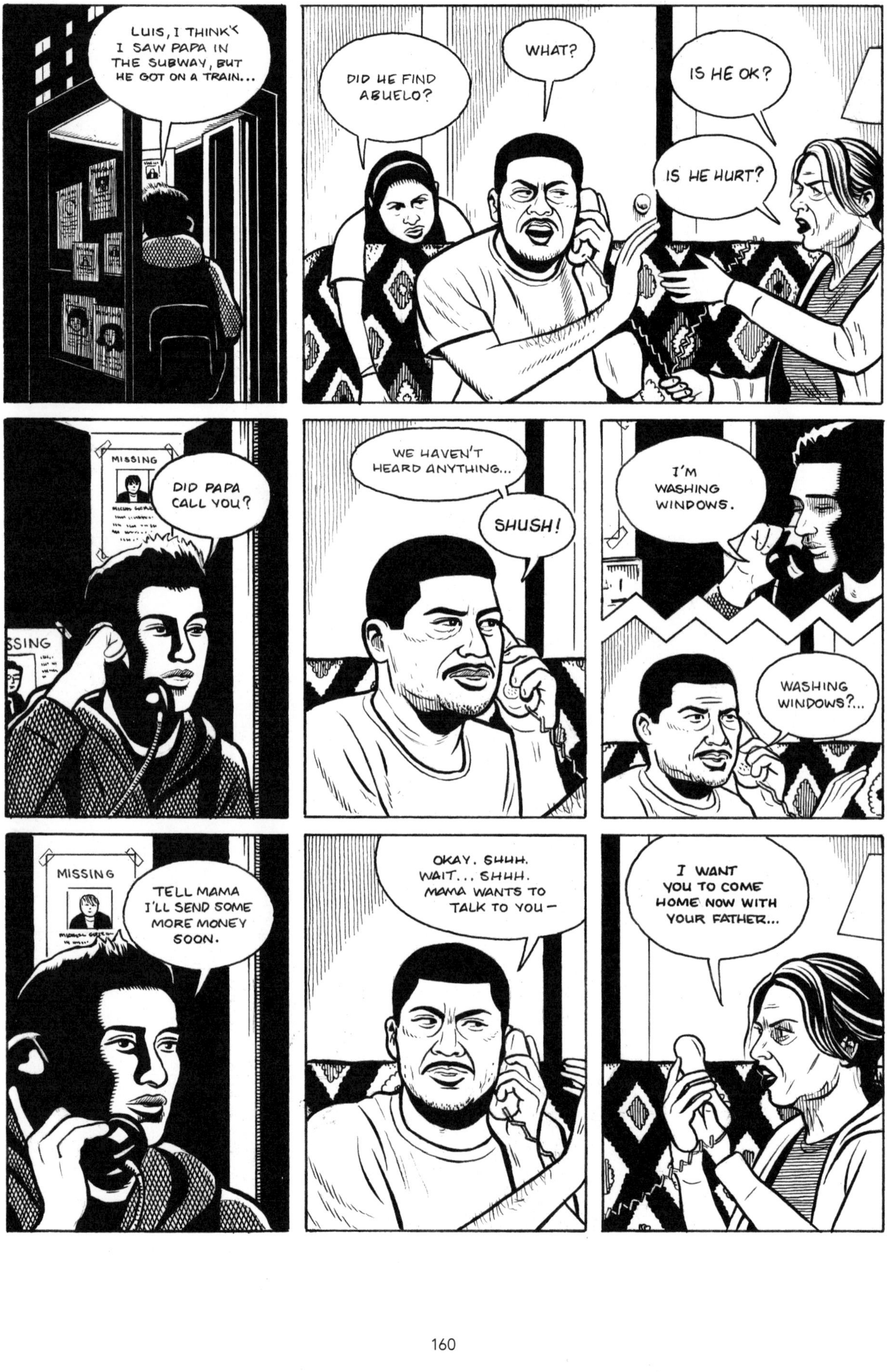
LUIS, I THINK I SAW PAPA IN THE SUBWAY, BUT HE GOT ON A TRAIN...
DID HE FIND ABUELO?
WHAT?
IS HE OK?
IS HE HURT?
MISSING
DID PAPA CALL YOU?
WE HAVEN'T HEARD ANYTHING...
SHUSH!
I'M WASHING WINDOWS.
WASHING WINDOWS?...
MISSING
TELL MAMA I'LL SEND SOME MORE MONEY SOON.
OKAY. SHHH. WAIT... SHHH. MAMA WANTS TO TALK TO YOU—
I WANT YOU TO COME HOME NOW WITH YOUR FATHER...

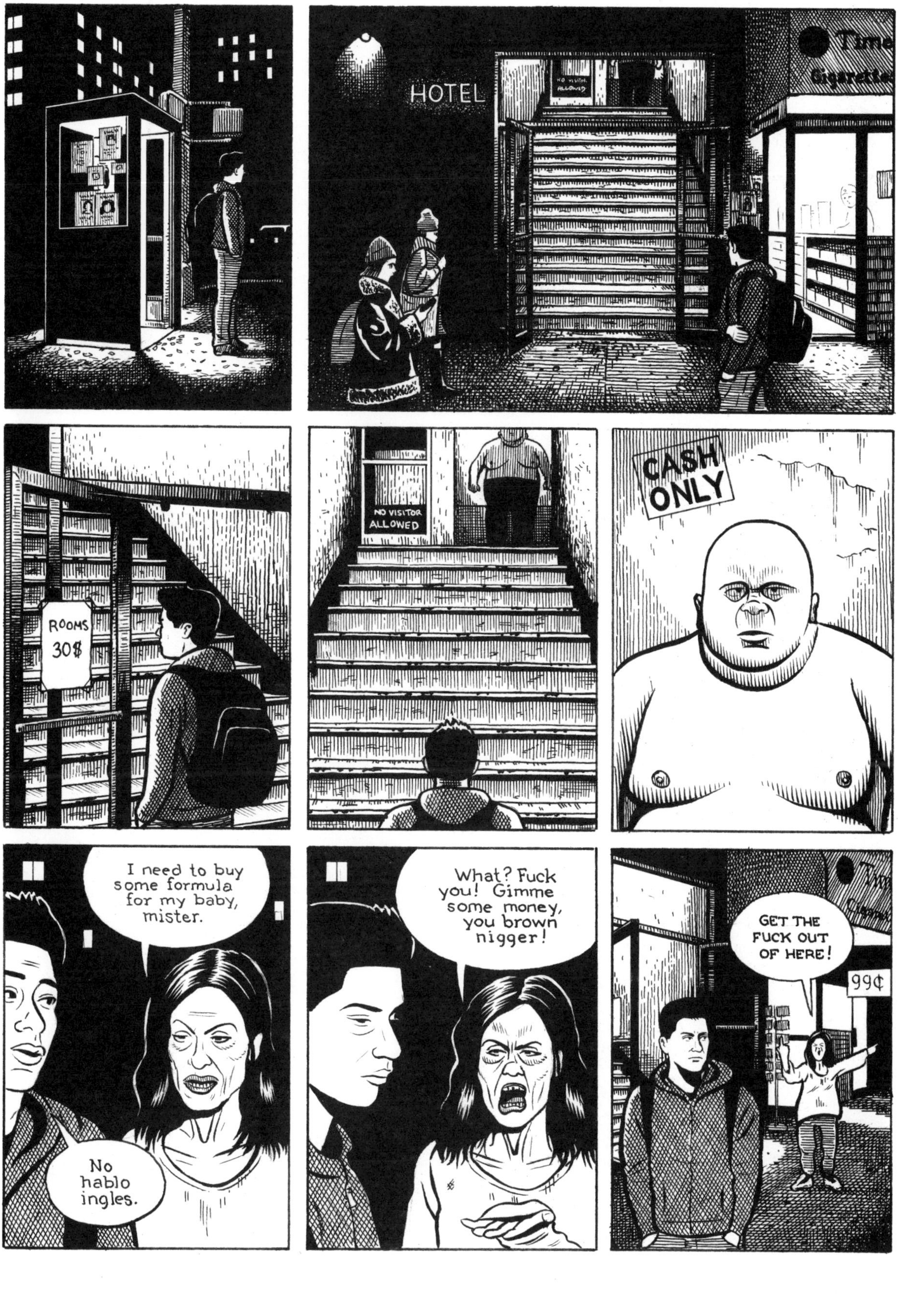
HOTEL
NO VISITOR ALLOWED
Time
Cigarettes
ROOMS 30$
NO VISITOR ALLOWED
CASH ONLY
I need to buy some formula for my baby, mister.
No hablo ingles.
What? Fuck you! Gimme some money, you brown nigger!
GET THE FUCK OUT OF HERE!
99¢

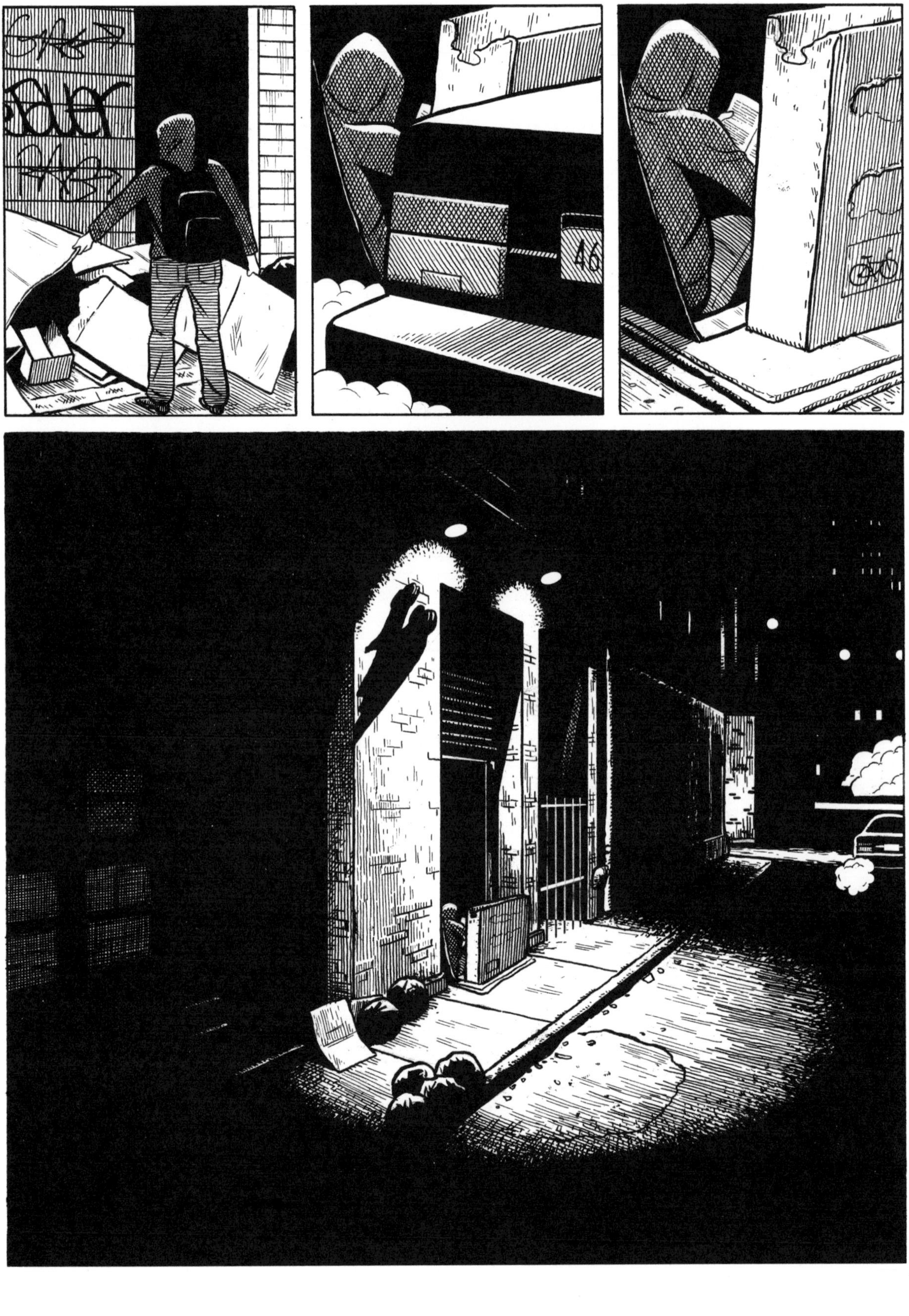
46

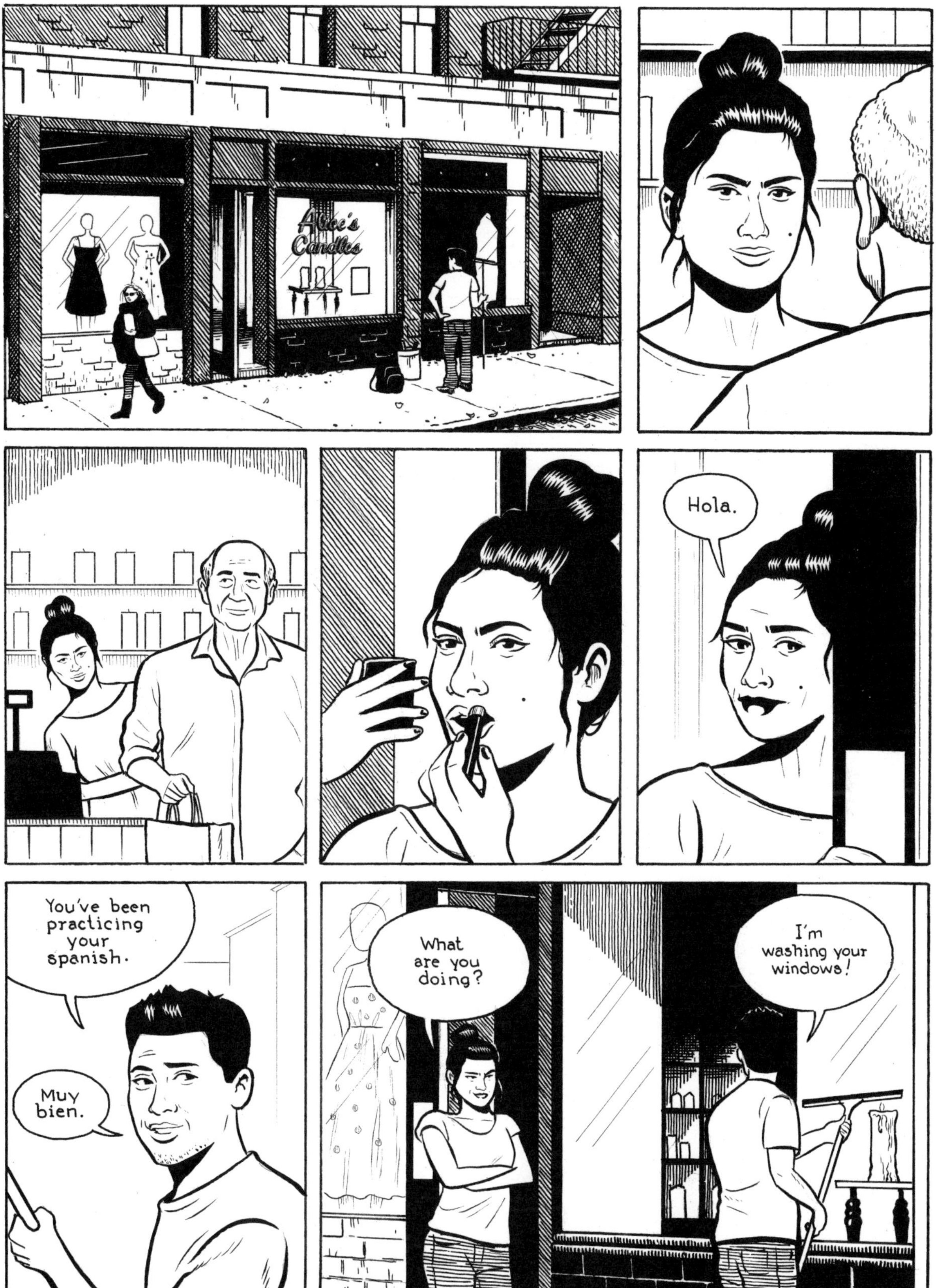
Alice's Candles
Hola.
You've been practicing your spanish.
Muy bien.
What are you doing?
I'm washing your windows!

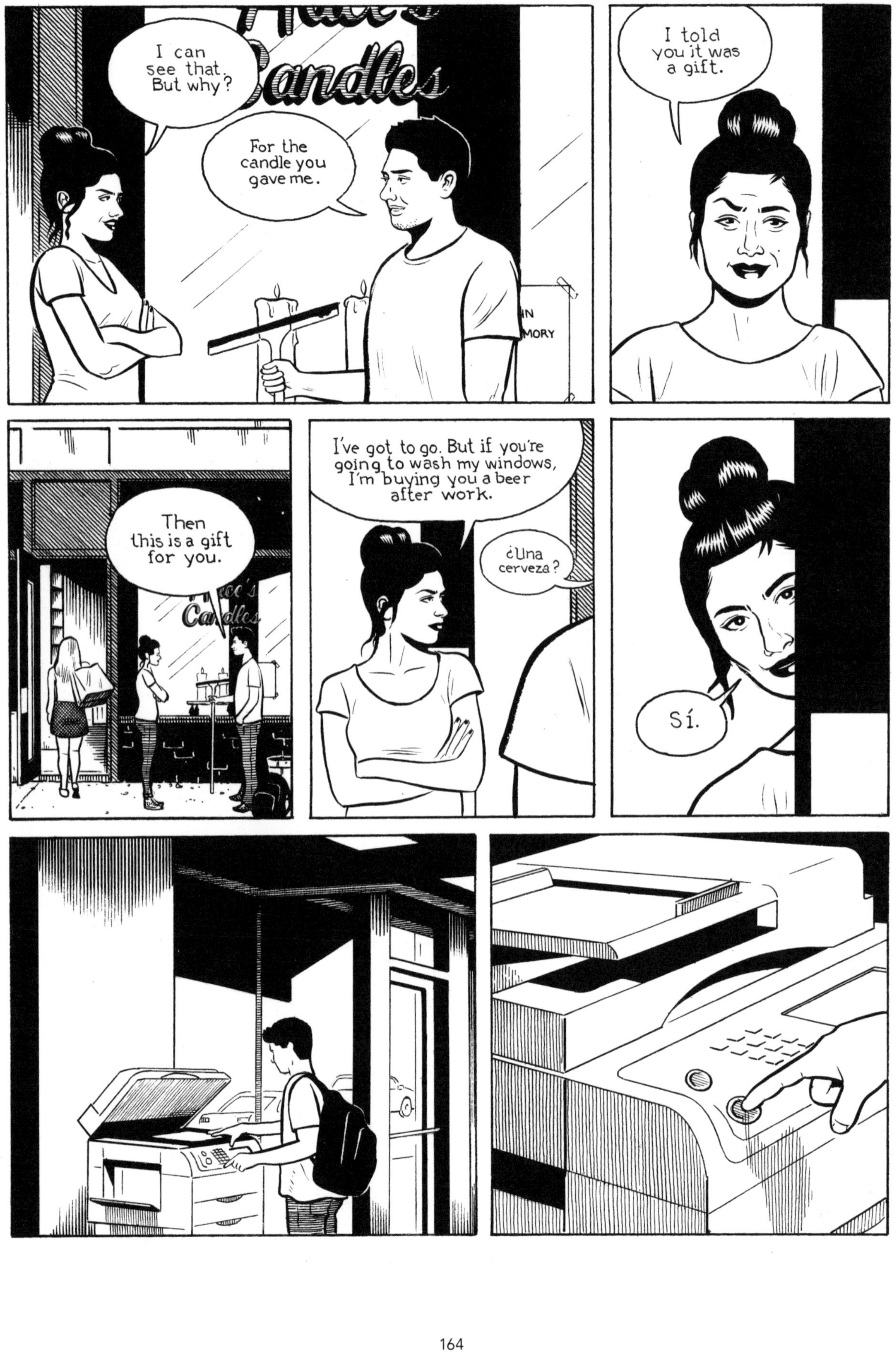
I can see that. But why?
Candles
For the candle you gave me.
I told you it was a gift.
Then this is a gift for you.
I've got to go. But if you're going to wash my windows, I'm buying you a beer after work.
¿Una cerveza?
Sí.

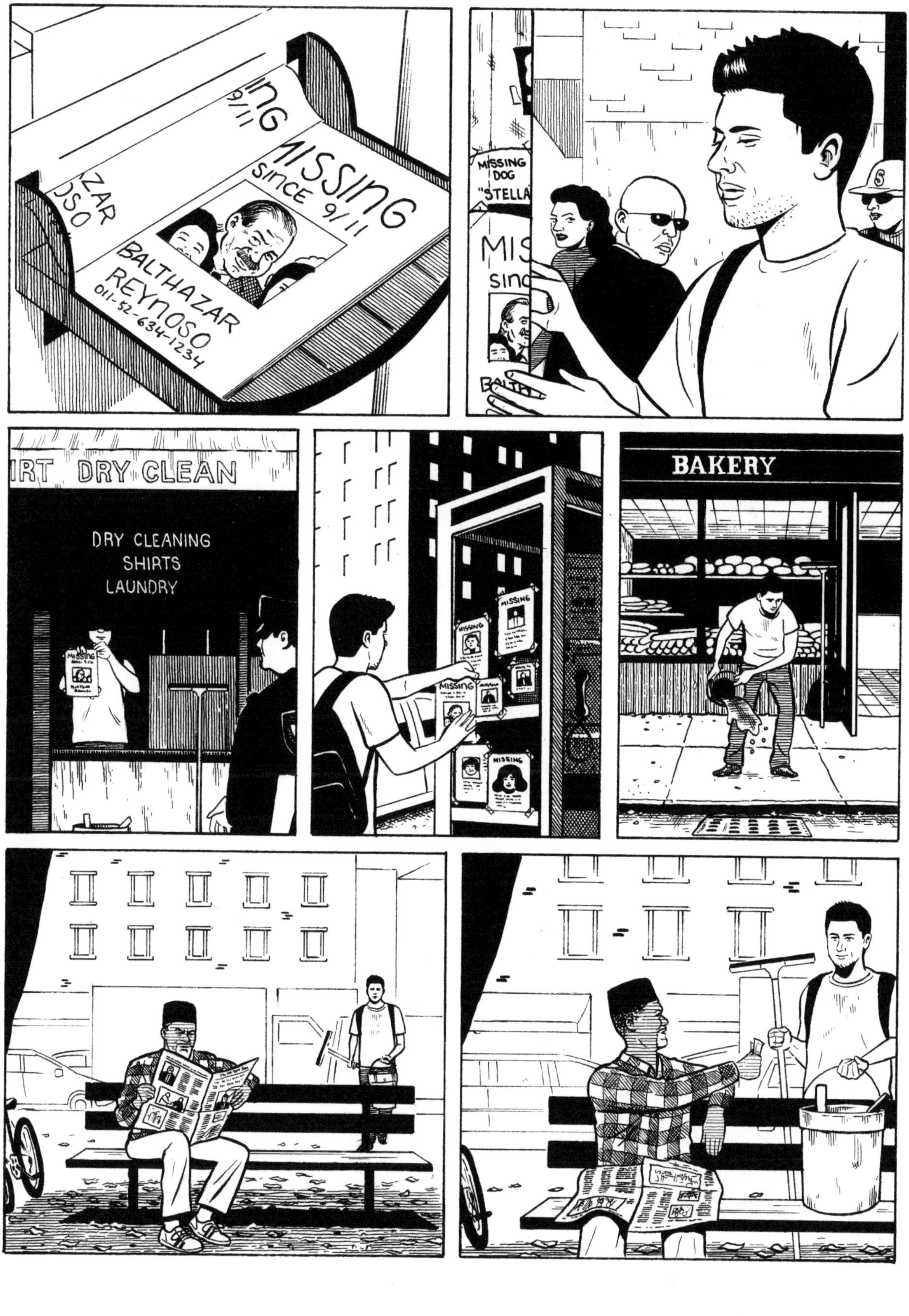
MISSING
SINCE 9/11
BALTHAZAR
REYNOSO
011-52-634-1234
MISSING
DOG
DRY CLEAN
DRY CLEANING
SHIRTS
LAUNDRY
MISSING
MISSING
MISSING
BAKERY

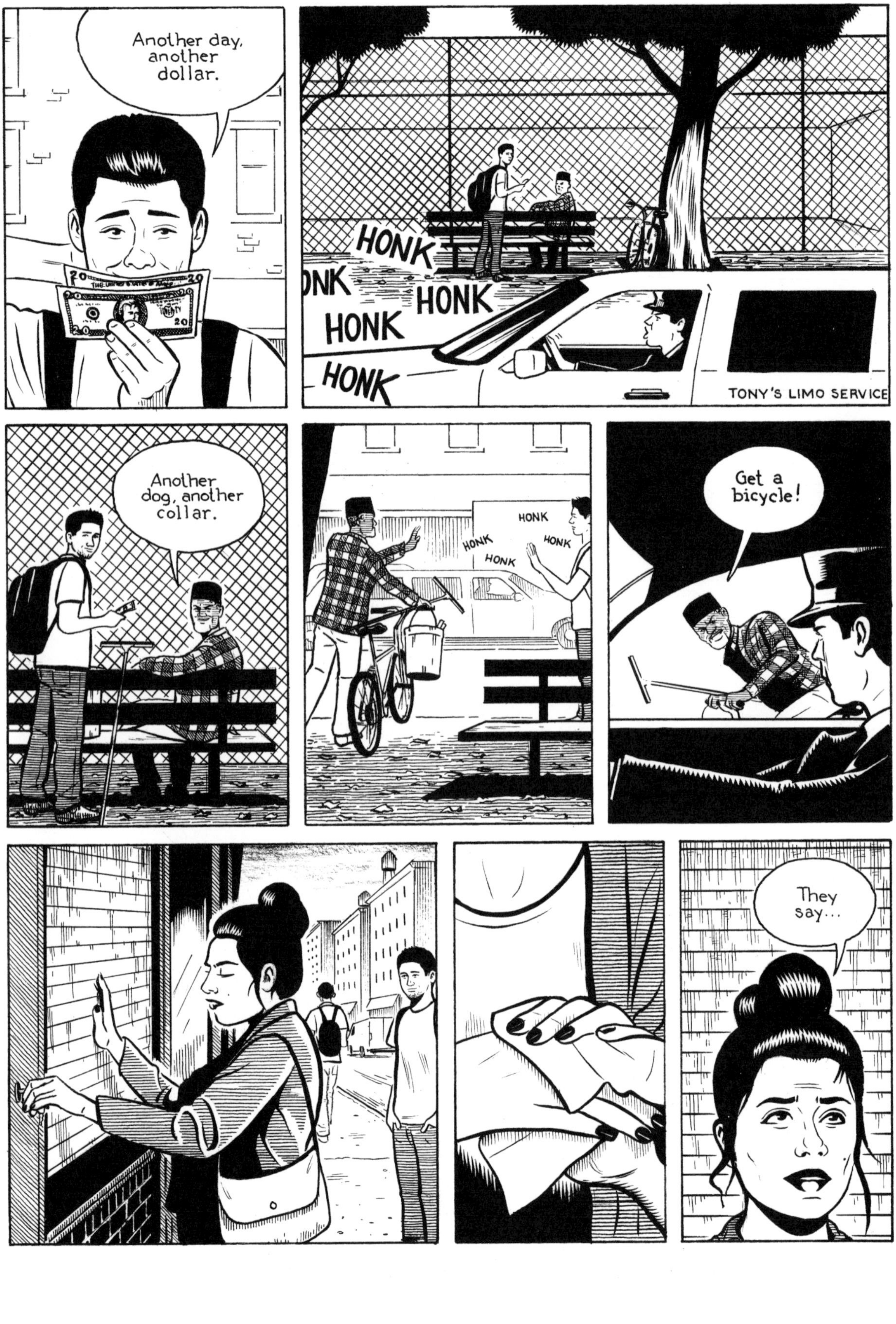
Another day, another dollar.
HONK
HONK
HONK
HONK
HONK
TONY'S LIMO SERVICE
Another dog, another collar.
HONK
HONK
HONK
HONK
Get a bicycle!
They say...

...the heat from all the burnt computers released billions of toxins and PCBs...

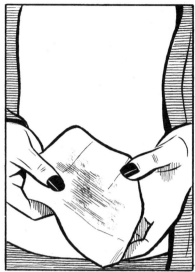

I'm sorry. That was completely insensitive.

That's ok. It's the truth.

Now I really owe you a drink.

STOP BED BUGS

REBUILD NEW YORK — REBUILD USA

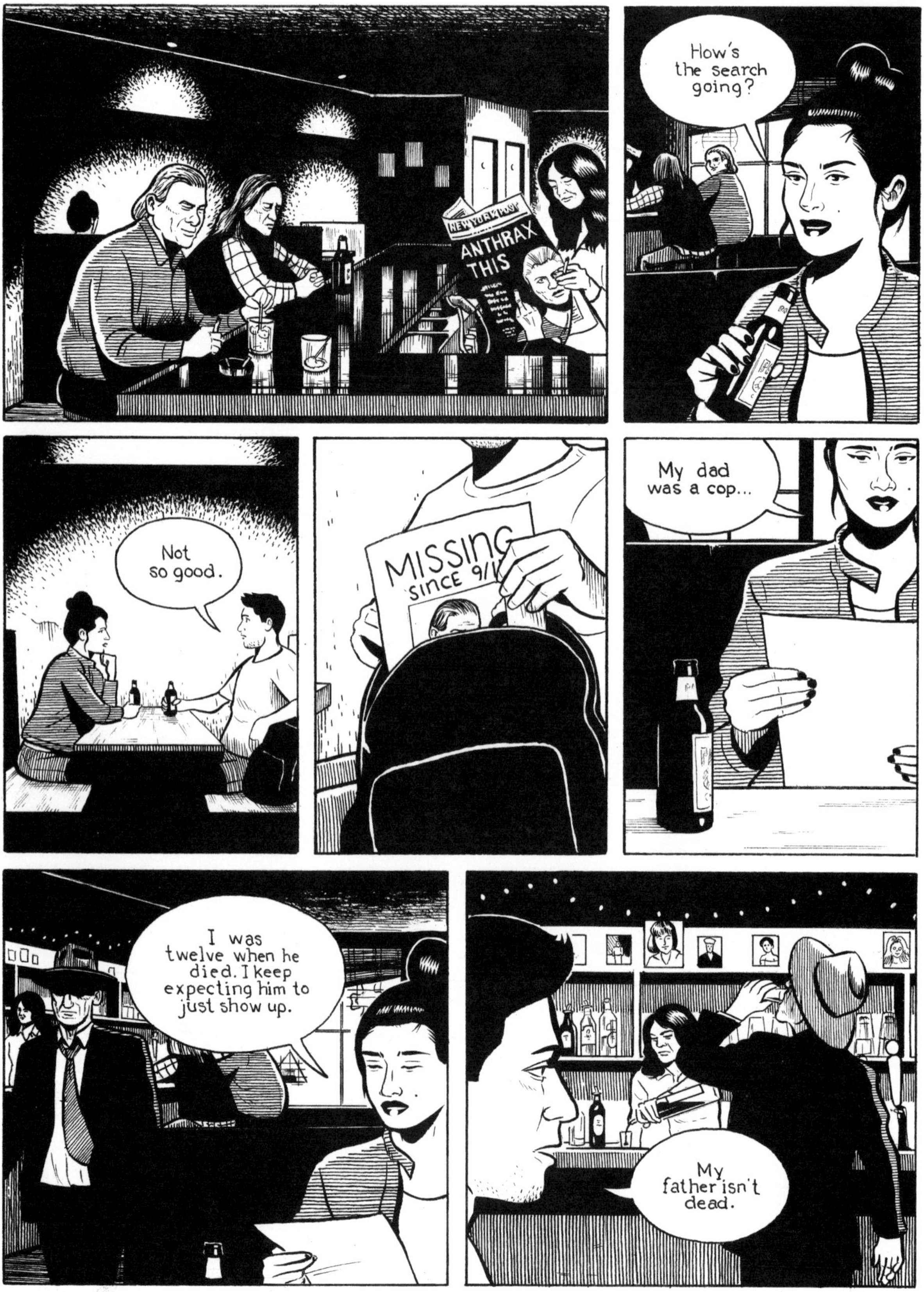
NEW YORK POST
ANTHRAX THIS
How's the search going?
Not so good.
MISSING SINCE 9/1
My dad was a cop...
I was twelve when he died. I keep expecting him to just show up.
My father isn't dead.

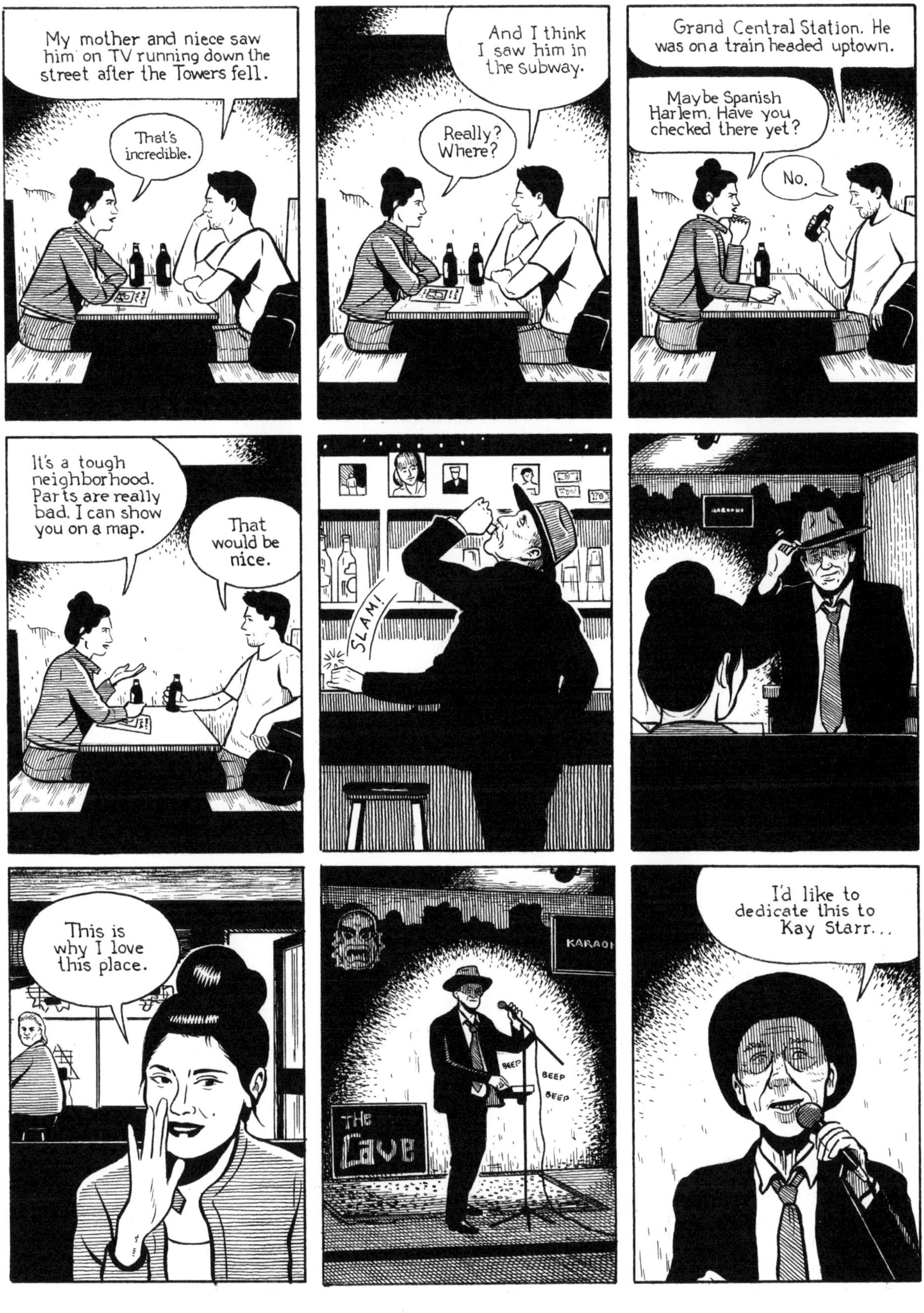
My mother and niece saw him on TV running down the street after the Towers fell.
That's incredible.
And I think I saw him in the subway.
Really? Where?
Grand Central Station. He was on a train headed uptown.
Maybe Spanish Harlem. Have you checked there yet?
No.
It's a tough neighborhood. Parts are really bad. I can show you on a map.
That would be nice.
SLAM!
This is why I love this place.
THE Cave
BEEP
BEEP
BEEP
I'd like to dedicate this to Kay Starr...

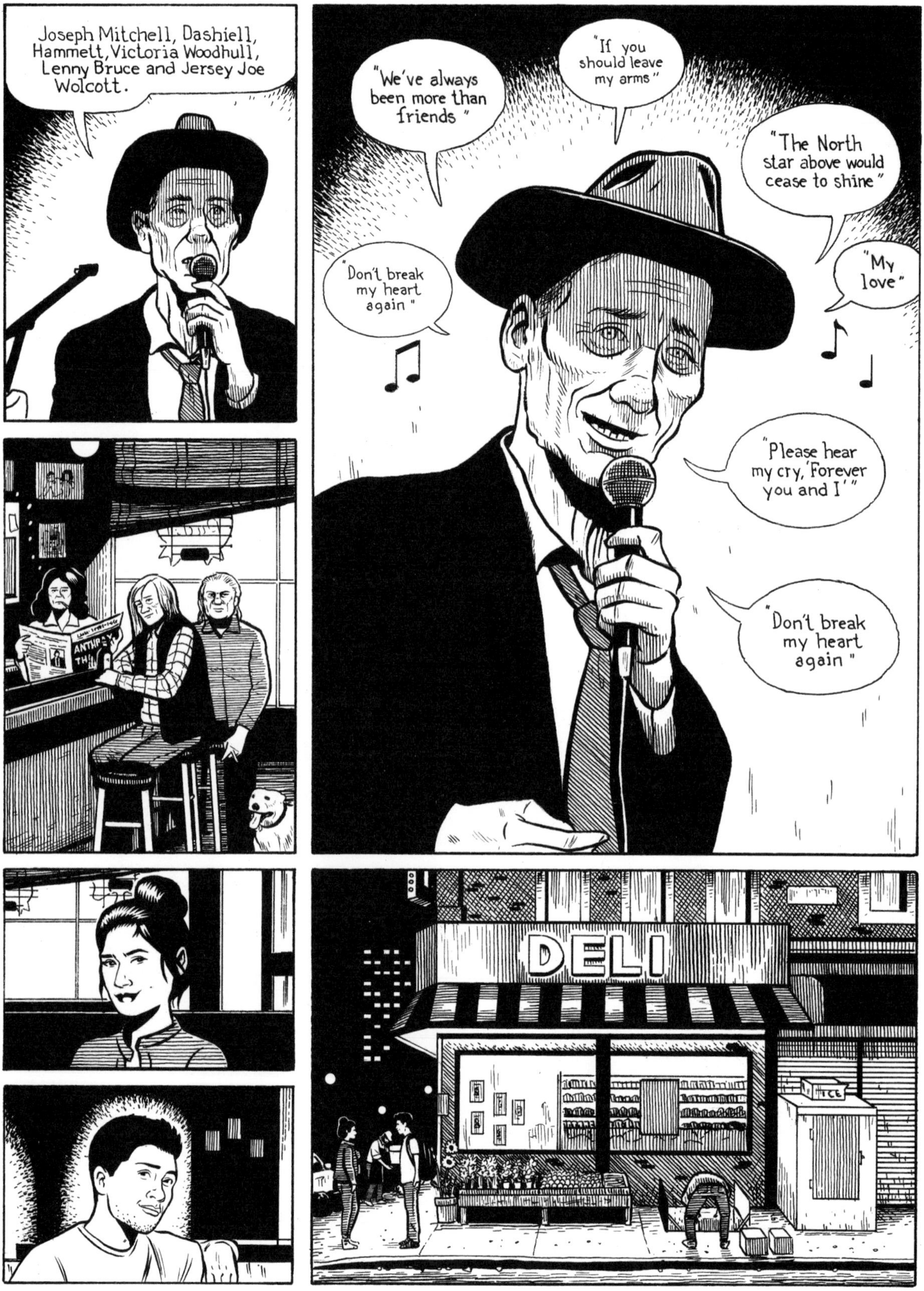

Joseph Mitchell, Dashiell, Hammett, Victoria Woodhull, Lenny Bruce and Jersey Joe Wolcott.
"We've always been more than friends"
"If you should leave my arms"
"The North star above would cease to shine"
"Don't break my heart again"
"My love"
"Please hear my cry, 'Forever you and I'"
"Don't break my heart again"
DELI
ICE

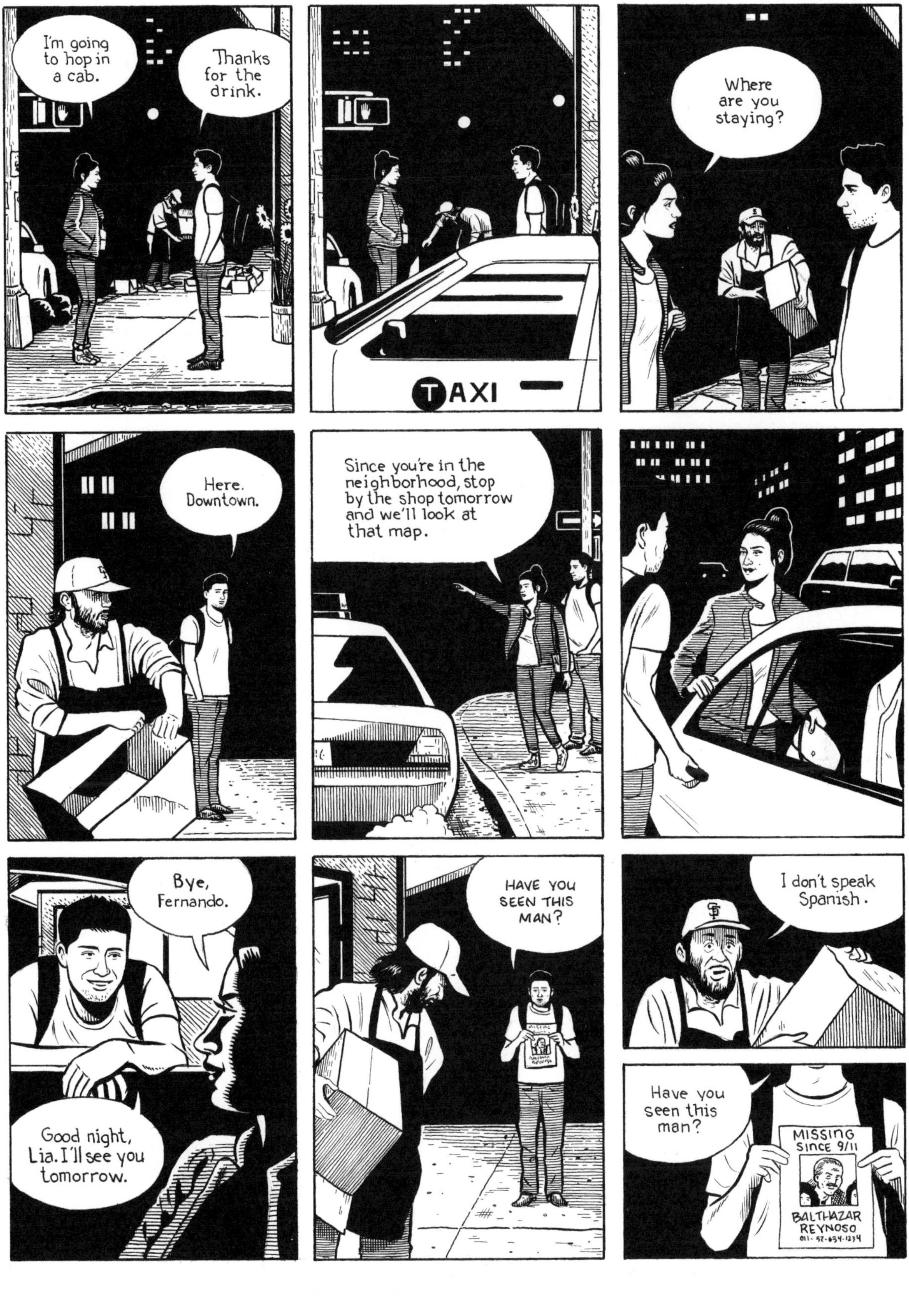
I'm going to hop in a cab.
Thanks for the drink.
TAXI
Where are you staying?
Here. Downtown.
Since you're in the neighborhood, stop by the shop tomorrow and we'll look at that map.
Bye, Fernando.
Good night, Lia. I'll see you tomorrow.
HAVE YOU SEEN THIS MAN?
I don't speak Spanish.
Have you seen this man?
MISSING SINCE 9/11
BALTHAZAR REYNOSO
011-52-634-1234

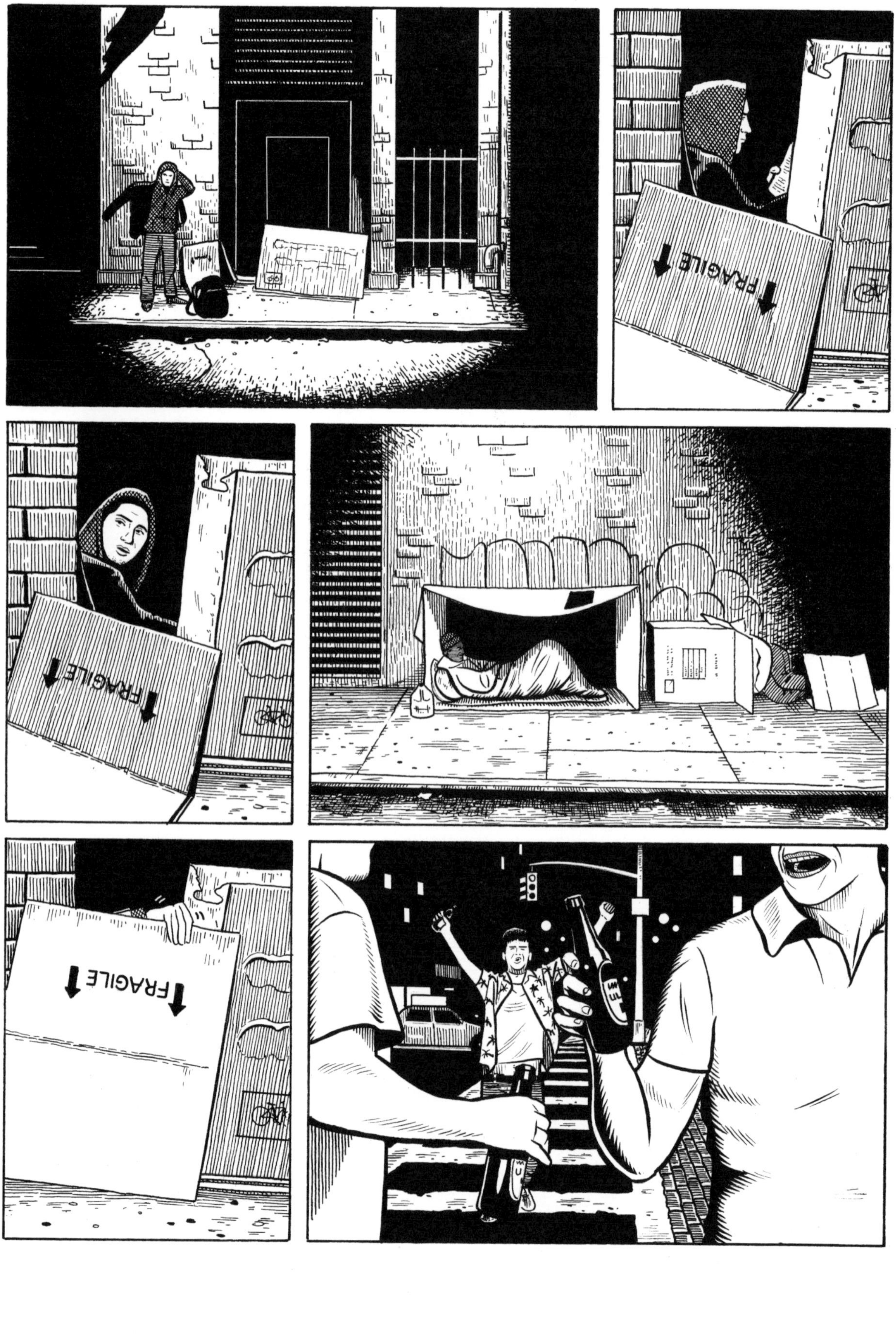
FRAGILE
FRAGILE
FRAGILE

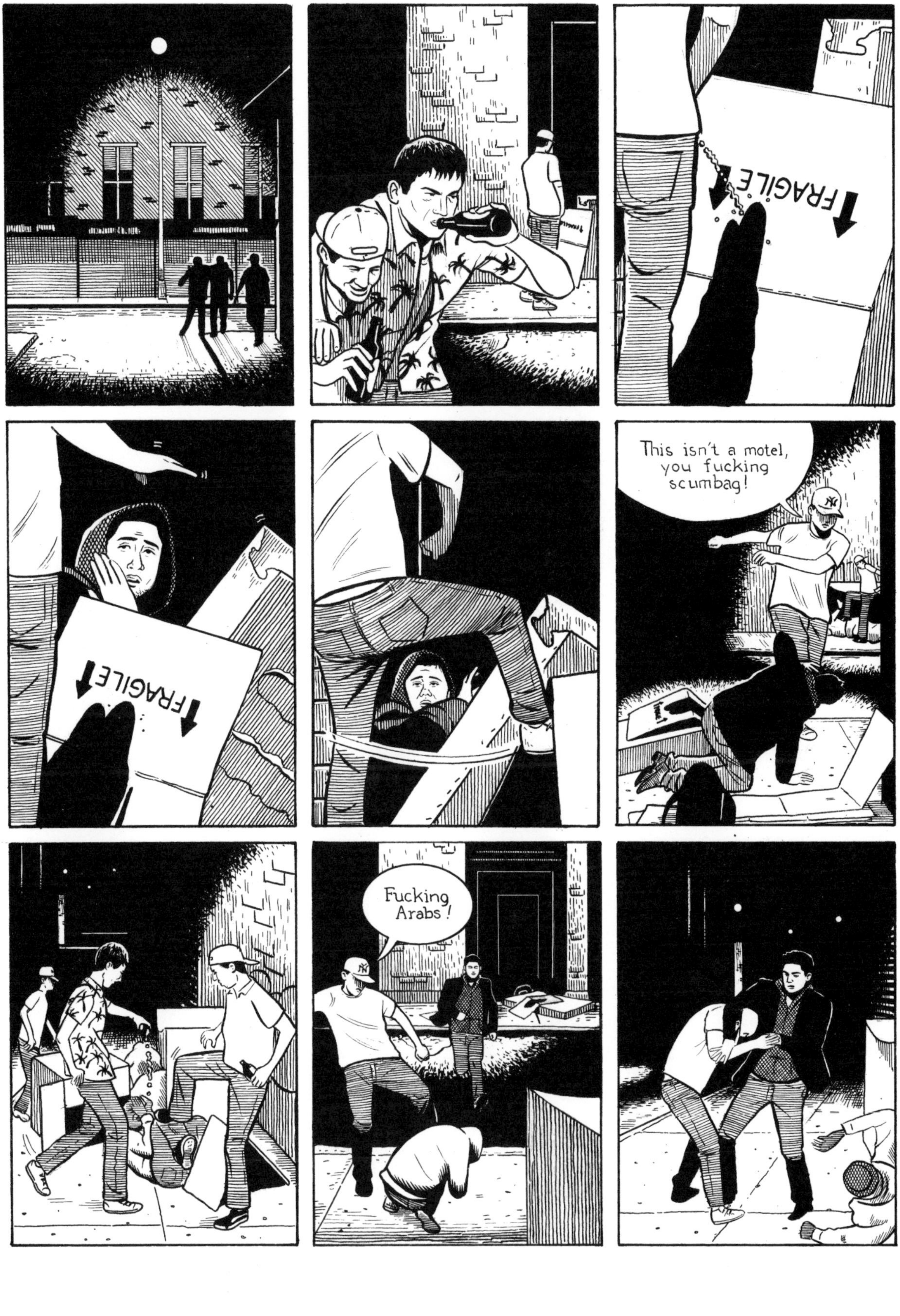
FRAGILE
FRAGILE
This isn't a motel, you fucking scumbag!
Fucking Arabs!

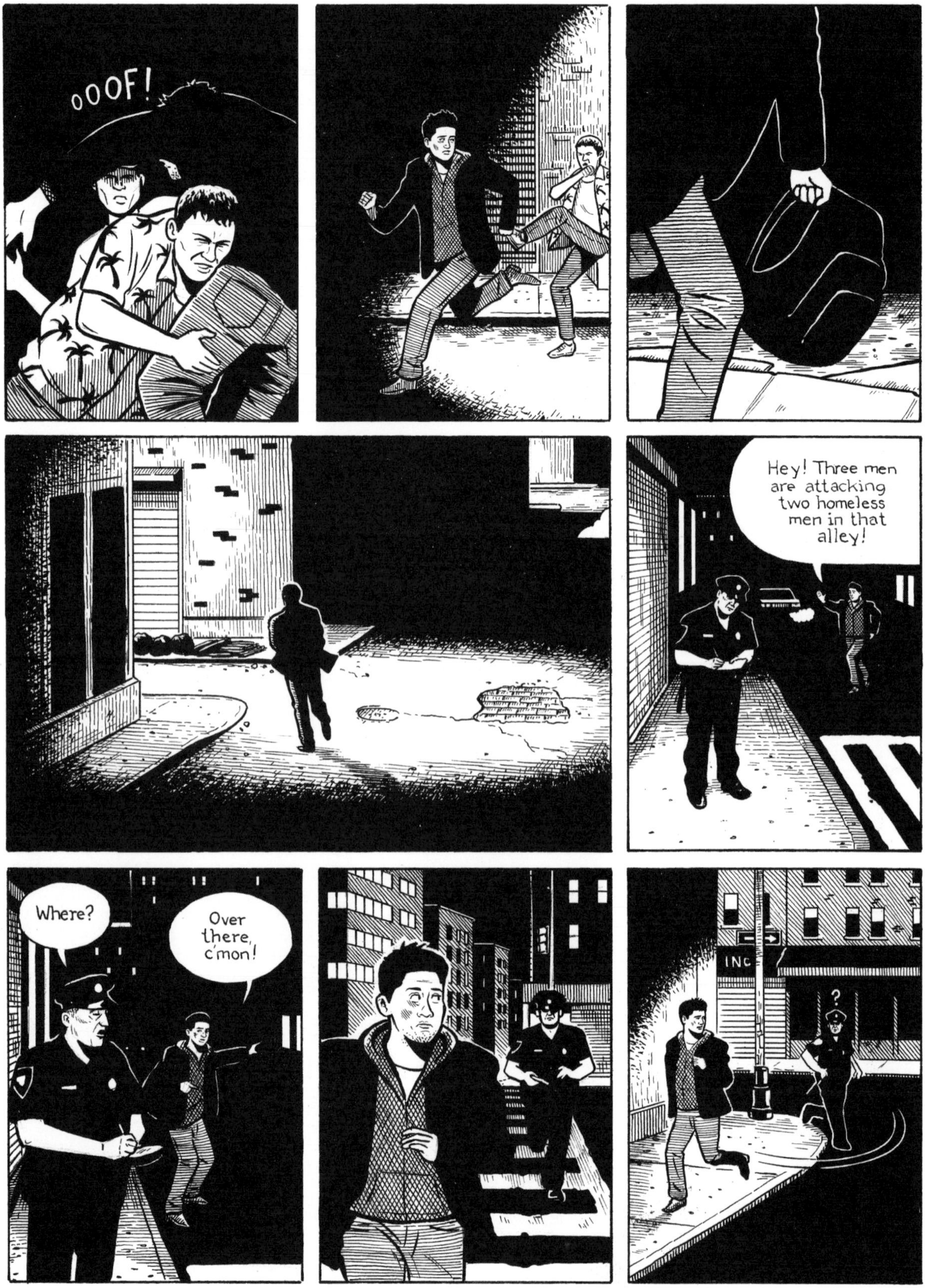
OOOF!
Hey! Three men are attacking two homeless men in that alley!
Where?
Over there, c'mon!
INC
?

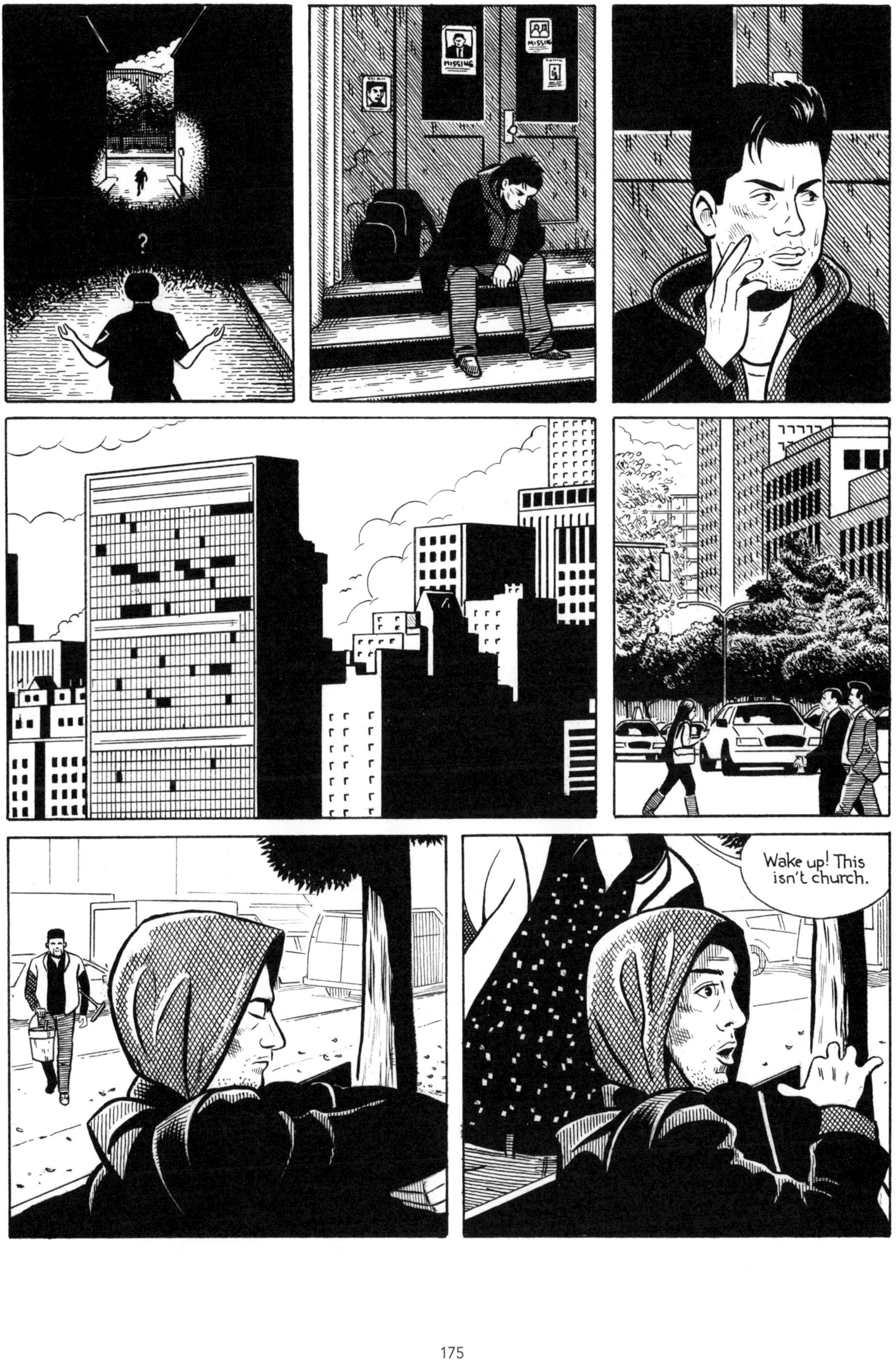
?
MISSING
MISSING
Wake up! This isn't church.

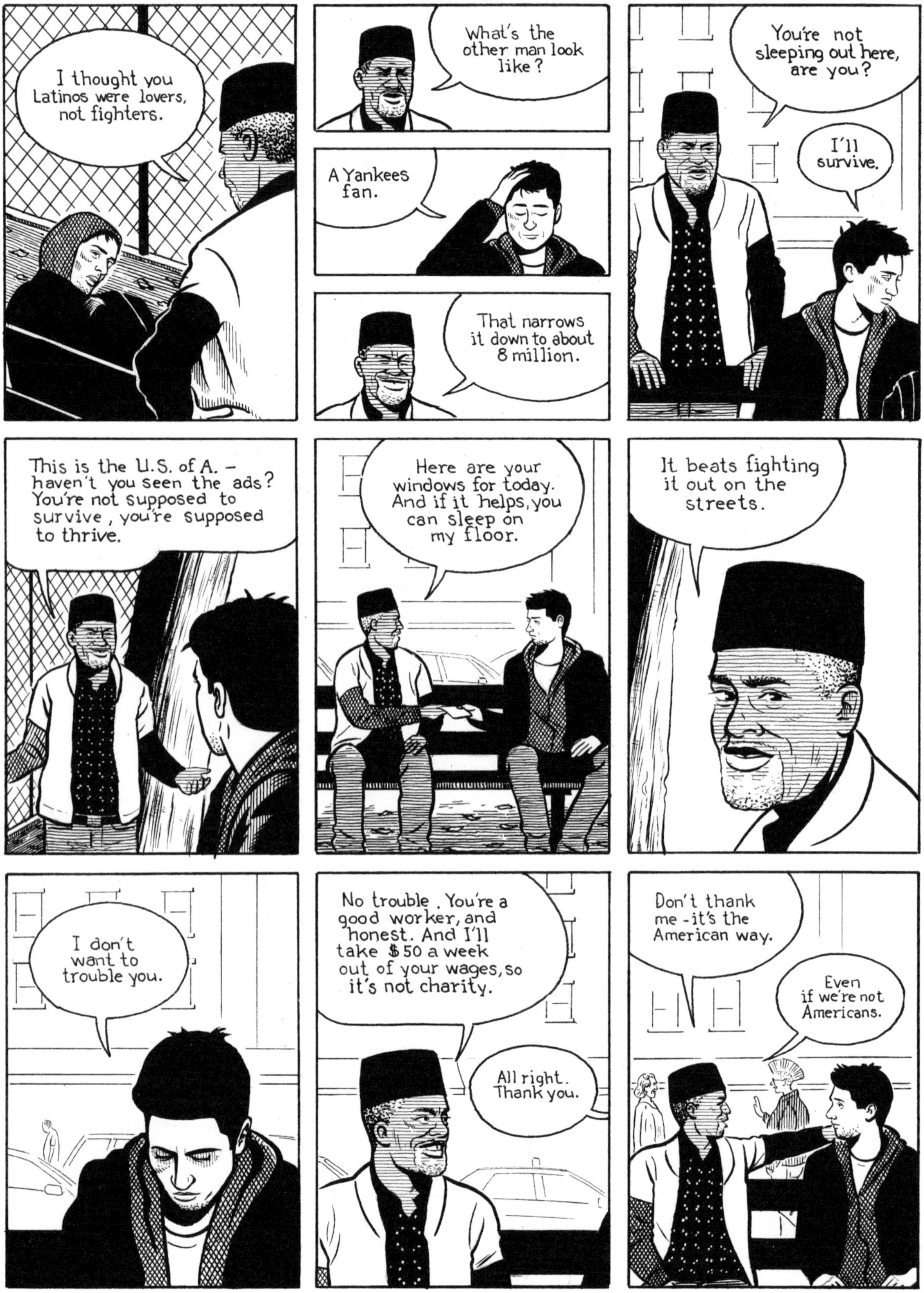
I thought you Latinos were lovers, not fighters.
What's the other man look like?
A Yankees fan.
That narrows it down to about 8 million.
You're not sleeping out here, are you?
I'll survive.
This is the U.S. of A. - haven't you seen the ads? You're not supposed to survive, you're supposed to thrive.
Here are your windows for today. And if it helps, you can sleep on my floor.
It beats fighting it out on the streets.
I don't want to trouble you.
No trouble. You're a good worker, and honest. And I'll take $50 a week out of your wages, so it's not charity.
All right. Thank you.
Don't thank me - it's the American way.
Even if we're not Americans.

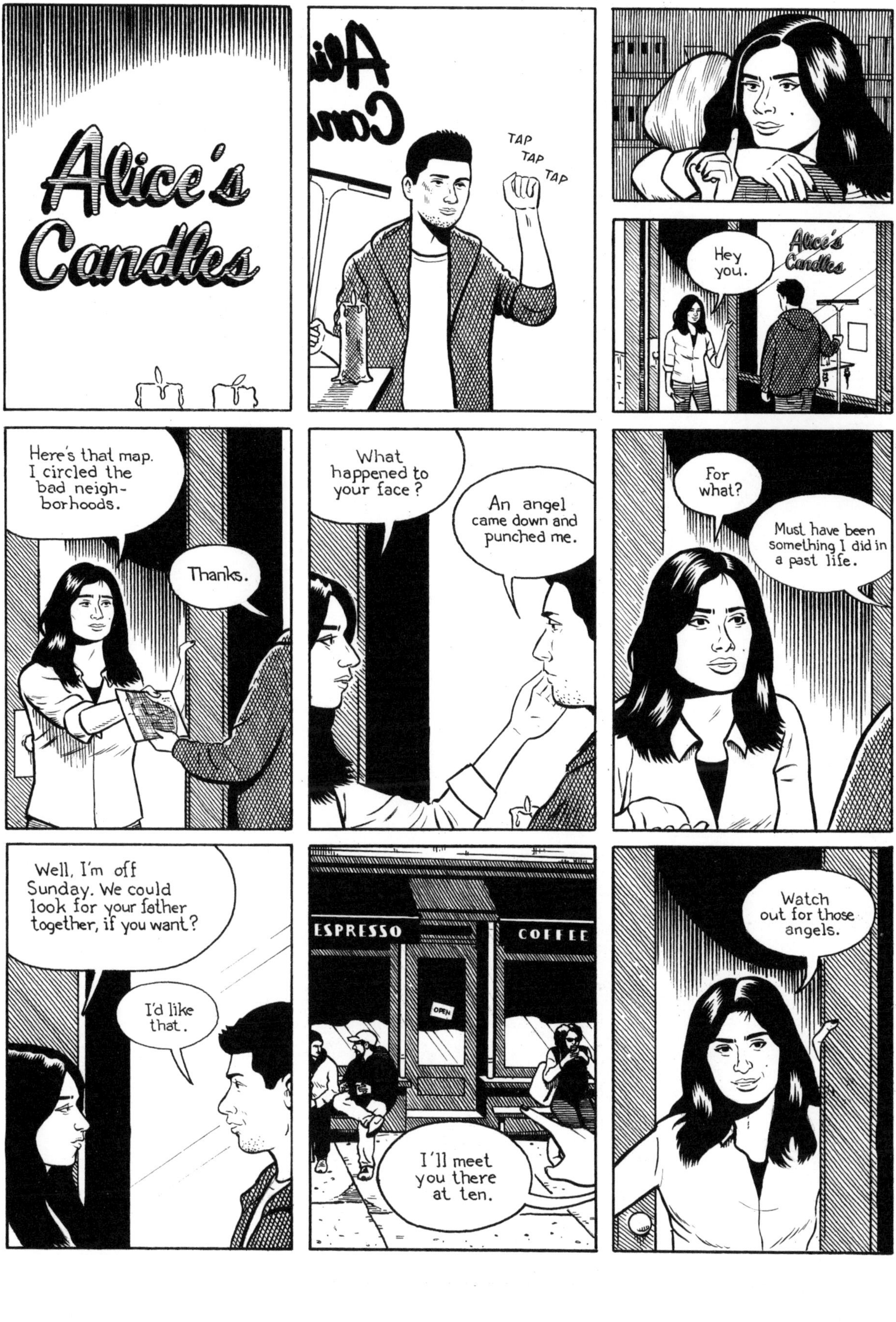
Alice's Candles
TAP TAP TAP
Hey you.
Alice's Candles
Here's that map. I circled the bad neigh-borhoods.
Thanks.
What happened to your face?
An angel came down and punched me.
For what?
Must have been something I did in a past life.
Well, I'm off Sunday. We could look for your father together, if you want?
I'd like that.
ESPRESSO
COFFEE
OPEN
I'll meet you there at ten.
Watch out for those angels.

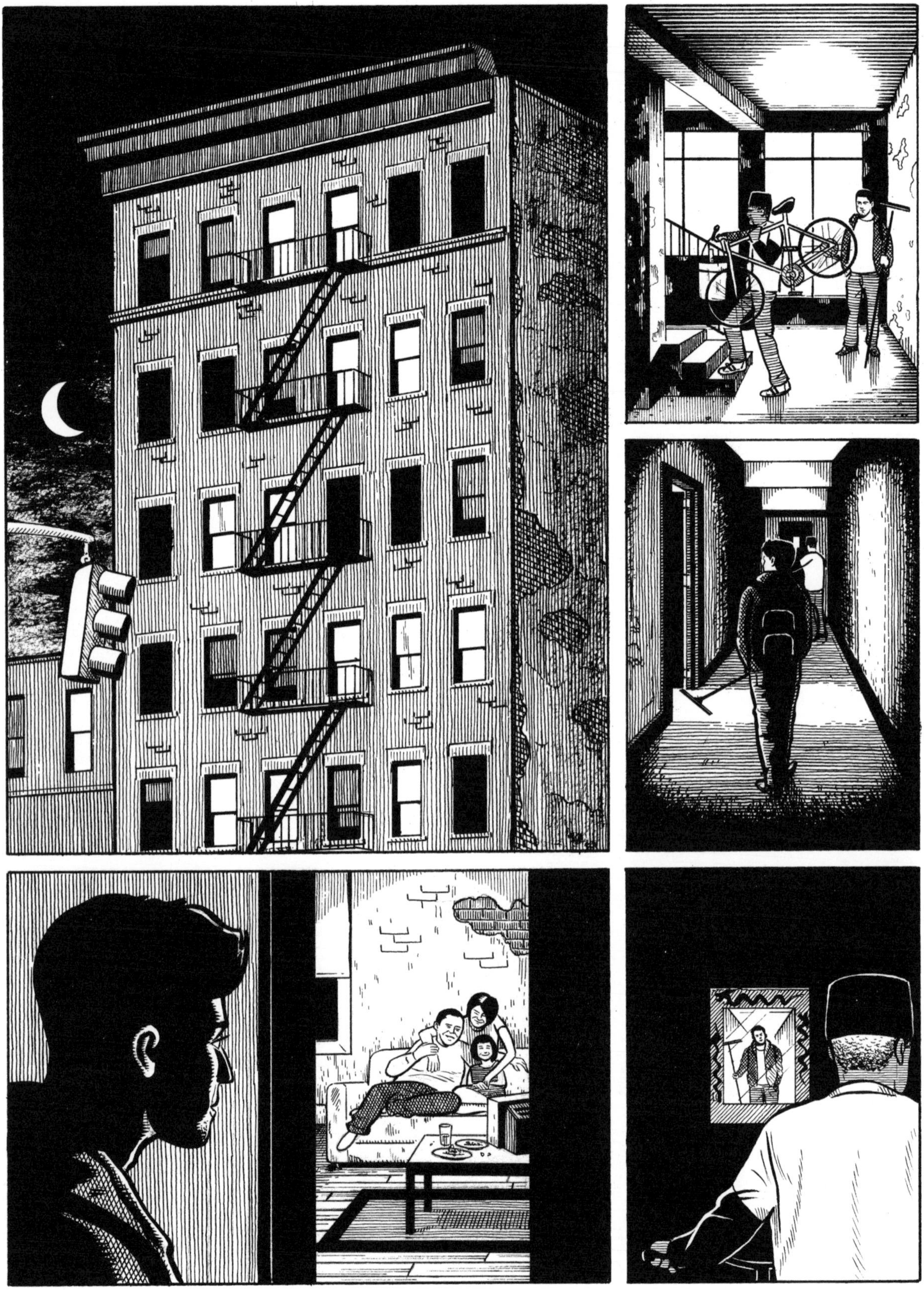

Feng Shui. Keeps out the bad spirits.

That's a lot of work for a little piece of glass.

Nik, Amos...

I ♡ NY UMBRELLA

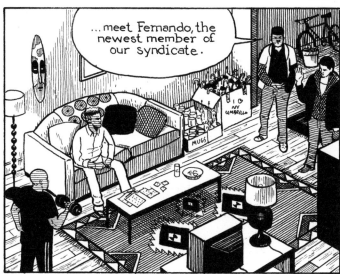

...meet Fernando, the newest member of our syndicate.

Welcome to little Lagos.

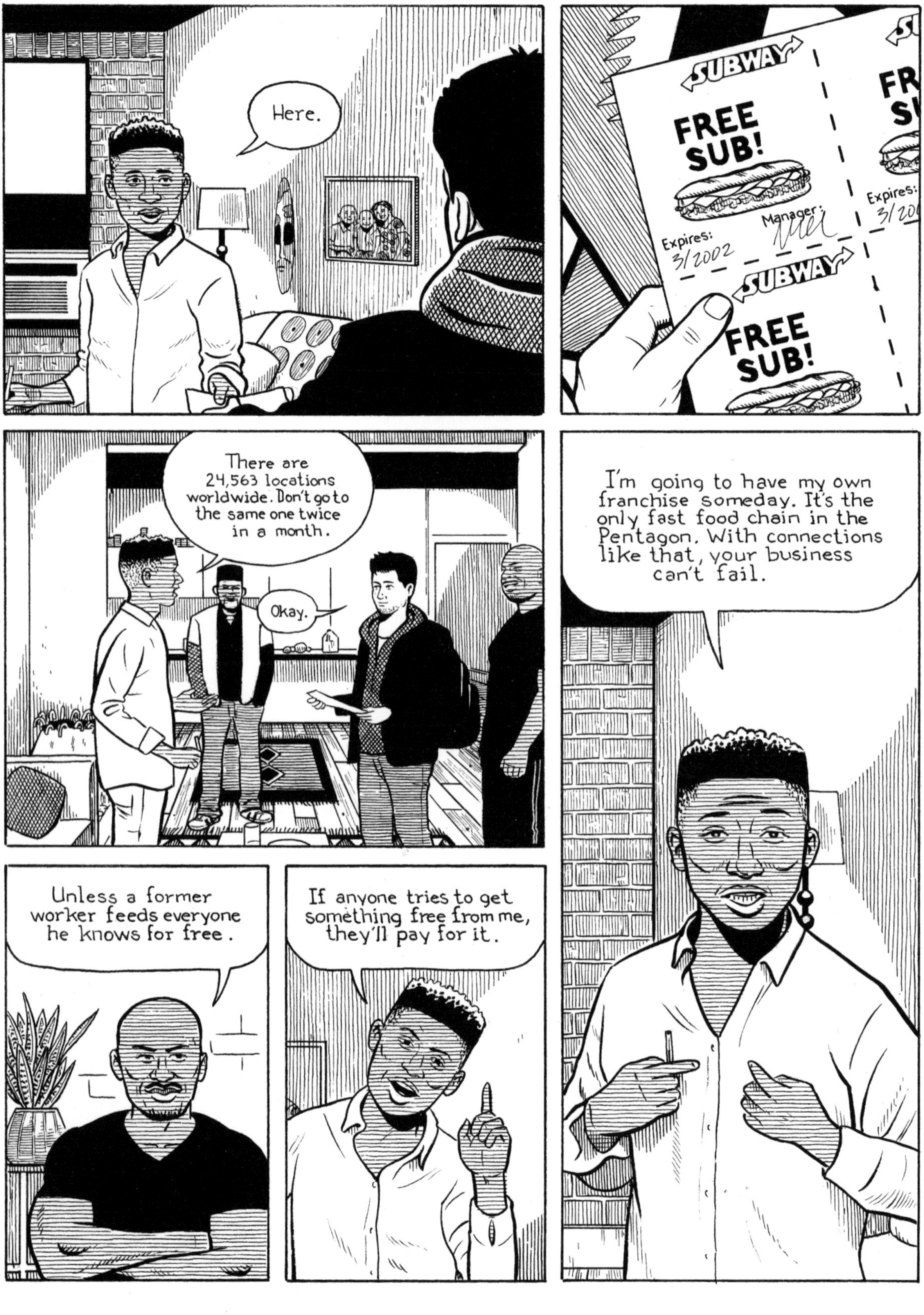
Here.
SUBWAY
FREE SUB!
Expires: 3/2002
Manager:
SUBWAY
FREE SUB!
There are 24,563 locations worldwide. Don't go to the same one twice in a month.
Okay.
I'm going to have my own franchise someday. It's the only fast food chain in the Pentagon. With connections like that, your business can't fail.
Unless a former worker feeds everyone he knows for free.
If anyone tries to get something free from me, they'll pay for it.

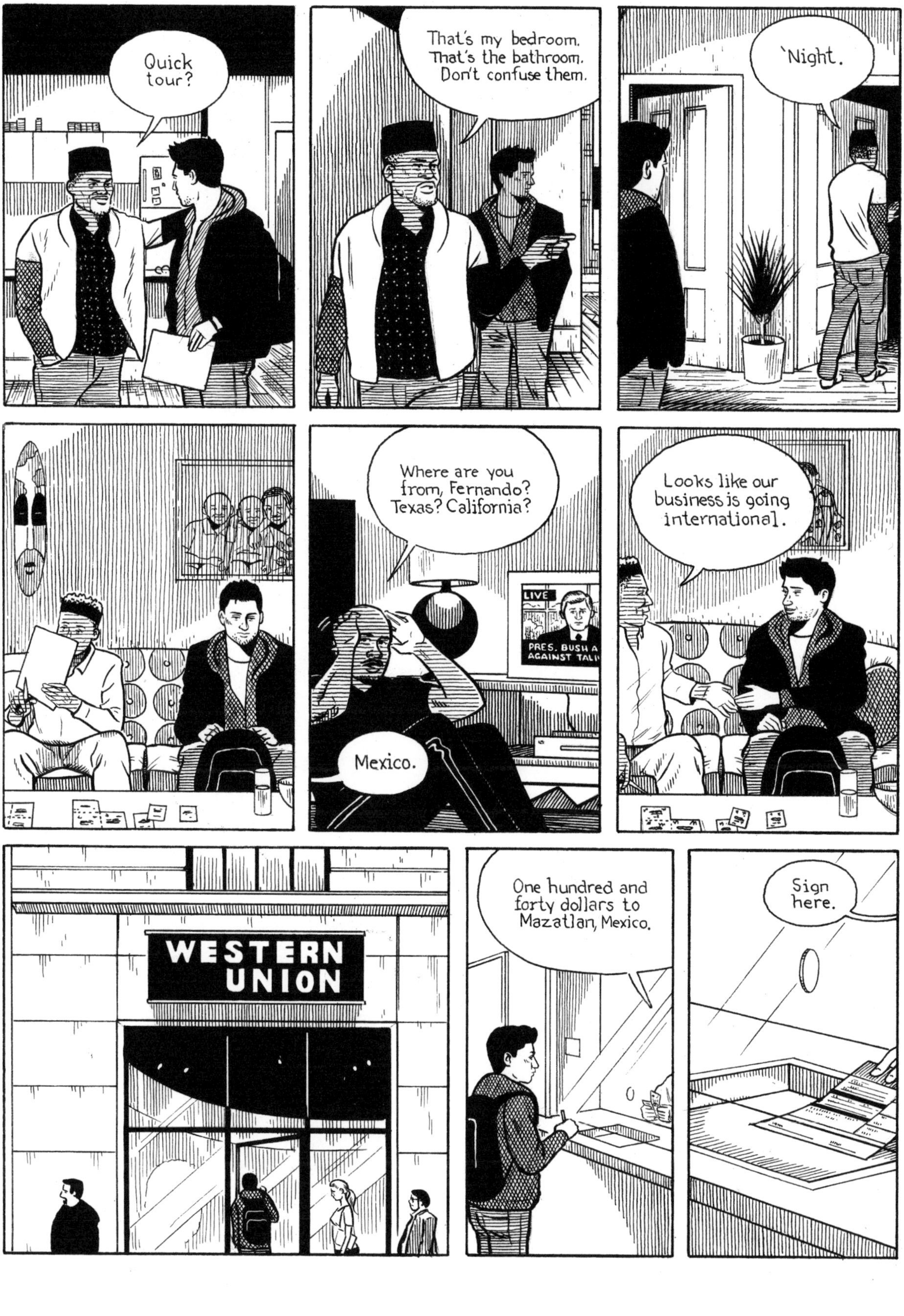
Quick tour?
That's my bedroom. That's the bathroom. Don't confuse them.
'Night.
Where are you from, Fernando? Texas? California?
LIVE
PRES. BUSH A
AGAINST TALI
Mexico.
Looks like our business is going international.
WESTERN UNION
One hundred and forty dollars to Mazatlan, Mexico.
Sign here.

t's on Pr
SALON
Wait a minute...
CAN YOU HEAR THE DRUMS, FERNANDO? I REMEMBER LONG AGO ANOTHER STARRY NIGHT LIKE THIS. IN THE FIRELIGHT, FERNANDO
That's much better.
"There was something in the air that night"
"The stars were bright"

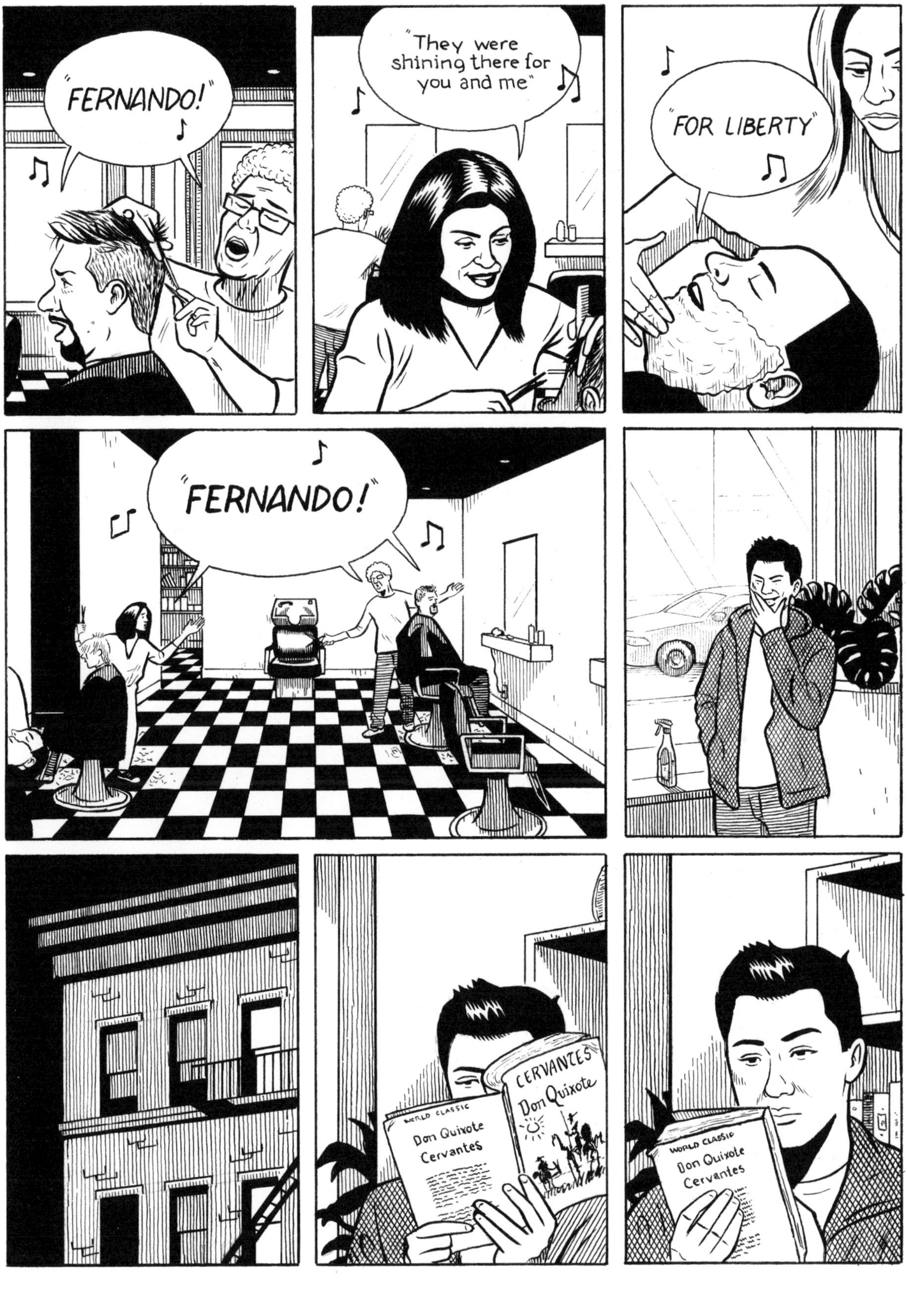
"FERNANDO!"
"They were shining there for you and me"
"FOR LIBERTY"
"FERNANDO!"
WORLD CLASSIC
Don Quixote
Cervantes
CERVANTES
Don Quixote
WORLD CLASSIC
Don Quixote
Cervantes

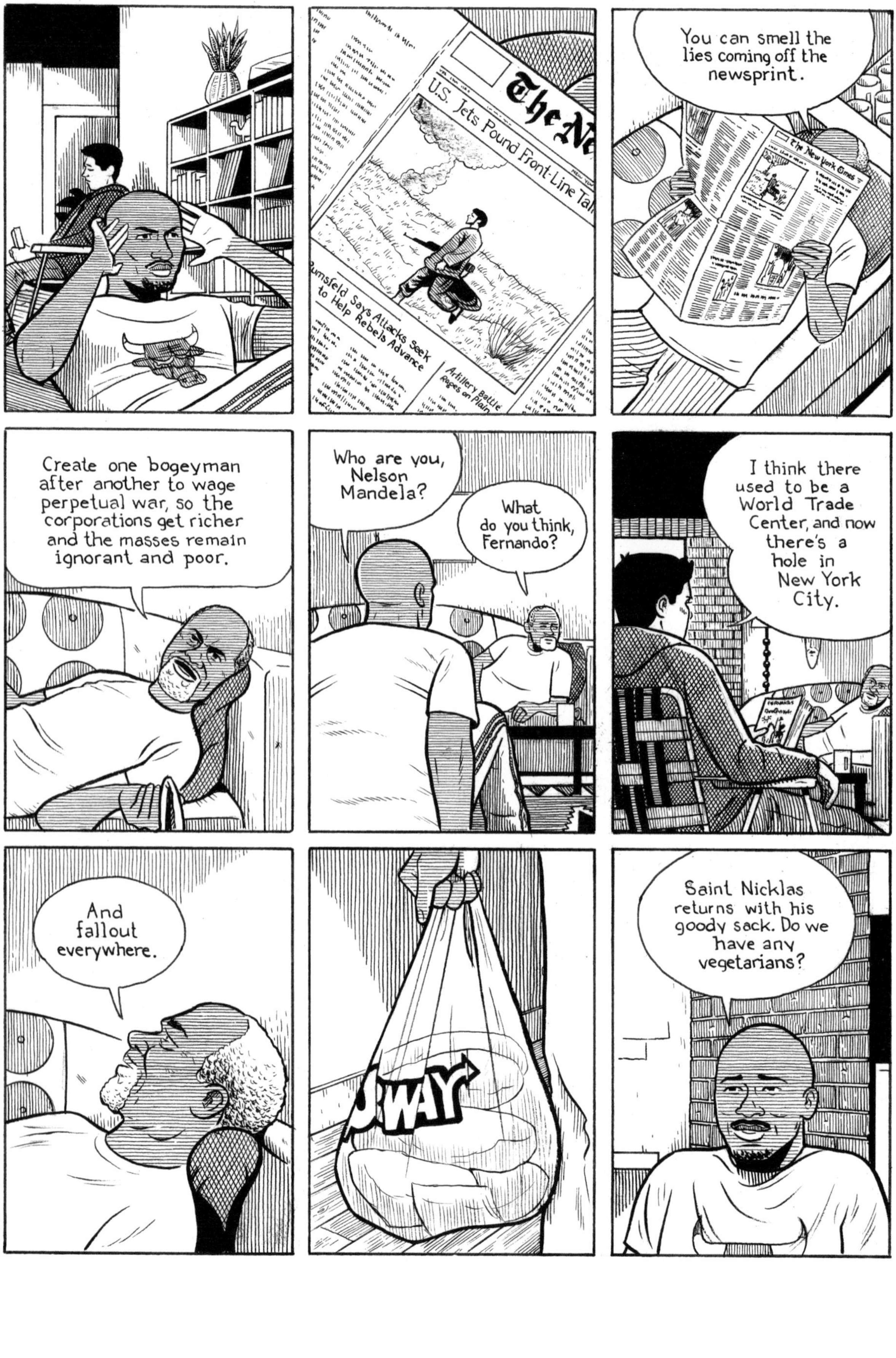

U.S. Jets Pound Front-Line
umsfeld Says Attacks Seek to Help Rebels Advance
Artillery Battle Rages on Plain
You can smell the lies coming off the newsprint.
Create one bogeyman after another to wage perpetual war, so the corporations get richer and the masses remain ignorant and poor.
Who are you, Nelson Mandela?
What do you think, Fernando?
I think there used to be a World Trade Center, and now there's a hole in New York City.
And fallout everywhere.
WAY
Saint Nicklas returns with his goody sack. Do we have any vegetarians?

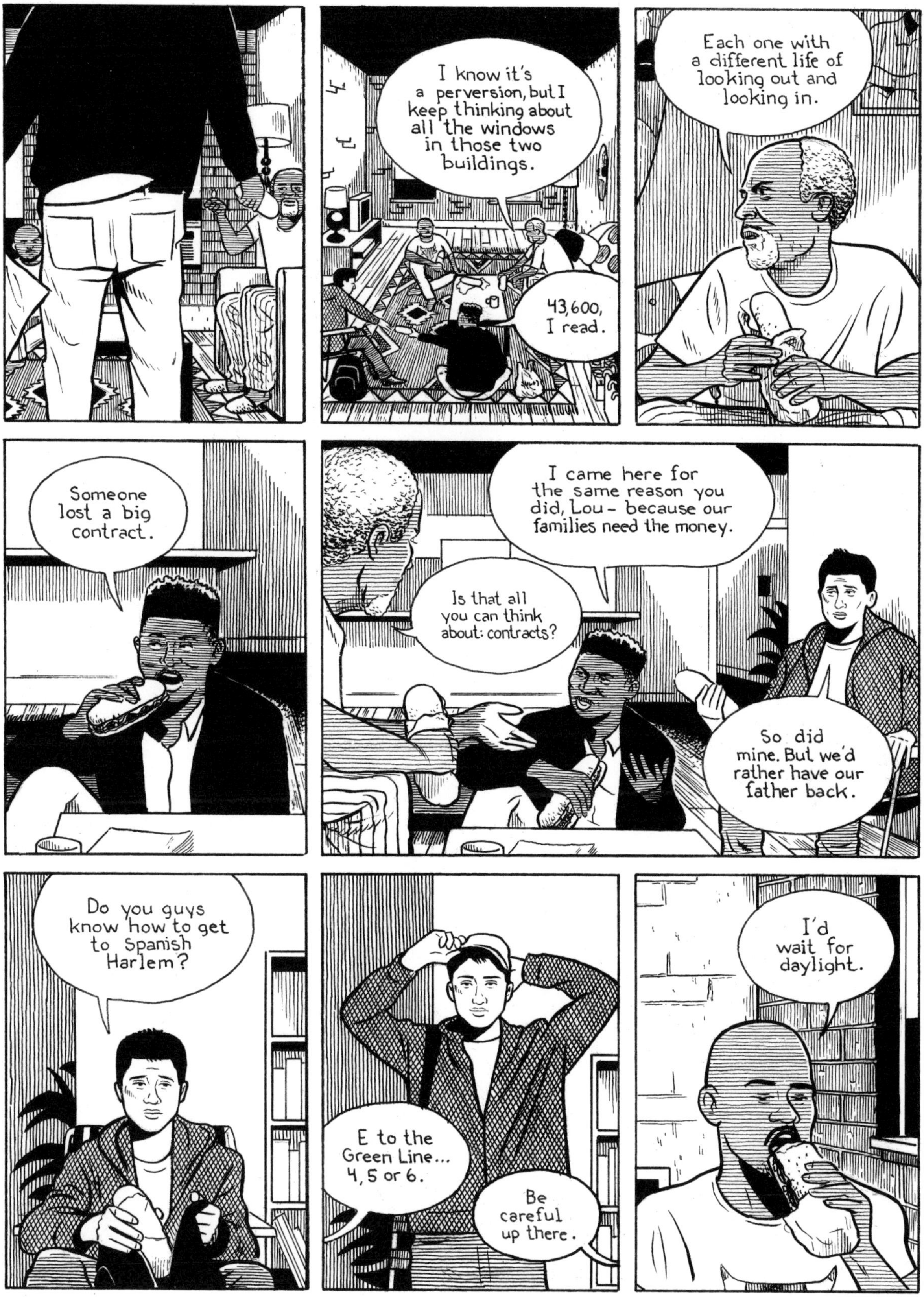
I know it's a perversion, but I keep thinking about all the windows in those two buildings.
43,600, I read.
Each one with a different life of looking out and looking in.
Someone lost a big contract.
I came here for the same reason you did, Lou - because our families need the money.
Is that all you can think about: contracts?
So did mine. But we'd rather have our father back.
Do you guys know how to get to Spanish Harlem?
E to the Green Line... 4, 5 or 6.
Be careful up there.
I'd wait for daylight.

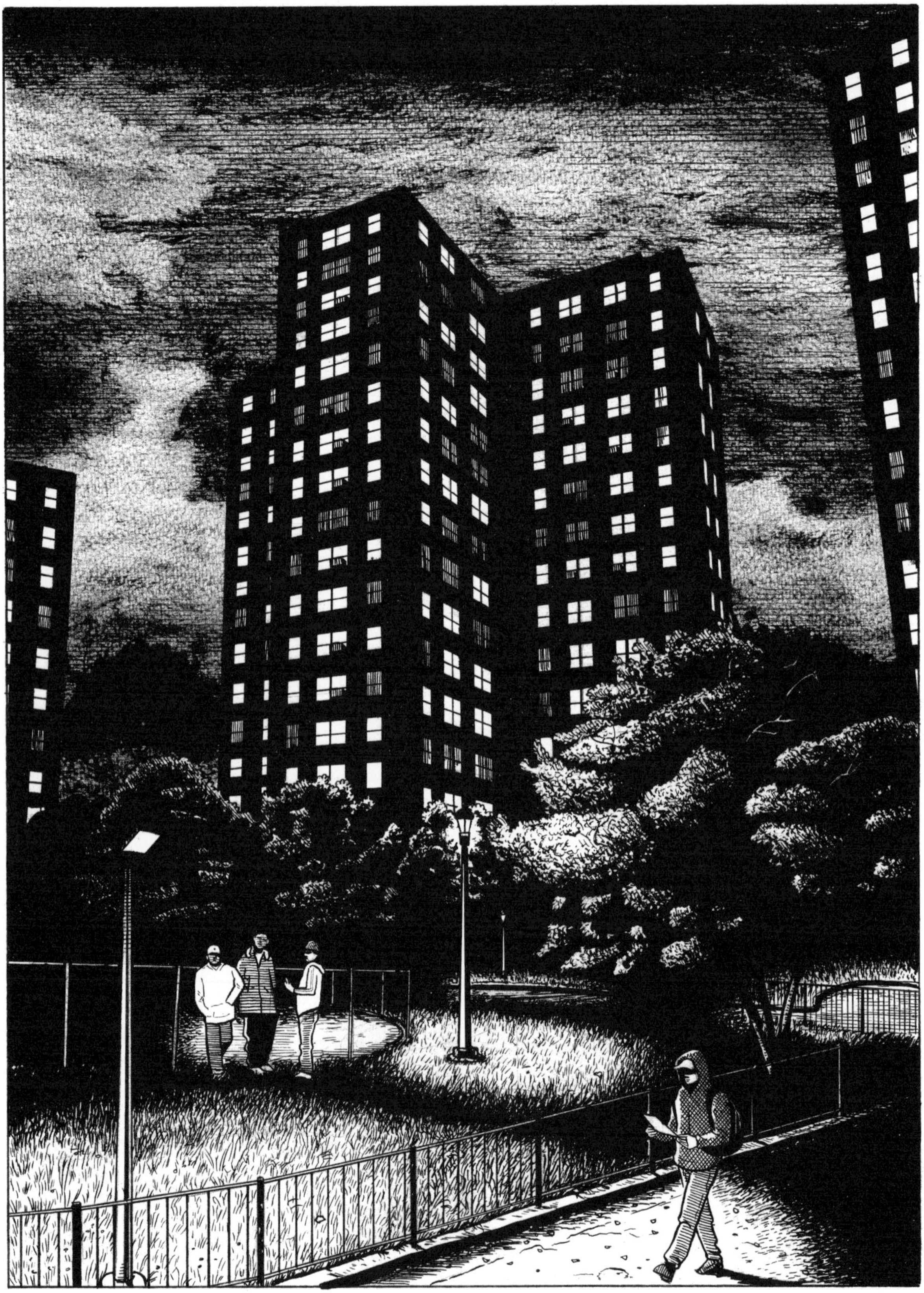

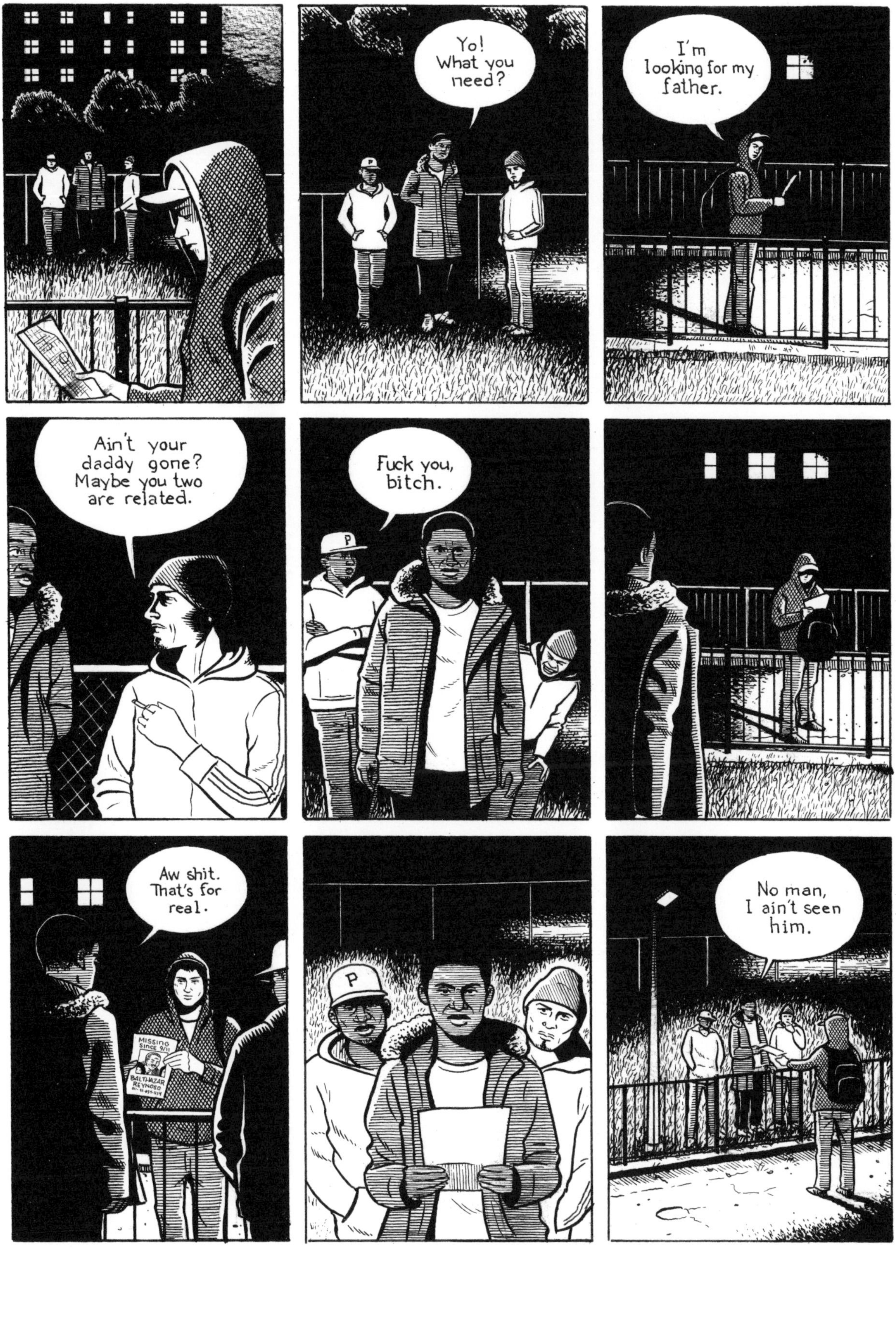
Yo! What you need?
I'm looking for my father.
Ain't your daddy gone? Maybe you two are related.
Fuck you, bitch.
Aw shit. That's for real.
MISSING SINCE 9/11
BALTHAZAR REYNOSO
No man, I ain't seen him.

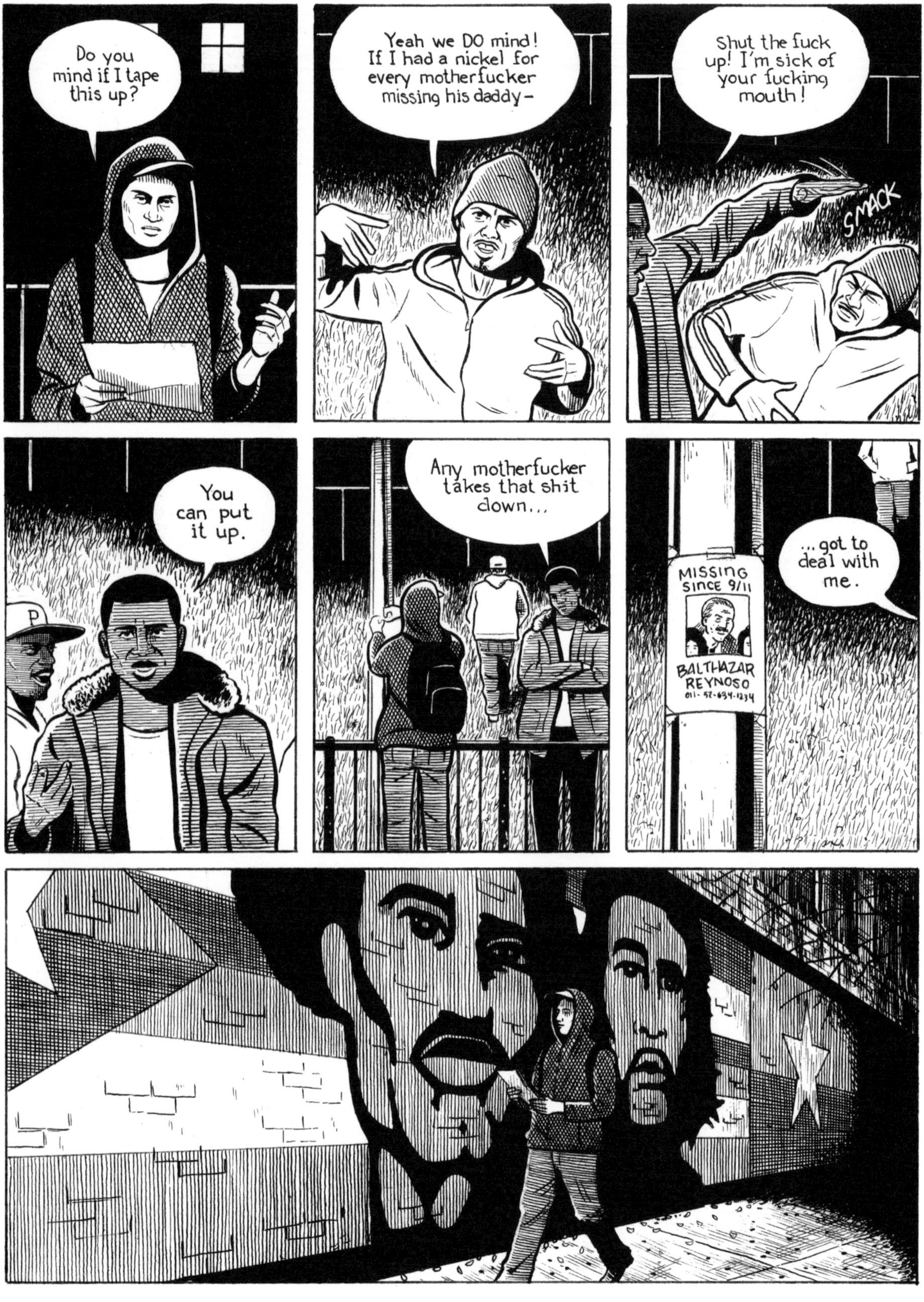
Do you mind if I tape this up?
Yeah we DO mind! If I had a nickel for every motherfucker missing his daddy-
Shut the fuck up! I'm sick of your fucking mouth!
SMACK
You can put it up.
Any motherfucker takes that shit down...
MISSING SINCE 9/11
BALTHAZAR REYNOSO
...got to deal with me.

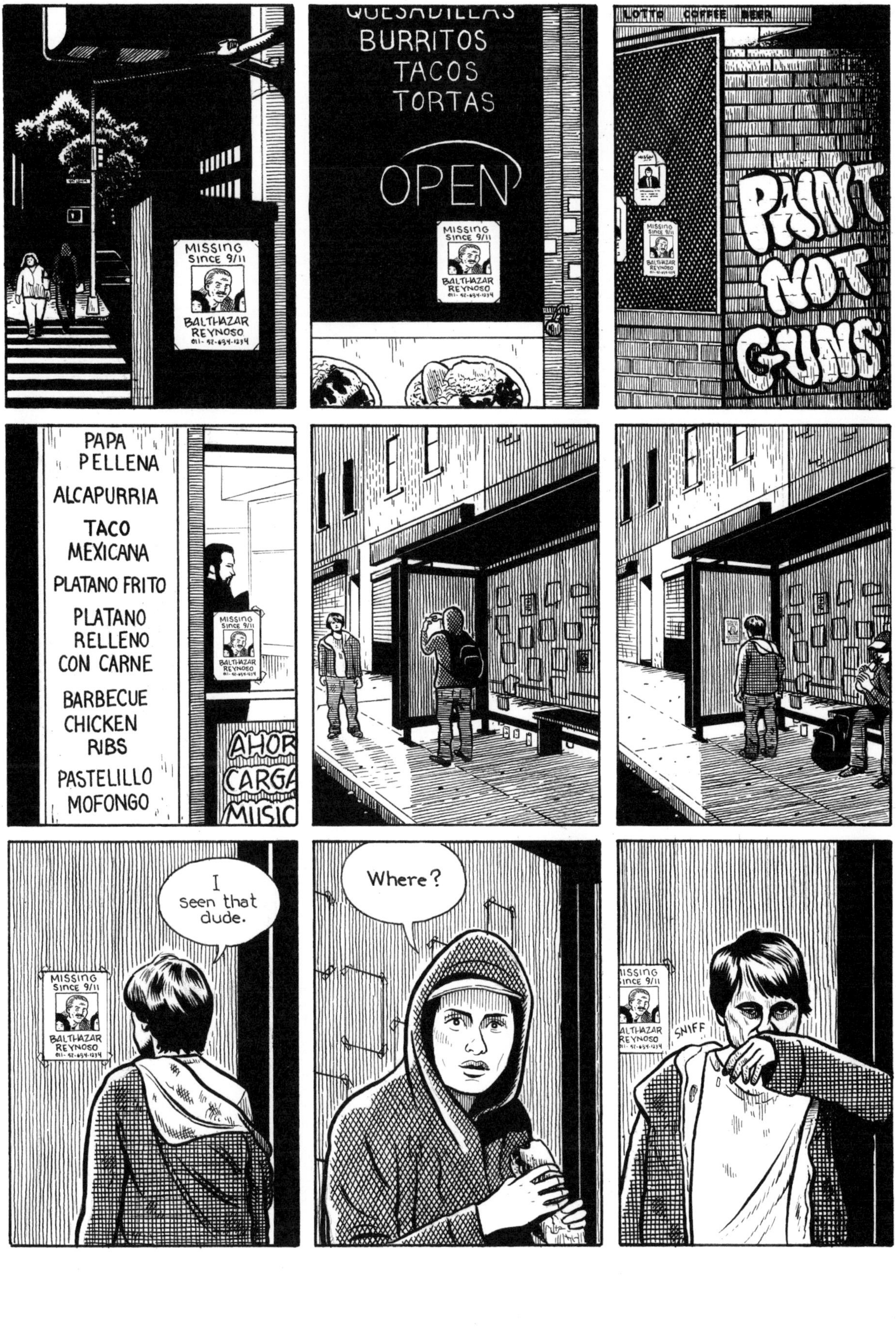
MISSING SINCE 9/11
BALTHAZAR REYNOSO
011-52-634-1234
BURRITOS
TACOS
TORTAS
OPEN
MISSING SINCE 9/11
BALTHAZAR REYNOSO
011-52-634-1234
LOTTO COFFEE BEER
MISSING SINCE 9/11
BALTHAZAR REYNOSO
PAINT NOT GUNS
PAPA PELLENA
ALCAPURRIA
TACO MEXICANA
PLATANO FRITO
PLATANO RELLENO CON CARNE
BARBECUE CHICKEN RIBS
PASTELILLO MOFONGO
MISSING SINCE 9/11
BALTHAZAR REYNOSO
AHOR
CARGA
MUSIC
MISSING SINCE 9/11
BALTHAZAR REYNOSO
011-52-634-1234
I seen that dude.
Where?
MISSING SINCE 9/11
ALTHAZAR REYNOSO
SNIFF

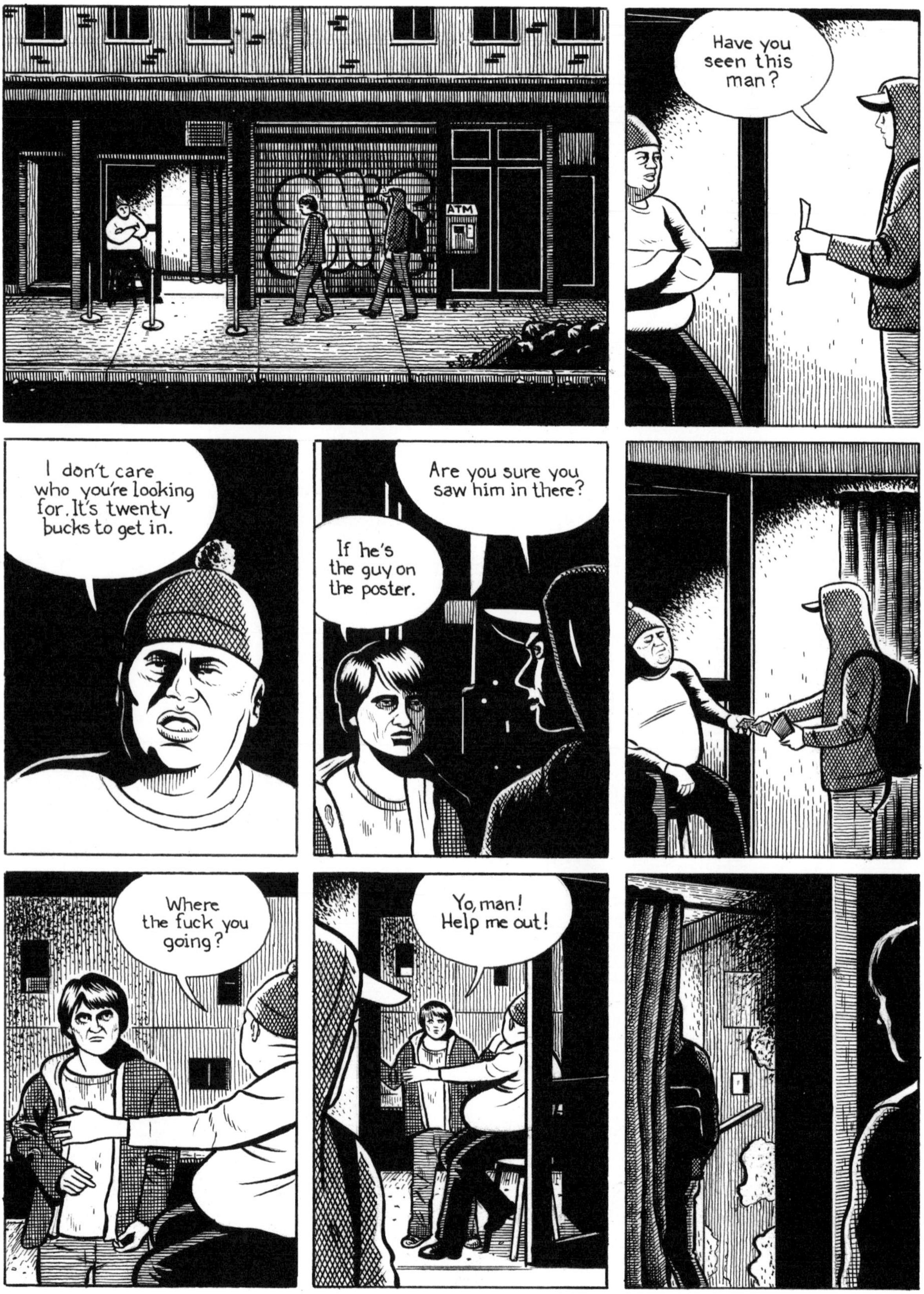
ATM
Have you seen this man?
I don't care who you're looking for. It's twenty bucks to get in.
Are you sure you saw him in there?
If he's the guy on the poster.
Where the fuck you going?
Yo, man! Help me out!

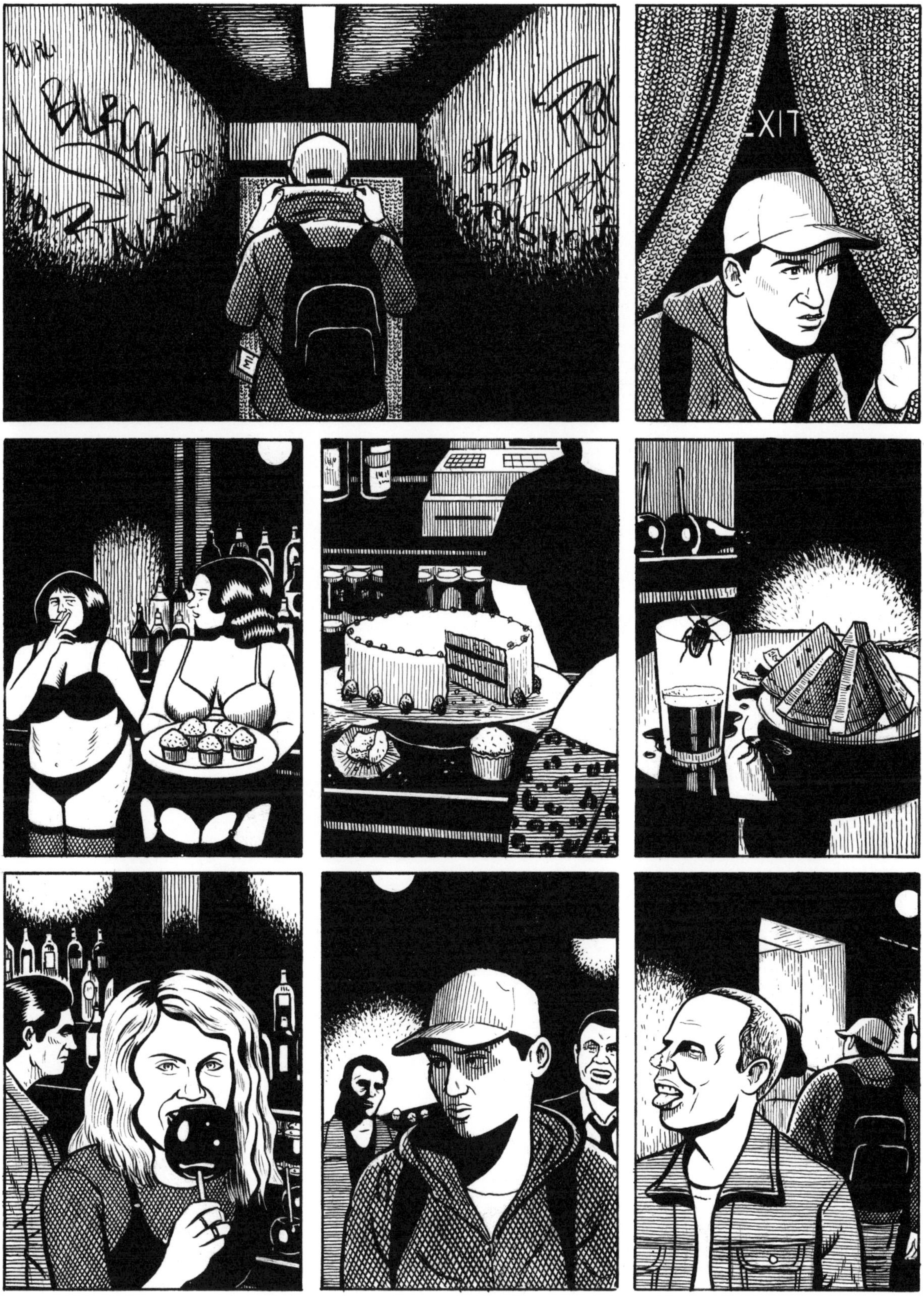
EXIT

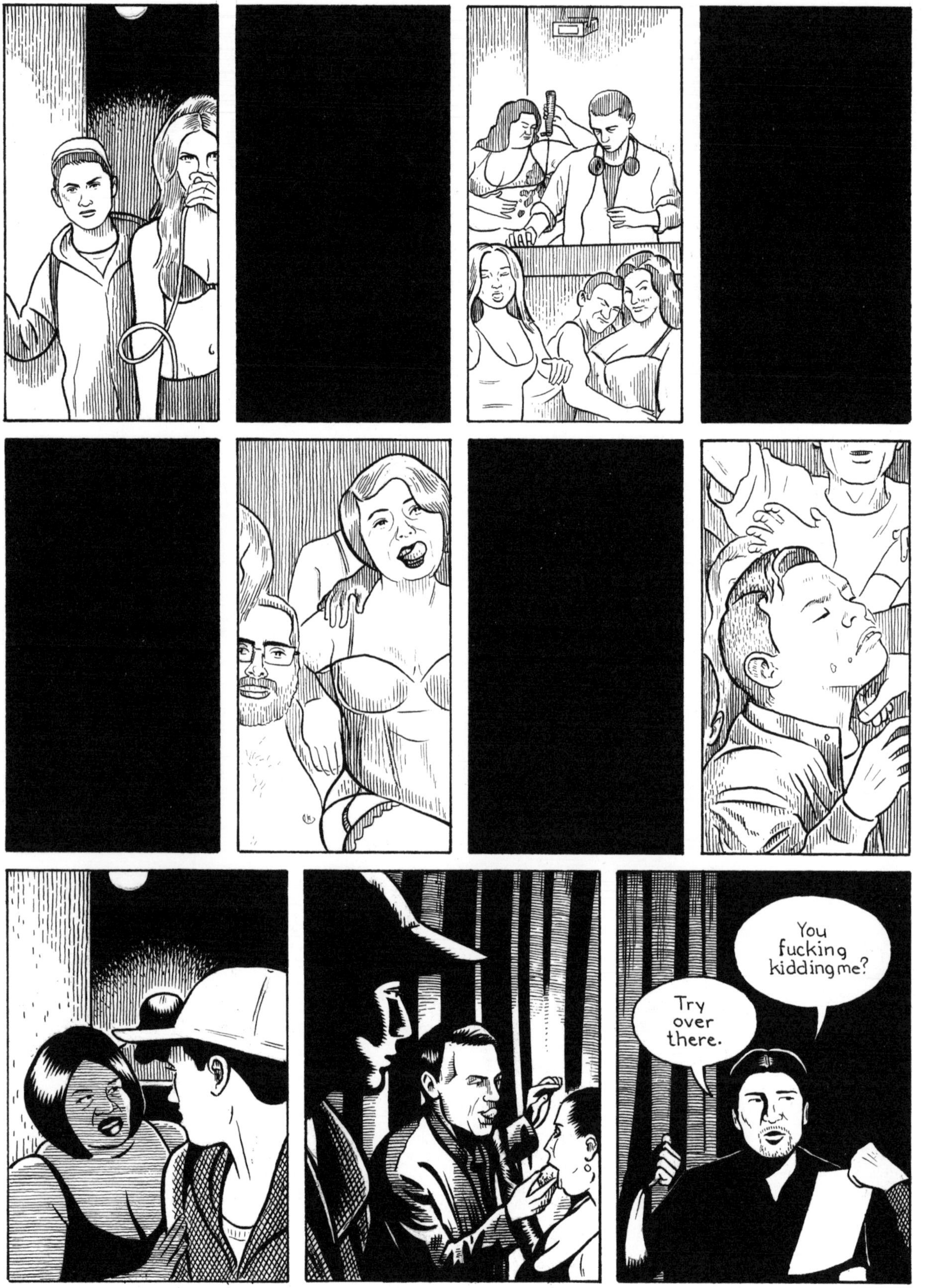
Try over there.
You fucking kidding me?

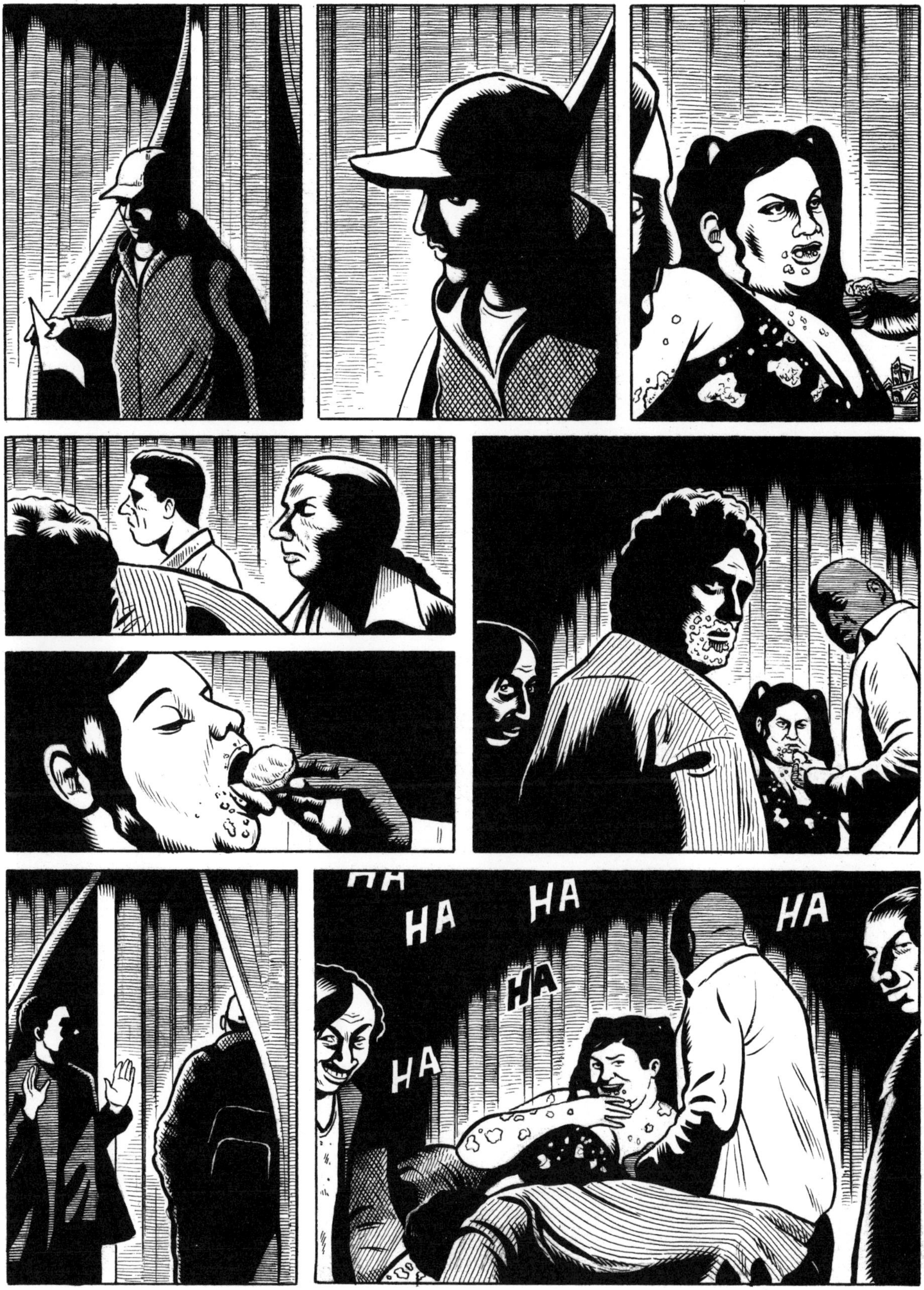
HA
HA
HA
HA
HA
HA

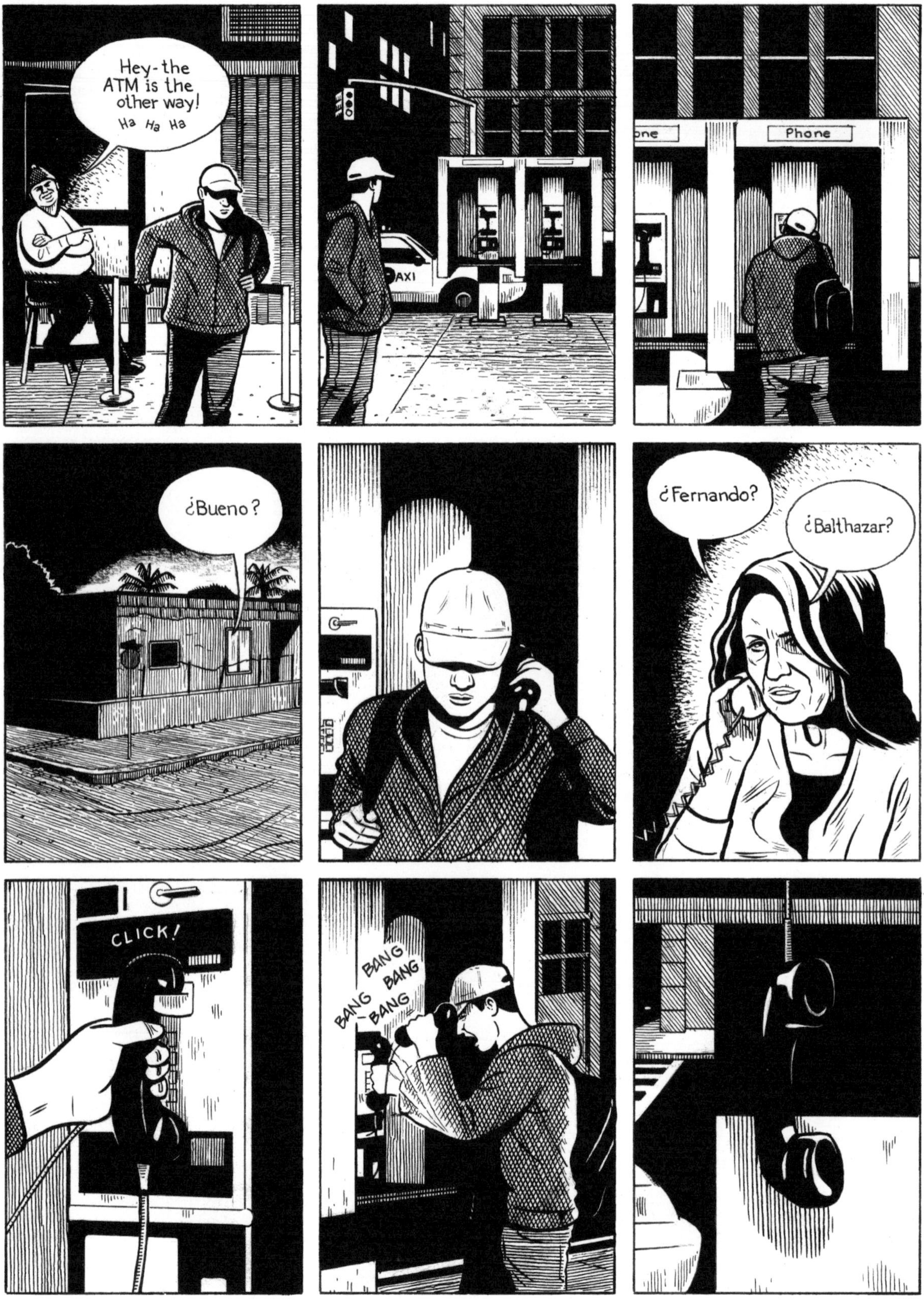
Hey-the ATM is the other way! Ha Ha Ha
¿Bueno?
¿Fernando?
¿Balthazar?
CLICK!
BANG BANG BANG BANG

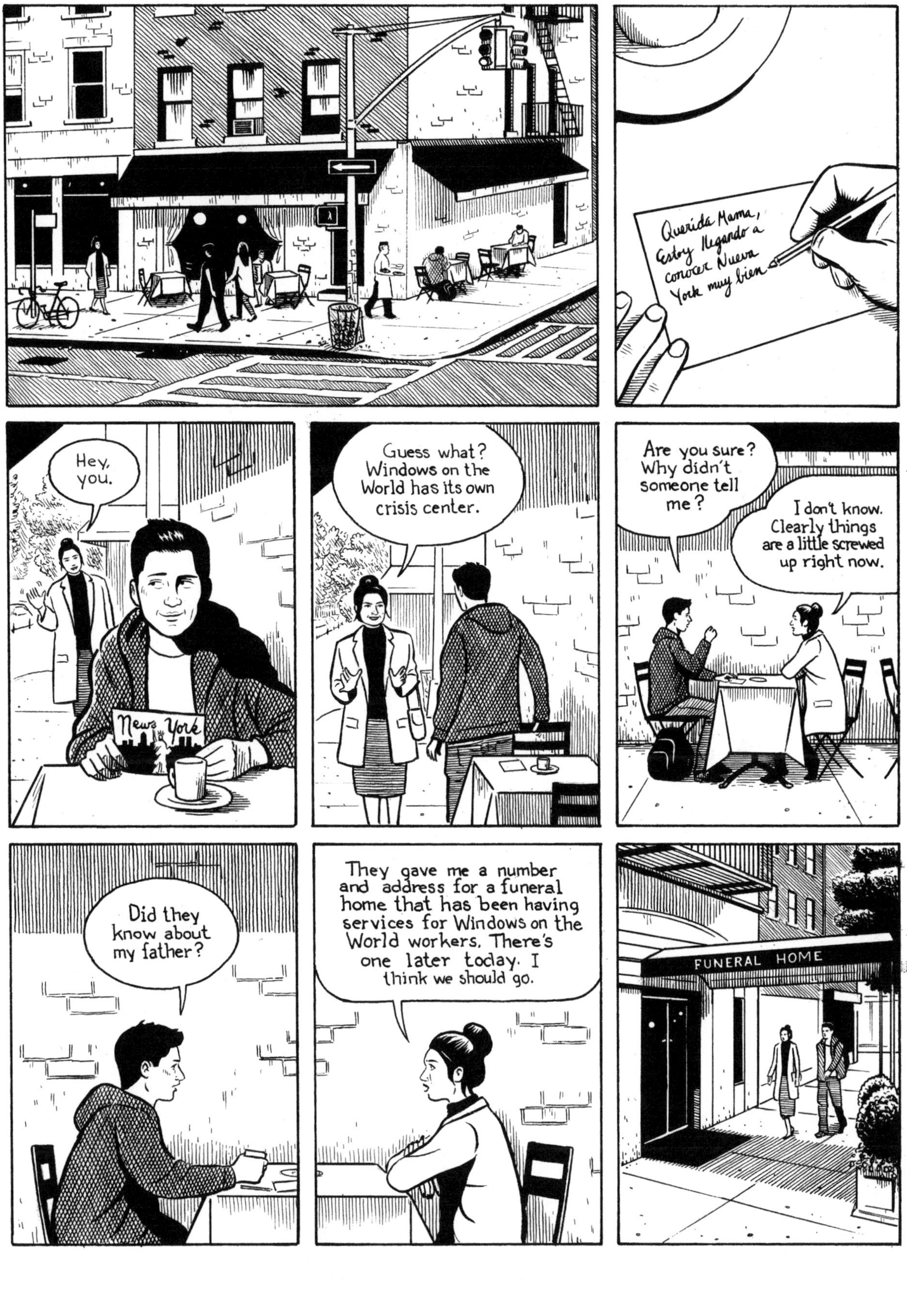
Querida Mama,
Estoy llegando a conocer Nueva York muy bien
Hey, you.
News York
Guess what? Windows on the World has its own crisis center.
Are you sure? Why didn't someone tell me?
I don't know. Clearly things are a little screwed up right now.
Did they know about my father?
They gave me a number and address for a funeral home that has been having services for Windows on the World workers. There's one later today. I think we should go.
FUNERAL HOME

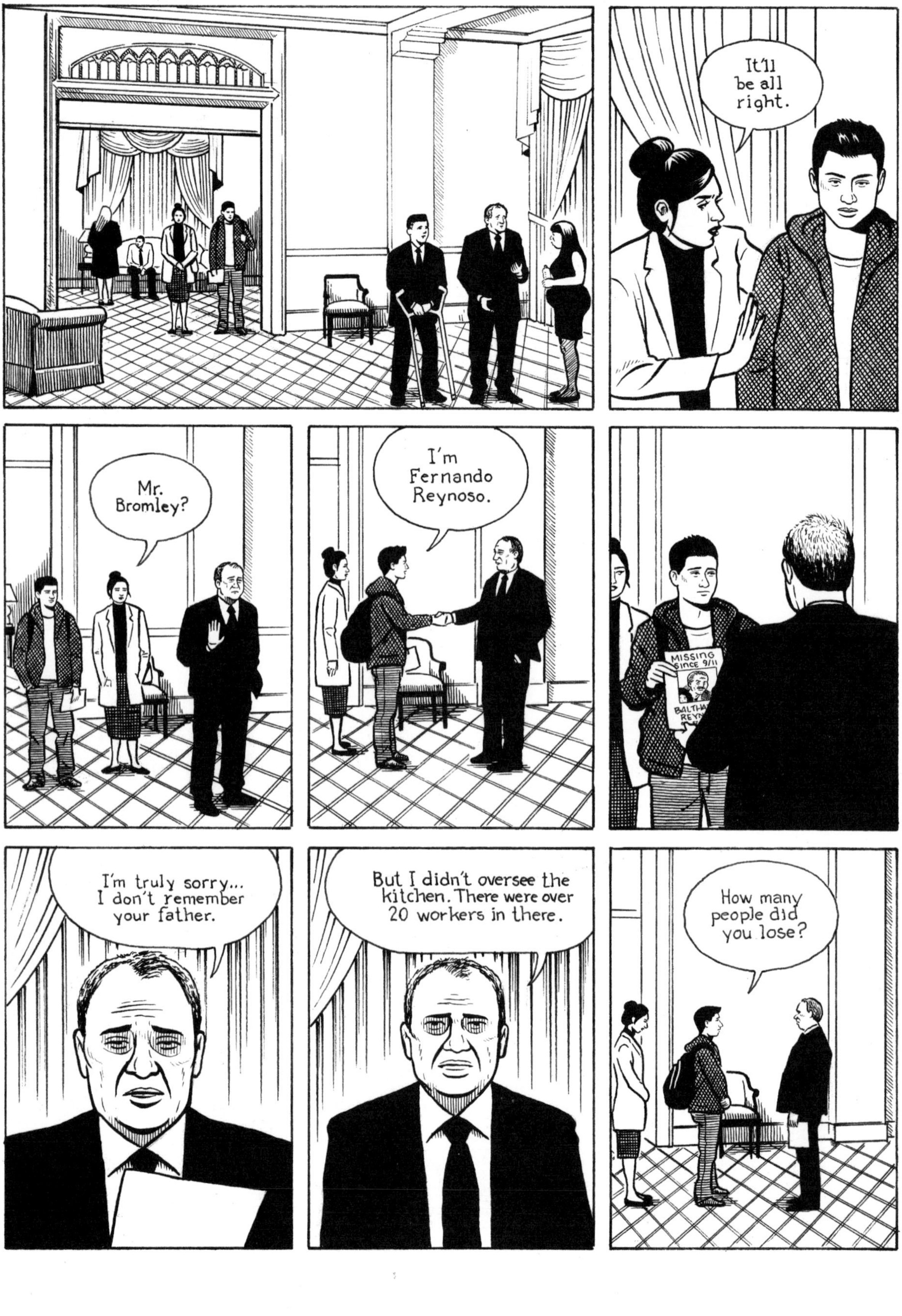
It'll be all right.
Mr. Bromley?
I'm Fernando Reynoso.
MISSING SINCE 9/11
I'm truly sorry... I don't remember your father.
But I didn't oversee the kitchen. There were over 20 workers in there.
How many people did you lose?

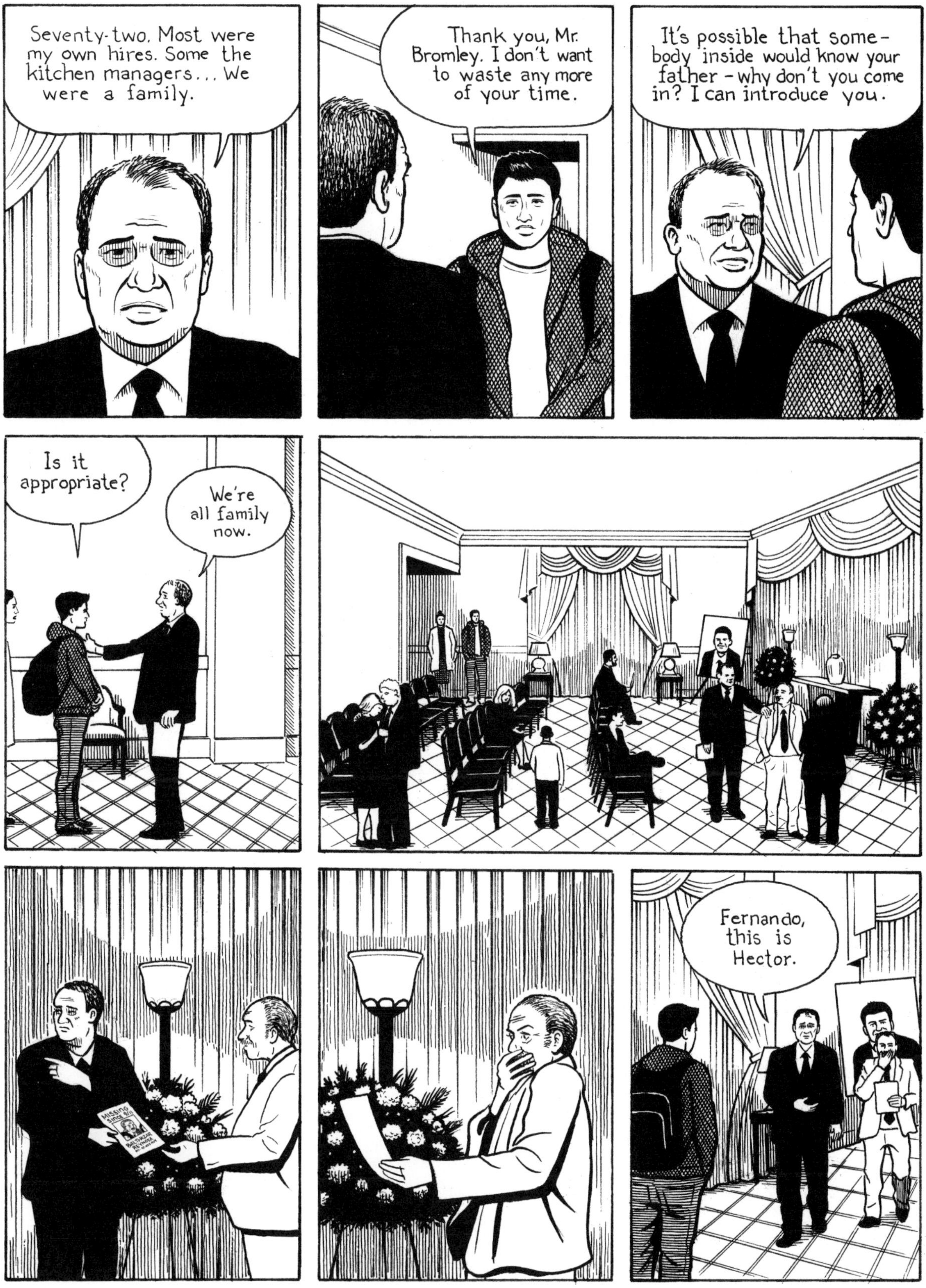
Seventy-two. Most were my own hires. Some the kitchen managers... We were a family.
Thank you, Mr. Bromley. I don't want to waste any more of your time.
It's possible that somebody inside would know your father - why don't you come in? I can introduce you.
Is it appropriate?
We're all family now.
Fernando, this is Hector.

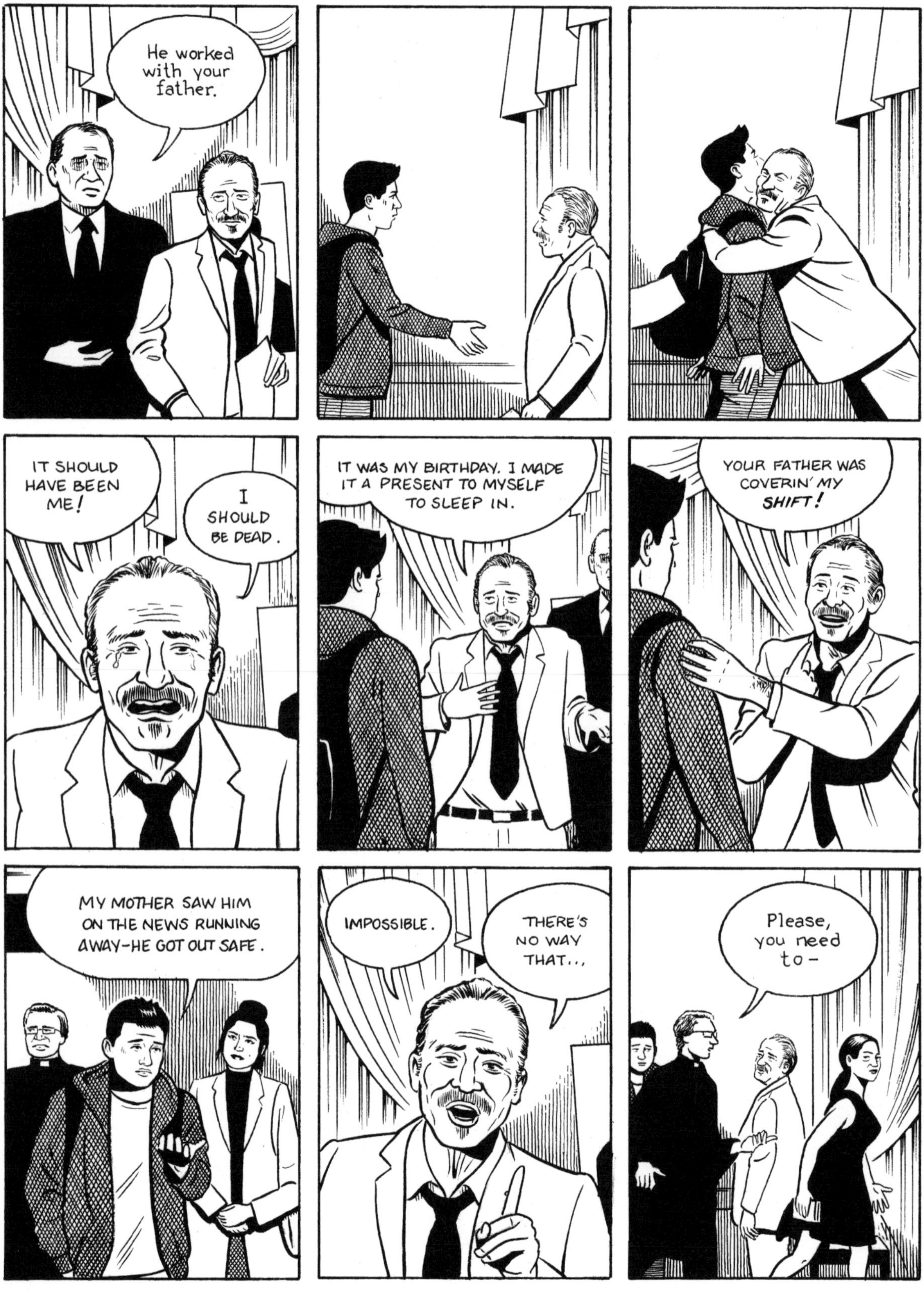
He worked with your father.
IT SHOULD HAVE BEEN ME!
I SHOULD BE DEAD.
IT WAS MY BIRTHDAY. I MADE IT A PRESENT TO MYSELF TO SLEEP IN.
YOUR FATHER WAS COVERIN' MY SHIFT!
MY MOTHER SAW HIM ON THE NEWS RUNNING AWAY-HE GOT OUT SAFE.
IMPOSSIBLE.
THERE'S NO WAY THAT...
Please, you need to-

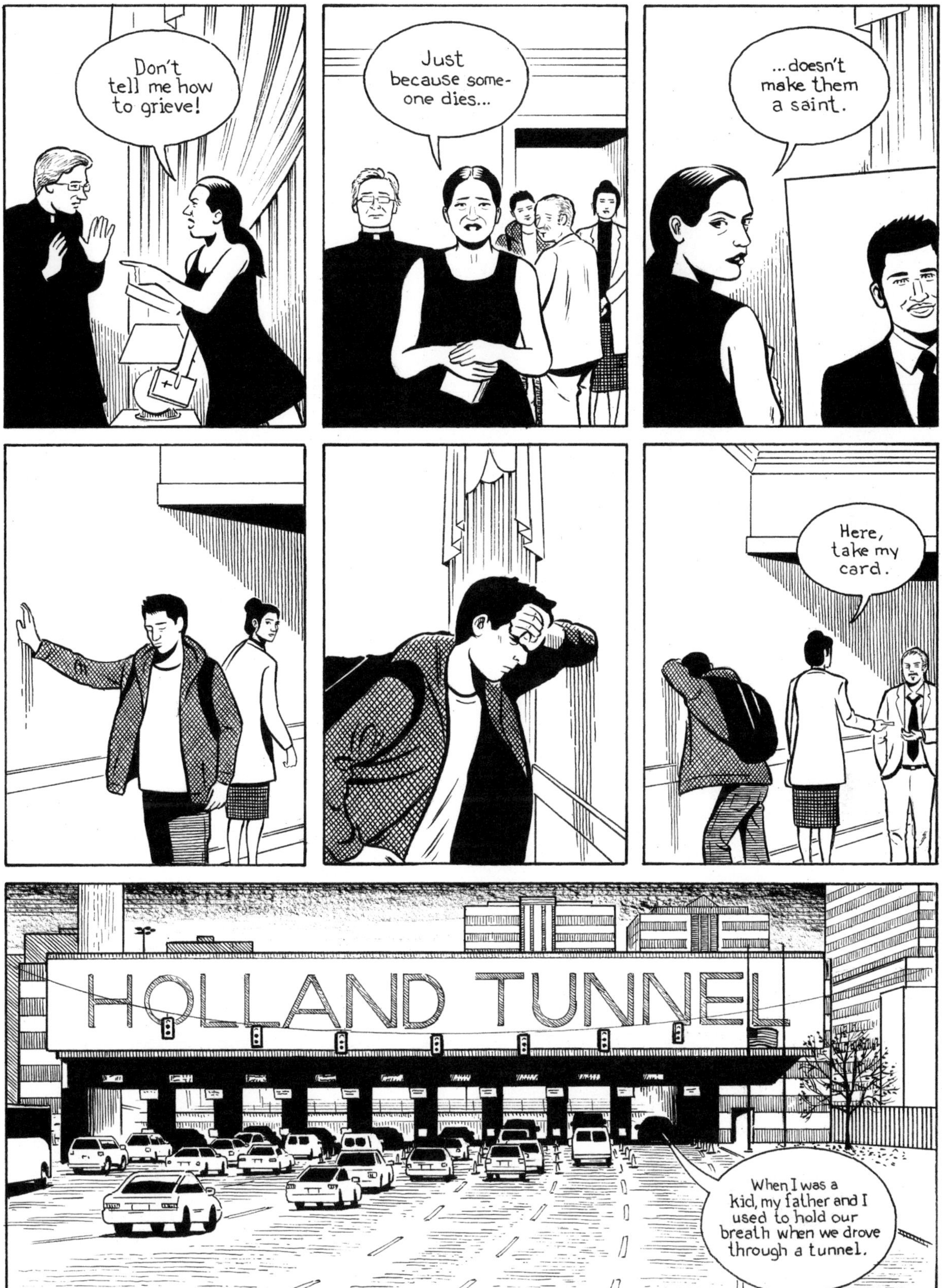
Don't tell me how to grieve!
Just because some-one dies...
...doesn't make them a saint.
Here, take my card.
HOLLAND TUNNEL
When I was a kid, my father and I used to hold our breath when we drove through a tunnel.

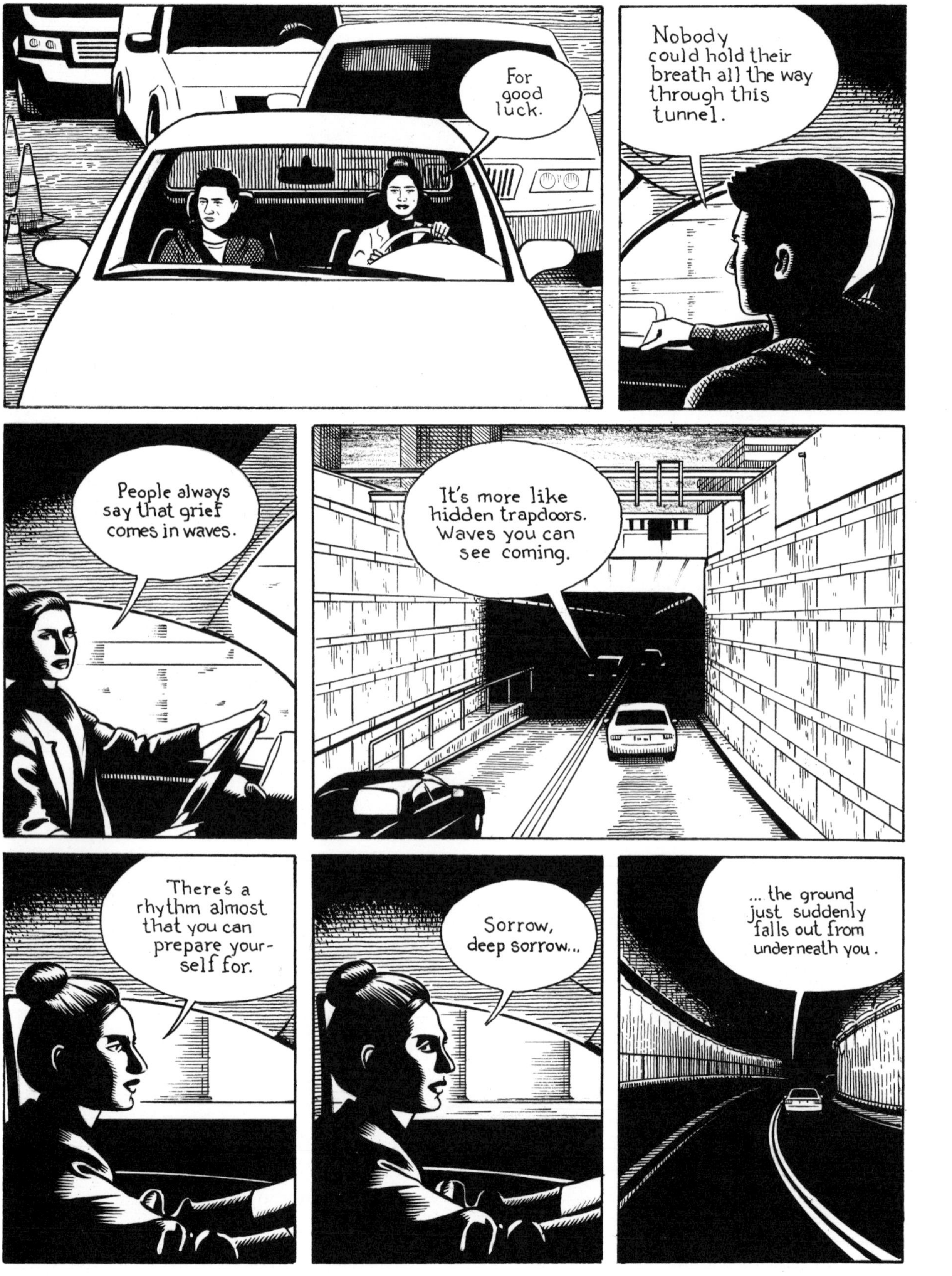
For good luck.
Nobody could hold their breath all the way through this tunnel.
People always say that grief comes in waves.
It's more like hidden trapdoors. Waves you can see coming.
There's a rhythm almost that you can prepare your-self for.
Sorrow, deep sorrow...
... the ground just suddenly falls out from underneath you.

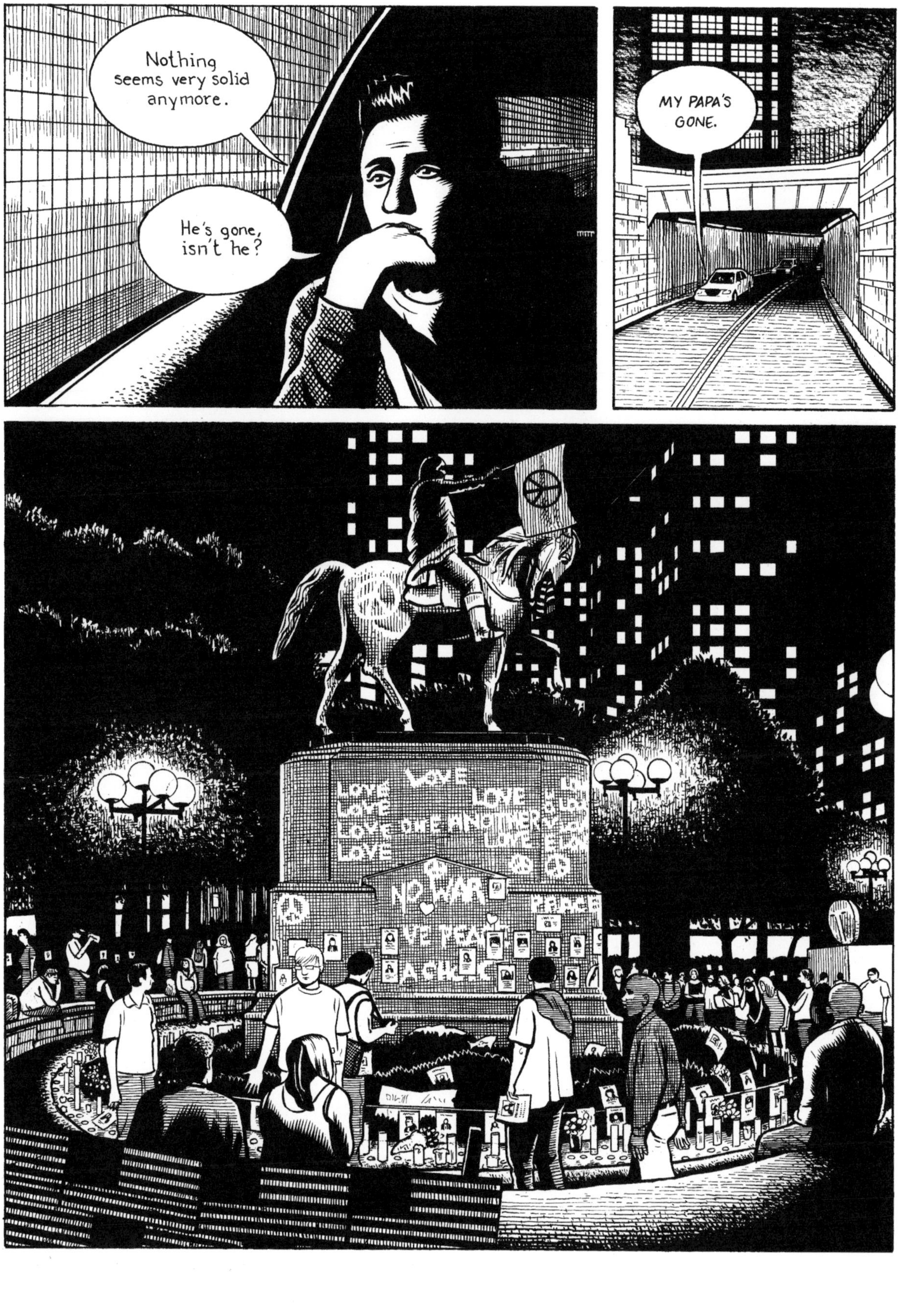
Nothing seems very solid anymore.
He's gone, isn't he?
MY PAPA'S GONE.
LOVE
LOVE
NO WAR
PEACE

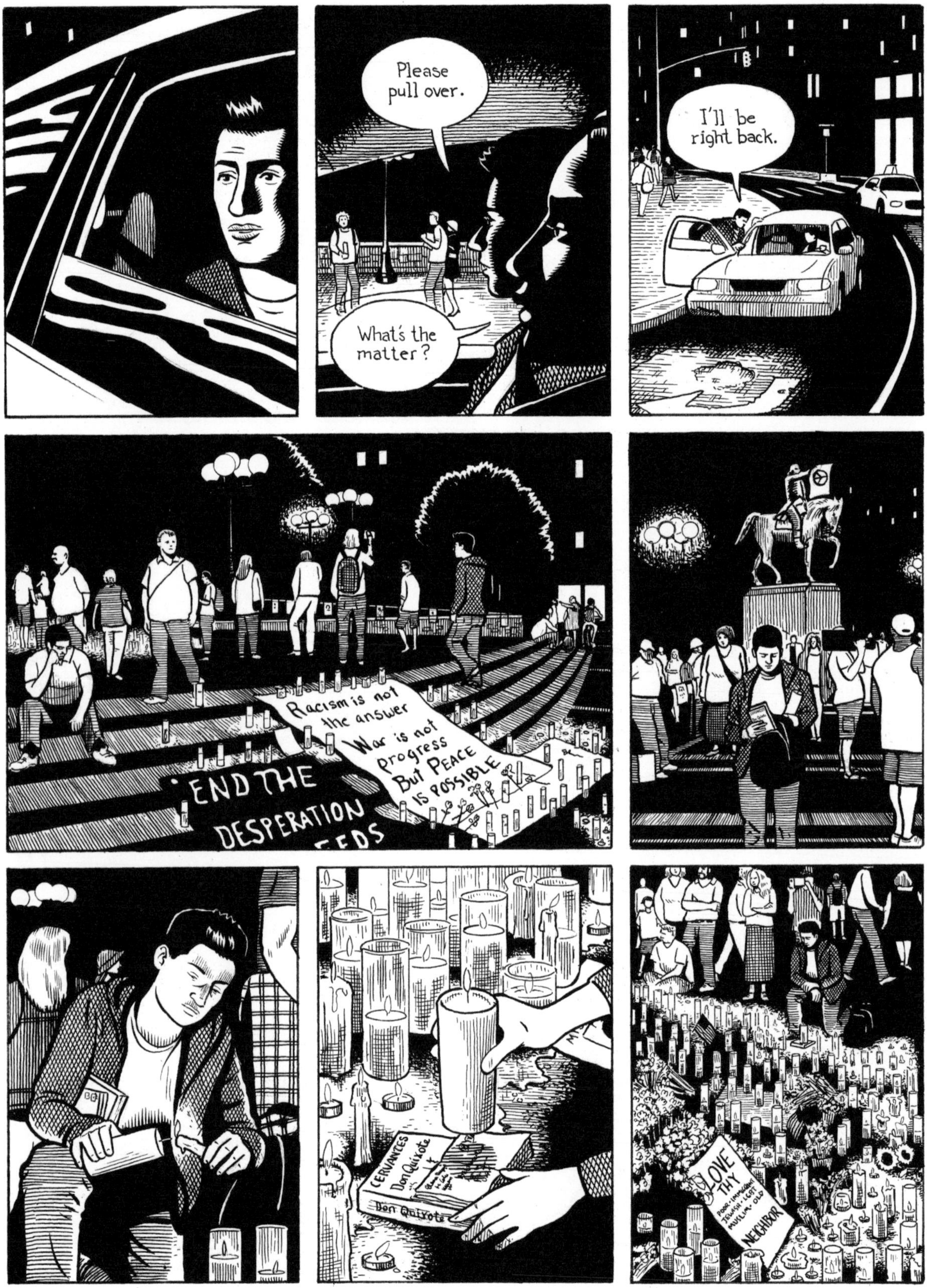
Please pull over.
What's the matter?
I'll be right back.
END THE
DESPERATION
Racism is not the answer
War is not progress
But PEACE IS POSSIBLE
CERVANTES
Don Quixote
Don Quixote
LOVE THY
POOR · IMMIGRANT
JEWISH · LGBT
MUSLIM · OLD
NEIGHBOR

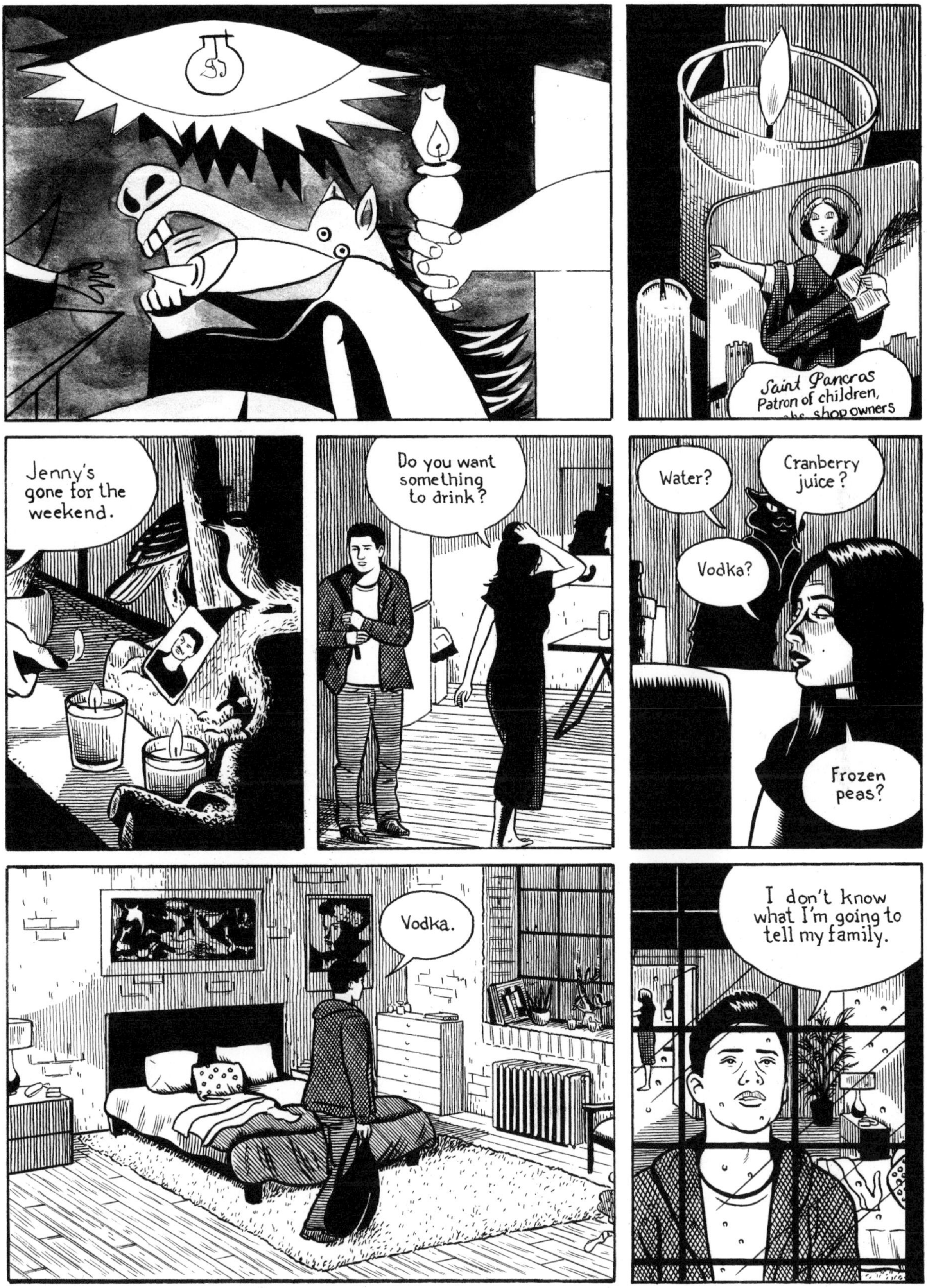
Saint Pancras
Patron of children,
shop owners
Jenny's gone for the weekend.
Do you want something to drink?
Water?
Cranberry juice?
Vodka?
Frozen peas?
Vodka.
I don't know what I'm going to tell my family.

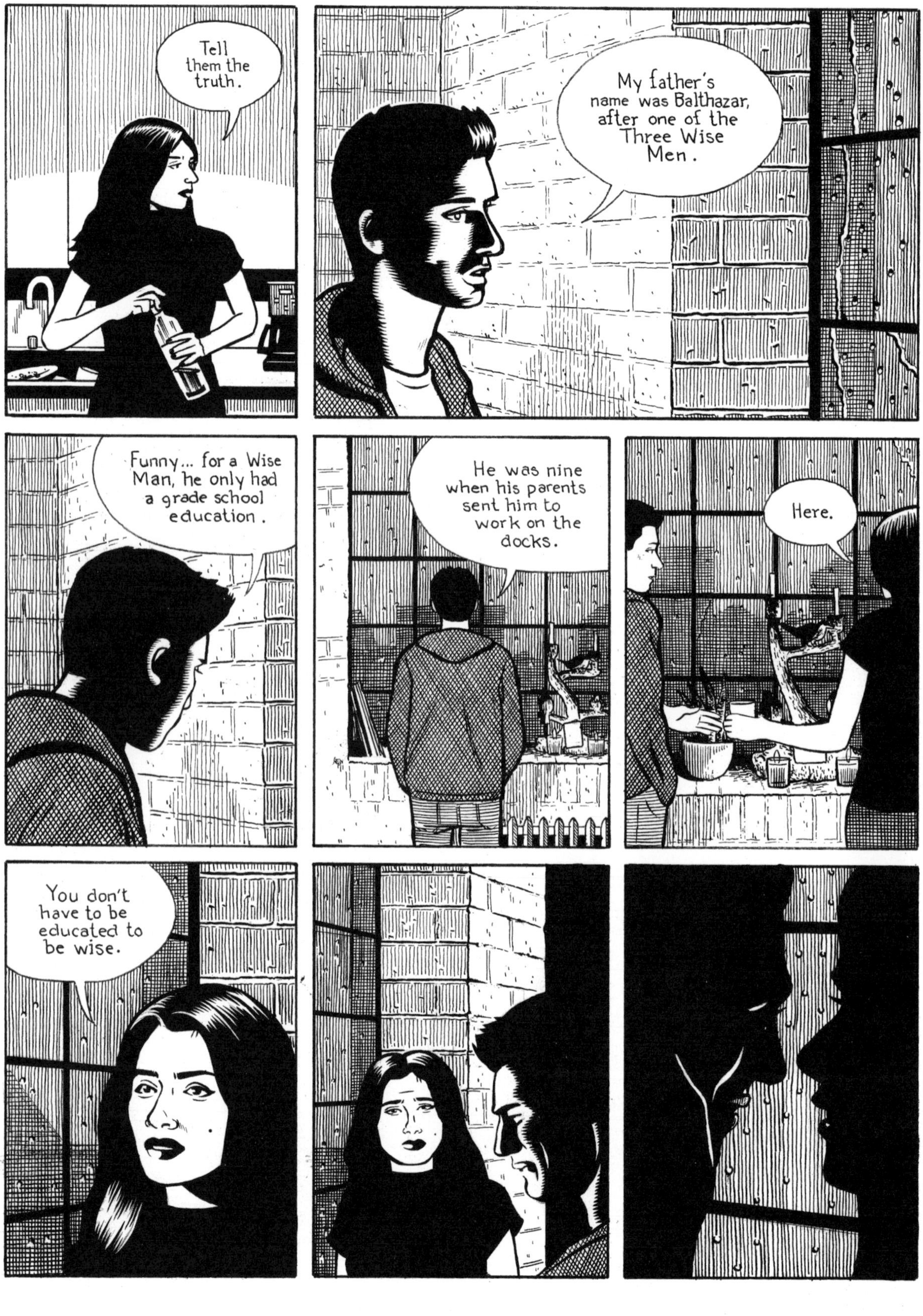
Tell them the truth.
My father's name was Balthazar, after one of the Three Wise Men.
Funny... for a Wise Man, he only had a grade school education.
He was nine when his parents sent him to work on the docks.
Here.
You don't have to be educated to be wise.

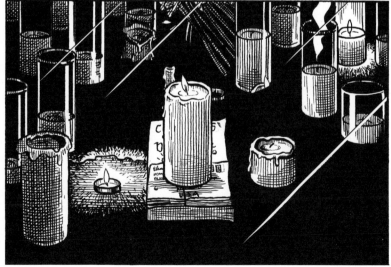

Let the machine get it.

Hi, I'm not here right now. Please leave a message.

Lia, this is Hector. We met at the service yesterday. I have some information for your friend...

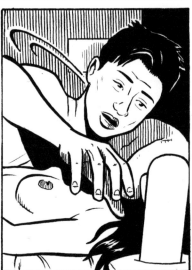

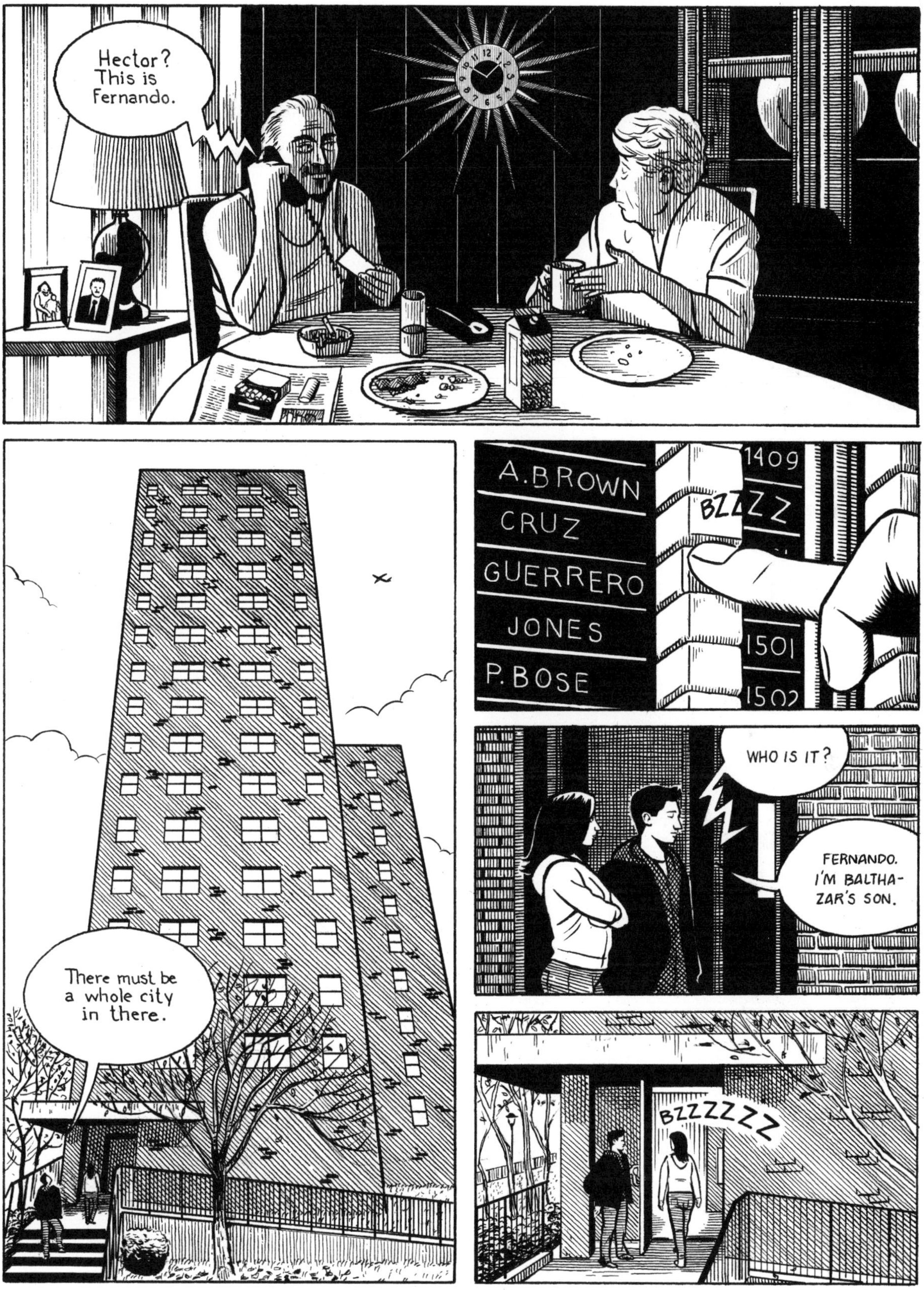
Hector? This is Fernando.
A.BROWN
CRUZ
GUERRERO
JONES
P.BOSE
1409
1501
1502
BZZZZ
There must be a whole city in there.
WHO IS IT?
FERNANDO. I'M BALTHAZAR'S SON.
BZZZZZZ

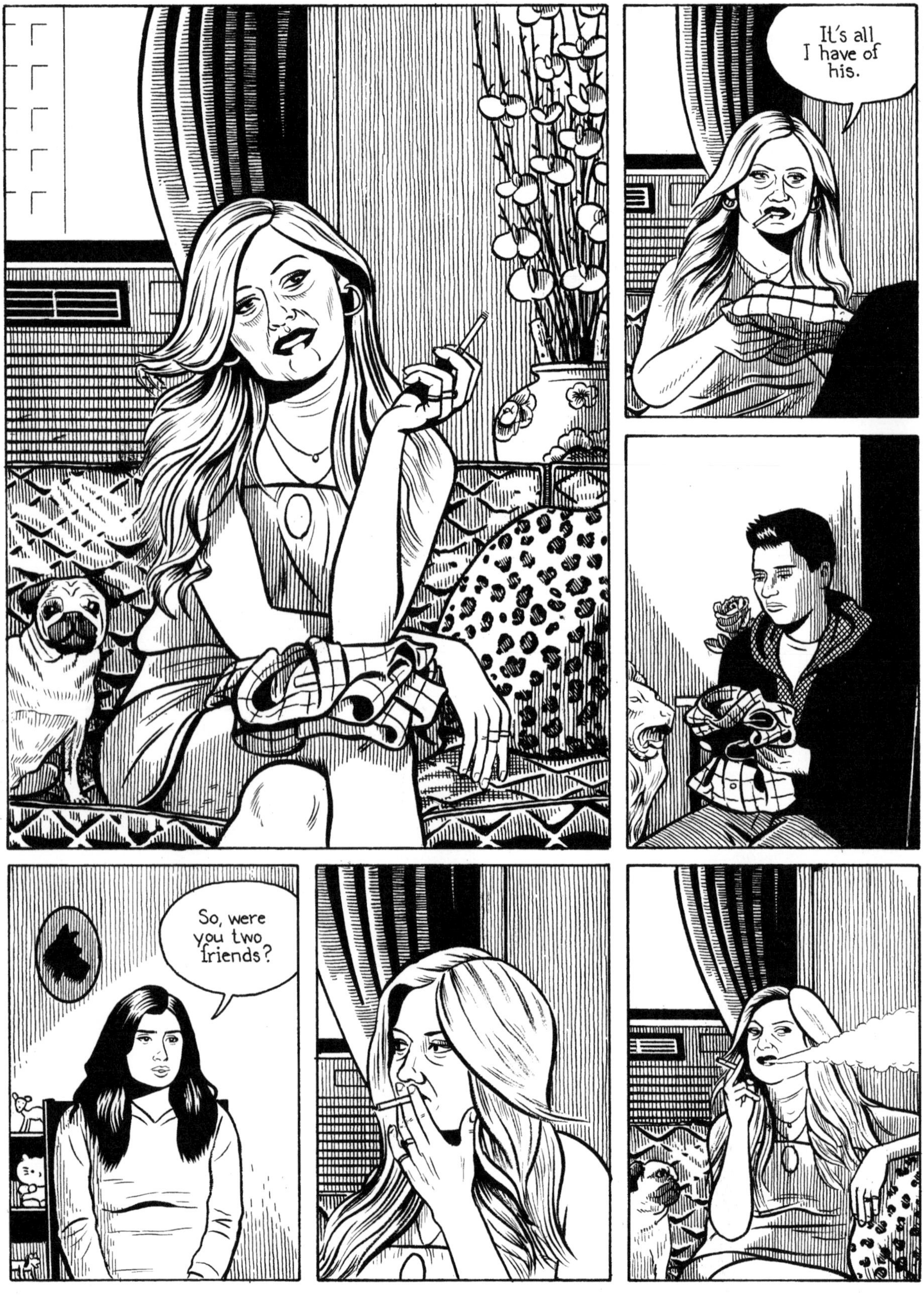
It's all I have of his.
So, were you two friends?

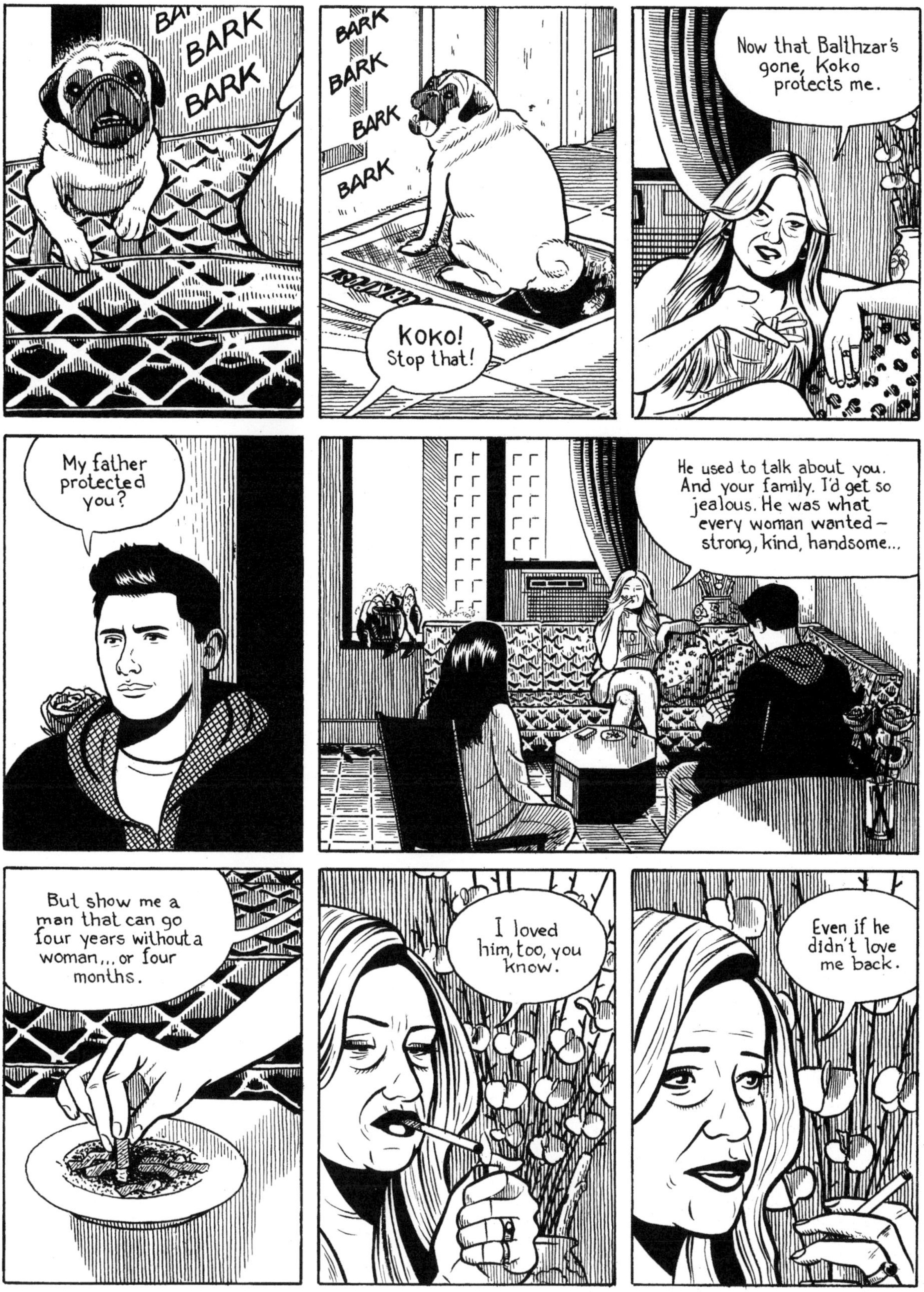
BAR
BARK
BARK
BARK
BARK
BARK
BARK
KOKO! Stop that!
Now that Balthzar's gone, Koko protects me.
My father protected you?
He used to talk about you. And your family. I'd get so jealous. He was what every woman wanted – strong, kind, handsome...
But show me a man that can go four years without a woman... or four months.
I loved him, too, you know.
Even if he didn't love me back.

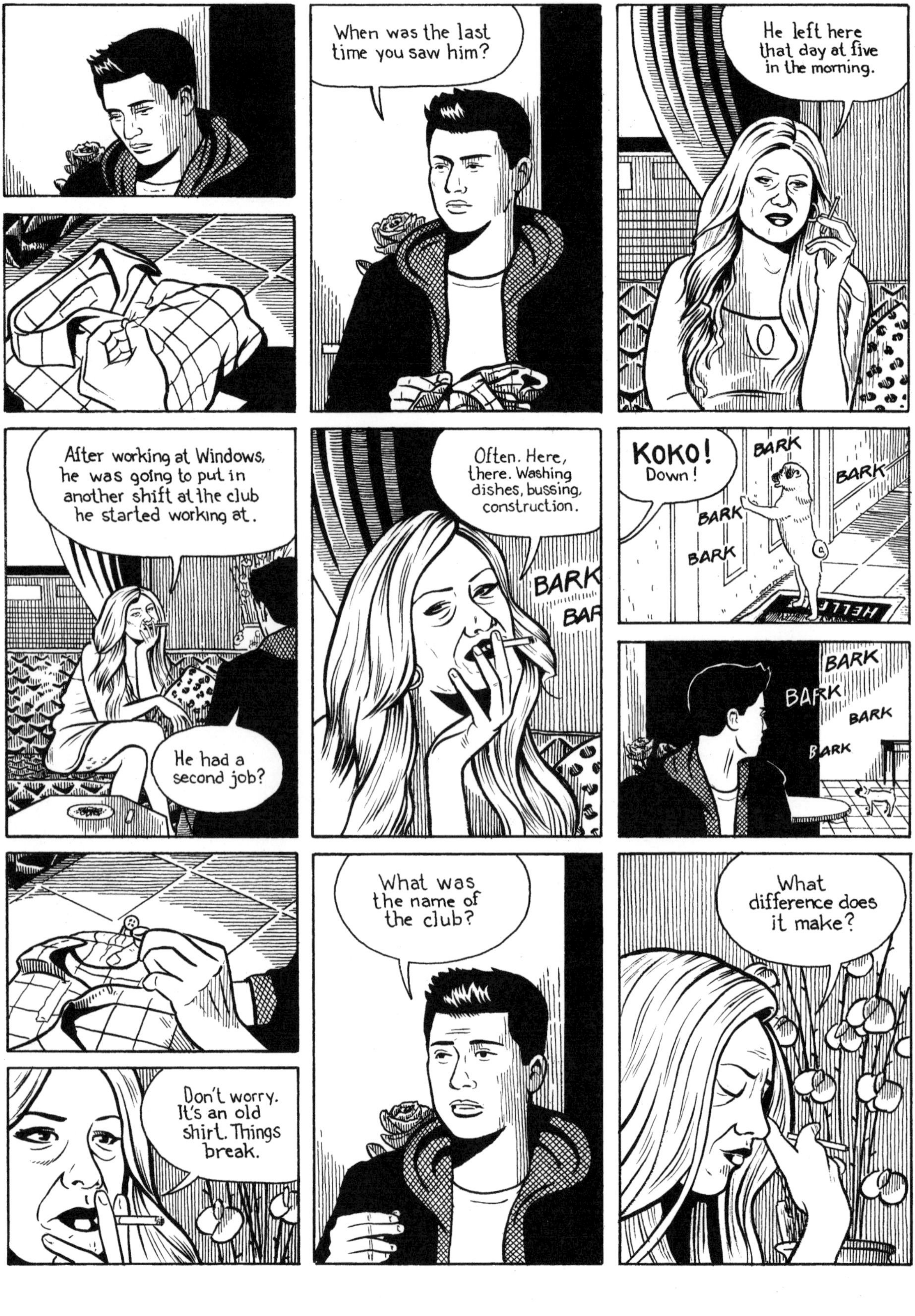

When was the last time you saw him?
He left here that day at five in the morning.
After working at Windows, he was going to put in another shift at the club he started working at.
He had a second job?
Often. Here, there. Washing dishes, bussing, construction.
BARK
BAR
KOKO! Down!
BARK
BARK
BARK
BARK
BARK
BARK
BARK
BARK
Don't worry. It's an old shirt. Things break.
What was the name of the club?
What difference does it make?

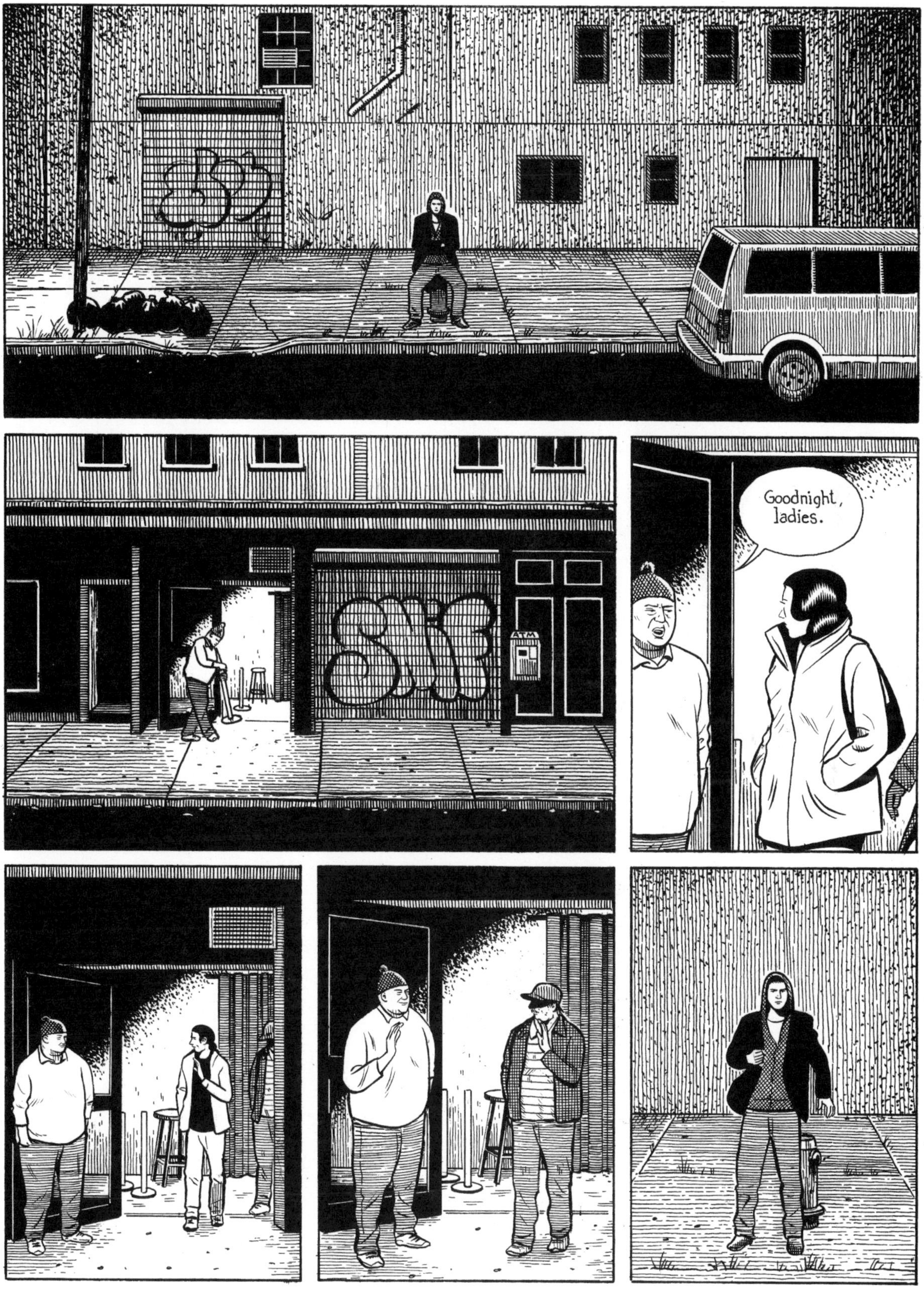
Goodnight, ladies.

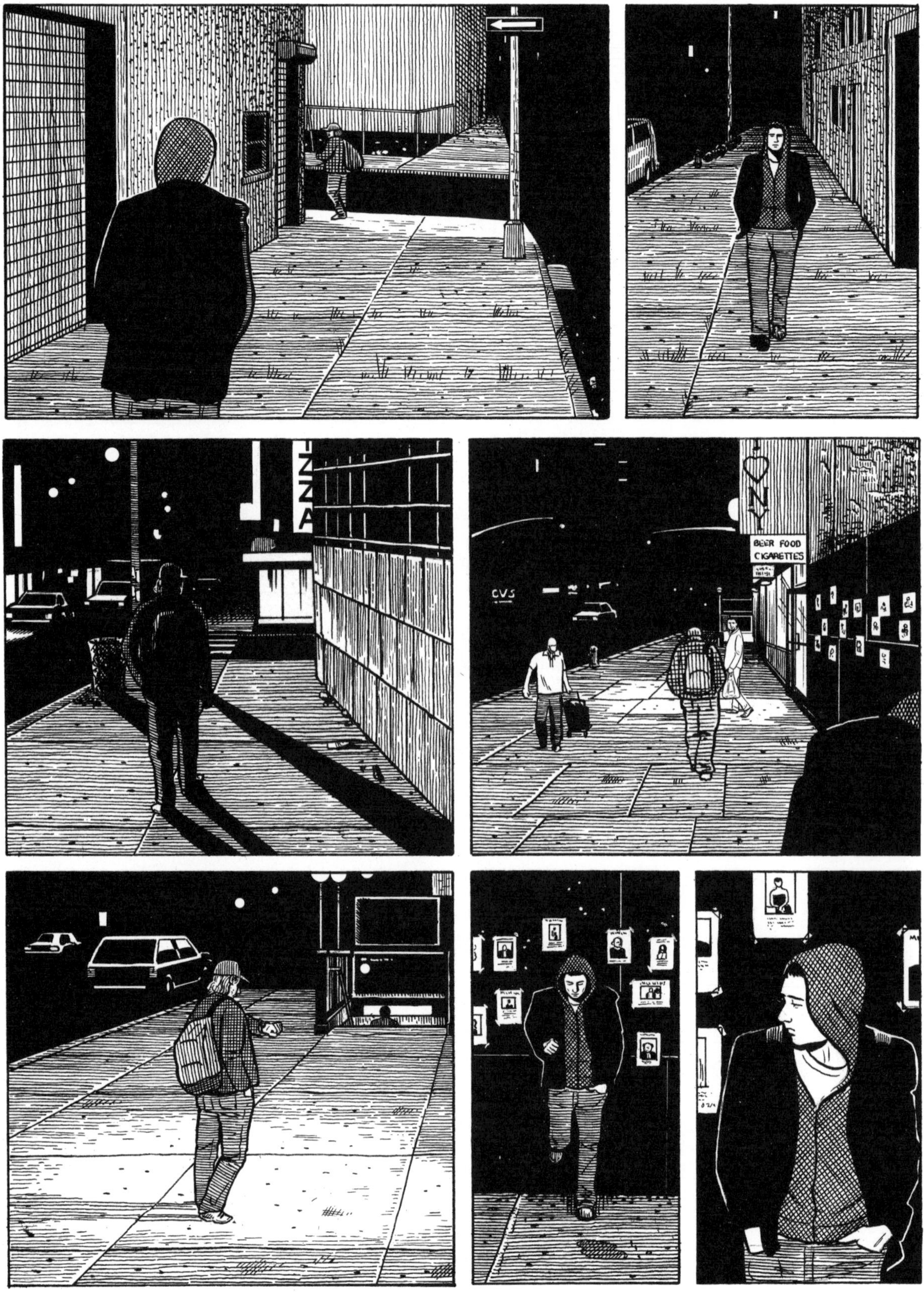
BEER FOOD
CIGARETTES
CVS

3 for $20.0
MISSING
RITZ DINER
HELP
SEEN ME?
MISSING

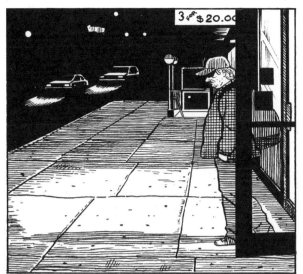

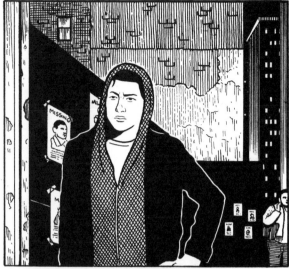

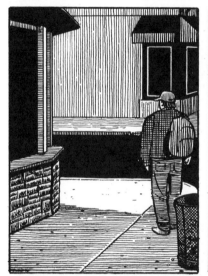

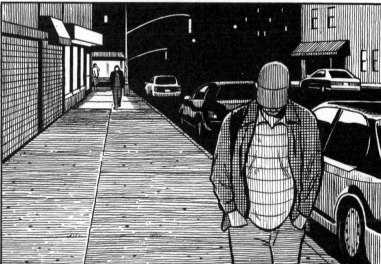

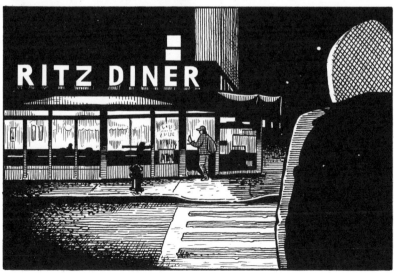

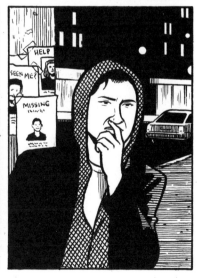

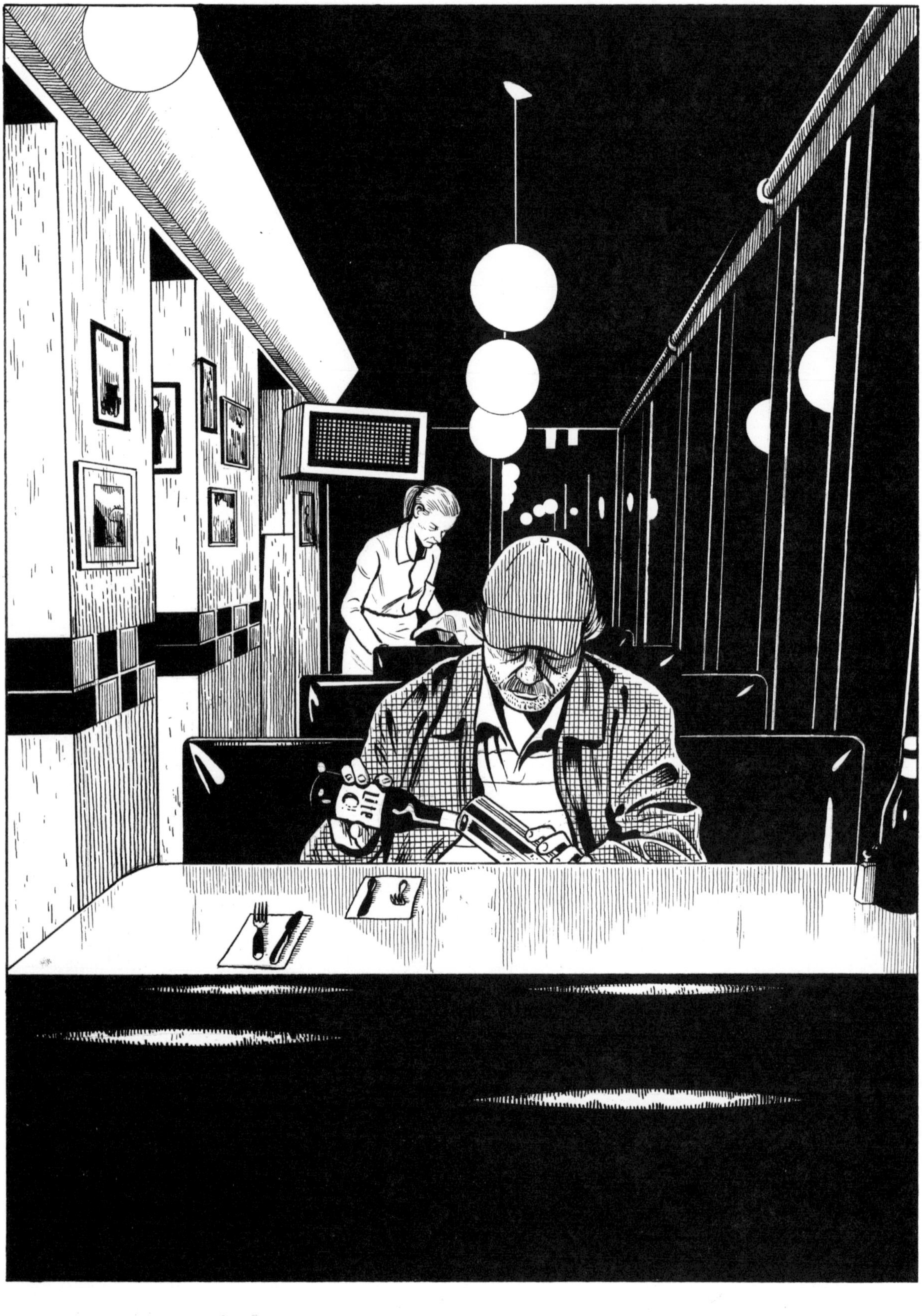

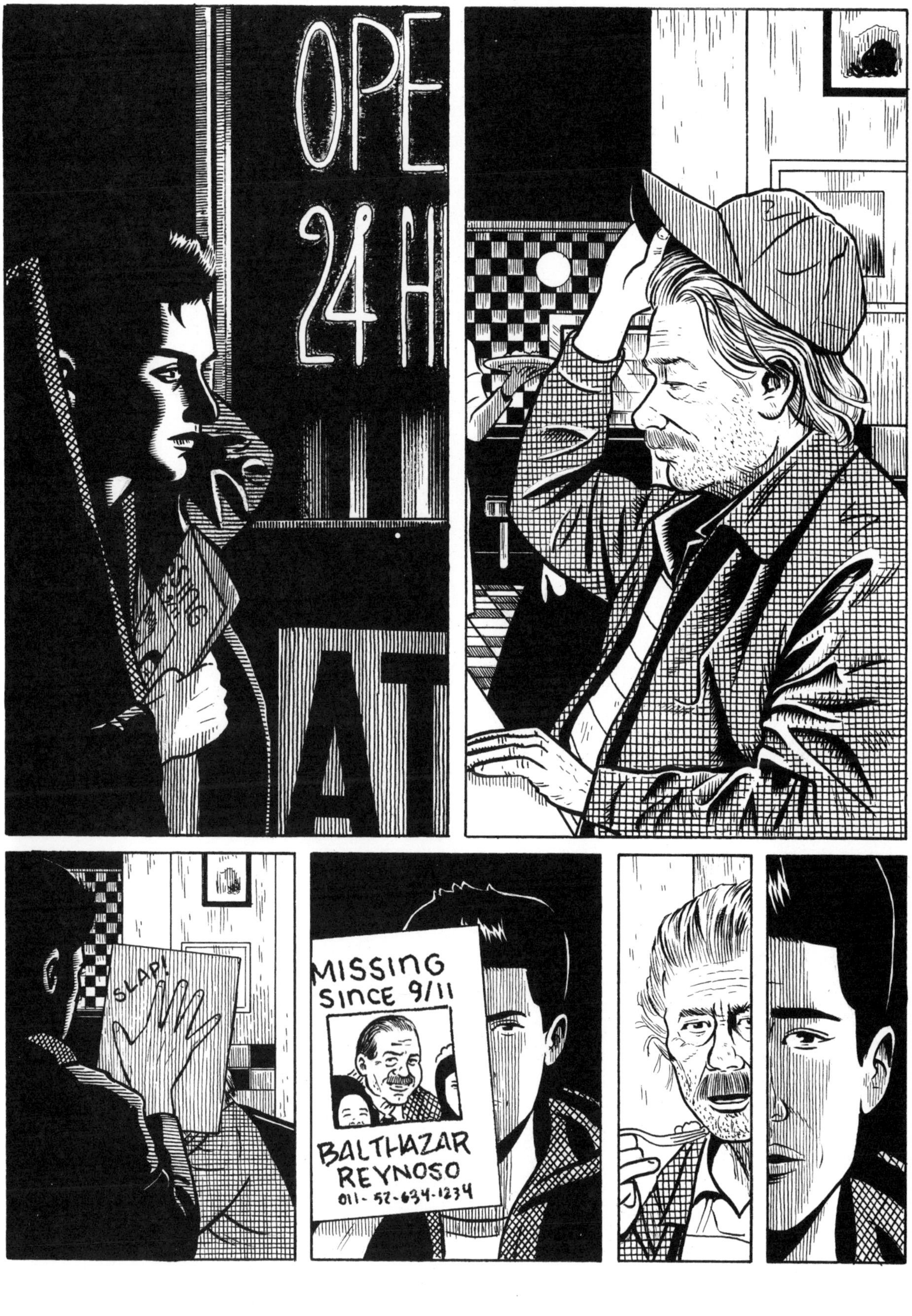
OPE
24 H
AT
SLAP!
MISSING
SINCE 9/11
BALTHAZAR
REYNOSO
011-52-634-1234

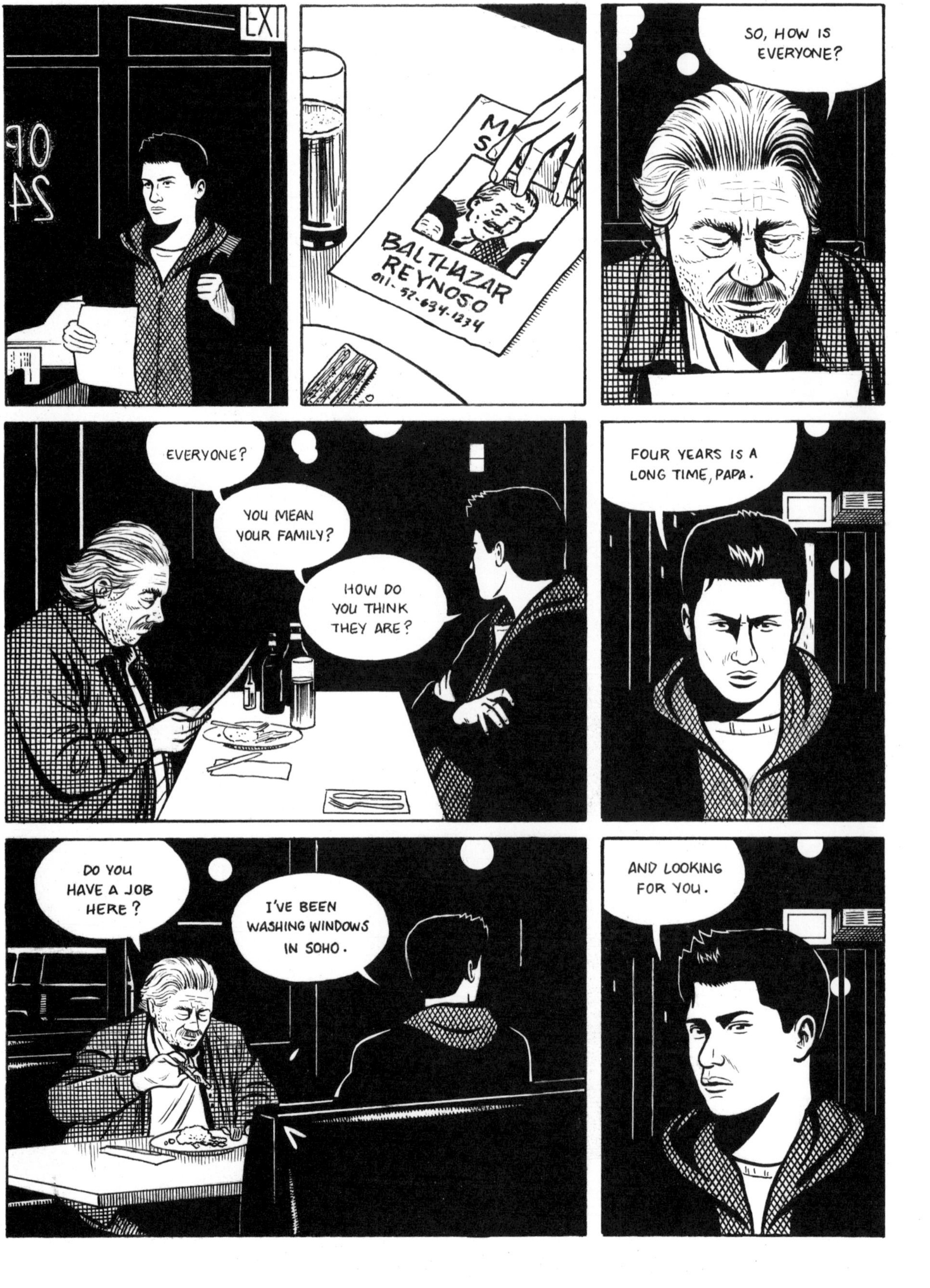
EXIT
BALTHAZAR REYNOSO
011-52-634-1234
SO, HOW IS EVERYONE?
EVERYONE?
YOU MEAN YOUR FAMILY?
HOW DO YOU THINK THEY ARE?
FOUR YEARS IS A LONG TIME, PAPA.
DO YOU HAVE A JOB HERE?
I'VE BEEN WASHING WINDOWS IN SOHO.
AND LOOKING FOR YOU.

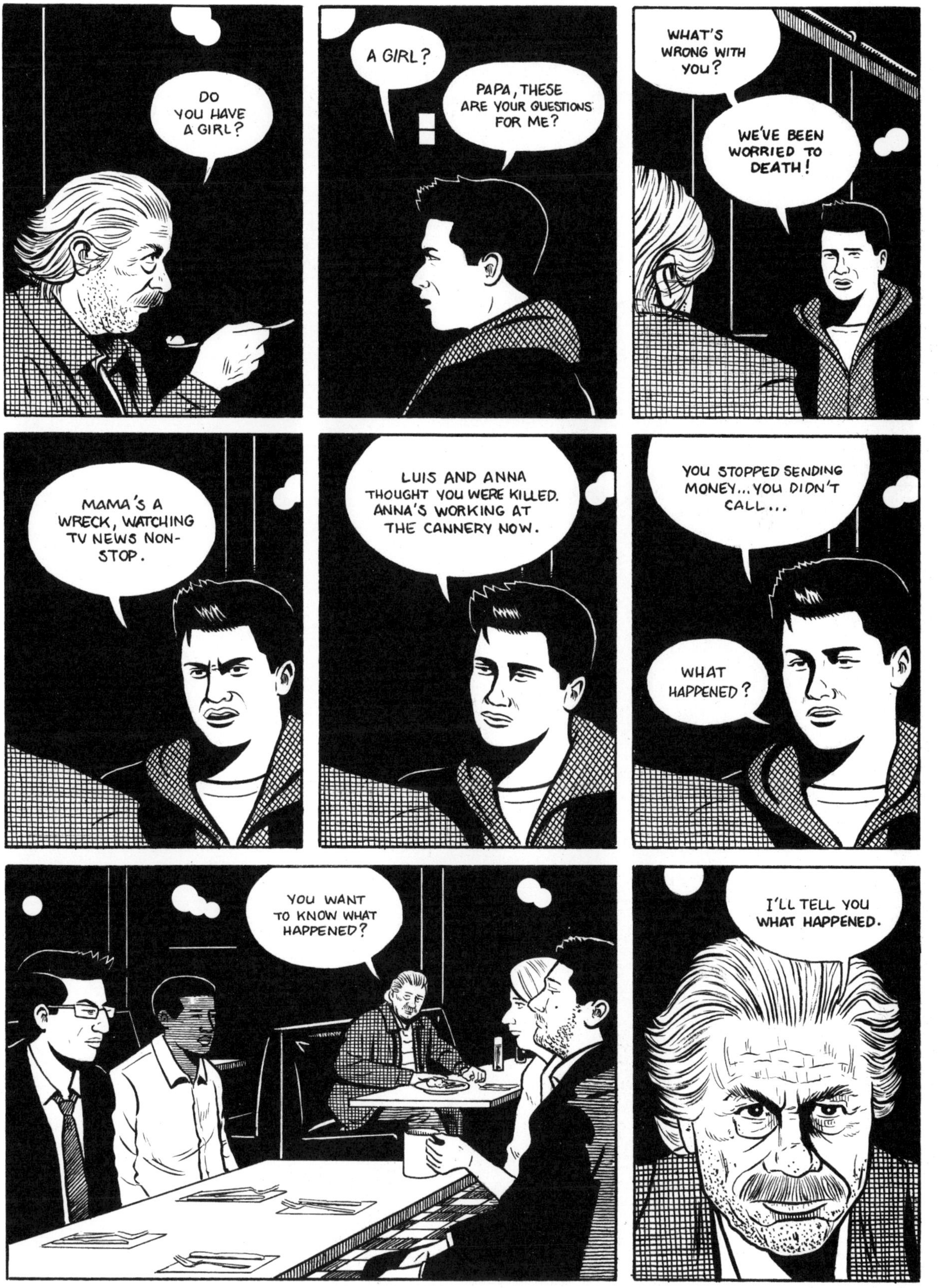
DO YOU HAVE A GIRL?
A GIRL?
PAPA, THESE ARE YOUR QUESTIONS FOR ME?
WHAT'S WRONG WITH YOU?
WE'VE BEEN WORRIED TO DEATH!
MAMA'S A WRECK, WATCHING TV NEWS NON-STOP.
LUIS AND ANNA THOUGHT YOU WERE KILLED. ANNA'S WORKING AT THE CANNERY NOW.
YOU STOPPED SENDING MONEY... YOU DIDN'T CALL...
WHAT HAPPENED?
YOU WANT TO KNOW WHAT HAPPENED?
I'LL TELL YOU WHAT HAPPENED.

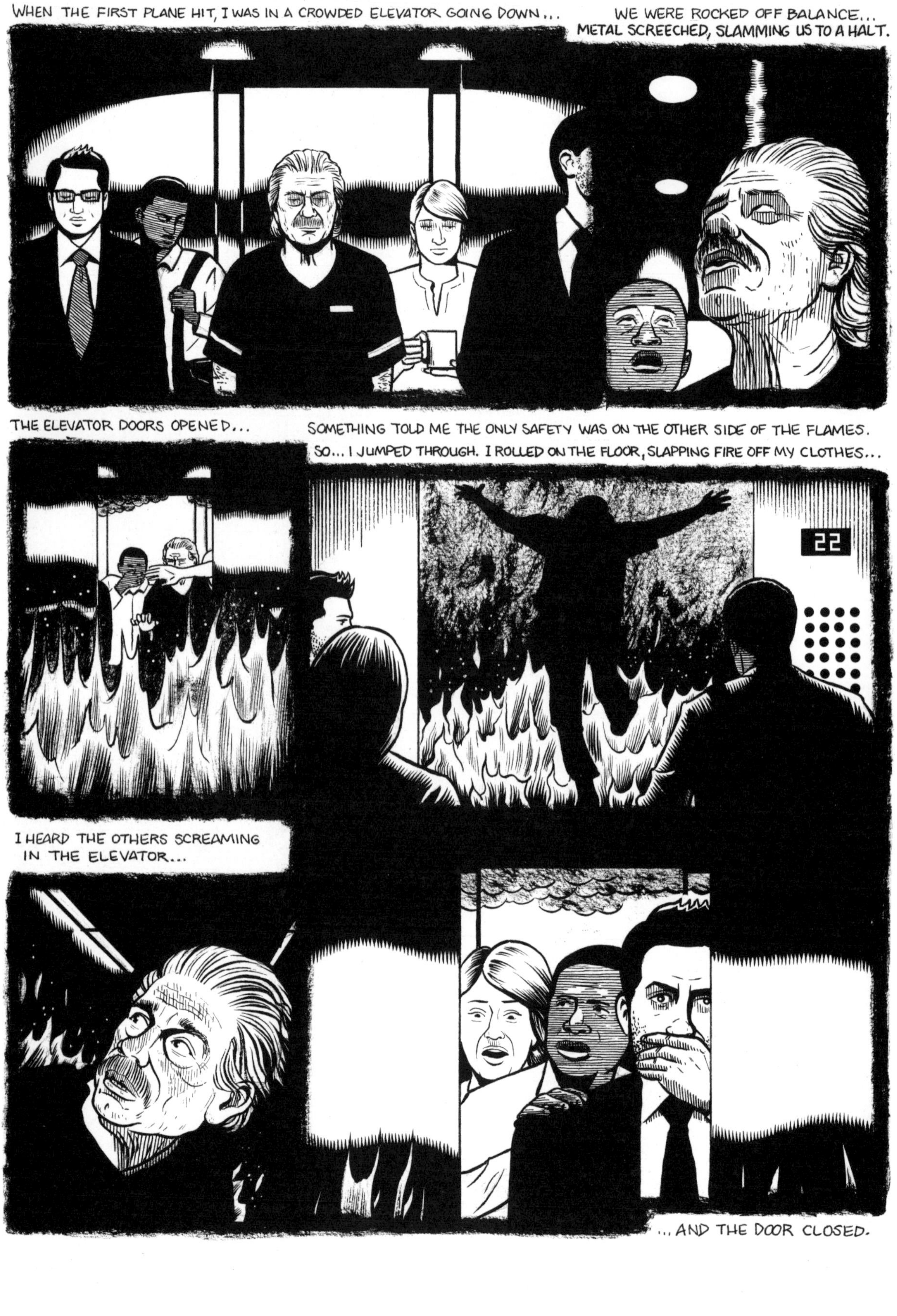
WHEN THE FIRST PLANE HIT, I WAS IN A CROWDED ELEVATOR GOING DOWN...
WE WERE ROCKED OFF BALANCE...
METAL SCREECHED, SLAMMING US TO A HALT.
THE ELEVATOR DOORS OPENED...
SOMETHING TOLD ME THE ONLY SAFETY WAS ON THE OTHER SIDE OF THE FLAMES.
SO... I JUMPED THROUGH. I ROLLED ON THE FLOOR, SLAPPING FIRE OFF MY CLOTHES...
22
I HEARD THE OTHERS SCREAMING IN THE ELEVATOR...
...AND THE DOOR CLOSED.

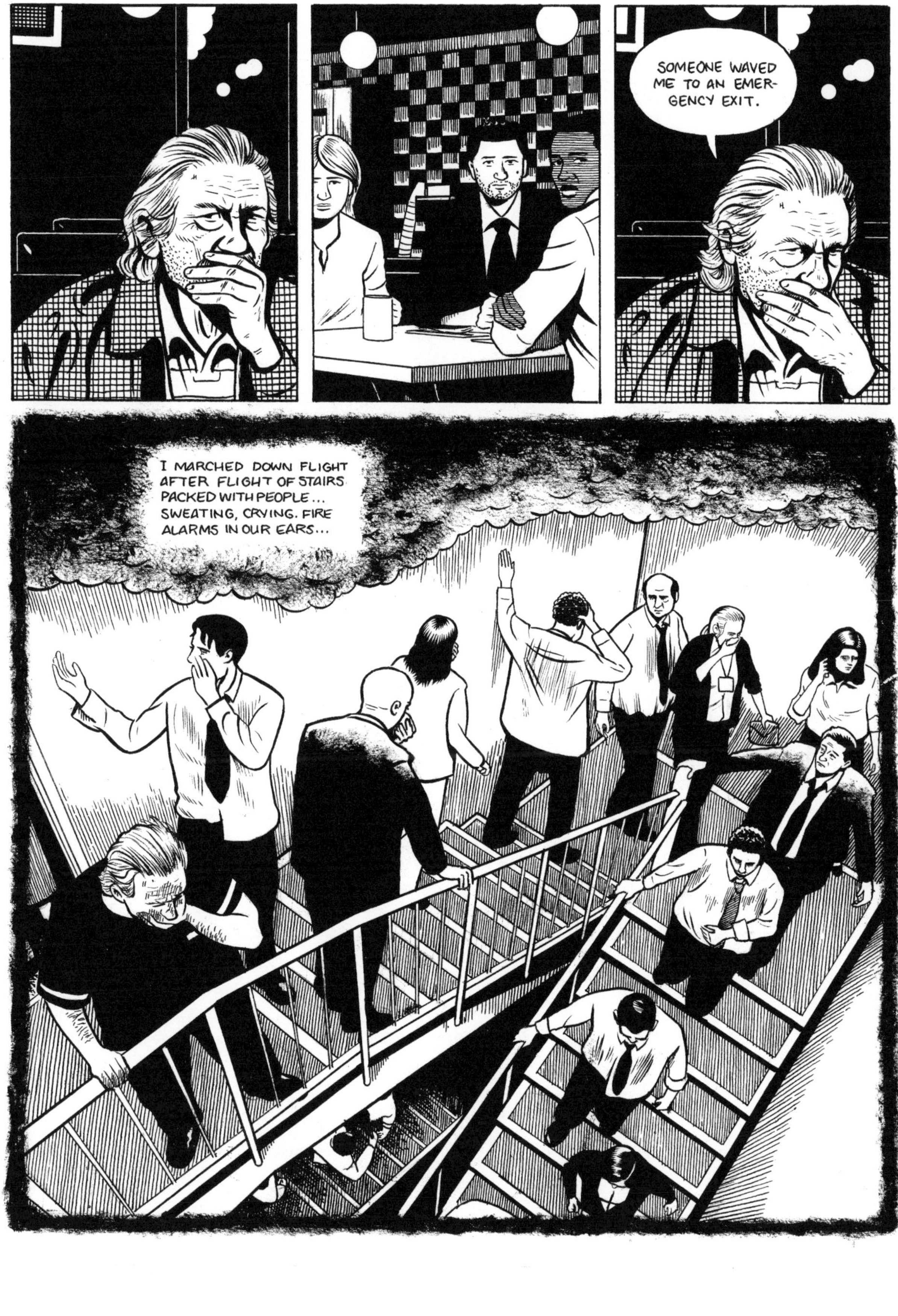
SOMEONE WAVED ME TO AN EMERGENCY EXIT.
I MARCHED DOWN FLIGHT AFTER FLIGHT OF STAIRS PACKED WITH PEOPLE... SWEATING, CRYING. FIRE ALARMS IN OUR EARS...

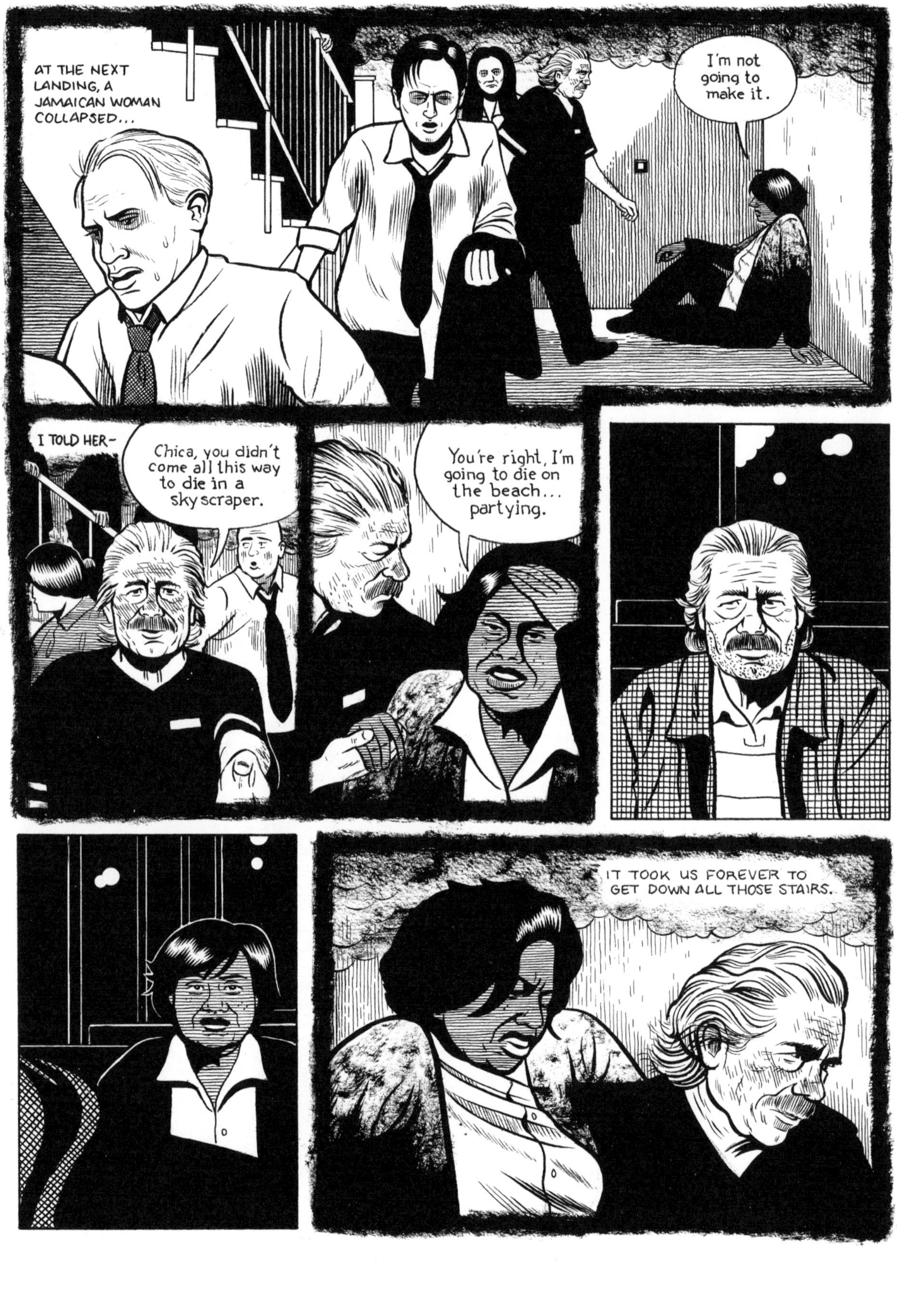
AT THE NEXT LANDING, A JAMAICAN WOMAN COLLAPSED...
I'm not going to make it.
I TOLD HER-
Chica, you didn't come all this way to die in a skyscraper.
You're right, I'm going to die on the beach... partying.
IT TOOK US FOREVER TO GET DOWN ALL THOSE STAIRS.

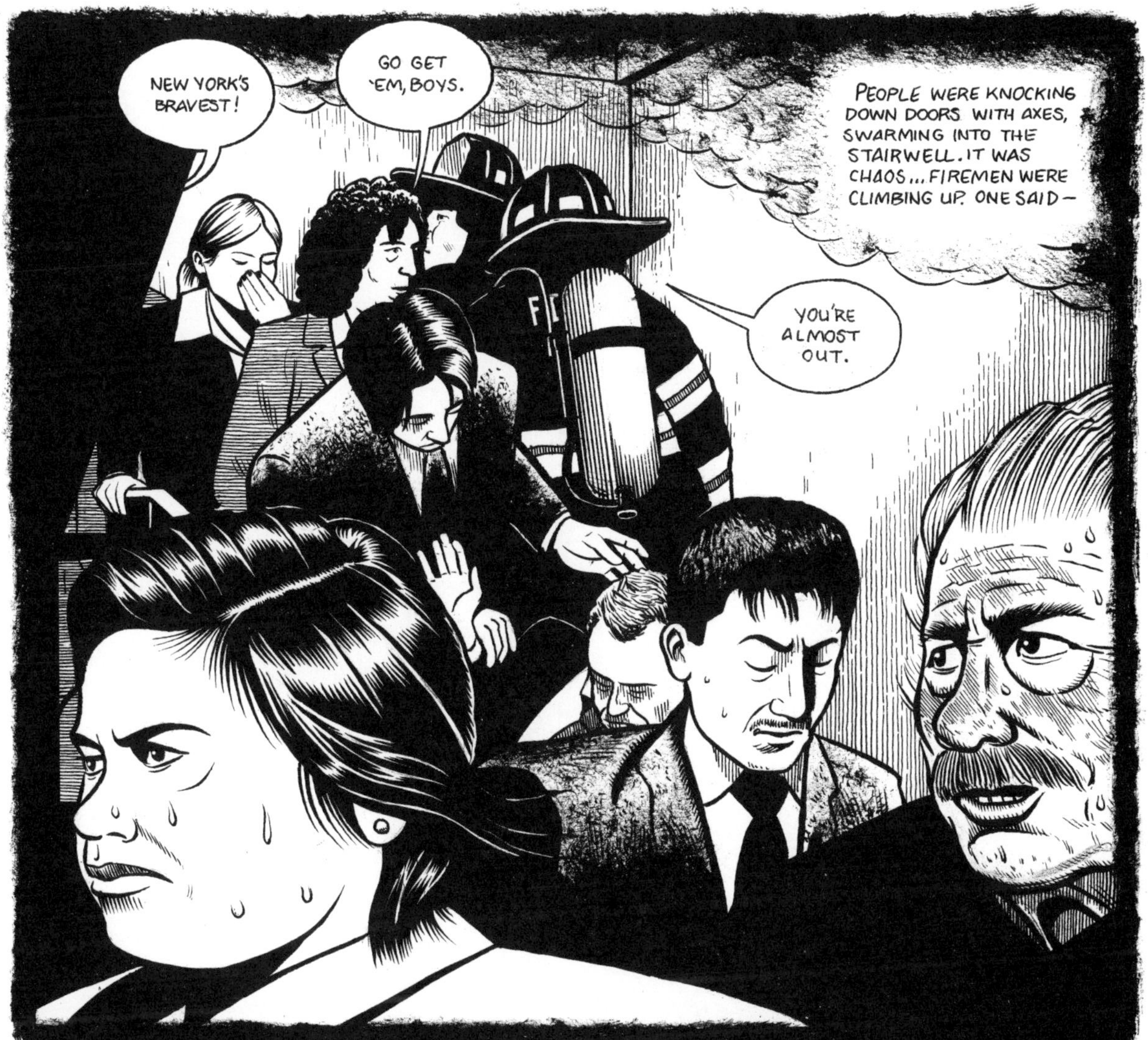
NEW YORK'S BRAVEST!
GO GET 'EM, BOYS.
PEOPLE WERE KNOCKING DOWN DOORS WITH AXES, SWARMING INTO THE STAIRWELL. IT WAS CHAOS... FIREMEN WERE CLIMBING UP. ONE SAID—
YOU'RE ALMOST OUT.
FD

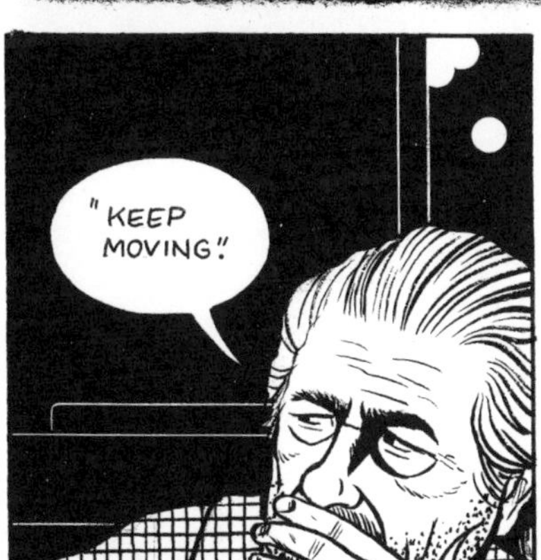
"KEEP MOVING!"

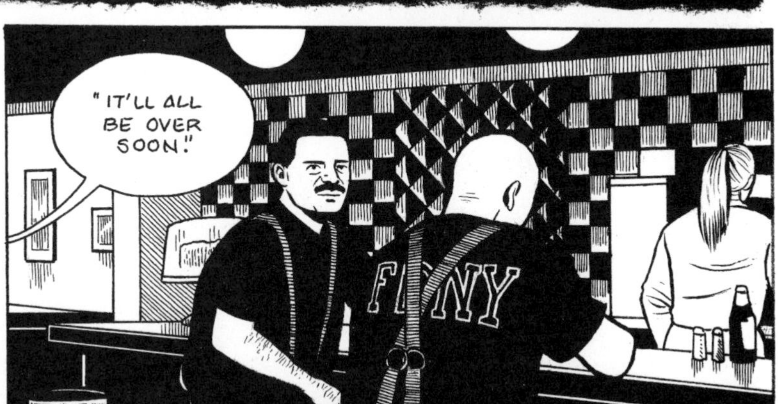
"IT'LL ALL BE OVER SOON!"
FDNY

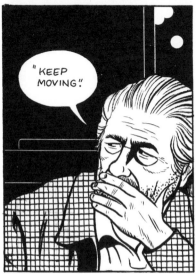

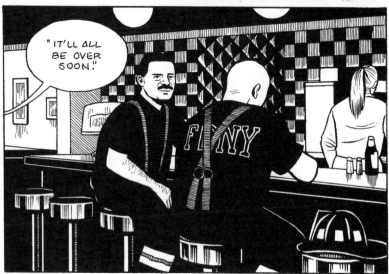

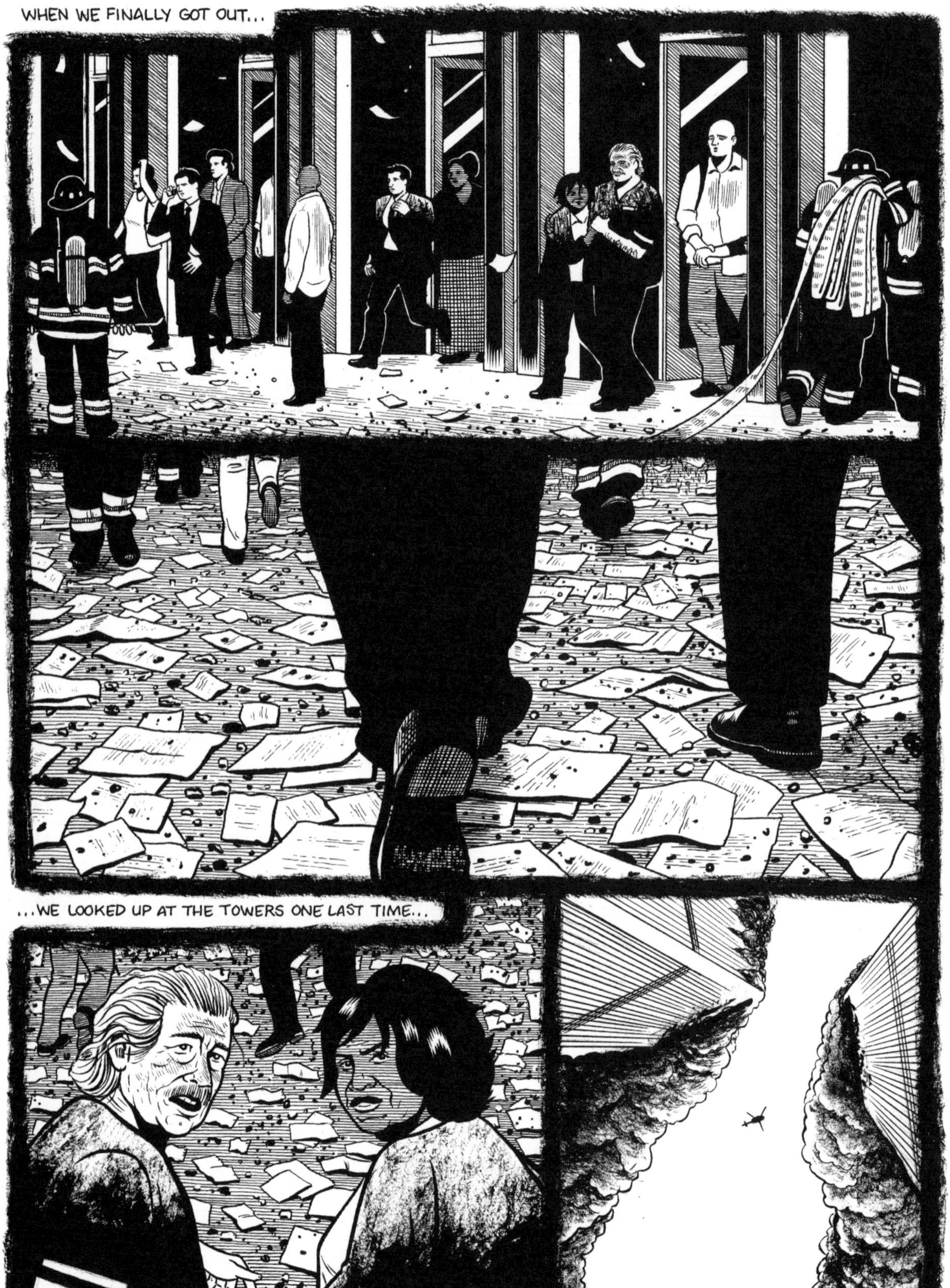
WHEN WE FINALLY GOT OUT...
...WE LOOKED UP AT THE TOWERS ONE LAST TIME...

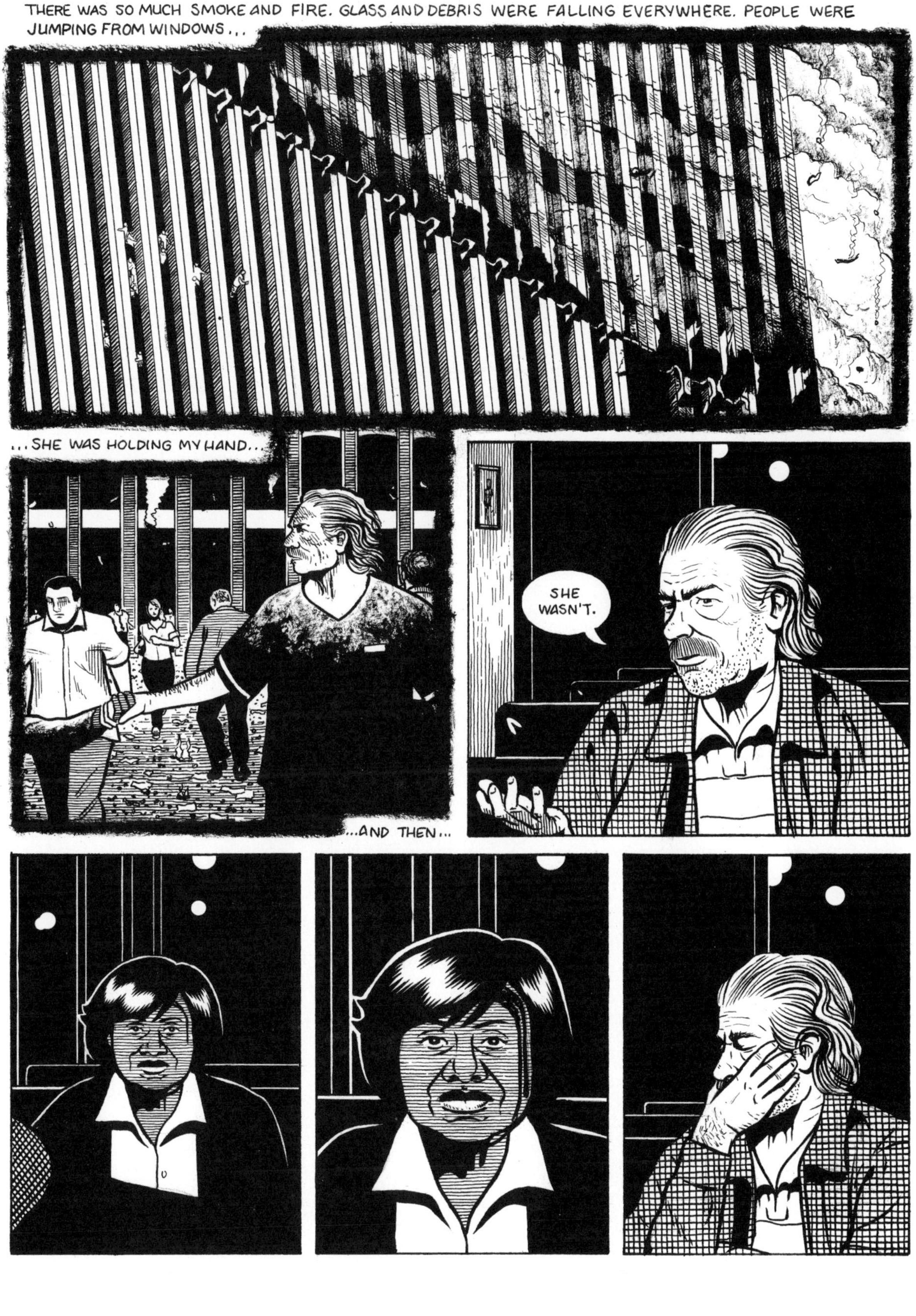
THERE WAS SO MUCH SMOKE AND FIRE. GLASS AND DEBRIS WERE FALLING EVERYWHERE. PEOPLE WERE JUMPING FROM WINDOWS...
...SHE WAS HOLDING MY HAND...
...AND THEN...
SHE WASN'T.

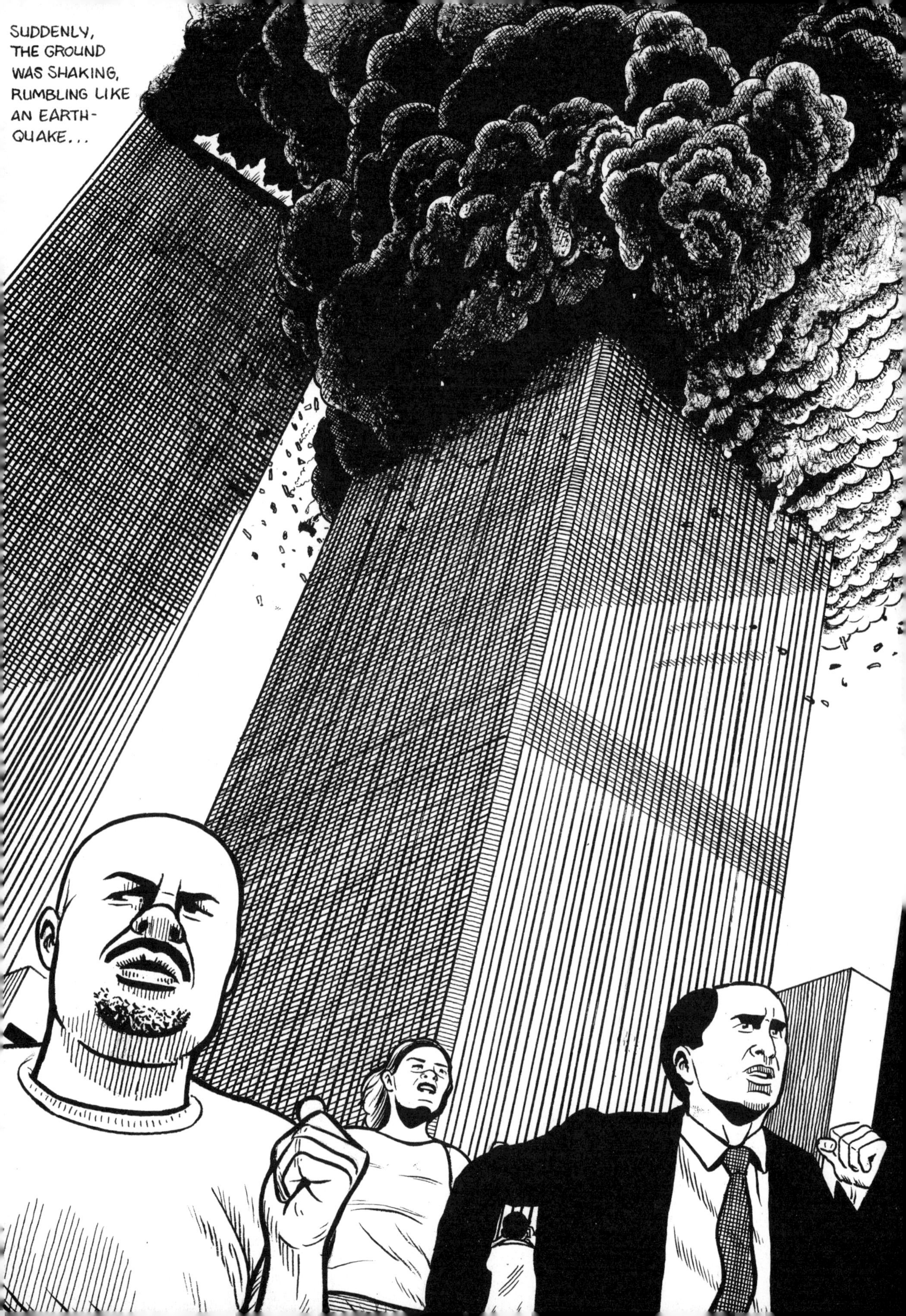
SUDDENLY, THE GROUND WAS SHAKING, RUMBLING LIKE AN EARTH-QUAKE...

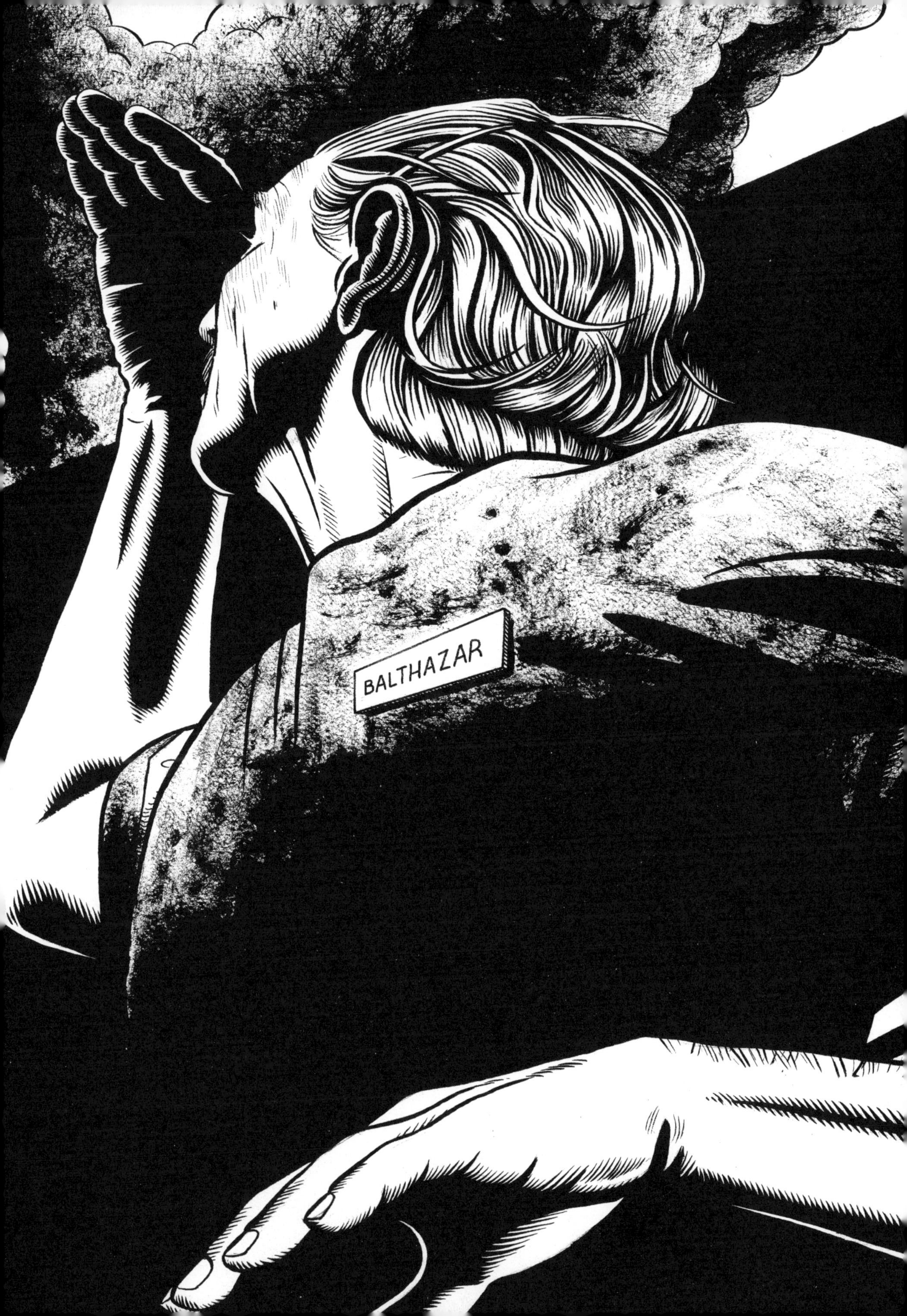
BALTHAZAR

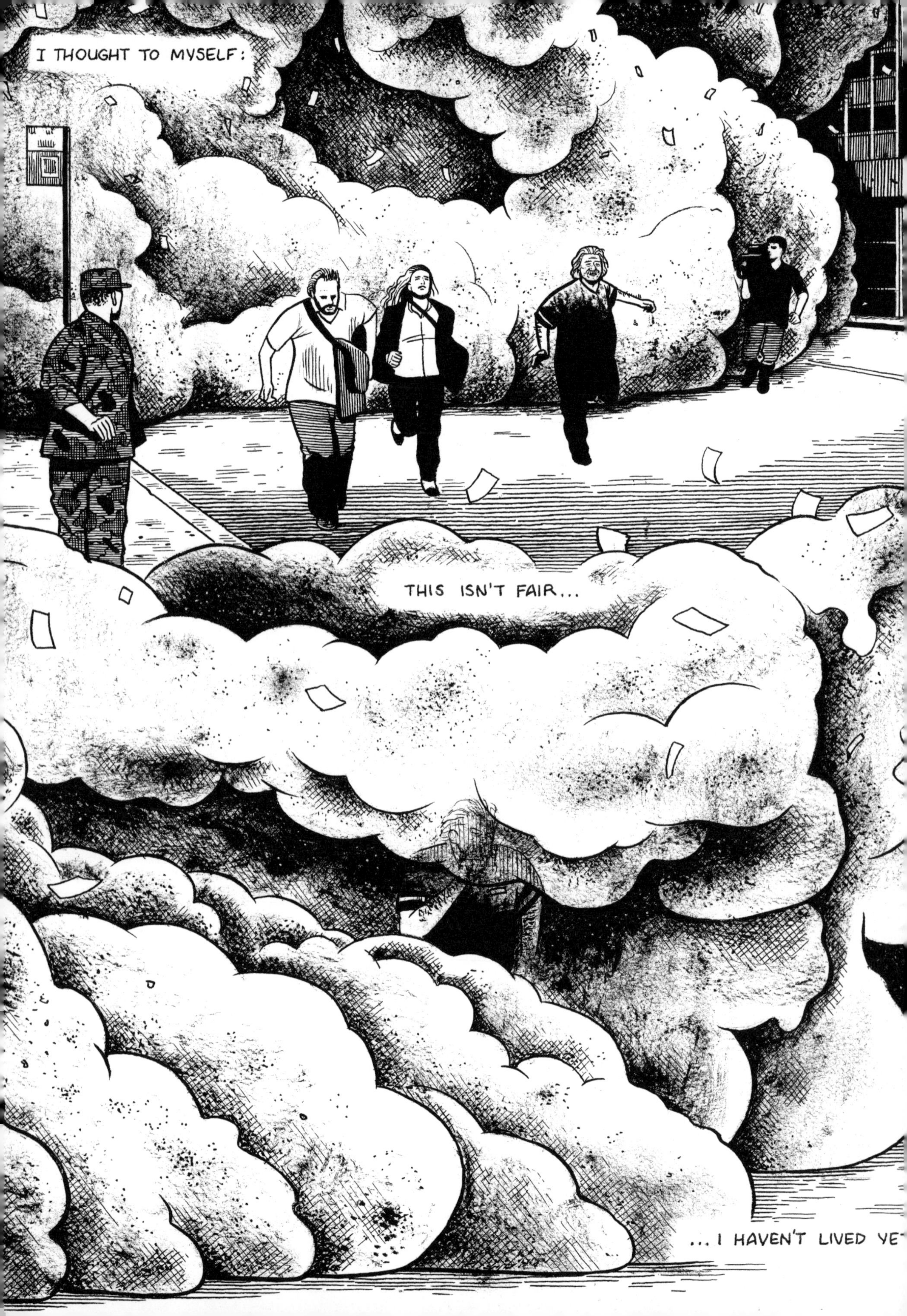
I THOUGHT TO MYSELF:
THIS ISN'T FAIR...
... I HAVEN'T LIVED YET

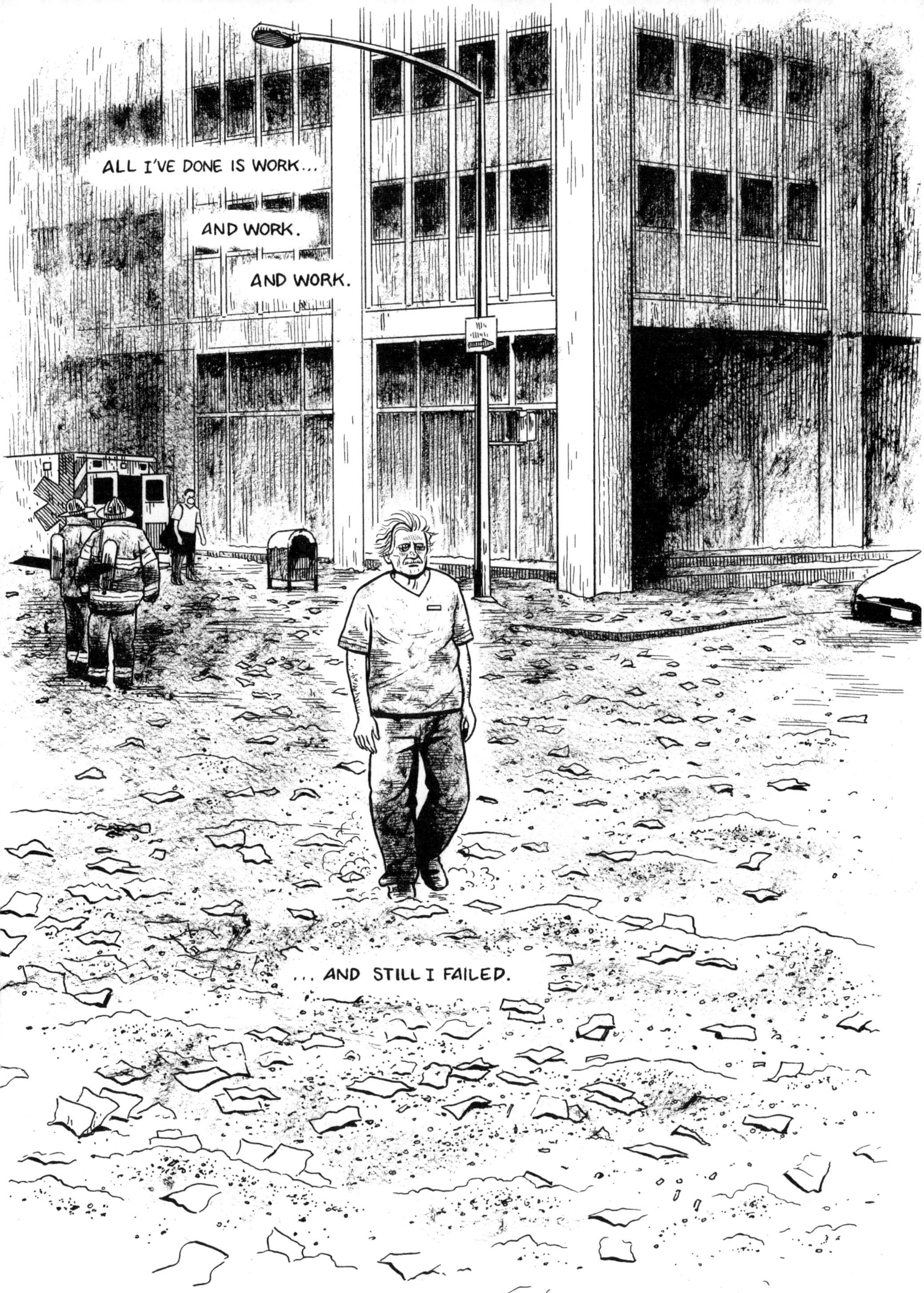
ALL I'VE DONE IS WORK...
AND WORK.
AND WORK.
... AND STILL I FAILED.

THEN I THOUGHT OF MY FAMILY. OF YOU, AND YOUR BROTHERS. MY GRAND-CHILDREN. YOUR MOTHER.

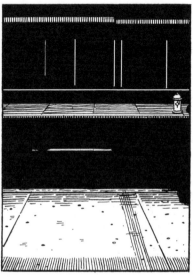

AND I REALIZED IT'S EASIER TO LEAVE IF YOU NEVER SAY GOODBYE.

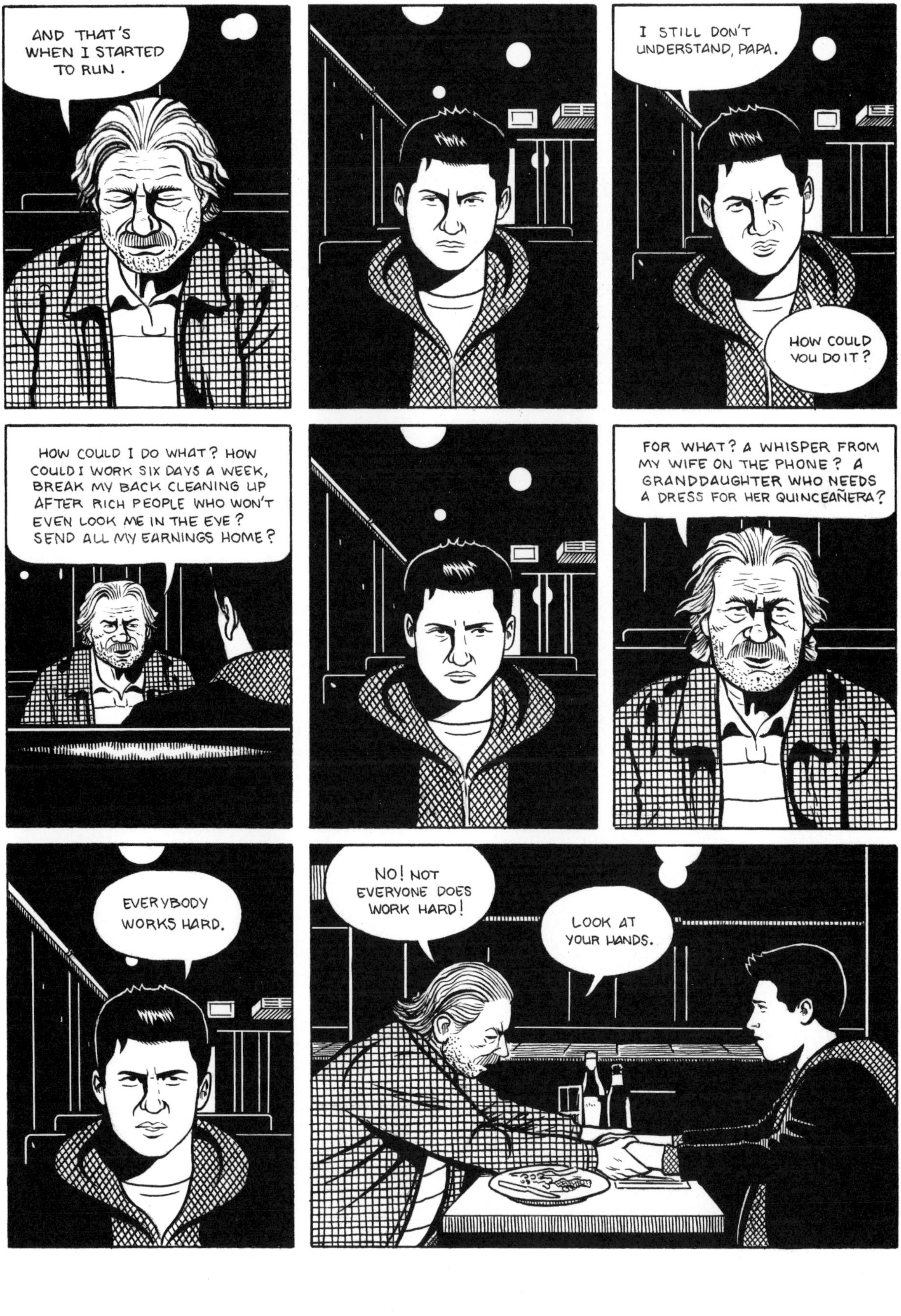
AND THAT'S WHEN I STARTED TO RUN.
I STILL DON'T UNDERSTAND, PAPA.
HOW COULD YOU DO IT?
HOW COULD I DO WHAT? HOW COULD I WORK SIX DAYS A WEEK, BREAK MY BACK CLEANING UP AFTER RICH PEOPLE WHO WON'T EVEN LOOK ME IN THE EYE? SEND ALL MY EARNINGS HOME?
FOR WHAT? A WHISPER FROM MY WIFE ON THE PHONE? A GRANDDAUGHTER WHO NEEDS A DRESS FOR HER QUINCEAÑERA?
EVERYBODY WORKS HARD.
NO! NOT EVERYONE DOES WORK HARD!
LOOK AT YOUR HANDS.

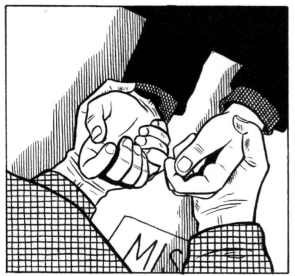

LOOK AT MINE.

SHRIMP, SHRIMP, SHRIMP. LOAD, UNLOAD, LOAD. CARRY, CARRY, CARRY. CRATES, NETS, HOSES, CRAP. HOW HARD HAVE YOU HAD TO WORK? MY SON, THE READER!

I WORK!

I WORKED SO YOU COULD GO TO COLLEGE, HAVE A BETTER LIFE.

SO TELL ME ABOUT YOUR WORK. AT YOUR HOTEL. HAVE YOU EVER SCRUBBED TOILETS ALL DAY? WIPED UP SHIT AND PISS AND GOD KNOWS WHAT?

HAVE YOU TORN OUT FIBREGLASS?

YOU LEFT US, PAPA.

TINY PARTICLES STABBING AT YOUR THROAT?

AND THEY WON'T GIVE YOU A MASK BECAUSE IF YOU'RE NOT AMERICAN, THEY THINK YOU'RE LESS THAN HUMAN!

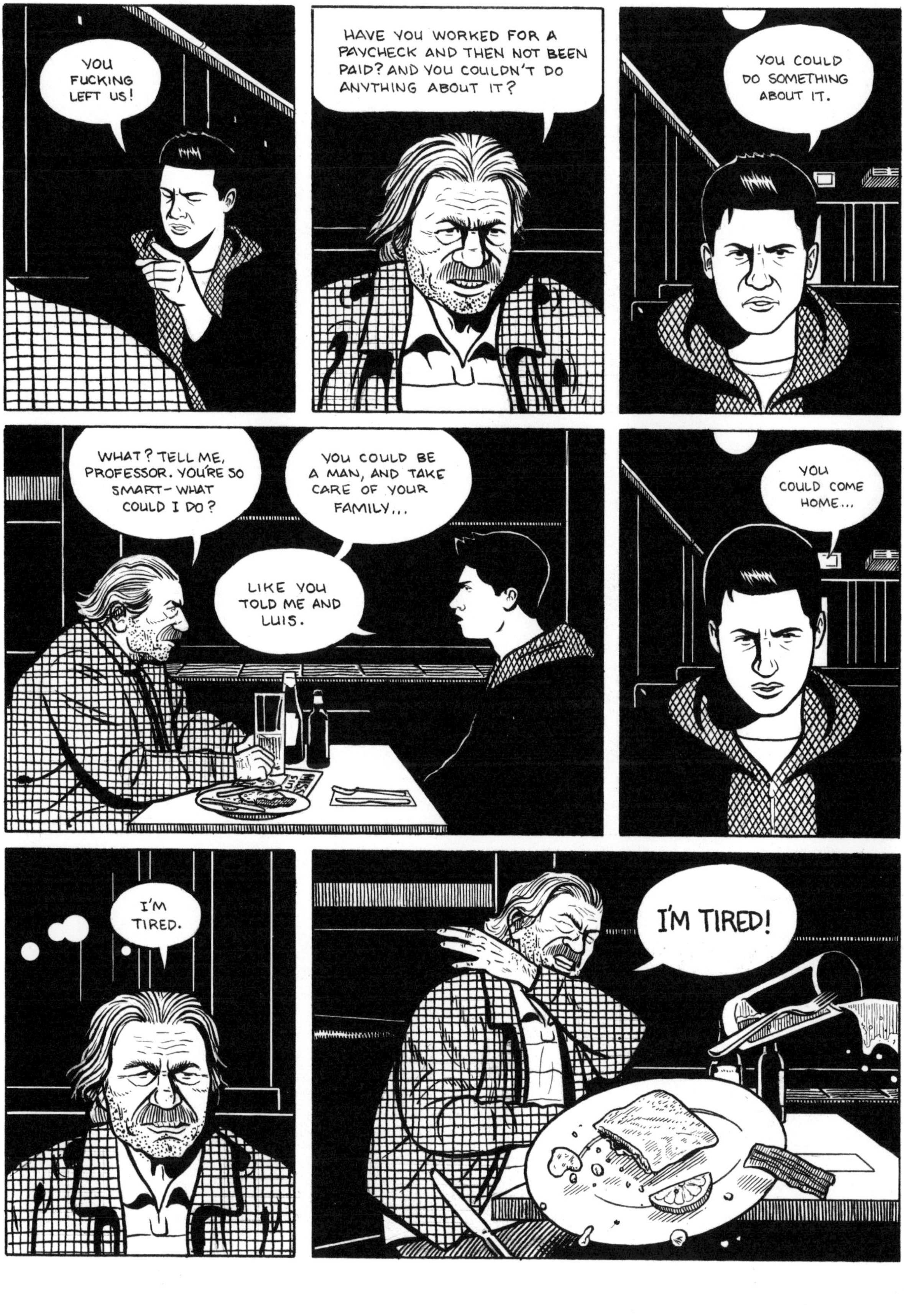
YOU FUCKING LEFT US!
HAVE YOU WORKED FOR A PAYCHECK AND THEN NOT BEEN PAID? AND YOU COULDN'T DO ANYTHING ABOUT IT?
YOU COULD DO SOMETHING ABOUT IT.
WHAT? TELL ME, PROFESSOR. YOU'RE SO SMART- WHAT COULD I DO?
YOU COULD BE A MAN, AND TAKE CARE OF YOUR FAMILY...
LIKE YOU TOLD ME AND LUIS.
YOU COULD COME HOME...
I'M TIRED.
I'M TIRED!

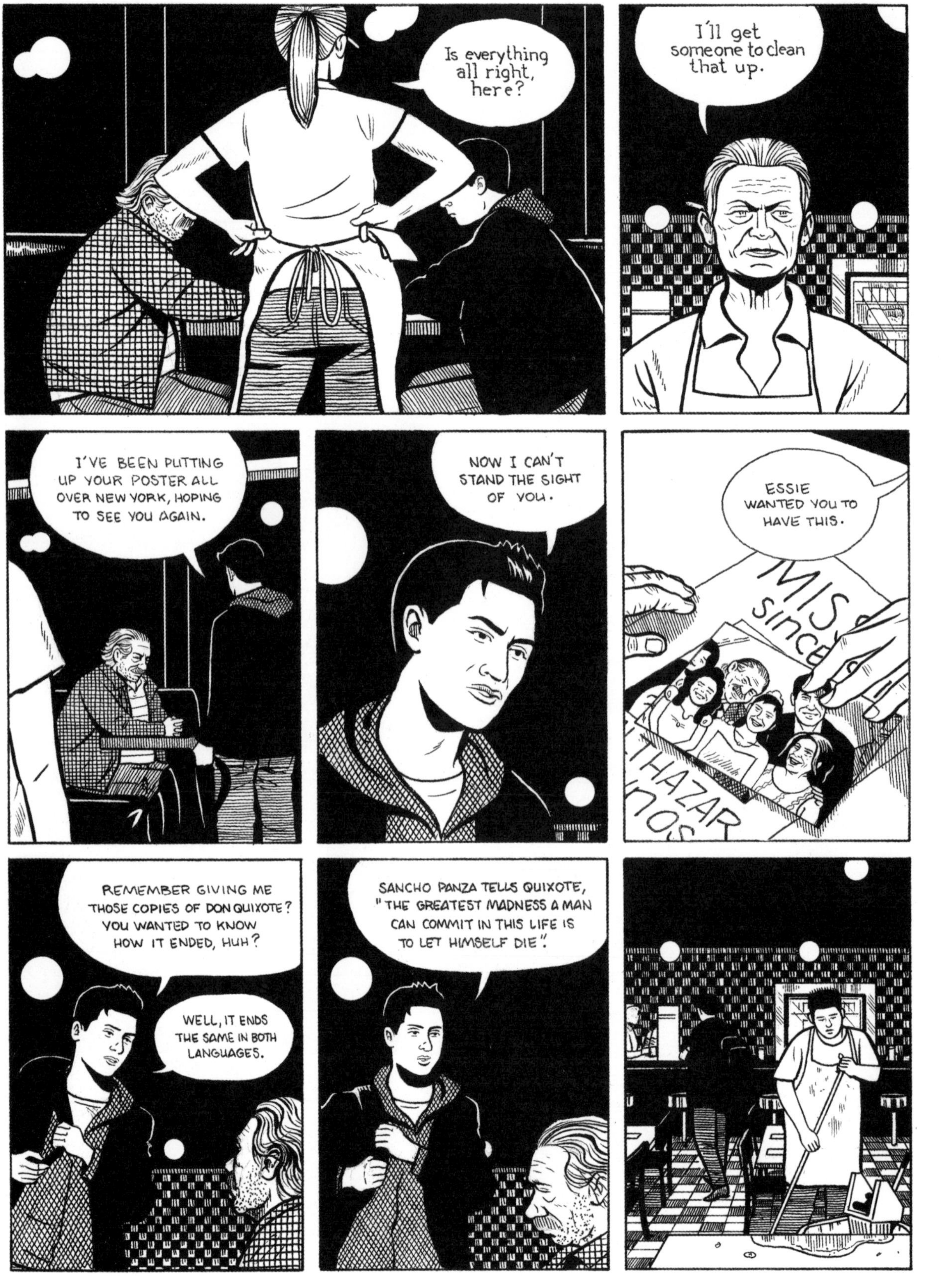
Is everything all right, here?
I'll get someone to clean that up.
I'VE BEEN PUTTING UP YOUR POSTER ALL OVER NEW YORK, HOPING TO SEE YOU AGAIN.
NOW I CAN'T STAND THE SIGHT OF YOU.
ESSIE WANTED YOU TO HAVE THIS.
REMEMBER GIVING ME THOSE COPIES OF DON QUIXOTE? YOU WANTED TO KNOW HOW IT ENDED, HUH?
WELL, IT ENDS THE SAME IN BOTH LANGUAGES.
SANCHO PANZA TELLS QUIXOTE, "THE GREATEST MADNESS A MAN CAN COMMIT IN THIS LIFE IS TO LET HIMSELF DIE".

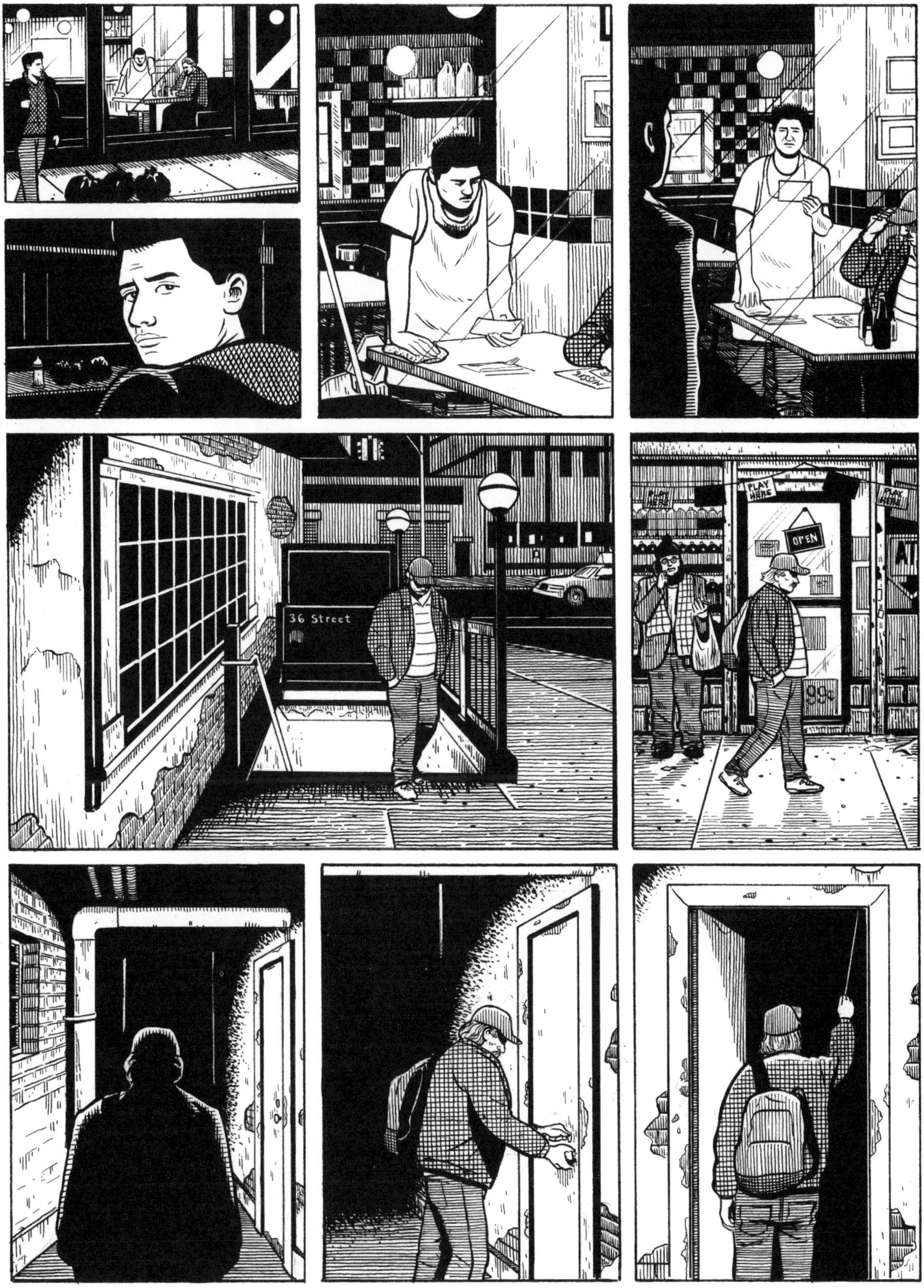
36 Street
PLAY HERE
PLAY HERE
OPEN
99¢

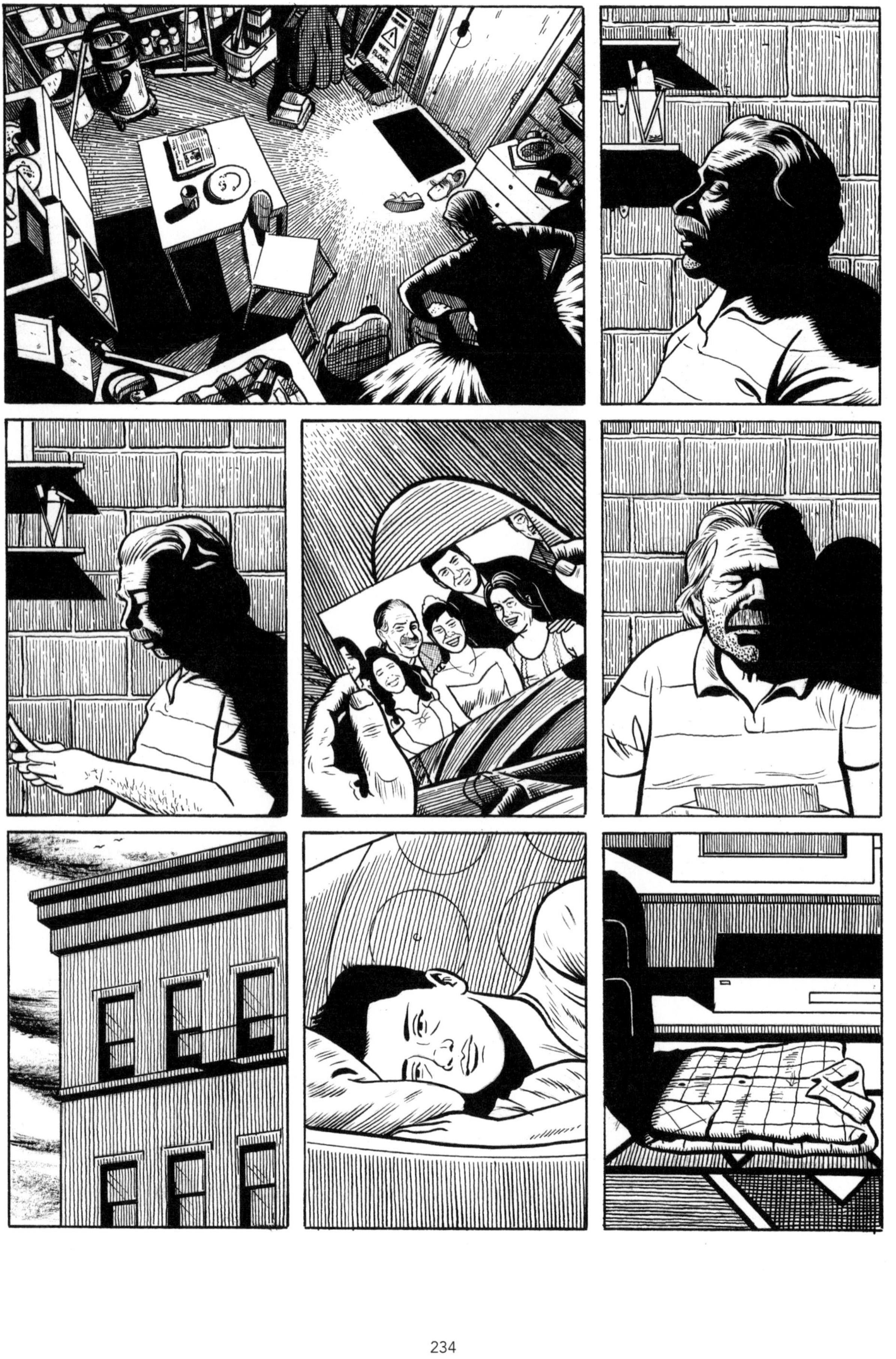
WET FLOOR

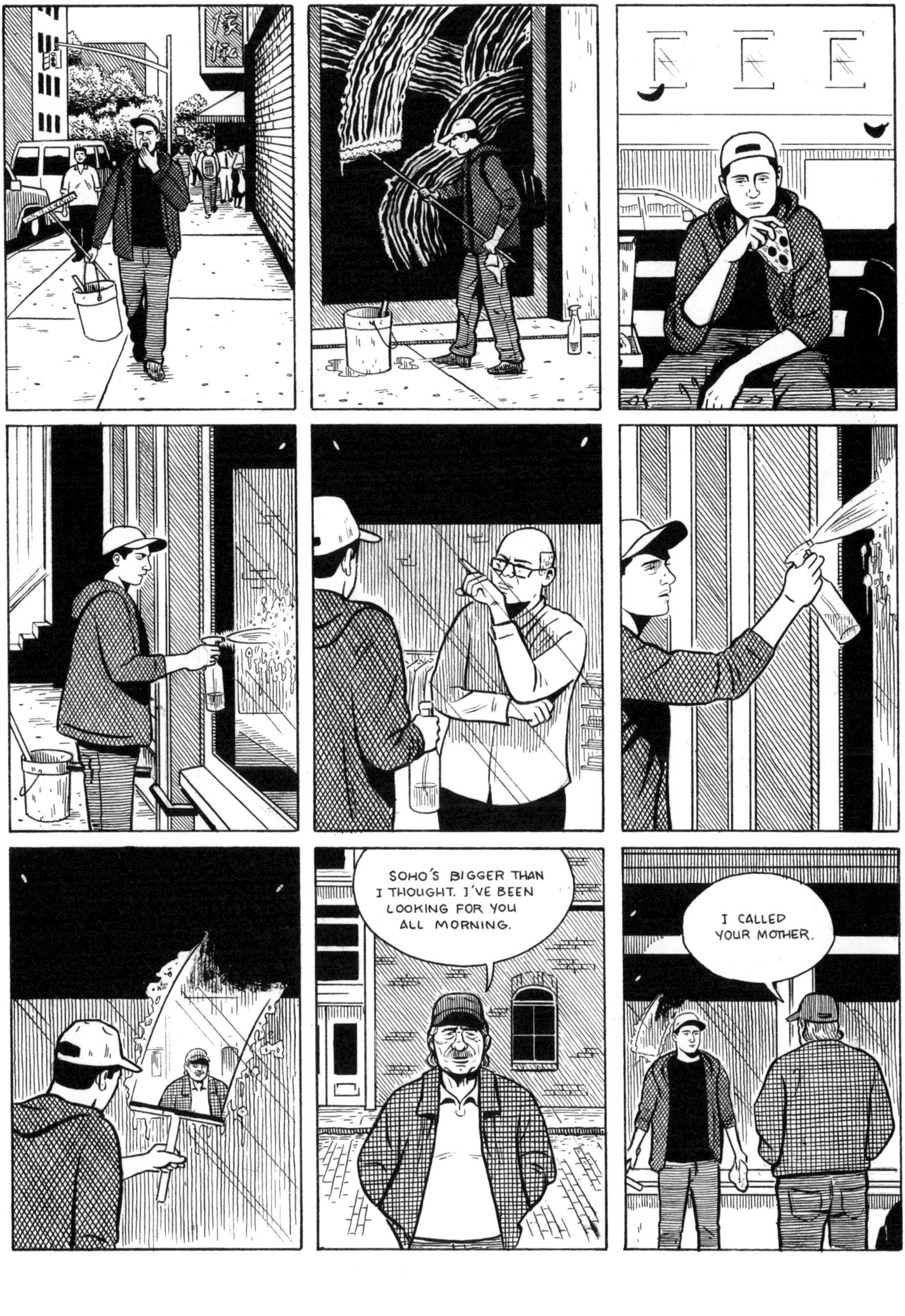
SOHO'S BIGGER THAN I THOUGHT. I'VE BEEN LOOKING FOR YOU ALL MORNING.
I CALLED YOUR MOTHER.

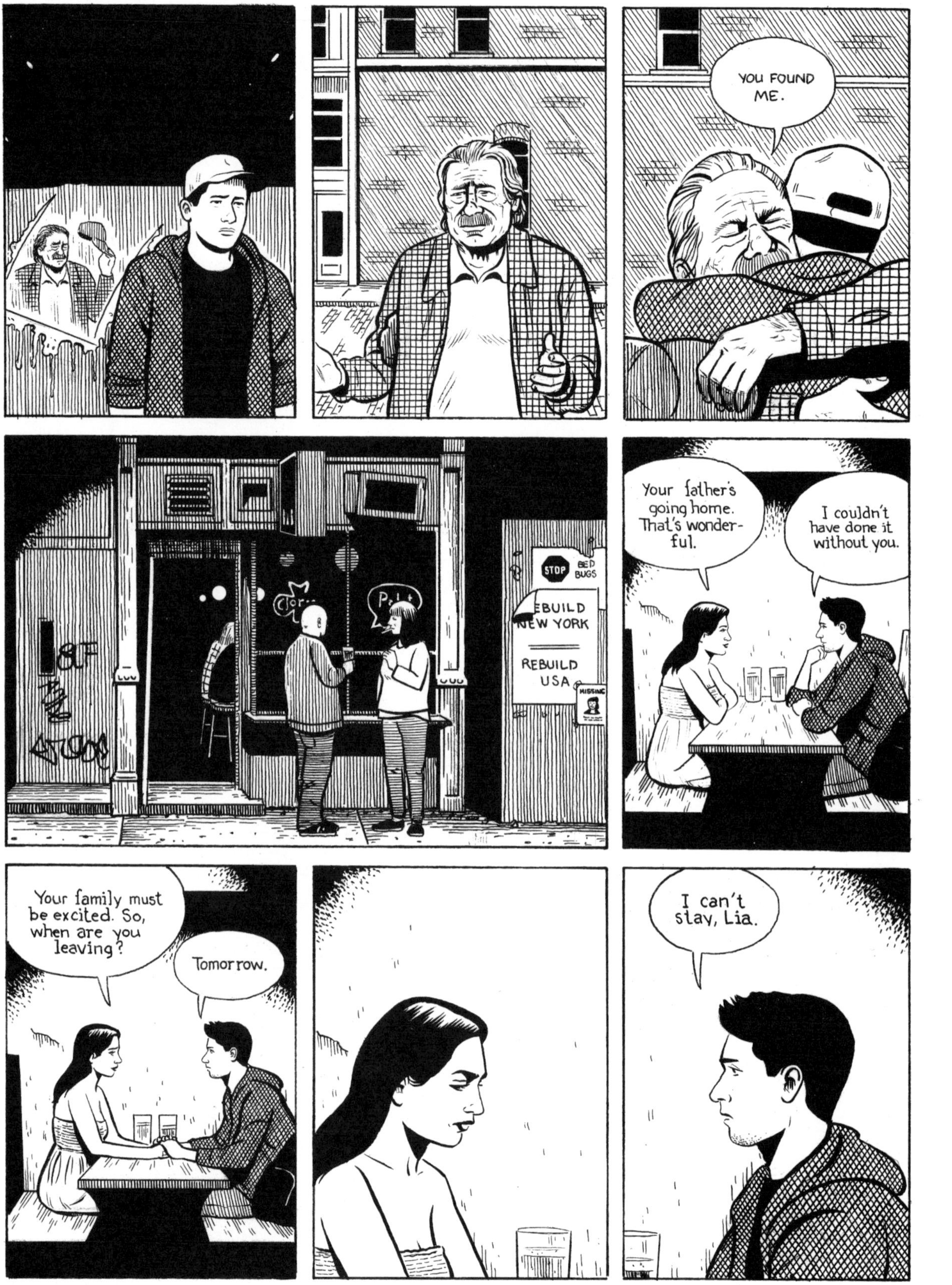
YOU FOUND ME.
STOP BED BUGS
EBUILD NEW YORK
REBUILD USA
MISSING
Your father's going home. That's wonderful.
I couldn't have done it without you.
Your family must be excited. So, when are you leaving?
Tomorrow.
I can't stay, Lia.

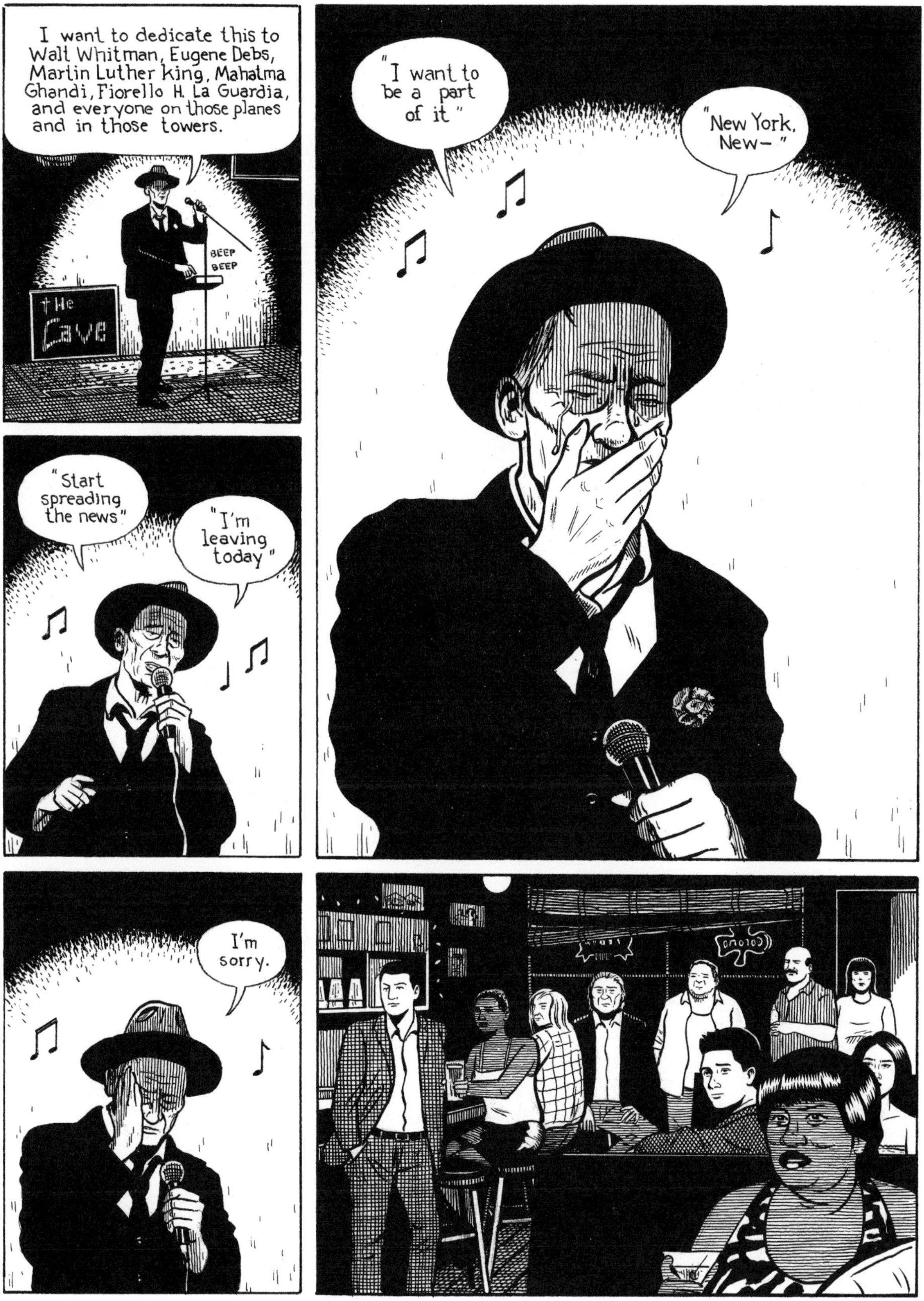
I want to dedicate this to Walt Whitman, Eugene Debs, Martin Luther king, Mahatma Ghandi, Fiorello H. La Guardia, and everyone on those planes and in those towers.
BEEP BEEP
THE CAVE
"Start spreading the news"
"I'm leaving today"
"I want to be a part of it"
"New York, New–"
I'm sorry.

"I wanna wake up in a city that doesn't sleep"
"And find I'm king of the hill"
"Top of the heap!"
"These little town blues"
"Are melting away"
"I'll make a brand new start of it, in old New York"
"If I can make it there, I'll make it anywhere It's up to you New York!"
"NEW YORK!"

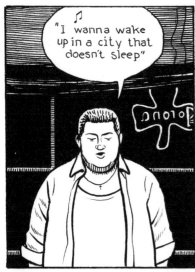

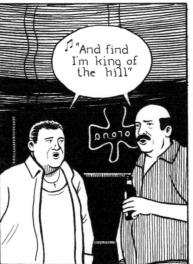

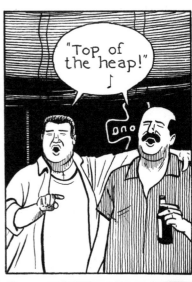

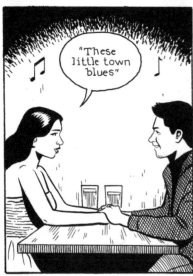

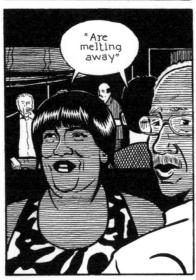

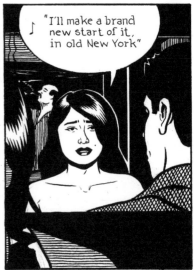

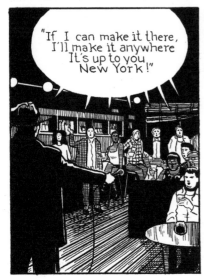

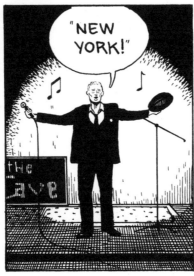

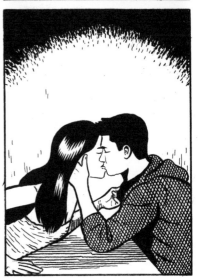

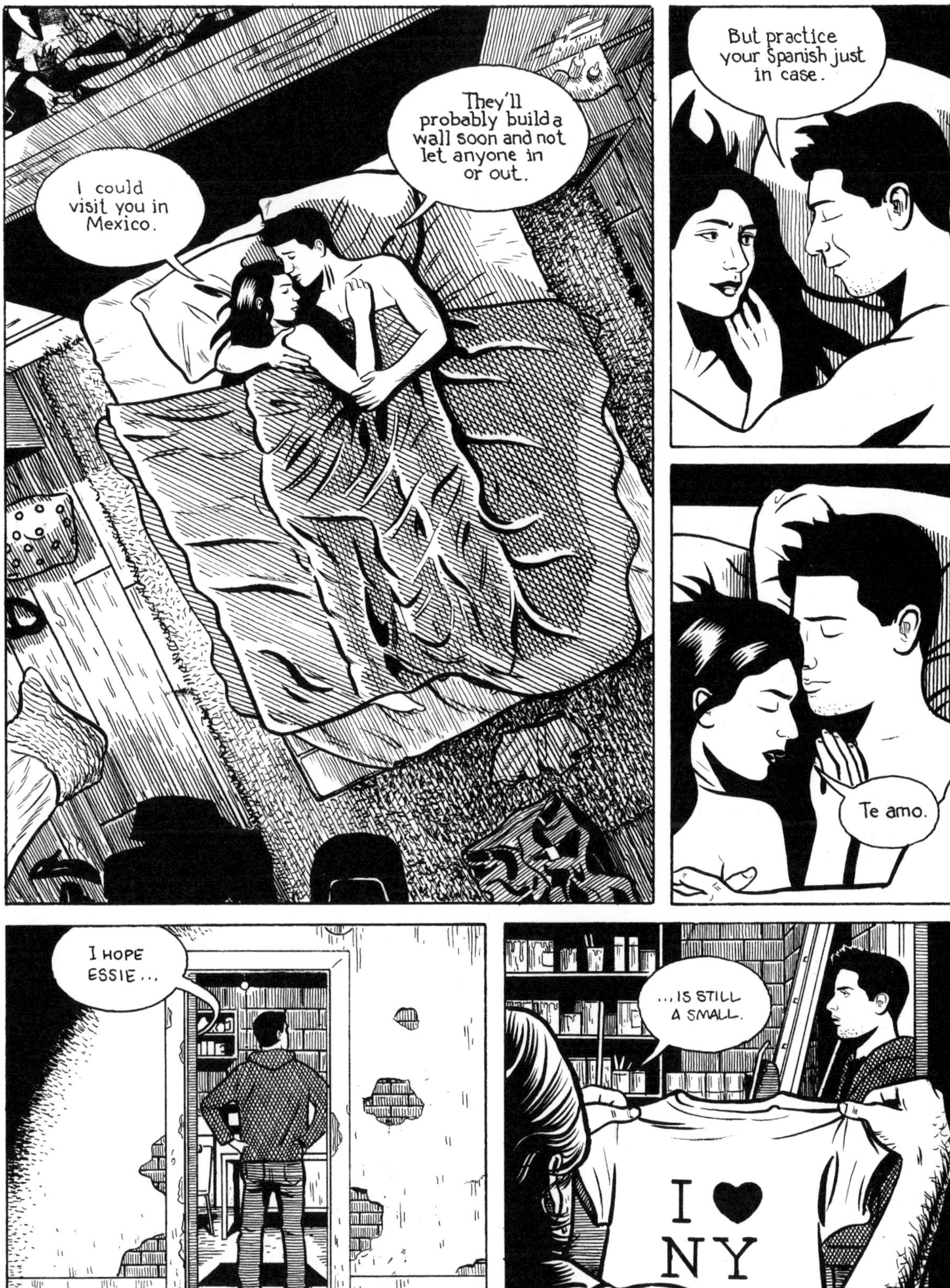
I could visit you in Mexico.
They'll probably build a wall soon and not let anyone in or out.
But practice your Spanish just in case.
Te amo.
I HOPE ESSIE...
...IS STILL A SMALL.
I ♥ NY

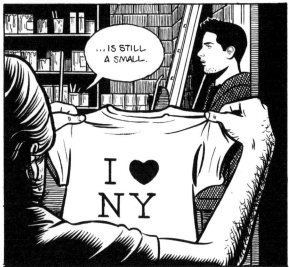

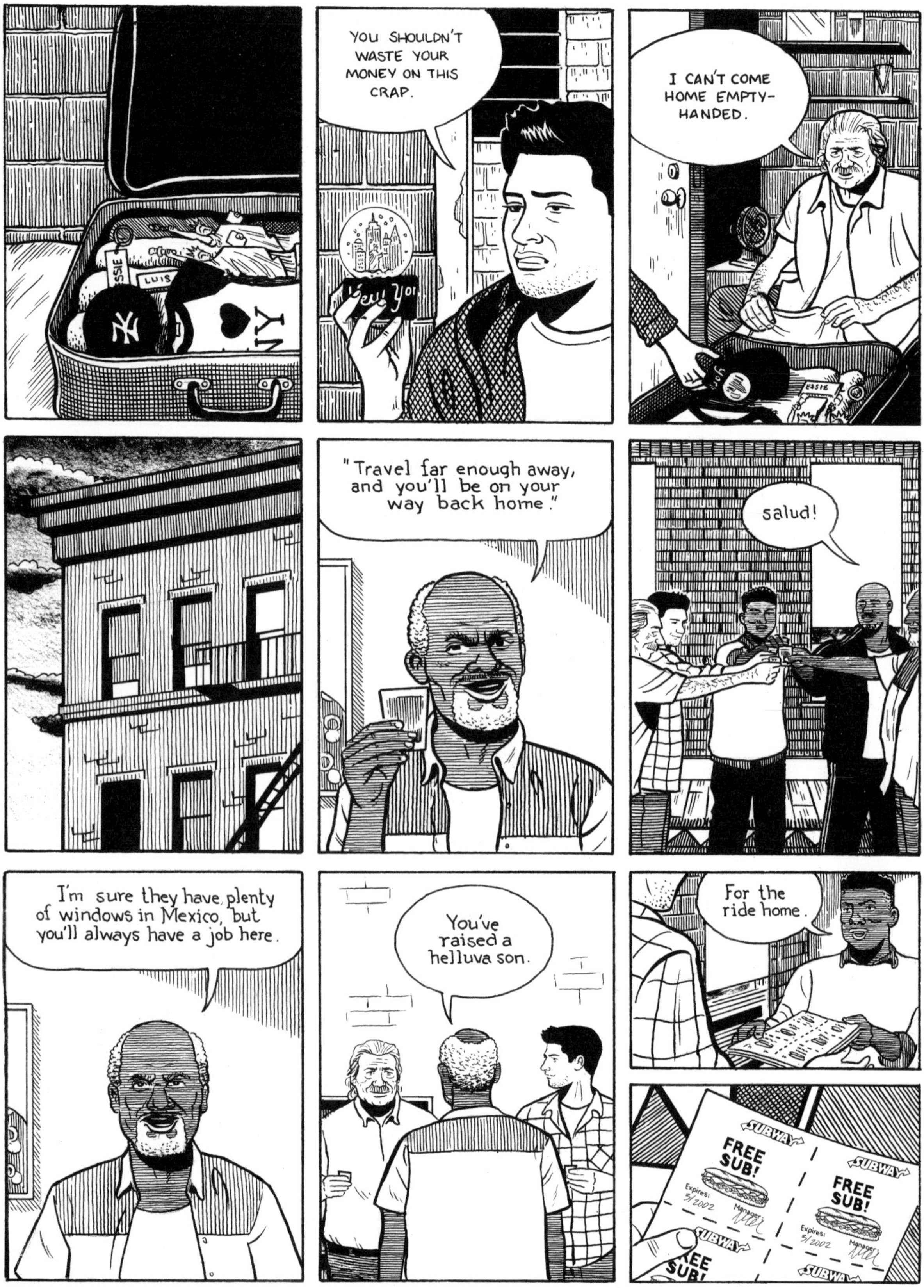

YOU SHOULDN'T WASTE YOUR MONEY ON THIS CRAP.
I CAN'T COME HOME EMPTY-HANDED.
"Travel far enough away, and you'll be on your way back home."
salud!
I'm sure they have plenty of windows in Mexico, but you'll always have a job here.
You've raised a helluva son.
For the ride home.
SUBWAY
FREE SUB!
Expires: 3/2002

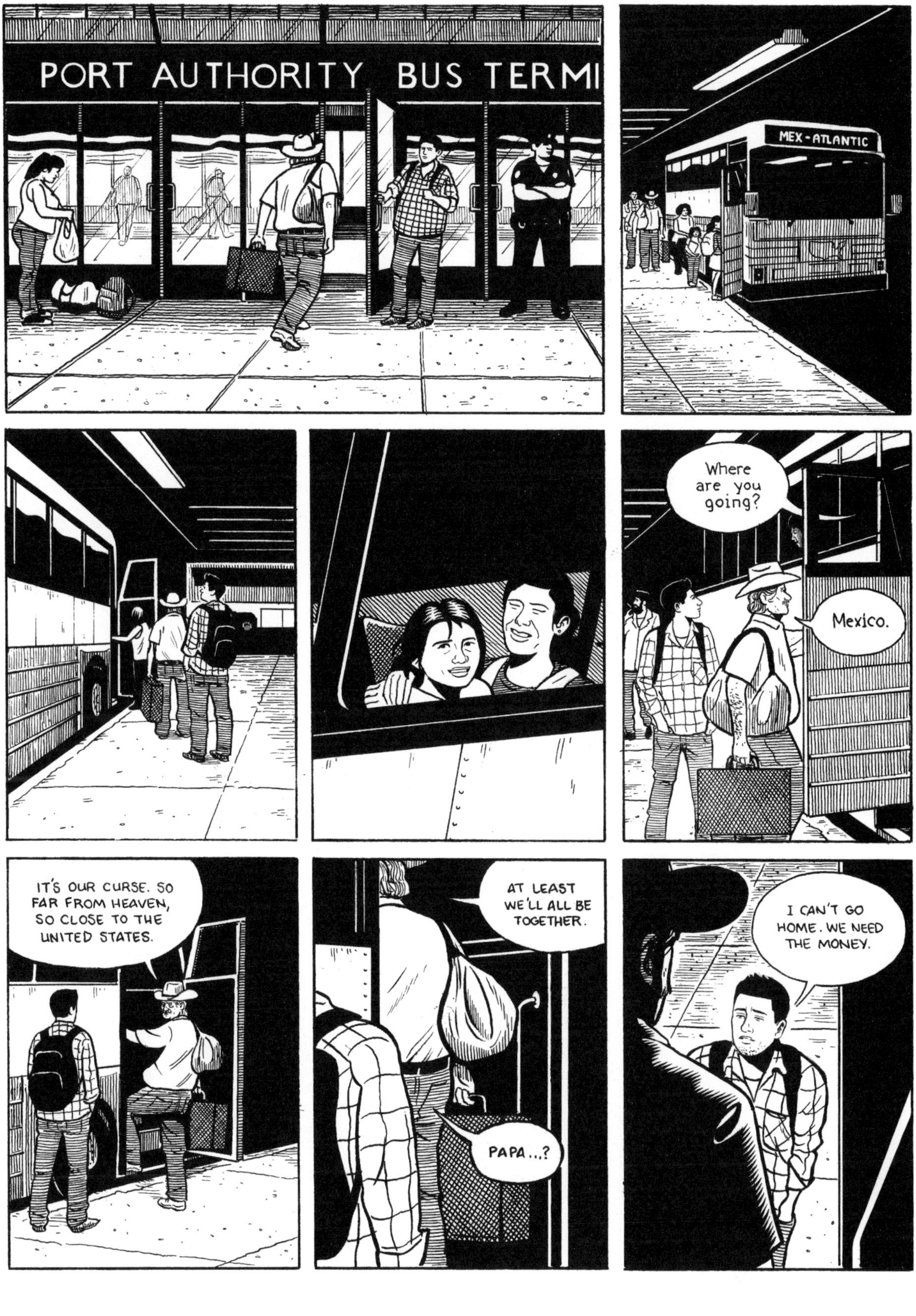
PORT AUTHORITY BUS TERMI
MEX-ATLANTIC
Where are you going?
Mexico.
IT'S OUR CURSE. SO FAR FROM HEAVEN, SO CLOSE TO THE UNITED STATES.
AT LEAST WE'LL ALL BE TOGETHER.
PAPA...?
I CAN'T GO HOME. WE NEED THE MONEY.

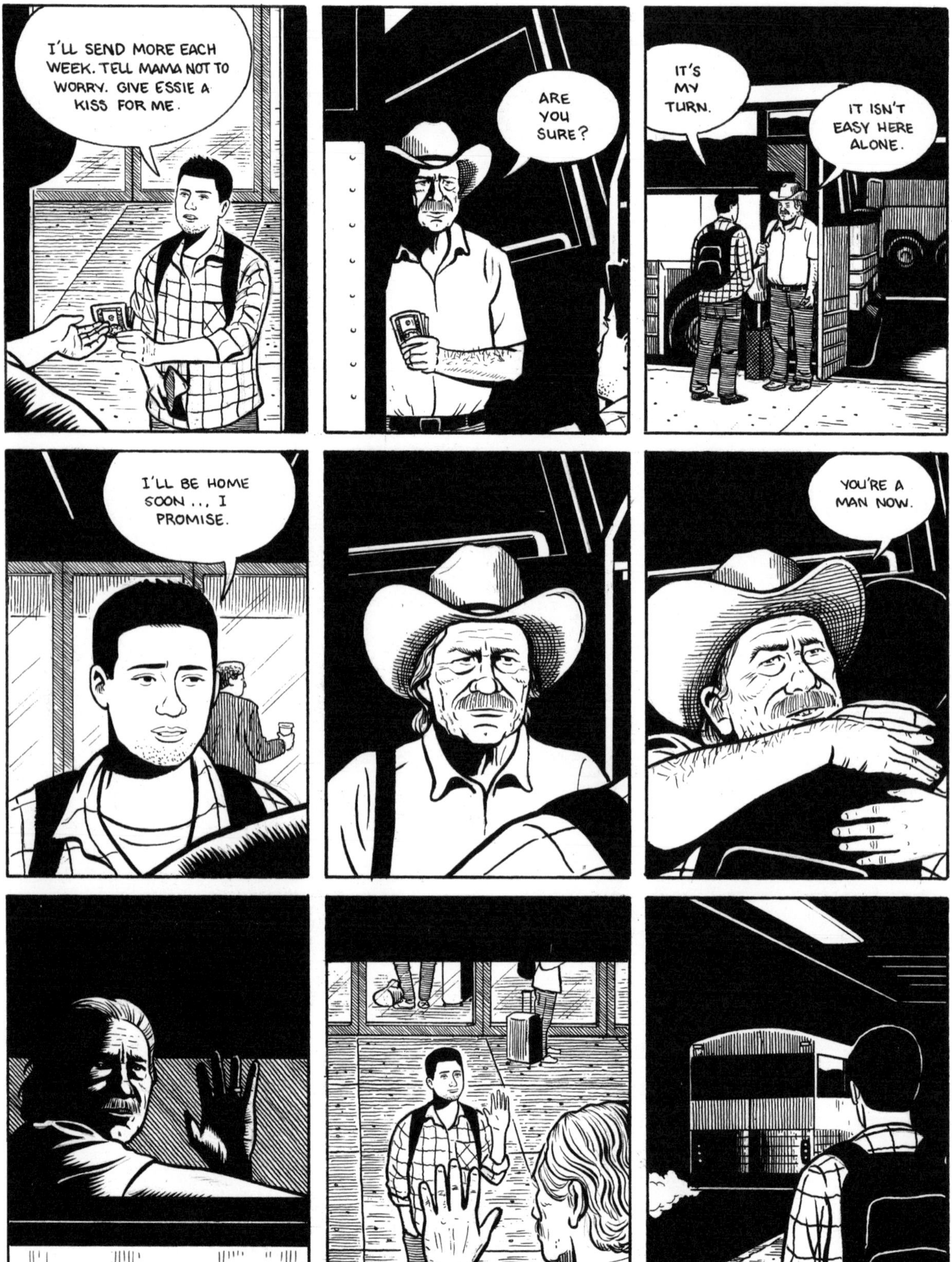
I'LL SEND MORE EACH WEEK. TELL MAMA NOT TO WORRY. GIVE ESSIE A KISS FOR ME.
ARE YOU SURE?
IT'S MY TURN.
IT ISN'T EASY HERE ALONE.
I'LL BE HOME SOON ..., I PROMISE.
YOU'RE A MAN NOW.

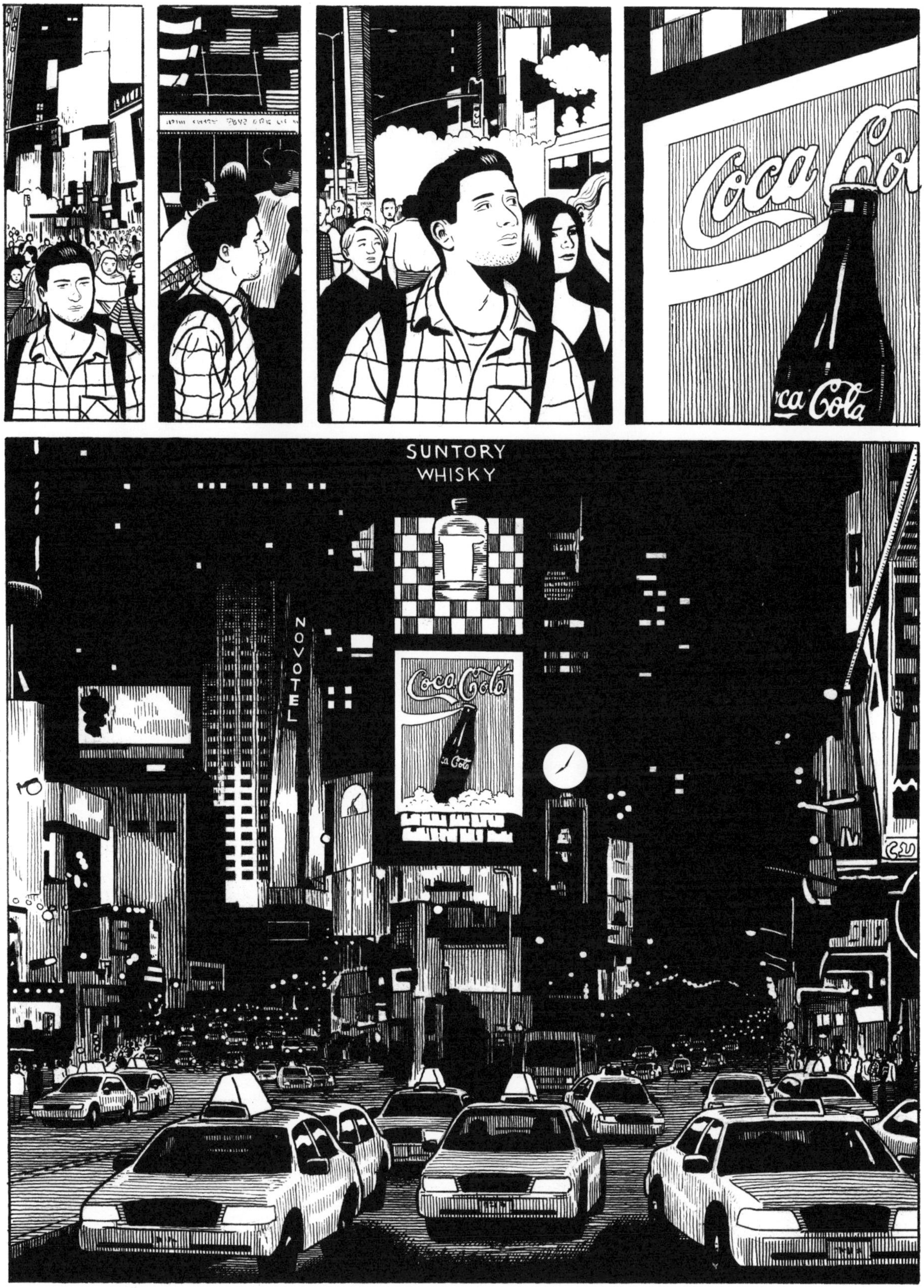
SUNTORY
WHISKY
NOVOTEL
Coca-Cola

OTHER WORKS BY THE AUTHORS:

Jon Sack:
La Lucha: The Story of Lucha Castro
and Human Rights in Mexico
(a graphic novel with Adam Shapiro)

Robert Mailer Anderson:
Boonville (a novel)
The Death of Teddy Ballgame (a play)
Pig Hunt (a screenplay)
Windows on the World (a screenplay)